Selected Short Works

by

Henry James

Selected Short Works by Henry James

THE ASPERN PAPERS
THE BEAST IN THE JUNGLE
THE JOLLY CORNER

THORNDIKE
CHIVERS

This Large Print edition is published by Thorndike Press®, Waterville, Maine USA and by BBC Audiobooks, Ltd, Bath, England.

The following titles are now in Public Domain in the United States and the United Kingdom, and were originally published as follows:

The Aspern Papers 1888
The Beast in the Jungle 1903
The Jolly Corner 1908

The present texts are from the New York Edition of The Novels and Tales of Henry James (1907–1917).

U.S. Hardcover 0-7862-6332-6 (Perennial Bestsellers)
U.K. Hardcover 0-7540-9871-0 (Chivers Large Print)

The text of this Large Print edition is unabridged.
Other aspects of the book may vary from the original edition.

Set in 16 pt. Plantin.

Printed in the United States on permanent paper.

British Library Cataloguing-in-Publication Data available

ISBN 0-7862-6332-6 (lg. print : hc : alk. paper)

Selected Short Works by Henry James

TABLE OF CONTENTS

The Aspern Papers

1

I had taken Mrs Prest into my confidence; without her in truth I should have made but little advance, for the fruitful idea in the whole business dropped from her friendly lips. It was she who found the short cut and loosed the Gordian knot. It is not supposed easy for women to rise to the large free view of anything, anything to be done; but they sometimes throw off a bold conception — such as a man wouldn't have risen to — with singular serenity. "Simply make them take you in on the footing of a lodger" — I don't think that unaided I should have risen to that. I was beating about the bush, trying to be ingenious, wondering by what combination of arts I might become an acquaintance, when she offered this happy suggestion that the way to become an acquaintance was first to become an intimate. Her actual knowledge of the Misses Bordereau was scarcely larger than mine, and indeed I had brought with me from England some definite facts that were new to her. Their name had been mixed up ages before with one of the greatest names of the century, and they now lived obscurely in Venice, lived on very small means, unvisited, unapproachable, in a sequestered and dilapidated old palace: this was the substance of my friend's impression of them. She herself had been established in Venice some fifteen years and had done a great deal of good there; but the circle of her benevolence had never embraced the two shy, mysterious and, as was somehow supposed, scarcely respectable Americans — they were believed to have lost in their long exile all national quality, besides being as their name implied of some remoter French affiliation — who asked no favours and desired no attention. In the early years of her residence she had made an attempt to see them, but this had been successful only as regards the little one, as Mrs Prest called the niece; though in fact I afterwards found her the bigger of the two in inches. She had heard Miss Bordereau was ill and had a suspicion she was in want, and had gone to the house to offer aid, so that if there were suffering, American suffering in particular, she shouldn't have it on her conscience. The "little one" had received her in the great cold tarnished Venetian *sala,* the central hall of the house, paved with marble and roofed with dim cross-beams, and hadn't even asked her to sit down. This was not encouraging for me, who wished to sit so fast, and I remarked as much to Mrs Prest. She replied, however, with profundity, "Ah, but there's all the difference: I went to confer a favour and you'll go to ask one. If they're proud you'll be on the right side." And she offered to show me their house to begin with — to row me thither in her gondola. I let her know I had already been to look at it half a dozen times; but I accepted her invitation, for it charmed me to hover about the place. I had made my way to it the day after my arrival in Venice — it had been described to me in advance by the friend in England to whom I owed definite information as to their possession of the papers — laying siege to it with my eyes while I considered my plan of campaign. Jeffrey Aspern had never been in it that I knew of, but some note of his voice seemed to abide there by a roundabout implication and in a "dying fall."

Mrs Prest knew nothing about the papers, but was interested in my curiosity, as always in the joys and sorrows of her friends. As we went, however, in her gondola, gliding there under the sociable hood with the bright Venetian picture framed on either side by the movable window, I saw how my eagerness amused her and that she found my interest in my possible spoil a fine case of monomania. "One would think you expected from it the answer to the riddle of the universe," she said; and I denied the impeachment only by replying that if I had to choose between that precious solution and a bundle of Jeffrey Aspern's letters I knew indeed which would appear to me the greater boon. She pretended to make light of his genius and I took no pains to defend him. One doesn't defend one's god: one's god is in himself a defence. Besides, to-day, after his long comparative obscuration, he hangs high in the heaven of our literature for all the world to see; he's a part of the light by which we walk. The most I said was that he was no doubt not a woman's poet; to which she rejoined aptly enough that he had been at least Miss Bordereau's. The strange thing had been for me to discover in England that she was still alive: it was as if I had been told Mrs Siddons was, or Queen Caroline, or the famous Lady Hamilton, for it seemed to me that she belonged to a generation as extinct. "Why she must be tremendously old — at least a hundred," I had said; but on coming to consider dates I saw it not strictly involved that she should have far exceeded the common span. None the less she was of venerable age and her relations with Jeffrey Aspern had occurred in her early womanhood. "That's her excuse," said Mrs Prest half-sententiously and yet also somewhat as if she were ashamed of making a speech so little in the real tone of Venice. As if a woman needed an excuse for having loved the divine poet! He had been not only one of the most brilliant minds of his day — and in those years, when the century was young, there were, as every one knows, many — but one of the most genial men and one of the handsomest.

The niece, according to Mrs Prest, was of minor antiquity, and the conjecture was risked that she was only a grand-niece. This was possible; I had nothing but my share in the very limited knowledge of my English fellow worshipper John Cumnor, who had never seen the couple. The world, as I say, had recognised Jeffrey Aspern, but Cumnor and I had recognised him most. The multitude to-day flocked to his temple, but of that temple he and I regarded ourselves as the appointed ministers. We held, justly, as I think, that we had done more for his memory than any one else, and had done it simply by opening lights into his life. He had nothing to fear from us because he had nothing to fear from the truth,

15

which alone at such a distance of time we could be interested in establishing. His early death had been the only dark spot, as it were, on his fame, unless the papers in Miss Bordereau's hands should perversely bring out others. There had been an impression about 1825 that he had "treated her badly," just as there had been an impression that he had "served," as the London populace says, several other ladies in the same masterful way. Each of these cases Cumnor and I had been able to investigate, and we had never failed to acquit him conscientiously of any grossness. I judged him perhaps more indulgently than my friend; certainly, at any rate, it appeared to me that no man could have walked straighter in the given circumstances. These had been almost always difficult and dangerous. Half the women of his time, to speak liberally, had flung themselves at his head, and while the fury raged — the more that it was very catching — accidents, some of them grave, had not failed to occur. He was not a woman's poet, as I had said to Mrs Prest, in the modern phase of his reputation; but the situation had been different when the man's own voice was mingled with his song. That voice, by every testimony, was one of the most charming ever heard. "Orpheus and the Mænads!" had been of course my foreseen judgement when first I turned over his correspondence. Almost all the Mænads were unreasonable and many of them unbearable; it struck me that he had been kinder and more considerate than in his place — if I could imagine myself in any such box — I should have found the trick of.

It was certainly strange beyond all strangeness, and I shall not take up space with attempting to explain it, that whereas among all these other relations and in these other directions of research we had to deal with phantoms and dust, the mere echoes of echoes, the one living source of information that had lingered on into our time had been unheeded by us. Every one of Aspern's contemporaries had, according to our belief, passed away; we had not been able to look into a single pair of eyes into which his had looked or to feel a transmitted contact in any aged hand that his had touched. Most dead of all did poor Miss Bordereau appear, and yet she alone had survived. We exhausted in the course of months our wonder that we had not found her out sooner, and the substance of our explanation was that she had kept so quiet. The poor lady on the whole had had reason for doing so. But it was a revelation to us that self-effacement on such a scale had been possible in the latter half of the nineteenth century — the age of newspapers and telegrams and photographs and interviewers. She had taken no great trouble for it either — hadn't hidden herself away in an undiscoverable hole, had boldly settled down in a city of exhibition. The one apparent secret of her safety had been that Venice contained so many much greater curiosities. And then accident had somehow favoured her, as was shown for example in the fact that Mrs Prest had never happened to name her to me, though I had spent three weeks in Venice — under her nose, as it were — five years before. My friend indeed had not named her much to any one; she appeared almost to have forgotten the fact of her continuance. Of course Mrs Prest hadn't the nerves of an editor. It was meanwhile no explanation of the old woman's having eluded us to say that she lived abroad, for our researches had again and again taken us — not only by correspondence but by personal inquiry — to France, to Germany, to Italy, in which countries, not counting his important stay in England, so many of the too few years of Aspern's career had been spent. We were glad to think at least that in all our promulgations — some people now consider I believe that we have overdone them — we had only touched in passing and in the most discreet manner on Miss Bordereau's connexion. Oddly enough, even if we had had the material — and we had often wondered what could have become of it — this would have been the most difficult episode to handle.

The gondola stopped, the old palace was there; it was a house of the class which in Venice carries even in extreme dilapidation the dignified name. "How charming! It's grey and pink!" my companion exclaimed; and that is the most comprehensive description of it. It was not particularly old, only two or three centuries; and it had an air not so much of decay as of quiet discouragement, as if it had rather missed its career. But its wide front, with a stone balcony from end to end of the *piano nobile* or most important floor, was architectural enough, with the aid of various pilasters and arches; and the stucco with which in the intervals it had long ago been endued was rosy in the April afternoon. It overlooked a clean melancholy rather lonely canal, which had a narrow *riva* or convenient footway on either side. "I don't know why — there are no brick gables," said Mrs Prest, "but this corner has seemed to me before more Dutch than Italian, more like Amsterdam than like Venice. It's eccentrically neat, for reasons of its own; and though you may pass on foot scarcely any one ever thinks of doing so. It's as negative — considering *where* it is — as a Protestant Sunday. Perhaps the people are afraid of the Misses Bordereau. I daresay they have the reputation of witches."

I forget what answer I made to this — I was given up to two other reflexions. The first of these was that if the old lady lived in such a big and imposing house she couldn't be in any sort of misery and therefore wouldn't be tempted by a chance to let a couple of rooms. I expressed this fear to Mrs Prest, who gave me a very straight answer. "If she didn't live in a big house how could it be a question of her having rooms to spare? If she were not amply lodged you'd lack ground to approach her. Besides, a big house here, and especially in this *quartier perdu,* proves nothing at all: it's perfectly consistent with a state of penury. Dilapidated old palazzi, if you'll go out of the way for them, are to be had for five shillings a year. And as for the people who live in them — no, until you've explored Venice socially as much as I have, you can form no idea of their domestic desolation. They live on nothing, for they've nothing to live on." The other idea that had come into my head was connected with a high blank wall which appeared to confine an expanse of ground on one side of the house. Blank I call it, but it was figured over with the patches that please a painter, repaired breaches, crumblings of plaster, extrusions of brick that had turned pink with time; while a few thin trees, with the poles of certain rickety trellises, were visible over the top. The place was a garden and apparently attached to the house. I suddenly felt that so attached it gave me my pretext.

I sat looking out on all this with Mrs Prest (it was covered with the golden glow of Venice) from the shade of our *felze*, and she asked me if I would go in then, while she waited for me, or come back another time. At first I couldn't decide — it was doubtless very weak of me. I wanted still to think I *might* get a footing, and was afraid to meet failure, for it would leave me, as I remarked to my companion, without another arrow for my bow. "Why not another?" she inquired as I sat there hesitating and thinking it over; and she wished to know

21

why even now and before taking the trouble of becoming an inmate — which might be wretchedly uncomfortable after all, even if it succeeded — I hadn't the resource of simply offering them a sum of money down. In that way I might get what I wanted without bad nights.

"Dearest lady," I exclaimed, "excuse the impatience of my tone when I suggest that you must have forgotten the very fact — surely I communicated it to you — which threw me on your ingenuity. The old woman won't have her relics and tokens so much as spoken of; they're personal, delicate, intimate, and she hasn't the feelings of the day, God bless her! If I should sound that note first I should certainly spoil the game. I can arrive at my spoils only by putting her off her guard, and I can put her off her guard only by ingratiating diplomatic arts. Hypocrisy, duplicity are my only chance. I'm sorry for it, but there's no baseness I wouldn't commit for Jeffrey Aspern's sake. First I must take tea with her — then tackle the main job." And I told over what had happened to John Cumnor on his respectfully writing to her. No notice whatever had been taken of his first letter, and the second had been answered very sharply, in six lines, by the niece. "Miss Bordereau requested her to say that she couldn't imagine what he meant by troubling them. They had none of Mr Aspern's 'literary remains,' and if they *had* had wouldn't have dreamed of showing them to any one on any account whatever. She couldn't imagine what he was talking about and begged he would let her alone." I certainly didn't want to be met that way.

"Well," said Mrs Prest after a moment and all provokingly, "perhaps they really haven't anything. If they deny it flat how are you sure?"

"John Cumnor's sure, and it would take me long to tell you how his conviction, or his very strong presumption — strong enough to stand against the old lady's not unnatural fib — has built itself up. Besides, he makes much of the internal evidence of the niece's letter."

"The internal evidence?"

"Her calling him 'Mr Aspern.' "

"I don't see what that proves."

"It proves familiarity, and familiarity implies the possession of mementoes, of tangible objects. I can't tell you how that 'Mr' affects me — how it bridges over the gulf of time and brings our hero near to me — nor what an edge it gives to my desire to see

Juliana. You don't say 'Mr' Shakespeare."

"Would I, any more, if I had a box full of his letters?"

"Yes, if he had been your lover and some one wanted them." And I added that John Cumnor was so convinced, and so all the more convinced by Miss Bordereau's tone, that he would have come himself to Venice on the undertaking were it not for the obstacle of his having, for any confidence, to disprove his identity with the person who had written to them, which the old ladies would be sure to suspect in spite of dissimulation and a change of name. If they were to ask him point-blank if he were not their snubbed correspondent it would be too awkward for him to lie; whereas I was fortunately not tied in that way. I was a fresh hand — I could protest without lying.

"But you'll have to take a false name," said Mrs Prest. "Juliana lives out of the world as much as it is possible to live, but she has none the less probably heard of Mr Aspern's editors. She perhaps possesses what you've published."

"I've thought of that," I returned; and I drew out of my pocketbook a visiting-card neatly engraved with a well-chosen *nom de guerre*.

"You're very extravagant — it adds to your immorality. You might have done it in pencil or ink," said my companion.

"This looks more genuine."

"Certainly you've the courage of your curiosity. But it will be awkward about your letters; they won't come to you in that mask."

"My banker will take them in and I shall go every day to get them. It will give me a little walk."

"Shall you depend all on that?" asked Mrs Prest. "Aren't you coming to see me?"

"Oh you'll have left Venice for the hot months long before there are any results. I'm prepared to roast all summer — as well as through the long hereafter per-haps you'll say! Meanwhile John Cumnor will bombard me with letters addressed, in my feigned name, to the care of the padrona."

"She'll recognise his hand," my companion suggested.

"On the envelope he can disguise it."

"Well, you're a precious pair! Doesn't it occur to you that even if you're able to say you're not Mr Cumnor in person they may still suspect you of being his emissary?"

"Certainly, and I see only one way to parry that."

"And what may that be?"

I hesitated a moment. "To make love to the niece."

"Ah," cried my friend, "wait till you see her!"

2

"I must work the garden — I must work the garden," I said to myself five minutes later and while I waited, upstairs, in the long, dusky sala, where the bare scagliola floor gleamed vaguely in a chink of the closed shutters. The place was impressive, yet looked somehow cold and cautious. Mrs Prest had floated away, giving me a rendez-vous at the end of half an hour by some neighbouring water-steps; and I had been let into the house, after pulling the rusty bell-wire, by a small red-headed and white-faced maid-servant, who was very young and not ugly and wore clicking pattens and a shawl in the fashion of a hood. She had not contented herself with opening the door from above by the usual arrangement of a creaking pulley, though she had looked down at me first from an upper window, dropping the cautious challenge which in Italy precedes the act of admission. I was irritated as a general thing by this survival of medieval manners, though as so fond, if yet so special, an antiquarian I suppose I ought to have liked it; but, with my resolve to be genial from the threshold at any price, I took my false card out of my pocket and held it up to her, smiling as if it were a magic token. It had the effect of one indeed, for it brought her, as I say, all the way down. I begged her to hand it to her mistress, having first written on it in Italian the words: "Could you very kindly see a gentleman, a travelling American, for a moment?" The little maid wasn't hostile — even that was perhaps something gained. She coloured, she smiled and looked both frightened and pleased. I could see that my arrival was a great affair, that visits in such a house were rare and that she was a person who would have liked a bustling place. When she pushed forward the heavy door behind me I felt my foot in the citadel and promised myself ever so firmly to keep it there. She pattered across the damp stony lower hall and I followed her up the high staircase — stonier still, as it seemed — without an invitation. I think she had meant I should wait for her below, but such was not my idea, and I took up my station in the sala. She flitted, at the far end of it, into impenetrable regions, and I looked at the place with my heart beating as

I had known it to do in dentists' parlours. It had a gloomy grandeur, but owed its character almost all to its noble shape and to the fine architectural doors, as high as those of grand frontages, which, leading into the various rooms, repeated themselves on either side at intervals. They were surmounted with old faded painted escutcheons and here and there in the spaces between them hung brown pictures, which I noted as speciously bad, in battered and tarnished frames that were yet more desirable than the canvases themselves. With the exception of several straw-bottomed chairs that kept their backs to the wall the grand obscure vista contained little else to minister to effect. It was evidently never used save as a passage, and scantly even as that. I may add that by the time the door through which the maid-servant had escaped opened again my eyes had grown used to the want of light.

I hadn't meanwhile meant by my private ejaculation that I must myself cultivate the soil of the tangled enclosure which lay beneath the windows, but the lady who came toward me from the distance over the hard shining floor might have supposed as much from the way in which, as I went rapidly to meet her, I exclaimed, taking care to speak Italian: "The garden, the garden —

do me the pleasure to tell me if it's yours!"

She stopped short, looking at me with wonder; and then, "Nothing here is mine," she answered in English, coldly and sadly.

"Oh you're English; how delightful!" I ingenuously cried. "But surely the garden belongs to the house?"

"Yes, but the house doesn't belong to me." She was a long lean pale person, habited apparently in a dull-coloured dressing-gown, and she spoke very simply and mildly. She didn't ask me to sit down, any more than years before — if she were the niece — she had asked Mrs Prest, and we stood face to face in the empty pompous hall.

"Well then, would you kindly tell me to whom I must address myself? I'm afraid you'll think me horribly intrusive, but you know I *must* have a garden — upon my honour I must!"

Her face was not young, but it was candid; it was not fresh, but it was clear. She had large eyes which were not bright, and a great deal of hair which was not "dressed," and long fine hands which were — possibly — not clean. She clasped these members almost convulsively as, with a confused alarmed look, she broke out: "Oh don't take it away from us; we like it ourselves!"

"You have the use of it then?"

"Oh yes. If it wasn't for that — !" And she gave a wan vague smile.

"Isn't it a luxury, precisely? That's why, intending to be in Venice some weeks, possibly all summer, and having some literary work, some reading and writing to do, so that I must be quiet and yet if possible a great deal in the open air — that's why I've felt a garden to be really indispensable. I appeal to your own experience," I went on with as sociable a smile as I could risk. "Now can't I look at yours?"

"I don't know, I don't understand," the poor woman murmured, planted there and letting her weak wonder deal — helplessly enough, as I felt — with my strangeness.

"I mean only from one of those windows — such grand ones as you have here — if you'll let me open the shutters." And I walked toward the back of the house. When I had advanced halfway I stopped and waited as in the belief she would accompany me. I had been of necessity quite abrupt, but I strove at the same time to give her the impression of extreme courtesy. "I've looked at furnished rooms all over the place, and it seems impossible to find any with a garden attached. Naturally in a place like Venice gardens are rare. It's absurd if you like, for a man, but I can't live without flowers."

"There are none to speak of down there." She came nearer, as if, though she mistrusted me, I had drawn her by an invisible thread. I went on again, and she continued as she followed me: "We've a few, but they're very common. It costs too much to cultivate them; one has to have a man."

"Why shouldn't I be the man?" I asked. "I'll work without wages; or rather I'll put in a gardener. You shall have the sweetest flowers in Venice."

She protested against this with a small quaver of sound that might have been at the same time a gush of rapture for my free sketch. Then she gasped: "We don't know you — we don't know you."

"You know me as much as I know you; or rather much more, because you know my name. And if you're English I'm almost a countryman."

"We're not English," said my companion, watching me in practical submission while I threw open the shutters of one of the divisions of the wide high window.

"You speak the language so beautifully: might I ask what you are?" Seen from above the garden was in truth shabby, yet I

31

felt at a glance that it had great capabilities. She made no rejoinder, she was so lost in her blankness and gentleness, and I exclaimed: "You don't mean to say you're also by chance American?"

"I don't know. We used to be."

"Used to be? Surely you haven't changed?"

"It's so many years ago. We don't seem to be anything now."

"So many years that you've been living here? Well, I don't wonder at that; it's a grand old house. I suppose you all use the garden," I went on, "but I assure you I shouldn't be in your way. I'd be very quiet and stay quite in one corner."

"We all use it?" she repeated after me vaguely, not coming close to the window but looking at my shoes. She appeared to think me capable of throwing her out.

"I mean all your family — as many as you are."

"There's only one other than me. She's very old. She never goes down."

I feel again my thrill at this close identification of Juliana; in spite of which, however, I kept my head. "Only one other in all this great house!" I feigned to be not only amazed but almost scandalised. "Dear lady, you must have space then to spare!"

"To spare?" she repeated — almost as for the rich unwonted joy to her of spoken words.

"Why you surely don't live (two quiet women — I see *you* are quiet, at any rate) in fifty rooms!" Then with a burst of hope and cheer I put the question straight. "Couldn't you for a good rent *let* me two or three? That would set me up!"

I had now struck the note that translated my purpose, and I needn't reproduce the whole of the tune I played. I ended by making my entertainer believe me an undesigning person, though of course I didn't even attempt to persuade her I was not an eccentric one. I repeated that I had studies to pursue; that I wanted quiet; that I delighted in a garden and had vainly sought one up and down the city: that I would undertake that before another month was over the dear old house should be smothered in flowers. I think it was the flowers that won my suit, for I afterwards found that Miss Tina — for such the name of this high tremulous spinster proved somewhat incongruously to be — had an insatiable appetite for them. When I speak of my suit as won I mean that before I left her she had promised me she would refer the question to her aunt. I invited information as to who her aunt might be and she answered, "Why Miss Bordereau!" with an air of surprise, as if I might have been expected to know. There were contradictions like this in Miss Tina which, as I observed later, contributed to make her rather pleasingly incalculable and interesting. It was the study of the two ladies to live so that the world shouldn't talk of them or touch them, and yet they had never altogether accepted the idea that it didn't hear of them. In Miss Tina at any rate a grateful susceptibility to human contact had not died out, and contact of a limited order there would be if I should come to live in the house.

"We've never done anything of the sort; we've never had a lodger or any kind of inmate." So much as this she made a point of saying to me. "We're very poor, we live very badly — almost on nothing. The rooms are very bare — those you might take; they've nothing at all in them. I don't know how you'd sleep, how you'd eat."

"With your permission I could easily put in a bed and a few tables and chairs. *C'est la moindre des choses* and the affair of an hour or two. I know a little man from whom I can hire for a trifle what I should so briefly want, what I should use; my gondolier can bring the things round in his boat. Of course in this great house you must have a second kitchen, and my servant, who's a wonderfully handy fellow" — this personage was an evocation of the moment — "can easily cook me a chop there. My tastes and habits are of the simplest: I live on flowers!" And then I ventured to add that if they were very poor it was all the more reason they should let their rooms. They were bad economists — I had never heard of such a waste of material.

I saw in a moment my good lady had never before been spoken to in any such fashion — with a humorous firmness that didn't exclude sympathy, that was quite founded on it. She might easily have told me that my sympathy was impertinent, but this by good fortune didn't occur to her. I left her with the understanding that she would submit the question to her aunt and that I might come back the next day for their decision.

"The aunt will refuse; she'll think the whole proceeding very *louche!*" Mrs Prest declared shortly after this, when I had resumed my place in her gondola. She had put the idea into my head and now — so little are women to be counted on — she appeared to take a despondent view of it. Her pessimism provoked me and I pretended to have the best hopes; I went so far as to boast of a distinct prevision of success. Upon this Mrs Prest broke out: "Oh I see what's in your head! You fancy you've made such an impression in five minutes that she's dying for you to come and can be depended on to bring the old one round. If you do get in you'll count it as a triumph."

I did count it as a triumph, but only for the commentator — in the last analysis — not for the man, who had not the tradition of personal conquest. When I went back on the morrow the little maid-servant conducted me straight through the long sala — it opened there as before in large perspective and was lighter now, which I thought a good omen — into the apartment from which the recipient of my former visit had emerged on that occasion. It was a spacious shabby parlour with a fine old painted ceiling under which a strange figure sat alone at one of the windows. They come back to me now almost with the palpitation they caused, the successive states marking my consciousness that as the door of the room closed behind me I was really face to face with the Juliana of some of Aspern's most exquisite and most renowned lyrics. I grew used to her afterwards, though never completely; but as she sat there before me my heart beat as fast as if the miracle of resurrection had taken place for my benefit. Her presence seemed somehow to contain and express his own, and I felt nearer to him at that first moment of seeing her than I ever had been before or ever have been since. Yes, I remember my emotions in their order, even including a curious little tremor that took me when I saw the niece not to be there. With her, the day before, I had become sufficiently familiar, but it almost exceeded my courage — much as I had longed for the event — to be left alone with so terrible a relic as the aunt. She was too strange, too literally resurgent. Then came a check from the perception that we weren't really face to face, inasmuch as she had over her eyes a horrible green shade which served for her almost as a mask. I believed for the instant that she had put it on expressly, so that from underneath it she might take me all in without my getting at herself. At the same time it created a presumption of some ghastly death's-head lurking behind it. The divine Juliana as a grinning skull — the vision hung there until it passed. Then it came to me that she *was* tremendously old — so old that death might take her at any moment, before I should have time to compass my end. The next thought was a correction to that; it lighted up the situation. She would die next week, she would die tomorrow — then I could pounce on her possessions and ransack her drawers. Meanwhile she sat there neither moving nor speaking. She was very small and shrunken, bent forward with her hands in her lap. She was dressed in black and her head was wrapped in a piece of old black lace which showed no hair.

My emotion keeping me silent she spoke first, and the remark she made was exactly the most unexpected.

3

"Our house is very far from the centre, but the little canal is very *comme il faut*."

"It's the sweetest corner of Venice and I can imagine nothing more charming," I hastened to reply. The old lady's voice was very thin and weak, but it had an agreeable, cultivated murmur and there was wonder in the thought that that individual note had been in Jeffrey Aspern's ear.

"Please to sit down there. I hear very

well," she said quietly, as if perhaps I had been shouting; and the chair she pointed to was at a certain distance. I took possession of it, assuring her I was perfectly aware of my intrusion and of my not having been properly introduced, and that I could but throw myself on her indulgence. Perhaps the other lady, the one I had had the honour of seeing the day before, would have explained to her about the garden. That was literally what had given me courage to take a step so unconventional. I had fallen in love at sight with the whole place — she herself was probably so used to it that she didn't know the impression it was capable of making on a stranger — and I had felt it really a case to risk something. Was her own kindness in receiving me a sign that I was not wholly out in my calculation? It would make me extremely happy to think so. I could give her my word of honour that I was a most respectable inoffensive person and that as a co-tenant of the palace, so to speak, they would be barely conscious of my existence. I would conform to any regulations, any restrictions, if they would only let me enjoy the garden. Moreover I should be delighted to give her references, guarantees; they would be of the very best, both in

Venice and in England, as well as in America.

She listened to me in perfect stillness and I felt her look at me with great penetration, though I could see only the lower part of her bleached and shrivelled face. Independently of the refining process of old age it had a delicacy which once must have been great. She had been very fair, she had had a wonderful complexion. She was silent a little after I had ceased speaking; then she began: "If you're so fond of a garden why don't you go to *terra firma*, where there are so many far better than this?"

"Oh it's the combination!" I answered, smiling; and then with rather a flight of fancy: "It's the idea of a garden in the middle of the sea."

"This isn't the middle of the sea; you can't so much as see the water."

I stared a moment, wondering if she wished to convict me of fraud. "Can't see the water? Why, dear madam, I can come up to the very gate in my boat."

She appeared inconsequent, for she said vaguely in reply to this: "Yes, if you've got a boat. I haven't any; it's many years since I've been in one of the *gondole*." She uttered these words as if they designed a curious far-away craft known to her only by hearsay.

"Let me assure you of the pleasure with which I would put mine at your service!" I returned. I had scarcely said this, however, before I became aware that the speech was in questionable taste and might also do me the injury of making me appear too eager, too possessed of a hidden motive. But the old woman remained impenetrable and her attitude worried me by suggesting that she had a fuller vision of me than I had of her. She gave me no thanks for my somewhat extravagant offer, but remarked that the lady I had seen the day before was her niece; she would presently come in. She had asked her to stay away a little on purpose — had had her reasons for seeing me first alone. She relapsed into silence and I turned over the fact of these unmentioned reasons and the question of what might come yet; also that of whether I might venture on some judicious remark in praise of her companion. I went so far as to say I should be delighted to see our absent friend again: she had been so very patient with me, considering how odd she must have thought me — a declaration which drew from Miss Bordereau another of her whimsical speeches.

"She has very good manners; I bred her up myself!" I was on the point of saying that that accounted for the easy grace of the niece, but I arrested myself in time, and the next moment the old woman went on: "I don't care who you may be — I don't want to know; it signifies very little to-day." This had all the air of being a formula of dismissal, as if her next words would be that I might take myself off now that she had had the amusement of looking on the face of such a monster of indiscretion. Therefore I was all the more surprised when she added in her soft venerable quaver: "You may have as many rooms as you like — if you'll pay me a good deal of money."

I hesitated but an instant, long enough to measure what she meant in particular by this condition. First it struck me that she must have really a large sum in her mind; then I reasoned quickly that her idea of a large sum would probably not correspond to my own. My deliberation, I think, was not so visible as to diminish the promptitude with which I replied: "I will pay with pleasure and of course in advance whatever you may think it proper to ask me."

"Well then, a thousand francs a month," she said instantly, while her baffling green shade continued to cover her attitude.

The figure, as they say, was startling and my logic had been at fault. The sum she had mentioned was, by the Venetian measure of such matters, exceedingly large; there was many an old palace in an out-of-the-way corner that I might on such terms have enjoyed the whole of by the year. But so far as my resources allowed I was prepared to spend money, and my decision was quickly taken. I would pay her with a smiling face what she asked, but in that case I would make it up by getting hold of my "spoils" for nothing. Moreover if she had asked five times as much I should have risen to the occasion, so odious would it have seemed to me to stand chaffering with Aspern's Juliana. It was queer enough to have a question of money with her at all. I assured her that her views perfectly met my own and that on the morrow I should have the pleasure of putting three months' rent into her hand. She received this announcement with apparent complacency and with no discoverable sense that after all it would become her to say that I ought to see the rooms first. This didn't occur to her, and indeed her serenity was mainly what I wanted. Our little agreement was just concluded when the door opened and the younger lady appeared on the threshold. As soon as Miss Bordereau saw her niece she cried out almost gaily: "He'll give three thousand — three thousand tomorrow!"

Miss Tina stood still, her patient eyes turning from one of us to the other; then she brought out, scarcely above her breath: "Do you mean francs?"

"Did you mean francs or dollars?" the old woman asked of me at this.

"I think francs were what you said," I sturdily smiled.

"That's very good," said Miss Tina, as if she had felt how overreaching her own question might have looked.

"What do *you* know? You're ignorant," Miss Bordereau remarked; not with acerbity but with a strange soft coldness.

"Yes, of money — certainly of money!" Miss Tina hastened to concede.

"I'm sure you've your own fine branches of knowledge," I took the liberty of saying genially. There was something painful to me, somehow, in the turn the conversation had taken, in the discussion of dollars and francs.

"She had a very good education when she was young. I looked into that myself," said Miss Bordereau. Then she added:

"But she has learned nothing since."

"I've always been with *you*," Miss Tina rejoined very mildly, and of a certainty with no intention of an epigram.

"Yes, but for that — !" her aunt declared with more satirical force. She evidently meant that but for this her niece would never have got on at all; the point of the observation, however, being lost on Miss Tina, though she blushed at hearing her history revealed to a stranger. Miss Bordereau went on, addressing herself to me: "And what time will you come to-morrow with the money?"

"The sooner the better. If it suits you I'll come at noon."

"I'm always here, but I have my hours," said the old woman as if her convenience were not to be taken for granted.

"You mean the times when you receive?"

"I never receive. But I'll see you at noon, when you come with the money."

"Very good, I shall be punctual." To which I added: "May I shake hands with you on our contract?" I thought there ought to be some little form; it would make me really feel easier, for I was sure there would be no other. Besides, though Miss Bordereau couldn't to-day be called personally attractive and there was something even in her wasted antiquity that bade one stand at one's distance, I felt an irresistible desire to hold in my own for a moment the hand Jeffrey Aspern had pressed.

For a minute she made no answer, and I saw that my proposal failed to meet with her approbation. She indulged in no movement of withdrawal, which I half-expected; she only said coldly: "I belong to a time when that was not the custom."

I felt rather snubbed but I exclaimed good-humouredly to Miss Tina, "Oh you'll do as well!" I shook hands with her while she assented with a small flutter. "Yes, yes, to show it's all arranged!"

"Shall you bring the money in gold?" Miss Bordereau demanded as I was turning to the door.

I looked at her a moment. "Aren't you a little afraid, after all, of keeping such a sum as that in the house?" It was not that I was annoyed at her avidity, but was truly struck with the disparity between such a treasure and such scanty means of guarding it.

"Whom should I be afraid of if I'm not afraid of you?" she asked with her shrunken grimness.

"Ah well," I laughed, "I shall be in point of fact a protector and I'll bring gold if you prefer."

"Thank you," the old woman returned with dignity and with an inclination of her head which evidently signified my dismissal. I passed out of the room, thinking how hard it would be to circumvent her. As I stood in the sala again I saw that Miss Tina had followed me, and I supposed that as her aunt had neglected to suggest I should take a look at my quarters it was her purpose to repair the omission. But she made no such overture; she only stood there with a dim, though not a languid smile, and with an effect of irresponsible incompetent youth almost comically at variance with the faded facts of her person. She was not infirm, like her aunt, but she struck me as more deeply futile, because her inefficiency was inward, which was not the case with Miss Bordereau's. I waited to see if she would offer to show me the rest of the house, but I didn't precipitate the question, inasmuch as my plan was from this moment to spend as much of my time as possible in her society. A minute indeed elapsed before I committed myself.

"I've had better fortune than I hoped. It was very kind of her to see me. Perhaps you said a good word for me."

"It was the idea of the money," said Miss Tina.

"And did you suggest that?"

"I told her you'd perhaps pay largely."

"What made you think that?"

"I told her I thought you were rich."

"And what put that into your head?"

"I don't know; the way you talked."

"Dear me, I must talk differently now," I returned. "I'm sorry to say it's not the case."

"Well," said Miss Tina, "I think that in Venice the *forestieri* in general often give a great deal for something that after all isn't much." She appeared to make this remark with a comforting intention, to wish to remind me that if I had been extravagant I wasn't foolishly singular. We walked together along the sala, and as I took its magnificent measure I observed that I was afraid it wouldn't form a part of my *quartiere*. Were my rooms by chance to be among those that opened into it? "Not if you go above — to the second floor," she answered as if she had rather taken for granted I would know my proper place.

"And I infer that that's where your aunt would like me to be."

"She said your apartments ought to be very distinct."

"That certainly would be best." And I listened with respect while she told me that above I should be free to take whatever I might like; that there was another staircase, but only from the floor on which we stood, and that to pass from it to the garden-level or to come up to my lodging I should have in effect to cross the great hall. This was an immense point gained; I foresaw that it would constitute my whole leverage in my relations with the two ladies. When I asked Miss Tina how I was to manage at present to find my way up she replied with an access of that sociable shyness which constantly marked her manner:

"Perhaps you can't. I don't see — unless I should go with you." She evidently hadn't thought of this before.

We ascended to the upper floor and visited a long succession of empty rooms. The best of them looked over the garden; some of the others had above the opposite rough-tiled house-tops a view of the blue lagoon. They were all dusty and even a little disfigured with long neglect, but I saw that by spending a few hundred francs I should be able to make three or four of them habitable enough. My experiment was turning out costly, yet now that I had all but taken possession I ceased to allow this to trouble me. I mentioned to my companion a few of the things I should put in, but she replied rather more precipitately than usual that I might do exactly what I liked: she seemed to wish to notify me that the Misses Bordereau would take none but the most veiled interest in my proceedings. I guessed that her aunt had instructed her to adopt this tone, and I may as well say now that I came afterwards to distinguish perfectly (as I believed) between the speeches she made on her own responsibility and those the old woman imposed upon her. She took no notice of the unswept condition of the rooms and indulged neither in explanations nor in apologies. I said to myself that this was a sign Juliana and her niece — disenchanting idea! — were untidy persons with a low Italian standard; but I afterwards recognised that a lodger who had forced an entrance had no *locus standi* as a critic. We looked out of a good many windows, for there was nothing within the rooms to look at, and still I wanted to linger. I asked her what several different objects in the prospect might be, but in no case did she appear to know. She was evidently not familiar with the view — it was as if she had not looked at it for years — and I presently saw that she was too preoccupied with something else to pretend to care for it. Suddenly she said — the remark was not suggested:

"I don't know whether it will make any difference to you, but the money is for me."

"The money — ?"

"The money you're going to bring."

"Why you'll make me wish to stay here two or three years!" I spoke as benevolently as possible, though it had begun to act on my nerves that these women so associated with Aspern should so constantly bring the pecuniary question back.

"That would be very good for me," she answered almost gaily.

"You put me on my honour!"

She looked as if she failed to understand this, but went on: "She wants me to have more. She thinks she's going to die."

"Ah not soon I hope!" I cried with genuine feeling. I had perfectly considered the possibility of her destroying her documents on the day she should feel her end at hand. I believed that she would cling to them till then, and I was as convinced of her reading Aspern's letters over every night or at least pressing them to her withered lips. I would have given a good deal for some view of those solemnities. I asked Miss Tina if her venerable relative were seriously ill, and she replied that she was only very tired — she had lived so extraordinarily long. That was what she said herself — she wanted to die for a change. Besides, all her friends had been dead for ages; either they ought to have remained or she ought to have gone. That was another thing her aunt often said: she was not at all resigned — resigned, that is, to life.

"But people don't die when they like, do they?" Miss Tina inquired. I took the liberty of asking why, if there was actually enough money to maintain both of them, there would not be more than enough in case of her being left alone. She considered this difficult problem a moment and then said: "Oh well, you know, she takes care of me. She thinks that when I'm alone I shall be a great fool and shan't know how to manage."

"I should have supposed rather that you took care of *her*. I'm afraid she's very proud."

"Why, have you discovered that already?" Miss Tina cried with a dimness of glad surprise.

"I was shut up with her there for a considerable time and she struck me, she interested me extremely. It didn't take me long to make my discovery. She won't have much to say to me while I'm here."

"No, I don't think she will," my companion averred.

"Do you suppose she has some suspicion of me?"

Miss Tina's honest eyes gave me no sign I had touched a mark. "I shouldn't think so — letting you in after all so easily."

"You call it easily? She has covered her risk," I said. "But where is it one could take an advantage of her?"

"I oughtn't to tell you if I knew, ought I?" And Miss Tina added, before I had time to reply to this, smiling dolefully: "Do you think we've any weak points?"

"That's exactly what I'm asking. You'd only have to mention them for me to respect them religiously."

She looked at me hereupon with that air of timid but candid and even gratified curiosity with which she had confronted me from the first; after which she said: "There's nothing to tell. We're terribly quiet. I don't know how the days pass. We've no life."

"I wish I might think I should bring you a little."

"Oh, we know what we want," she went on. "It's all right."

There were twenty things I desired to ask her: how in the world they did live; whether they had any friends or visitors, any relations in America or in other countries. But I judged such probings premature; I must leave it to a later chance. "Well, don't *you* be proud," I contented myself with saying. "Don't hide from me altogether."

"Oh I must stay with my aunt," she returned without looking at me. And at the same moment, abruptly, without any ceremony of parting, she quitted me and disappeared, leaving me to make my own way downstairs. I stayed a while longer, wandering about the bright desert — the sun was pouring in — of the old house, thinking the situation over on the spot. Not even the pattering little *serva* came to look after me, and I reflected that after all this treatment showed confidence.

4

Perhaps it did, but all the same, six weeks later, towards the middle of June, the moment when Mrs Prest undertook her annual migration, I had made no measurable advance. I was obliged to confess to her that I had no results to speak of. My first step had been unexpectedly rapid, but there was no appearance it would be followed by a second. I was a thousand miles from taking tea with my hostesses — that privilege of which, as I reminded my good friend, we both had had a vision. She reproached me with lacking boldness and I answered that even to be bold you must have an opportunity: you may push on through a breach, but you can't batter down a dead wall. She returned that the breach I had already made was big enough to admit an army, and accused me of wasting precious hours in whimpering in her salon when I ought to have been carrying on the struggle in the field. It is true that I went to see her very often — all on the theory that it would console me (I freely expressed my discouragement) for my want of success on my own premises. But I began to feel that it didn't console me to be perpetually chaffed for my scruples, especially since I was really so vigilant; and I was rather glad when my ironic friend closed her house for the summer. She had expected to draw amusement from the drama of my intercourse with the Misses Bordereau, and was disappointed that the intercourse, and consequently the drama, had not come off. "They'll lead you on to your ruin," she said before she left Venice. "They'll get all your money without showing you a scrap." I think I settled down to my business with more concentration after her departure.

It was a fact that up to that time I had not, save on a single brief occasion, had even a moment's contact with my queer hostesses. The exception had occurred when I carried them according to my promise the terrible three thousand francs. Then I found Miss Tina awaiting me in the hall, and she took the money from my hand with a promptitude that prevented my seeing her aunt. The old lady had promised to receive me, yet apparently thought nothing of breaking that vow. The money was contained in a bag of chamois leather, of respectable dimensions, which my banker had given me, and Miss Tina had to make a big fist to receive it. This she did with extreme solemnity, though I tried to treat the affair a little as a joke. It was in no jocular strain, yet it was with a clearness akin to a brightness that she inquired, weighing the money in her two palms: "Don't you think it's too much?" To which I replied that this would depend on the amount of pleasure I should get for it. Hereupon she turned away from me quickly, as she had done the day before, murmuring in a tone different from any she had used hitherto: "Oh pleasure, pleasure — there's no pleasure in this house!"

After that, for a long time, I never saw her, and I wondered the common chances of the day shouldn't have helped us to meet. It could only be evident that she was immensely on her guard against them; and in addition to this the house was so big that for each other we were lost in it. I used to look out for her hopefully as I crossed the sala in my comings and goings, but I was not rewarded with a glimpse of the tail of her dress. It was as if she never peeped out of her aunt's apartment. I used to wonder what she did there week after week and year after year. I had never met so stiff a policy of seclusion; it was more than keeping quiet — it was like hunted creatures feigning death. The two ladies appeared to have no visitors whatever and no sort of contact with the world. I judged at least that people couldn't have come to the house and that Miss Tina couldn't have gone out without my catching some view of it. I did what I disliked myself for doing — considering it but as once in a way: I questioned my servant about their habits and let him infer that I should be interested in any information he might glean. But he gleaned amazingly little for a knowing Venetian: it must be added that where there is a perpetual fast there are very few crumbs on the floor. His ability in other ways was sufficient, if not quite all I had attributed to him on the occasion of my first interview with Miss Tina. He had helped my gondolier to bring me round a boat-load of furniture; and when these articles had been carried to the top of the palace and distributed according to our associated wisdom he organised my household with such dignity as answered to its being composed exclusively of himself. He made me in short as comfortable as I could be with my indifferent prospects. I should have been glad if he had fallen in love with Miss Bordereau's maid, or, failing this, had taken her in aversion: either event might have brought about some catastrophe, and a catastrophe might have led to some parley. It was my idea that she would have been sociable, and I myself on various occasions saw her flit to and fro on domestic errands, so that I was sure she was accessible. But I tasted of no gossip from that fountain, and I afterwards learned that Pasquale's affections were fixed upon an object that made him heedless of other women. This was a young lady with a powdered face, a yellow cotton gown and much leisure, who used often to come to see him. She practised, at her convenience, the art of a stringer of beads — these ornaments are made in Venice to profusion; she had her pocket full of them and I used to find them on the floor of my apartment — and kept an eye on the possible rival in the house. It was not for me of course to make the domestics tattle, and I never said a word to Miss Bordereau's cook.

It struck me as a proof of the old woman's resolve to have nothing to do with me that she should never have sent me a receipt for my three months' rent. For some days I looked out for it and then, when I had given it up, wasted a good deal of time in wondering what her reason had been for neglecting so indispensable and familiar a form. At first I was tempted to send her a reminder; after which I put by the idea — against my judgement as to what was right in the particular case — on the general ground of wishing to keep quiet. If Miss Bordereau suspected me of ulterior aims she would suspect me less if I should be businesslike, and yet I consented not to be. It was possible she intended her omission as an impertinence, a visible irony, to show how she could overreach people who attempted to overreach her. On that hypothesis it was well to let her see that one didn't notice her little tricks. The real reading of the matter, I afterwards gathered, was simply the poor lady's desire to emphasise the fact that I was in the enjoyment of a favour as rigidly limited as it had been liberally bestowed. She had given me part of her house, but she wouldn't add to that so much as a morsel of paper with her name on it. Let me say that even at first this didn't make me too miserable, for the whole situation had the charm of its oddity. I foresaw that I should have a summer after my own literary heart, and the sense of playing with my opportunity was much greater after all than any sense of being played with. There could be no Venetian business without patience, and since I adored the place I was much more in the spirit of it for having laid in a large provision. That spirit kept me perpetual company and seemed to look out at me from the revived immortal face — in which all his genius shone — of the great poet who was my prompter. I had invoked him and he had come; he hovered before me half the time; it was as if his bright ghost had returned to earth to assure me he regarded the affair as his own no less than as mine and that we should see it fraternally and fondly to a conclusion. It was as if he had said: "Poor dear, be easy with her; she has some natural prejudices; only give her time. Strange as it may appear to you she was very attractive in 1820. Meanwhile, aren't we in Venice together, and what better place is there for the meeting of dear friends? See how it glows with the advancing summer; how the sky and the sea and the rosy air and the marble of the palaces all shimmer and melt together." My eccentric private errand became a part of the general romance and the general glory — I felt even a mystic companionship, a moral fraternity with all those who in the past had been in the service of art. They had worked for beauty, for a devotion; and what else was I doing? That element was in everything that Jeffrey Aspern had written, and I was only bringing it to light.

I lingered in the sala when I went to and fro; I used to watch — as long as I thought decent — the door that led to Miss Bordereau's part of the house. A person observing me might have supposed I was trying to cast a spell on it or attempting some odd experiment in hypnotism. But I was only praying it might open or thinking what treasure probably lurked behind it. I hold it singular, as I look back, that I should never have doubted for a moment that the sacred relics were there; never have failed to know the joy of being beneath the same roof with them. After all they were under my hand — they had not escaped me yet — and they made my life continuous, in a fashion, with the illustrious life they had touched at the other end. I lost myself in this satisfaction to the point of assuming — in my quiet extravagance — that poor Miss Tina also went back, and still went back, as I used to phrase it. She did indeed, the gentle spinster, but not quite so far as Jeffrey Aspern, who was simple hearsay to her quite as he was to me. Only she had lived for years with Juliana, she had seen and handled all mementoes and — even though she was stupid — some esoteric knowledge had rubbed off on her. That was what the old woman represented — esoteric knowledge; and this was the idea with which my critical heart used to thrill. It literally beat faster often of an evening when I had been out, as I stopped with my candle in the re-echoing hall on my way up to bed. It was as if at such a moment as that, in the stillness and after the long contradiction of the day, Miss Bordereau's secrets were in the air, the wonder of her survival more vivid. These were the acute impressions. I had them in another form, with more of a certain shade of reciprocity, during the hours I sat in the garden looking up over the top of my book at the closed windows of my hostess. In these windows no sign of life ever appeared; it was as if, for fear of my catching a glimpse of them, the two ladies passed their days in the dark. But this only emphasised their having matters to conceal; which was what I had wished to prove. Their motionless shutters became as expressive as eyes consciously closed, and I took comfort in the probability that, though invisible themselves, they kept me in view between the lashes.

I made a point of spending as much time as possible in the garden, to justify the picture I had originally given of my horticultural passion. And I not only spent time, but (hang it! as I said) spent precious money. As soon as I had got my rooms arranged and could give the question proper thought I surveyed the place with a clever expert and made terms for having it put in order. I was sorry to do this, for personally I liked it better as it was, with its weeds and its wild rich tangle, its sweet characteristic Venetian shabbiness. I had to be consistent, to keep my promise that I would smother the house in flowers. Moreover I clung to the fond fancy that by flowers I should make my way — I should succeed by big nosegays. I would batter the old women with lilies — I would bombard their citadel with roses. Their door would have to yield to the pressure when a mound of fragrance should be heaped against it. The place in truth had been brutally neglected. The Venetian capacity for dawdling is of the largest, and for a good many days unlimited litter was all my gardener had to show for his ministrations. There was a great digging of holes and carting about of earth, and after a while I grew so impatient that I had thoughts of sending for my "results" to the nearest stand. But I felt sure my friends would see through the chinks of their shutters where such tribute *couldn't* have been gathered, and might so make up their minds against my veracity. I possessed my soul, and finally, though the delay was long, perceived some appearances of bloom. This encouraged me, and I waited serenely enough till they multiplied. Meanwhile the real summer days arrived and began to pass, and as I look back upon them they seem to me almost the happiest of my life. I took more and more care to be in the garden whenever it was not too hot. I had an arbour arranged and a low table and an armchair put into it; and I carried out books and portfolios — I had always some business of writing in hand — and worked and waited and mused and hoped, while the golden hours elapsed and the plants drank in the light and the inscrutable old palace turned pale and then, as the day waned, began to recover and flush and my papers rustled in the wandering breeze of the Adriatic.

Considering how little satisfaction I got from it at first it is wonderful I shouldn't have grown more tired of trying to guess what mystic rites of ennui the Misses Bordereau celebrated in their darkened rooms; whether this had always been the tenor of their life and how in previous years they had escaped elbowing their neighbours. It was supposable they had then had other habits, forms and resources; that they must once have been young or at least middle-aged. There was no end to the questions it was possible to ask about them and no end to the answers it was not possible to frame. I had known many of my country-people in Europe and was familiar with the strange ways they were liable to take up there; but the Misses Bordereau formed altogether a new type of the American absentee. Indeed it was clear the American name had ceased to have any application to them — I had seen this in the ten minutes I spent in the old woman's room. You could never have said whence they came from the appearance of either of them; wherever it was they had long ago shed and unlearned all native marks and notes. There was nothing in them one recognised or fitted, and, putting the question of speech aside, they might have been Norwegians or Spaniards. Miss Bordereau, after all had been in Europe nearly three-quarters of a century; it appeared by some verses addressed to her by Aspern on the occasion of his own second absence from America — verses of which Cumnor and I had after infinite conjecture established solidly enough the date — that she was even then, as a girl of twenty, on the foreign side of the sea. There was a profession in the poem — I hope not just for the phrase — that he had come back for her sake. We had no real light on her circumstances at that moment, any more than we had upon her origin, which we believed to be of the sort usually spoken of as modest. Cumnor had a theory that she had been a governess in some family in which the poet visited and that, in consequence of her position, there was from the first something un-avowed, or rather something quite clandes-tine, in their relations. I on the other hand had hatched a little romance according to which she was the daughter of an artist, a painter or a sculptor, who had left the Western world, when the century was fresh, to study in the ancient schools. It was essential to my hypothesis that this amiable man should have lost his wife, should have been poor and unsuccessful and should have had a second daughter of a disposition quite different from Juliana's. It was also indispensable that he should have been accompanied to Europe by these young ladies and should have established himself there for the remainder of a struggling saddened life. There was a further implication that Miss Bordereau had had in her youth a perverse and reckless, albeit a generous and fascinating character, and that she had braved some wondrous chances. By what passions had she been ravaged, by what adventures and sufferings had she been blanched, what store of memories had she laid away for the monotonous future?

I asked myself these things as I sat spinning theories about her in my arbour and the bees droned in the flowers. It was incontestable that, whether for right or for wrong, most readers of certain of Aspern's poems (poems not as ambiguous as the sonnets — scarcely more divine, I think — of Shakespeare) had taken for granted that

Juliana had not always adhered to the steep footway of renunciation. There hovered about her name a perfume of impenitent passion, an intimation that she had not been exactly as the respectable young person in general. Was this a sign that her singer had betrayed her, had given her away, as we say nowadays, to posterity? Certain it is that it would have been difficult to put one's finger on the passage in which her fair fame suffered injury. Moreover was not any fame fair enough that was so sure of duration and was associated with works immortal through their beauty? It was a part of my idea that the young lady had had a foreign lover — and say an unedifying tragical rupture — before her meeting with Jeffrey Aspern. She had lived with her father and sister in a queer old-fashioned expatriated artistic Bohemia of the days when the esthetic was only the academic and the painters who knew the best models for *contadina* and *pifferaro* wore peaked hats and long hair. It was a society less awake than the coteries of to-day — in its ignorance of the wonderful chances, the opportunities of the early bird, with which its path was strewn — to tatters of old stuff and fragments of old crockery; so that Miss Bordereau appeared not to have picked up or have inherited many objects of importance. There was no enviable *bric-à-brac,* with its provoking legend of cheapness, in the room in which I had seen her. Such a fact as that suggested bareness, but none the less it worked happily into the sentimental interest I had always taken in the early movements of my countrymen as visitors to Europe. When Americans went abroad in 1820 there was something romantic, almost heroic in it, as compared with the perpetual ferryings of the present hour, the hour at which photography and other conveniences have annihilated surprise. Miss Bordereau had sailed with her family on a tossing brig in the days of long voyages and sharp differences; she had had her emotions on the top of yellow diligences, passed the night at inns where she dreamed of travellers' tales, and was most struck, on reaching the Eternal City, with the elegance of Roman pearls and scarfs and mosaic brooches. There was something touching to me in all that, and my imagination frequently went back to the period. If Miss Bordereau carried it there of course Jeffrey Aspern had at other times done so with greater force. It was a much more important fact, if one was looking at his genius critically, that he had lived in the days before the general transfusion. It had happened to me to regret that he had known Europe at all; I should have liked to see what he would have written without that experience, by which he had incontestably been enriched. But as his fate had ruled otherwise I went with him — I tried to judge how the general old order would have struck him. It was not only there, however, I watched him; the relations he had entertained with the special new had even a livelier interest. His own country after all had had most of his life, and his muse, as they said at that time, was essentially American. That was originally what I had prized him for: that at a period when our native land was nude and crude and provincial, when the famous "atmosphere" it is supposed to lack was not even missed, when literature was lonely there and art and form almost impossible, he had found means to live and write like one of the first; to be free and general and not at all afraid; to feel, understand and express everything.

5

I was seldom at home in the evening, for when I attempted to occupy myself in my apartments the lamplight brought in a swarm of noxious insects, and it was too hot for closed windows. Accordingly I spent the late hours either on the water — the moon-lights of Venice are famous — or in the splendid square which serves as a vast fore-court to the strange old church of Saint Mark. I sat in front of Florian's café eating ices, listening to music, talking with acquain-tances: the traveller will remember how the immense cluster of tables and little chairs stretches like a promontory into the smooth lake of the Piazza. The whole place, of a summer's evening, under the stars and with all the lamps, all the voices and light foot-steps on marble — the only sounds of the immense arcade that encloses it — is an open-air saloon dedicated to cooling drinks and to a still finer degustation, that of the splendid impressions received during the day. When I didn't prefer to keep mine to myself there was always a stray tourist, dis-encumbered of his Bädeker, to discuss them with, or some domesticated painter rejoicing in the return of the season of strong effects. The great basilica, with its low domes and bristling embroideries, the mystery of its mosaic and sculpture, looked ghostly in the tempered gloom, and the sea-breeze passed between the twin columns of the Piazzetta, the lintels of a door no longer guarded, as gently as if a rich curtain swayed there. I used sometimes on these occasions to think of the Misses Bordereau and of the pity of their being shut up in apartments which in the Venetian July even Venetian vastness couldn't relieve of some stuffiness. Their life seemed miles away from the life of the Piazza, and no doubt it was really too late to make the austere Juliana change her habits. But poor Miss Tina would have enjoyed one of Florian's ices, I was sure; sometimes I even had thoughts of carrying one home to her. Fortunately my patience bore fruit and I was not obliged to do anything so ridiculous.

One evening about the middle of July I came in earlier than usual — I forget what chance had led to this — and instead of going up to my quarters made my way into the garden. The temperature was very high; it was such a night as one would gladly have spent in the open air, and I was in no hurry to go to bed. I had floated home in my gondola, listening to the slow splash of the oar in the dark narrow canals, and now the only thought that occupied me was that it would be good to recline at one's length in the fragrant darkness on a garden-bench. The odour of the canal was doubtless at the bottom of that aspiration, and the breath of the garden, as I entered it, gave consistency to my purpose. It was delicious — just such an air as must have trembled with Romeo's vows when he stood among the thick flowers and raised his arms to his mistress's balcony. I looked at the windows of the palace to see if by chance the example of Verona — Verona being not far off — had been followed; but everything was dim, as usual, and everything was still. Juliana might on the summer nights of her youth have murmured down from open windows at Jeffrey Aspern, but Miss Tina was not a poet's mistress any more than I was a poet. This, however, didn't prevent my gratification from being great as I became aware on reaching the end of the garden that my younger padrona was seated in one of the bowers. At first I made out but an indistinct figure, not in the least counting on such an overture from one of my hostesses; it even occurred to me that some enamoured maid-servant had stolen in to keep a tryst with her sweetheart. I was going to turn away, not to frighten her, when the figure rose to its height and I recognised Miss Bordereau's niece. I must do myself the justice that I didn't wish to frighten her either, and much as I had longed for some such accident I should have been capable of retreating. It was as if I had laid a trap for her by coming home earlier than usual and by adding to that oddity my invasion of the garden. As she rose she spoke to me, and then I guessed that perhaps, secure in my almost inveterate absence, it was her nightly practice to take a lonely airing. There was no trap in truth, because I had had no suspicion. At first I took the words she uttered for an impatience of my arrival; but as she repeated them — I hadn't caught them clearly — I had the surprise of hearing her say: "Oh dear, I'm so glad you've come!" She and her aunt had in common the property of unexpected speeches. She came out of the arbour almost as if to throw herself in my arms.

I hasten to add that I escaped this ordeal and that she didn't even shake hands with me. It was an ease to her to see me and presently she told me why — because she was nervous when out-of-doors at night alone. The plants and shrubs looked so strange in the dark, and there were all sorts of queer sounds — she couldn't tell me what they were — like the noises of animals. She stood close to me, looking about her with an air of greater security but without any demonstration of interest in me as an individual. Then I felt how little nocturnal prowlings could have been her habit, and I was also reminded — I had been afflicted by the same in talking with her before I took possession — that it was impossible to allow too much for her simplicity.

"You speak as if you were lost in the backwoods," I cheeringly laughed. "How you manage to keep out of this charming place when you've only three steps to take to get into it is more than I've yet been able to discover. You hide away amazingly so long as I'm on the premises, I know; but I had a hope you peeped out a little at other times. You and your poor aunt are worse off than Carmelite nuns in their cells. Should you mind telling me how you exist without air, without exercise, without any sort of human contact? I don't see how you carry on the common business of life."

She looked at me as if I had spoken a strange tongue, and her answer was so little of one that I felt it make for irritation. "We go to bed very early — earlier than you'd believe." I was on the point of saying that this only deepened the mystery, but she gave me some relief by adding: "Before you came we weren't so private. But I've never been out at night."

"Never in these fragrant alleys, blooming here under your nose?"

"Ah," said Miss Tina, "they were never nice till now!" There was a finer sense in this and a flattering comparison, so that it seemed to me I had gained some advantage. As I might follow that further by establishing a good grievance I asked her why, since she thought my garden nice, she had never thanked me in any way for the flowers I had been sending up in such quantities for the previous three weeks. I had not been discouraged — there had been, as she would have observed, a daily armful; but I had been brought up in the common forms and a word of recognition now and then would have touched me in the right place.

"Why, I didn't know they were for me!"

"They were for both of you. Why should I make a difference?"

Miss Tina reflected as if she might be thinking of a reason for that, but she failed to produce one. Instead of this she asked abruptly: "Why in the world do you want so much to know us?"

"I ought after all to make a difference," I replied. "That question's your aunt's; it isn't yours. You wouldn't ask it if you hadn't been put up to it."

"She didn't tell me to ask you," Miss Tina replied without confusion. She was indeed the oddest mixture of shyness and straightness.

"Well, she has often wondered about it herself and expressed her wonder to you. She has insisted on it, so that she has put the idea into your head that I'm insufferably pushing. Upon my word I think I've been very discreet. And how completely your aunt must have lost every tradition of sociability, to see anything out of the way in the idea that respectable intelligent people, living as we do under the same roof, should occasionally exchange a remark! What could be more natural? We're of the same country and have at least some of the same tastes, since, like you, I'm intensely fond of Venice."

My friend seemed incapable of grasping more than one clause in any proposition, and she now spoke quickly, eagerly, as if she were answering my whole speech. "I'm not in the least fond of Venice. I should like to go far away!"

"Has she always kept you back so?" I went on, to show her I could be as irrelevant as herself.

"She told me to come out to-night; she has told me very often," said Miss Tina.

"It is I who wouldn't come. I don't like to leave her."

"Is she too weak, is she really failing?" I demanded, with more emotion, I think, than I meant to betray. I measured this by the way her eyes rested on me in the darkness. It embarrassed me a little, and to turn the matter off I continued genially: "Do let us sit down together comfortably somewhere — while you tell me all about her."

Miss Tina made no resistance to this. We found a bench less secluded, less confidential, as it were, than the one in the arbour; and we were still sitting there when I heard midnight ring out from those clear bells of Venice which vibrate with a solemnity of their own over the lagoon and hold the air so much more than the chimes of other places. We were together more than an hour, and our interview gave, as it struck me, a great lift to my undertaking. Miss Tina accepted the situation without a protest; she had avoided me for three months, yet now she treated me almost as if these three months had made me an old friend. If I had chosen I might have gathered from this that though she had avoided me she had given a good deal of consideration to doing so. She paid no attention to the flight of time — never worried at my keeping her so long away from her aunt. We talked freely, answering questions and asking them and not even taking advantage of certain longish pauses by which they were naturally broken to say she thought she had better go in. It was almost as if she were waiting for something — something I might say to her — and intended to give me my opportunity. I was the more struck by this as she told me how much less well her aunt had been for a good many days, and in a way that was rather new. She was markedly weaker; at moments she showed no strength at all; yet more than ever before she wished to be left alone. That was why she had told her to come out — not even to remain in her own room, which was alongside; she pronounced poor Miss Tina "a worry, a bore and a source of aggravation." She sat still for hours together, as if for long sleep; she had always done that, musing and dozing; but at such times formerly she gave, in breaks, some small sign of life, of interest, liking her companion to be near her with her work. This sad personage confided to me that at present her aunt was so motionless as to create the fear she was dead; moreover she scarce ate or drank — one couldn't see what she lived on. The great thing was that she still on most days got up; the serious job was to dress her, to wheel her out of her bedroom. She clung to as many of her old habits as possible and had always, little company as they had received for years, made a point of sitting in the great parlour.

I scarce knew what to think of all this — of Miss Tina's sudden conversion to sociability and of the strange fact that the more the old woman appeared to decline to her end the less she should desire to be looked after. The story hung indifferently together, and I even asked myself if it mightn't be a trap laid for me, the result of a design to make me show my hand. I couldn't have told why my companions (as they could only by courtesy be called) should have this purpose — why they should try to trip up so lucrative a lodger. But at any hazard I kept on my guard, so that Miss Tina shouldn't have occasion again to ask me what I might really be "up to." Poor woman, before we parted for the night my mind was at rest as to what *she* might be. She was up to nothing at all.

She told me more about their affairs than I had hoped; there was no need to be prying, for it evidently drew her out simply to feel me listen and care. She ceased wondering why I *should,* and at last, while describing the brilliant life they had led years before, she almost chattered. It was Miss Tina who judged it brilliant; she said that when they first came to live in Venice, years and years back — I found her essentially vague about dates and the order in which events had occurred — there was never a week they hadn't some visitor or didn't make some pleasant *passeggio* in the town. They had seen all the curiosities; they had even been to the Lido in a boat — she spoke as if I might think there was a way on foot; they had had a collation there, brought in three baskets and spread out on the grass. I asked her what people they had known and she said, Oh very nice ones — the Cavaliere Bombicci and the Contessa Altemura, with whom they had had a great friendship! Also English people — the Churtons and the Goldies and Mrs Stock-Stock, whom they had loved dearly; she was dead and gone, poor dear. That was the case with most of their kind circle — this expression was Miss Tina's own; though a few were left, which was a wonder considering how they had neglected them. She mentioned the names of two or three Venetian old women; of a certain doctor, very clever, who was so attentive — he came as a friend, he had really given up practice; of the *avvocato* Pochintesta, who wrote beautiful poems and had addressed one to her aunt. These people came to see them without fail every year, usually at the *capo d'anno,* and of old her aunt used to make them some little present — her aunt and she together: small things that she, Miss Tina, turned out with her own hand, paper lamp-shades, or mats for the decanters of wine at dinner, or those woollen things that in cold weather are worn on the wrists. The last few years there hadn't been many presents; she couldn't think what to make and her aunt had lost interest and never suggested. But the people came all the same; if the good Venetians liked you once they liked you for ever.

There was affecting matter enough in the good faith of this sketch of former social glories; the picnic at the Lido had remained vivid through the ages and poor Miss Tina evidently was of the impression that she had had a dashing youth. She had in fact had a glimpse of the Venetian world in its gossiping home-keeping parsimonious professional walks; for I noted for the first time how nearly she had acquired by contact the trick of the familiar soft-sounding almost infantile prattle of the place. I judged her to have imbibed this invertebrate dialect from the natural way the names of things and people — mostly purely local — rose to her lips. If she knew little of what they represented she knew still less of anything else. Her aunt had drawn in — the failure of interest in the table-mats and lamp-shades was a sign of that — and she hadn't been able to mingle in society or to entertain it alone; so that her range of reminiscence struck one as an old world altogether. Her tone, hadn't it been so decent, would have seemed to carry one back to the queer rococo Venice of Goldoni and Casanova. I found myself mistakenly think of her too as one of Jeffrey Aspern's contemporaries; this came from her having so little in common with my own. It was possible, I indeed reasoned, that she hadn't even heard of him; it might very well be that Juliana had forborne to lift for innocent eyes the veil that covered the temple of her glory. In this case she perhaps wouldn't know of the existence of the papers, and I welcomed that presumption — it made me feel more safe with her — till I remembered we had believed the letter of disavowal received by Cumnor to be in the handwriting of the niece. If it had been dictated to her she had of course to know what it was about;

though the effect of it withal was to repudiate the idea of any connexion with the poet. I held it probable at all events that Miss Tina hadn't read a word of his poetry. Moreover if, with her companion, she had always escaped invasion and research, there was little occasion for her having got it into her head that people were "after" the letters. People had not been after them, for people hadn't heard of them. Cumnor's fruitless feeler would have been a solitary accident.

When midnight sounded Miss Tina got up; but she stopped at the door of the house only after she had wandered two or three times with me round the garden. "When shall I see you again?" I asked before she went in; to which she replied with promptness that she should like to come out the next night. She added, however, that she shouldn't come — she was so far from doing everything she liked.

"You might do a few things *I* like," I quite sincerely sighed.

"Oh you — I don't believe you!" she murmured at this, facing me with her simple solemnity.

"Why don't you believe me?"

"Because I don't understand you."

"That's just the sort of occasion to have

faith." I couldn't say more, though I should have liked to, as I saw I only mystified her; for I had no wish to have it on my conscience that I might pass for having made love to her. Nothing less should I have seemed to do had I continued to beg a lady to "believe in me" in an Italian garden on a midsummer night. There was some merit in my scruples, for Miss Tina lingered and lingered: I made out in her the conviction that she shouldn't really soon come down again and the wish therefore to protract the present. She insisted, too, on making the talk between us personal to ourselves; and altogether her behaviour was such as would have been possible only to a perfectly artless and a considerably witless woman.

"I shall like the flowers better now that I know them also meant for me."

"How could you have doubted it? If you'll tell me the kind you like best I'll send a double lot."

"Oh I like them all best!" Then she went on familiarly: "Shall you study — shall you read and write — when you go up to your rooms?"

"I don't do that at night — at this season. The lamplight brings in the animals."

"You might have known that when you came."

"I did know it!"

"And in winter do you work at night?"

"I read a good deal, but I don't often write." She listened as if these details had a rare interest, and suddenly a temptation quite at odds with all the prudence I had been teaching myself glimmered at me in her plain mild face. Ah yes, she was safe and I could make her safer! It seemed to me from one moment to another that I couldn't wait longer — that I really must take a sounding. So I went on: "In general before I go to sleep (very often in bed; it's a bad habit, but I confess to it) I read some great poet. In nine cases out of ten it's a volume of Jeffrey Aspern."

I watched her well as I pronounced that name, but I saw nothing wonderful. Why should I indeed? Wasn't Jeffrey Aspern the property of the human race?

"Oh *we* read him — we *have* read him," she quietly replied.

"He's my poet of poets — I know him almost by heart."

For an instant Miss Tina hesitated; then her sociability was too much for her. "Oh by heart — that's nothing;" and, though dimly, she quite lighted. "My aunt used to know him, to know him" — she paused an instant and I wondered what she was going to say — "to know him as a visitor."

"As a visitor?" I guarded my tone.

"He used to call on her and take her out."

I continued to stare. "My dear lady, he died a hundred years ago!"

"Well," she said amusingly, "my aunt's a hundred and fifty."

"Mercy on us!" I cried; "why didn't you tell me before? I should like so to ask her about him."

"She wouldn't care for that — she wouldn't tell you," Miss Tina returned.

"I don't care what she cares for! She *must* tell me — it's not a chance to be lost."

"Oh you should have come twenty years ago. Then she still talked about him."

"And what did she say?" I eagerly asked.

"I don't know — that he liked her immensely."

"And she — didn't she like *him?*"

"She said he was a god." Miss Tina gave me this information flatly, without expression; her tone might have made it a piece of trivial gossip. But it stirred me deeply as she dropped the words into the summer night; their sound might have been the light rustle of an old unfolded love-letter.

"Fancy, fancy!" I murmured. And then:

"Tell me this, please — has she got a portrait of him? They're distressingly rare."

"A portrait? I don't know," said Miss Tina; and now there was discomfiture in her face. "Well, good-night!" she added; and she turned into the house.

I accompanied her into the wide dusky stone-paved passage that corresponded on the ground floor with our great sala. It opened at one end into the garden, at the other upon the canal, and was lighted now only by the small lamp always left for me to take up as I went to bed. An extinguished candle which Miss Tina apparently had brought down with her stood on the same table with it. "Good-night, good-night!" I replied, keeping beside her as she went to get her light. "Surely you'd know, shouldn't you, if she had one?"

"If she had what?" the poor lady asked, looking at me queerly over the flame of her candle.

"A portrait of the god. I don't know what I wouldn't give to see it."

"I don't know what she has got. She keeps her things locked up." And Miss Tina went away toward the staircase with the sense evidently of having said too much.

I let her go — I wished not to frighten

her — and I contented myself with re-marking that Miss Bordereau wouldn't have locked up such a glorious possession as that: a thing a person would be proud of and hang up in a prominent place on the parlour-wall. Therefore of course she hadn't any portrait. Miss Tina made no direct answer to this and, candle in hand, with her back to me, mounted two or three degrees. Then she stopped short and turned round, looking at me across the dusky space.

"Do you write — do you write?" There was a shake in her voice — she could scarcely bring it out.

"Do I write? Oh don't speak of my writing on the same day with Aspern's!"

"Do you write about *him* — do you pry into his life?"

"Ah that's your aunt's question; it can't be yours!" I said in a tone of slightly wounded sensibility.

"All the more reason then that you should answer it. Do you, please?"

I thought I had allowed for the falsehoods I should have to tell, but I found that in fact when it came to the point I hadn't. Be-sides, now that I had an opening there was a kind of relief in being frank. Lastly — it was perhaps fanciful, even fatuous — I guessed that Miss Tina personally wouldn't in the last resort be less my friend. So after a moment's hesitation I answered: "Yes, I've written about him and I'm looking for more material. In heaven's name have you got any?"

"Santo Dio!" she exclaimed without heeding my question; and she hurried upstairs and out of sight. I might count upon her in the last resort, but for the present she was visibly alarmed. The proof of it was that she began to hide again, so that for a fortnight I kept missing her. I found my patience ebbing, and after four or five days of this I told the gardener to stop the "floral tributes."

6

One afternoon, at last, however, as I came down from my quarters to go out, I found her in the sala: it was our first encounter on that ground since I had come to the house. She put on no air of being there by accident; there was an ignorance of such arts in her honest angular diffidence. That I might be quite sure she was waiting for me she mentioned it at once, but telling me with it that Miss Bordereau wished to see me: she would take me into the room at that moment if I had time. If I had been late for a love-tryst I would have stayed for this, and I quickly signified that I should be delighted to wait on my benefactress. "She wants to talk with you — to know you," Miss Tina said, smiling as if she herself appreciated that idea; and she led me to the door of her aunt's apartment. I stopped her a moment before she had opened it, looking at her with some curiosity. I told her that this was a great satisfaction to me and a great honour; but all the same I should like to ask what had made Miss Bordereau so markedly and suddenly change. It had been only the other day that she wouldn't suffer me near her. Miss Tina was not embarrassed by my question; she had as many little unexpected serenities, plausibilities almost, as if she told fibs, but the odd part of them was that they had on the contrary their source in her truthfulness.

"Oh my aunt varies," she answered; "it's so terribly dull — I suppose she's tired."

"But you told me she wanted more and more to be alone."

Poor Miss Tina coloured as if she found me too pushing. "Well, if you don't believe she wants to see you, I haven't invented it! I think people often are capricious when they're very old."

"That's perfectly true. I only wanted to be clear as to whether you've repeated to her what I told you the other night."

"What you told me?"

"About Jeffrey Aspern — that I'm looking for materials."

"If I had told her do you think she'd have sent for you?"

"That's exactly what I want to know. If she wants to keep him to herself she might have sent for me to tell me so."

"She won't speak of him," said Miss Tina. Then as she opened the door she added in a lower tone: "I told her nothing."

The old woman was sitting in the same place in which I had seen her last, in the same position, with the same mystifying bandage over her eyes. Her welcome was to turn her almost invisible face to me and show me that while she sat silent she saw me clearly. I made no motion to shake hands with her; I now felt too well that this was out of place for ever. It had been sufficiently enjoined on me that she was too sacred for trivial modernisms — too venerable to touch. There was something so grim in her aspect — it was partly the accident of her green shade — as I stood there to be measured, that I ceased on the spot to doubt her suspecting me, though I didn't in the least myself suspect that Miss Tina hadn't just spoken the truth. She hadn't betrayed me, but the old woman's brooding instinct had served her; she had turned me over and over in the long still hours and had guessed. The worst of it was that she looked terribly like an old woman who at a pinch would, even like Sardanapalus, burn her treasure. Miss Tina pushed a chair forward, saying to me, "This will be a good place for you to sit." As I took possession of it I asked after Miss Bordereau's health; expressed the hope that in spite of the very hot weather it was satisfactory. She answered that it was good enough — good enough; that it was a great thing to be alive.

"Oh as to that, it depends upon what you compare it with!" I returned with a laugh.

"I don't compare — I don't compare. If I did that I should have given everything up long ago."

I liked to take this for a subtle allusion to the rapture she had known in the society of Jeffrey Aspern — though it was true that such an allusion would have accorded ill with the wish I imputed to her to keep him buried in her soul. What it accorded with

93

was my constant conviction that no human being had ever had a happier social gift than his, and what it seemed to convey was that nothing in the world was worth speaking of if one pretended to speak of that. But one didn't pretend! Miss Tina sat down beside her aunt, looking as if she had reason to believe some wonderful talk would come off between us.

"It's about the beautiful flowers," said the old lady; "you sent us so many — I ought to have thanked you for them before. But I don't write letters and I receive company but at long intervals."

She hadn't thanked me while the flowers continued to come, but she departed from her custom so far as to send for me as soon as she began to fear they wouldn't come any more. I noted this; I remembered what an acquisitive propensity she had shown when it was a question of extracting gold from me, and I privately rejoiced at the happy thought I had had in suspending my tribute. She had missed it and was willing to make a concession to bring it back. At the first sign of this concession I could only go to meet her. "I'm afraid you haven't had many, of late, but they shall begin again immediately — to-morrow, to-night."

"Oh do send us some to-night!" Miss

Tina cried as if it were a great affair.

"What else should you do with them? It isn't a manly taste to make a bower of your room," the old woman remarked.

"I don't make a bower of my room, but I'm exceedingly fond of growing flowers, of watching their ways. There's nothing unmanly in that; it has been the amusement of philosophers, of statesmen in retirement; even, I think, of great captains."

"I suppose you know you can sell them — those you don't use," Miss Bordereau went on. "I daresay they wouldn't give you much for them; still, you could make a bargain."

"Oh I've never in my life made a bargain, as you ought pretty well to have gathered. My gardener disposes of them and I ask no questions."

"I'd ask a few, I can promise you!" said Miss Bordereau; and it was so I first heard the strange sound of her laugh, which was as if the faint "walking" ghost of her old-time tone had suddenly cut a caper. I couldn't get used to the idea that this vision of pecuniary profit was most what drew out the divine Juliana.

"Come into the garden yourself and pick them; come as often as you like; come every day. The flowers are all for you," I pursued, addressing Miss Tina and carrying off this veracious statement by treating it as an innocent joke. "I can't imagine why she doesn't come down," I added for Miss Bordereau's benefit.

"You must make her come; you must come up and fetch her," the old woman said to my stupefaction. "That odd thing you've made in the corner will do very well for her to sit in."

The allusion to the most elaborate of my shady coverts, a sketchy "summer-house," was irreverent; it confirmed the impression I had already received that there was a flicker of impertinence in Miss Bordereau's talk, a vague echo of the boldness or the archness of her adventurous youth and which had somehow automatically outlived passions and faculties. None the less I asked: "Wouldn't it be possible for you to come down there yourself? Wouldn't it do you good to sit there in the shade and the sweet air?"

"Oh sir, when I move out of this it won't be to sit in the air, and I'm afraid that any that may be stirring around me won't be particularly sweet! It will be a very dark shade indeed. But that won't be just yet," Miss Bordereau continued cannily, as if to correct any hopes this free glance at the last receptacle of her mortality might lead me to entertain. "I've sat here many a day and have had enough of arbours in my time. But I'm not afraid to wait till I'm called."

Miss Tina had expected, as I felt, rare conversation, but perhaps she found it less gracious on her aunt's side — considering I had been sent for with a civil intention — than she had hoped. As to give the position a turn that would put our companion in a light more favourable she said to me: "Didn't I tell you the other night that she had sent me out? You see I can do what I like!"

"Do you pity her — do you teach her to pity herself?" Miss Bordereau demanded, before I had time to answer this appeal. "She has a much easier life than I had at her age."

"You must remember it has been quite open to me," I said, "to think you rather inhuman."

"Inhuman? That's what the poets used to call the women a hundred years ago. Don't try that; you won't do as well as they!" Juliana went on. "There's no more poetry in the world — that *I* know of at least. But I won't bandy words with you," she said, and I well remember the old-fashioned artificial sound she gave the speech. "You make me talk, talk, talk! It isn't good for me at all." I got up at this and told her I would take no more of her time; but she detained me to put a question. "Do you remember, the day I saw you about the rooms, that you offered us the use of your gondola?" And when I assented promptly, struck again with her disposition to make a "good thing" of my being there and wondering what she now had in her eye, she produced: "Why don't you take that girl out in it and show her the place?"

"Oh dear aunt, what do you want to do with me?" cried the "girl" with a piteous quaver. "I know all about the place!"

"Well then go with him and explain!" said Miss Bordereau, who gave an effect of cruelty to her implacable power of retort. This showed her as a sarcastic profane cynical old woman. "Haven't we heard that there have been all sorts of changes in all these years? You ought to see them, and at your age — I don't mean because you're so young — you ought to take the chances that come. You're old enough, my dear, and this gentleman won't hurt you. He'll show you the famous sunsets, if they still go on — *do* they go on? The sun set for me so long ago. But that's not a reason. Besides,

I shall never miss you; you think you're too important. Take her to the Piazza; it used to be very pretty," Miss Bordereau continued, addressing herself to me. "What have they done with the funny old church? I hope it hasn't tumbled down. Let her look at the shops; she may take some money, she may buy what she likes."

Poor Miss Tina had got up, discountenanced and helpless, and as we stood there before her aunt it would certainly have struck a spectator of the scene that our venerable friend was making rare sport of us. Miss Tina protested in a confusion of exclamations and murmurs; but I lost no time in saying that if she would do me the honour to accept the hospitality of my boat I would engage she really shouldn't be bored. Or if she didn't want so much of my company the boat itself, with the gondolier, was at her service; he was a capital oar and she might have every confidence. Miss Tina, without definitely answering this speech, looked away from me and out of the window, quite as if about to weep, and I remarked that once we had Miss Bordereau's approval we could easily come to an understanding. We would take an hour, whichever she liked, one of the very next days. As I made my obeisance to the old lady I asked her if she would kindly permit me to see her again.

For a moment she kept me; then she said: "Is it very necessary to your happiness?"

"It diverts me more than I can say."

"You're wonderfully civil. Don't you know it almost kills me?"

"How can I believe that when I see you more animated, more brilliant than when I came in?"

"That's very true, aunt," said Miss Tina. "I think it does you good."

"Isn't it touching, the solicitude we each have that the other shall enjoy herself?" sneered Miss Bordereau. "If you think me brilliant to-day you don't know what you're talking about; you've never seen an agreeable woman. What do you people know about good society?" she cried; but before I could tell her, "Don't try to pay me a compliment; I've been spoiled," she went on. "My door's shut, but you may sometimes knock."

With this she dismissed me and I left the room. The latch closed behind me, but Miss Tina, contrary to my hope, had remained within. I passed slowly across the hall and before taking my way downstairs waited a little. My hope was answered; after a minute my conductress followed me.

"That's a delightful idea about the Piazza," I said. "When will you go — to-night, to-morrow?"

She had been disconcerted, as I have mentioned, but I had already perceived, and I was to observe again, that when Miss Tina was embarrassed she didn't — as most women would have in like case — turn away, floundering and hedging, but came closer, as it were, with a deprecating, a clinging appeal to be spared, to be protected. Her attitude was a constant prayer for aid and explanation, and yet no woman in the world could have been less of a comedian. From the moment you were kind to her she depended on you absolutely; her self-consciousness dropped and she took the greatest intimacy, the innocent intimacy that was all she could conceive, for granted. She didn't know, she now declared, what possessed her aunt, who had changed so quickly, who had got some idea. I replied that she must catch the idea and let me have it: we would go and take an ice together at Florian's and she should report while we listened to the band.

"Oh it will take me a long time to be able to 'report'!" she said rather ruefully; and she could promise me this satisfaction neither for that night nor for the next. I

101

was patient now, however, for I felt I had only to wait; and in fact at the end of the week, one lovely evening after dinner, she stepped into my gondola, to which in honour of the occasion I had attached a second oar.

We swept in the course of five minutes into the Grand Canal; whereupon she uttered a murmur of ecstasy as fresh as if she had been a tourist just arrived. She had forgotten the splendour of the great water-way on a clear summer evening, and how the sense of floating between marble palaces and reflected lights disposed the mind to freedom and ease. We floated long and far, and though my friend gave no high-pitched voice to her glee I was sure of her full surrender. She was more than pleased, she was transported; the whole thing was an immense liberation. The gondola moved with slow strokes, to give her time to enjoy it, and she listened to the splash of the oars, which grew louder and more musically liquid as we passed into narrow canals, as if it were a revelation of Venice. When I asked her how long it was since she had thus floated she answered: "Oh I don't know; a long time — not since my aunt began to be ill." This was not the only show of her extreme vagueness about the previous years and the line marking off the period of Miss Bordereau's eminence. I was not at liberty to keep her out long, but we took a considerable *giro* before going to the Piazza. I asked her no questions, holding off by design from her life at home and the things I wanted to know; I poured, rather, treasures of information about the objects before and around us into her ears, describing also Florence and Rome, discoursing on the charms and advantages of travel. She reclined, receptive, on the deep leather cushions, turned her eyes conscientiously to everything I noted and never mentioned to me till some time afterwards that she might be supposed to know Florence better than I, as she had lived there for years with her kinswoman. At last she said with the shy impatience of a child: "Are we not really going to the Piazza? That's what I want to see!" I immediately gave the order that we should go straight after which we sat silent with the expectation of arrival. As some time still passed, however, she broke out of her own movement: "I've found out what's the matter with my aunt: she's afraid you'll go!"

I quite gasped. "What has put that into her head?"

"She has had an idea you've not been

happy. That's why she's different now."

"You mean she wants to make me happier?"

"Well, she wants you not to go. She wants you to stay."

"I suppose you mean on account of the rent," I remarked candidly.

Miss Tina's candour but profited. "Yes, you know; so that I shall have more."

"How much does she want you to have?" I asked with all the gaiety I now felt. "She ought to fix the sum, so that I may stay till it's made up."

"Oh that wouldn't please me," said Miss Tina. "It would be unheard of, your taking that trouble."

"But suppose I should have my own reasons for staying in Venice?"

"Then it would be better for you to stay in some other house."

"And what would your aunt say to that?"

"She wouldn't like it at all. But I should think you'd do well to give up your reasons and go away altogether."

"Dear Miss Tina," I said, "it's not so easy to give up my reasons!"

She made no immediate answer to this, but after a moment broke out afresh: "I think I know what your reasons are!"

"I daresay, because the other night I

almost told you how I wished you'd help me to make them good."

"I can't do that without being false to my aunt."

"What do you mean by being false to her?"

"Why, she would never consent to what you want. She has been asked, she has been written to. It makes her fearfully angry."

"Then she *has* papers of value?" I precipitately cried.

"Oh she has everything!" sighed Miss Tina with a curious weariness, a sudden lapse into gloom.

These words caused all my pulses to throb, for I regarded them as precious evidence. I felt them too deeply to speak, and in the interval the gondola approached the Piazzetta. After we had disembarked I asked my companion if she would rather walk round the square or go and sit before the great café; to which she replied that she would do whichever I liked best — I must only remember again how little time she had. I assured her there was plenty to do both, and we made the circuit of the long arcades. Her spirits revived at the sight of the bright shop-windows, and she lingered and stopped, admiring or disapproving of their contents, asking me what I thought of things, theorising about prices. My attention wandered from her; her words of a while before, "Oh she has everything!" echoed so in my consciousness. We sat down at last in the crowded circle at Florian's, finding an unoccupied table among those that were ranged in the square. It was a splendid night and all the world out-of-doors; Miss Tina couldn't have wished the elements more auspicious for her return to society. I saw she felt it all even more than she told, but her impressions were well-nigh too many for her. She had forgotten the attraction of the world and was learning that she had for the best years of her life been rather mercilessly cheated of it. This didn't make her angry; but as she took in the charming scene her face had, in spite of its smile of appreciation, the flush of a wounded surprise. She didn't speak, sunk in the sense of opportunities, for ever lost, that ought to have been easy; and this gave me a chance to say to her: "Did you mean a while ago that your aunt has a plan of keeping me on by admitting me occasionally to her presence?"

"She thinks it will make a difference with you if you sometimes see her. She wants you so much to stay that she's willing to make that concession."

"And what good does she consider I think it will do me to see her?"

"I don't know; it must be interesting," said Miss Tina simply. "You told her you found it so."

"So I did; but every one doesn't think that."

"No, of course not, or more people would try."

"Well, if she's capable of making that reflexion she's capable also of making this further one," I went on: "that I must have a particular reason for not doing as others do, in spite of the interest she offers — for not leaving her alone." Miss Tina looked as if she failed to grasp this rather complicated proposition; so I continued: "If you've not told her what I said to you the other night may she not at least have guessed it?"

"I don't know — she's very suspicious."

"But she hasn't been made so by indiscreet curiosity, by persecution?"

"No, no; it isn't that," said Miss Tina, turning on me a troubled face. "I don't know how to say it: it's on account of something — ages ago, before I was born — in her life."

"Something? What sort of thing?" — and

I asked it as if I could have no idea.

"Oh she has never told me." And I was sure my friend spoke the truth.

Her extreme limpidity was almost provoking, and I felt for the moment that she would have been more satisfactory if she had been less ingenuous. "Do you suppose it's something to which Jeffrey Aspern's letters and papers — I mean the things in her possession — have reference?"

"I daresay it is!" my companion exclaimed as if this were a very happy suggestion. "I've never looked at any of those things."

"None of them? Then how do you know what they are?"

"I don't," said Miss Tina placidly. "I've never had them in my hands. But I've seen them when she has had them out."

"Does she have them out often?"

"Not now, but she used to. She's very fond of them."

"In spite of their being compromising?"

"Compromising?" Miss Tina repeated as if vague as to what that meant. I felt almost as one who corrupts the innocence of youth.

"I allude to their containing painful memories."

"Oh I don't think anything's painful."

"You mean there's nothing to affect her reputation?"

An odder look even than usual came at this into the face of Miss Bordereau's niece — a confession, it seemed, of helplessness, an appeal to me to deal fairly, generously with her. I had brought her to the Piazza, placed her among charming influences, paid her an attention she appreciated, and now I appeared to show it all as a bribe — a bribe to make her turn in some way against her aunt. She was of a yielding nature and capable of doing almost anything to please a person markedly kind to her; but the greatest kindness of all would be not to presume too much on this. It was strange enough, as I afterwards thought, that she had not the least air of resenting my want of consideration for her aunt's character, which would have been in the worst possible taste if anything less vital — from my point of view — had been at stake. I don't think she really measured it. "Do you mean she ever did something bad?" she asked in a moment.

"Heaven forbid I should say so, and it's none of my business. Besides, if she did," I agreeably put it, "that was in other ages, in another world. But why shouldn't she destroy her papers?"

"Oh she loves them too much."

"Even now, when she may be near her end?"

"Perhaps when she's sure of that she will."

"Well, Miss Tina," I said, "that's just what I should like you to prevent."

"How can I prevent it?"

"Couldn't you get them away from her?"

"And give them to you?"

This put the case, superficially, with sharp irony, but I was sure of her not intending that. "Oh I mean that you might let me see them and look them over. It isn't for myself, or that I should want them at any cost to any one else. It's simply that they would be of such immense interest to the public, such immeasurable importance as a contribution to Jeffrey Aspern's history."

She listened to me in her usual way, as if I abounded in matters she had never heard of, and I felt almost as base as the reporter of a newspaper who forces his way into a house of mourning. This was marked when she presently said: "There was a gentleman who some time ago wrote to her in very much those words. He also wanted her papers."

"And did she answer him?" I asked, rather ashamed of not having my friend's rectitude.

"Only when he had written two or three times. He made her very angry."

"And what did she say?"

"She said he was a devil," Miss Tina replied categorically.

"She used that expression in her letter?"

"Oh no; she said it to me. She made me write to him."

"And what did you say?"

"I told him there were no papers at all."

"Ah poor gentleman!" I groaned.

"I knew there were, but I wrote what she bade me."

"Of course you had to do that. But I hope I shan't pass for a devil."

"It will depend upon what you ask me to do for you," my companion smiled.

"Oh if there's a chance of *your* thinking so my affair's in a bad way! I shan't ask you to steal for me, nor even to fib — for you *can't* fib, unless on paper. But the principal thing is this — to prevent her destroying the papers."

"Why, I've no control of her," said Miss Tina. "It's she who controls me."

"But she doesn't control her own arms and legs, does she? The way she would naturally destroy her letters would be to burn them. Now she can't burn them without fire, and she can't get fire unless you give it her."

"I've always done everything she has asked," my poor friend pleaded. "Besides, there's Olimpia."

I was on the point of saying that Olimpia was probably corruptible, but I thought it best not to sound that note. So I simply put it that this frail creature might perhaps be managed.

"Every one can be managed by my aunt," said Miss Tina. And then she remembered that her holiday was over; she must go home.

I laid my hand on her arm, across the table, to stay her a moment. "What I want of you is a general promise to help me."

"Oh how *can* I, how *can* I?" she asked, wondering and troubled. She was half-surprised, half-frightened at my attaching that importance to her, at my calling on her for action.

"This is the main thing: to watch our friend carefully and warn me in time, before she commits that dreadful sacrilege."

"I can't watch her when she makes me go out."

"That's very true."

"And when you do too."

"Mercy on us — do you think she'll have done anything tonight?"

"I don't know. She's very cunning."

"Are you trying to frighten me?" I asked.

I felt this question sufficiently answered when my companion murmured in a musing, almost envious way: "Oh but she loves them — she loves them!"

This reflexion, repeated with such emphasis, gave me great comfort; but to obtain more of that balm I said: "If she shouldn't intend to destroy the objects we speak of before her death she'll probably have made some disposition by will."

"By will?"

"Hasn't she made a will for your benefit?"

"Ah she has so little to leave. That's why she likes money," said Miss Tina.

"Might I ask, since we're really talking things over, what you and she live on?"

"On some money that comes from America, from a gentleman — I think a lawyer — in New York. He sends it every quarter. It isn't much!"

"And won't she have disposed of that?"

My companion hesitated — I saw she was blushing. "I believe it's mine," she said; and the look and tone which accompanied these words betrayed so the absence of the habit of thinking of herself that I almost thought her charming. The next instant she added: "But she had in an *avvocato* here once, ever so long ago. And some people came and signed something."

"They were probably witnesses. And you weren't asked to sign? Well then," I argued, rapidly and hopefully, "it's because you're the legatee. She must have left all her documents to you!"

"If she has it's with very strict conditions," Miss Tina responded, rising quickly, while the movement gave the words a small character of decision. They seemed to imply that the bequest would be accompanied with a proviso that the articles bequeathed should remain concealed from every inquisitive eye, and that I was very much mistaken if I thought her the person to depart from an injunction so absolute.

"Oh of course you'll have to abide by the terms," I said; and she uttered nothing to mitigate the rigour of this conclusion. None the less, later on, just before we disembarked at her own door after a return which had taken place almost in silence, she said to me abruptly: "I'll do what I can to help you." I was grateful for this — it was very well so far as it went; but it didn't keep me from remembering that night in a worried waking hour that I now had her word for it to re-enforce my own impression that the old woman was full of craft.

7

The fear of what this side of her character might have led her to do made me nervous for days afterwards. I waited for an intimation from Miss Tina; I almost read it as her duty to keep me informed, to let me know definitely whether or not Miss Bordereau had sacrificed her treasures. But as she gave no sign I lost patience and determined to put the case to the very touch of my own senses. I sent late one afternoon to ask if I might pay the ladies a visit, and my servant came back with surprising news. Miss Bordereau could be approached without the least difficulty; she had been moved out into the sala and was sitting by the window that overlooked the garden. I descended and found this picture correct; the old lady had been wheeled forth into the world and had a certain air, which came mainly perhaps from some brighter element in her dress, of being prepared again to have converse with it. It had not yet, however, begun to flock about her; she was perfectly alone and, though the door leading to her own quarters stood open, I had at first no glimpse of Miss Tina. The window at which she sat had the afternoon shade and, one of the shutters having been pushed back, she could see the pleasant garden, where the summer sun had by this time dried up too many of the plants — she could see the yellow light and the long shadows.

"Have you come to tell me you'll take the rooms for six months more?" she asked as I approached her, startling me by something coarse in her cupidity almost as much as if she hadn't already given me a specimen of it. Juliana's desire to make our acquaintance lucrative had been, as I have sufficiently indicated, a false note in my image of the woman who had inspired a great poet with immortal lines; but I may say here definitely that I after all recognised large allowance to be made for her. It was I who had kindled the unholy flame; it was I who had put into her head that she had the means of making money. She appeared never to have thought of that; she had been living wastefully for years, in a house five times too big for her, on a footing that I could explain only by the presumption that, excessive as it was, the space she enjoyed cost her next to nothing and that, small as were her revenues, they left her, for Venice, an appreciable margin. I had descended on her one day and taught her to calculate, and my almost extravagant comedy on the subject of the garden had presented me irresistibly in the light of a victim. Like all persons who achieve the miracle of changing their point of view late in life, she had been intensely converted: she had seized my hint with a desperate tremulous clutch.

I invited myself to go and get one of the chairs that stood, at a distance, against the wall — she had given herself no concern as to whether I should sit or stand; and while I placed it near her I began gaily:

"Oh dear madam, what an imagination you have, what an intellectual sweep! I'm a poor devil of a man of letters who lives from day to day. How can I take palaces by the year? My existence is precarious. I don't know whether six months hence I shall have bread to put in my mouth. I've treated myself for once; it has been an immense luxury. But when it comes to going on — !"

"Are your rooms too dear? If they are you can have more for the same money," Juliana responded. "We can arrange, we can *combinare*, as they say here."

"Well yes, since you ask me, they're too

dear, much too dear," I said. "Evidently you suppose me richer than I am."

She looked at me as from the mouth of her cave. "If you write books don't you sell them?"

"Do you mean don't people buy them? A little, a very little — not so much as I could wish. Writing books, unless one be a great genius — and even then! — is the last road to fortune. I think there's no more money to be made by good letters."

"Perhaps you don't choose nice subjects. What do you write about?" Miss Bordereau implacably pursued.

"About the books of other people. I'm a critic, a commentator, an historian, in a small way." I wondered what she was coming to.

"And what other people now?"

"Oh better ones than myself: the great writers mainly — the great philosophers and poets of the past; those who are dead and gone and can't, poor darlings, speak for themselves."

"And what do you say about them?"

"I say they sometimes attached themselves to very clever women!" I replied as for pleasantness. I had measured, as I thought, my risk, but as my words fell upon the air they were to strike me as imprudent.

However, I had launched them and I wasn't sorry, for perhaps after all the old woman would be willing to treat. It seemed tolerably obvious that she knew my secret: why therefore drag the process out? But she didn't take what I had said as a confession; she only asked:

"Do you think it's right to rake up the past?"

"I don't feel that I know what you mean by raking it up. How can we get at it unless we dig a little? The present has such a rough way of treading it down."

"Oh I like the past, but I don't like critics," my hostess declared with her hard complacency.

"Neither do I, but I like their discoveries."

"Aren't they mostly lies?"

"The lies are what they sometimes discover," I said, smiling at the quiet impertinence of this. "They often lay bare the truth."

"The truth is God's, it isn't man's: we had better leave it alone. Who can judge of it? — who can say?"

"We're terribly in the dark, I know," I admitted; "but if we give up trying what becomes of all the fine things? What becomes of the work I just mentioned, that of the great philosophers and poets? It's all vain words if there's nothing to measure it by."

"You talk as if you were a tailor," said Miss Bordereau whimsically; and then she added quickly and in a different manner: "This house is very fine; the proportions are magnificent. To-day I wanted to look at this part again. I made them bring me out here. When your man came just now to learn if I would see you I was on the point of sending for you to ask if you didn't mean to go on. I wanted to judge what I'm letting you have. This sala is very grand," she pursued like an auctioneer, moving a little, as I guessed, her invisible eyes. "I don't believe you often have lived in such a house, eh?"

"I can't often afford to!" I said.

"Well then how much will you give me for six months?"

I was on the point of exclaiming — and the air of excruciation in my face would have denoted a moral fact — "Don't, Juliana; for *his* sake, don't!" But I controlled myself and asked less passionately: "Why should I remain so long as that?"

"I thought you liked it," said Miss Bordereau with her shrivelled dignity.

"So I thought I should."

For a moment she said nothing more,

and I left my own words to suggest to her what they might. I half-expected her to say, coldly enough, that if I had been disappointed we needn't continue the discussion, and this in spite of the fact that I believed her now to have in her mind — however it had come there — what would have told her that my disappointment was natural. But to my extreme surprise she ended by observing: "If you don't think we've treated you well enough perhaps we can discover some way of treating you better." This speech was somehow so incongruous that it made me laugh again, and I excused myself by saying that she talked as if I were a sulky boy pouting in the corner and having to be "brought round." I hadn't a grain of complaint to make; and could anything have exceeded Miss Tina's graciousness in accompanying me a few nights before to the Piazza? At this the old woman went on: "Well, you brought it on yourself!" And then in a different tone: "She's a very fine girl." I assented cordially to this proposition, and she expressed the hope that I did so not merely to be obliging, but that I really liked her. Meanwhile I wondered still more what Miss Bordereau was coming to. "Except for me, to-day," she said, "she hasn't a relation in the world." Did she by describing her niece as amiable and unencumbered wish to represent her as a *parti?*

It was perfectly true that I couldn't afford to go on with my rooms at a fancy price and that I had already devoted to my undertaking almost all the hard cash I had set apart for it. My patience and my time were by no means exhausted, but I should be able to draw upon them only on a more usual Venetian basis. I was willing to pay the precious personage with whom my pecuniary dealings were such a discord twice as much as any other *padrona di casa* would have asked, but I wasn't willing to pay her twenty times as much. I told her so plainly, and my plainness appeared to have some success, for she exclaimed: "Very good; you've done what I asked — you've made an offer!"

"Yes, but not for half a year. Only by the month."

"Oh I must think of that then." She seemed disappointed that I wouldn't tie myself to a period, and I guessed that she wished both to secure me and to discourage me; to say severely: "Do you dream that you can get off with less than six months? Do you dream that even by the end of that time you'll be appreciably nearer your victory?" What was most in my mind was that she had a fancy to play me the trick of making me engage myself when in fact she had sacrificed her treasure. There was a moment when my suspense on this point was so acute that I all but broke out with the question, and what kept it back was but an instinctive recoil — lest it should be a mistake — from the last violence of self-exposure. She was such a subtle old witch that one could never tell where one stood with her. You may imagine whether it cleared up the puzzle when, just after she had said she would think of my proposal and without any formal transition, she drew out of her pocket with an embarrassed hand a small object wrapped in crumpled white paper. She held it there a moment and then resumed: "Do you know much about curiosities?"

"About curiosities?"

"About antiquities, the old gimcracks that people pay so much for to-day. Do you know the kind of price they bring?"

I thought I saw what was coming, but I said ingenuously: "Do you want to buy something?"

"No, I want to sell. What would an amateur give me for that?" She unfolded the white paper and made a motion for me to take from her a small oval portrait. I possessed myself of it with fingers of which I could only hope that they didn't betray the intensity of their clutch, and she added: "I would part with it only for a good price."

At the first glance I recognised Jeffrey Aspern, and was well aware that I flushed with the act. As she was watching me, however, I had the consistency to exclaim: "What a striking face! Do tell me who he is."

"He's an old friend of mine, a very distinguished man in his day. He gave it me himself, but I'm afraid to mention his name, lest you never should have heard of him, critic and historian as you are. I know the world goes fast and one generation forgets another. He was all the fashion when I was young."

She was perhaps amazed at my assurance, but I was surprised at hers; at her having the energy, in her state of health and at her time of life, to wish to sport with me to that tune simply for her private entertainment — the humour to test me and practise on me and befool me. This at least was the interpretation that I put upon her production of the relic, for I couldn't believe she really desired to sell it or cared for any information I might give her. What she wished was to dangle it before my eyes and put a prohibitive price on it. "The face comes back to me, it torments me," I said, turning the object this way and that and looking at it very critically. It was a careful but not a supreme work of art, larger than the ordinary miniature and representing a young man with a remarkably handsome face, in a high-collared green coat and a buff waistcoat. I felt in the little work a virtue of likeness and judged it to have been painted when the model was about twenty-five. There are, as all the world knows, three other portraits of the poet in existence, but none of so early a date as this elegant image. "I've never seen the original, clearly a man of a past age, but I've seen other reproductions of this face," I went on. "You expressed doubt of this generation's having heard of the gentleman, but he strikes me for all the world as a celebrity. Now who is he? I can't put my finger on him — I can't give him a label. Wasn't he a writer? Surely he's a poet." I was determined that it should be she, not I, who should first pronounce Jeffrey Aspern's name.

My resolution was taken in ignorance of Miss Bordereau's extremely resolute character, and her lips never formed in my hearing the syllables that meant so much for her. She neglected to answer my question, but raised her hand to take back the picture, using a gesture which though impotent was in a high degree peremptory. "It's only a person who should know for himself that would give me my price," she said with a certain dryness.

"Oh then you have a price?" I didn't restore the charming thing; not from any vindictive purpose, but because I instinctively clung to it. We looked at each other hard while I retained it.

"I know the least I would take. What it occurred to me to ask you about is the most I shall be able to get."

She made a movement, drawing herself together as if in a spasm of dread at having lost her prize, she had been impelled to the immense effort of rising to snatch it from me. I instantly placed it in her hand again, saying as I did so: "I should like to have it myself, but with your ideas it would be quite beyond my mark."

She turned the small oval plate over in her lap, with its face down, and I heard her catch her breath as after a strain or an escape. This, however, did not prevent her saying in a moment: "You'd buy a likeness of a person you don't know by an artist who has no reputation?"

"The artist may have no reputation, but that thing's wonderfully well painted," I replied, to give myself a reason.

"It's lucky you thought of saying that, because the painter was my father."

"That makes the picture indeed precious!" I returned with gaiety; and I may add that a part of my cheer came from this proof I had been right in my theory of Miss Bordereau's origin. Aspern had of course met the young lady on his going to her father's studio as a sitter. I observed to Miss Bordereau that if she would entrust me with her property for twenty-four hours I should be happy to take advice on it; but she made no other reply than to slip it in silence into her pocket. This convinced me still more that she had no sincere intention of selling it during her lifetime, though she may have desired to satisfy herself as to the sum her niece, should she leave it to her, might expect eventually to obtain for it. "Well, at any rate, I hope you won't offer it without giving me notice," I said as she remained irresponsive. "Remember me as a possible purchaser."

"I should want your money first!" she returned with unexpected rudeness; and then, as if she bethought herself that I might well complain of such a tone and wished to turn the matter off, asked abruptly what I talked about with her niece when I went out with her that way of an evening.

"You speak as if we had set up the habit," I replied. "Certainly I should be very glad if it were to become our pleasant custom. But in that case I should feel a still greater scruple at betraying a lady's confidence."

"Her confidence? Has my niece confidence?"

"Here she is — she can tell you herself," I said; for Miss Tina now appeared on the threshold of the old woman's parlour. "Have you confidence, Miss Tina? Your aunt wants very much to know."

"Not in her, not in her!" the younger lady declared, shaking her head with a dolefulness that was neither jocular nor affected. "I don't know what to do with her; she has fits of horrid imprudence. She's so easily tired — and yet she has begun to roam, to drag herself about the house." And she looked down at her yoke-fellow of long years with a vacancy of wonder, as if all their contact and custom hadn't made her perversities, on occasion, any more easy to follow.

"I know what I'm about. I'm not losing my mind. I daresay you'd like to think so," said Miss Bordereau with a crudity of cynicism.

"I don't suppose you came out here yourself. Miss Tina must have had to lend you a hand," I interposed for conciliation.

"Oh she insisted we should push her; and when she insists!" said Miss Tina, in the same tone of apprehension: as if there were no knowing what service she disapproved of her aunt might force her next to render.

"I've always got most things done I wanted, thank God! The people I've lived with have humoured me," the old woman continued, speaking out of the white ashes of her vanity.

I took it pleasantly up. "I suppose you mean they've obeyed you."

"Well, whatever it is — when they like one."

"It's just because I like you that I want to resist," said Miss Tina with a nervous laugh.

"Oh I suspect you'll bring Miss Bordereau upstairs next to pay me a visit," I went on; to which the old lady replied: "Oh no; I can keep an eye on you from here!"

"You're very tired; you'll certainly be ill to-night!" cried Miss Tina.

"Nonsense, dear; I feel better at this moment than I've done for a month. To-morrow I shall come out again. I want to be where I can see this clever gentleman."

"Shouldn't you perhaps see me better in your sitting-room?" I asked.

"Don't you mean shouldn't you have a better chance at *me?*" she returned, fixing me a moment with her green shade.

"Ah I haven't that anywhere! I look at you but don't see you."

"You agitate her dreadfully — and that's not good," said Miss Tina, giving me a reproachful deterrent headshake.

"I want to watch you — I want to watch you!" Miss Bordereau went on.

"Well then let us spend as much of our time together as possible — I don't care where. That will give you every facility."

"Oh I've seen you enough for to-day. I'm satisfied. Now I'll go home," Juliana said. Miss Tina laid her hands on the back of the wheeled chair and began to push, but I begged her to let me take her place. "Oh yes, you may move me this way — you shan't in any other!" the old woman cried as she felt herself propelled firmly and easily over the smooth hard floor. Before we reached the door of her own apartment she bade me stop, and she took a long last look up and down the noble sala. "Oh it's a prodigious house!" she murmured; after which I pushed her forward. When we had entered the parlour Miss Tina let me know she should now be able to manage, and at the same moment the little red-haired *donna* came to meet her mistress. Miss Tina's idea was evidently to get her aunt immediately back to bed. I confess that in spite of this urgency I was guilty of the indiscretion of lingering; it held me there to feel myself so close to the objects I coveted — which would be probably put away somewhere in the faded unsociable room. The place had indeed a bareness that suggested no hidden values; there were neither dusky nooks nor curtained corners, neither massive cabinets nor chests with iron bands. Moreover it was possible, it was perhaps even likely, that the old lady had consigned her relics to her bedroom, to some battered box that was shoved under the bed, to the drawer of some lame dressing-table, where they would be in the range of vision by the dim night-lamp. None the less I turned an eye on every article of furniture, on every conceivable cover for a hoard, and noticed that there were half a dozen things with drawers, and in particular a tall old secretary with brass ornaments of the style of the Empire — a receptacle somewhat infirm but still capable of keeping rare secrets. I don't know why this article so engaged me, small purpose as I had of breaking into it; but I stared at it so hard that Miss Tina noticed me and changed colour. Her doing this made me think I was right and that, wherever they might have been before, the Aspern papers at that moment languished behind the peevish little lock of the secretary. It was hard to turn my attention from the dull mahogany front when I reflected that a plain panel divided me from the goal of my hopes; but I gathered up my slightly scattered prudence and with an effort took leave of my hostess. To make the effort graceful I said to her that I should certainly bring her an opinion about the little picture.

"The little picture?" Miss Tina asked in surprise.

"What do *you* know about it, my dear?" the old woman demanded. "You needn't mind. I've fixed my price."

"And what may that be?"

"A thousand pounds."

"Oh Lord!" cried poor Miss Tina irrepressibly.

"Is that what she talks to you about?" said Miss Bordereau.

"Imagine your aunt's wanting to know!" I had to separate from my younger friend with only those words, though I should have liked immensely to add: "For heaven's sake meet me to-night in the garden!"

8

As it turned out the precaution had not been needed, for three hours later, just as I had finished my dinner, Miss Tina appeared, unannounced, in the open doorway of the room in which my simple repasts were served. I remember well that I felt no surprise at seeing her; which is not a proof of my not believing in her timidity. It was immense, but in a case in which there was a particular reason for boldness it never would have prevented her from running up to my floor. I saw that she was not quite full of a particular reason; it threw her forward — made her seize me, as I rose to meet her, by the arm.

"My aunt's very ill; I think she's dying!"

"Never in the world," I answered bitterly. "Don't you be afraid!"

"Do go for a doctor — do, do! Olimpia's gone for the one we always have, but she doesn't come back; I don't know what has happened to her. I told her that if he wasn't at home she was to follow him where he had gone; but apparently she's following him all over Venice. I don't know what to do — she looks so as if she were sinking."

"May I see her, may I judge?" I asked. "Of course I shall be delighted to bring some one; but hadn't we better send my man instead, so that I may stay with you?"

Miss Tina assented to this and I despatched my servant for the best doctor in the neighbourhood. I hurried downstairs with her, and on the way she told me that an hour after I quitted them in the afternoon Miss Bordereau had had an attack of "oppression," a terrible difficulty in breathing. This had subsided, but had left her so exhausted that she didn't come up; she seemed all spent and gone. I repeated that she wasn't gone, that she wouldn't go yet; whereupon Miss Tina gave me a sharper sidelong glance than she had ever favoured me withal and said: "Really, what do you mean? I suppose you don't accuse her of making-believe!" I forget what reply I made to this, but I fear that in my heart I thought the old woman capable of any weird manœuvre. Miss Tina wanted to know what I had done to her; her aunt had told her I had made her so angry. I declared I had done nothing whatever — I had been exceedingly careful; to which my companion rejoined that our friend had assured her she had had a scene with me — a scene that had upset her. I answered with some resentment that the scene had been of *her* making — that I couldn't think what she was angry with me for unless for not seeing my way to give a thousand pounds for the portrait of Jeffrey Aspern. "And did she show you that? Oh gracious — oh deary me!" groaned Miss Tina, who seemed to feel the situation pass out of her control and the elements of her fate thicken round her. I answered her I'd give anything to possess it, yet that I had no thousand pounds; but I stopped when we came to the door of Miss Bordereau's room. I had an immense curiosity to pass it, but I thought it my duty to represent to Miss Tina that if I made the invalid angry she ought perhaps to be spared the sight of me. "The sight of you? Do you think she can *see?*" my companion demanded almost with indignation. I did think so but forebore to say it, and I softly followed my conductress.

I remember that what I said to her as I

stood for a moment beside the old woman's bed was: "Does she never show you her eyes then? Have you never seen them?" Miss Bordereau had been divested of her green shade, but — it was not my fortune to behold Juliana in her nightcap — the upper half of her face was covered by the fall of a piece of dingy lace-like muslin, a sort of extemporised hood which, wound round her head, descended to the end of her nose, leaving nothing visible but her white withered cheeks and puckered mouth, closed tightly and, as it were, consciously. Miss Tina gave me a glance of surprise, evidently not seeing a reason for my impatience. "You mean she always wears something? She does it to preserve them."

"Because they're so fine?"

"Oh to-day, to-day!" And Miss Tina shook her head speaking very low. "But they used to be magnificent!"

"Yes indeed — we've Aspern's word for that." And as I looked again at the old woman's wrappings I could imagine her not having wished to allow any supposition that the great poet had overdone it. But I didn't waste my time in considering Juliana, in whom the appearance of respiration was so slight as to suggest that no human attention could ever help her more. I turned my eyes once more all over the room, rummaging with them the closets, the chests of drawers, the tables. Miss Tina at once noted their direction and read, I think, what was in them; but she didn't answer it, turning away restlessly, anxiously, so that I felt rebuked, with reason, for an appetite well-nigh indecent in the presence of our dying companion. All the same I took another view, endeavouring to pick out mentally the receptacle to try first, for a person who should wish to put his hand on Miss Bordereau's papers directly after her death. The place was a dire confusion; it looked like the dressing-room of an old actress. There were clothes hanging over chairs, odd-looking shabby bundles here and there, and various pasteboard boxes piled together, battered, bulging and discoloured, which might have been fifty years old. Miss Tina after a moment noticed the direction of my eyes again, and, as if she guessed how I judged such appearances — forgetting I had no business to judge them at all — said, perhaps to defend herself from the imputation of complicity in the disorder:

"She likes it this way; we can't move things. There are old bandboxes she has had most of her life." Then she added, half-taking pity on my real thought: "Those things were there." And she pointed to a small low trunk which stood under a sofa that just allowed room for it. It struck me as a queer superannuated coffer, of painted wood, with elaborate handles and shrivelled straps and with the colour — it had last been endued with a coat of light green — much rubbed off. It evidently had travelled with Juliana in the olden time — in the days of adventures, which it had shared. It would have made a strange figure arriving at a modern hotel.

"*Were* there — they aren't now?" I asked, startled by Miss Tina's implication.

She was going to answer, but at that moment the doctor came in — the doctor whom the little maid had been sent to fetch and whom she had at last overtaken. My servant, going on his own errand, had met her with her companion in tow, and in the sociable Venetian spirit, retracing his steps with them, had also come up to the threshold of the padrona's room, where I saw him peep over the doctor's shoulder. I motioned him away the more instantly that the sight of his prying face reminded me how little I myself had to do there — an admonition confirmed by the sharp way the little doctor eyed me, his air of taking me for a rival who had the field before him. He was a short fat brisk gentleman who wore the tall hat of his profession and seemed to look at everything but his patient. He kept me still in range as if it struck him I too should be better for a dose, so that I bowed to him and left him with the women, going down to smoke a cigar in the garden. I was nervous; I couldn't go further; I couldn't leave the place. I don't know exactly what I thought might happen, but I felt it important to be there. I wandered about the alleys — the warm night had come on — smoking cigar after cigar and studying the light in Miss Bordereau's windows. They were open now, I could see; the situation was different. Sometimes the light moved, but not quickly; it didn't suggest the hurry of a crisis. Was the old woman dying or was she already dead? Had the doctor said that there was nothing to be done at her tremendous age but to let her quietly pass away? Or had he simply announced with a look a little more conventional that the end of the end had come? Were the other two women just going and coming over the offices that follow in such a case? It made me uneasy not to be nearer, as if I thought the doctor himself might carry away the papers with him. I bit my cigar hard while it assailed me again that perhaps there were now no papers to carry!

I wandered about an hour and more. I looked out for Miss Tina at one of the windows, having a vague idea that she might come there to give me some sign. Wouldn't she see the red tip of my cigar in the dark and feel sure I was hanging on to know what the doctor had said? I'm afraid it's a proof of the grossness of my anxieties that I should have taken in some degree for granted at such an hour, in the midst of the greatest change that could fall on her, poor Miss Tina's having also a free mind for them. My servant came down and spoke to me; he knew nothing save that the doctor had gone after a visit of half an hour. If he had stayed half an hour then Miss Bordereau was still alive: it couldn't have taken so long to attest her decease. I sent the man out of the house; there were moments when the sense of his curiosity annoyed me, and this was one of them. *He* had been watching my cigar-tip from an upper window, if Miss Tina hadn't; he couldn't know what I was after and I couldn't tell him, though I suspected in him fantastic private theories about me which he thought fine and which, had I more exactly known them, I should have thought offensive.

I went upstairs at last, but I mounted no higher than the sala. The door of Miss Bordereau's apartment was open, showing from the parlour the dimness of a poor candle. I went toward it with a light tread, and at the same moment Miss Tina appeared and stood looking at me as I approached. "She's better, she's better," she said even before I had asked. "The doctor has given her something; she woke up, came back to life while he was there. He says there's no immediate danger."

"No immediate danger? Surely he thinks her condition serious."

"Yes, because she had been excited. That affects her dreadfully."

"It will do so again then, because she works herself up. She did so this afternoon."

"Yes, she mustn't come out any more," said Miss Tina with one of her lapses into a deeper detachment.

"What's the use of making such a remark as that," I permitted myself to ask, "if you begin to rattle her about again the first time she bids you?"

"I won't — I won't do it any more."

"You must learn to resist her," I went on.

141

"Oh yes, I shall; I shall do so better if you tell me it's right."

"You mustn't do it for me — you must do it for yourself. It all comes back to you, if you're scared and upset."

"Well, I'm not upset now," said Miss Tina placidly enough. "She's very quiet."

"Is she conscious again — does she speak?"

"No, she doesn't speak, but she takes my hand. She holds it fast."

"Yes," I returned, "I can see what force she still has by the way she grabbed that picture this afternoon. But if she holds you fast how comes it that you're here?"

Miss Tina waited a little; though her face was in deep shadow — she had her back to the light in the parlour and I had put down my own candle far off, near the door of the sala — I thought I saw her smile ingenuously. "I came on purpose — I had heard your step."

"Why, I came on tiptoe, as soundlessly as possible."

"Well, I had heard you," said Miss Tina.

"And is your aunt alone now?"

"Oh no — Olimpia sits there."

On my side I debated. "Shall we then pass in there?" And I nodded at the parlour; I wanted more and more to be on the spot.

"We can't talk there — she'll hear us."

I was on the point of replying that in that case we'd sit silent, but I felt too much this wouldn't do, there was something I desired so immensely to ask her. Thus I hinted we might walk a little in the sala, keeping more at the other end, where we shouldn't disturb our friend. Miss Tina assented unconditionally; the doctor was coming again, she said, and she would be there to meet him at the door. We strolled through the fine superfluous hall, where on the marble floor — particularly as at first we said nothing — our footsteps were more audible than I had expected. When we reached the other end — the wide window, inveterately closed, connecting with the balcony that overhung the canal — I submitted that we had best remain there, as she would see the doctor arrive the sooner. I opened the window and we passed out on the balcony. The air of the canal seemed even heavier, hotter than that of the sala. The place was hushed and void; the quiet neighbourhood had gone to sleep. A lamp, here and there, over the narrow black water, glimmered in double; the voice of a man going homeward singing, his jacket on his shoulder and his hat on his ear, came to us from a distance. This didn't prevent the scene from being very *comme il faut,* as Miss Bordereau had called it the first time I saw her. Presently a gondola passed along the canal with its slow rhythmical plash, and as we listened we watched it in silence. It didn't stop, it didn't carry the doctor; and after it had gone on I said to Miss Tina:

"And where are they now — the things that were in the trunk?"

"In the trunk?"

"That green box you pointed out to me in her room. You said her papers had been there; you seemed to mean she had transferred them."

"Oh yes; they're not in the trunk," said Miss Tina.

"May I ask if you've looked?"

"Yes, I've looked — for you."

"How for me, dear Miss Tina? Do you mean you'd have given them to me if you had found them?" — and I fairly trembled with the question.

She delayed to reply and I waited. Suddenly she broke out: "I don't know what I'd do — what I wouldn't!"

"Would you look again — somewhere else?"

She had spoken with a strange unexpected emotion, and she went on in the same

144

tone: "I can't — I can't — while she lies there. It isn't decent."

"No, it isn't decent," I replied gravely. "Let the poor lady rest in peace." And the words, on my lips, were not hypocritical, for I felt reprimanded and shamed.

Miss Tina added in a moment, as if she had guessed this and were sorry for me, but at the same time wished to explain that I did push her, or at least harp on the chord, too much: "I can't deceive her that way. I can't deceive her — perhaps on her deathbed."

"Heaven forbid I should ask you, though I've been guilty myself!"

"You've been guilty?"

"I've sailed under false colours." I felt now I must make a clean breast of it, must tell her I had given her an invented name on account of my fear her aunt would have heard of me and so refuse to take me in. I explained this as well as that I had really been a party to the letter addressed them by John Cumnor months before.

She listened with great attention, almost in fact gaping for wonder, and when I had made my confession she said: "Then your real name — what is it?" She repeated it over twice when I had told her, accompanying it with the exclamation, "Gracious,

gracious!" Then she added: "I like your own best."

"So do I" — and I felt my laugh rueful. "Ouf! it's a relief to get rid of the other."

"So it was a regular plot — a kind of conspiracy?"

"Oh a conspiracy — we were only two," I replied, leaving out of course Mrs Prest.

She considered; I thought she was perhaps going to pronounce us very base. But this was not her way, and she remarked after a moment, as in candid impartial contemplation: "How much you must want them!"

"Oh I do, passionately!" I grinned, I fear, to admit. And this chance made me go on, forgetting my compunction of a moment before. "How can she possibly have changed their place herself? How can she walk? How can she arrive at that sort of muscular exertion? How can she lift and carry things?"

"Oh when one wants and when one has so much will!" said Miss Tina as if she had thought over my question already herself and had simply had no choice but that answer — the idea that in the dead of night, or at some moment when the coast was clear, the old woman had been capable of a miraculous effort.

"Have you questioned Olimpia? Hasn't she helped her — hasn't she done it for her?" I asked; to which my friend replied promptly and positively that their servant had had nothing to do with the matter, though without admitting definitely that she had spoken to her. It was as if she were a little shy, a little ashamed now, of letting me see how much she had entered into my uneasiness and had me on her mind. Suddenly she said to me without any immediate relevance:

"I rather feel you a new person, you know, now that you've a new name."

"It isn't a new one; it's a very good old one, thank fortune!"

She looked at me a moment. "Well, I do like it better."

"Oh if you didn't I would almost go on with the other!"

"Would you really?"

I laughed again, but I returned for all answer: "Of course if she can rummage about that way she can perfectly have burnt them."

"You must wait — you must wait," Miss Tina mournfully moralised; and her tone ministered little to my patience, for it seemed after all to accept that wretched possibility. I would teach myself to wait, I declared nevertheless; because in the first place I couldn't do otherwise and in the second I had her promise, given me the other night, that she would help me.

"Of course if the papers are gone that's no use," she said; not as if she wished to recede, but only to be conscientious.

"Naturally. But if you could only find out!" I groaned, quivering again.

"I thought you promised you'd wait."

"Oh you mean wait even for that?"

"For what then?"

"Ah nothing," I answered rather foolishly, being ashamed to tell her what had been implied in my acceptance of delay — the idea that she would perhaps do more for me than merely find out.

I know not if she guessed this; at all events she seemed to bethink herself of some propriety of showing me more rigour. "I didn't promise to deceive, did I? I don't think I did."

"It doesn't much matter whether you did or not, for you couldn't!"

Nothing is more possible than that she wouldn't have contested this even hadn't she been diverted by our seeing the doctor's gondola shoot into the little canal and approach the house. I noted that he came as fast as if he believed our proprietress still in danger. We looked down at him while he disembarked and then went back into the sala to meet him. When he came up, however, I naturally left Miss Tina to go off with him alone, only asking her leave to come back later for news.

I went out of the house and walked far, as far as the Piazza, where my restlessness declined to quit me. I was unable to sit down; it was very late now though there were people still at the little tables in front of the cafés: I could but uneasily revolve, and I did so half a dozen times. The only comfort, none the less, was in my having told Miss Tina who I really was. At last I took my way home again, getting gradually and all but inextricably lost, as I did whenever I went out in Venice: so that it was considerably past midnight when I reached my door. The sala, upstairs, was as dark as usual, and my lamp as I crossed it found nothing satisfactory to show me. I was disappointed, for I had notified Miss Tina that I would come back for a report, and I thought she might have left a light there as a sign. The door of the ladies' apartment was closed; which seemed a hint that my faltering friend had gone to bed in impatience of waiting for me. I stood in the middle of the place, considering, hoping she would hear me and perhaps peep out, saying to myself too that she would never go to bed with her aunt in a state so critical; she would sit up and watch — she would be in a chair, in her dressing-gown. I went nearer the door; I stopped there and listened. I heard nothing at all and at last I tapped gently. No answer came, and after another minute I turned the handle. There was no light in the room; this ought to have prevented my entrance, but it had no such effect. If I have frankly stated the importunities, the indelicacies, of which my desire to possess myself of Jeffrey Aspern's papers had made me capable I needn't shrink, it seems to me, from confessing this last indiscretion. I regard it as the worst thing I did, yet there were extenuating circumstances. I was deeply though doubtless not disinterestedly anxious for more news of Juliana, and Miss Tina had accepted from me, as it were, a rendezvous which it might have been a point of honour with me to keep. It may be objected that her leaving the place dark was a positive sign that she released me, and to this I can only reply that I wished not to be released.

The door of Miss Bordereau's room was open and I could see beyond it the faintness of a taper. There was no sound — my footstep caused no one to stir. I came farther into the room; I lingered there lamp in hand. I wanted to give Miss Tina a chance to come to me if, as I couldn't doubt, she were still with her aunt. I made no noise to call her; I only waited to see if she wouldn't notice my light. She didn't, and I explained this — I found afterwards I was right — by the idea that she had fallen asleep. If she had fallen asleep her aunt was not on her mind, and my explanation ought to have led me to go out as I had come. I must repeat again that it didn't, for I found myself at the same moment given up to something else. I had no definite purpose, no bad intention, but felt myself held to the spot by an acute, though absurd, sense of opportunity. Opportunity for what I couldn't have said, inasmuch as it wasn't in my mind that I might proceed to thievery. Even had this tempted me I was confronted with the evident fact that Miss Bordereau didn't leave her secretary, her cupboard and the drawers of her tables gaping. I had no keys, no tools and no ambition to smash her furniture. None the less it came to me that I was now, perhaps, alone, unmolested, at the hour of freedom and safety, nearer to the source of my hopes than I had ever been. I held up my lamp, let the light play on the different objects as if it could tell me something. Still there came no movement from the other room. If Miss Tina was sleeping she was sleeping sound. Was she doing so — generous creature — on purpose to leave me the field? Did she know I was there and was she just keeping quiet to see what I would do — what I *could* do? Yet might I, when it came to that? She herself knew even better than I how little.

I stopped in front of the secretary, gaping at it vainly and no doubt grotesquely; for what had it to say to me after all? In the first place it was locked, and in the second it almost surely contained nothing in which I was interested. Ten to one the papers had been destroyed, and even if they hadn't the keen old woman wouldn't have put them in such a place as that after removing them from the green trunk — wouldn't have transferred them, with the idea of their safety on her brain, from the better hiding-place to the worse. The secretary was more conspicuous, more exposed in a room in which she could no longer mount guard. It opened with a key, but there was a small brass handle, like a button, as well: I saw this as I played my lamp over it. I did something more, for the climax of my crisis; I caught a glimpse of the possibility that Miss Tina wished me really to understand. If she didn't so wish me, if she wished me to keep away, why hadn't she locked the door of communication between the sitting-room and the sala? That would have been a definite sign that I was to leave them alone. If I didn't leave them alone she meant me to come for a purpose — a purpose now represented by the super-subtle inference that to oblige me she had unlocked the secretary. She hadn't left the key, but the lid would probably move if I touched the button. This possibility pressed me hard and I bent very close to judge. I didn't propose to do anything, not even — not in the least — to let down the lid; I only wanted to test my theory, to see if the cover *would* move. I touched the button with my hand — a mere touch would tell me; and as I did so — it is embarrassing for me to relate it — I looked over my shoulder. It was a chance, an instinct, for I had really heard nothing. I almost let my luminary drop and certainly I stepped back, straightening myself up at what I saw. Juliana stood there in her night-dress, by the doorway of her room, watching me; her hands were raised, she had lifted the everlasting curtain that covered half her face, and for the first, the last, the only time I beheld her extraordinary eyes. They glared at me; they were like the sudden drench, for a caught burglar, of a flood of gaslight; they made me horribly ashamed. I never shall forget her strange little bent white tottering figure, with its lifted head, her attitude, her expression; neither shall I forget the tone in which as I turned, looking at her, she hissed out passionately, furiously:

"Ah you publishing scoundrel!"

I can't now say what I stammered to excuse myself, to explain; but I went toward her to tell her I meant no harm. She waved me off with her old hands, retreating before me in horror; and the next thing I knew she had fallen back with a quick spasm, as if death had descended on her, into Miss Tina's arms.

9

I left Venice the next morning, directly on learning that my hostess had not succumbed, as I feared at the moment, to the shock I had given her — the shock I may also say she had given me. How in the world could I have supposed her capable of getting out of bed by herself? I failed to see Miss

Tina before going; I only saw the *donna*, whom I entrusted with a note for her younger mistress. In this note I mentioned that I should be absent but a few days. I went to Treviso, to Bassano, to Castelfranco; I took walks and drives and looked at musty old churches with ill-lighted pictures; I spent hours seated smoking at the doors of cafés, where there were flies and yellow curtains, on the shady side of sleepy little squares. In spite of these pastimes, which were mechanical and perfunctory, I scantly enjoyed my travels: I had had to gulp down a bitter draught and couldn't get rid of the taste. It had been devilish awkward, as the young men say, to be found by Juliana in the dead of night examining the attachment of her bureau; and it had not been less so to have to believe for a good many hours after that it was highly probable I had killed her. My humiliation galled me, but I had to make the best of it, had, in writing to Miss Tina, to minimise it, as well as account for the posture in which I had been discovered. As she gave me no word of answer I couldn't know what impression I made on her. It rankled for me that I had been called a publishing scoundrel, since certainly I did publish and no less certainly hadn't been very delicate. There was a moment when I stood convinced that the only way to purge my dishonour was to take myself straight away on the instant; to sacrifice my hopes and relieve the two poor women for ever of the oppression of my intercourse. Then I reflected that I had better try a short absence first, for I must already have had a sense (unexpressed and dim) that in disappearing completely it wouldn't be merely my own hopes I should condemn to extinction. It would perhaps answer if I kept dark long enough to give the elder lady time to believe herself rid of me. That she would wish to be rid of me after this — if I wasn't rid of her — was now not to be doubted: that midnight monstrosity would have cured her of the disposition to put up with my company for the sake of my dollars. I said to myself that after all I couldn't abandon Miss Tina, and I continued to say this even while I noted that she quite ignored my earnest request — I had given her two or three addresses, at little towns, *poste restante* — for some sign of her actual state. I would have made my servant write me news but that he was unable to manage a pen. Couldn't I measure the scorn of Miss Tina's silence — little disdainful as she had ever been? Really the soreness pressed; yet if I had scruples about going back I had others about not doing so, and I wanted to put myself on a better footing. The end of it was that I did return to Venice on the twelfth day; and as my gondola gently bumped against our palace steps a fine palpitation of suspense showed me the violence my absence had done me.

I had faced about so abruptly that I hadn't even telegraphed to my servant. He was therefore not at the station to meet me, but he poked out his head from an upper window when I reached the house. "They have put her into earth, *quella vecchia*," he said to me in the lower hall while he shouldered my valise; and he grinned and almost winked as if he knew I should be pleased with his news.

"She's dead!" I cried, giving him a very different look.

"So it appears, since they've buried her."

"It's all over then? When was the funeral?"

"The other yesterday. But a funeral you could scarcely call it, signore: *roba da niente — un piccolo passeggio brutto* of two gondolas. *Poveretta!*" the man continued, referring apparently to Miss Tina. His conception of funerals was that they were mainly to amuse the living.

I wanted to know about Miss Tina, how she might be and generally where; but I asked him no more questions till we had got upstairs. Now that the fact had met me I took a bad view of it, especially of the idea that poor Miss Tina had had to manage by herself after the end. What did she know about arrangements, about the steps to take in such a case? Poveretta indeed! I could only hope the doctor had given her support and that she hadn't been neglected by the old friends of whom she had told me, the little band of the faithful whose fidelity consisted in coming to the house once a year. I elicited from my servant that two old ladies and an old gentleman had in fact rallied round Miss Tina and had supported her — they had come for her in a gondola of their own — during the journey to the cemetery, the little red-walled island of tombs which lies to the north of the town and on the way to Murano. It appeared from these signs that the Misses Bordereau were Catholics, a discovery I had never made, as the old woman couldn't go to church and her niece, so far as I perceived, either didn't, or went only to early mass in the parish before I was stirring. Certainly even the priests respected their seclusion; I had never caught the whisk of the curato's skirt. That evening, an hour later, I sent my servant down with five words on a card to ask if Miss Tina would see me a few moments. She was not in the house, where he had sought her, he told me when he came back, but in the garden walking about to refresh herself and picking the flowers quite as if they belonged to her. He had found her there and she would be happy to see me.

I went down and passed half an hour with poor Miss Tina. She had always had a look of musty mourning, as if she were wearing out old robes of sorrow that wouldn't come to an end; and in this particular she made no different show. But she clearly had been crying, crying a great deal — simply, satisfyingly, refreshingly, with a primitive retarded sense of solitude and violence. But she had none of the airs or graces of grief, and I was almost surprised to see her stand there in the first dusk with her hands full of admirable roses and smile at me with reddened eyes. Her white face, in the frame of her mantilla, looked longer, leaner than usual. I hadn't doubted her being irreconcilably disgusted with me, her considering I ought to have been on the spot to advise her, to help her; and, though I believed there was no rancour in her composition and no great conviction of the importance of her affairs, I had prepared myself for a change in her manner, for some air of injury and estrangement, which should say to my conscience: "Well, you're a nice person to have professed things!" But historic truth compels me to declare that this poor lady's dull face ceased to be dull, almost ceased to be plain, as she turned it gladly to her late aunt's lodger. That touched him extremely, and he thought it simplified his situation until he found it didn't. I was as kind to her that evening as I knew how to be, and I walked about the garden with her as long as seemed good. There was no explanation of any sort between us; I didn't ask her why she hadn't answered my letter. Still less did I repeat what I had said to her in that communication; if she chose to let me suppose she had forgotten the position in which Miss Bordereau had surprised me and the effect of the discovery on the old woman, I was quite willing to take it that way: I was grateful to her for not treating me as if I had killed her aunt.

We strolled and strolled, though really not much passed between us save the recognition of her bereavement, conveyed in my manner and in the expression she had of depending on me now, since I let her see

I still took an interest in her. Miss Tina's was no breast for the pride or the pretence of independence; she didn't in the least suggest that she knew at present what would become of her. I forbore to press on that question, however, for I certainly was not prepared to say that I would take charge of her. I was cautious; not ignobly, I think, for I felt her knowledge of life to be so small that in her unsophisticated vision there would be no reason why — since I seemed to pity her — I shouldn't somehow look after her. She told me how her aunt had died, very peacefully at the last, and how everything had been done afterwards by the care of her good friends — fortunately, thanks to me, she said, smiling, there was money in the house. She repeated that when once the "nice" Italians like you they are your friends for life, and when we had gone into this she asked me about my *giro*, my impressions, my adventures, the places I had seen. I told her what I could, making it up partly, I'm afraid, as in my discon-certed state I had taken little in; and after she had heard me she exclaimed, quite as if she had forgotten her aunt and her sorrow, "Dear, dear, how much I should like to do such things — to take an amusing little journey!" It came over me for the moment that I ought to propose some enterprise, say I would accompany her anywhere she liked; and I remarked at any rate that a pleasant excursion — to give her a change — might be managed: we would think of it, talk it over. I spoke never a word of the Aspern documents, asked no question as to what she had ascertained or what had otherwise happened with regard to them before Juliana's death. It wasn't that I wasn't on pins and needles to know, but that I thought it more decent not to show greed again so soon after the catastrophe. I hoped she herself would say something, but she never glanced that way, and I thought this natural at the time. Later on, however, that night, it occurred to me that her silence was matter for suspicion; since if she had talked of my movements, of anything so detached as the Giorgione at Castelfranco, she might have alluded to what she could easily remember was in my mind. It was not to be supposed the emotion produced by her aunt's death had blotted out the recollection that I was interested in that lady's relics, and I fidgeted afterwards as it came to me that her reticence might very possibly just mean that no relics survived. We separated in the garden — it was she who said she must go in; now that she was alone on the *piano nobile* I felt that (judged at any rate by Venetian ideas) I was on rather a different footing in regard to the invasion of it. As I shook hands with her for good-night I asked if she had some general plan, had thought over what she had best do. "Oh yes, oh yes, but I haven't settled anything yet," she replied quite cheerfully. Was her cheerfulness explained by the impression that I would settle for her?

I was glad the next morning that we had neglected practical questions, as this gave me a pretext for seeing her again immediately. There was a practical enough question now to be touched on. I owed it to her to let her know formally that of course I didn't expect her to keep me on as a lodger, as also to show some interest in her own tenure, what she might have on her hands in the way of a lease. But I was not destined, as befell, to converse with her for more than an instant on either of these points. I sent her no message; I simply went down to the sala and walked to and fro there. I knew she would come out; she would promptly see me accessible. Somehow I preferred not to be shut up with her; gardens and big halls seemed better places to talk. It was a splendid morning, with something in the air that told of the waning of the long Venetian summer; a freshness from the sea that stirred the flowers in the garden and made a pleasant draught in the house, less shuttered and darkened now than when the old woman was alive. It was the beginning of autumn, of the end of the golden months. With this it was the end of my experiment — or would be in the course of half an hour, when I should really have learned that my dream had been reduced to ashes. After that there would be nothing left for me but to go to the station; for seriously — and as it struck me in the morning light — I couldn't linger there to act as guardian to a piece of middle-aged female helplessness. If she hadn't saved the papers wherein should I be indebted to her? I think I winced a little as I asked myself how much, if she *had* saved them, I should have to recognise and, as it were, reward such a courtesy. Mightn't that service after all saddle me with a guardianship? If this idea didn't make me more uncomfortable as I walked up and down it was because I was convinced I had nothing to look to. If the old woman hadn't destroyed everything before she pounced on me in the parlour she had done so the next day.

It took Miss Tina rather longer than I had expected to act on my calculation; but when at last she came out she looked at me without surprise. I mentioned I had been waiting for her and she asked why I hadn't let her know. I was glad a few hours later on that I had checked myself before remarking that a friendly intuition might have told her: it turned to comfort for me that I hadn't played even to that mild extent on her sensibility. What I did say was virtually the truth — that I was too nervous, since I expected her now to settle my fate.

"Your fate?" said Miss Tina, giving me a queer look; and as she spoke I noticed a rare change in her. Yes, she was other than she had been the evening before — less natural and less easy. She had been crying the day before and was not crying now, yet she struck me as less confident. It was as if something had happened to her during the night, or at least as if she had thought of something that troubled her — something in particular that affected her relations with me, made them more embarrassing and more complicated. Had she simply begun to feel that her aunt's not being there now altered my position?

"I mean about our papers. *Are* there any? You must know now."

"Yes, there are a great many; more than I supposed." I was struck with the way her voice trembled as she told me this.

"Do you mean you've got them in there — and that I may see them?"

"I don't think you can see them," said Miss Tina with an extraordinary expression of entreaty in her eyes, as if the dearest hope she had in the world now was that I wouldn't take them from her. But how could she expect me to make such a sacrifice as that after all that had passed between us? What had I come back to Venice for but to see them, to take them? My joy at learning they were still in existence was such that if the poor woman had gone down on her knees to beseech me never to mention them again I would have treated the proceedings as a bad joke. "I've got them but I can't show them," she lamentably added.

"Not even to me? Ah Miss Tina!" I broke into a tone of infinite remonstrance and reproach.

She coloured and the tears came back to her eyes; I measured the anguish it cost her to take such a stand, which a dreadful sense of duty had imposed on her. It made me quite sick to find myself confronted with that particular obstacle; all the more that it seemed to me I had been distinctly encouraged to leave it out of account. I quite held Miss Tina to have assured me that if she had no greater hindrance than that — ! "You don't mean to say you made her a deathbed promise? It was precisely against your doing anything of that sort that I thought I was safe. Oh I would rather she had burnt the papers outright than have to reckon with such a treachery as that."

"No, it isn't a promise," said Miss Tina.

"Pray what is it then?"

She hung fire, but finally said: "She tried to burn them, but I prevented it. She had hid them in her bed."

"In her bed — ?"

"Between the mattresses. That's where she put them when she took them out of the trunk. I can't understand how she did it, because Olimpia didn't help her. She tells me so and I believe her. My aunt only told her afterwards, so that she shouldn't undo the bed — anything but the sheets. So it was very badly made," added Miss Tina simply.

"I should think so! And how did she try to burn them?"

"She didn't try much; she was too weak those last days. But she told me — she charged me. Oh it was terrible! She couldn't speak after that night. She could only make signs."

"And what did you do?"

"I took them away. I locked them up."

"In the secretary?"

"Yes, in the secretary," said Miss Tina, reddening again.

"Did you tell her you'd burn them?"

"No, I didn't — on purpose."

"On purpose to gratify me?"

"Yes, only for that."

"And what good will you have done me if after all you won't show them?"

"Oh none. I know that — I know that," she dismally sounded.

"And did she believe you had destroyed them?"

"I don't know what she believed at the last. I couldn't tell — she was too far gone."

"Then if there was no promise and no assurance I can't see what ties you."

"Oh she hated it so — she hated it so! She was so jealous. But here's the portrait — you may have that," the poor woman announced, taking the little picture, wrapped up in the same manner in which her aunt had wrapped it, out of her pocket.

"I may have it — do you mean you give

it to me?" I gasped as it passed into my hand.

"Oh yes."

"But it's worth money — a large sum."

"Well!" said Miss Tina, still with her strange look.

I didn't know what to make of it, for it could scarcely mean that she wanted to bargain like her aunt. She spoke as for making me a present. "I can't take it from you as a gift," I said, "and yet I can't afford to pay you for it according to the idea Miss Bordereau had of its value. She rated it at a thousand pounds."

"Couldn't we sell it?" my friend threw off.

"God forbid! I prefer the picture to the money."

"Well then keep it."

"You're very generous."

"So are you."

"I don't know why you should think so," I returned; and this was true enough, for the good creature appeared to have it in her mind some rich reference that I didn't in the least seize.

"Well, you've made a great difference for me," she said.

I looked at Jeffrey Aspern's face in the little picture, partly in order not to look at that of my companion, which had begun to trouble me, even to frighten me a little — it had taken so very odd, so strained and unnatural a cast. I made no answer to this last declaration; I but privately consulted Jeffrey Aspern's delightful eyes with my own — they were so young and brilliant and yet so wise and so deep: I asked him what on earth was the matter with Miss Tina. He seemed to smile at me with mild mockery; he might have been amused at my case. I had got into a pickle for him — as if he needed it! He was unsatisfactory for the only moment since I had known him. Nevertheless, now that I held the little picture in my hand I felt it would be a precious possession. "Is this a bribe to make me give up the papers?" I presently and all perversely asked. "Much as I value this, you know, if I were to be obliged to choose, the papers are what I should prefer. Ah but ever so much!"

"How can you choose — how can you choose?" Miss Tina returned slowly and woefully.

"I see! Of course there's nothing to be said if you regard the interdiction that rests on you as quite insurmountable. In this case it must seem to you that to part with them would be an impiety of the worst kind, a simple sacrilege!"

She shook her head, only lost in the queerness of her case. "You'd understand if you had known her. I'm afraid," she quavered suddenly — "I'm afraid! She was terrible when she was angry."

"Yes, I saw something of that, that night. She was terrible. Then I saw her eyes. Lord, they were fine!"

"I see them — they stare at me in the dark!" said Miss Tina.

"You've grown nervous with all you've been through."

"Oh yes, very — very!"

"You mustn't mind; that will pass away," I said kindly. Then I added resignedly, for it really seemed to me that I must accept the situation: "Well, so it is, and it can't be helped. I must renounce." My friend, at this, with her eyes on me, gave a low soft moan, and I went on: "I only wish to goodness she had destroyed them: then there would be nothing more to say. And I can't understand why, with her ideas, she didn't."

"Oh she lived on them!" said Miss Tina.

"You can imagine whether that makes me want less to see them," I returned not quite so desperately. "But don't let me stand here as if I had it in my soul to tempt you to anything base. Naturally, you understand, I give up my rooms. I leave Venice immediately." And I took up my hat, which I had placed on a chair. We were still rather awkwardly on our feet in the middle of the sala. She had left the door of the apartments open behind her, but had not led me that way.

A strange spasm came into her face as she saw me take my hat. "Immediately — do you mean to-day?" The tone of the words was tragic — they were a cry of desolation.

"Oh no; not so long as I can be of the least service to you."

"Well, just a day or two more — just two or three days," she panted. Then controlling herself she added in another manner: "She wanted to say something to me — the last day — something very particular. But she couldn't."

"Something very particular?"

"Something more about the papers."

"And did you guess — have you any idea?"

"No, I've tried to think — but I don't know. I've thought all kinds of things."

"As for instance?"

"Well, that if you were a relation it would be different."

I wondered. "If I were a relation — ?"

"If you weren't a stranger. Then it would be the same for you as for me. Anything that's mine would be yours, and you could do what you like. I shouldn't be able to prevent you — and you'd have no responsibility."

She brought out this droll explanation with a nervous rush and as if speaking words got by heart. They gave me the impression of a subtlety which at first I failed to follow. But after a moment her face helped me to see farther, and then the queerest of lights came to me. It was embarrassing, and I bent my head over Jeffrey Aspern's portrait. What an odd expression was in his face! "Get out of it as you can, my dear fellow!" I put the picture into the pocket of my coat and said to Miss Tina: "Yes, I'll sell it for you. I shan't get a thousand pounds by any means, but I shall get something good."

She looked at me through pitiful tears, but seemed to try to smile as she returned: "We can divide the money."

"No, no, it shall be all yours." Then I went on: "I think I know what your poor aunt wanted to say. She wanted to give directions that her papers should be buried with her."

Miss Tina appeared to weigh this suggestion; after which she answered with striking decision, "Oh no, she wouldn't have thought that safe!"

"It seems to me nothing could be safer."

"She had an idea that when people want to publish they're capable — !" And she paused, very red.

"Of violating a tomb? Mercy on us, what must she have thought of me!"

"She wasn't just, she wasn't generous!" my companion cried with sudden passion.

The light that had come into my mind a moment before spread farther. "Ah don't say that, for we *are* a dreadful race." Then I pursued: "If she left a will, that may give you some idea."

"I've found nothing of the sort — she destroyed it. She was very fond of me." Miss Tina added with an effect of extreme inconsequence. "She wanted me to be happy. And if any person should be kind to me — she wanted to speak of that."

I was almost awestricken by the astuteness with which the good lady found herself inspired, transparent astuteness as it was and stitching, as the phrase is, with white thread. "Depend upon it she didn't want to make any provision that would be agreeable to *me*."

"No, not to you, but quite to me. She knew I should like it if you could carry out your idea. Not because she cared for you, but because she did think of me," Miss Tina went on with her unexpected persuasive volubility. "You could see the things — you could use them." She stopped, seeing I grasped the sense of her conditional — stopped long enough for me to give some sign that I didn't give. She must have been conscious, however, that though my face showed the greatest embarrassment ever painted on a human countenance it was not set as a stone, it was also full of compassion. It was a comfort to me a long time afterwards to consider that she couldn't have seen in me the smallest symptom of disrespect. "I don't know what to do; I'm too tormented, I'm too ashamed!" she continued with vehemence. Then turning away from me and burying her face in her hands she burst into a flood of tears. If she didn't know what to do it may be imagined whether I knew better. I stood there dumb, watching her while her sobs resounded in the great empty hall. In a moment she was up at me again with her streaming eyes. "I'd give you everything, and she'd understand, where she is — she'd forgive me!"

"Ah Miss Tina — ah Miss Tina," I

stammered for all reply. I didn't know what to do, as I say, but at a venture I made a wild vague movement in consequence of which I found myself at the door. I remember standing there and saying, "It wouldn't do, it wouldn't do!" — saying it pensively, awkwardly, grotesquely, while I looked away to the opposite end of the sala as at something very interesting. The next thing I remember is that I was downstairs and out of the house. My gondola was there and my gondolier, reclining on the cushions, sprang up as soon as he saw me. I jumped in and to his usual *"Dove comanda?"* replied, in a tone that made him stare: "Anywhere, anywhere; out into the lagoon!"

He rowed me away and I sat there prostrate, groaning softly to myself, my hat pulled over my brow. What in the name of the preposterous did she mean if she didn't mean to offer me her hand? That was the price — that was the price! And did she think I wanted it, poor deluded infatuated extravagant lady? My gondolier, behind me, must have seen my ears red as I wondered, motionless there under the fluttering *tenda* with my hidden face, noticing nothing as we passed — wondered whether her delusion, her infatuation had been my own reckless work. Did she think

I had made love to her even to get the papers? I hadn't, I hadn't; I repeated that over to myself for an hour, for two hours, till I was wearied if not convinced. I don't know where, on the lagoon, my gondolier took me; we floated aimlessly and with slow rare strokes. At last I became conscious that we were near the Lido, far up, on the right hand, as you turn your back to Venice, and I made him put me ashore. I wanted to walk, to move, to shed some of my bewilderment. I crossed the narrow strip and got to the sea-beach — I took my way toward Malamocco. But presently I flung myself down again on the warm sand, in the breeze, on the coarse dry grass. It took it out of me to think I had been so much at fault, that I had unwittingly, but none the less deplorably trifled. But I hadn't given her cause — distinctly I hadn't. I had said to Mrs Prest that I would make love to her; but it had been a joke without consequences and I had never said it to my victim. I had been as kind as possible because I really liked her; but since when had that become a crime where a woman of such an age and such an appearance was concerned? I am far from remembering clearly the succession of events and feelings during this long day of confusion, which I spent entirely in wandering about, without going home, until late at night: it only comes back to me that there were moments when I pacified my conscience and others when I lashed it into pain. I didn't laugh all day — that I do recollect; the case, however, it might have struck others, seemed to me so little amusing. I should have been better employed perhaps in taking in the comic side of it. At any rate, whether I had given cause or not, there was no doubt whatever that I couldn't pay the price. I couldn't accept the proposal. I couldn't, for a bundle of tattered papers, marry a ridiculous pathetic provincial old woman. It was a proof of how little she supposed the idea would come to me that she should have decided to suggest it herself in that practical argumentative heroic way — with the timidity, however, so much more striking than the boldness, that her reasons appeared to come first and her feelings afterward.

As the day went on I grew to wish I had never heard of Aspern's relics, and I cursed the extravagant curiosity that had put John Cumnor on the scent of them. We had more than enough material without them, and my predicament was the just punishment of that most fatal of human follies, our not having known when to stop. It was very well to say it was no predicament, but the way out was simple, that I had only to leave Venice by the first train in the morning, after addressing Miss Tina a note which should be placed in her hand as soon as I got clear of the house; for it was strong proof of my quandary that when I tried to make up the note to my taste in advance — I would put it on paper as soon as I got home, before going to bed — I couldn't think of anything but "How can I thank you for the rare confidence you've placed in me?" That would never do; it sounded exactly as if an acceptance were to follow. Of course I might get off without writing at all, but that would be brutal, and my idea was still to exclude brutal solutions. As my confusion cooled I lost myself in wonder at the importance I had attached to Juliana's crumpled scraps; the thought of them became odious to me and I was as vexed with the old witch for the superstition that had prevented her from destroying them as I was with myself for having already spent more money than I could afford in attempting to control their fate. I forget what I did, where I went after leaving the Lido and at what hour or with what recovery of composure I made my way back to my boat. I only know that in the afternoon, when the air was aglow with the sunset, I was standing before the church of Saints John and Paul and looking up at the small square-jawed face of Bartolomeo Colleoni, the terrible *condottiere* who sits so sturdily astride of his huge bronze horse on the high pedestal on which Venetian gratitude maintains him. The statue is incomparable, the finest of all mounted figures, unless that of Marcus Aurelius, who rides benignant before the Roman Capitol, be finer: but I was not thinking of that; I only found myself staring at the triumphant captain as if he had had an oracle on his lips. The western light shines into all his grimness at that hour and makes it wonderfully personal. But he continued to look far over my head, at the red immersion of another day — he had seen so many go down into the lagoon through the centuries — and if he were thinking of battles and stratagems they were of a different quality from any I had to tell him of. He couldn't direct me what to do, gaze up at him as I might. Was it before this or after that I wandered about for an hour in the small canals, to the continued stupefaction of my gondolier, who had never seen me so restless and yet so void of purpose and could extract from me no order but "Go anywhere — everywhere — all over the place"? He reminded me that I had not lunched, and expressed therefore respectfully the hope that I would dine earlier. He had had long periods of leisure during the day, when I had left the boat and rambled, so that I was not obliged to consider him, and I told him that till the morrow, for reasons, I should touch no meat. It was an effect of poor Miss Tina's proposal, not altogether auspicious, that I had quite lost my appetite. I don't know why it happened that on this occasion I was more than ever struck with that queer air of sociability, of cousinship and family life, which makes up half the expression of Venice. Without streets and vehicles, the uproar of wheels, the brutality of horses, and with its little winding ways where people crowd together, where voices sound as in the corridors of a house, where the human step circulates as if it skirted the angles of furniture and shoes never wear out, the place has the character of an immense collective apartment, in which Piazzo San Marco is the most ornamented corner, and palaces and churches, for the rest, play the part of great divans of repose, tables of entertainment, expanses of decoration. And somehow the splendid common domicile, familiar, domestic and resonant, also resembles a theatre with its actors clicking over bridges and, in straggling processions, tripping along fondamentas. As you sit in your gondola the foot-ways that in certain parts edge the canals assume to the eye the importance of a stage, meeting it at the same angle, and the Venetian figures, moving to and fro against the battered scenery of their little houses of comedy, strike you as members of an endless dramatic troupe.

I went to bed that night very tired and without being able to compose an address to Miss Tina. Was this failure the reason why I became conscious the next morning as soon as I awoke of a determination to see the poor lady again the first moment she would receive me? That had something to do with it, but what had still more was the fact that during my sleep the oddest revulsion had taken place in my spirit. I found myself aware of this almost as soon as I opened my eyes: it made me jump out of my bed with the movement of a man who remembers that he has left the house-door ajar or a candle burning under a shelf. Was I still in time to save my goods? That question was in my heart; for what had now come to pass was that in the un-conscious cerebration of sleep I had swung back to a passionate appreciation of Juliana's treasure. The pieces composing it were now more precious than ever and a positive ferocity had come into my need to acquire them. The condition Miss Tina had attached to that act no longer appeared an obstacle worth thinking of, and for an hour this morning my repentant imagination brushed it aside. It was absurd I should be able to invent nothing; absurd to renounce so easily and turn away helpless from the idea that the only way to become possessed was to unite myself to her for life. I mightn't unite myself, yet I might still have what she had. I must add that by the time I sent down to ask if she would see me I had invented no alternative, though in fact I drew out my dressing in the interest of my wit. This failure was humiliating, yet what could the alternative be? Miss Tina sent back word I might come; and as I descended the stairs and crossed the sala to her door — this time she received me in her aunt's forlorn parlour — I hoped she wouldn't think my announcement was to be "favourable." She certainly would have understood my recoil of the day before.

As soon as I came into the room I saw

that she had done so, but I also saw something which had not been in my forecast. Poor Miss Tina's sense of her failure had produced a rare alteration in her, but I had been too full of stratagems and spoils to think of that. Now I took it in; I can scarcely tell how it startled me. She stood in the middle of the room with a face of mildness bent upon me, and her look of forgiveness, of absolution, made her angelic. It beautified her; she was younger; she was not a ridiculous old woman. This trick of her expression, this magic of her spirit, transfigured her, and while I still noted it I heard a whisper somewhere in the depths of my conscience: "Why not, after all — why not?" It seemed to me I *could* pay the price. Still more distinctly, however, than the whisper I heard Miss Tina's own voice. I was so struck with the different effect she made on me that at first I wasn't clearly aware of what she was saying; then I recognised she had bade me good-bye — she said something about hoping I should be very happy.

"Good-bye — good-bye?" I repeated with an inflexion interrogative and probably foolish.

I saw she didn't feel the interrogation, she only heard the words: she had strung herself up to accepting our separation and they fell upon her ear as a proof. "Are you going to-day?" she asked. "But it doesn't matter, for whenever you go I shall not see you again. I don't want to." And she smiled strangely, with an infinite gentleness. She had never doubted my having left her the day before in horror. How *could* she, since I hadn't come back before night to contradict, even as a simple form, even as an act of common humanity, such an idea? And now she had the force of soul — Miss Tina with force of soul was a new conception — to smile at me in her abjection.

"What shall you do — where shall you go?" I asked.

"Oh I don't know. I've done the great thing. I've destroyed the papers."

"Destroyed them?" I wailed.

"Yes; what was I to keep them for? I burnt them last night, one by one, in the kitchen."

"One by one?" I coldly echoed it.

"It took a long time — there were so many." The room seemed to go round me as she said this and a real darkness for a moment descended on my eyes. When it passed Miss Tina was there still, but the transfiguration was over and she had changed back to a plain dingy elderly person. It was in this character she spoke as she said, "I can't stay with you longer, I can't"; and it was in this character she turned her back upon me, as I had turned mine upon her twenty-four hours before, and moved to the door of her room. Here she did what I hadn't done when I quitted her — she paused long enough to give me one look. I have never forgotten it, and I sometimes still suffer from it, though it was not resentful. No, there was no resentment, nothing hard or vindictive in poor Miss Tina; for when, later, I sent her, as the price of the portrait of Jeffrey Aspern, a larger sum of money than I had hoped to be able to gather for her, writing to her that I had sold the picture, she kept it with thanks; she never sent it back. I wrote her that I had sold the picture, but I admitted to Mrs Prest at the time — I met this other friend in London that autumn — that it hangs above my writing-table. When I look at it I can scarcely bear my loss — I mean of the precious papers.

The Beast
in the
Jungle

1

What determined the speech that startled him in the course of their encounter scarcely matters, being probably but some words spoken by himself quite without intention — spoken as they lingered and slowly moved together after their renewal of acquaintance. He had been conveyed by friends an hour or two before to the house at which she was staying; the party of visitors at the other house, of whom he was one, and thanks to whom it was his theory, as always, that he was lost in the crowd, had been invited over to luncheon. There had been after luncheon much dispersal, all in the interest of the original motive, a view of Weatherend itself and the fine things, intrinsic features, pictures, heirlooms, treasures of all the arts, that made the place almost famous; and the great rooms were so numerous that guests could wander at their will, hang back from the principal group and in cases where they took such matters with the last seriousness give themselves up to mysterious appreciations and measurements. There were persons to be observed, singly or in couples, bending toward objects in out-of-the-way corners with their hands on their knees and their heads nodding quite as with the emphasis of an excited sense of smell. When they were two they either mingled their sounds of ecstasy or melted into silences of even deeper import, so that there were aspects of the occasion that gave it for Marcher much the air of the "look round," previous to a sale highly advertised, that excites or quenches, as may be, the dream of acquisition. The dream of acquisition at Weatherend would have had to be wild indeed, and John Marcher found himself, among such suggestions, disconcerted almost equally by the presence of those who knew too much and by that of those who knew nothing. The great rooms caused so much poetry and history to press upon him that he needed some straying apart to feel in a proper relation with them, though this impulse was not, as happened, like the gloating of some of his companions, to be compared to the movements of a dog sniffing a cupboard. It had an issue promptly enough in a direction that was not to have been calculated.

It led, briefly, in the course of the October afternoon, to his closer meeting with May Bartram, whose face, a reminder, yet not quite a remembrance, as they sat much separated at a very long table, had begun merely by troubling him rather pleasantly. It affected him as the sequel of something of which he had lost the beginning. He knew it, and for the time quite welcomed it, as a continuation, but didn't know what it continued, which was an interest or an amusement the greater as he was also somehow aware — yet without a direct sign from her — that the young woman herself hadn't lost the thread. She hadn't lost it, but she wouldn't give it back to him, he saw, without some putting forth of his hand for it; and he not only saw that, but saw several things more, things odd enough in the light of the fact that at the moment some accident of grouping brought them face to face he was still merely fumbling with the idea that any contact between them in the past would have had no importance. If it had had no importance he scarcely knew why his actual impression of her should so seem to have so much; the answer to which, however, was that in such a life as they all appeared to be leading for the moment one could but take things as they came. He was satisfied, without in the least being able to say why, that this young lady might roughly have ranked in the house as a poor relation; satisfied also that she was not there on a brief visit, but was more or less a part of the establishment — almost a working, a remunerated part. Didn't she enjoy at periods a protection that she paid for by helping, among other services, to show the place and explain it, deal with the tiresome people, answer questions about the dates of the building, the styles of the furniture, the authorship of the pictures, the favourite haunts of the ghost? It wasn't that she looked as if you could have given her shillings — it was impossible to look less so. Yet when she finally drifted toward him, distinctly handsome, though ever so much older — older than when he had seen her before — it might have been as an effect of her guessing that he had, within the couple of hours, devoted more imagination to her than to all the others put together, and had thereby penetrated to a kind of truth that the others were too stupid for. She *was* there on harder terms than any one; she was there as a consequence of things suffered, one way and another, in the interval of years; and she remembered him very much as she was remembered — only a good deal better.

By the time they at last thus came to

speech they were alone in one of the rooms — remarkable for a fine portrait over the chimney-place — out of which their friends had passed, and the charm of it was that even before they had spoken they had practically arranged with each other to stay behind for talk. The charm, happily, was in other things too — partly in there being scarce a spot at Weatherend without something to stay behind for. It was in the way the autumn day looked into the high windows as it waned; the way the red light, breaking at the close from under a low sombre sky, reached out in a long shaft and played over old wainscots, old tapestry, old gold, old colour. It was most of all perhaps in the way she came to him as if, since she had been turned on to deal with the simpler sort, he might, should he choose to keep the whole thing down, just take her mild attention for a part of her general business. As soon as he heard her voice, however, the gap was filled up and the missing link supplied; the slight irony he divined in her attitude lost its advantage. He almost jumped at it to get there before her. "I met you years and years ago in Rome. I remember all about it." She confessed to disappointment — she had been so sure he didn't; and to prove how well he did he began to pour forth the particular recollections that popped up as he called for them. Her face and her voice, all at his service now, worked the miracle — the impression operating like the torch of a lamplighter who touches into flame, one by one, a long row of gas-jets. Marcher flattered himself the illumination was brilliant, yet he was really still more pleased on her showing him, with amusement, that in his haste to make everything right he had got most things rather wrong. It hadn't been at Rome — it had been at Naples; and it hadn't been eight years before — it had been more nearly ten. She hadn't been, either, with her uncle and aunt, but with her mother and her brother; in addition to which it was not with the Pembles *he* had been, but with the Boyers, coming down in their company from Rome — a point on which she insisted, a little to his confusion, and as to which she had her evidence in hand. The Boyers she had known, but didn't know the Pembles, though she had heard of them, and it was the people he was with who had made them acquainted. The incident of the thunderstorm that had raged round them with such violence as to drive them for refuge into an excavation — this incident had not occurred at the Palace of the Caesars, but at Pompeii, on an occasion when they had been present there at an important find.

He accepted her amendments, he enjoyed her corrections, though the moral of them was, she pointed out, that he *really* didn't remember the least thing about her; and he only felt it as a drawback that when all was made strictly historic there didn't appear much of anything left. They lingered together still, she neglecting her office — for from the moment he was so clever she had no proper right to him — and both neglecting the house, just waiting as to see if a memory or two more wouldn't again breathe on them. It hadn't taken them many minutes, after all, to put down on the table, like the cards of a pack, those that constituted their respective hands; only what came out was that the pack was unfortunately not perfect — that the past, invoked, invited, encouraged, could give them, naturally, no more than it had. It had made them anciently meet — her at twenty, him at twenty-five; but nothing was so strange, they seemed to say to each other, as that, while so occupied, it hadn't done a little more for them. They looked at each other as with the feeling of an occasion missed; the present would have been so much better if the other, in the far distance, in the foreign land, hadn't been so stupidly meagre. There weren't apparently, all counted, more than a dozen little old things that had succeeded in coming to pass between them; trivialities of youth, simplicities of freshness, stupidities of ignorance, small possible germs, but too deeply buried — too deeply (didn't it seem?) to sprout after so many years. Marcher could only feel he ought to have rendered her some service — saved her from a capsized boat in the Bay or at least recovered her dressing-bag, filched from her cab in the streets of Naples by a lazzarone with a stiletto. Or it would have been nice if he could have been taken with fever all alone at his hotel, and she could have come to look after him, to write to his people, to drive him out in convalescence. *Then* they would be in possession of the something or other that their actual show seemed to lack. It yet somehow presented itself, this show, as too good to be spoiled; so that they were reduced for a few minutes more to wondering a little helplessly why — since they seemed to know a certain number of the same people — their reunion had been so long averted. They didn't use that name for it, but their delay from minute to minute to join the others was a kind of confession that they didn't quite want it to be a failure. Their attempted supposition of reasons for their not having met but showed how little they knew of each other. There came in fact a moment when Marcher felt a positive pang. It was vain to pretend she was an old friend, for all the communities were wanting, in spite of which it was as an old friend that he saw she would have suited him. He had new ones enough — was surrounded with them for instance on the stage of the other house; as a new one he probably wouldn't have so much as noticed her. He would have liked to invent something, get her to make-believe with him that some passage of a romantic or critical kind *had* originally occurred. He was really almost reaching out in imagination — as against time — for something that would do, and saying to himself that if it didn't come this sketch of a fresh start would show for quite awkwardly bungled. They would separate, and now for no second or no third chance. They would have tried and not succeeded. Then it was, just at the turn, as he afterwards made it out to himself, that, everything else failing, she herself decided to take up the case and, as it were, save the situation. He felt as soon as she spoke that she had been consciously keeping back what she said and hoping to get on without it; a scruple in her that immensely touched him when, by the end of three or four minutes more, he was able to measure it. What she brought out, at any rate, quite cleared the air and supplied the link — the link it was so odd he should frivolously have managed to lose.

"You know you told me something I've never forgotten and that again and again has made me think of you since; it was that tremendously hot day when we went to Sorrento, across the bay, for the breeze. What I allude to was what you said to me, on the way back, as we sat under the awning of the boat enjoying the cool. Have you forgotten?"

He had forgotten and was even more surprised than ashamed. But the great thing was that he saw in this no vulgar reminder of any "sweet" speech. The vanity of women had long memories, but she was making no claim on him of a compliment or a mistake. With another woman, a totally different one, he might have feared the recall possibly even of some imbecile "offer." So, in having to say that he had indeed forgotten, he was conscious rather of a loss than of a gain; he already saw an interest in the matter of her mention. "I try to think — but I give it up. Yet I remember the Sorrento day."

"I'm not very sure you do," May Bartram after a moment said; "and I'm not very sure I ought to want you to. It's dreadful to bring a person back at any time to what he was ten years before. If you've lived away from it," she smiled, "so much the better."

"Ah if *you* haven't why should I?" he asked.

"Lived away, you mean, from what I myself was?"

"From what *I* was. I was of course an ass," Marcher went on; "but I would rather know from you just the sort of ass I was than — from the moment you have something in your mind — not know anything."

Still, however, she hesitated. "But if you've completely ceased to be that sort — ?"

"Why I can then all the more bear to know. Besides, perhaps I haven't."

"Perhaps. Yet if you haven't," she added, "I should suppose you'd remember. Not indeed that *I* in the least connect with my impression the invidious name you use. If I had only thought you foolish," she explained, "the thing I speak of wouldn't so have remained with me. It was about yourself." She waited as if it might come to him; but as, only meeting her eyes in wonder, he gave no sign, she burnt her ships. "Has it ever happened?"

Then it was that, while he continued to stare, a light broke for him and the blood slowly came to his face, which began to burn with recognition. "Do you mean I told you — ?" But he faltered, lest what came to him shouldn't be right, lest he should only give himself away.

"It was something about yourself that it was natural one shouldn't forget — that is if one remembered you at all. That's why I ask you," she smiled, "if the thing you then spoke of has ever come to pass?"

Oh then he saw, but he was lost in wonder and found himself embarrassed. This, he also saw, made her sorry for him, as if her allusion had been a mistake. It took him but a moment, however, to feel it hadn't been, much as it had been a surprise. After the first little shock of it her knowledge on the contrary began, even if rather strangely, to taste sweet to him. She was the only other person in the world then who would have it, and she had had it all these years, while the fact of his having so breathed his secret had unaccountably faded from him. No wonder they couldn't have met as if nothing had happened. "I judge," he finally said, "that I know what you mean. Only I had strangely enough lost any sense of having taken you so far into my confidence."

"Is it because you've taken so many others as well?"

"I've taken nobody. Not a creature since then."

"So that I'm the only person who knows?"

"The only person in the world."

"Well," she quickly replied, "I myself have never spoken. I've never, never repeated of you what you told me." She looked at him so that he perfectly believed her. Their eyes met over it in such a way that he was without a doubt. "And I never will."

She spoke with an earnestness that, as if almost excessive, put him at ease about her possible derision. Somehow the whole question was a new luxury to him — that is from the moment she was in possession. If she didn't take the sarcastic view she clearly took the sympathetic, and that was what he had had, in all the long time, from no one whomsoever. What he felt was that he couldn't at present have begun to tell her, and yet could profit perhaps exquisitely by the accident of having done so of old. "Please don't then. We're just right as it is."

"Oh I am," she laughed, "if you are!" To which she added: "Then you do still feel in the same way?"

It was impossible he shouldn't take to himself that she was really interested, though it all kept coming as perfect surprise. He had thought of himself so long as abominably alone, and lo he wasn't alone a bit. He hadn't been, it appeared, for an hour — since those moments on the Sorrento boat. It was *she* who had been, he seemed to see as he looked at her — she who had been made so by the graceless fact of his lapse of fidelity. To tell her what he had told her — what had it been but to ask something of her? something that she had given, in her charity, without his having, by a remembrance, by a return of the spirit, failing another encounter, so much as thanked her. What he had asked of her had been simply at first not to laugh at him. She had beautifully not done so for ten years, and she was not doing so now. So he had endless gratitude to make up. Only for that he must see just how he had figured to her. "What, exactly, was the account I gave — ?"

"Of the way you did feel? Well, it was very simple. You said you had had from your earliest time, as the deepest thing within you, the sense of being kept for something rare and strange, possibly prodigious and terrible, that was sooner or later to happen to you, that you had in your bones the foreboding and the conviction of, and that would perhaps overwhelm you."

"Do you call that very simple?" John Marcher asked.

She thought a moment. "It was perhaps because I seemed, as you spoke, to understand it."

"You do understand it?" he eagerly asked.

Again she kept her kind eyes on him. "You still have the belief?"

"Oh!" he exclaimed helplessly. There was too much to say.

"Whatever it's to be," she clearly made out, "it hasn't yet come."

He shook his head in complete surrender now. "It hasn't yet come. Only, you know, it isn't anything I'm to *do*, to achieve in the world, to be distinguished or admired for. I'm not such an ass as *that*. It would be much better, no doubt, if I were."

"It's to be something you're merely to suffer?"

"Well, say to wait for — to have to meet,

to face, to see suddenly break out in my life; possibly destroying all further consciousness, possibly annihilating me; possibly, on the other hand, only altering everything, striking at the root of all my world and leaving me to the consequences, however they shape themselves."

She took this in, but the light in her eyes continued for him not to be that of mockery. "Isn't what you describe perhaps but the expectation — or at any rate the sense of danger, familiar to so many people — of falling in love?"

John Marcher wondered. "Did you ask me that before?"

"No — I wasn't so free-and-easy then. But it's what strikes me now."

"Of course," he said after a moment, "it strikes you. Of course it strikes *me*. Of course what's in store for me may be no more than that. The only thing is," he went on, "that I think if it had been that I should by this time know."

"Do you mean because you've *been* in love?" And then as he but looked at her in silence: "You've been in love, and it hasn't meant such a cataclysm, hasn't proved the great affair?"

"Here I am, you see. It hasn't been overwhelming."

"Then it hasn't been love," said May Bartram.

"Well, I at least thought it was. I took it for that — I've taken it till now. It was agreeable, it was delightful, it was miserable," he explained. "But it wasn't strange. It wasn't what *my* affair's to be."

"You want something all to yourself — something that nobody else knows or *has* known?"

"It isn't a question of what I 'want' — God knows I don't want anything. It's only a question of the apprehension that haunts me — that I live with day by day."

He said this so lucidly and consistently that he could see it further impose itself. If she hadn't been interested before she'd have been interested now. "Is it a sense of coming violence?"

Evidently now too again he liked to talk of it. "I don't think of it as — when it does come — necessarily violent. I only think of it as natural and as of course above all unmistakeable. I think of it simply as *the* thing. *The* thing will of itself appear natural."

"Then how will it appear strange?"

Marcher bethought himself. "It won't — to *me*."

"To whom then?"

"Well," he replied, smiling at last, "say to you."

"Oh then I'm to be present?"

"Why you *are* present — since you know."

"I see." She turned it over. "But I mean at the catastrophe."

At this, for a minute, their lightness gave way to their gravity; it was as if the long look they exchanged held them together. "It will only depend on yourself — if you'll watch with me."

"Are you afraid?" she asked.

"Don't leave me *now*," he went on.

"Are you afraid?" she repeated.

"Do you think me simply out of my mind?" he pursued instead of answering. "Do I merely strike you as a harmless lunatic?"

"No," said May Bartram. "I understand you. I believe you."

"You mean you feel how my obsession — poor old thing! — may correspond to some possible reality?"

"To some possible reality."

"Then you *will* watch with me?"

She hesitated, then for the third time put her question. "Are you afraid?"

"Did I tell you I was — at Naples?"

"No, you said nothing about it."

"Then I don't know. And I should *like* to

know," said John Marcher. "You'll tell me yourself whether you think so. If you'll watch with me you'll see."

"Very good then." They had been moving by this time across the room, and at the door, before passing out, they paused as for the full wind-up of their understanding. "I'll watch with you," said May Bartram.

2

The fact that she "knew" — knew and yet neither chaffed him nor betrayed him — had in a short time begun to constitute between them a goodly bond, which became more marked when, within the year that followed their afternoon at Weatherend, the opportunities for meeting multiplied. The event that thus promoted these occasions was the death of the ancient lady her great-aunt, under whose wing, since losing her mother, she had to such an extent found shelter, and who, though but the widowed mother of the new successor to the property, had succeeded — thanks to a high tone and a high temper — in not forfeiting the supreme position at the great house. The deposition of this personage arrived but with her death, which, followed by many changes, made in particular a difference for the young woman in whom Marcher's expert attention had recognised from the first a dependent with a pride that might ache though it didn't bristle. Nothing for a long time had made him easier than the thought that the aching must have been much soothed by Miss Bartram's now finding herself able to set up a small home in London. She had acquired property, to an amount that made that luxury just possible, under her aunt's extremely complicated will, and when the whole matter began to be straightened out, which indeed took time, she let him know that the happy issue was at last in view. He had seen her again before that day, both because she had more than once accompanied the ancient lady to town and because he had paid another visit to the friends who so conveniently made of Weatherend one of the charms of their own hospitality. These friends had taken him back there; he had achieved there again with Miss Bartram some quiet detachment; and he had in London succeeded in persuading her to more than one brief absence from her aunt. They went together, on these latter occasions, to the National Gallery and the South Kensington Museum, where, among vivid reminders, they talked of Italy at large — not now attempting to recover, as at first, the taste of their youth and their ignorance. That recovery, the first day at Weatherend, had served its purpose well, had given them quite enough; so that they were, to Marcher's sense, no longer hovering about the headwaters of their stream, but had felt their boat pushed sharply off and down the current.

They were literally afloat together; for our gentleman this was marked, quite as marked as that the fortunate cause of it was just the buried treasure of her knowledge. He had with his own hands dug up this little hoard, brought to light — that is to within reach of the dim day constituted by their discretions and privacies — the object of value the hiding-place of which he had, after putting it into the ground himself, so strangely, so long forgotten. The rare luck of having again just stumbled on the spot made him indifferent to any other question; he would doubtless have devoted more time to the odd accident of his lapse of memory if he hadn't been moved to devote so much to the sweetness, the comfort, as he felt, for the future, that this accident itself had helped to keep fresh. It had never entered into his plan that any one should "know," and mainly for the reason that it wasn't in him to tell any one. That would have been impossible, for nothing but the amusement of a cold world would have waited on it. Since, however, a mysterious fate had opened his mouth betimes, in spite of him, he would count that a compensation and profit by it to the utmost. That the right person *should* know tempered the asperity of his secret more even than his shyness had permitted him to imagine; and May Bartram was clearly right, because — well, because there she was. Her knowledge simply settled it; he would have been sure enough by this time had she been wrong. There was that in his situation, no doubt, that disposed him too much to see her as a mere confidant, taking all her light for him from the fact — the fact only — of her interest in his predicament; from her mercy, sympathy, seriousness, her consent not to regard him as the funniest of the funny. Aware, in fine, that her price for him was just in her giving him this constant sense of his being admirably spared, he was careful to remember that she had also a life of her own, with things that might happen to *her*, things that in friendship one should likewise take account of. Something fairly remarkable came to pass with him, for that matter, in this connexion — something represented by a certain passage of his consciousness, in the suddenest way, from one extreme to the other.

He had thought himself, so long as nobody knew, the most disinterested person in the world, carrying his concentrated burden, his perpetual suspense, ever so quietly, holding his tongue about it, giving others no glimpse of it nor of its effect upon his life, asking of them no allowance and only making on his side all those that were asked. He hadn't disturbed people with the queerness of their having to know a haunted man, though he had had moments of rather special temptation on hearing them say they were forsooth "unsettled." If they were as unsettled as he was — he who had never been settled for an hour in his life — they would know what it meant. Yet it wasn't, all the same, for him to make them, and he listened to them civilly enough. This was why he had such good — though possibly such rather colourless — manners; this was why, above all, he could regard himself, in a greedy world, as decently — as in fact perhaps even a little sublimely — unselfish. Our point is accordingly that he valued this character quite sufficiently to measure his present danger of letting it lapse, against which he promised himself to be much on his guard. He was quite ready, none the less, to be selfish just a little, since surely no more charming occasion for it had come to him. "Just a little," in a word, was just as much as Miss Bartram, taking one day with another, would let him. He never would be in the least coercive and would keep well before him the lines on which consideration for her — the very highest — ought to proceed. He would thoroughly establish the heads under which her affairs, her requirements, her peculiarities — he went so far as to give them the latitude of that name — would come into their intercourse. All this naturally was a sign of how much he took the intercourse itself for granted. There was nothing more to be done about *that*. It simply existed; had sprung into being with her first penetrating question to him in the autumn light there at Weatherend. The real form it should have taken on the basis that stood out large was the form of their marrying. But the devil in this was that the very basis itself put marrying out of the question. His conviction, his apprehension, his obsession, in short, wasn't a privilege he could invite a woman to share; and that consequence of it was precisely what was the matter with him. Something or other lay in wait for him, amid the twists and the turns of the months and the years, like a crouching beast in the jungle. It signified little whether the crouching beast were destined to slay him or to be slain. The definite point was the inevitable spring of the creature; and the definite lesson from that was that a man of feeling didn't cause himself to be accompanied by a lady on a tiger-hunt. Such was the image under which he had ended by figuring his life.

They had at first, none the less, in the scattered hours spent together, made no allusion to that view of it; which was a sign he was handsomely alert to give that he didn't expect, that he in fact didn't care, always to be talking about it. Such a feature in one's outlook was really like a hump on one's back. The difference it made every minute of the day existed quite independently of discussion. One discussed of course *like* a hunchback, for there was always, if nothing else, the hunchback face. That remained, and she was watching him; but people watched best, as a general thing, in silence, so that such would be predominantly the manner of their vigil.

Yet he didn't want, at the same time, to be tense and solemn; tense and solemn was what he imagined he too much showed for with other people. The thing to be, with the one person who knew, was easy and natural — to make the reference rather than be seeming to avoid it, to avoid it rather than be seeming to make it, and to keep it, in any case, familiar, facetious even, rather than pedantic and portentous. Some such consideration as the latter was doubtless in his mind for instance when he wrote pleasantly to Miss Bartram that perhaps the great thing he had so long felt as in the lap of the gods was no more than this circumstance, which touched him so nearly, of her acquiring a house in London. It was the first allusion they had yet again made, needing any other hitherto so little; but when she replied, after having given him the news, that she was by no means satisfied with such a trifle as the climax to so special a suspense, she almost set him wondering if she hadn't even a larger conception of singularity for him than he had for himself. He was at all events destined to become aware little by little, as time went by, that she was all the while looking at his life, judging it, measuring it, in the light of the thing she knew, which grew to be at last, with the consecration of the years, never mentioned between them save as "the real truth" about him. That had always been his own form of reference to it, but she adopted the form so quietly that, looking back at the end of a period, he knew there was no moment at which it was traceable that she had, as he might say, got inside his idea, or exchanged the attitude of beautifully indulging for that of still more beautifully believing him.

It was always open to him to accuse her of seeing him but as the most harmless of maniacs, and this, in the long run — since it covered so much ground — was his easiest description of their friendship. He had a screw loose for her, but she liked him in spite of it and was practically, against the rest of the world, his kind wise keeper, unremunerated but fairly amused and, in the absence of other near ties, not disreputably occupied. The rest of the world of course thought him queer, but she, she only, knew how, and above all why, queer; which was precisely what enabled her to dispose the concealing veil in the right folds. She took his gaiety from him — since it had to pass with them for gaiety — as she took everything else; but she certainly so far justified by her unerring touch his finer sense of the degree to which he had ended by convincing her. *She* at least never spoke of the secret of his life except as "the real truth about you," and she had in fact a wonderful way of making it seem, as such, the secret of her own life too. That was in fine how he so constantly felt her as allowing for him; he couldn't on the whole call it anything else. He allowed for himself, but she, exactly, allowed still more; partly because, better placed for a sight of the matter, she traced his unhappy perversion through reaches of its course into which he could scarce follow it. He knew how he felt, but, besides knowing that, she knew how he *looked* as well; he knew each of the things of importance he was insidiously kept from doing, but she could add up the amount they made, understand how much, with a lighter weight on his spirit, he might have done, and thereby establish how, clever as he was, he fell short. Above all she was in the secret of the difference between the forms he went through — those of his little office under Government, those of caring for his modest patrimony, for his library, for his garden in the country, for the people in London whose invitations he accepted and repaid — and the detachment that reigned beneath them and that made of all behaviour, all that could in the least be called behaviour, a long act of dissimulation. What it had come to was that he wore a mask painted with the social simper, out of the eye-holes of which there looked eyes of an expression not in the least matching the other features. This the stupid world, even after years, had never more than half-discovered. It was only May Bartram who had, and she achieved, by an art indescribable, the feat of at once — or perhaps it was only alternately — meeting the eyes from in front and mingling her own vision, as from over his shoulder, with their peep through the apertures.

So while they grew older together she did watch with him, and so she let this association give shape and colour to her own existence. Beneath *her* forms as well detachment had learned to sit, and behaviour had become for her, in the social sense, a false account of herself. There was but one account of her that would have been true all the while and that she could give straight to nobody, least of all to John Marcher. Her whole attitude was a virtual statement, but the perception of that only seemed called to take its place for him as one of the many things necessarily crowded out of his consciousness. If she had moreover, like himself, to make sacrifices to their real truth, it was to be granted that her compensation might have affected her as more prompt and more natural. They had long periods, in this London time, during which, when they were together, a stranger might have listened to them without in the least pricking up his ears; on the other hand the real truth was equally liable at any moment to rise to the surface, and the auditor would then have wondered indeed what they were talking about. They had from an early hour made up their mind that society was, luckily, unintelligent, and the margin allowed them by this had fairly become one of their commonplaces. Yet there were still moments when the situation turned almost fresh — usually under the effect of some expression drawn from herself. Her expressions doubtless repeated themselves, but her intervals were generous. "What saves us, you know, is that we answer so completely to so usual an appearance: that of the man and woman whose friendship has become such a daily habit — or almost — as to be at last indispensable." That for instance was a remark she had frequently enough had occasion to make, though she had given it at different times different developments. What we are especially concerned with is the turn it happened to take from her one afternoon when he had come to see her in honour of her birthday. This anniversary had fallen on a Sunday, at a season of thick fog and general outward gloom; but he had brought her his customary offering, having known her now long enough to have established a hundred small traditions. It was one of his proofs to himself, the present he made her on her birthday, that he hadn't sunk into real selfishness. It was mostly nothing more than a small trinket, but it was always fine of its kind, and he was regularly careful to pay for it more than he thought he could afford. "Our habit saves you at least, don't you see? because it makes you, after all, for the vulgar, indistinguishable from other men. What's the most inveterate mark of men in general? Why the capacity to spend endless time with dull women — to spend it I won't say without being bored, but without minding that they are, without being driven off at a tangent by it; which comes to the same thing. I'm your dull woman, a part of the daily bread for which you pray at church. That covers your tracks more than anything."

"And what covers yours?" asked Marcher, whom his dull woman could mostly to this extent amuse. "I see of course what you mean by your saving me, in this way and that, so far as other people are concerned — I've seen it all along. Only what is it that saves *you?* I often think, you know, of that."

She looked as if she sometimes thought of that too, but rather in a different way. "Where other people, you mean, are concerned?"

"Well, you're really so in with me, you know — as a sort of result of my being so in with yourself. I mean of my having such an immense regard for you, being so tremendously mindful of all you've done for me. I sometimes ask myself if it's quite fair. Fair I mean to have so involved and — since one may say it — interested you. I almost feel as if you hadn't really had time to do anything else."

"Anything else but be interested?" she asked. "Ah what else does one ever want to be? If I've been 'watching' with you, as we long ago agreed I was to do, watching's always in itself an absorption."

"Oh certainly," John Marcher said, "if you hadn't had your curiosity — ! Only doesn't it sometimes come to you as time goes on that your curiosity isn't being particularly repaid?"

May Bartram had a pause. "Do you ask that, by any chance, because you feel at all that yours isn't? I mean because you have to wait so long."

Oh he understood what she meant! "For the thing to happen that never does happen? For the beast to jump out? No, I'm just where I was about it. It isn't a matter as to which I can *choose,* I can decide for a change. It isn't one as to which there *can* be a change. It's in the lap of the gods. One's in the hands of one's law — there one is. As to the form the law will take, the way it will operate, that's its own affair."

"Yes," Miss Bartram replied; "of course one's fate's coming, of course it *has* come in its own form and its own way, all the while. Only, you know, the form and the way in your case were to have been — well, something so exceptional and, as one may say, so particularly *your* own."

Something in this made him look at her with suspicion. "You say 'were to *have* been,' as if in your heart you had begun to doubt."

"Oh!" she vaguely protested.

"As if you believe," he went on, "that nothing will now take place."

She shook her head slowly but rather inscrutably. "You're far from my thought."

He continued to look at her. "What then is the matter with you?"

"Well," she said after another wait, "the matter with me is simply that I'm more sure than ever my curiosity, as you call it, will be but too well repaid."

They were frankly grave now; he had got up from his seat, had turned once more about the little drawing-room to which, year after year, he brought his inevitable topic; in which he had, as he might have said, tasted their intimate community with every sauce, where every object was as familiar to him as the things of his own house and the very carpets were worn with his fitful walk very much as the desks in old counting-houses are worn by the elbows of generations of clerks. The generations of his nervous moods had been at work there, and the place was the written history of his whole middle life. Under the impression of what his friend had just said he knew himself, for some reason, more aware of these things; which made him, after a moment, stop again before her. "Is it possibly that you've grown afraid?"

"Afraid?" He thought, as she repeated the word, that his question had made her, a little, change colour; so that, lest he should have touched on a truth, he explained very kindly: "You remember that that was what you asked *me* long ago — that first day at Weatherend."

"Oh yes, and you told me you didn't know — that I was to see for myself. We've said little about it since, even in so long a time."

"Precisely," Marcher interposed — "quite as if it were too delicate a matter for us to make free with. Quite as if we might find, on pressure, that I *am* afraid. For then," he said, "we shouldn't, should we? quite know what to do."

She had for the time no answer to this question. "There have been days when I thought you were. Only, of course," she added, "there have been days when we have thought almost anything."

"Everything. Oh!" Marcher softly groaned as with a gasp, half-spent, at the face, more uncovered just then than it had been for a long while, of the imagination always with them. It had always had its incalculable moments of glaring out, quite as with the very eyes of the very Beast, and, used as he was to them, they could still draw from him the tribute of a sigh that rose from the depths of his being. All they had thought, first and last, rolled over him; the past seemed to have been reduced to mere barren speculation. This in fact was what the place had just struck him as so full of — the simplification of everything but the state of suspense. That remained only by seeming to hang in the void surrounding it. Even his original fear, if fear it had been, had lost itself in the desert. "I judge, however," he continued, "that you see I'm not afraid now."

"What I see, as I make it out, is that you've achieved something almost unprecedented in the way of getting used to danger. Living with it so long and so closely you've lost your sense of it; you know it's there, but you're indifferent, and you cease even, as of old, to have to whistle in the dark. Considering what the danger is," May Bartram wound up, "I'm bound to say I don't think your attitude could well be surpassed."

John Marcher faintly smiled. "It's heroic?"

"Certainly — call it that."

It was what he would have liked indeed to call it. "I *am* then a man of courage?"

"That's what you were to show me."

He still, however, wondered. "But doesn't the man of courage know what he's afraid of — or *not* afraid of? I don't know *that,* you see. I don't focus it. I can't name it. I only know I'm exposed."

"Yes, but exposed — how shall I say? — so directly. So intimately. That's surely enough."

"Enough to make you feel then — as what we may call the end and the upshot of our watch — that I'm not afraid?"

"You're not afraid. But it isn't," she said, "the end of our watch. That is it isn't the end of yours. You've everything still to see."

"Then why haven't *you?*" he asked. He had had, all along, today, the sense of her keeping something back, and he still had it. As this was his first impression of that it quite made a date. The case was the more marked as she didn't at first answer; which in turn made him go on. "You know something I don't." Then his voice, for that of a man of courage, trembled a little. "You know what's to happen." Her silence, with the face she showed, was almost a confession — it made him sure. "You know, and you're afraid to tell me. It's so bad that you're afraid I'll find out."

All this might be true, for she did look as if, unexpectedly to her, he had crossed some mystic line that she had secretly drawn round her. Yet she might, after all, not have worried; and the real climax was that he himself, at all events, needn't. "You'll never find out."

3

It was all to have made, none the less, as I have said, a date; which came out in the fact that again and again, even after long intervals, other things that passed between them wore in relation to this hour but the character of recalls and results. Its immediate effect had been indeed rather to lighten insistence — almost to provoke a reaction; as if their topic had dropped by its own weight and as if moreover, for that matter, Marcher had been visited by one of his occasional warnings against egotism. He had kept up, he felt, and very decently on the whole, his consciousness of the importance of not being selfish, and it was true that he had never sinned in that direction without promptly enough trying to press the scales the other way. He often repaired his fault, the season permitting, by inviting his friend to accompany him to the opera: and it not infrequently thus happened that, to show he didn't wish her to have but one sort of food for her mind, he was the cause of her appearing there with him a dozen nights in the month. It even happened that, seeing her home at such times, he occasionally went in with her to finish, as he called it, the evening, and, the better to make his point, sat down to the frugal but always careful little supper that awaited his pleasure. His point was made, he thought, by his not eternally insisting with her on himself; made for instance, at such hours, when it befell that, her piano at hand and each of them familiar with it, they went over passages of the opera together. It chanced to be on one of these occasions, however, that he reminded her of her not having answered a certain question he had put to her during the talk that had taken place between them on her last birthday. "What is it that saves *you?*" — saved her, he meant, from that appearance of variation from the usual human type. If he had practically escaped remark, as she pretended, by doing, in the most important particular, what most men do — find the answer to life in patching up an alliance of a sort with a woman no better than himself — how had she escaped it, and how could the alliance, such as it was, since they must suppose it had been more or less noticed, have failed to make her rather positively talked about?

"I never said," May Bartram replied, "that it hadn't made me a good deal talked about."

"Ah well then you're not 'saved.'"

"It hasn't been a question for me. If you've had your woman I've had," she said, "my man."

"And you mean that makes you all right?"

Oh it was always as if there were so much to say! "I don't know why it shouldn't make me — humanly, which is what we're speaking of — as right as it makes you."

"I see," Marcher returned. "'Humanly,' no doubt, as showing that you're living for something. Not, that is, just for me and my secret."

May Bartram smiled. "I don't pretend it exactly shows that I'm not living for you. It's my intimacy with you that's in question."

He laughed as he saw what she meant. "Yes, but since, as you say, I'm only, so far as people make out, ordinary, you're — aren't you? — no more than ordinary either. You help me to pass for a man like another. So if I *am*, as I understand you, you're not compromised. Is that it?"

She had another of her waits, but she

spoke clearly enough. "That's it. It's all that concerns me — to help you to pass for a man like another."

He was careful to acknowledge the remark handsomely. "How kind, how beautiful, you are to me! How shall I ever repay you?"

She had her last grave pause, as if there might be a choice of ways. But she chose. "By going on as you are."

It was into this going on as he was that they relapsed, and really for so long a time that the day inevitably came for a further sounding of their depths. These depths, constantly bridged over by a structure firm enough in spite of its lightness and of its occasional oscillation in the somewhat vertiginous air, invited on occasion, in the interest of their nerves, a dropping of the plummet and a measurement of the abyss. A difference had been made moreover, once for all, by the fact that she had all the while not appeared to feel the need of rebutting his charge of an idea within her that she didn't dare to express — a charge uttered just before one of the fullest of their later discussions ended. It had come up for him then that she "knew" something and that what she knew was bad — too bad to tell him. When he had spoken of it as visibly so bad that she was afraid he might find it out, her reply had left the matter too equivocal to be let alone and yet, for Marcher's special sensibility, almost too formidable again to touch. He circled about it at a distance that alternately narrowed and widened and that still wasn't much affected by the consciousness in him that there was nothing she could "know," after all, any better than he did. She had no source of knowledge he hadn't equally — except of course that she might have finer nerves. That was what women had where they were interested; they made out things, where people were concerned, that the people often couldn't have made out for themselves. Their nerves, their sensibility, their imagination, were conductors and revealers, and the beauty of May Bartram was in particular that she had given herself so to his case. He felt in these days what, oddly enough, he had never felt before, the growth of a dread of losing her by some catastrophe — some catastrophe that yet wouldn't at all be *the* catastrophe: partly because she had almost of a sudden begun to strike him as more useful to him than ever yet, and partly by reason of an appearance of uncertainty in her health, coincident and equally new. It was characteristic of the inner detachment he had hitherto so successfully cultivated and to which our whole account of him is a reference, it was characteristic that his complications, such as they were, had never yet seemed so as at this crisis to thicken about him, even to the point of making him ask himself if he were, by any chance, of a truth, within sight or sound, within touch or reach, within the immediate jurisdiction, of the thing that waited.

When the day came, as come it had to, that his friend confessed to him her fear of a deep disorder in her blood, he felt somehow the shadow of a change and the chill of a shock. He immediately began to imagine aggravations and disasters, and above all to think of her peril as the direct menace for himself of personal privation. This indeed gave him one of those partial recoveries of equanimity that were agreeable to him — it showed him that what was still first in his mind was the loss she herself might suffer. "What if she should have to die before knowing, before seeing — ?" It would have been brutal, in the early stages of her trouble, to put that question to her; but it had immediately sounded for him to his own concern, and the possibility was what most made him sorry for her. If she did "know," moreover, in the sense of

her having had some — what should he
think? — mystical irresistible light, this
would make the matter not better, but
worse, inasmuch as her original adoption
of his own curiosity had quite become the
basis of her life. She had been living to see
what would *be* to be seen, and it would
quite lacerate her to have to give up before
the accomplishment of the vision. These
reflexions, as I say, quickened his gener-
osity; yet, make them as he might, he saw
himself, with the lapse of the period, more
and more disconcerted. It lapsed for him
with a strange steady sweep, and the
oddest oddity was that it gave him, independently of the threat of much inconve-
nience, almost the only positive surprise
his career, if career it could be called, had
yet offered him. She kept the house as she
had never done; he had to go to her to see
her — she could meet him nowhere now,
though there was scarce a corner of their
loved old London in which she hadn't in
the past, at one time or another, done so;
and he found her always seated by her fire
in the deep old-fashioned chair she was
less and less able to leave. He had been
struck one day, after an absence exceeding
his usual measure, with her suddenly
looking much older to him than he had

ever thought of her being; then he recognised that the suddenness was all on his side — he had just simply and suddenly noticed. She looked older because inevitably, after so many years, she *was* old, or almost; which was of course true in still greater measure of her companion. If she was old, or almost, John Marcher assuredly was, and yet it was her showing of the lesson, not his own, that brought the truth home to him. His surprises began here; when once they had begun they multiplied; they came rather with a rush: it was as if, in the oddest way in the world, they had all been kept back, sown in a thick cluster, for the late afternoon of life, the time at which for people in general the unexpected has died out.

One of them was that he should have caught himself — for he *had* so done — *really* wondering if the great accident would take form now as nothing more than his being condemned to see this charming woman, this admirable friend, pass away from him. He had never so unreservedly qualified her as while confronted in thought with such a possibility; in spite of which there was small doubt for him that as an answer to his long riddle the mere effacement of even so fine a feature of his situation would be an abject anti-climax. It would represent, as connected with his past attitude, a drop of dignity under the shadow of which his existence could only become the most grotesque of failures. He had been far from holding it a failure — long as he had waited for the appearance that was to make it a success. He had waited for quite another thing, not for such a thing as that. The breath of his good faith came short, however, as he recognised how long he had waited, or how long at least his companion had. That she, at all events, might be recorded as having waited in vain — this affected him sharply, and all the more because of his at first having done little more than amuse himself with the idea. It grew more grave as the gravity of her condition grew, and the state of mind it produced in him, which he himself ended by watching as if it had been some definite disfigurement of his outer person, may pass for another of his surprises. This conjoined itself still with another, the really stupefying consciousness of a question that he would have allowed to shape itself had he dared. What did everything mean — what, that is, did *she* mean, she and her vain waiting and her probable death and the soundless admonition of it all — unless that, at this time of day, it was simply, it was overwhelmingly too late? He had never at any stage of his queer consciousness admitted the whisper of such a correction; he had never till within these last few months been so false to his conviction as not to hold that what was to come to him had time, whether *he* struck himself as having it or not. That at last, at last, he certainly hadn't it, to speak of, or had it but in the scantiest measure — such, soon enough, as things went with him, became the inference with which his old obsession had to reckon: and this it was not helped to do by the more and more confirmed appearance that the great vagueness casting the long shadow in which he had lived had, to attest itself, almost no margin left. Since it was in Time that he was to have met his fate, so it was in Time that his fate was to have acted; and as he waked up to the sense of no longer being young, which was exactly the sense of being stale, just as that, in turn, was the sense of being weak, he waked up to another matter beside. It all hung together; they were subject, he and the great vagueness, to an equal and indivisible law. When the possibilities themselves had accordingly turned stale, when the secret of the gods had grown faint, had perhaps even quite evaporated, that, and that only, was failure. It wouldn't have been failure to be bankrupt, dishonoured, pilloried, hanged; it was failure not to be anything. And so, in the dark valley into which his path had taken its unlooked-for twist, he wondered not a little as he groped. He didn't care what awful crash might overtake him, with what ignominy or what monstrosity he might yet be associated — since he wasn't after all too utterly old to suffer — if it would only be decently proportionate to the posture he had kept, all his life, in the threatened presence of it. He had but one desire left — that he shouldn't have been "sold."

4

Then it was that, one afternoon, while the spring of the year was young and new she met all in her own way his frankest betrayal of these alarms. He had gone in late to see her, but evening hadn't settled and she was presented to him in that long fresh light of waning April days which affects us often with a sadness sharper than the greyest hours of autumn. The week had been warm, the spring was supposed to have begun early, and May Bartram sat, for the first time in the year, without a fire; a fact that, to Marcher's sense, gave the scene of which she formed part a smooth and ultimate look, an air of knowing, in its immaculate order and cold meaningless cheer, that it would never see a fire again. Her own aspect — he could scarce have said why — intensified this note. Almost as white as wax, with the marks and signs in her face as numerous and as fine as if they had been etched by a needle, with soft white draperies relieved by a faded green scarf on the delicate tone of which the years had further refined, she was the picture of a serene and exquisite but impenetrable sphinx, whose head, or indeed all whose person, might have been powdered with silver. She was a sphinx, yet with her white petals and green fronds she might have been a lily too — only an artificial lily, wonderfully imitated and constantly kept, without dust or stain, though not exempt from a slight droop and a complexity of faint creases, under some clear glass bell. The perfection of household care, of high polish and finish, always reigned in her rooms, but they now looked most as if everything had been wound up, tucked in, put away, so that she might sit with folded hands and with nothing more to do. She was "out of it," to

Marcher's vision; her work was over; she communicated with him as across some gulf or from some island of rest that she had already reached, and it made him feel strangely abandoned. Was it — or rather wasn't it — that if for so long she had been watching with him the answer to their question must have swum into her ken and taken on its name, so that her occupation was verily gone? He had as much as charged her with this in saying to her, many months before, that she even then knew something she was keeping from him. It was a point he had never since ventured to press, vaguely fearing as he did that it might become a difference, perhaps a disagreement, between them. He had in this later time turned nervous, which was what he in all the other years had never been; and the oddity was that his nervousness should have waited till he had begun to doubt, should have held off so long as he was sure. There was something, it seemed to him, that the wrong word would bring down on his head, something that would so at least ease off his tension. But he wanted not to speak the wrong word; that would make everything ugly. He wanted the knowledge he lacked to drop on him, if drop it could, by its own august weight. If she was to forsake him it was surely for her to take leave. This was why he didn't directly ask her again what she knew; but it was also why, approaching the matter from another side, he said to her in the course of his visit: "What do you regard as the very worst that at this time of day *can* happen to me?"

He had asked her that in the past often enough; they had, with the odd irregular rhythm of their intensities and avoidances, exchanged ideas about it and then had seen the ideas washed away by cool intervals, washed like figures traced in sea-sand. It had ever been the mark of their talk that the oldest allusions in it required but a little dismissal and reaction to come out again, sounding for the hour as new. She could thus at present meet his enquiry quite freshly and patiently. "Oh yes, I've repeatedly thought, only it always seemed to me of old that I couldn't quite make up my mind. I thought of dreadful things, between which it was difficult to choose; and so must you have done."

"Rather! I feel now as if I had scarce done anything else. I appear to myself to have spent my life in thinking of nothing *but* dreadful things. A great many of them I've at different times named to you, but there were others I couldn't name."

"They were too, too dreadful?"

"Too, too dreadful — some of them."

She looked at him a minute, and there came to him as he met it an inconsequent sense that her eyes, when one got their full clearness, were still as beautiful as they had been in youth, only beautiful with a strange cold light — a light that somehow was a part of the effect, if it wasn't rather a part of the cause, of the pale hard sweetness of the season and the hour. "And yet," she said at last, "there are horrors we've mentioned."

It deepened the strangeness to see her, as such a figure in such a picture, talk of "horrors," but she was to do in a few minutes something stranger yet — though even of this he was to take the full measure but afterwards — and the note of it already trembled. It was, for the matter of that, one of the signs that her eyes were having again the high flicker of their prime. He had to admit, however, what she said. "Oh yes, there were times when we did go far." He caught himself in the act of speaking as if it all were over. Well, he wished it were; and the consummation depended for him clearly more and more on his friend.

But she had now a soft smile. "Oh far — !"

It was oddly ironic. "Do you mean you're prepared to go further?"

She was frail and ancient and charming as she continued to look at him, yet it was rather as if she had lost the thread. "Do you consider that we went far?"

"Why I thought it the point you were just making — that we *had* looked most things in the face."

"Including each other?" She still smiled. "But you're quite right. We've had together great imaginations, often great fears; but some of them have been unspoken."

"Then the worst — we haven't faced that. I *could* face it, I believe, if I knew what you think it. I feel," he explained, "as if I had lost my power to conceive such things." And he wondered if he looked as blank as he sounded. "It's spent."

"Then why do you assume," she asked, "that mine isn't?"

"Because you've given me signs to the contrary. It isn't a question for you of conceiving, imagining, comparing. It isn't a question now of choosing." At last he came out with it. "You know something I don't. You've shown me that before."

These last words had affected her, he made out in a moment, exceedingly, and she spoke with firmness. "I've shown you, my dear, nothing."

He shook his head. "You can't hide it."

"Oh, oh!" May Bartram sounded over what she couldn't hide. It was almost a smothered groan.

"You admitted it months ago, when I spoke of it to you as of something you were afraid I should find out. Your answer was that I couldn't, that I wouldn't, and I don't pretend I have. But you had something therefore in mind, and I now see how it must have been, how it still is, the possibility that, of all possibilities, has settled itself for you as the worst. This," he went on, "is why I appeal to you. I'm only afraid of ignorance to-day — I'm not afraid of knowledge." And then as for a while she said nothing: "What makes me sure is that I see in your face and feel here, in this air and amid these appearances, that you're out of it. You've done. You've had your experience. You leave me to my fate."

Well, she listened, motionless and white in her chair, as on a decision to be made, so that her manner was fairly an avowal, though still, with a small fine inner stiffness, an imperfect surrender. "It *would* be the worst," she finally let herself say. "I mean the thing I've never said."

It hushed him a moment. "More monstrous than all the monstrosities we've named?"

"More monstrous. Isn't that what you sufficiently express," she asked, "in calling it the worst?"

Marcher thought. "Assuredly — if you mean, as I do, something that includes all the loss and all the shame that are thinkable."

"It would if it *should* happen," said May Bartram. "What we're speaking of, remember, is only my idea."

"It's your belief," Marcher returned. "That's enough for me. I feel your beliefs are right. Therefore if, having this one, you give me no more light on it, you abandon me."

"No, no!" she repeated. "I'm with you — don't you see? — still." And as to make it more vivid to him she rose from her chair — a movement she seldom risked in these days — and showed herself, all draped and all soft, in her fairness and slimness. "I haven't forsaken you."

It was really, in its effort against weakness, a generous assurance, and had the success of the impulse not, happily, been great, it would have touched him to pain more than to pleasure. But the cold charm in her eyes had spread, as she hovered before him, to all the rest of her person, so that it was for the minute almost a recovery of youth. He couldn't pity her for that; he could only take her as she showed — as capable even yet of helping him. It was as if, at the same time, her light might at any instant go out; wherefore he must make the most of it. There passed before him with intensity the three or four things he wanted most to know; but the question that came of itself to his lips really covered the others. "Then tell me if I shall consciously suffer."

She promptly shook her head. "Never!"

It confirmed the authority he imputed to her, and it produced on him an extraordinary effect. "Well, what's better than that? Do you call that the worst?"

"You think nothing is better?" she asked.

She seemed to mean something so special that he again sharply wondered, though still with the dawn of a prospect of relief. "Why not, if one doesn't *know?*" After which, as their eyes, over his question, met in a silence, the dawn deepened and something to his purpose came prodigiously out of her very face. His own, as he took it in, suddenly flushed to the forehead, and he gasped with the force of a perception to which, on the instant, everything fitted. The sound of his gasp filled the air; then he became articulate. "I see — if I don't suffer!"

In her own look, however, was doubt. "You see what?"

"Why what you mean — what you've always meant."

She again shook her head. "What I mean isn't what I've always meant. It's different."

"It's something new?"

She hung back from it a little. "Something new. It's not what you think. I see what you think."

His divination drew breath then; only her correction might be wrong. "It isn't that I *am* a blockhead?" he asked between faintness and grimness. "It isn't that it's all a mistake?"

"A mistake?" she pityingly echoed. *That* possibility, for her, he saw, would be monstrous; and if she guaranteed him the immunity from pain it would accordingly not be what she had in mind. "Oh no," she declared; "it's nothing of that sort. You've been right."

Yet he couldn't help asking himself if she weren't, thus pressed, speaking but to save him. It seemed to him he should be most in a hole if his history should prove all a platitude. "Are you telling me the truth, so that I shan't have been a bigger idiot than I can bear to know? I *haven't* lived with a vain imagination, in the most besotted illusion? I haven't waited but to see the door shut in my face?"

She shook her head again. "However the case stands *that* isn't the truth. Whatever the reality, it *is* a reality. The door isn't shut. The door's open," said May Bartram.

"Then something's to come?"

She waited once again, always with her cold sweet eyes on him. "It's never too late." She had, with her gliding step, diminished the distance between them, and she stood nearer to him, close to him, a minute, as if still charged with the unspoken: Her movement might have been for some finer emphasis of what she was at once hesitating and deciding to say. He had been standing by the chimney-piece, fireless and sparely adorned, a small perfect old French clock and two morsels of rosy Dresden constituting all its furniture; and her hand grasped the shelf while she kept him waiting, grasped it a little as for support and encouragement. She only kept him waiting, however; that is he only waited. It had become suddenly, from her movement and attitude, beautiful and vivid to him that she had something more to give him; her wasted face delicately shone with it — it glittered almost as with the white lustre of silver in her expression. She was right, incontestably, for what he saw in her face was the truth, and strangely, without consequence, while their talk of it as dreadful was still in the air, she appeared to present it as inordinately soft. This, prompting bewilderment, made him but gape the more gratefully for her revelation, so that they continued for some minutes silent, her face shining at him, her contact imponderably pressing, and his stare all kind but all expectant. The end, none the less, was that what he had expected failed to come to him. Something else took place instead, which seemed to consist at first in the mere closing of her eyes. She gave way at the same instant to a slow fine shudder, and though he remained staring — though he stared in fact but the harder — turned off and regained her chair. It was the end of what she had been intending, but it left him thinking only of that.

"Well, you don't say — ?"

She had touched in her passage a bell near the chimney and had sunk back strangely pale. "I'm afraid I'm too ill."

"Too ill to tell me?" It sprang up sharp to him, and almost to his lips, the fear she might die without giving him light. He checked himself in time from so expressing his question, but she answered as if she had heard the words.

"Don't you know — now?"

" 'Now' — ?" She had spoken as if some difference had been made within the moment. But her maid, quickly obedient to her bell, was already with them. "I know nothing." And he was afterwards to say to himself that he must have spoken with odious impatience, such an impatience as to show that, supremely disconcerted, he washed his hands of the whole question.

"Oh!" said May Bartram.

"Are you in pain?" he asked as the woman went to her.

"No," said May Bartram.

Her maid, who had put an arm round her as if to take her to her room, fixed on him eyes that appealingly contradicted her; in spite of which, however, he showed once more his mystification. "What then has happened?"

She was once more, with her companion's help, on her feet, and, feeling withdrawal imposed on him, he had blankly found his hat and gloves and had reached the door. Yet he waited for her answer. "What *was* to," she said.

5

He came back the next day, but she was then unable to see him, and as it was literally the first time this had occurred in the long stretch of their acquaintance he turned away, defeated and sore, almost angry — or feeling at least that such a break in their custom was really the beginning of the end — and wandered alone with his thoughts, especially with the one he was least able to keep down. She was dying and he would lose her; she was dying and his life would end. He stopped in the Park, into which he had passed, and stared before him at his recurrent doubt. Away from her the doubt pressed again; in her presence he had believed her, but as he felt his forlornness he threw himself into the explanation that, nearest at hand, had most of a miserable warmth for him and least of a cold torment. She had deceived him to save him — to put him off with something in which he should be able to rest. What could the thing that was to happen to him be, after all, but just this thing that had begun to happen? Her dying, her death, his consequent solitude — *that* was what he had figured as the Beast in the Jungle, that was what had been in the lap of the gods. He had had her word for it as he left her — what else on earth could she have meant? It wasn't a thing of a monstrous order; not a fate rare and distinguished; not a stroke of fortune that overwhelmed and immortalised; it had only the stamp of the common doom. But poor Marcher at this hour judged the common doom sufficient. It would serve his turn, and even as the consummation of infinite waiting he would bend his pride to accept it. He sat down on a bench in the twilight. He hadn't been a fool. Something had *been,* as she had said, to come. Before he rose indeed it had quite struck him that the final fact really matched with the long avenue through which he had had to reach it. As sharing his suspense and as giving herself all, giving her life, to bring it to an end, she had come with him every step of the way. He had lived by her aid, and to leave her behind would be cruelly, damnably to miss her. What could be more overwhelming than that?

Well, he was to know within the week, for though she kept him a while at bay, left him restless and wretched during a series of days on each of which he asked about her only again to have to turn away, she ended his trial by receiving him where she had always received him. Yet she had been brought out at some hazard into the presence of so many of the things that were, consciously, vainly, half their past, and there was scant service left in the gentleness of her mere desire, all too visible, to check his obsession and wind up his long trouble. That was clearly what she wanted; the one thing more, her own peace, while she could still put out her hand. He was so affected by her state that, once seated by her chair, he was moved to let everything go; it was she herself therefore who brought him back, took up again, before she dismissed him, her last word of the other time. She showed how she wished to leave their business in order. "I'm not sure you understood. You've nothing to wait for more. It *has* come."

Oh how he looked at her! "Really?"

"Really."

"The thing that, as you said, *was* to?"

"The thing that we began in our youth to watch for."

Face to face with her once more he believed her; it was a claim to which he had so abjectly little to oppose. "You mean that it has come as a positive definite occurrence, with a name and a date?"

"Positive. Definite. I don't know about the 'name,' but oh with a date!"

He found himself again too helplessly at sea. "But come in the night — come and passed me by?"

May Bartram had her strange faint smile. "Oh no, it hasn't passed you by!"

"But if I haven't been aware of it and it

hasn't touched me — ?"

"Ah your not being aware of it" — and she seemed to hesitate an instant to deal with this — "your not being aware of it is the strangeness *in* the strangeness. It's the wonder *of* the wonder." She spoke as with the softness almost of a sick child, yet now at last, at the end of all, with the perfect straightness of a sibyl. She visibly knew that she knew, and the effect on him was of something coordinate, in its high character, with the law that had ruled him. It was the true voice of the law; so on her lips would the law itself have sounded. "It *has* touched you," she went on. "It has done its office. It has made you all its own."

"So utterly without my knowing it?"

"So utterly without your knowing it." His hand, as he leaned to her, was on the arm of her chair, and, dimly smiling always now, she placed her own on it. "It's enough if *I* know it."

"Oh!" he confusedly breathed, as she herself of late so often had done.

"What I long ago said is true. You'll never know now, and I think you ought to be content. You've *had* it," said May Bartram.

"But had what?"

"Why what was to have marked you out.

The proof of your law. It has acted. I'm too glad," she then bravely added, "to have been able to see what it's *not*."

He continued to attach his eyes to her, and with the sense that it was all beyond him, and that *she* was too, he would still have sharply challenged her hadn't he so felt it an abuse of her weakness to do more than take devoutly what she gave him, take it hushed as to a revelation. If he did speak, it was out of the foreknowledge of his loneliness to come. "If you're glad of what it's 'not' it might then have been worse?"

She turned her eyes away, she looked straight before her; with which after a moment: "Well, you know our fears."

He wondered. "It's something then we never feared?"

On this slowly she turned to him. "Did we ever dream, with all our dreams, that we should sit and talk of it thus?"

He tried for a little to make out that they had; but it was as if their dreams, numberless enough, were in solution in some thick cold mist through which thought lost itself. "It might have been that we couldn't talk?"

"Well" — she did her best for him — "not from this side. This, you see," she said, "is the *other* side."

"I think," poor Marcher returned, "that

253

all sides are the same to me." Then, however, as she gently shook her head in correction: "We mightn't, as it were, have got across — ?"

"To where we are — no. We're *here*" — she made her weak emphasis.

"And much good does it do us!" was her friend's frank comment.

"It does us the good it can. It does us the good that *it* isn't here. It's past. It's behind," said May Bartram. "Before —" but her voice dropped.

He had got up, not to tire her, but it was hard to combat his yearning. She after all told him nothing but that his light had failed — which he knew well enough without her. "Before — ?" he blankly echoed.

"Before, you see, it was always to *come*. That kept it present."

"Oh I don't care what comes now! Besides," Marcher added, "it seems to me I liked it better present, as you say, than I can like it absent with *your* absence."

"Oh mine!" — and her pale hands made light of it.

"With the absence of everything." He had a dreadful sense of standing there before her for — so far as anything but this proved, this bottomless drop was concerned — the last time of their life. It rested on him with a weight he felt he could scarce bear, and this weight it apparently was that still pressed out what remained in him of speakable protest. "I believe you; but I can't begin to pretend I understand. *Nothing*, for me, is past; nothing *will* pass till I pass myself, which I pray my stars may be as soon as possible. Say, however," he added, "that I've eaten my cake, as you contend, to the last crumb — how can the thing I've never felt at all be the thing I was marked out to feel?"

She met him perhaps less directly, but she met him unperturbed. "You take your 'feelings' for granted. You were to suffer your fate. That was not necessarily to know it."

"How in the world — when what is such knowledge but suffering?"

She looked up at him a while in silence. "No — you don't understand."

"I suffer," said John Marcher.

"Don't, don't!"

"How can I help at least *that?*"

"*Don't!*" May Bartram repeated.

She spoke it in a tone so special, in spite of her weakness, that he stared an instant — stared as if some light, hitherto hidden, had shimmered across his vision. Darkness again closed over it, but the gleam had already become for him an idea. "Because I haven't the right — ?"

"Don't *know* — when you needn't," she mercifully urged. "You needn't — for we shouldn't."

"Shouldn't?" If he could but know what she meant!

"No — it's too much."

"Too much?" he still asked but, with a mystification that was the next moment of a sudden to give way. Her words, if they meant something, affected him in this light — the light also of her wasted face — as meaning *all*, and the sense of what knowledge had been for herself came over him with a rush which broke through into a question. "Is it of that then you're dying?"

She but watched him, gravely at first, as to see, with this, where he was, and she might have seen something or feared something that moved her sympathy. "I would live for you still — if I could." Her eyes closed for a little, as if, withdrawn into herself, she were for a last time trying. "But I can't!" she said as she raised them again to take leave of him.

She couldn't indeed, as but too promptly and sharply appeared, and he had no vision of her after this that was anything but darkness and doom. They had parted for ever in that strange talk; access to her chamber of pain, rigidly guarded, was almost wholly forbidden him; he was feeling now moreover, in the face of doctors, nurses, the two or three relatives attracted doubtless by the presumption of what she had to "leave," how few were the rights, as they were called in such cases, that he had to put forward, and how odd it might even seem that their intimacy shouldn't have given him more of them. The stupidest fourth cousin had more, even though she had been nothing in such a person's life. She had been a feature of features in *his*, for what else was it to have been so indispensable? Strange beyond saying were the ways of existence, baffling for him the anomaly of his lack, as he felt it to be, of producible claim. A woman might have been, as it were, everything to him, and it might yet present him in no connexion that any one seemed held to recognise. If this was the case in these closing weeks it was the case more sharply on the occasion of the last offices rendered, in the great grey London cemetery, to what had been mortal, to what had been precious, in his friend. The concourse at her grave was not numerous, but he saw himself treated as scarce more nearly concerned with it than if there had been a thousand others. He was in short from this moment face to face with the fact that he was to profit extraordinarily little by the interest May Bartram had taken in him. He couldn't quite have said what he expected, but he hadn't surely expected this approach to a double privation. Not only had her interest failed him, but he seemed to feel himself unattended — and for a reason he couldn't seize — by the distinction, the dignity, the propriety, if nothing else, of the man markedly bereaved. It was as if in the view of society he had not *been* markedly bereaved, as if there still failed some sign or proof of it, and as if none the less his character could never be affirmed nor the deficiency ever made up. There were moments as the weeks went by when he would have liked, by some almost aggressive act, to take his stand on the intimacy of his loss, in order that it *might* be questioned and his retort, to the relief of his spirit, so recorded; but the moments of an irritation more helpless followed fast on these, the moments during which, turning things over with a good conscience but with a bare horizon, he found himself wondering if he oughtn't to have begun, so to speak, further back.

He found himself wondering indeed at many things, and this last speculation had others to keep it company. What could he have done, after all, in her lifetime, without giving them both, as it were, away? He couldn't have made known she was watching him, for that would have published the superstition of the Beast. This was what closed his mouth now — now that the Jungle had been threshed to vacancy and that the Beast had stolen away. It sounded too foolish and too flat; the difference for him in this particular, the extinction in his life of the element of suspense, was such as in fact to surprise him. He could scarce have said what the effect resembled; the abrupt cessation, the positive prohibition, of music perhaps, more than anything else, in some place all adjusted and all accustomed to sonority and to attention. If he could at any rate have conceived lifting the veil from his image at some moment of the past (what had he done, after all, if not lift it to *her?*) so to do this to-day, to talk to people at large of the Jungle cleared and confide to them that he now felt it as safe, would have been not only to see them listen as to a goodwife's tale, but really to hear himself tell one. What it presently came to in truth was that poor Marcher waded through his beaten grass, where no life stirred, where no breath sounded, where no evil eye seemed to gleam from a possible lair, very much as if vaguely looking for the Beast, and still more as if acutely missing it. He walked about in an existence that had grown strangely more spacious and, stopping fitfully in places where the undergrowth of life struck him as closer, asked himself yearningly, wondered secretly and sorely, if it would have lurked here or there. It would have at all events *sprung;* what was at least complete was his belief in the truth itself of the assurance given him. The change from his old sense to his new was absolute and final: what was to happen *had* so absolutely and finally happened that he was as little able to know a fear for his future as to know a hope; so absent in short was any question of anything still to come. He was to live entirely with the other question, that of his unidentified past, that of his having to see his fortune impenetrably muffled and masked.

The torment of this vision became then his occupation; he couldn't perhaps have consented to live but for the possibility of guessing. She had told him, his friend, not to guess; she had forbidden him, so far as he might, to know, and she had even in a sort denied the power in him to learn: which were so many things precisely, to deprive him of rest. It wasn't that he wanted, he argued for fairness, that anything past and done should repeat itself; it was only that he shouldn't, as an anticlimax, have been taken sleeping so sound as not to be able to win back by an effort of thought the lost stuff of consciousness. He declared to himself at moments that he would either win it back or have done with consciousness for ever; he made this idea his one motive in fine, made it so much his passion that none other, to compare with it, seemed ever to have touched him. The lost stuff of consciousness became thus for him as a strayed or stolen child to an unappeasable father; he hunted it up and down very much as if he were knocking at doors and enquiring of the police. This was the spirit in which, inevitably, he set himself to travel; he started on a journey that was to be as long as he could make it; it danced before him that, as the other side of the globe couldn't possibly have less to say to him, it might, by a possibility of suggestion, have more. Before he quitted London, however, he made a pilgrimage to May Bartram's grave, took his way to it through the endless avenues of the grim suburban metropolis, sought it out in the wilderness of tombs, and, though he had come but for the renewal of the act of farewell, found himself, when he had at last stood by it, beguiled into long intensities. He stood for an hour, powerless to turn away and yet powerless to penetrate the darkness of death; fixing with his eyes her inscribed name and date, beating his forehead against the fact of the secret they kept, drawing his breath, while he waited, as if some sense would in pity of him rise from the stones. He kneeled on the stones, however, in vain; they kept what they concealed; and if the face of the tomb did become a face for him it was because her two names became a pair of eyes that didn't know him. He gave them a last long look, but no palest light broke.

6

He stayed away, after this, for a year; he visited the depths of Asia, spending himself on scenes of romantic interest, of superlative sanctity; but what was present to him everywhere was that for a man who had known what *he* had known the world was vulgar and vain. The state of mind in which he had lived for so many years shone out to him, in reflexion, as a light that coloured and refined, a light beside which the glow of the East was garish cheap and thin. The terrible truth was that he had lost — with everything else — a distinction as well; the things he saw couldn't help being common when he had become common to look at them. He was simply now one of them himself — he was in the dust, without a peg for the sense of difference; and there were hours when, before the temples of gods and the sepulchres of kings, his spirit turned for nobleness of association to the barely discriminated slab in the London suburb. That had become for him, and more intensely with time and distance, his one witness of a past glory. It was all that was left to him for proof or pride, yet the past glories of Pharaohs were nothing to him as he thought of it. Small wonder then that he came back to it on the morrow of his return. He was drawn there this time as irresistibly as the other, yet with a confidence, almost, that was doubtless the effect of the many months that had elapsed. He had lived, in spite of himself, into his change of feeling, and in wandering over the earth had wandered, as might be said, from the circumference to the centre of his desert. He had settled to his safety and accepted perforce his extinction; figuring to himself, with some colour, in the likeness of certain little old men he remembered to have seen, of whom, all meagre and wizened as they might look, it was related that they had in their time fought twenty duels or been loved by ten princesses. They indeed had been wondrous for others while he was but wondrous for himself, which, however, was exactly the cause of his haste to renew the wonder by getting back, as he might put it, into his own presence. That had quickened his steps and checked his delay. If his visit was prompt it was because he had been separated so long from the part of himself that alone he now valued.

It's accordingly not false to say that he reached his goal with a certain elation and stood there again with a certain assurance. The creature beneath the sod *knew* of his rare experience, so that, strangely now, the place had lost for him its mere blankness of expression. It met him in mildness — not, as before, in mockery; it wore for him the air of conscious greeting that we find, after absence, in things that have closely belonged to us and which seem to confess of themselves to the connexion. The plot of ground, the graven tablet, the tended flowers affected him so as belonging to him that he resembled for the hour a contented landlord reviewing a piece of property. Whatever had happened — well, had happened. He had not come back this time with the vanity of that question, his former worrying "what, *what?*" now practically so spent. Yet he would none the less never again so cut himself off from the spot; he would come back to it every month, for if he did nothing else by its aid he at least held up his head. It thus grew for him, in the oddest way, a positive resource; he carried out his idea of periodical returns, which took their place at last among the most inveterate of his habits. What it all amounted to, oddly enough, was that in his finally so simplified world this garden of death gave him the few square feet of earth on which he could still most live. It was as if, being nothing anywhere else for any one, nothing even for himself, he were just everything here, and if not for a crowd of witnesses or indeed for any witness but John Marcher, then by clear right of the register that he could scan like an open page. The open page was the tomb of his friend, and *there* were the facts of the past, there the truth of his life, there the backward reaches in which he could lose himself. He did this from time to time with such effect that he seemed to wander through the old years with his hand in the arm of a companion who was, in the most extraordinary manner, his other, his younger self; and to wander, which was more extraordinary yet, round and round a third presence — not wandering she, but stationary, still, whose eyes, turning with his revolution, never ceased to follow him, and whose seat was his point, so to speak, of orientation. Thus in short he settled to live — feeding all on the sense that he once *had* lived, and dependent on it not alone for a support but for an identity.

It sufficed him in its way for months and the year elapsed; it would doubtless even have carried him further but for an accident, superficially slight, which moved him, quite in another direction, with a force beyond any of his impressions of Egypt or of India. It was a thing of the merest chance — the turn, as he afterwards felt, of a hair, though he was indeed to live to believe that if light hadn't come to him in this particular fashion it would still have come in another. He was to live to believe this, I say, though he was not to live, I may not less definitely mention, to do much else. We allow him at any rate the benefit of the conviction, struggling up for him at the end, that, whatever might have happened or not happened, he would have come round of himself to the light. The incident of an autumn day had put the match to the train laid from of old by his misery. With the light before him he knew that even of late his ache had only been smothered. It was strangely drugged, but it throbbed; at the touch it began to bleed. And the touch, in the event, was the face of a fellow mortal. This face, one grey afternoon when the leaves were thick in the alleys, looked into Marcher's own, at the cemetery, with an expression like the cut of a blade. He felt it, that is, so deep down that he winced at the steady thrust. The person who so mutely assaulted him was a figure he had noticed, on reaching his own goal, absorbed by a grave a short distance away, a grave apparently fresh, so that the emotion of the visitor would probably match it for frankness. This fact alone forbade further attention, though during the time he stayed he remained vaguely conscious of his neighbour, a middle-aged man apparently, in mourning, whose bowed back, among the clustered monuments and mortuary yews, was constantly presented. Marcher's theory that these were elements in contact with which he himself revived, had suffered, on this occasion, it may be granted, a marked, an excessive check. The autumn day was dire for him as none had recently been, and he rested with a heaviness he had not yet known on the low stone table that bore May Bartram's name. He rested without power to move, as if some spring in him, some spell vouchsafed, had suddenly been broken for ever. If he could have done that moment as he wanted he would simply have stretched himself on the slab that was ready to take him, treating it as a place prepared to receive his last sleep. What in all the wide world had he now to keep awake for? He stared before him with the question, and it was then that, as one of the cemetery walks passed near him, he caught the shock of the face.

His neighbour at the other grave had withdrawn, as he himself, with force enough in him, would have done by now, and was advancing along the path on his way to one of the gates. This brought him close, and his pace was slow, so that — and all the more as there was a kind of hunger in his look — the two men were for a minute directly confronted. Marcher knew him at once for one of the deeply stricken — a perception so sharp that nothing else in the picture comparatively lived, neither his dress, his age, nor his presumable character and class; nothing lived but the deep ravage of the features he showed. He *showed* them — that was the point; he was moved, as he passed, by some impulse that was either a signal for sympathy or, more possibly, a challenge to an opposed sorrow. He might already have been aware of our friend, might at some previous hour have noticed in him the smooth habit of the scene, with which the state of his own senses so scantly consorted, and might thereby have been stirred as by an overt discord. What Marcher was at all events conscious of was in the first place that the image of scarred passion presented to him was conscious too — of something that profaned the air; and in the second that, roused, startled, shocked, he was yet the next moment looking after it, as it went, with envy. The most extraordinary thing that had happened to him — though he had given that name to other matters as well — took place, after his immediate vague stare, as a consequence of this impression. The stranger passed, but the raw glare of his grief remained, making our friend wonder in pity what wrong, what wound it expressed, what injury not to be healed. What had the man *had*, to make him by the loss of it so bleed and yet live?

Something — and this reached him with a pang — that *he*, John Marcher, hadn't; the proof of which was precisely John Marcher's arid end. No passion had ever touched him, for this was what passion meant; he had survived and maundered and pined, but where had been *his* deep ravage? The extraordinary thing we speak of was the sudden rush of the result of this question. The sight that had just met his eyes named to him, as in letters of quick flame, something he had utterly, insanely missed, and what he had missed made these things a train of fire, made them mark themselves in an anguish of inward throbs. He had seen *outside* of his life, not learned it within, the way a woman was mourned when she had been loved for herself: such was the force of his conviction of the meaning of the stranger's face, which still flared for him as a smoky torch. It hadn't come to him, the knowledge, on the wings of experience; it had brushed him, jostled him, upset him, with the disrespect of chance, the insolence of accident. Now that the illumination had begun, however, it blazed to the zenith, and what he presently stood there gazing at was the sounded void of his life. He gazed, he drew breath, in pain; he turned in his dismay, and, turning, he had before him in sharper incision than ever the open page of his story. The name on the table smote him as the passage of his neighbour had done, and what it said to him, full in the face, was that *she* was what he had missed. This was the awful thought, the answer to all the past, the vision at the dread clearness of which he grew as cold as the stone beneath him. Everything fell together, confessed, explained, overwhelmed; leaving him most of all stupefied at the blindness he had cherished. The fate he had been marked for he had met with a vengeance — he had emptied the cup to the lees; he had been the man of his time, *the* man, to whom nothing on earth was to have happened. That was the rare stroke — that was his visitation. So he saw it, as we say, in pale horror, while the pieces fitted and fitted. So *she* had seen it while he didn't, and so she served at this hour to drive the truth home. It was the truth, vivid and monstrous, that all the while he had waited the wait was itself his portion. This the companion of his vigil had at a given moment made out, and she had then offered him the chance to baffle his doom. One's doom, however, was never baffled, and on the day she told him his own had come down she had seen him but stupidly stare at the escape she offered him.

The escape would have been to love her; then, *then* he would have lived. *She* had lived — who could say now with what passion? — since she had loved him for himself, whereas he had never thought of her (ah how it hugely glared at him!) but in the chill of his egotism and the light of her use. Her spoken words came back to him — the chain stretched and stretched. The Beast had lurked indeed, and the Beast, at its hour, had sprung; it had sprung in that twilight of the cold April when, pale, ill, wasted, but all beautiful, and perhaps even then recoverable, she had risen from her chair to stand before him and let him imaginably guess. It had sprung as he didn't guess; it had sprung as she hopelessly turned from him, and the mark, by the time he left her, had fallen where it *was* to fall. He had justified his fear and achieved his fate; he had failed, with the last exactitude, of all he was to fail of; and a moan now rose to his lips as he remembered she had prayed he mightn't know. This horror of waking — *this* was knowledge, knowledge under the breath of which the very tears in his eyes seemed to freeze. Through them, none the less, he tried to fix it and hold it; he kept it there before him so that he might feel the pain. That at least, belated and bitter, had something of the taste of life. But the bitterness suddenly sickened him, and it was as if, horribly, he saw, in the truth, in the cruelty of his image, what had been appointed and done. He saw the Jungle of his life and saw the lurking Beast; then, while he looked, perceived it, as by a stir of the air, rise, huge and hideous, for the leap that was to settle him. His eyes darkened — it was close; and, instinctively turning, in his hallucination, to avoid it, he flung himself, face down, on the tomb.

The Jolly Corner

1

"Every one asks me what I 'think' of every-thing," said Spencer Brydon; "and I make answer as I can — begging or dodging the question, putting them off with any nonsense. It wouldn't matter to any of them really," he went on, "for, even were it possible to meet in that stand-and-deliver way so silly a demand on so big a subject, my 'thoughts' would still be almost altogether about something that concerns only myself." He was talking to Miss Staverton, with whom for a couple of months now he had availed himself of every possible occasion to talk; this disposition and this resource, this comfort and support, as the situation in fact presented itself, having promptly enough taken the first place in the considerable array of rather unattenuated surprises attending his so strangely belated return to America. Every-thing was somehow a surprise; and that might be natural when one had so long and so consistently neglected everything, taken pains to give surprises so much margin for play. He had given them more than thirty years — thirty-three, to be exact; and they now seemed to him to have organised their performance quite on the scale of that licence. He had been twenty-three on leaving New York — he was fifty-six today: unless indeed he were to reckon as he had sometimes, since his repatriation, found himself feeling; in which case he would have lived longer than is often allotted to man. It would have taken a century, he repeatedly said to himself, and said also to Alice Staverton, it would have taken a longer absence and a more averted mind than those even of which he had been guilty, to pile up the differences, the newnesses, the queernesses, above all the bignesses, for the better or the worse, that at present assaulted his vision wherever he looked.

The great fact all the while however had been the incalculability; since he *had* supposed himself, from decade to decade, to be allowing, and in the most liberal and intelligent manner, for brilliancy of change. He actually saw that he had allowed for nothing; he missed what he would have been sure of finding, he found what he would never have imagined. Proportions and values were upside-down; the ugly things he had expected, the ugly things of his far-away youth, when he had too promptly waked up to a sense of the ugly — these uncanny phenomena placed him rather, as it happened, under the charm; whereas the "swagger" things, the modern, the monstrous, the famous things, those he had more particularly, like thousands of ingenuous enquirers every year, come over to see, were exactly his sources of dismay. They were as so many set traps for displeasure, above all for reaction, of which his restless tread was constantly pressing the spring. It was interesting, doubtless, the whole show, but it would have been too disconcerting hadn't a certain finer truth saved the situation. He had distinctly not, in this steadier light, come over *all* for the monstrosities; he had come, not only in the last analysis but quite on the face of the act, under an impulse with which they had nothing to do. He had come — putting the thing pompously — to look at his "property," which he had thus for a third of a century not been within four thousand miles of, or, expressing it less sordidly, he had yielded to the humour of seeing again his house on the jolly corner, as he usually, and quite fondly, described it — the one in which he had first seen the light, in which various members of his family had lived and had died, in which the holidays of his over-schooled boyhood had been passed and the few social flowers of his chilled adolescence gathered, and which, alienated then for so long a period, had, through the successive deaths of his two brothers and the termination of old arrangements, come wholly into his hands. He was the owner of another, not quite so "good" — the jolly corner having been, from far back, superlatively extended and consecrated; and the value of the pair represented his main capital, with an income consisting, in these later years, of their respective rents which (thanks precisely to their original excellent type) had never been depressingly low. He could live in "Europe," as he had been in the habit of living, on the product of these flourishing New York leases, and all the better since, that of the second structure, the mere number in its long row, having within a twelvemonth fallen in, renovation at a high advance had proved beautifully possible.

These were items of property indeed, but he had found himself since his arrival distinguishing more than ever between them. The house within the street, two bristling blocks westward, was already in course of reconstruction as a tall mass of flats; he had acceded, some time before, to overtures for this conversion — in which, now that it was going forward, it had been not the least of his astonishments to find himself able, on the spot, and though without a previous ounce of such experience, to participate with a certain intelligence, almost with a certain authority. He had lived his life with his back so turned to such concerns and his face addressed to those of so different an order that he scarce knew what to make of this lively stir, in a compartment of his mind never yet penetrated, of a capacity for business and a sense for construction. These virtues, so common all round him now, had been dormant in his own organism — where it might be said of them perhaps that they had slept the sleep of the just. At present, in the splendid autumn weather — the autumn at least was a pure boon in the terrible place — he loafed about his "work" undeterred, secretly agitated; not in the least "minding" that the whole proposition, as they said, was vulgar and sordid, and ready to climb ladders, to walk the plank, to handle materials and look wise about them, to ask questions, in fine, and challenge explanations and really "go into" figures.

It amused, it verily quite charmed him; and, by the same stroke, it amused, and even more, Alice Staverton, though perhaps charming her perceptibly less. She wasn't however going to be better off for it, as *he* was — and so astonishingly much: nothing was now likely, he knew, ever to make her better off than she found herself, in the afternoon of life, as the delicately frugal possessor and tenant of the small house in Irving Place to which she had subtly managed to cling through her almost unbroken New York career. If he knew the way to it now better than to any other address among the dreadful multiplied numberings which seemed to him to reduce the whole place to some vast ledger-page, overgrown, fantastic, of ruled and criss-crossed lines and figures — if he had formed, for his consolation, that habit, it was really not a little because of the charm of his having encountered and recognised, in the vast wilderness of the wholesale, breaking through the mere gross generalisation of wealth and force and success, a small still scene where items and shades, all delicate things, kept the sharpness of the notes of a high voice perfectly trained, and where economy hung about like the scent of a garden. His old friend lived with one maid and herself dusted her relics and trimmed her lamps and polished her silver; she stood off, in the awful modern crush, when she could, but she sallied forth and did battle when the challenge was really to "spirit," the spirit she after all confessed to, proudly and a little shyly, as to that of the better time, that of *their* common, their quite far-away and antediluvian social period and order. She made use of the street-cars when need be, the terrible things that people scrambled for as the panic-stricken at sea scramble for the boats; she affronted, inscrutably, under stress, all the public concussions and ordeals; and yet, with that slim mystifying grace of her appearance, which defied you to say if she were a fair young woman who looked older through trouble, or a fine smooth older one who looked young through successful indifference; with her precious reference, above all, to memories and histories into which he could enter, she was as exquisite for him as some pale pressed flower (a rarity to begin with), and, failing other sweetnesses, she was a sufficient reward of his effort. They had communities of knowledge, "their" knowledge (this discriminating possessive was always on her lips) of presences of the other age, presences all overlaid, in his case, by the experience of a man and the freedom of a wanderer, overlaid by pleasure, by infidelity, by passages of life that were strange and dim to her, just by "Europe" in short, but still unobscured, still exposed and cherished, under that pious visitation of the spirit from which she had never been diverted.

She had come with him one day to see how his "apartment-house" was rising; he had helped her over gaps and explained to her plans, and while they were there had happened to have, before her, a brief but lively discussion with the man in charge, the representative of the building-firm that had undertaken his work. He had found himself quite "standing-up" to this personage over a failure on the latter's part to observe some detail of one of their noted conditions, and had so lucidly urged his case that, besides ever so prettily flushing, at the time, for sympathy in his triumph, she had afterwards said to him (though to a slightly greater effect of irony) that he had clearly for too many years neglected a real gift. If he had but stayed at home he would have anticipated the inventor of the sky-scraper. If he had but stayed at home he would have discovered his genius in time really to start some new variety of awful architectural hare and run it till it burrowed in a goldmine. He was to remember these words, while the weeks elapsed, for the small silver ring they had sounded over the queerest and deepest of his own lately most disguised and most muffled vibrations.

It had begun to be present to him after the first fortnight, it had broken out with the oddest abruptness, this particular wanton wonderment: it met him there — and this was the image under which he himself judged the matter, or at least, not a little, thrilled and flushed with it — very much as he might have been met by some strange figure, some unexpected occupant, at a turn of one of the dim passages of an empty house. The quaint analogy quite hauntingly remained with him, when he didn't indeed rather improve it by a still intenser form: that of his opening a door behind which he would have made sure of finding nothing, a door into a room shuttered and void, and yet so coming, with a great suppressed start, on some quite erect confronting presence, something planted in the middle of the place and facing him through the dusk. After that visit to the house in construction he walked with his companion to see the other and always so much the better one, which in the eastward direction formed one of the corners, the "jolly" one precisely, of the street now so generally dishonoured and disfigured in its westward reaches, and of the comparatively conservative Avenue. The Avenue still had pretensions, as Miss Staverton said, to decency; the old people had mostly gone, the old names were unknown, and here and there an old association seemed to stray, all vaguely, like some very aged person, out too late, whom you might meet and feel the impulse to watch or follow, in kindness, for safe restoration to shelter.

They went in together, our friends; he admitted himself with his key, as he kept no one there, he explained, preferring, for his reasons, to leave the place empty, under a simple arrangement with a good woman living in the neighbourhood and who came for a daily hour to open windows and dust and sweep. Spencer Brydon had his reasons and was growingly aware of them; they seemed to him better each time he was there, though he didn't name them all to his companion, any more than he told her as yet how often, how quite absurdly often, he himself came. He only let her see for the present, while they walked through the great blank rooms, that absolute vacancy reigned and that, from top to bottom, there was nothing but Mrs.

Muldoon's broomstick, in a corner, to tempt the burglar. Mrs. Muldoon was then on the premises, and she loquaciously attended the visitors, preceding them from room to room and pushing back shutters and throwing up sashes — all to show them, as she remarked, how little there was to see. There was little indeed to see in the great gaunt shell where the main dispositions and the general apportionment of space, the style of an age of ampler allowances, had nevertheless for its master their honest pleading message, affecting him as some good old servant's, some lifelong retainer's appeal for a character, or even for a retiring-pension; yet it was also a remark of Mrs. Muldoon's that, glad as she was to oblige him by her noonday round, there was a request she greatly hoped he would never make of her. If he should wish her for any reason to come in after dark she would just tell him, if he "plased" that he must ask it of somebody else.

The fact that there was nothing to see didn't militate for the worthy woman against what one *might* see, and she put it frankly to Miss Staverton that no lady could be expected to like, could she? "craping up to thim top storeys in the ayvil hours." The gas and the electric light were

287

off the house, and she fairly evoked a gruesome vision of her march through the great grey rooms — so many of them as there were too! — with her glimmering taper. Miss Staverton met her honest glare with a smile and the profession that she herself certainly would recoil from such an adventure. Spencer Brydon meanwhile held his peace — for the moment; the question of the "evil" hours in his old home had already become too grave for him. He had begun some time since to "crape," and he knew just why a packet of candles addressed to that pursuit had been stowed by his own hand, three weeks before, at the back of a drawer of the fine old sideboard that occupied, as a "fixture," the deep recess in the dining-room. Just now he laughed at his companions — quickly however changing the subject; for the reason that, in the first place, his laugh struck him even at that moment as starting the odd echo, the conscious human resonance (he scarce knew how to qualify it) that sounds made while he was there alone sent back to his ear or his fancy; and that, in the second, he imagined Alice Staverton for the instant on the point of asking him, with a divination, if he ever so prowled. There were divinations he was unprepared for, and he had at all events averted enquiry by the time Mrs. Muldoon had left them, passing on to other parts.

There was happily enough to say, on so consecrated a spot, that could be said freely and fairly; so that a whole train of declarations was precipitated by his friend's having herself broken out, after a yearning look round: "But I hope you don't mean they want you to pull *this* to pieces!" His answer came, promptly, with his reawakened wrath: it was of course exactly what they wanted, and what they were "at" him for, daily, with the iteration of people who couldn't for their life understand a man's liability to decent feelings. He had found the place, just as it stood and beyond what he could express, an interest and a joy. There were values other than the beastly rent-values, and in short, in short — ! But it was thus Miss Staverton took him up. "In short you're to make so good a thing of your sky-scraper that, living in luxury on *those* ill-gotten gains, you can afford for a while to be sentimental here!" Her smile had for him, with the words, the particular mild irony with which he found half her talk suffused; an irony without bitterness and that came, exactly, from her having so much imagination —

not, like the cheap sarcasms with which one heard most people, about the world of "society," bid for the reputation of cleverness, from nobody's really having any. It was agreeable to him at this very moment to be sure that when he had answered, after a brief demur, "Well yes: so, precisely, you may put it!" her imagination would still do him justice. He explained that even if never a dollar were to come to him from the other house he would nevertheless cherish this one; and he dwelt, further, while they lingered and wandered, on the fact of the stupefaction he was already exciting, the positive mystification he felt himself create.

He spoke of the value of all he read into it, into the mere sight of the walls, mere shapes of the rooms, mere sound of the floors, mere feel, in his hand, of the old silver-plated knobs of the several mahogany doors, which suggested the pressure of the palms of the dead; the seventy years of the past in fine that these things represented, the annals of nearly three generations, counting his grandfather's, the one that had ended there, and the impalpable ashes of his long-extinct youth, afloat in the very air like microscopic motes. She listened to everything; she was a woman who answered intimately but who utterly didn't chatter. She scattered abroad therefore no cloud of words; she could assent, she could agree, above all she could encourage, without doing that. Only at the last she went a little further than he had done himself. "And then how do you know? You may still, after all, want to live here." It rather indeed pulled him up, for it wasn't what he had been thinking, at least in her sense of the words. "You mean I may decide to stay on for the sake of it?"

"Well, *with* such a home — !" But, quite beautifully, she had too much tact to dot so monstrous an *i*, and it was precisely an illustration of the way she didn't rattle. How could any one — of any wit — insist on any one else's "wanting" to live in New York?

"Oh," he said, "I *might* have lived here (since I had my opportunity early in life); I might have put in here all these years. Then everything would have been different enough — and, I dare say, 'funny' enough. But that's another matter. And then the beauty of it — I mean of my perversity, of my refusal to agree to a 'deal' — is just in the total absence of a reason. Don't you see that if I had a reason about the matter at all it would *have* to be the other way, and would then be inevitably a reason of dollars? There are no reasons here *but* of dollars. Let us therefore have none whatever — not the ghost of one."

They were back in the hall then for departure, but from where they stood the vista was large, through an open door, into the great square main saloon, with its almost antique felicity of brave spaces between windows. Her eyes came back from that reach and met his own a moment. "Are you very sure the 'ghost' of one doesn't, much rather, serve — ?"

He had a positive sense of turning pale. But it was as near as they were then to come. For he made answer, he believed, between a glare and a grin: "Oh ghosts — of course the place must swarm with them! I should be ashamed of it if it didn't. Poor Mrs. Muldoon's right, and it's why I haven't asked her to do more than look in."

Miss Staverton's gaze again lost itself, and things she didn't utter, it was clear, came and went in her mind. She might even for the minute, off there in the fine room, have imagined some element dimly gathering. Simplified like the death-mask of a handsome face, it perhaps produced for her just then an effect akin to the stir of an expression in the "set" commemorative plaster. Yet whatever her impression may have been she produced instead a vague platitude. "Well, if it were only furnished and lived in — !"

She appeared to imply that in case of its being still furnished he might have been a little less opposed to the idea of a return. But she passed straight into the vestibule, as if to leave her words behind her, and the next moment he had opened the house-door and was standing with her on the steps. He closed the door and, while he re-pocketed his key, looking up and down, they took in the comparatively harsh actuality of the Avenue, which reminded him of the assault of the outer light of the Desert on the traveller emerging from an Egyptian tomb. But he risked before they stepped into the street his gathered answer to her speech. "For me it *is* lived in. For me it *is* furnished." At which it was easy for her to sigh "Ah yes — !" all vaguely and discreetly; since his parents and his favourite sister, to say nothing of other kin, in numbers, had run their course and met their end there. That represented, within the walls, ineffaceable life.

It was a few days after this that, during an hour passed with her again, he had expressed his impatience of the too flattering curiosity — among the people he met — about his appreciation of New York. He had arrived at none at all that was socially producible, and as for that matter of his "thinking" (thinking the better or the worse of anything there) he was wholly taken up with one subject of thought. It was mere vain egoism, and it was moreover, if she liked, a morbid obsession. He found all things come back to the question of what he personally might have been, how he might have led his life and "turned out," if he had not so, at the outset, given it up. And confessing for the first time to the intensity within him of this absurd speculation — which but proved also, no doubt, the habit of too selfishly thinking — he affirmed the impotence there of any other source of interest, any other native appeal. "What would it have made of me, what would it have made of me? I keep for ever wondering, all idiotically; as if I could possibly know! I see what it has made of dozens of others, those I meet, and it positively aches within me, to the point of exasperation, that it would have made something of me as well. Only I can't make out *what*, and the worry of it, the small rage of curiosity never to be satisfied, brings back what I remember to have felt, once or twice, after judging best, for reasons, to burn some important letter unopened. I've been sorry, I've hated it — I've never known what was in the letter. You may of course say it's a trifle — !"

"I don't say it's a trifle," Miss Staverton gravely interrupted.

She was seated by her fire, and before her, on his feet and restless, he turned to and fro between this intensity of his idea and a fitful and unseeing inspection, through his single eyeglass, of the dear little old objects on her chimney-piece. Her interruption made him for an instant look at her harder. "I shouldn't care if you did!" he laughed, however; "and it's only a figure, at any rate, for the way I now feel. *Not* to have followed my perverse young course — and almost in the teeth of my father's curse, as I may say; not to have kept it up, so, 'over there,' from that day to this, without a doubt or a pang; not, above all, to have liked it, to have loved it, so much, loved it, no doubt, with such an abysmal conceit of my own preference: some variation from *that*, I say, must have produced some different effect for my life and for my 'form.' I should have stuck here — if it had been possible; and I was too young, at twenty-three, to judge, *pour deux sous*, whether it *were* possible. If I had waited I might have seen it was, and then I might have been, by staying here, something nearer to one of these types who have been hammered so hard and made so keen by their conditions. It isn't that I admire them so much — the question of any charm in them, or of any charm, beyond that of the rank money-passion, exerted by their conditions *for* them, has nothing to do with the matter: it's only a question of what fantastic, yet perfectly possible, development of my own nature I mayn't have missed. It comes over me that I had then a strange *alter ego* deep down somewhere within me, as the full-blown flower is in the small tight bud, and that I just took the course, I just transferred him to the climate, that blighted him for once and for ever."

"And you wonder about the flower," Miss Staverton said. "So do I, if you want to know; and so I've been wondering these several weeks. I believe in the flower," she continued, "I feel it would have been quite splendid, quite huge and monstrous."

"Monstrous above all!" her visitor echoed; "and I imagine, by the same stroke, quite hideous and offensive."

"You don't believe that," she returned;

"if you did you wouldn't wonder. You'd know, and that would be enough for you. What you feel — and what I feel *for* you — is that you'd have had power."

"You'd have liked me that way?" he asked.

She barely hung fire. "How should I not have liked you?"

"I see. You'd have liked me, have preferred me, a billionaire!"

"How should I not have liked you?" she simply again asked.

He stood before her still — her question kept him motionless. He took it in, so much there was of it; and indeed his not otherwise meeting it testified to that. "I know at least what I am," he simply went on; "the other side of the medal's clear enough. I've not been edifying — I believe I'm thought in a hundred quarters to have been barely decent. I've followed strange paths and worshipped strange gods; it must have come to you again and again — in fact you've admitted to me as much — that I was leading, at any time these thirty years, a selfish frivolous scandalous life. And you see what it has made of me."

She just waited, smiling at him. "You see what it has made of *me*."

"Oh you're a person whom nothing can

have altered. You were born to be what you are, anywhere, anyway: you've the perfection nothing else could have blighted. And don't you see how, without my exile, I shouldn't have been waiting till now — ?" But he pulled up for the strange pang.

"The great thing to see," she presently said, "seems to me to be that it has spoiled nothing. It hasn't spoiled your being here at last. It hasn't spoiled this. It hasn't spoiled your speaking —" She also however faltered.

He wondered at everything her controlled emotion might mean. "Do you believe then — too dreadfully! — that I *am* as good as I might ever have been?"

"Oh no! Far from it!" With which she got up from her chair and was nearer to him. "But I don't care," she smiled.

"You mean I'm good enough?"

She considered a little. "Will you believe it if I say so? I mean will you let that settle your question for you?" And then as if making out in his face that he drew back from this, that he had some idea which, however absurd, he couldn't yet bargain away: "Oh you don't care either — but very differently: you don't care for anything but yourself."

Spencer Brydon recognised it — it was

in fact what he had absolutely professed. Yet he importantly qualified. "*He* isn't myself. He's the just so totally other person. But I do want to see him," he added. "And I can. And I shall."

Their eyes met for a minute while he guessed from something in hers that she divined his strange sense. But neither of them otherwise expressed it, and her apparent understanding, with no protesting shock, no easy derision, touched him more deeply than anything yet, constituting for his stifled perversity, on the spot, an element that was like breatheable air. What she said however was unexpected. "Well, *I've* seen him."

"You — ?"

"I've seen him in a dream."

"Oh a 'dream' — !" It let him down.

"But twice over," she continued. "I saw him as I see you now."

"You've dreamed the same dream — ?"

"Twice over," she repeated. "The very same."

This did somehow a little speak to him, as it also gratified him. "You dream about me at that rate?"

"Ah about *him!*" she smiled.

His eyes again sounded her. "Then you know all about him." And as she said nothing more: "What's the wretch like?"

She hesitated, and it was as if he were pressing her so hard that, resisting for reasons of her own, she had to turn away. "I'll tell you some other time!"

2

It was after this that there was most of a virtue for him, most of a cultivated charm, most of a preposterous secret thrill, in the particular form of surrender to his obsession and of address to what he more and more believed to be his privilege. It was what in these weeks he was living for — since he really felt life to begin but after Mrs. Muldoon had retired from the scene and, visiting the ample house from attic to cellar, making sure he was alone, he knew himself in safe possession and, as he tacitly expressed it, let himself go. He sometimes came twice in the twenty-four hours; the moments he liked best were those of gathering dusk, of the short autumn twilight; this was the time of which, again and again, he found himself hoping most. Then he could, as seemed to him, most intimately wander and wait, linger and listen, feel his fine attention, never in his life before so fine, on the pulse of the great vague place: he preferred the lampless hour and only wished he might have prolonged each day the deep crepuscular spell. Later — rarely much before midnight, but then for a considerable vigil — he watched with his glimmering light; moving slowly, holding it high, playing it far, rejoicing above all, as much as he might, in open vistas, reaches of communication between rooms and by passages; the long straight chance or show, as he would have called it, for the revelation he pretended to invite. It was practice he found he could perfectly "work" without exciting remark; no one was in the least the wiser for it; even Alice Staverton, who was moreover a well of discretion, didn't quite fully imagine.

He let himself in and let himself out with the assurance of calm proprietorship; and accident so far favoured him that, if a fat Avenue "officer" had happened on occasion to see him entering at eleven-thirty, he had never yet, to the best of his belief, been noticed as emerging at two. He walked there on the crisp November nights, arrived regularly at the evening's end; it was as easy to do this after dining out as to take his way to a club or to his hotel. When he left his club, if he hadn't been dining out, it was ostensibly to go to his hotel; and when he left his hotel, if he had spent a part of the evening there, it was ostensibly to go to his club. Everything was easy in fine; everything conspired and promoted: there was truly even in the strain of his experience something that glossed over, something that salved and simplified, all the rest of consciousness. He circulated, talked, renewed, loosely and pleasantly, old relations — met indeed, so far as he could, new expectations and seemed to make out on the whole that in spite of the career, of such different contacts, which he had spoken of to Miss Staverton as ministering so little, for those who might have watched it, to edification, he was positively rather liked than not. He was a dim secondary social success — and all with people who had truly not an idea of him. It was all mere surface sound, this murmur of their welcome, this popping of their corks — just as his gestures of response were the extravagant shadows, emphatic in proportion as they meant little, of some game of *ombres chinoises*. He projected himself all day, in thought, straight over the bristling line of hard unconscious heads and into the other, the real, the waiting life; the life that, as soon as he had heard behind him the click of his great house-door, began for him, on the jolly corner, as beguilingly as the slow opening bars of some rich music follows the tap of the conductor's wand.

He always caught the first effect of the steel point of his stick on the old marble of the hall pavement, large black-and-white squares that he remembered as the admiration of his childhood and that had then made in him, as he now saw, for the growth of an early conception of style. This effect was the dim reverberating tinkle as of some far-off bell hung who should say where? — in the depths of the house, of the past, of that mystical other world that might have flourished for him had he not, for weal or woe, abandoned it. On this impression he did ever the same thing; he put his stick noiselessly away in a corner — feeling the place once more in the likeness of some great glass bowl, all precious concave crystal, set delicately humming by the play of a moist finger round its edge. The concave crystal held, as it were, this mystical other world, and the indescribably fine murmur of its rim was the sigh there, the scarce audible pathetic wail to his strained ear, of all the old baffled forsworn possibilities. What he did therefore by this appeal of his hushed presence was to wake them into such measure of ghostly life as they might still enjoy. They were shy, all but unappeasably shy, but they weren't really sinister; at least they weren't as he had hitherto felt them — before they had taken the Form he so yearned to make them take, the Form he at moments saw himself in the light of fairly hunting on tiptoe, the points of his evening-shoes, from room to room and from storey to storey.

That was the essence of his vision — which was all rank folly, if one would, while he was out of the house and otherwise occupied, but which took on the last verisimilitude as soon as he was placed and posted. He knew what he meant and what he wanted; it was as clear as the figure on a cheque presented in demand for cash. His *alter ego* "walked" — that was the note of his image of him, while his image of his motive for his own odd pastime was the desire to waylay him and meet him. He roamed, slowly, warily, but all restlessly, he himself did — Mrs. Muldoon had been right, absolutely, with her figure of their "craping"; and the presence he watched for would roam restlessly too. But it would be as cautious and as shifty; the conviction of its probable, in fact its already quite sensible, quite audible evasion of pursuit grew for him from night to night, laying on him finally a rigour to which nothing in his life had been comparable. It had been the theory of many superficially-judging persons, he knew, that he was wasting that life in a surrender to sensations, but he had tasted of no pleasure so fine as his actual tension, had been introduced to no sport that demanded at once the patience and the nerve of this stalking of a creature more subtle, yet at bay perhaps more formidable, than any beast of the forest. The terms, the comparisons, the very practices of the chase positively came again into play; there were even moments when passages of his occasional experience as a sportsman, stirred memories, from his younger time, of moor and mountain and desert, revived for him — and to the increase of his keenness — by the tremendous force of analogy. He found himself at moments — once he had placed his single light on some mantel-shelf or in some recess — stepping back into shelter or shade, effacing himself behind a door or in an embrasure, as he had sought of old the vantage of rock and tree; he found himself holding his breath and living in the joy of the instant, the supreme suspense created by big game alone.

He wasn't afraid (though putting himself

the question as he believed gentlemen on Bengal tiger-shoots or in close quarters with the great bear of the Rockies had been known to confess to having put it); and this indeed — since here at least he might be frank! — because of the impression, so intimate and so strange, that he himself produced as yet a dread, produced certainly a strain, beyond the liveliest he was likely to feel. They fell for him into categories, they fairly became familiar, the signs, for his own perception, of the alarm his presence and his vigilance created; though leaving him always to remark, portentously, on his probably having formed a relation, his probably enjoying a consciousness, unique in the experience of man. People enough, first and last, had been in terror of apparitions, but who had ever before so turned the tables and become himself, in the apparitional world, an incalculable terror? He might have found this sublime had he quite dared to think of it; but he didn't too much insist, truly, on that side of his privilege. With habit and repetition he gained to an extraordinary degree the power to penetrate the dusk of distances and the darkness of corners, to resolve back into their innocence the treacheries of uncertain light, the evil-looking forms taken in the gloom by mere shadows, by accidents of the air, by shifting effects of perspective; putting down his dim luminary he could still wander on without it, pass into other rooms and, only knowing it was there behind him in case of need, see his way about, visually project for his purpose a comparative clearness. It made him feel, this acquired faculty, like some monstrous stealthy cat; he wondered if he would have glared at these moments with large shining yellow eyes, and what it mightn't verily be, for the poor hard-pressed *alter ego*, to be confronted with such a type.

He liked however the open shutters; he opened everywhere those Mrs. Muldoon had closed, closing them as carefully afterwards, so that she shouldn't notice: he liked — oh this he did like, and above all in the upper rooms! — the sense of the hard silver of the autumn stars through the window-panes, and scarcely less the flare of the street-lamps below, the white electric lustre which it would have taken curtains to keep out. This was human actual social; this was of the world he had lived in, and he was more at his ease certainly for the countenance, coldly general and impersonal, that all the while and in spite of his detachment it seemed to give him. He had support of course mostly in the rooms at the wide front and the prolonged side; it failed him considerably in the central shades and the parts at the back. But if he sometimes, on his rounds, was glad of his optical reach, so none the less often the rear of the house affected him as the very jungle of his prey. The place was there more subdivided; a large "extension" in particular, where small rooms for servants had been multiplied, abounded in nooks and corners, in closets and passages, in the ramifications especially of an ample back staircase over which he leaned, many a time, to look far down — not deterred from his gravity even while aware that he might, for a spectator, have figured some solemn simpleton playing at hide-and-seek. Outside in fact he might himself make that ironic *rapprochement;* but within the walls, and in spite of the clear windows, his consistency was proof against the cynical light of New York.

It had belonged to that idea of the exasperated consciousness of his victim to become a real test for him; since he had quite put it to himself from the first that, oh distinctly! he could "cultivate" his whole perception. He had felt it as above all open to cultivation — which indeed was but another name for his manner of spending his time. He was bringing it on, bringing it to perfection, by practice; in consequence of which it had grown so fine that he was now aware of impressions, attestations of his general postulate, that couldn't have broken upon him at once. This was the case more specifically with a phenomenon at last quite frequent for him in the upper rooms, the recognition — absolutely unmistakeable, and by a turn dating from a particular hour, his resumption of his campaign after a diplomatic drop, a calculated absence of three nights — of his being definitely followed, tracked at a distance carefully taken and to the express end that he should the less confidently, less arrogantly, appear to himself merely to pursue. It worried, it finally quite broke him up, for it proved, of all the conceivable impressions, the one least suited to his book. He was kept in sight while remaining himself — as regards the essence of his position — sightless, and his only recourse then was in abrupt turns, rapid recoveries of ground. He wheeled about, retracing his steps, as if he might so catch in his face at least the stirred air of some other quick revolution. It was indeed true that his fully dislocalised thought of these manœuvres recalled to him Pantaloon, at the Christmas farce, buffeted and tricked from behind by ubiquitous Harlequin; but it left intact the influence of the conditions themselves each time he was re-exposed to them, so that in fact this association, had he suffered it to become constant, would on a certain side have but ministered to his intenser gravity. He had made, as I have said, to create on the premises the baseless sense of a reprieve, his three absences; and the result of the third was to confirm the after-effect of the second.

On his return, that night — the night succeeding his last intermission — he stood in the hall and looked up the staircase with a certainty more intimate than any he had yet known. "He's *there,* at the top, and waiting — not, as in general, falling back for disappearance. He's holding his ground, and it's the first time — which is a proof, isn't it? that something has happened for him." So Brydon argued with his hand on the banister and his foot on the lowest stair; in which position he felt as never before the air chilled by his logic. He himself turned cold in it, for he seemed of a sudden to know what now was involved. "Harder pressed? — yes, he takes it in, with its thus making clear to him that I've come, as they say, 'to stay.' He finally doesn't like and can't bear it, in the sense, I mean, that his wrath, his menaced interest, now balances with his dread. I've hunted him till he has 'turned': that, up there, is what has happened — he's the fanged or the antlered animal brought at last to bay." There came to him, as I say — but determined by an influence beyond my notation! — the acuteness of this certainty; under which however the next moment he had broken into a sweat that he would as little have consented to attribute to fear as he would have dared immediately to act upon it for enterprise. It marked none the less a prodigious thrill, a thrill that represented sudden dismay, no doubt, but also represented, and with the selfsame throb, the strangest, the most joyous, possibly the next minute almost the proudest, duplication of consciousness.

"He has been dodging, retreating, hiding, but now, worked up to anger, he'll fight!" — this intense impression made a single mouthful, as it were, of terror and applause. But what was wondrous was that the applause, for the felt fact, was so eager, since, if it was his other self he was running to earth, this ineffable identity was thus in the last resort not unworthy of him. It bristled there — somewhere near at hand, however unseen still — as the hunted thing, even as the trodden worm of the adage *must* at last bristle; and Brydon at this instant tasted probably of a sensation more complex than had ever before found itself consistent with sanity. It was as if it would have shamed him that a character so associated with his own should triumphantly succeed in just skulking, should to the end not risk the open, so that the drop of this danger was, on the spot, a great lift of the whole situation. Yet with another rare shift of the same subtlety he was already trying to measure by how much more he himself might now be in peril of fear; so rejoicing that he could, in another form, actively inspire that fear, and simultaneously quaking for the form in which he might passively know it.

The apprehension of knowing it must after a little have grown in him, and the strangest moment of his adventure perhaps, the most memorable or really most interesting, afterwards, of his crisis, was the lapse of certain instants of concentrated conscious *combat*, the sense of a need to hold on to something, even after the manner of a man slipping and slipping on some awful incline; the vivid impulse, above all, to move, to act, to charge, somehow and upon something — to show himself, in a word, that he wasn't afraid. The state of "holding-on" was thus the state to which he was momentarily reduced; if there had been anything, in the great vacancy, to seize, he would presently have been aware of having clutched it as he might under a shock at home have clutched the nearest chair-back. He had been surprised at any rate — of this he *was* aware — into something unprecedented since his original appropriation of the place; he had closed his eyes, held them tight, for a long minute, as with that instinct of dismay and that terror of vision. When he opened them the room, the other contiguous rooms, extraordinarily, seemed lighter — so light, almost, that at first he took the change for day. He stood firm, however that might be, just where he had paused; his resistance had helped him — it was as if there were something he had tided over. He knew after a little what this was — it had been in the imminent danger of flight. He had stiffened his will against going; without this he would have made for the stairs, and it seemed to him that, still with his eyes closed, he would have descended them, would have known how, straight and swiftly, to the bottom.

Well, as he had held out, here he was — still at the top, among the more intricate upper rooms and with the gauntlet of the others, of all the rest of the house, still to run when it should be his time to go. He would go at his time — only at his time: didn't he go every night very much at the same hour? He took out his watch — there was light for that: it was scarcely a quarter past one, and he had never withdrawn so soon. He reached his lodgings for the most part at two — with his walk of a quarter of an hour. He would wait for the last quarter — he wouldn't stir till then; and he kept his watch there with his eyes on it, reflecting while he held it that this deliberate wait, a wait with an effort, which he recognised, would serve perfectly for the attestation he desired to make. It would prove his courage — unless indeed the latter might most be proved by his budging at last from his place. What he mainly felt now was that, since he hadn't originally scuttled, he had his dignities — which had never in his life seemed so many — all to preserve and to carry aloft. This was before him in truth as a physical image, an image almost worthy of an age of greater romance. That remark indeed glimmered for him only to glow the next instant with a finer light; since what age of romance, after all, could have matched either the state of his mind or, "objectively," as they said, the wonder of his situation? The only difference would have been that, brandishing his dignities over his head as in a parchment scroll, he might then — that is in the heroic time — have proceeded downstairs with a drawn sword in his other grasp.

At present, really, the light he had set down on the mantel of the next room would have to figure his sword; which utensil, in the course of a minute, he had taken the requisite number of steps to possess himself of. The door between the rooms was open, and from the second another door opened to a third. These rooms, as he remembered, gave all three upon a common corridor as well, but there was a fourth, beyond them, without issue save through the preceding. To have moved, to have heard his step again, was appreciably a help; though even in recognising this he lingered once more a little by the chimney-piece on which his light had rested. When he next moved, just hesitating where to turn, he found himself considering a circumstance that, after his first and comparatively vague apprehension of it, produced in him the start that often attends some pang of recollection, the violent shock of having ceased happily to forget. He had come into sight of the door in which the brief chain of communication ended and which he now surveyed from the nearer threshold, the one not directly facing it. Placed at some distance to the left of this point, it would have admitted him to the last room of the four, the room without other approach or egress, had it not, to his intimate conviction, been closed *since* his former visitation, the matter probably of a quarter of an hour before. He stared with all his eyes at the wonder of the fact, arrested again where he stood and again holding his breath while he sounded its sense. Surely it had been *subsequently* closed — that is it had been on his previous passage indubitably open!

He took it full in the face that something had happened between — that he couldn't not have noticed before (by which he meant on his original tour of all the rooms that evening) that such a barrier had exceptionally presented itself. He had indeed since that moment undergone an agitation so extraordinary that it might have muddled for him any earlier view; and he tried to convince himself that he might perhaps then have gone into the room and, inadvertently, automatically, on coming out, have drawn the door after him. The difficulty was that this exactly was what he never did; it was against his whole policy, as he might have said, the essence of which was to keep vistas clear. He had them from the first, as he was well aware, quite on the brain: the strange apparition, at the far end of one of them, of his baffled "prey" (which had become by so sharp an irony so little the term now to apply!) was the form of success his imagination had most cherished, projecting into it always a refinement of beauty. He had known fifty times the start of perception that had afterwards dropped; had fifty times gasped to himself "There!" under some fond brief hallucination. The house, as the case stood, admirably lent itself; he might wonder at the taste, the native architecture of the particular time, which could rejoice so in the multiplication of doors — the opposite extreme to the modern, the actual almost complete proscription of them; but it had fairly contributed to provoke this obsession of the presence encountered telescopically, as he might say, focussed and studied in diminishing perspective and as by a rest for the elbow.

It was with these considerations that his present attention was charged — they perfectly availed to make what he saw portentous. He *couldn't,* by any lapse, have blocked that aperture; and if he hadn't, if it was unthinkable, why what else was clear but that there had been another agent? Another agent? — he had been catching, as he felt, a moment back, the very breath of him; but when had he been so close as in this simple, this logical, this completely personal act? It was so logical, that is, that one might have *taken* it for personal; yet for what did Brydon take it, he asked himself, while, softly panting, he felt his eyes almost leave their sockets. Ah this time at last they *were,* the two, the opposed projections of him, in presence; and this time, as much as one would, the question of danger loomed. With it rose, as not before, the question of courage — for what he knew the blank face of the door to say to him was "Show us how much you have!" It stared, it glared back at him with that challenge; it put to him the two alternatives: should he just push it open or not? Oh to have this consciousness was to *think* — and to think, Brydon knew, as he stood there, was, with the lapsing moments, not to have acted! Not to have acted — that was the misery and the pang — was even still not to act; was in fact *all* to feel the thing in another, in a new and terrible way. How long did he pause and how long did he debate? There was presently nothing to measure it; for his vibration had already changed — as just by the effect of its intensity. Shut up there, at bay, defiant, and with the prodigy of the thing palpably proveably *done,* thus giving notice like some stark signboard — under that accession of accent the situation itself had turned; and Brydon at last remarkably made up his mind on what it had turned to.

It had turned altogether to a different admonition; to a supreme hint, for him, of the value of Discretion! This slowly dawned, no doubt — for it could take its time; so perfectly, on his threshold, had he been stayed, so little as yet had he either advanced or retreated. It was the strangest of all things that now when, by his taking ten steps and applying his hand to a latch, or even his shoulder and his knee, if necessary, to a panel, all the hunger of his prime need might have been met, his high curiosity crowned, his unrest assuaged — it was amazing, but it was also exquisite and rare, that insistence should have, at a touch, quite dropped from him. Discretion

— he jumped at that; and yet not, verily, at such a pitch, because it saved his nerves or his skin, but because, much more valuably, it saved the situation. When I say he "jumped" at it I feel the consonance of this term with the fact that — at the end indeed of I know not how long — he did move again, he crossed straight to the door. He wouldn't touch it — it seemed now that he might *if* he would: he would only just wait there a little, to show, to prove, that he wouldn't. He had thus another station, close to the thin partition by which revelation was denied him; but with his eyes bent and his hands held off in a mere intensity of stillness. He listened as if there had been something to hear, but this attitude, while it lasted, was his own communication. "If you won't then — good: I spare you and I give up. You affect me as by the appeal positively for pity: you convince me that for reasons rigid and sublime — what do I know? — we both of us should have suffered. I respect them then, and, though moved and privileged as, I believe, it has never been given to man, I retire, I renounce — never, on my honour, to try again. So rest for ever — and let *me!*"

That, for Brydon, was the deep sense of this last demonstration — solemn, measured, directed, as he felt it to be. He brought it to a close, he turned away; and now verily he knew how deeply he had been stirred. He retraced his steps, taking up his candle, burnt, he observed, well-nigh to the socket, and marking again, lighten it as he would, the distinctness of his footfall; after which, in a moment, he knew himself at the other side of the house. He did here what he had not yet done at these hours — he opened half a casement, one of those in the front, and let in the air of the night; a thing he would have taken at any time previous for a sharp rupture of his spell. His spell was broken now, and it didn't matter — broken by his concession and his surrender, which made it idle henceforth that he should ever come back. The empty street — its other life so marked even by the great lamplit vacancy — was within call, within touch; he stayed there as to be in it again, high above it though he was still perched; he watched as for some comforting common fact, some vulgar human note, the passage of a scavenger or a thief, some night-bird however base. He would have blessed that sign of life; he would have welcomed positively the slow approach of his friend the policeman, whom he had hitherto only sought to avoid, and was not sure that if

the patrol had come into sight he mightn't
have felt the impulse to get into relation
with it, to hail it, on some pretext, from his
fourth floor.

The pretext that wouldn't have been too
silly or too compromising, the explanation
that would have saved his dignity and kept
his name, in such a case, out of the papers,
was not definite to him: he was so occupied with the thought of recording his Discretion — as an effect of the vow he had
just uttered to his intimate adversary —
that the importance of this loomed large
and something had overtaken all ironically
his sense of proportion. If there had been a
ladder applied to the front of the house,
even one of the vertiginous perpendiculars
employed by painters and roofers and
sometimes left standing overnight, he
would have managed somehow, astride of
the window-sill, to compass by outstretched
leg and arm that mode of descent. If there
had been some such uncanny thing as he
had found in his room at hotels, a workable
fire-escape in the form of notched cable or
a canvas shoot, he would have availed himself of it as a proof — well, of his present
delicacy. He nursed that sentiment, as the
question stood, a little in vain, and even —
at the end of he scarce knew, once more,

how long — found it, as by the action on his mind of the failure of response of the outer world, sinking back to vague anguish. It seemed to him he had waited an age for some stir of the great grim hush; the life of the town was itself under a spell — so unnaturally, up and down the whole prospect of known and rather ugly objects, the blankness and the silence lasted. Had they ever, he asked himself, the hard-faced houses, which had begun to look livid in the dim dawn, had they ever spoken so little to any need of his spirit? Great builded voids, great crowded stillnesses put on, often, in the heart of cities, for the small hours, a sort of sinister mask, and it was of this large collective negation that Brydon presently became conscious — all the more that the break of day was, almost incredibly, now at hand, proving to him what a night he had made of it.

He looked again at his watch, saw what had become of his time-values (he had taken hours for minutes — not, as in other tense situations, minutes for hours) and the strange air of the streets was but the weak, the sullen flush of a dawn in which everything was still locked up. His choked appeal from his own open window had been the sole note of life, and he could but break off at last as for a worse despair. Yet while so deeply demoralised he was capable again of an impulse denoting — at least by his present measure — extraordinary resolution; of retracing his steps to the spot where he had turned cold with the extinction of his last pulse of doubt as to there being in the place another presence than his own. This required an effort strong enough to sicken him; but he had his reason, which overmastered for the moment everything else. There was the whole of the rest of the house to traverse, and how should he screw himself to that if the door he had seen closed were at present open? He could hold to the idea that the closing had practically been for him an act of mercy, a chance offered him to descend, depart, get off the ground and never again profane it. This conception held together, it worked; but what it meant for him depended now clearly on the amount of forbearance his recent action, or rather his recent inaction, had engendered. The image of the "presence," whatever it was, waiting there for him to go — this image had not yet been so concrete for his nerves as when he stopped short of the point at which certainty would have come to him. For, with all his resolution, or more exactly with all his dread, he did stop short — he hung back from really seeing. The risk was too great and his fear too definite: it took at this moment an awful specific form.

He knew — yes, as he had never known anything — that, *should* he see the door open, it would all too abjectly be the end of him. It would mean that the agent of his shame — for his shame was the deep abjection — was once more at large and in general possession; and what glared him thus in the face was the act that this would determine for him. It would send him straight about to the window he had left open, and by that window, be long ladder and dangling rope as absent as they would, he saw himself uncontrollably insanely fatally take his way to the street. The hideous chance of this he at least could avert; but he could only avert it by recoiling in time from assurance. He had the whole house to deal with, this fact was still there; only he now knew that uncertainty alone could start him. He stole back from where he had checked himself — merely to do so was suddenly like safety — and, making blindly for the greater staircase, left gaping rooms and sounding passages behind. Here was the top of the stairs, with a fine large dim descent and three spacious landings to mark off. His instinct was all for mildness, but his feet were harsh on the floors, and, strangely, when he had in a couple of minutes become aware of this, it counted somehow for help. He couldn't have spoken, the tone of his voice would have scared him, and the common conceit or resource of "whistling in the dark" (whether literally or figuratively) have appeared basely vulgar; yet he liked none the less to hear himself go, and when he had reached his first landing — taking it all with no rush, but quite steadily — that stage of success drew from him a gasp of relief.

The house, withal, seemed immense, the scale of space again inordinate; the open rooms to no one of which his eyes deflected, gloomed in their shuttered state like mouths of caverns; only the high skylight that formed the crown of the deep well created for him a medium in which he could advance, but which might have been, for queerness of colour, some watery under-world. He tried to think of something noble, as that his property was really grand, a splendid possession; but this nobleness took the form too of the clear delight with which he was finally to sacrifice it. They might come in now, the builders, the destroyers — they might come as soon as they would. At the end of two flights he had dropped to another zone, and from the middle of the third, with only one more left, he recognised the influence of the lower windows, of half-drawn blinds, of the occasional gleam of street-lamps, of the glazed spaces of the vestibule. This was the bottom of the sea, which showed an illumination of its own and which he even saw paved — when at a given moment he drew up to sink a long look over the banisters — with the marble squares of his childhood. By that time indubitably he felt, as he might have said in a commoner cause, better; it had allowed him to stop and draw breath, and the ease increased with the sight of the old black-and-white slabs. But what he most felt was that now surely, with the element of impunity pulling him as by hard firm hands, the case was settled for what he might have seen above had he dared that last look. The closed door, blessedly remote now, was still closed — and he had only in short to reach that of the house.

He came down further, he crossed the passage forming the access to the last flight; and if here again he stopped an instant it was almost for the sharpness of the thrill of assured escape. It made him shut his eyes — which opened again to the straight slope of the remainder of the stairs. Here was impunity still, but impunity almost excessive; inasmuch as the side-lights and the high fan-tracery of the entrance were glimmering straight into the hall; an appearance produced, he the next instant saw, by the fact that the vestibule gaped wide, that the hinged halves of the inner door had been thrown far back. Out of that again the *question* sprang at him, making his eyes, as he felt, half-start from his head, as they had done, at the top of the house, before the sign of the other door. If he had left that one open, hadn't he left this one closed, and wasn't he now in *most* immediate presence of some inconceivable occult activity? It was as sharp, the question, as a knife in his side, but the answer hung fire still and seemed to lose itself in the vague darkness to which the thin admitted dawn, glimmering archwise over the whole outer door, made a semicircular margin, a cold silvery nimbus that seemed to play a little as he looked — to shift and expand and contract.

It was as if there had been something within it, protected by indistinctness and corresponding in extent with the opaque surface behind, the painted panels of the

328

last barrier to his escape, of which the key was in his pocket. The indistinctness mocked him even while he stared, affected him as somehow shrouding or challenging certitude, so that after faltering an instant on his step he let himself go with the sense that here *was* at last something to meet, to touch, to take, to know — something all unnatural and dreadful, but to advance upon which was the condition for him either of liberation or of supreme defeat. The penumbra, dense and dark, was the virtual screen of a figure which stood in it as still as some image erect in a niche or as some black-vizored sentinel guarding a treasure. Brydon was to know afterwards, was to recall and make out, the particular thing he had believed during the rest of his descent. He saw, in its great grey glimmering margin, the central vagueness diminish, and he felt it to be taking the very form toward which, for so many days, the passion of his curiosity had yearned. It gloomed, it loomed, it was something, it was somebody, the prodigy of a personal presence.

Rigid and conscious, spectral yet human, a man of his own substance and stature waited there to measure himself with his power to dismay. This only could it be — this only till he recognised, with his advance, that what made the face dim was the pair of raised hands that covered it and in which, so far from being offered in defiance, it was buried as for dark deprecation. So Brydon, before him, took him in; with every fact of him now, in the higher light, hard and acute — his planted stillness, his vivid truth, his grizzled bent head and white masking hands, his queer actuality of evening-dress, of dangling double eye-glass, of gleaming silk lappet and white linen, of pearl button and gold watch-guard and polished shoe. No portrait by a great modern master could have presented him with more intensity, thrust him out of his frame with more art, as if there had been "treatment," of the consummate sort, in his every shade and salience. The revulsion, for our friend, had become, before he knew it, immense — this drop, in the act of apprehension, to the sense of his adversary's inscrutable manœuvre. That meaning at least, while he gaped, it offered him; for he could but gape at his other self in this other anguish, gape as a proof that *he,* standing there for the achieved, the enjoyed, the triumphant life, couldn't be faced in his triumph. Wasn't the proof in the splendid covering hands, strong and completely spread? — so spread and so intentional that, in spite of a special verity that surpassed every other, the fact that one of these hands had lost two fingers, which were reduced to stumps, as if accidentally shot away, the face was effectually guarded and saved.

"Saved," though, *would* it be? — Brydon breathed his wonder till the very impunity of his attitude and the very insistence of his eyes produced, as he felt, a sudden stir which showed the next instant as a deeper portent, while the head raised itself, the betrayal of a braver purpose. The hands, as he looked, began to move, to open; then, as if deciding in a flash, dropped from the face and left it uncovered and presented. Horror, with the sight, had leaped into Brydon's throat, gasping there in a sound he couldn't utter; for the bared identity was too hideous as *his,* and his glare was the passion of his protest. The face, *that* face, Spencer Brydon's? — he searched it still, but looking away from it in dismay and denial, falling straight from his height of sublimity. It was unknown, inconceivable, awful, disconnected from any possibility — ! He had been "sold," he inwardly moaned, stalking such game as this: the presence before him was a presence, the horror within him a horror, but the waste of his nights had been only grotesque and the success of his adventure an irony. Such an identity fitted his at *no* point, made its alternative monstrous. A thousand times yes, as it came upon him nearer now — the face was the face of a stranger. It came upon him nearer now, quite as one of those expanding fantastic images projected by the magic lantern of childhood; for the stranger, whoever he might be, evil, odious, blatant, vulgar, had advanced as for aggression, and he knew himself give ground. Then harder pressed still, sick with the force of his shock, and falling back as under the hot breath and the roused passion of a life larger than his own, a rage of personality before which his own collapsed, he felt the whole vision turn to darkness and his very feet give way. His head went round; he was going; he had gone.

3

What had next brought him back, clearly — though after how long? — was Mrs. Muldoon's voice, coming to him from quite near, from so near that he seemed presently to see her as kneeling on the ground before him while he lay looking up at her; himself not wholly on the ground, but half-raised and upheld — conscious, yes, of tenderness of support and, more particularly, of a head pillowed in extraordinary softness and faintly refreshing fragrance. He considered, he wondered, his wit but half at his service; then another face intervened, bending more directly over him, and he finally knew that Alice Staverton had made her lap an ample and perfect cushion to him, and that she had to this end seated herself on the lowest degree of the staircase, the rest of his long person remaining stretched on his old black-and-white slabs. They were cold, these marble squares of his youth; but *he* somehow was not, in this rich return of consciousness — the most wonderful hour, little by little, that he had ever known, leaving him, as it did, so gratefully, so abysmally passive, and yet as with a treasure of intelligence waiting all round him for quiet appropriation; dissolved, he might call it, in the air of the place and producing the golden glow of a late autumn afternoon. He had come back, yes — come back from further away than any man but himself had ever travelled; but it was strange how with this sense what he had come back *to* seemed really the great thing, and as if his prodigious journey had been all for the sake of it. Slowly but surely his consciousness grew, his vision of his state thus completing itself: he had been miraculously *carried* back — lifted and carefully borne as from where he had been picked up, the uttermost end of an interminable grey passage. Even with this he was suffered to rest, and what had now brought him to knowledge was the break in the long mild motion.

It had brought him to knowledge, to knowledge — yes, this was the beauty of his state; which came to resemble more and more that of a man who has gone to sleep on some news of a great inheritance, and then, after dreaming it away, after profaning it with matters strange to it, has waked up again to serenity of certitude and has only to lie and watch it grow. This was the drift of his patience — that he had only to let it shine on him. He must moreover, with intermissions, still have been lifted and borne; since why and how else should he have known himself, later on, with the afternoon glow intenser, no longer at the foot of his stairs — situated as these now seemed at that dark other end of his tunnel — but on a deep window-bench of his high saloon, over which had been spread, couch-fashion, a mantle of soft stuff lined with grey fur that was familiar to his eyes and that one of his hands kept fondly feeling as for its pledge of truth. Mrs. Muldoon's face had gone, but the other, the second he had recognised, hung over him in a way that showed how he was still propped and pillowed. He took it all in, and the more he took it the more it seemed to suffice: he was as much at peace as if he had had food and drink. It was the two women who had found him, on Mrs. Muldoon's having plied, at her usual hour, her latch-key — and on her having above all arrived while Miss Staverton still lingered near the house. She had been turning away, all anxiety, from worrying the vain bell-handle — her calculation having been of the hour of the good woman's visit; but the latter, blessedly, had come up while she was still there, and they had entered together. He had then lain, beyond the vestibule, very much as he was lying now — quite, that is, as he appeared to have fallen, but all so wondrously without bruise or gash; only in a depth of stupor. What he most took in, however, at present, with the steadier clearance, was that Alice Staverton had for a long unspeakable moment not doubted he was dead.

"It must have been that I *was*." He made

it out as she held him. "Yes — I can only have died. You brought me literally to life. Only," he wondered, his eyes rising to her, "only, in the name of all the benedictions, how?"

It took her but an instant to bend her face and kiss him, and something in the manner of it, and in the way her hands clasped and locked his head while he felt the cool charity and virtue of her lips, something in all this beatitude somehow answered everything. "And now I keep you," she said.

"Oh keep me, keep me!" he pleaded while her face still hung over him: in response to which it dropped again and stayed close, clingingly close. It was the seal of their situation — of which he tasted the impress for a long blissful moment in silence. But he came back. "Yet how did you know — ?"

"I was uneasy. You were to have come, you remember — and you had sent no word."

"Yes, I remember — I was to have gone to you at one today." It caught on to their "old" life and relation — which were so near and so far. "I was still out there in my strange darkness — where was it, what was it? I must have stayed there so long." He

336

could but wonder at the depth and the duration of his swoon.

"Since last night?" she asked with a shade of fear for her possible indiscretion.

"Since this morning — it must have been: the cold dim dawn of today. Where have I been," he vaguely wailed, "where have I been?" He felt her hold him close, and it was as if this helped him now to make in all security his mild moan. "What a long dark day!"

All in her tenderness she had waited a moment. "In the cold dim dawn?" she quavered.

But he had already gone on piecing together the parts of the whole prodigy. "As I didn't turn up you came straight — ?"

She barely cast about. "I went first to your hotel — where they told me of your absence. You had dined out last evening and hadn't been back since. But they appeared to know you had been at your club."

"So you had the idea of *this* — ?"

"Of what?" she asked in a moment.

"Well — of what has happened."

"I believed at least you'd have been here. I've known, all along," she said, "that you've been coming."

" 'Known' it — ?"

"Well, I've believed it. I said nothing to you

after that talk we had a month ago — but I felt sure. I knew you *would*," she declared.

"That I'd persist, you mean?"

"That you'd see him."

"Ah but I didn't!" cried Brydon with his long wail. "There's somebody — an awful beast; whom I brought, too horribly, to bay. But it's not me."

At this she bent over him again, and her eyes were in his eyes. "No — it's not you." And it was as if, while her face hovered, he might have made out in it, hadn't it been so near, some particular meaning blurred by a smile. "No, thank heaven," she repeated — "it's not you! Of course it wasn't to have been."

"Ah but it *was*," he gently insisted. And he stared before him now as he had been staring for so many weeks. "I was to have known myself."

"You couldn't!" she returned consolingly. And then reverting, and as if to account further for what she had herself done, "But it wasn't only *that*, that you hadn't been at home," she went on. "I waited till the hour at which we had found Mrs. Muldoon that day of my going with you; and she arrived, as I've told you, while, failing to bring any one to the door, I lingered in my despair on the steps. After a little, if she hadn't come, by such a mercy, I should have found means to hunt her up. But it wasn't," said Alice Staverton, as if once more with her fine intention — "it wasn't only that."

His eyes, as he lay, turned back to her. "What more then?"

She met it, the wonder she had stirred. "In the cold dim dawn, you say? Well, in the cold dim dawn of this morning I too saw you."

"Saw *me* — ?"

"Saw *him*," said Alice Staverton. "It must have been at the same moment."

He lay an instant taking it in — as if he wished to be quite reasonable. "At the same moment?"

"Yes — in my dream again, the same one I've named to you. He came back to me. Then I knew it for a sign. He had come to you."

At this Brydon raised himself; he had to see her better. She helped him when she understood his movement, and he sat up, steadying himself beside her there on the window-bench and with his right hand grasping her left. "*He* didn't come to me."

"You came to yourself," she beautifully smiled.

"Ah I've come to myself now — thanks

to you, dearest. But this brute, with his awful face — this brute's a black stranger. He's none of *me,* even as I *might* have been," Brydon sturdily declared.

But she kept the clearness that was like the breath of infallibility. "Isn't the whole point that you'd have been different?"

He almost scowled for it. "As different as *that* — ?"

Her look again was more beautiful to him than the things of this world. "Haven't you exactly wanted to know *how* different? So this morning," she said, "you appeared to me."

"Like *him?*"

"A black stranger!"

"Then how did you know it was I?"

"Because, as I told you weeks ago, my mind, my imagination, had worked so over what you might, what you mightn't have been — to show you, you see, how I've thought of you. In the midst of that you came to me — that my wonder might be answered. So I knew," she went on; "and believed that, since the question held you too so fast, as you told me that day, you too would see for yourself. And when this morning I again saw I knew it would be because you had — and also then, from the first moment, because you somehow

340

wanted me. *He* seemed to tell me of that. So why," she strangely smiled, "shouldn't I like him?"

It brought Spencer Brydon to his feet. "You 'like' that horror — ?"

"I *could* have liked him. And to me," she said, "he was no horror. I had accepted him."

" 'Accepted' — ?" Brydon oddly sounded.

"Before, for the interest of his difference — yes. And as *I* didn't disown him, as *I* knew him — which you at last, confronted with him in his difference, so cruelly didn't, my dear — well, he must have been, you see, less dreadful to me. And it may have pleased him that I pitied him."

She was beside him on her feet, but still holding his hand — still with her arm supporting him. But though it all brought for him thus a dim light, "You 'pitied' him?" he grudgingly, resentfully asked.

"He has been unhappy; he has been ravaged," she said.

"And haven't I been unhappy? Am not I — you've only to look at me! — ravaged?"

"Ah I don't say I like him *better,*" she granted after a thought. "But he's grim, he's worn — and things have happened to him. He doesn't make shift, for sight, with your charming monocle."

"No" — it struck Brydon: "I couldn't have sported mine 'downtown.' They'd have guyed me there."

"His great convex pince-nez — I saw it, I recognised the kind — is for his poor ruined sight. And his poor right hand — !"

"Ah!" Brydon winced — whether for his proved identity or for his lost fingers. Then, "He has a million a year," he lucidly added. "But he hasn't you."

"And he isn't — no, he isn't — *you!*" she murmured as he drew her to his breast.

We hope you have enjoyed this Large Print book. Other Thorndike, Wheeler or Chivers Press Large Print books are available at your library or directly from the publishers.

For more information about current and upcoming titles, please call or write, without obligation, to:

Publisher
Thorndike Press
295 Kennedy Memorial Drive
Waterville, ME 04901
Tel. (800) 223-1244

Or visit our Web site at:
www.gale.com/thorndike
www.gale.com/wheeler

OR

Chivers Large Print
published by BBC Audiobooks Ltd
St James House, The Square
Lower Bristol Road
Bath BA2 3SB
England
Tel. +44(0) 800 136919
email: bbcaudiobooks@bbc.co.uk
www.bbcaudiobooks.co.uk

All our Large Print titles are designed for easy reading, and all our books are made to last.

AGRARIAN SOCIALISM

S. M. Lipset

AGRARIAN SOCIALISM

THE COÖPERATIVE COMMONWEALTH FEDERATION
IN SASKATCHEWAN

A Study in Political Sociology

UNIVERSITY OF CALIFORNIA PRESS
Berkeley and Los Angeles · 1967

UNIVERSITY OF CALIFORNIA PRESS
BERKELEY AND LOS ANGELES, CALIFORNIA

CAMBRIDGE UNIVERSITY PRESS
LONDON, ENGLAND

PRINTED IN THE UNITED STATES OF AMERICA

TO THE MEMORY OF MY FATHER
MAX LIPSET
WHO HAD THE SAME DREAMS
AS THE FARMERS OF SASKATCHEWAN

Foreword

N<small>O PHENOMENON</small> is more urgently in need of study today than the conditions under which new social movements may emerge in our society. Man's fate in societies living by big technology, urbanization, and division of labor is from now on a collective one. But social atomism has deeply corrupted our capacity to live together; and both personally and collectively our helplessness grows as democracy wanes. The recovery of democracy, if indeed it can occur, can happen only through men thinking together of what it is they want and organizing to move together. As a study at first hand of such a contemporary people's movement on our continent, Professor Lipset's deeply perceptive study is of first-rate importance.

We people on the North American continent have been bemused by our favored circumstances. We came to a new continent rich in resources coincidentally with the upsurge of the machine age. Protected by continental isolation, we have been able to take ourselves and our institutions for granted while we spread out westward in the pursuit of wealth. The abundance of our good fortune relative to older, crowded nations abroad has encouraged in us a pragmatic, unspeculative temper; and as a result today we watch with skepticism and not a little impatience the innovations of nations across the world that have forsaken liberal go-as-you-please and are attempting to discover new and more effective ways of living together.

History will probably look back on the twentieth century as one of the great eras of institutional change, comparable in magnitude to the shifts from feudalism to capitalism and the age of power-driven machinery. Industrial society is being forced toward one or another form of collective organization because the effort to operate modern technology under rules appropriate to the eighteenth century is wracking society to pieces.

As liberal society resists this change, it is taking on more and more the form of what in Europe is called "mass society." This does not mean "big" in the numerical sense, but the attrition of strong, spontaneous ties among men and the resulting loss of durable, autonomous standards of thinking and feeling and acting. Men in mass society become social atoms suspended in insignificance, acted upon but incapable of initiative save in the narrowest personal sense. Hitler deliberately exploited and speeded up this movement in German industrial society, as a necessary condition for the imposition of Nazi controls, by seeking to capture, neutralize, or destroy vocational and recreational organizations, the churches, and even the autonomy of the family.

Among us, the tendency to mass society accompanies the growth in the business world of bigness and power without responsibility, of urban propinquity careless of social belonging, and the resulting depersonalizing of all social processes. So much of decision making has ceased to go forward at the level of a man's eye and subject to local relevance and control that democracy is becoming a form increasingly devoid of feeling tone and is denied in action. As persons we are blurred; as citizens we become helpless participants in actions we do not understand. It is difficult to sustain the personal tensions of such living as social irrelevants in the midst of large issues that dominate our lives. So, as our public lives become more helpless, we seek escape and the sense of personal recovery through turning away from the issues themselves. We give over to others the search for solutions to our social dilemmas, while we concentrate on means to momentary self-identity, seeking a sense of personal idiom through such specious spontaneities as rivalrous consumer spending.

In such circumstances, those solicitous for the welfare of democracy search the horizons for signs of genuine democratic organization. And it is precisely such a movement that Professor Lipset here analyzes. That a regathering of the forces of democracy should appear on the agricultural periphery of industrial society is significant. Farmers, especially those in the one-crop economy of the Great Plains, embody in an extreme form the modern anachronism of the independent enterpriser bereft of control over his market, a stranger in the ruling institutional world of organized urban big business. And yet the farmer retains, better than the urban man, sources of resistance to the mass tendency: he produces a product that men indubitably need, and he accordingly respects his crop, the land that produces it, and his own labor. He and his family, especially in regions remote from large cities, know the value of coöperative social living, and they are relatively less distracted by the impersonal substitute activities that accompany competitive urban getting and spending. Here is a stance from which a man may still believe in the democratic right to stand and fight.

And yet even this show of independence may be a passing phase. The farmer owns or aspires to own land, and Hitler found massive support among German farmers by exploiting this desire. Our own world of industrial controls has discovered the political power of crop subsidies, and, presumably, the party of big business will not again overlook, as did the Republican Party in 1948, the clamor of farmers for storage facilities for their crops. In the present era, in which progress may no longer be taken for granted as a built-in feature of liberal democracy, and in which the volume and finesse of controls from the top of a class-stratified social system are rapidly increasing, it becomes more than ever important to study the conditions under which men can and will cease to "grin and bear it" and can and will organize to make their wants politically effective.

The urban middle class may not be looked to for democratic leadership. They have, it seems probable, learned far less than both the upper class and labor about the meaning of events since the First World War. Their nostalgia for a vanishing way of life is deep and genuine, whereas the upper class of big business uses these now primitive symbols only as convenient political weapons.

Today, democratic leadership can come, if it comes at all, only from labor, if possible in collaboration with farmers. And the growth of organized labor in the United States in the past decade and a half would seem to suggest, as does the Labor government in Britain, that labor is on the offensive. But labor itself has become big business in the managerial struggle of business unionism for a widening share of the capitalist "take"; and it remains to be seen whether big profit-oriented labor, operating under narrow bureaucracies habituated to managing the rank and file, will or can become more than a junior partner within a limited welfare capitalism. Those who view the fountain of progressive social legislation as inexhaustible should bear in mind the historic "ransom" character of such legislation, and the prospect that capitalism may reach the point where it neither can nor will continue to grant such concessions. Perhaps only then will labor on this abundant continent recognize its true class position and prepare to fight. But in this extremity, if the lessons of fascism have been learned, it may be too late.

Can the fire spread from the prairies? I do not know how far Professor Lipset would go in agreement with my appraisal of the position in which we appear now to find ourselves. But I have read and reread his close analysis for clues as to the larger potentialities of this "provincial socialist beachhead within capitalism." Here exists as clear and clean a democratic base as yet remains on this continent: a pervasive web of organization and participation. In wheat pools and other coöperatives and local services there is one elective position for every two or three farmers in Saskatchewan. After nearly fifty years of agrarian organization, "The C.C.F. has succeeded in involving more people in direct political activities than any other party in American and Canadian history, with the possible exception of certain similar farmers' parties." In 1945, 8 per cent of the electorate belonged to the party.

Here indeed is healthy democratic tissue, democracy living as it has largely ceased to live among urban men. But the apparent singleness of the pressure on the farmer living by a one-crop economy deceives him even as it unites him; for, as Professor Lipset so well shows, it fails to equip him for the bold extension of his somewhat parochial version of democracy to other elements in a wider population living predominantly by urban industry and trade. As the coöperating farmer's ideology meets the factory worker and the middle-class businessman, it wavers, blurs, and recedes. An agrarian socialist party becomes a liberal agrarian protest movement, and programs for the socialization of industry falter. Truly, he who sets out to make significant reforms should never hesitate or compromise!

As this is written, the Coöperative Commonwealth Federation as a national party in Canada has been thrown into retreat. In June, 1948, its systematic work at the level of municipal politics, in addition to its provincial and national campaigning and trade-union support in urban areas, was bearing fruit; and observers were speaking openly of the prospect of its superseding the Conservative Party as the official opposition to the Liberals in Ottawa. But the national election in June, 1949, brought crushing defeat. The C.C.F. captured only 13 seats in the national Parliament, a scant 3 more than the Social Credit Party, while the Liberals won 190 seats and the Conservatives 42. Even in Saskatchewan, where a C.C.F. government had been in power for five years, the Liberals won 14 of the 20 seats in the national Parliament. There was evidence that many voters throughout Canada voted in a "Stop Socialism" mood. How much the election reflected Canadian reaction to the Labor government in Britain and to anti-left propaganda from the United States it is difficult to say.

Likewise, it is hard to estimate the impact of the new mineral and industrial prosperity that has come to the Prairie Provinces since the war. They now realize the advantages of diversifying their economic base by inviting new industry. Coal and natural gas abound in Alberta, next door to Saskatchewan, and since 1947 Imperial Oil (a Standard Oil subsidiary) has found oil in abundance in Alberta and to a somewhat lesser extent in Saskatchewan. This casts a dangerous light on socialism in Saskatchewan and is likely to invite serious pressures upon the C.C.F.

It is difficult for one who has lived among men engaged in a noble and hopeful movement and shared their hopes and frustrations to reveal to them in cold print the full measure of one's sober conclusions. Am I mistaken in sensing in Professor Lipset's concluding chapter more disappointment with the prospects of the Coöperative Commonwealth Federation than he explicitly states? I hope I am. It may be that we are reduced to taking comfort from the reflection that, as he says, "As long as there are social organizations that produce men who do not accept the *status quo*, who see 'the inhumanity of man to man' as a crime, there will be hope in the human race."

I, too, am confident of the long future. And that future will gain immeasurably from the candid realism of this truly sophisticated study. But for the immediate future, our lifetime and that of our children, I fear it is later than we and the men of Saskatchewan think. We on this side of the Atlantic Ocean live in an angry world dominated by power committed to reaction. And we too, despite our knowledge and resources, perhaps shall only learn at long last, and the hard way.

ROBERT S. LYND

Columbia University
January, 1950

Author's Preface

I<small>T IS OBVIOUS</small> that research studies are not a simple reporting of all the facts, or the relationships that exist within the area analyzed. A study can deal only with the questions which the researcher raises, and it is possible to ask an almost infinite number of questions about any sociological problem. Some sociologists unfortunately do not recognize this, and present their research reports as definitive and "correct" studies of class, race relations, the family, and so on.

The theoretical framework within which one operates determines in large measure the results obtained. This does not mean that it is impossible to be objective because all the variables in a situation are not studied. Within the context of a given theoretical system and set of research questions it is possible to measure objectively the relationship among the variables that seem significant. One can, for example, study class structure by raising the question, as W. Lloyd Warner has done, of the relation between the status structure and the customs and institutions of society. It is equally possible to study the implications of a hierarchical societal structure in terms of its organized power and influence, as the Lynds did in their *Middletown* studies.

I personally believe that the problems raised by the Lynds are more important for an understanding of the way in which our society operates; but, regardless of how different sociologists look at the problem of class structure, each can make an "objective" study. This does not suggest that one conceptual scheme is as good as any other, but it does mean that many of them are not mutually exclusive and that there is room for different approaches to the analysis of the same phenomena. It is necessary, therefore, that the sociologist make clear the nature of the theoretical system he uses in research, that is, through which set of theoretical spectacles he views a problem.

My own theoretical framework is derived largely from the sociologists who have been concerned with problems of power, influence, class, organization, social change, and functional analysis. In terms of the "classical" sociologists, I have been most influenced by Karl Marx, Max Weber, and Emil Durkheim, and by Robert S. Lynd and Robert K. Merton among contemporary sociologists. I have not integrated the various theoretical systems into one system. The task of developing and integrating a systematic sociology is one which the entire discipline faces and which few persons pretend to have resolved. I have deliberately avoided explicit discussions of sociological theory in this study, though I believe that the reader will recognize the conceptual schemes used.

Intellectual honesty impels me to make explicit the political assumptions underlying this study of a socialist movement. I am a supporter of the democratic socialist movement of which the C.C.F. is a part, but I have been concerned with the wide discrepancy between the ideology and behavior of most present-day democratic socialist governments. As the Western world moves increasingly in a collectivist or statist direction, whether it is called "a fair deal," socialism, communism, or fascism, I believe that the social scientists operating in the relatively free atmosphere of Western democratic society must increasingly turn to the analysis of the operation and development of such systems. Our lack of knowledge of the social forces determining the actions of governments means that the people called upon to do the planning in present-day society are often engaged in logically contradictory behavior—planning without knowledge.

A gradually increasing body of sociological literature is developing in studies of organizations, political and private. Much of this research is, however, conducted in the context of the theory of organization, that is, using the concept of bureaucracy as the key analytical variable, and analyzing the behavior of different groups as related to the needs of the bureaucratic structure. I believe that such research is extremely valuable and fruitful but that it tends to oversimplify and overdetermine the process of social change. The needs of the organization and the individuals inhabiting the bureaucratic structure are only part of the cluster of factors that determine organizational action. It is impossible, as I see it, to understand the activities of a government political party without relating them to the structure of the community within which the movement arose, the opposition and support it received at different stages, the nature of the bureaucratic structure which the party develops, the ideological framework of the party, the climate of opinion within which it operates, the nature of the governmental bureaucratic structure which it is called upon to administer, and the immediate socioeconomic problems it faces when taking office. Behavior and institutional patterns should be discussed in functional terms, that is, related to the specific needs of specific groups and structures; but no one structure, like the party or governmental bureaucracy, can be singled out as the principal variable to which other behavior is functional. This study, therefore, was begun with the conscious decision not to use this approach, though I recognize the important contributions which men using it have made to the understanding of bureaucracy.

The preface of a book is traditionally used to express the indebtedness of the writer to those who aided him in obtaining and assembling the data. To do so for this study would be a herculean and almost impossible task. I spent almost fourteen months in Saskatchewan, and during that time was assisted by thousands of people in and out of the C.C.F.

Saskatchewan is a unique and rewarding place for a social scientist to do research, for the province contains a larger proportion of lay social scientists than any other area I have visited. The farmers are interested in their society and its relations to the rest of the world. Winter after winter, when the wheat crop is in, thousands of meetings are held throughout the province by political parties, churches, farmers' educational associations, and coöperatives. There are informal gatherings, also, in which farmers discuss economic and political problems. Not hedged in by the necessity of punching a time clock daily, these farmers, who have come from every part of Europe and North America, have frequent sessions in which they consider the ideas of Adam Smith, Karl Marx, William Morris, Henry George, James Keir Hardie, William Jennings Bryan, Thorstein Veblen, and others.

Almost every English-speaking farmer subscribes to three or four farm weeklies, which are veritable storehouses of economic and political debate. In their correspondence columns the more literate and vociferous farmers argue the merits of religion, systems of government, the Soviet Union, socialism, socialized medicine, Social Credit, and schemes for marketing wheat. In traveling about the province I soon learned not to be surprised when a farmer whom I was interviewing would open a book by Morris, Henry George, Veblen, Major C. H. Douglas, or some technical social scientist.

The role of the social scientist was, therefore, a definable one to the leaders of organized rural activity in the province, as well as to many farmers. They knew, at least, that people made studies of economic and social problems. I was someone who was trying to discover why Saskatchewan alone among the major governmental units of the United States and Canada had elected a socialist party to office, and who was interested in finding out what that party was now doing. I think I can safely say that this activity was not regarded as "queer." Obviously, those whom I met in the course of the study defined it in different ways, but all were extremely coöperative.

A one-man study of a large social movement is necessarily limited in scope, but its limitations were overcome, in part at least, by the large measure of coöperation freely granted by leaders and members of the C.C.F. and other Saskatchewan groups. Questionnaires were distributed by the C.C.F. and two other Saskatchewan farm organizations to their leaders. Permission to use documentary materials was easily obtainable. Leaders and members of the three major political parties—the C.C.F., the Progressive Conservatives, and the Liberals,—trade-unions, coöperatives, and farm organizations were generous indeed with both time and information. Members of the government, cabinet members, members of the legislature, and civil servants were equally helpful.

There are certain persons, however, whose aid must be individually acknowledged. These include Premier T. C. Douglas and the entire membership of his cabinet; Dr. Morris C. Shumiatcher and Thomas McLeod of the Premier's staff; Professor Carlyle King, president of the C.C.F., Saskatchewan Section; Gladys Strum, Dr. Cecil Sheps, Dr. Mindel Sheps, M. F. Allore, Gertrude Telford, Frank Hanson, Mr. and Mrs. Charles Pfeiffer, "Em" Allore, and

Marion Bryden. I am especially indebted to Mrs. Austin Bothwell, Legislative Librarian, who made possible much of the documentary research.

It is impossible to end this preface without acknowledging the great debt I owe to my friend and teacher, Robert S. Lynd. His insight into the problem of class and political power was of great assistance in the organizing of my work. I should also like to thank Robert K. Merton for his invaluable help. Whatever methodological acumen and statistical background this study possesses can be attributed primarily to Paul Lazarsfeld. I am indebted also to my former colleagues at the University of Toronto, Professor S. D. Clark and Dr. Jean Burnet, who know more about western Canada than I can ever hope to learn, and who gave me the benefit of their knowledge.

I am especially indebted to the Social Science Research Council of the United States for making this study possible through the award of a predoctoral research fellowship, and to the Canadian Social Science Research Council for a grant-in-aid for statistical analysis of election data.

The major acknowledgment has been left to the end. Elsie Braun Lipset collaborated in every stage of this study. It would never have assumed its present form without her participation.

Berkeley, California   SEYMOUR MARTIN LIPSET
October, 1949

Contents

Chapter I

THE BACKGROUND
OF AGRARIAN RADICALISM

ADICAL POLITICAL movements are assuming a dominant position in the world today. England, France, Norway, Israel, Russia, China, Hungary, Poland, are but some of the countries in which political parties whose avowed goal is a "socialist" society control or form part of the government. In many other countries in Europe, South America, and Asia, democratic leftist or totalitarian communist parties are major political forces.[1]

The United States and Canada are the foremost exceptions to the growing collectivist trend. Capitalist democracy, which attained its greatest heights on this continent, has not been challenged by a significant nation-wide socialist movement. The immense material wealth of North America, which has given workers and farmers a higher living standard than in any other place on earth, has apparently prevented any organized threat to the capitalist system.

Various attempts have been made to explain why there is no socialism in the United States or Canada. For the most part, these have tried to answer the question by comparing the social and

[1] For notes to chapter i see pages 287–289.

[1]

economic structures of North America and of Europe. Among the factors differentiating the American scene from that of Europe, the following have been suggested:

1. The absence of a feudal tradition prevented fixed social strata and explicit institutionalization of class lines.[2]

2. A richly endowed and sparsely settled continent encouraged an economically expanding capitalist society in which many could rise in the economic and social structure after this became impossible in Europe.[3]

3. The emergence of the United States as a nation coincidently with the Industrial Revolution has meant that the institutions of this new, sprawling, loosely structured population have been associated in the popular mind as the cause of the country's prosperity. So long as the level of living rose, there seemed no reason to make radical changes in "the American way."[4]

4. The open frontier absorbed malcontents and acted as a safety valve to prevent organized radicalism.[5]

5. The steady influx of foreign-born constituted the labor floor and distracted the attention of American-born labor from the fact that it was part of the "lower class." This also resulted in cleavages along national, racial, and religious lines rather than along class lines.[6]

6. The conflicting interests and different rates of development of the various regions channeled internal conflicts along geographical lines and made most of the social protest movements regional rather than national.[7]

7. The political system typical of the United States concentrated power in a popularly elected executive and made third parties much more difficult to launch in America than in parliamentary countries.

These factors have probably been important, but both radicals and conservatives have accepted too automatically the assumption that North American political radicalism must develop under conditions similar to those in Europe. The tactics of radicals and the theoretical approach of social scientists have both been biased by an implicit assumption that American radicalism, when and if it developed, would be a simple repetition of European working-class movements. Few have focused on the forces in North American culture that might create native patterns of organized discontent.

There have, in fact, been large and significant class movements for social and economic change in the United States which have attempted to challenge the business control of society. It is in order, then, to analyze the problem of American radicalism by studying the conditions under which class-conscious protest movements have arisen, as well as the factors that account for their success or failure. Such studies would be more fruitful for an understanding of why North America has no significant socialist movement than would general discussions of differences between American and European social structures.

If American social and political history is examined from this point of view, a significant pattern emerges. The history of American political class consciousness has been primarily a story of agrarian upheavals. From Shay's Rebellion through the Jeffersonian and Jacksonian movements in the United States and the "Clear Grits" in Canada, American farmers have been in the forefront of the battle against the control of society by business. The agrarian revolt became significant as part of the world-wide movements for economic collectivism after the Civil War, when western wheat-belt farmers had to resort to various collectivist schemes to alleviate the coercions of a growing monopoly capitalism.

It is significant that the first electorally successful North American socialist movement, the Coöperative Commonwealth Federation (C.C.F.), came to power in the almost completely rural province of Saskatchewan in 1944. It is impossible to understand why an avowedly socialist party should have won a majority vote among supposedly conservative farmers unless one recognizes how often the social and economic position of the American wheat-belt farmer, in the United States as in Canada, has made him the American radical.

Agrarian radicalism after the Civil War developed with the extension of the railroad west of the Mississippi. The western frontier continued to advance as the railroads supplied a steady horde of new settlers from the East and from Europe. A new population striving for freedom and security pushed west with the railroads, only to find themselves bound hand and foot to the coercions of the new transportation in attempting to market their crops. Once settled on their raw new farms and deeply in debt to the bankers for equipment, the farmers' whole existence rested precariously on the weather and the world price of wheat. "The farmers were as a

class *a priori* unprotected, the victims of a system of free trade selling and protected purchasing—in their economic relation as consumers paying heavy prices for high tariff goods, and as producers most of them selling against the competition of the world's markets."[8]

To the frontier farmer the business tactics of the local banker seemed erratic and ruthless. When times were good the farmer was urged to expand his use of bank credit, but in periods of depression he found himself caught helplessly in a vise. He faced chronic high freight rates and a grain-elevator monopoly. He was forced to sell his wheat to the local grain elevator and to accept the prices and grades arbitrarily set by the elevator agent.

As John D. Hicks, a historian of American Populism, pointed out, farmers "suffered from the railroads, from the trusts and the middlemen, from the money lenders and the bankers, and from the muddled currency. . . . Hence arose the veritable chorus of denunciation directed against those individuals and those corporations who considered only their own advantage without regard to the effect their actions might have upon the farmer and his interests."[9]

Organized rural protest took three forms: educational organization, such as the Patrons of Husbandry and the Farmers' Alliance, to put pressure on government to aid farmers; coöperative organization to eliminate the profits of middlemen; and, after these two methods failed, political parties seeking control of the state in the interest of organized agriculture.

The first major agrarian upheaval after the Civil War developed during the great depression of 1873–1878. The price of wheat fell 49 per cent between 1868 and 1878. Capital became scarce in the West, while the costs of distribution and of the goods which the farmers bought remained relatively high. The gradualist solution of coöperation and political pressure that had been practiced by the Patrons of Husbandry, then the dominant educational group among farmers, seemed futile, and the various state organizations of the Patrons began to organize local political parties to obtain direct control of state governments.[10]

The Independent (or Reform) parties concentrated on controlling the railroads and the middlemen; later came the Greenback parties, which focused on monetary reform. These parties expressed the frustrations of the frontier farmers who had seen their years of toil

come to nought while railroads and businessmen continued to make profits. From the start, therefore, the programs and propaganda of the agrarians were explicitly opposed to big business.

The Independents, who organized in 1873, demanded "the subjection of corporations, and especially of the railroad corporations, to the control of the state."[11] They also called for reductions in tariffs that aided eastern manufacturers, and the elimination of the middleman's profits. "Coöperation" and "Down with Monopolies" were their popular slogans.[12] In some areas, especially in the more radical northwestern wheat belt, government ownership of railroads was advocated. In order to break the power of the middleman, cooperatives were formed, including

local, county, and state agencies for the purchase of implements and supplies and the sale of farm products, local grain elevators, and coöperative stores, the manufacture of farm machinery, banking, insurance, and even organizations for bringing direct trade between the American producer and the European consumer.... [The farmers] believed it possible to regain their economic independence by themselves assuming the management of those industries which touched them most closely.[13]

Such collectivist agrarian programs recurred in the American Northwest until the explicit formulation of socialism as a goal in the C.C.F. program of the 1930's.

The Independent parties were extremely short-lived. Most of them disappeared within two or three years, before the presidential election of 1876. Their major proposal—government regulation of railroads—proved a failure, as the laws passed in various states to control the railroads were invalidated in the courts. Their disappearance, however, was not a result of a decline in agrarian protest. The continuing and deepening depression of the 1870's led many farm leaders to the conviction that a more fundamental change in economic structure was needed; and accordingly they turned to monetary reform as a solution.

The frontier settlers, who carried a heavy load of debt, believed that an increase in the circulation of money, with consequent higher farm prices, would enable them to get rid of their debts. To do this required a frontal attack on the banks and their power to issue credit. This took the organized form of Greenback parties, demanding that the federal government should issue all money and regulate its value, and that "there be an adequate supply of money fixing a minimum amount per capita of the population."[14]

Continuing rural antagonism to large-scale wealth was expressed in the demand that government bonds be taxed and that "a graduated income tax should be levied for the support of the government and the payment of its debts." The Greenbackers felt that the adoption of their program "would muster out of service the vast army of idlers who, under the existing system, grow rich upon the earnings of others, that every man and woman may by their own efforts secure a competency, so that overgrown fortunes and extreme poverty will seldom be found within the limits of our republic."[15]

The Greenback movement represented a significant advance in the thinking of agrarian leaders. The failures of local Independent parties had taught them that economic evils could not be controlled by influencing local state governments. They thought that they had located the nucleus of the problem in the operations of the banking system; but it would be impossible to reform the national banking system without control of the federal government. So the Greenbackers soon realized that they needed urban allies. An alliance with eastern business groups was obviously impossible, in view of the program of the movement; therefore they sought an alliance with various radical labor groups in the East, and renamed their organization the Greenback Labor Party. The common antagonism of rural and urban radicals to the power of big business and their need for mutual support to win electoral majorities led both groups to overlook temporarily any divergences of outlook or interest. This effort by agrarian leaders to find labor allies who would support the demands of the farmers in return for rural support of labor's program is characteristic of American agrarianism.

In the congressional elections of 1878 the Greenback Party received 1,000,065 votes. This was the high point of the movement. In 1880, the next presidential election year, their strength declined to 308,578 votes. The main support of the movement came from the western agrarian states.[16]

The return of prosperity, with consequent higher prices for wheat and other farm goods, increased the circulation of money. "As prosperity returned, the strength of the Greenback Party waned."[17] Its rapid decline indicated the lack of any fundamental desire for basic social and economic change on the part of the farmers. The Party leaders had concentrated on the need for cheap

money, which, they argued, required control of the bankers. But when prosperity gave the farmers what the Party advocated, the latter lost interest in monetary reform. This transitory character of organized rural protest was to prove characteristic of subsequent agrarian movements.

The next upswing in the cycle of agrarian protest followed the economic crisis of 1887. Credit had again become very difficult to obtain in the West. The old cry of the Greenbackers for monetary reform revived.

> In the rural portions of the central regions, where farmers stayed and struggled with failing crops and low prices, with unyielding debts and relentless taxes, where they fought a battle, now successful, now unavailing, to retain the land they had bought and to redeem the high hopes with which they had come to the West—in this region unrest and discontent prevailed . . . finally to break forth in a program of open revolt.[18]

A new economic and educational organization, the National Farmers' Alliance, grew up in the old Independent Party states. Simultaneously, the Southern Alliance emerged in the South. The programs of both called for "financial reform of an inflationist nature, . . . and asked that the government take over and operate all means of transportation and communication."[19] It was not until 1890, when crop prices again began to fall drastically, that various state Alliances organized independent political parties, called People's parties. Kansas started a new party in June, 1890. Nebraska and the middle border joined the movement. North and South Dakota, Colorado, and even Michigan and Indiana nominated state tickets. In the South, the Southern Alliance operated through Democratic Party primaries. Much of the propaganda of these groups was directed at Wall Street, the banks, the railroads, and big business.[20]

Like the Greenbackers before them, the supporters of Populism attempted to obtain the backing of the labor movement. The Knights of Labor agreed to work with the organized farm movement, but the growing American Federation of Labor refused, because the Alliances were "composed of employing farmers."[21] In spite of opposition from A. F. of L. leaders who were under Socialist influence, the Northern Alliance stated its sympathy for "the just demands of labor of every grade"; and it recognized "that many of the evils from which the farming community suffers op-

press universal labor, and that therefore producers should unite in a demand for the reform of unjust systems and the repeal of laws that bear unequally upon the people."[22] The Northern Alliance called for farmer-labor unity to gain control of the government.

The political Populist movement became a loose coalition of three separate groups: Rocky Mountain Populism, which was interested primarily in the free coinage of silver and was neither agrarian nor radical; southern Populism, which could not make a radical break because of the necessity of upholding "white supremacy"; and wheat-belt Populism, which was the agrarian radical wing of the movement.[23]

The Populists won a number of important local victories in 1890, but when the price of wheat declined further, they realized that they needed a national victory.[24] In 1892 the party nominated James B. Weaver as its presidential candidate and adopted a platform designed to appeal to farmers, workers, and the silver interests of the mountain states:

Wealth belongs to him who creates it and every dollar taken from industry without an equivalent is robbery. If any will not work, neither shall he eat. The interests of rural and civil labor are the same, their enemies are identical. . . .

. . . The time has come when the railroad corporations will either own the people or the people will own the railroads . . . the telegraphs and the telephones . . . should be owned and operated by the government in the interests of the people. . . .

[We demand:] (1) free and unlimited coinage of silver at the present legal ratio of 16 to 1; (2) the amount of circulating medium be speedily increased to not less than $50 per capita; (3). . . . a graduated income tax.[25]

The most important agrarian part of the platform, however, was the so-called subtreasury plan to require the federal government to store nonperishable farm products and to advance money up to 80 per cent of their market value at 1 or 2 per cent interest. "The farmers believed that through this subtreasury plan the volume of money would become adequate and elastic enough at harvest time and the rates of interest low enough to permit of their moving their crops at a good profit."[26]

Weaver succeeded in polling over a million votes, and he actually carried Colorado, Idaho, and Kansas. In the congressional elections of 1894 the Populists won 1,500,000 votes, which virtually

eliminated the Democrats as a major party in the West and the Northwest. In 1896 the Democratic Party saved itself from possible extinction by taking over that part of the Populist program which advocated free coinage of silver, and succeeded in getting the majority of the Populist Party to fuse with it behind the candidacy of William Jennings Bryan.[27]

The wheat-belt agrarians had resisted the merger of the Populists with the Democrats, but they lost control of the party to the free silverites, who were not interested in the radical economic phases of the Populist platform. Many of the radicals were bitter at this "betrayal" of their earlier hopes of building a new radical party that would destroy the growing power of eastern monopoly; but their original compromise in joining with the nonradical mining interests had destroyed the force of their criticism. As prosperity returned in the late 'nineties, even the wheat-belt farmers lost interest in building a new party, and all efforts to revive the movement on a purely agrarian basis failed.

The lack of a long-term program for social change accounted, in part, for the failure of Populism to become a permanent radical protest movement. The farmers struck out at random at the most visible economic evils that affected them. They opposed the banks, the railroads, the wheat-elevator companies, and the shortage of money, but they saw each evil as an evil in itself, not as part of the total economic system. They accepted without question the support of any group that would join them. By focusing on specific transitory evils, the agrarian leaders failed to lay the educational base for a new radical movement, and they were unable to hold their followers in line when the manifestations of these evils disappeared during the upswings of the business cycle.

The weakness of elected Populist officials contributed also to the downfall of the Party, as John D. Hicks has pointed out.

Populist legislation was all too frequently found defective and unconstitutional. In administrative affairs the Populists were even less successful. Evidently their genius lay in protest rather than in performance. The third party men who took office were often inexperienced as administrators and it is not surprising that they were baffled by the difficulties that confronted them, difficulties that, incidentally, were made just as baffling as the opponents of Populism knew how to make them. . . . From the men they elected to office the Populists expected more than was humanly possible; and when the millennium failed to arrive they turned promptly from ardent supporters to disappointed critics.[28]

An examination of the electoral support of these agrarian movements reveals a consistent pattern. It was the economic and cli-
matically vulnerable wheat belt that formed the backbone of all
the protest movements, from the Independent parties of the 1870's
down to the contemporary C.C.F. in Canada.

The Independent parties had their main source of strength in
the Northwest of the 1870's, in Illinois, Iowa, Wisconsin, and
Minnesota. In the order named, these were the greatest wheat-
producing states in the Union at that time: they produced more
than one-third of all the wheat raised in the United States.[29] Similarly, Oregon and California, the two western states that joined
the movement, were largely grain-growing states in the 1870's.
All these areas were following a one-crop type of agriculture, with
very little mixed farming, and therefore were almost completely
exposed to the fluctuations of the world' wheat market.

The same conditions were associated with the rise of the Independent and Greenback movements. In Iowa and Wisconsin, "the
year of the poorest yield per acre of wheat in the history of both
states was the year of the organization of the Greenback Party . . .
[and] the years of the lowest prices and the greatest agricultural
depression were also the years of the greatest strength of the
Greenback Party."[30] A comparison of election returns by counties
with the census data on agricultural production reveals distinct
differences between rural supporters and opponents of the Greenbackers. The dairy and mixed farmers of both states "paid but
little attention to the Greenback movement."[31] In the leading
Greenback counties, however, "there was little stress upon . . .
diversified farming and dairy, and marked concentration upon
grain farming."[32]

Agrarian Populism also arose in the wheat belt.

The driving force for a new party came from the wheat-belt, although
many other forces were eventually rallied around the idea and the organization. Populist expression was strongest and clearest in the wheat
states. The degree of Populist strength in other sections can be gauged
with amazing accuracy by an examination of the type of farming. The
stresses inherent in the economy of cotton were not less severe than
those in wheat, but the organizational and political expression of southern agriculture was poisoned by the vestiges of feudalism. The agriculture of the middle and eastern states was diversified in character, a
fact which cushioned the shock of the clash with monopoly and thwarted
clear-cut expression of the farmers' needs.[33]

An analysis of the Populist vote reveals clearly the role of the grain growers as the backbone of the Populist revolt.[34] During the Populist agitation there were three farming sections in the upper Mississippi Valley: "corn-livestock farming in a wide belt stretching from Ohio westward through Iowa and gradually pushing into eastern Kansas and Nebraska; dairy farming, found principally in Wisconsin and southeastern Minnesota; and grain farming, predominantly wheat, which had pushed out into a broad crescent sweeping from Kansas, through Nebraska, the Dakotas, and western Minnesota."[35] It was the latter area that backed the Populists.

In Minnesota the wheat areas supplied the greater part of the Populist vote. ". . . there was throughout the farmer agitation of the period a distinct cleavage between that part of the state where dairying had developed and the western counties which were predominantly given over to wheat production."[36] The Populist strength in Kansas was in the central part of the state, which was predominantly a wheat region; the older, settled portion had changed over in part to the corn-livestock system and remained solidly conservative Republican.[37] Similar conditions prevailed in Nebraska. ". . . the western counties, which were still cattle country, and the eastern counties, where the corn-livestock system had gained a foothold, were least affected, while the center of Populist power was in the central part . . . where grain farming was still the dominant system."[38] The same tendency existed in Iowa, for the chief strength of the Populists was in the northwestern grain-growing section, where "the Populists made important gains over the Greenback vote of 1880."[39] Other sections of Iowa, which had earlier supported the Greenbackers but had changed in the intervening decade from wheat to hogs and cattle, were uninfluenced by the new agrarianism.[40]

It is apparent, therefore, that agrarianism remained essentially the same throughout the latter half of the nineteenth century. The wheat-growing and frontier areas were most vulnerable economically, and had the newest and least-integrated social structure. These areas formed the basic core of all the movements.

The Socialist Party, which was the major third-party movement in the United States from 1900 to the First World War, was the sole major radical political movement that did not follow the pattern of agrarian revolt. The organizers of the Party were almost entirely urban workers or intellectuals, and its platform and lead-

ers made their major appeal to the urban working class. But the major strength of the Socialist Party vote at its high point in 1912, when it received 5.9 per cent of the national vote for president, was not in the manufacturing centers but in the western states.

As the *New Republic* commented at the time:

> In certain agricultural states, where there are few wage earners, and where farm-owners and tenants who wish to become farm-owners do not know what wage slavery is, the Socialist vote is comparatively strong. In Kansas, in Minnesota, in Texas, in several other preponderately agricultural states, the proportionate Socialist vote is much larger than in New York, Pennsylvania, New Jersey, and other industrial states.[41]

Robert F. Hoxie, who made a study of Socialist Party electoral victories in 1911, found a pattern of Socialist success

> based on Socialist organization and agitation, but occurring for the large part in small agricultural or semiagricultural communities. Victories of this kind are pretty generally diffused, but their special habitat seems to be in the old stronghold of Populism. The brand of socialism which they represent tends to be in outer seeming of the ultra-theoretical blood-and-thunder variety; but an examination of the party membership in these areas often discloses a surprisingly high proportion of farmers.[42]

The Socialist Party was strongest in Oklahoma, which was then a wheat state. "At the height of the movement, the Socialist Party commanded close to one-third of the total vote of Oklahoma, elected six members of the state legislature, and a number of county officers."[43] Virtually all this vote came from the wheat-growing regions. Substantial support for the Socialist Party was obtained from farmers, in spite of the fact that a large section of the Party opposed such recruiting. At the first convention of the Party in 1900, the delegates were unable to decide whether they should even make an appeal to farmers. As Job Harrison, a Party leader, stated, "We are building in this convention a working-class platform; the farmers do not belong to the working class, because the farmers own the farms."[44] In 1910, after a bitter fight, the Party reversed itself on the land question. The program adopted, however, advocated that existing government lands should be used for "model state farms and various forms of collective agricultural enterprise."[45]

In view of the antagonism felt by a large section of the Socialists toward the farmers as a class, one may wonder how much more rural support the Party might have gained if it had really attempted to present a farm program designed to protect the farmer on his land and aimed at the elimination of the middleman and the socialization of monopolies, as earlier agrarian parties had advocated. In North Dakota, the heart of the wheat belt, A. C. Townley, who subsequently founded the Non-Partisan League, recruited hundreds of farmers to the Socialist Party, but he was forced to break with the Party in 1914 when its doctrinaire leaders opposed the mass recruitment of farmers. "[The orthodox Socialists] feared—and apparently with good reason—that it wasn't dyed-in-the-wool Socialism that Townley was spreading among the farmers. They were inclined to believe that his converts weren't really Socialist at all. This man Townley, with his talk of a 'state program,' evidently was only an opportunist, a 'yellow-belly,' a hated 'reformer.' "[46]

The destruction of the Socialist Party during and after the First World War by a combination of government persecution and Communist splits prevented the development of an American agrarian socialism. If the Party had not been destroyed by the war, the wheat farmers of Oklahoma or North Dakota might have taken the lead in establishing a strong socialist movement on this continent. The Saskatchewan Coöperative Commonwealth Federation, as we shall see later, follows directly in this tradition of North American socialism.

The most important radical agrarian movement after the First World War was the Non-Partisan League, which attained great influence in the western Great Plains region of the United States from 1916 to 1922. The League was organized in the wheat state of North Dakota in 1915 by A. C. Townley and a small group of socialist farmers. They attacked existing political parties as "useless for the farmers' purpose" and called for a farmers' alliance "to grapple with organized 'big business' greed."[47]

Many wheat farmers had again become convinced that the system of marketing grain was unfair to the producers. They believed that "bankers, merchants, and professional politicians were in league with the millers to exploit them."[48] In 1911 farmers in North Dakota organized a marketing coöperative designed to eliminate the profits of elevator companies, grain traders, and speculators

in futures on the Grain Exchange; but business struck back by refusing trading rights on the Minneapolis Exchange to this farmers' Equity Coöperative Exchange.[49] Farm organizations thereupon demanded in 1913 that North Dakota build a state-owned "terminal elevator, which it was hoped would be able to store enough wheat to create the independent market so earnestly desired."[50] But the Republican-controlled legislature refused. This action by the dominant political party in the state gave impetus to the Non-Partisan League drive to build a radical class-conscious agrarian movement.

The program of the League, drawn up by socialists, dealt in the main with proposals for government ownership and control of various enterprises:

1. State ownership of terminal elevators, flour mills, packing houses, and cold-storage plants.
2. State inspection of grain and grain dockage.
3. Exemption of farm improvements from taxation.
4. State hail insurance on the acreage tax basis.
5. Rural credit banks operated at cost.[51]

The strategy of the League was to attempt to capture the North Dakota Republican Party by entering a League slate in the primaries rather than by starting a new party. In 1916, the first election contested by the League, it elected the governor and all the other state officials. After winning control of both houses of the legislature in 1918, it enacted a large part of its program into law: a state bank; a Home Building Association to lend money at low rates of interest; a graduated state income tax distinguishing between earned and unearned income; a state hail-insurance fund; a workmen's compensation act that assessed employers for its support; the eight-hour day for working women; and regulation of working conditions in the mines.[52]

Such forthright action in North Dakota alerted many members of the national Socialist Party, for they felt that the agrarian organization was carrying out the Socialist program. Many members of the Socialist Party were accordingly brought in from outside the state to assist the League's work. This move was openly defended in the Socialist Party's national organ by Arthur LeSeur, Townley's legal adviser, and himself a Socialist. "While the Non-Partisan League in North Dakota is composed exclusively of farmers, the Labor unions of the state have stood as one man with the

League . . . [and] its program is composed of precisely the points included in the Socialist Party platform for the last six years."[53]

In 1917 the League began to organize in neighboring states, and eventually enrolled more than 200,000 members.[54] Almost all its support, however, was in the wheat area tributary to Minneapolis and St. Paul. It never completely captured any other state than North Dakota, though the old Republican machine in South Dakota adopted much of its program and set up a "state rural credits system, a state-owned coal mine, and a state cement plant," and promised that if the North Dakota flour mill and packing plant were successful, South Dakota would adopt them also.[55]

The agricultural depression of 1920 damaged the League, as the decline in the price of wheat reduced the state's finances and embarrassed the state-owned industries and the state bank. The state attempted to raise funds by selling state bonds; but private bankers seized this opportunity to bring the agrarian reformers to their knees. A report of a committee of the North Dakota Bankers' Association to the general body makes this clear:

It was urged by your committee that the construction and operation of mills, elevators, and banks by the State was an experiment, was theoretical, was without precedent, and its success far from assured; that investors now proposing to buy the State's bonds were naturally cautious; that if these industries should prove gross failures, and the people of the future feel aggrieved, the ultimate payment of these bonds might be questioned, and therefore they would not pay the bonds, unless some assurance is given that no large similar indebtedness is to be created until it is determined whether or not these ventures are a success; in short, that $3,000,000 was enough with which to experiment.

Your committee is reminded that there is no law by which a state can be compelled to pay its indebtedness. If coming generations, when the bonds mature, should have found that these experiments were unsound and these millions wasted, it is not inconceivable that they might hesitate to pay an enormous debt for which they never received any value. If the experiments proved successful the contrary would be the case. It would take at least two or three years to determine the question by actual experience.[56]

The bankers' committee demanded that the state "Provide some assurance to the public that the so-called farmers' industrial program will be confined to the Grand Forks mill and elevator, to the Drake mill, and the Bank of North Dakota."[57] The Non-Partisan State Industrial Commission refused to accept the bankers' terms.

The proposition . . . cannot honorably be considered by the Commission for the reason that it is a plain attempt on the part of the financial interests, presumably Wall Street financiers, to dictate the political, financial and industrial policies of the State of North Dakota, and requiring a surrender of the sovereign powers of the State. The time has not yet arrived when any group, no matter how powerful financially, can dictate to this State how to manage its own affairs. Every State in the Union is guaranteed a republican form of government under our constitution. The officers of the State, even though elected by the people, have no authority to surrender its sovereignty. . . . We are satisfied that any group of men that would exact such a surrender and arrogate to themselves the prerogative of making the laws for the people of the State would rule with a tyrannical hand.[58]

North Dakota then tried to get out-of-state bankers to handle the bonds, "but the financial houses of Minneapolis and Chicago were unwilling to undertake the sale of the state's bonds."[59] An investigation of the state bank in 1921 revealed its insolvency. The conservative opposition to the League thereupon initiated a recall election. The League officials were defeated by a small majority, though in the same election a majority of the voters cast their ballots in favor of maintaining the state industries.[60]

The failure of the Non-Partisan League indicates one of the crucial difficulties facing all agrarian protest movements that attempt to solve the farmers' ills on a local or regional level. The economic and financial system of a nation involves a single web of power, and any part severs itself from the whole at its own peril. This was especially true in the unbalanced single-crop wheat economy of North Dakota. Like the Independents of the 1870's, the Non-Partisans were attacking giants with a slingshot.

An analysis of the voting strength of the Non-Partisan League reveals the same geographical pattern of agrarian radicalism that was exhibited by earlier farm parties: the one-crop wheat-growing regions gave the movement its greatest support. In Minnesota the League candidates "received heavy support from northwestern wheat counties and very light support from the southern and corn-growing counties."[61] The Non-Partisan vote in South Dakota in 1920 "was determined by sectional differences associated with crop-producing areas,"[62] the main support coming from wheat-producing areas. The greatest vote of the Non-Partisan League was received, of course, in North Dakota, which is the second most highly rural state in the Union and raises only wheat.

The hard-times, "grudge" character of agrarian movements within the prevailing North American optimism was borne out by the sharp decline of the Non-Partisan League in the prosperous 1920's.[63] After 1929 the League revived and returned to power in North Dakota in 1932. An offshoot of the League, the Minnesota Farmer-Labor Party, also succeeded in electing state officials and United States senators in the 'thirties. The revived protest movement did not, however, succeed in permanently rebuilding a strong national movement, though there seemed to be popular sentiment for it in the early 'thirties. The New Deal program, setting a floor under agricultural prices and providing crop insurance and extensive federal government aid projects, gave farmers what they wanted and destroyed the embryonic radicalism. Had Roosevelt not headed off the potential radical revolt by making sharp concessions to the farmers, North Dakota and its neighbors might again have challenged the two-party system. It should be noted that North Dakota lies directly south of Saskatchewan and is the state most comparable to it, both geographically and economically.

Farmers are customarily considered a slow-moving group, long on stability and short on innovation. Both conservatives and radicals have agreed that the farmer is too individualistic to be a natural "joiner" and too "set in his ways" to become a sustained radical. As Veblen remarked of the farmer,

> ... he is, on the whole, an obstinately loyal supporter of the system of law and custom which so makes the conditions of life for him.

His unwavering loyalty to the system is in part a holdover from that obsolete past when he was the Independent Farmer of the poets; but in part it is also due to the still surviving persuasion that he is on the way, by hard work and shrewd management, to acquire a "competence"; such as will enable him some day to take his due place among the absentee owners of the land and so come in for an easy livelihood at the cost of the rest of the community; and in part it is also due to the persistent though fantastic opinion that his own present interest is tied up with the system of absentee ownership, in that he is himself an absentee owner by so much as he owns land and equipment which he works with hired help,—always presuming that he is such an owner in effect or in prospect.[64]

The role of revolutionary catalyst, which might eventually lead to an overthrow of existing capitalist society, has commonly been

assigned to the working classes. In the United States and Canada, however, workers as a group have never fulfilled either the hopes of Marxists or the fears of conservatives. On the contrary, certain groups of farmers have been more wont to seek redress for their economic grievances through class-conscious political action.

Agrarian radicalism, although it rarely is explicitly socialist, has directed its attack against big-business domination. In certain economic areas farmers have openly challenged private ownership and control of industry. American agrarians have attempted, either through government or coöperative ownership, to eliminate private control of banking, insurance, transportation, natural resources, public utilities, manufacture of farm implements, wholesale and retail distribution of consumers' goods, and food commodity exchanges. The large measure of "socialism without doctrine" that can be found in the programs of agrarian political and economic organizations is in many respects more socialistic than the nationalization policies of some explicitly socialist parties.

Agrarian radicalism has developed within the same American cultural framework that has proved so great a stumbling block to the organization of working-class radicalism. The farmers, like the workers, have been exposed to the material benefits of American society, to ethnic heterogeneity, to the American creed of opportunity and classlessness, and to similar social pressures. This suggests that some of the explanations cited earlier for the failure of American socialism may be oversimplified in that they neglect significant variables that may cause a lower economic class to turn against the *status quo*.

In Saskatchewan a new agrarian social movement, the Coöperative Commonwealth Federation, which is avowedly socialist, has won majority power in an almost completely rural area. It is highly significant that the first electorally successful socialist party in the United States or Canada should have developed in the same Great Plains wheat belt that earlier produced the Greenbackers, the Populists, the Non-Partisans, and other agrarian upheavals. The existence of a socialist government in rural Saskatchewan confounds those who would perpetuate the myth of the conservative farmer.

The success of the C.C.F. to date presents us with a dynamic experiment-in-process in the development of radical class consciousness. It offers a significant opportunity for a detailed study

of the factors in North American society that are conducive to the development of organized radicalism. It should be possible from its study to cast light on the relationship between economic pressures and organized class action. To recognize that depressions result in agrarian protest in the wheat belt tells little of the process by which economic reverses produce class action; for many rural and urban groups have been exposed to depressions without forming any large protest movement. Obviously, some important variables must intervene between the economic factor and organized social action.

Chapter II

THE SOCIAL AND ECONOMIC SETTING

T HE GREAT PLAINS region of Canada is the last settled agricultural frontier on the North American continent. Lying directly north of the wheat belt of Dakota and Montana, it is in every major respect similar to those regions in geographic appearance and economic structure.

Until 1870 the area that now comprises Alberta and Saskatchewan was governed as the private property of the Hudson's Bay Company. Its population consisted of Indian tribes and small groups of whites and half-breeds who worked for "the Company." In 1869 the newly formed Dominion of Canada purchased the rights to this gigantic territory, including what is now the province of Manitoba.

The land was thrown open to agricultural development after 1870. Settlement was encouraged on a homestead basis similar to the manner in which the western United States was occupied. Despite the fertility of the land, however, settlement lagged. By 1891 only 251,473 people lived in the entire region, while the much smaller Territory of Dakota, directly south, had a population of 510,000. The major reason for the failure to attract settlers was

the existence of free homestead land south of the border. The United States had a greater appeal to European immigrants than did the unknown Canada, and it also had a larger population in the East to draw upon for western settlement.[1]

The turn of the century, however, witnessed the beginnings of a flood of immigration into the Canadian North-West Territories. Free fertile lands in the United States were becoming exhausted, and the world wheat price had begun a gradual but steady rise. These economic factors, combined with the aggressive immigration policy fostered by the Laurier administration, brought immigrants from England, Europe, eastern Canada, and the United States. Expansion was continuous and rapid. Most of this new settlement occurred between 1900 and 1914. "An area larger than Vermont was 'entered' in free homesteads in 1909; twice the area of Connecticut in 1910; more than Delaware and New Hampshire in 1911; nearly the area of Maryland in 1912; more than Massachusetts in 1913; and more than the area of Wales in 1914."[2] The First World War slowed the rate of expansion, but in less than a decade almost the whole "last best West" was occupied.

More than 1,000,000 people settled on the Canadian prairies between 1896 and 1913, and the population constituted 20 per cent of the total population of Canada in 1913, as over against only 7 per cent in 1896. Occupied land rose from 10,000,000 to 70,000,000 acres. Wheat production increased from 20,000,000 to 209,000,000 bushels. In the three Prairie Provinces the total value of agricultural production amounted to between $300,000,000 and $400,000,000 annually by the end of this period.[3] Settlers came from every part of Europe and America and soon destroyed the ethnic homogeneity of Canada as a British and French nation. Saskatchewan in 1911 had about 275,000 immigrants from parts of Europe other than Britain and France.

In 1905 the North-West Territories were divided into the provinces of Alberta and Saskatchewan.[4] The relative recency of their frontier period is an important factor in the contemporary social and political history of the two provinces. Much of rural western Canada is still in the semifrontier stage from which the Great Plains agrarian states of the United States emerged at the end of the nineteenth century. Thus Saskatchewan and Alberta today are comparable to the frontier areas of Kansas and Nebraska in the

---

[1] For notes to chapter ii see pages 289–290.

late nineteenth century when these states were strongholds of Greenbackism and Populism. The Canadian West still lacks a static social structure, and in this respect it is characteristic of frontier areas.

Along with this open social system before the depression of the 1930's went unlimited optimism. Those who moved to the Western Provinces were attracted by the hope of bettering their lot. Sub-

TABLE 1

Occupational Backgrounds of Farm Operators in Sample Areas, 1930–1931

District	Total farm operators	Farming experience only		Nonagricultural experience	
		Number	Per cent	Number	Per cent
Saskatchewan:					
Davidson..................	136	71	52.2	64	47.1
Kindersley................	204	84	41.2	114	55.9
Turtleford................	174	78	44.8	94	54.0
Alberta:					
Medicine Hat.............	290	143	49.3	139	48.0
Olds.....................	125	53	42.4	72	57.7
Peace River..............	332	94	28.3	238	71.7
Totals....................	1,261	523	41.5	721	57.2

Source: Canadian Pioneer Problems Committee Surveys, quoted in C. A. Dawson and Eva A. Younge, *Pioneering in the Prairie Provinces* (Toronto, 1940), p. 318.

sequent failure to attain their original goals and the absence of strong, settled ties to a traditional pattern of economic, political, and social behavior have made the frontier farmers of Canada, like the frontier farmers of the United States before them, receptive to new ideas, to panaceas that promise the opportunities they seek. First-generation frontier settlers still form a large proportion of the farm heads of the province. Many of the men who came to Saskatchewan before the First World War are still vigorous and influential in the life of the province. One still senses in Saskatchewan today the meaning of frontier restlessness, the desire of these farmers for change, and the gropings for new horizons.

The readiness to improvise and adopt new ideas has not been limited to political behavior. In the 1920's many local rural governments in Saskatchewan developed an indigenous system of

TABLE 2

Nonagricultural Occupations Previously Engaged in by Farm Operators, 1930–1931

District	Farm operators who had nonagricultural occupations	Total number of nonagricultural occupations	Professional men	Business proprietors	Clerical and service workers	Skilled workers	Semiskilled and unskilled workers
					Percentage distribution		
Saskatchewan:							
Davidson	64	102	5	18	16	15	46
Kindersley	114	163	4	3	20	24	49
Turtleford	94	133	3	9	26	26	36
Alberta:							
Medicine Hat	139	206	3	7	16	17	57
Olds	72	111	6	11	11	13	59
Peace River	238	365	5	8	31	13	43

Source: Canadian Pioneer Problems Committee Surveys, quoted in C. A. Dawson and Eva R. Younge, *Pioneering in the Prairie Provinces* (Toronto, 1940), p. 123.

socialized medicine. The movement for Protestant church unity, which resulted in the formation of the United Church of Canada from a merger of Methodist, Presbyterian, and Congregational churches, was largely a movement of the Canadian West. The sparsely settled frontier regions could not support competing Protestant sects, and the farmers insisted that theological differences be sacrificed to the needs of the people.[5]

There is one significant difference, however, between frontier settlement in the United States in the nineteenth century and that of Saskatchewan in the early twentieth century. Saskatchewan was settled in part by working-class immigrants during a period of rising trade-unionism, a growing world socialist movement, and an active coöperative movement in England, Germany, and Scandinavia. Tables 1 and 2 indicate, for a sample of Saskatchewan and Alberta farm heads in 1930–1931, the class origins of frontier farmers. Of the farmers in the sample, 37 per cent had been laborers—skilled, semiskilled, or unskilled—before going to the frontier. Some had been trade-union members and even socialists at home. Fred Green, the secretary of the Saskatchewan Grain Growers' Association (S.G.G.A.), the first large agrarian movement before the First World War, and George Langley, one of its major leaders, had both been members of the British Labor Party.[6] Langley had been one of the first members of the Fabian Society.[7] The two most important permanent officials of the United Farmers of Canada (Saskatchewan Section), the present-day successor to the S.G.G.A., were members of the Independent Labor Party of England and the Socialist Party of the United States, respectively.[8]

The role of an open frontier as a safety valve preventing the growth of a large organized radical movement in the United States and Canada has often been stressed. Unfortunately, no statistical data are available on the political backgrounds of the pioneers. One gains the impression in Saskatchewan that at least one aspect of this hypothesis is correct—namely, that a considerable number of those whose discontent with social and economic conditions at home had led them to join radical parties were attracted to the new world of the frontier. In virtually every area visited in the course of this study, one or more old-country socialists were encountered. This was true not only for the farmers who came from Europe but for many of the American and eastern Canadian

settlers as well. Three of the C.C.F. members of the 1944–1948 legislature, previously residents in the United States, had voted for Eugene V. Debs for president of the United States. One had been a supporter of the I.W.W. The reverses suffered by the socialist movements back home helped create the environmental basis for Saskatchewan's socialist movement in the 1930's.[9]

The frontier character alone would not have created or maintained the conditions for rapid social change. Most North American frontier areas that were once centers of agrarian radicalism became strongholds of political and economic conservatism within a few decades after their original settlement as economic conditions became more stable. A clue, therefore, to understanding the continued unrest on the Canadian prairies lies in the perpetuation of an extremely unstable agricultural economy.

Like the neighboring state of North Dakota, the stronghold of American agrarianism, the life of the Prairie Provinces of Canada still depends on the frontier crop, wheat. Saskatchewan has never been able to develop a mature, stable economy, either industrially or agriculturally.

To an unique extent, the economic history of Saskatchewan is that of wheat. No other governmental unit in the world attempting to maintain a modern civilization is so completely dependent on the production and marketing of one commodity—a commodity which under even normal conditions is subject to wide variations in production and price. *On the average, about 85 per cent of the value of all net production in Saskatchewan is supplied by the agricultural industry, and about 80 per cent of the cash income of the agricultural industry is derived from wheat.*[10]

As in frontier days, almost every person in the province today is in agriculture or in an occupation servicing farmers. The occupational structure of the region reveals this fact clearly. As table 3 shows, only 3 per cent of the total working force was engaged in manufacturing in 1936, when the C.C.F. emerged as a large socialist party.

The lack of important secondary industries means that any change in the fortunes of wheat necessarily affects almost everyone in the province. The implications of this fact for the continuation of organized unrest can easily be seen from table 4, which presents the fluctuations in yield and price of wheat from year to year. These variations are caused by three factors: weather varia-

tions in wheat yield, price fluctuations, and variations in grade of wheat. In Saskatchewan all three factors are extremely variable.

Year after year, Saskatchewan wheat farmers have perforce lived the life of gamblers. They invest their money and labor on the same plot of land in an enterprise that may arbitrarily leave them either poverty-stricken or comparatively well to do at the end of the harvest. Actually, the wheat yields of Saskatchewan are

TABLE 3

OCCUPATIONS OF SASKATCHEWAN RESIDENTS FOURTEEN YEARS OF AGE AND OVER

Group	1936		1941	
	Number	Percentage	Number	Percentage
Agriculture................	217,315	62.7	197,009	58.3
Service....................	46,960	13.5	48,371	14.3
Trade and finance.........	21,084	6.1	24,249	7.2
Transport.................	15,649	4.5	15,868	4.7
Manufacturing............	11,116	3.2	16,184	4.8
Clerical..................	10,625	3.1	13,233	3.9
Laborers..................	9,310	2.7	9,424	2.8
Other occupations.........	8,759	2.5	11,267	3.3
All occupations..........	346,604	100.0	337,881	100.0

SOURCE: Dominion Bureau of Statistics, *Census of Saskatchewan, 1936*, pp. 518–527; *Eighth Census of Canada, 1941*, Vol. 7, pp. 316–317.

more variable "than those of the Argentine, Australia, the United States, ... India, ... and Canada as a whole."[11] The wheat lands of the province are part of the dust bowl of North America, and thus are subject to recurrent droughts. The absence of rain or the coming of insect pests spells financial ruin for the entire year. Even in years of sufficient average rainfall in the province as a whole, many farms suffer crop failure. "In the period 1918 to 1935, there were only three years, 1922, 1923, and 1928, when the average yield of wheat did not fall to 5 bushels per acre or less in any one [rural] municipality of the province, and even in those years ... crop failure was experienced on a considerable number of individual farms."[12]

As table 4 indicates, a good crop is no guaranty of a decent income for the wheat farmer. Wheat prices are even more variable than crop yields. Canadian wheat is primarily an export crop.

Since more wheat per capita of total population is grown in Canada than in any of the other major exporting countries—Argentina, Australia, and the United States—the price received by the Canadian farmer is more closely determined by world market conditions. Twice within a decade, in 1921 and in 1930, the price

TABLE 4

YIELD AND PRICE OF WHEAT IN SASKATCHEWAN BY YEARS

Year	Av. yield (bu. per acre)	Price per bu.	Year	Av. yield (bu. per acre)	Price per bu.
1900	8.8	....	1927	19.5	0.97
1905	23.1	....	1928	23.3	0.77
1906	....	....	1929	11.1	1.03
1908	14.5	....	1930	14.0	0.47
1909	23.1	....	1931	8.8	0.38
1910	15.8	0.69	1932	13.6	0.35
1911	20.8	0.58	1933	8.7	0.47
1912	19.2	0.56	1934	8.6	0.61
1913	21.3	0.64	1935	10.8	0.60
1914	13.7	1.48	1936	7.5	0.92
1915	25.1	0.91	1937	2.7	1.05
1916	16.3	1.28	1938	10.0	0.58
1917	14.3	1.95	1939	19.1	0.54
1918	10.0	1.99	1940	17.1	0.53
1919	8.5	2.32	1941	12.0	0.53
1920	11.3	1.55	1942	24.7	0.69
1921	13.8	0.76	1943	15.2	1.02
1922	20.3	0.85	1944	18.9	1.06
1923	21.3	0.65	1945	12.4	1.16
1924	10.2	1.21	1946	14.6	1.14
1925	18.8	1.25	1947	12.2	1.15
1926	16.2	1.08			

SOURCE: Records of Secretary of Statistics, Department of Agriculture, Regina.

of Canadian wheat fell to less than half of the previous year's price. No other nongrain crop varies so much in price.[13]

Variations in grade of wheat are not so important as price and yield in affecting income. There are, nevertheless, wide fluctuations in the grade of wheat from year to year because of changing weather conditions, and these variations directly affect the price received.

More than any other rural group, the wheat farmer is economically naked, completely exposed to the vagaries of the price

system. There is no doubt that many farmers in other parts of Canada and the world are in a worse financial position, but few experience the chronic alternation between wealth and poverty of the farmers of Saskatchewan. It is possible to adjust to a continuously low income and standard of living, as do many farmers in the Maritime Provinces; for one can plan one's life ahead, make provision for future expenditures, and adjust community institutions to the economic possibilities of an area. The pattern of life of the mixed-crop farmer may be upset by severe depression, but food, clothing, and shelter are secure, and price fluctuations are not so great as in the wheat belt. But it is the "boom and bust" character of wheat production that unhinges life's plans.

The oscillating character of the Saskatchewan economy went far toward preventing the emergence of an integrated, conservative rural society. The farmers continued to be a marginal frontier group in relation to the total society, and developed attitudes characteristic of outcast groups, believing that they did not receive their just or "parity" share of the national wealth and culture. The cleavage that developed early in the history of the province between the economically dominant urban world and the insecure rural areas was sharpened by the fluctuations of the business cycle; and this encouraged conflict between the urban middle class and the farmers.

Farm owners have traditionally been lumped by many sociologists with the middle class, along with urban business and professional groups. This broad concept of the middle class not only blurs significant class differences in urban areas; it also disguises the most significant social cleavage in the Great Plains farming region—that between the farm world and the world of the towns and cities linked to urban eastern business. Farmers and middle-class businessmen in western Canada are groups apart, with different patterns of life, and they are in many ways hostile to each other.[14]

Economic class differences tend to be played down in the local community, though every farmer is aware that some of his neighbors are big and powerful, and others are small and weak. Actually, some farmers have life chances that in prosperous periods are typical of the middle class, whereas others will remain as helpless economically as the urban working class. Economic classes, therefore, do exist among Saskatchewan farmers, though the pres-

sure of outside circumstances on the grain market makes farmers stand together. The conflict between urban and agricultural worlds involves first, the grip of the eastern urban world of grain trading, distribution, and credit on *all* grain farmers, and second, the traditional immediate exploitative relation of the town to its rural hinterland, which Veblen has pointed out:

> The country town is an organization of business concerns engaged in buying things from the farmers in order to sell at an advance to the central markets, and in buying from the central markets in order to sell at an advance to the farmers. The country town is an organization of "middlemen" and it is out of this difference between the buying price and the selling price that the entire town gets its living. . . .
>
> . . . it is to be admitted without argument or hesitation that these country-town merchants, bankers, and buyers are by law and custom entitled to all the profits which they can get, and as long as they can get them. . . . It is the time-honored customary right of the townsman to turn an honest penny at the cost of the countrymen.[15]

External business controls tend to make farmers hostile—the degree of hostility varying with the price of wheat—to the entire urban world, including the cities and towns of Saskatchewan. Some big farmers, of course, are treated with deference in the banks of Regina, for here the urban group and middle-class farmers meet as members of a common class. Both farmers and townspeople in Saskatchewan belong to the same economic class, if class position is determined by the amount of property owned and the chance of getting ahead. But economic class consciousness is prevented from developing by the fact that the obvious power of the absentee eastern grain brokers, bankers, and railroad companies over the lives of western farmers encourages strategic solidarity among Saskatchewan farmers vis-à-vis an urban world in which all business and some urban labor are lumped together.

This cleavage between farmers and the urban middle class is accentuated by the fact that the organized community life of the rural population is carried on independently of social activities in the neighboring towns and cities. There are very few institutions which bind farmers and townspeople together in a common enterprise.[16] The farmers have their own economic organizations and their own marketing and consumers' coöperatives. The coöperative movement, which today includes the majority of Saskatchewan farmers, is an indication of the desire to stabilize rural

economy by eliminating the middleman.[17] This movement is also a cause of increased tension between the urban middle class and the farmers.

Very little intermingling occurs between the cliques of the towns and those of the countryside; each has an independent social life. A recent study of town-country relations in a district in Alberta comparable to Saskatchewan reports that townspeople and country people shop at different times, patronize different restaurants and hotels, and do not belong to the same churches or organizations. Few of the townspeople reported personal acquaintances among the neighboring farmers.[18]

Saskatchewan has few cities, and no large urban center dominates the life of the province. There are only four widely scattered cities: Regina, the provincial capital, with a population of 58,000; Moose Jaw, forty miles west of Regina, with 20,000; Saskatoon, the site of the provincial university, with 43,000; and Prince Albert, in northern Saskatchewan, with 13,000. Only 16 per cent of the population of the province lives in these urban centers, with another 10 per cent living in towns or villages of more than 1,000 population.[19]

The cities are only larger versions of the country towns; they are primarily trading centers serving rural areas. Transportation and wholesale and retail trade employ most of the urban population.[20] Little economic or political power is concentrated in the cities. The urban upper class, to the extent that such a class exists at all, is composed of branch managers of national banks and corporations or heads of small local manufacturing or trading organizations. The visitor is struck by the number of banks bearing such names as the Royal Bank of Canada, the Bank of Montreal, the Bank of Toronto. The large department stores and mail-order houses are owned by national chains: Eaton's, Simpson's, the Hudson's Bay Company. These signify the extent to which the local commercial life is a branch of the urban world "back East." To the farmer they symbolize the world of eastern business that controls his fate.

Unlike the situation of farmers in Michigan or Ontario, there is little in Saskatchewan to array farmers psychologically against labor. Well under 5 per cent of the population is industrial labor, excluding railroad workers, as against 58 per cent in agriculture. Urban labor is, then, a negligible factor in the life of the province.

Most of its workers are employed in retail stores or small shops. Until the 1940's the organized labor movement was limited to the Railroad Brotherhoods and small locals of skilled craftsmen, such as printers and carpenters.

The lack of powerful urban centers means that the basically rural character of the province dominates its social and political life. The provincial government, the newspapers, and the university must all be oriented toward the farmer. This has made it difficult for professional politicians and urban newspapers to eliminate the group consciousness of the farmer.

The development of agrarian group consciousness over against the urban world has been further strengthened by the social structure created by the wheat economy. It is difficult to apply class terminology to these farmers. The sparsity of population, because of the large size of wheat farms, means that most of the farm communities contain not more than a hundred families.

Mechanization has reduced the importance of the traditional lower class, the farm laborer. "Technological advance in farm machinery has, within a generation, hurried the plains region farmer from ox-drawn plough to four-horse binder, . . . to today's rubber-tired power combine and one-way seeder with which one man can farm a section [640 acres] of grain land."[21] Two-thirds of the farmers of Saskatchewan did not employ anyone outside their own families in 1941. This stands in interesting contrast to mixed farming in Ontario, where almost half of the farms had hired help.[22] A large part of Saskatchewan farm labor is hired only for August and September, when additional help, composed primarily of students, is required for the harvest.

Within the farm operators' group, variations in size of farm and income usually reflect class differences. Sharp variations exist in Saskatchewan as a whole; but they exist mainly *between* areas rather than *within* individual rural communities. Farmers in districts of good soil are generally more well to do than those in poor regions. Large farms of 640 acres to double that size are to be found on the rich Regina plains and in the Rosetown district west of Saskatoon, while small farms of 160 to 320 acres are clustered in the poor-soil regions of northern Saskatchewan. Within the province the average assessment per acre of land varies from an index of 9 for the poorest rural municipality to 76 for the wealthiest.[23] Within any one community, however, variations in the value

of land are necessarily small, for with few exceptions farms have the same conditions of soil and rainfall. Differences in income do exist within individual rural communities, but they are not large enough to result in the emergence of distinct social classes.

Although tenancy was a growing phenomenon in Saskatchewan before the Second World War, it does not constitute a predominant class difference as it does in many other agricultural regions on this continent. This is due to the fact that poor land yields a cash return so low that tenancy is unprofitable, and when an owner dies or is foreclosed the property is resold at any price it will bring.

TABLE 5

DISTRIBUTION OF SASKATCHEWAN TENANTS BY AGE, 1943

(Percentages)

Under 20	21–30	31–40	41–50	51–60	61–70	71–80	Total
1.1	32.8	31.0	18.2	12.2	4.2	0.5	100.0

SOURCE: Provincial Mediation Board, *A Survey of Agricultural Land Debt and of Ownership and Tenancy in Saskatchewan, as at December 31, 1943* (1944), p. 31.

On the other hand, when land falls vacant in regions of highly productive soil, the owner of an adjoining farm usually rents or buys it, or an energetic young farmer occupies it as a tenant. Tenant farmers, therefore, are often among the more well-to-do members of the farming population in the province as a whole. Second, and more important, is the following fact:

Tenancy in this Province is not a permanent factor . . . but is rather a part of the progress pattern of Ownership—young farmers with a limited capital renting land until they are able to purchase land through Agreement of Sale, or by the acceptance of a Mortgage for the unpaid balance, achieving titled ownership at higher ages, depending on the speed made possible by favourable, or unfavourable, economic conditions.[24]

A comparison of a large random sample of owners and tenants revealed that the average age of farm owners in Saskatchewan in 1943 was 51 years, while that of tenants was 39. The median age of tenants was 36.5 years, and, as table 5 shows, 64 per cent of them were under 41 years of age. Tenancy, therefore, would appear to be largely an age rather than a class difference, a transitional phase in a farmer's career.

Cleavages in ethnic background and religion have been more important than economic class divisions in separating agrarians into distinct social groups. Ethnically, the three Prairie Provinces of Canada are more comparable to the heterogeneity found in many areas south of the border than to the rest of Canada. As table 6 shows, only 41.9 per cent of the population of rural Sas-

TABLE 6

Total Population of Saskatchewan by Ethnic
Origins, 1941

Ethnic origin	Number	Percentage
British..............	397,905	44.9
English...........	205,519	23.2
Irish..............	104,072	11.7
Scottish..........	108,919	12.3
Others............	2,995	0.4
French..............	50,530	5.7
Austrian............	10,655	1.2
German..............	130,258	14.7
Hungarian..........	14,578	1.6
Dutch..............	35,894	4.1
Polish..............	27,902	3.1
Russian............	25,933	2.9
Scandinavian.......	68,806	7.8
Ukrainian..........	79,777	9.0
Others.............	26,962	3.0
Asiatic............	3,420	0.4
Indian and Eskimo...	13,388	1.5

Source: Dominion Bureau of Statistics, *Eighth Census of Canada, 1941*, Bulletin B-7, p. 3.

katchewan is of English, Scotch, and Irish origin. Much of this settlement has been in distinct ethnic enclaves. Saskatchewan has many Ukrainian, German, French, and Polish settlements. Dwelling together, settlers from non-English-speaking countries have not participated as much in rural community organizations as have English-speaking farmers. There is considerable prejudice against non-Anglo-Saxon groups, especially those from central and eastern Europe.

Ethnic differences are accompanied by religious cleavages. Most of the central European groups, Ukrainian, Russian, Polish, German, and Hungarian, as well as the French Canadians, are Roman Catholics. A small minority are Greek Orthodox. The majority of

the Saskatchewan citizens, however, belong to one of the Protestant denominations, as shown in table 7. Religious differences have at times created serious conflicts, especially between Protestants and Roman Catholics. The strength of this feeling was evident in the late 1920's, when the Ku Klux Klan entered the province and gained support for its anti-Catholic program.

We have seen that the similarity of climate, crops, markets, and agricultural technology has provided the wheat farmers of Sas-

TABLE 7

TOTAL POPULATION OF SASKATCHEWAN BY RELIGIOUS AFFILIATIONS, 1941

Religion	Number	Percentage
United Church.......	230,495	25.7
Roman Catholic.....	243,734	27.2
Anglican............	117,674	13.1
Lutheran...........	104,717	11.7
Presbyterian........	54,856	6.1
Mennonite..........	32,511	3.6
Greek Orthodox......	37,699	4.2
Baptist.............	19,460	2.2
Others.............	54,846	6.1
Totals............	895,992	100.0

SOURCE: Dominion Bureau of Statistics, *Eighth Census of Canada, 1941*, Bulletin A-5, pp. 2-3.

katchewan with the structural basis for collective action. "Though these men and women are of varied national and racial backgrounds, and many religious beliefs, their common, day-to-day problems, their persistent economic struggle for 'better price for wheat,' 'lower freight rates,' 'parity prices for farm crops,' have, within one generation, brought about a unity of purpose that seems a perpetual source of surprise to the residents of older provinces wherein there is much greater diversification of industrial and financial activity, readier access to markets—and more rain."[25]

The recent frontier background has meant that agrarians were comparatively free to adopt new and seemingly radical solutions for social and economic problems. There have been few tradition-bound patterns of political and economic action. In the last three decades two predominantly agrarian political parties, the Progres-

sives in the 1920's and the C.C.F. in the 1930's and 1940's, have won sweeping support.

The sparse settlement and lack of large urban centers, which made various community and social services economically unprofitable, have also increased local coöperative endeavors. Farmers have been forced to unite coöperatively to obtain telephone service, local roads, medical and hospital facilities, and other social services. Today 125,000 farmers hold almost 500,000 coöperative memberships; that is, on the average a farmer belongs to four or five coöperatives. Through coöperative and political action, grain growers have attempted to resist the coercions of a fluctuating market economy. The resulting widespread community participation has facilitated the rapid development and acceptance of new community institutions as events demonstrated the need for them. In succeeding chapters an attempt will be made to show how a radical agrarianism emerged as a direct and logical expression of the problems of the Saskatchewan wheat economy.

Chapter III

THE EMERGENCE OF AGRARIAN CLASS CONSCIOUSNESS

E conomic and political class consciousness obviously does not emerge as a simple reaction to the position of a group in the economic and social structure. The transformation of a group from a large mass of individuals, who do not recognize the existence of a basic, common class interest, to a self-conscious class occurs through the intervening factor of organized group action. Max Weber has well described the conditions that give rise to this development.

... the factor that creates "class" is unambiguously economic interest, and indeed only those interests involved in the existence of the "market"....

The degree in which "communal action" and possibly "societal action," emerges from the "mass actions" of the members of a class is linked to ... the extent of the [economic] contrasts that have already evolved, and is especially linked to the *transparency* of the connections between the causes and the consequences of the "class situation." For however different [economic] life chances may be, this fact in itself ... by no means gives birth to "class action". .... The fact of being conditioned must be distinctly recognizable. For only then the contrasts of life chances can be felt ... as a resultant from either (1) the given

distribution of property, or (2) the structure of the concrete economic order. It is only then that people may react against the class structure not only through acts of an intermittent and irrational protest, but in form of rational association.[1]

The development of economic class consciousness on the Canadian prairies dates from the first large-scale settlement at the turn of the century. Tens of thousands of farmers were scattered throughout the immense prairie region. They grew wheat which they sold at various railroad points to the representatives of the grain companies. This situation placed them at the mercy of these large companies and the railroads, which dictated the conditions of sale.

The Canadian Pacific Railway (C.P.R.), then the only line in western Canada, gave monopolies to individual trading companies at various railroad stops in order to encourage them to build grain elevators. In 1897 the C.P.R. ruled that no grain would be received for shipment except through the trading companies' elevators. This monopoly prevented farmers from selling to small individual buyers who did not have an elevator, or from shipping directly to the market in Winnipeg without having to store their wheat in a grain elevator.[2]

By the year 1900, almost three-quarters of the grain elevators in western Canada were owned by five companies. Monopoly control of elevator and grain companies was further strengthened by the formation of the Manitoba and North-West Grain Dealers' Association, which included most of the grain dealers and "soon had command of the situation from the buyers' standpoint."[3]

The monopoly eliminated competitive bidding for the farmers' wheat and permitted the trading companies to set the conditions of sale. As a result of the uneven distribution of bargaining power, many farmers maintained that the private companies were making exorbitant profits and could force them to accept less than the market price. The grain growers also asserted that the elevator agents undergraded wheat and thereby made additional unearned profits for the companies. Other common complaints were that the elevator agents deducted unnecessarily for unclean wheat and that they short-weighted the grain.

The trade practices of the railroads and grain companies aroused bitter resentment in the farmers.

---

[1] For notes to chapter iii see pages 291–294.

After all, they were the men who provided the golden stream out of which others were dipping repeatedly and making fortunes. It was all very well to pay for services rendered, but farmers complained that they were paying entirely too much. The townsmen were fleecing them, was their bitter reflection as they sweated in the prairie heat. Whether entirely justified or not, in those years a hostility toward middlemen was born that has never since expired.[4]

As long as the scattered farmers suffered one by one, with the sense that nothing could be done about their plight, they had no effective basis for action. They could only vote their individual protests at the next election. How did organization among them come about?

The year 1901 witnessed a major economic crisis in the West which resulted in the formation of the first powerful farmers' movement in western Canada. In that year the prairies produced 60,000,000 bushels of wheat—almost twice as much as had ever before been harvested. The railroads were unprepared to handle a crop of that size, and almost half of it was lost because there were not enough freight cars to move it before winter. The farmers complained bitterly that the railroads gave preference to the elevator companies in allotting cars. Spontaneous meetings of protest were held in many places. The temper of the times is described in the following statement by W. R. Motherwell, a subsequent leader of Saskatchewan farmers:

There was incipient rebellion when we organized. It's too late for organization; it's bullets we want, men were saying. But we really didn't know what we wanted; we were in despair. It was not a question of growing crops but of marketing them. In the fall when the elevator opened, you would see a rush of wagons, wheel to wheel, to see who would get there first. . . .

Well, we grew the wheat, which was valueless unless marketed. Wheat was regarded as gold by Easterners, but it had no value for us unless shipped out of the country. . . . Such conditions engendered bitterness and the country was ready for anything.[5]

A group of farmers around the town of Indian Head in the southwestern part of what is now Saskatchewan, where the wheat blockade had caused a loss of three-quarters of the crop, decided to form a farmers' organization to protect their rights. The Indian Head district was one of the oldest and richest in the then North-West Territories, as it was on the main line of the C.P.R. close

to the Manitoba border. On December 18, 1901, these farmers formed the Territorial Grain Growers' Association (T.G.G.A.), called the Saskatchewan Grain Growers' Association (S.G.G.A.) after 1905. This was the first permanent agrarian organization in what is now Saskatchewan and Alberta.[6]

The idea of an organized farmers' movement caught on quickly, and within two months the Association was able to hold its first convention. Delegates were present from sixteen local organizations with a total of 500 members. The delegates established a permanent organization and passed resolutions condemning the C.P.R. for its failure to supply railroad cars and its refusal to load wheat directly from farmers' wagons instead of from grain elevators. The convention also attacked the elevator companies for depressing the price of wheat through their monopoly control. The assembled agrarians hoped to bring pressure on Parliament to change railroad regulations.[7]

The convention also decided on a major plan which was to prove crucial in the later development of the movement: the inauguration of regular meetings of Association members in every locality for discussion of common problems. Here was the beginning of an activity fundamental to the continued vitality and growth of any movement. By 1916, fifteen years after its founding, the S.G.G.A. had 1,300 locals and a membership of 28,000.[8] The locals met once or twice a month to discuss rural, national, and world problems. They sent delegates to annual conventions of the Association where political problems were thrashed out in heated debate. These meetings came to be known as the "Farmers' Parliament"; and the provincial and federal governments not only recognized them as an authentic expression of rural opinion but adopted many of their proposals.

Soon after the first T.G.G.A. convention, the farmers seemed to have tangible evidence of the power of organization. The federal government passed remedial legislation requiring railway shipping agents to assign freight cars in the order in which they were applied for, regardless of whether the applicant was a farmer or an elevator company.[9] But this victory proved short-lived, for in the fall of 1902 a new wheat blockade developed as a result of another record-breaking crop. Instead of abiding by the new federal legislation, the railroad continued to coöperate with the private elevator companies by giving them most of the available

freight cars. At the 1902 convention of the T.G.G.A., the president, W. R. Motherwell, asserted, "The plain provisions of the car distribution clause are disregarded at every shipping point. . . . Of sixty-seven spotted cars at Sintaluta only seven have been assigned to farmers."[10] This monopoly enabled the elevator agents again to buy wheat on their own terms. The farmers maintained that local elevator prices were ten cents a bushel beneath the price they could receive after paying the freight to ship direct to the open market in Winnipeg.[11]

The T.G.G.A. now brought suit against the railroad, although many members were skeptical about the possibility of taming the mighty C.P.R. The Association charged one of the agents of the company with breaking the federal law by making preferential assignment of freight cars to the elevator companies. The T.G.G.A. not only won its suit in court, but, as a result, the railroad dropped its efforts to bolster the monopoly position of the grain companies.[12]

The victory of the T.G.G.A. over the railroad gave tremendous prestige to the farmers' organization. The Association began to form new locals in the more densely settled parts of what were then the North-West Territories, and a Manitoba Association was organized in 1903. The influence of the new organization was strongest in areas that had been settled for ten years or more, for the older pioneers were the ones who had lost their illusions about the West and accepted the necessity for group organization.[13]

The victory over the railroad did not end the farmers' suspicions that the elevator monopoly was still cheating them. The grain buyers continued to classify into different grades wheat that the farmers believed to be identical, and the day-to-day fluctuations on the Grain Exchange looked to the farmers more like the results of gambling in wheat than the orderly operation of a market. In 1905 the T.G.G.A. sent E. A. Partridge, one of its leaders, to Winnipeg to investigate the activities of the trading companies and of the Grain Exchange. His report to the Association was typical of agrarian feeling at the time.

. . . the North West Grain Dealers Association [of Winnipeg], which sets "street prices," [reduces] charges wherever a farmers' elevator or an independent dealer operates. The object of the elevator companies was to give the farmer the lowest price possible and get the largest amount of wheat through the elevators. More powerful than the line elevators, however, were the exporters and millers. The large amount

of capital and credit required, the difficulties of establishing trade connections . . . put limitations on competition, and the "wheat business is thus practically in the hands of three milling companies and five exporting firms." The Grain Exchange itself [is] "a combine" with a "gambling hell thrown in."[14]

Farmers were rapidly learning the advantages of group action. Partridge now set out to organize a farmer-owned coöperative grain company with its own elevators and flour mills, which would eventually eliminate middlemen in the grain trade. The top officials of the Grain Growers' Associations opposed the suggestion at first, because, as they said, they feared that the farmers would not support such a company and that its failure would endanger the existence of the Associations. This opposition by the executive of the Grain Growers was the first of many attempts by the elected leaders of prairie farm organizations to block the formation of new institutions to meet agrarian needs. But, in the end, antagonism to the private grain companies overrode the bureaucratic conservatism of the leaders; and Partridge was able to secure enough money from a large number of well-to-do farmers to start a farmers' company.[15]

This new venture, the Grain Growers' Grain Company, Ltd. (G.G.G.C.), was set up in 1906 as a coöperatively owned grain agency to receive grain from members and sell it directly on the Grain Exchange. To insure democratic control, no farmer was permitted to buy more than four of the $25 shares or to cast more than one vote at meetings. Six weeks after the G.G.G.C. started to operate, the Winnipeg Grain Exchange suspended the right of the new company to trade on the Exchange on the ground that the company had issued pamphlets "offending against the honour and dignity of the Exchange and reflecting on the methods adopted by certain members of the trade."[16] The farmers' company was charged also with paying patronage dividends to its clients, which violated the rules of the Exchange.

This open attack by the hated Grain Exchange spurred farmers to take another step in the direction of class-conscious action. It was evident that coöperative economic action was not enough to control the power of the grain monopoly. Only government intervention against the Exchange could save the company. In Manitoba, where the Exchange was incorporated, the Manitoba Grain Growers' Association threatened to take political action against

the provincial government unless it forced the Exchange to re-admit the company. The provincial cabinet attempted to dodge responsibility on the issue, but, with an election approaching, it finally prevailed upon the Exchange to take the company back.[17] The Exchange agreed to do so if the company would drop its plans for coöperative distribution of profits and would elect a new president in place of E. A. Partridge, who had been particularly violent in his attacks on the grain companies.[18]

The heads of the Grain Exchange recognized in Partridge a permanent and dangerous menace to their security. From the time of his arrival in the West from Ontario in 1883, as a young man of twenty-one, to his death in 1931, Partridge had the reputation of being a radical and a visionary. In an older, more stable society such a man would have been simply another "crackpot" agitator. In the newly settled, loosely structured society of the West, with its numerous unsolved economic and social problems, a man with ideas could command a hearing, and Partridge did so from the formation of the Grain Growers' Grain Company to his speeches urging socialism, in 1930 and 1931. "More ideas ... originated with him affecting the farmers' social and economic welfare than with any other dweller in the grain country."[19]

From the very first, Partridge saw the emerging farmers' move-ment as part of a world-wide conflict between capital and labor. The reforms that he advocated were part of a conscious, long-range program to get the agrarians to accept Ruskinian socialism, as he once made clear in an interview: "Coöperation provided a temporary remedy for the existing abuses of the grain trade. It would provide out of its revenues a great educational fund which would finance a newspaper and a campaign which would culmi-nate in the domination of the legislature by the common man, and in the introduction of state ownership of public utilities and natural resources. Then would come true coöperation based on the ethics of Ruskin."[20]

The G.G.G.C. refused the demand of the Grain Exchange for Partridge's removal as president of the company. In 1907, however, when a permanent organization of the company was established, Partridge refused to run again for the presidency. Essentially, he was an agitator who had to engage in new battles, but who withdrew from the administrative scene as soon as the fight was won.[21] The replacement of the aggressive fighting leader by a

more conservative bureaucratic type is characteristic in organizations such as trade-unions, political movements, and coöperatives.[22] Partridge's career was peculiar only in the fact that he consciously recognized the pressure for such change and stepped down willingly. This left him free to take on new battles.[23]

The attack by the Exchange on the young farmers' company was as important for it as the earlier victory of the Territorial Grain Growers' Association over the C.P.R. had been for that organization. The Exchange had explicitly recognized that the Grain Growers' Grain Company was a menace to its power. The economic enemy of the agrarians was becoming clearly identified. Publicity and interest were easier to obtain on a concrete issue than through abstract propaganda against the private companies and the Exchange. T. A. Crerar, who had succeeded Partridge as president of the G.G.G.C., "expressed the view that the company might never have survived had it not been for the publicity it was given by expulsion from the Exchange."[24]

The financial stability of the company enabled its directors to take another step in organizing and unifying agrarian opinion. In 1908 they decided to issue their own weekly newspaper. This paper, the *Grain Growers' Guide*, was supported also by the interprovincial council of the three Grain Growers' associations in Alberta, Saskatchewan, and Manitoba. Partridge, the foremost exponent of education in the movement, was chosen as its first editor. He hoped to make the paper the joint organ of the organized farmer and labor movements in the battle against organized capital, but the rest of the officials objected. Again the "agitator" dropped out of responsibility to resume his gadfly role, declaring, "I'm too irritable to get along with anybody in an office."[25] Partridge left behind him, however, a new means of solidifying rural opinion and action. The movement now had a newspaper to point out to the farmers the evils of the commercial system, advocating coöperation and, later, government ownership as the solution.[26]

But the stability of the G.G.G.C. was short-lived, as could have been expected in a contest with an institution so powerfully entrenched as the Grain Exchange. The company was growing steadily. Despite its inexperience and the lack of grain elevators of its own, it handled 3 per cent of the total grain crop in its first year of operation, 1907. This rose to 8 per cent by 1909.[27] These percentages may appear small, but it must be remembered that the

company was not yet able to do business at most country points, and many farmers preferred to sell directly to elevator companies who paid immediately upon delivery rather than to wait until the G.G.G.C. sold their crop.

In 1909–1910 the private companies struck back at the economic taproot of the farmers' company. The Exchange abolished its rule that a one-cent commission must be paid to companies handling wheat. This did not greatly affect the private elevator companies, as most of their profits were secured from storage charges and trading grain on the market. The farmers' company was, however, completely dependent on the commission to pay all its expenses.[28] The company organized a campaign among the farmers, pointing out that unless they agreed to continue paying the one-cent commission which underwrote its operating costs, the elevator combine would be able to destroy the company, and again have a complete monopoly. The *Grain Growers' Guide* rallied the farmers to the support of the company through arguments such as the following:

As we have often pointed out . . . the Exchange is being used by the Elevator Interests that seem to dominate it, to further their own particular ends with the result that the nefarious methods of the Elevator Trust bring suspicion and condemnation upon the Exchange and its members.

The pooling of receipts at country points is not forgotten by the farmers; heavy dockage and unfair grading and low prices paid when the farmers were compelled to sell and could not help themselves, are also not forgotten.

Every injustice and disturbance in the trade that has taken place since grain commenced to be marketed in Manitoba, can be traced to the Elevator Monopoly.

The farmers in this country owe nothing to the Elevator Trust and we have confidence in them to believe that they will not be bought over by them now.[29]

When the question of the farmers assuming the cost of the G.G.G.C. was put to the test in a shareholders' referendum, 98 per cent backed the company.[30] Thousands of letters poured into the head office, many of them expressing willingness to pay more than one cent a bushel rather than sell to the monopolies.[31] The aroused farmers voted with their wheat that fall, sending 16,332,645 bushels to the company, more than twice the amount in the year before.[32] This figure actually represented only 15 per

cent of the total wheat marketed in western Canada that year, for the coverage of the G.G.G.C. was still spotty. But 16,000,000 bushels constituted a powerful symbol.

This conflict and partial victory convinced the more militant of the organized farmers that their economic position would not be secure until they had successfully eliminated the middlemen all along the line. Although E. A. Partridge had refused to continue as a full-time officer, he had remained on the board of directors of the company; and he now began agitating for government ownership of all grain elevators to prevent a recurrence of attacks on the farmers by the elevator companies. Through the *Grain Growers' Guide* and the annual conventions of the provincial associations he was able to reach the farmers. Between 1907 and 1908, all three associations adopted the Partridge Plan for government ownership.[33] The *Guide* argued that "the large elevator interests, supported by many strong financial interests and working in harmony with large milling interests, were becoming dangerously strong. . . . they can steadily undersell competitors [such as the G.G.G.C.] having no storage facilities until such competitors are out of business."[34]

The Liberal governments of the three Prairie Provinces attempted to circumvent the suggestions of the farmers by proposing increased government regulation of the elevators, arguing that it would be unconstitutional for them to operate an elevator monopoly.[35] These arguments were ridiculed by the Grain Growers, who inaugurated a public campaign which obtained tens of thousands of petitions demanding government action. A conference of the reeves (heads) of the Manitoba rural municipalities also supported government ownership.[36] Faced by this challenge, the governments began to retreat. Saskatchewan appointed a Royal Commission to make a "searching inquiry into proposals looking to the creation and operation of a system of elevators to effect the objects outlined by the Grain Growers' Association,"[37] while the Manitoba government, facing an early election, agreed, in December, 1909, to set up a line of elevators as a public utility.[38]

Unfortunately for the success of the scheme, the provincial governments were making only superficial concessions to appease the electorate. The Manitoba cabinet refused to implement the plan, which called for an independent elevator commission named by the Grain Growers, and for the purchase of private elevators at

their replacement cost. The Manitoba Elevator Act, which placed the elevators under the supervision of a government-appointed commission, required "A petition signed by sixty per cent of the farmers contributory to a proposed elevator . . . before it could be purchased," and subjected the purchase price of elevators to arbitration.[39]

As the Grain Growers' leaders had predicted, the Manitoba experiment in government ownership ended in complete failure. The elevators lost money and in 1912 the government decided to go out of the elevator business. The *Grain Growers' Guide* charged that "the 'elevator fiasco' was due to the government's lack of sympathy for the scheme; seemingly it had been intended that the enterprise should fail. The elevators purchased . . . were worth only one-half the sum that had been paid for them."[40] The G.G.G.C. thereupon took over the elevators and operated them as a farmer-owned chain.

In Saskatchewan the government also disappointed the farmers who had believed that the appointment of a Royal Commission was the first step toward obtaining government-owned elevators. The Commission, however, recommended a farmer-owned coöperative system.[41] After a long debate at its 1911 convention, the S.G.G.A. approved the Commission's plan, stating that it would rather have a "coöperative system within the reach of their hand than one publicly-owned over which they had no influence."[42] The Saskatchewan Coöperative Elevator Company was organized in that year. By 1913 it owned 133 elevators and was supported by 13,156 members from among a total of 95,013 farmers in the province.[43]

It must be remembered that the agrarian organizations involved only a minority of the farmers. These organizations developed during the period of the greatest migration to the West. The tens of thousands of new settlers were interested in establishing farms, not in political or economic protest. Except for the convinced radicals, disillusion with existing economic practices probably came only as a result of personal misfortune. The S.G.G.A. and the Coöperative Elevator Company, for example, received most of their support from the earliest settled regions, where farmers had gradually learned the lessons of monopoly control of the grain trade. It is significant that the two most important centers of organized action in this early period were Indian Head and Sinta-

luta, in the southern part of the province on the first rail line that
entered Saskatchewan. These areas had been settled as early as
the 1880's.

A second influence negating the rapid growth of the agrarian
movement was the presence of large numbers of immigrants from
non-English-speaking countries. These farmers usually settled in
ethnic enclaves and had little to do with the English-speaking
settlers.

A third factor accounting for the spotty support of coöperatives
was the fact that their organization required financial investment
by members. Money was difficult to obtain in the newly settled
districts, where farmers were usually in debt. The fact that the
farmer-owned companies were handling 20 per cent of all wheat
grown on the prairies by the outbreak of the First World War is,
therefore, more significant than it first appears.

The first twelve years of the century had witnessed a growing
awareness by western farmers of the nature of their economic
problem. They had fought for government regulation of the grain
trade, coöperative marketing of wheat, and government ownership of elevators. They had succeeded in building the largest co-
operative elevator system in the world, which both bought and
sold grain. In the process, farmers were developing an increasingly critical attitude toward all middlemen in the distribution
process. A common economic class situation was resulting in
heightened consciousness and sharpened class attitudes. Out of
economic conflict, agrarian class unity was emerging.

The collectivist ideas, which were to mature in the C.C.F. in
the 1930's, were based directly on the farmers' day-to-day experiences. The experiences of two of the foremost leaders of the movement were typical of many western farmers.

He [Crerar] could not forget his own early experiences in marketing
grain when the elevators offered him fifty-nine cents per bushel, nine-
teen cents under the price at the terminal at the time. The freight rate
on his No. 1 Northern wheat he knew to be only nine cents per bushel
and when he was docked a bushel and a half to a load of fifty bushels
on top of it he had been aroused to protest.

. . . But when . . . he had pointed out the injustice of the price offered
and the dockage taken—the elevator man, quite calmly, had told him to
go to the devil!

"There's no use going to the other elevators, for you're all alike," said
young Crerar hotly.

"Then take your damned grain home again!" grinned the elevator operator insolently.

So the young farmer was compelled to sell his first wheat for what he could get. He was prepared to pay three cents per bushel on the spread, that being a reasonable charge; but although plenty of cars were available at the time, the spread cost him ten cents, a direct loss of seven cents per bushel.⁴⁴

Roderick McKenzie, who succeeded Partridge as editor of the *Guide,* had similar experiences.

He disposed of two loads of wheat at one of the elevators in Brandon one day and was given a grade and a price which he considered fair enough. When he came in with two more loads of the same kind of wheat next day, however, the elevator man told him that he had sent a sample to Winnipeg and found out that it was not grading the grade he had given him the day before.

"The train service wouldn't allow of such fast work, sir," said Roderick McKenzie. "I suppose you sent it by wire. . . . That five cents a bushel you want me to give you looks just as good in my pocket as in yours."

So he drove up town where the other buyers were and three of them looked at the wheat but refused to give a price for it. One of them was a son of the first elevator man to whom he had gone and, said he, "The Old Man gave you a knockdown for it, didn't he?"

"Yes, but—!"

"Well, we're not going to bid against him and if you want to sell it at all, haul it back to him."⁴⁵

Long before most of them had ever heard of socialism, western farmers believed that they were economically oppressed and exploited by the large commercial organizations. The report of the Saskatchewan Royal Commission, set up in 1910 to investigate the elevator situation, summarized the opinions of hundreds of rural leaders who had testified before it as follows:

Against the Initial Elevators.

1. Weights. That they give lower weights than the farmer is entitled to.

2. Dockage. That they take too large a percentage as against claiming the grain to grade. . . .

3. Grades. That in buying the grain they give lower grades than the grain is entitled to.

4. Prices. That they give too low prices even for the grades allowed. . . .

7. Substituting grain. That they often give the farmer inferior grain, taking his superior lot instead. . . .

Against the Banks.

1. That by restricting or refusing credit to many farmers, they force these to put their grain upon the market as soon as it is threshed, depriving them of the opportunity to hold it for a raise in price and compelling them to sell when the market is glutted and the price tends to be lowest. . . .

2. That in giving lines of credit for moving the crops they favor the larger companies and at times favor a few such companies. Thus giving these a virtual monopoly of bank credit, and assisting them in monopolizing the grain business.

Against the Railway Companies.

2. That they construct loading platforms as if the object was to render the use of them by the farmers as difficult as possible.

3. That in the past they helped to create elevator monopolies and assisted them, and that at present they favor the large milling and elevator companies wherever they can. . . .

Against the Terminal Elevator.

1. That they take too much dockage as against the shrinkage of the grain in handling. . . .

2. That they mix the different grades of grain, selling grain of the lower grade at the price of the higher grade, and that, the grain being dirty and lowered in grade by mixing, export prices are lowered and the prices paid to the farmers are also lowered. . . .

Against the Grading System.

1. That the grades do not represent the different values of the grain for milling purposes. . . .

Against the large Western Milling Companies.

4. That besides lowering the prices by lowering the grades, they artificially depress prices.

(a) By spreading false reports about crops.

(b) By juggling in options and especially by selling below market value early in the season in the Liverpool market quantities of grain for future delivery.

Against the Winnipeg Grain Exchange.

The large milling and elevator companies . . . exercise a controlling influence in the Exchange. . . . If the dominating interests maintain several elevators and buyers at any shipping point, and if they tolerate in the Exchange a number of apparently independent and competing commission men and exporters, it is only to deceive the public into believing that there is real competition in the trade.

And the dominating companies can make full use of the speculative

market of trading in futures, of hedging . . . of profiting by the rise and fall of the price in their own market, and of dealing in spreads when they occur between prices in different markets. Most important of all, they can complete the work of fixing the prices paid to the farmer.[46]

To this list of rural grievances against the big interests can be added the protests against the protective tariff, which, farmers felt, aided the manufacturing corporations of the East.

The highly visible character of economic constraints on the wheat farmers was an effective teacher. It was just one short step from wheat to the rest of the business system. An early history of the western farmers' movement described the reaction of a typical farmer of the time to the middleman.

The fellow who made that stove paid a profit to the Iron an' Steel Trust who supplied the raw iron ore. Then, he turned around and added a profit of his own before he let the wholesaler have it. Then the wholesaler chalked up more profit before he shipped it along to Joe Green over in town an' Joe just naturally had to soak me something before I got her aboard for home. That's profits on the profits! It's a hot proposition and it's my money that goes up the flue![47]

The conventions of the Grain Growers' Association gave recurrent expression to the deep-rooted antagonism of organized farmers to profits. They kept hitting out, almost at random, at the sore spots in the economy, and began saying, "There ought to be a law" to alleviate one or another evil. As yet there was no realization of the fact that they were actually challenging the fundamental economic base of the society, that this was a power fight between organized agrarians and organized business.

The 1907 convention passed a resolution "That the time has arrived for the installation of a provincial telephone system owned and operated by the government."[48] That same convention suggested that "oil fields and coal lands not at present exploited should be owned and controlled in the interests of the people."[49] It became very clear that the delegates were motivated by the desire to lower prices through eliminating profits. As one delegate put it, "We pay considerably too much for our fuel and if the government controlled the mines, it could control the price as well. . . . We discussed this question at our local meeting and there is a growing sentiment in this country for government ownership of the railroads."[50]

In 1909 the S.G.G.A. convention extended advocacy of government ownership to "timber, coal, oil or other mines," which should be operated so that "the profits and benefits be shared by all alike."[51] Public utilities, transportation, and banking were added to the list by the 1913 convention.[52] The receptivity of the provincial Liberal government to the farmers' demands is evidence of the strength of the farmers' movement. The province initiated government ownership of the telephones and of a coal mine. The coal mine proved unsuccessful and was later dropped, but the telephone lines continued under provincial ownership.

While agitating for increased government ownership, the organized farmers continued to push their coöperative elevators and other coöperative ventures. The *Grain Growers' Guide* turned its fire against the Retail Merchants' Association of Canada, which "is determined to keep the farmers and laboring classes subservient. They wish to keep all business in their own hands and thus take from the pockets of producers and consumers every cent."[53] In 1916 the S.G.G.A. organized a department to handle the wholesale purchase of supplies to be sold by the locals.[54]

By the time of the First World War the more militant farmers of Saskatchewan were organized as a fighting bloc. The S.G.G.A. continued to grow in size as well as in economic achievements. By 1916 it had over 1,300 separate locals, and 28,000 members, out of a possible 104,000 farmers.[55] This meant that there was an organized local of the S.G.G.A. with an average membership of twenty each in almost every farm community in the province. The fact that only one of every four farmers belonged to the organization did not mean that it was opposed by the majority of the rural community. The active members of the S.G.G.A. were leaders in the farming community. The officials of the rural municipalities, local school boards, and coöperative committees were members of the farmers' organization.

The same factors that led the farmers of Saskatchewan and western Canada to organize as a class for economic reform led to early support of direct political action. Many of the farmers' needs could be secured only with the aid of friendly governments, for, unlike the urban workers, the agrarians had no direct economic weapon such as the strike.

The first political movement in the West developed in the 1890's when the Patrons of Husbandry, with substantial support in Man-

itoba and the North-West Territories, elected a few independent farmers' candidates. The movement did not last, however, as it was based mainly on opposition to the high protective tariff and had, therefore, little to distinguish it from the low-tariff Liberals.[56]

In Saskatchewan the Grain Growers' Association first began to consider political action during the agitation for government-owned elevators. In 1909, when the Saskatchewan Liberal government hesitated to accede to the farmers' demands, Partridge, the principal advocate of government ownership, urged that

> every man get busy and, working within the party of his choice, make that party the instrument of his will . . . it is not necessary that a single man now occupying a seat in the local legislature who is opposed to Government ownership should be a member of the next legislature. The farmers are a majority of both parties. Let them go en masse to the councils of their respective parties and force the acceptance of this principle on both.[57]

The Liberal government appointed the Royal Commission to investigate government ownership of elevators.[58] This attempt to circumvent the desires of the farmers would have failed were it not for the fiasco of government-owned elevators in Manitoba. The S.G.G.A., therefore, accepted the suggestion that it start co-operative elevators rather than follow up Partridge's proposal for political action.

Interest in politics was strengthened from 1906 on by the desires of farmers to reduce the high protective tariff. Grain growers had to lower the costs of production as well as of marketing, after 1909 particularly, when "the world price of wheat began a downward trend, and the rising costs of transportation and of manufactured goods rose in conjunction to wipe out and reverse that favourable differential between the two on which the wheat boom of the early years of the century had been based."[59]

Farm organizations repeatedly petitioned the Ottawa government to reduce the tariffs on manufactured goods. The Liberal Party, the traditional low-tariff party, held power during this period, but like its Conservative protectionist predecessors, did little to reduce the tariff load on farmers. Opposition to the tariff reinforced the hostility of farmers to big business and the manufacturing interests. Resolutions of farmers' conventions and articles in the *Grain Growers' Guide* repeatedly denounced "the manufacturing interests [who] are continually using their influence with

our legislators to maintain, secure or increase their privilege to charge more for their products than the cost of production warrants through the instrumentality of the protective tariff."[60]

Growing discontent with agrarian dependence on favors from the traditional parties was evidenced from 1909 onward. The *Guide* editorialized against the two-party system. "[The big interests] realize that so long as the people are willing to endorse either of the old parties they are safe, but that if they send down to Ottawa insurgents or Progressives, then Special Privilege will not be able to plunder the people as in the past."[61] Letters to the editor urging political action appeared regularly after 1909.[62]

These murmurings of discontent did not receive much popular support. Farmers had not yet reached the point of recognizing a need for direct control of the government. The price of wheat held up and, with the exception of 1910, crops were good. Discontent with the tariff and the monopolistic distribution system was not great enough to create the basis for political action. Except for convinced radicals like Partridge, these evils were viewed not as the consequences of a total system, but rather as isolated problems that could be solved in time by coöperatives and remedial legislation. Farm leaders were still fumbling politically. They would strike out at visible economic evils, but did not yet realize that fundamental economic or political problems existed.

In 1913, however, a sharp drop in the price of wheat brought a demand for independent political action. Two resolutions were introduced at the S.G.G.A. convention of that year suggesting an "Independent party representing Agriculture and Labor similar to the [British] Labor Party."[63] The discussion of the resolutions revealed substantial support for the third-party idea. Many delegates objected to the low price of wheat, which they said was caused by high freight rates, and they urged a farmers' party that would nationalize the transportation system and thus increase the price of wheat. The resolutions favoring a third party were defeated only after C. C. Dunning, a leader in the S.G.G.A. and subsequently a Liberal Premier of the province, proposed in a substitute motion that "Direct legislation, the initiative and referendum and recall will more effectively bring about government of the people, by the people, for the people than any third party . . . [and therefore] this convention does not favor the establishment of a political third party."[64]

Proposals for a third party recurred at conventions during the war years, but were not adopted.[65] The debates indicated, however, that farmers in S.G.G.A. locals were discussing the need for a new party that would represent them. In 1915 the Non-Partisan League, which was then organizing just south of the border in North Dakota, made its way into Saskatchewan and received rural support. By 1917 it was publishing two weekly papers and had over 3,000 members in the province. The League's program in Saskatchewan was the same as the semisocialist one it was furthering in the United States.[66]

The new political movement encountered the carefully cultivated tie between S.G.G.A. leaders and the provincial Liberal Party. At conventions of the farm organization, Liberal leaders were careful to appear to be supporting farmers' demands. Several leaders of the S.G.G.A., W. R. Motherwell, the first president, J. A. Maharg, the second president, and George Langley and Charles Dunning, members of the board of directors of the S.G.G.A., became members of Liberal cabinets. The Grain Growers' leaders, who entered the provincial government, retained their membership and sometimes their official position in the organization. They appeared regularly as delegates to S.G.G.A. provincial conventions. The Liberals were therefore able to retain influence in the movement and to defeat any move toward class-conscious political action. Liberal leaders continually referred to the Liberal government as the farmers' government, and stressed the fact that a new political movement was not needed, as the agrarians controlled the existing government.[67] Premier Martin told the S.G.G.A. convention in 1919, "There are questions now coming before you affecting the welfare of the entire community of the province. It is the policy of the present government and will continue to be the policy of the present government to carry out these suggestions."[68]

On the whole, the claims of the provincial Liberals appear to be valid. They did implement most of the proposals of the S.G.G.A. which came under provincial jurisdiction. The Grain Growers were too strongly organized to be ignored by any government that hoped to retain power in a rural province. The conflict over government-owned elevators was the only significant point of difference between government and farmers. Unfortunately for the provincial Liberals, however, they were part of a national party, in which the influence of eastern business had more weight than

did the western farmers. Many farmers believed that the federal
Liberals in office had shown little more willingness than the Conservatives to yield to the farmers on issues such as the tariff and
reduced distribution costs.[69] This fact helped to negate the efforts
of Saskatchewan Liberals to prevent the emergence of an independent farmers' party.

Agrarian discontent continued during the First World War, a
period of sharp increase in the cost of goods and services that
farmers used. Farm leaders believed that high prices were a result
of the protective tariff designed to strengthen the position of eastern manufacturing companies. In 1917 the S.G.G.A. adopted, as its
political program, the "Farmers' Platform" of the Canadian Council of Agriculture, which called for elimination of virtually all
tariffs on the grounds that they were fleecing agriculture and
"making the rich richer and the poor poorer." The continued rural
antagonism to private industry and profits was clearly revealed in
the proposals for sharply graduated taxes on incomes over $4,000,
heavily graduated inheritance taxes on large estates, and graduated
profits taxes on large corporations. The convention of that year
asked also for nationalization of railroads, telegraphs, and express
companies, and opposed the alienation by the government of any
of its natural resources.[70]

The end of the First World War coincided with a sharp drop
in farm income as a result of declining wheat prices and a drought,
while the prices of manufactured goods remained at wartime
levels. To farm leaders this appeared to be another example of
big interests profiting at the expense of farmers. The Non-Partisan
League and other advocates of independent agrarian political
action, such as E. A. Partridge, began to win increasing support
among western grain growers. In March, 1919, the S.G.G.A. leaders
finally yielded to the pressure for a new party and began to organize for federal political action on the basis of the "Farmers'
Platform."[71] A federal by-election held in October, 1919, in the
Assiniboia constituency of southern Saskatchewan, gave concrete
evidence that the farmers wanted a new party. Oliver Gould, a
farmers' candidate, defeated W. R. Motherwell, the former president of the S.G.G.A. and now the Liberal nominee, by 5,224 votes.[72]

At the same time that Saskatchewan was forming a new farmers'
party, agrarians in the other Prairie Provinces and in Ontario began
organizing. Their candidates swept the polls in the provincial

election in Ontario just one week before Gould's election in Saskatchewan.[73] Ontario farmers were more conservative than those on the prairies, and their political action was largely a protest against the conscription of farmers' sons in the last months of the war, but the phenomenon of a farmers' government in conservative Ontario strengthened the hands of the advocates of political action in the West. The leaders of the farm organization in Alberta and Manitoba, facing the same rank-and-file pressures as the heads of the S.G.G.A., joined in the growing movement for a new party.[74]

On January 6, 1920, the National Progressive Party was formed under the leadership of T. A. Crerar, who had succeeded Partridge as head of the G.G.G.C. and who had been in the wartime union cabinet as the Grain Growers' representative.[75] This choice was to prove unfortunate for the young political movement, for Crerar, like most of the Grain Growers' leaders, had not been a supporter of agrarian political action until mass sentiment for it developed.[76] The presence of a large number of political opportunists in its top leadership prevented the Progressives from making a clean break with the old parties, especially with the Liberals.

The time was ripe for a new party in western Canada. The price the Saskatchewan farmer received for his wheat fell from $1.50 a bushel in 1920 to 76 cents a bushel in 1921. The disparity between the price of wheat and the price the farmer paid for other goods squeezed him hard. Between 1919 and 1920 the wholesale price index increased 16.3 per cent, while the price of wheat fell 31.7 per cent. In 1921 wheat fell exactly 50 per cent in price, and wholesale prices declined 29.5 per cent.[77]

The Progressives and the farmers' organizations were therefore able to win a tremendous response from the rural population on a program opposing business profiteering and the tariff. The western Progressives were insistent also on the reëstablishment of government marketing of wheat and the closing of the Grain Exchange. The farmers believed that if they could abolish gambling on the Exchange and eliminate private trading companies the price of wheat would go up.

In the federal election of 1921 the Progressives elected 65 members of Parliament out of a total of 245 in the House of Commons. Of these, 39 were from the prairie wheat belt, 15 of them from Saskatchewan. The only seat that was lost by the Progressives in Saskatchewan was the urban seat of Regina. The Party succeeded

in polling 62.6 per cent of the total vote in the 13 predominantly rural seats of Saskatchewan.[78] Its actual farm vote was probably higher, as the figures include the vote in towns and small villages, which were strongholds of the old parties.

This great victory of a party that was little more than a year old is an indication of the tightly organized nature of the Saskatchewan farming community. The S.G.G.A. had grown to a total of 36,000 members in 1919, which meant that almost one farmer in every three in the province belonged to the organization.[79] The Progressive victory was possible because of the educational and organizational work of the previous two decades. It was comparatively easy to create a new party in the grain belt, in a community that had had the experience of fighting for economic rights. The history of independent political action in Canada and the United States has shown the extent to which unified action to achieve economic goals can be quickly mobilized in the wheat belt. The absence of serious economic cleavages within the rural society and the common economic experiences of grain growers made this possible.

In the face of this agrarian success, the Liberal Party did what liberal parties on this continent tried to do in the past under similar circumstances: its new Prime Minister, W. L. Mackenzie King, sought to win back the agrarian radicals by offering them representation in the federal cabinet and promising to reduce the tariff. Unfortunately for the hopes of those who would build a permanent new party, many of the leaders had never been converted to the necessity for a class party. They had gone along with the tide until they thought that they could control it. Many Progressive members of Parliament, including T. A. Crerar, the national leader, had close ties with the Liberal machines in their areas, and favored accepting King's offer from the outset. The attempt to reach such unity after the elections in 1921 failed; there were too many newly elected agrarian members of Parliament who regarded such a proposal as a betrayal of their followers. Crerar was successful, however, in getting the Progressives to decline their rightful place as the official opposition to the Conservatives, who had fewer seats than the agrarians.[80]

Within two years the Progressive group in the House found themselves gradually led back into the Liberal fold by Crerar and others. They continually supported the government on controversial issues against the Conservatives, although they were able to

gain few concessions from the Liberals on the tariff and the government marketing of wheat. In 1924 a few of the more radical members from Alberta and Saskatchewan broke with the Progressive Party because it was too closely allied with the Liberals.[81]

The results of the Progressive experiment taught many Saskatchewan farmers a needed lesson. A new movement requires leaders who believe in it; if they are forced to act radically, they will revert to their original conservatism at the first opportunity. In interviewing members of the Saskatchewan C.C.F. who were active in the Progressive movement, I was struck by the number of old farmers who expressed the view that "you can't trust any politician, even those on our side," and then described the Progressive "betrayal."

In Saskatchewan the Liberal Party was even more successful in killing the agrarian threat. Recognizing that the farmers were behind the Progressives, Premier Martin announced that his provincial government was neutral in federal politics.[82] Early in 1921 he appointed J. A. Maharg, the president of the S.G.G.A., to the provincial cabinet, and called an election before the farmers' organization could decide whether to enter provincial politics.[83] These tactics succeeded in returning the Liberals to power. Twelve out of the thirteen independent farmers' candidates, who contested the election without any party or formal Grain Growers' support, were elected and formed the second largest group in the provincial House.[84] Had Premier Martin not called this "snap" election with the assistance of the Grain Growers' leaders, he would have been defeated, in all probability, as were the less politically astute old-party governments of Alberta and Manitoba. The lack of reality in the division between federal and provincial Liberals was made clear a few months later, when Martin dropped his neutrality on federal issues and backed the Liberals against the Progressives. Here was still another lesson for the Grain Growers to absorb.

A few Progressives continued to be elected federally and provincially in Saskatchewan until the 'thirties. The federal members joined with a similar farmers' group from Alberta and two socialist members from Winnipeg to form a small, independent left-wing group in the House of Commons opposed to the two old parties. This small "Ginger Group" was to keep alive the idea of a third party after the larger organization had collapsed, and was to help form the socialist C.C.F. of the 1930's.

It is difficult to explain why the Progressives hung on in a few constituencies, while disappearing almost completely in the rest. The constituency of Rosetown, which elected a Progressive until 1930, is one of the richest areas in Saskatchewan, while Mackenzie, which had a similar political record, is one of the poorest. One of the main factors seems to have been the political courage of the Progressive member of Parliament in a district. Where elected Progressives remained loyal to the third-party ideal and retained their ties with the local farm organizations, they could maintain strong electoral support, but where members of Parliament supported the Liberals, the Progressive movement died away.

The Progressive movement failed principally because it was more a product of immediate discontent than of long-term crisis. It was not the expression of a self-conscious class demanding deep-rooted changes. The farmers turned to independent political action because of the threat to their way of life posed by the postwar crisis. Once the conditions which produced the protest disappeared, the mass movement died.

Though unsuccessful in building a permanent agrarian party, the Progressive movement left deep roots in the Saskatchewan scene. It was the first important step in alienating farmers from their old party loyalties. Many who were active in the farmers' party never again supported the old parties, but continued to work for a new party. The success of the movement had proved that a third party could be built successfully within a short time.

The history of protest movements suggests that they have two elements: one is the formal organization; the other is the hard core of scattered adherents whose allegiance expresses a deep conviction of the need for change. The former tends to fall apart and disappear when protest is at the sporadic stage; the tougher supporters simply resume their earlier quest for a means of expressing their protest. The western frontier in the United States and Canada had a disproportionate share of such agitators. The protests of the Partridges of Saskatchewan arose not from a specific grievance but from the desire for a fundamental change in the social order. Movements rise and fall or grow conservative, but a nucleus of social innovators may hang on, waiting for the next opportunity to introduce change. They are the ones who attempt to learn from defeat. The Progressive experience did not permanently discourage the more politically militant of the Saskatchewan farmers, but

rather taught them that political action was a possibility. As we shall see later, when discussing the background of the C.C.F. leaders of the 'thirties, more than 30 per cent of them were active in the Progressive Party. The C.C.F. arose as a direct descendant of the earlier political movement.

Two forms of class action run through the agrarian movement: coöperative self-help in the strictly economic sphere through such devices as coöperatively run grain elevators; and, political action as an indirect device for achieving economic ends. At various periods one appears to be stressed more than the other. This has been as true in most of the Great Plains region as in Saskatchewan. Political action usually arises in a depression or during a major social crisis such as war, whereas coöperation occurs more frequently in periods of prosperity.

The reasons for this difference are twofold. Coöperation is a more gradualist approach to the problems of economic reform than political action. In a depression, farmers are less likely to accept gradualism when immediate action is called for. The problems of low prices, government relief, mortgage foreclosures, and credit become urgent, and only government action can remedy these conditions. A second reason for coöperation being weak in a depression is that the investment and share capital required to form a coöperative enterprise is not available during depressions. The depression effectively cancels out the alternative of coöperation and leaves political action as a weapon.

The same tendency of alternating class action can be seen in the organizational behavior of urban workers. Concentration on politics is most evident during a crisis, whereas trade-unionism is stressed in prosperous periods. In Europe, where the working class organized fairly early into trade-unions and political parties, the gradualist ideology of stressing trade-union gains tended to submerge the revolutionary aims of political parties during the periods of prosperity before and after the First World War. This was especially true in Germany. There has been, of course, a long-term secular trend in favor of class-conscious political action, in that workers or farmers who organize politically during one crisis rarely go back completely to the economic pressure-group stage. Basically, however, workers' and farmers' movements tend to drop objectives of far-reaching economic and political change if the *status quo* becomes stabilized over a period of years.

In Saskatchewan the postwar depression precipitated the tremendous sweep of the Progressive Party in 1921. Saskatchewan farmers hoped that the rural protest would compel the new government to restore government marketing of wheat through the Canadian Wheat Board, for wheat had reached its highest price level when the Board marketed the entire crop. The failure of both Conservative and Liberal governments to do anything about government marketing of wheat led many farmers to turn to the support of a proposal for a farmers' Wheat Pool, which would receive the grain from the farmers and market it coöperatively on the world market in a fashion similar to the work of the government board. The proposals for government and coöperative marketing of wheat renewed the perennial conflict between the agitators in the movement and heads of the farm organizations.

Many leaders of farm organizations feared that the idea of farmers taking complete control of their own crop was too radical, and would meet with such opposition from private elevator companies that it would fail. The officials of the farmers' companies, the Saskatchewan Coöperative Elevator Company, and the Grain Growers' Grain Company sought to delay the creation of a marketing pool for fear that it "would gradually encroach on the activities of the two companies."[85]

The bureaucratic conservatism of the leaders of the established farm organizations resulted finally in a split from the Saskatchewan Grain Growers' Association. In 1921 a small group of militant farmers, some of whom had had earlier experience in the trade-union movement, formed the Farmers' Union "with the object in view of supporting and affiliating with farmers' organizations in all the large producing countries to obtain control of all main farm produce, to regulate and obtain reasonable prices above cost of production, and also to protect the farmers' interests by the support and strength of their own organization!"[86] The new, more radical organization began a vigorous drive for a Wheat Pool.

The campaign of the Farmers' Union succeeded and the older S.G.G.A. agreed to work with the Union to build the Pool. Both organizations campaigned throughout the province, urging farmers to sign contracts agreeing to turn all their wheat over to the Wheat Pool for five years and thus completely eliminate the influence of middlemen. Thousands of volunteer organizers traveled from farmhouse to farmhouse throughout the province.

The new drive faced powerful opposition. The private grain companies vigorously propagandized against it. The daily press tried to convince the farmers that the Pool could not work. This resulted only in convincing the organized agrarians that they needed a paper of their own. The newspapers had earlier opposed the efforts of farmers to build an independent political movement. All four major papers, the Regina *Post*, the Regina *Leader*, the Saskatoon *Star*, and the Saskatoon *Phoenix*, were owned in 1923 by the Sifton Publishing Company, which was closely allied to the Liberal Party. The opposition of this one-company monopoly led many organized farmers to identify the daily press with the other "vested" business interests which they were fighting. This was a major step in the development of class consciousness and political sophistication. It was part of the emerging suspicion of one after another of the institutions of capitalism. "The farmers of the province were in no mood for anything that savoured of opposition. Considerable feeling was aroused and ere long the suspicion found expression . . . in the allegation that the *Morning Leader* was being financed by the grain trade."[87]

The 1923 convention of the S.G.G.A. instructed its executive to start a farmers' newspaper. The *Progressive*, later known as the *Western Producer*, began publication as a weekly on August 27, 1923, and has continued as the voice of the organized educational and coöperative movement of Saskatchewan.[88]

The resistance of the daily press and the grain trade to the Wheat Pool failed. The personal farm-to-farm canvass of Saskatchewan by members of the Farmers' Union and the S.G.G.A. enabled the Pool's supporters to overcome the superior economic power of their opponents. The organized agrarians were determined to take complete control of the marketing of their crops. Within one year, 45,000 farmers had signed contracts agreeing to sell all their wheat through the Pool for a period of five years, in spite of the fact that this meant an immediate financial sacrifice for many of them, as the private grain companies raised the price which they would pay above the Pool's price.[89]

The Wheat Pool campaign, like the earlier battles of the western farmers, must not be viewed as a conscious plan of radical leaders. Though there were hundreds of convinced socialists, monetary reformers, and coöperators among the leaders of the farm organizations, the overwhelming majority of farmers were never oriented

to any long-term goal of major social change. The active farm leaders learned from one fight to the next. In attempting to gain economic security, in fighting for concrete objectives as solutions to particular problems, the farmers gradually came to believe that they were fighting a total system, that the railroads, the Grain Exchange, the newspapers, all were pitted against them.

Following the successful Pool drive, the militant elements in the Farmers' Union initiated a campaign to merge the old Saskatchewan Coöperative Elevator Company with the Wheat Pool. The efforts to organize the Wheat Pool had been obstructed by the board of directors of the Elevator Company, who had rightly feared that the marketing coöperative would eventually attempt to absorb their organization. Local farm leaders, especially those in the Farmers' Union, felt that the Coöperative Elevator officials, many of them leaders in both the S.G.G.A. and the Liberal Party, had become profit-minded and preferred to hold their positions of power rather than involve their organization in the building of an experimental marketing pool.[90] The Union's drive against the old leaders succeeded when, in 1925, the majority of the shareholders of the Elevator Company voted to sell out to the Pool.[91] This victory was part of the recurrent struggle in the farm movement between the more militant, unpaid local leaders and the top officials.

It is difficult to overestimate the importance of the campaign for the Wheat Pool in the organization of farmers into a self-conscious class. The almost evangelical appeal for farmers finally to destroy the middlemen in the grain trade and control their own economic destiny activated more farmers than ever before in Saskatchewan history. More than half of the wheat growers of the province joined the new coöperative within two years after it was organized. As one observer of the prairie scene in the middle 'twenties commented, "The new coöperation has indeed become a veritable religion among the farmers."[92] The impetus for the development of the Wheat Pool resulted in the growth of coöperative marketing pools for livestock, dairies, and eggs. Consumers' coöperatives and purchasing associations made significant gains.

Another important step in the development of organized class consciousness was the great increase in educational activities. The coöperative and other agrarian organizations had been engaged in an extensive educational program almost from the start of the

coöperative movement. Partridge had helped launch the *Grain Growers' Guide* as a means of educating the farmers in regard to their economic problems. The coöperatives hired full-time men to travel around the province holding educational meetings and helping new local coöperatives to get started. These field men were usually hard-working enthusiasts, who left their farms to help further their economic ideals. The creation of the Wheat Pool meant that an educational program reached more farmers than ever before in the history of the farmers' movement.

Since the Pool had continually to face the effective opposition of the grain trade, which had a local representative in the person of the elevator agent in every Saskatchewan community, and since private grain companies continued to offer financial rewards of higher immediate prices to farmers who would not deal with the Pool, the Pool set up elected committees of about ten members each at every shipping point. These committees met from six to twelve times a year to discuss local Pool problems. In order to further the rural antagonism toward the private interests, the provincial office of the Pool sent study outlines to the committees on subjects such as the operation of the Grain Exchange, the effects of tariffs on agriculture, the profit structure of industries that affected farmers, and current legislation.[93]

The Pool organization became an effective educational agency. The most influential farmers were usually elected to the Pool committees. Through them, rural leaders were made aware of significant agricultural problems. To facilitate this work, the province was divided by the Pool into 16 large districts and 165 subdistricts. In each large district a full-time field man visited the committees and helped their work. Each of the subdistricts elected a delegate to the annual provincial convention. The delegates, who had to be farmers, were paid by the Pool to visit the Pool committees within their subdistrict during slack seasons.[94] This meant that there was one delegate for every eighty Pool committeemen, who in turn were responsible to about four hundred members.

The *Western Producer*, the weekly organ of the Pool, which went out to most of the farmhouses in the province, helped to maintain a unified agrarian opinion. It was edited by men who were hostile to many of the institutions of private capitalism. Farmers were encouraged to write for the paper on agrarian and political questions. An "Open Forum" carried discussions of political affairs,

socialism, currency reform, and problems of the coöperative movement.[95] Interviews with many local farm leaders indicate that it is still widely read.

Educational work was carried on also by the United Farmers of Canada (Saskatchewan Section) (U.F.C.), which had been formed in 1926 as a result of a merger of the S.G.G.A. and the Farmers' Union. The U.F.C. had about 20,000 members from the time it was founded until the depression. The leaders of the unified organization conceived of their association as a vanguard movement that would lead the farmers to new conquests. The educational movement had organized the coöperatives and the Progressive Party, and the leaders now saw their role as one of preventing conservatism in the coöperative movement. The vanguard conception is clearly indicated in the first pamphlet published by the U.F.C.:

Our leaders must always be in advance of the thought of the rank and file. . . . There is nothing to fear from the most radical ideas expressed on the platform, because . . . the body can move only as fast as the majority of the members are willing to go . . . [but] there must ever be leaders pointing out new paths to follow, stimulating the organizations with new hope and new conquests or rust and decay and rottenness will soon undermine its power.[96]

The new U.F.C. hoped to be in a better position to play this vanguard role by erecting constitutional barriers against multiple officeholding. Its constitution barred officers from holding executive positions in any other farm organization, or political office.[97] Many of the more conservative leaders in the farm movement who had retained their positions in the S.G.G.A. while becoming Liberal Party leaders or officers of the coöperatives had to resign. As a result, the Wheat Pool leaders were predominantly former members of the S.G.G.A., while the U.F.C. was controlled at the top by old Farmers' Union people.

At the grass-roots level there was considerable overlapping of the active members of the U.F.C. and of the Wheat Pool and other coöperatives. In general, however, the difference between the sections of the farm movement was the same as in the top leadership. The more radical participants devoted more time to educational activities than to the coöperatives. The agitators like Partridge, who was made the honorary president of the U.F.C., believed that coöperation was only a steppingstone in the long-

term fight against "vested interests." This emphasis can be seen in a pamphlet issued by the U.F.C. after unification.

First then we need a United Economic Farmers' Organization. This organization will supplement the efforts of the Wheat Pool and inspire it with courage and determination to win. But this is not the end, it is the beginning. . . .

When we farmers have organized our forces we shall have completed the organization of society on the individual basis. The next task will then be to work for the breakdown of all the conflicting forces by advocating the Coöperative Commonwealth. . . .

The private ownership of the machinery of production and the private control of currency and credit are the two great forces which prevent a coöperative society.[98]

Nineteenth-century liberal society accustomed men to constant change and to the expectation that change meant progress despite the industrial business cycles or the shifting price of wheat. The crisis in liberal democracy developed around growing doubts whether political democracy founded on capitalism could, in fact, continue to result in progress. These doubts led to restlessness under the old parties, efforts to dominate the latter by farmers electing their own men to the provincial legislature, sporadic new party movements, and self-help through direct interference in economic institutions through the setting up of farmers' grain elevators, a Wheat Pool, and an educational movement—all looking vaguely but with increasing self-confidence toward a coöperative commonwealth.

The factors that generated doubt in the old system and its institutions and prompted action were, first, the sense of helplessness of farmers before a remote business system of private grain elevators, middlemen, the Grain Exchange, the national banks, and the powerful railway system—all of which habitually dictated to farmers according to rules of their own; second, the recurrence of violent fluctuations in wheat prices and crop yield, the sole basis of the wheat farmers' standard of life; and third, the inability to get help fast enough and regularly enough from the reigning political parties.

This combination of old institutions and new doubts matured into a crisis. Because of the clarity of the relation between wheat prices and total welfare, the need for organized self-help was recognized earlier in the wheat area. In the more varied economy

of eastern Canada, industry, business, and finance were less simply related to welfare, and division of labor meant that different men had different perceptions of their relations to their institutions. Under such circumstances they worked along in the increasing complexity of industrial society with no clear sense of what and who were responsible for their fluctuating fate. Some drifted hopefully West to try their luck. But in the prairie frontier there was no place else to go. The issue could not be evaded. Men's fate narrowed to a single element—wheat. The crisis matured, therefore, in a simplified setting; the enemy was identified, and men began to think and act radically.

Conservative economists, Royal Commissions, and representatives of the institutions disliked by farmers have criticized the ideas and organized action of the agrarians on the ground that they were based on erroneous economic assumptions. Repeated attempts have been made to convince farmers that the handling of commodities involves intermediate steps, and that the middlemen are receiving only a fair return for necessary services. These logical arguments, however, ignore the fact that many of the charges of farmers are nonlogical. They have their basis not in the specific ills that farmers criticize, but in the totality of social and economic relations that bind the wheat grower to the railroads, the Grain Exchange, and the banks. The farmer saw the middlemen and said, "Let's abolish them." He was hitting out at the things he could see, not realizing that the problem was not these middling processes but the total system that determines how and by whom and for what they shall be operated.

The western farmer is in much the same position as the worker in large-scale industry. The price which each receives for his labor is determined by a complex of powerful factors of which only the part immediately impinging upon his life is visible.

It is not the rentier, the shareholder, and the banker who suffer the ill will of the workers, but almost exclusively the manufacturer and the business executive who are the direct opponents of workers in price wars. This is so in spite of the fact that it is precisely the cash boxes of the rentier, the shareholder, and the banker into which the more or less "unearned" gains flow, rather than into the pockets of the manufacturers or business executives.[99]

The situation in which all power is concentrated on one side can only lead to suspicion and conflict from the other side in a

society with democratic values. Workers and farmers are forced to accept the rules laid down by the possessors of economic power. Living in a society dominated by competitive pecuniary values, they come to believe that those with power are using it to exploit them.

The workers' reactions to this feeling of exploitation can be observed in their restriction of output.[100] Max Weber has called attention to the universality of this phenomenon: "the 'murmuring' of the workers known in ancient oriental ethics: the moral disapproval of the work-master's conduct, which in its practical significance was probably equivalent to an increasingly typical phenomenon of precisely the latest industrial development, namely, the 'slow down' of laborers by virtue of tacit agreement." The extent to which organized class action emerges "is especially linked to the *transparency* of the connections between the causes and the consequences of the 'class situation.' "[101] Among industrial workers, increasing recognition of the causes of their inferior, exploited situation leads to the organization of trade-unions and eventually class political parties seeking to acquire power from the business classes.

Similarly, farmers organize to cut down or eliminate, through government or coöperative action, the profits and power of those with whom they deal, either as producers or consumers. The more the farmer is involved as a small cog in a complex, fluctuating market economy, the more likely is he to become class-conscious and radical in his economic and political ideas. All over North America, the wheat farmers who are least involved in a subsistence rural economy, and are the most commercially oriented of the farmers, have been radical, while the poorer subsistence farmers, who are less subject to direct economic relations with big business organizations, have remained conservative.

Organized self-help was spurred on by the presence in western Canada of many settlers who had been active in socialist and coöperative movements in the old country. The instability of the frontier wheat economy offered these radicals a continuous forum in which to present their ideas. The records of farm organizations reveal a preoccupation with problems of debt, currency reform, tariff, railroad rates, and profits of manufacturers and distributors. This gave the comparatively small group of economic and political radicals an influence far out of proportion to their numbers.

The tendency toward radical change because of the economic crisis was counterbalanced by the institutionalization of the once-militant organizations. The bureaucratic summits of each new movement developed a vested interest in preserving the stability of its organization. The officials feared that support of new and untried ideas might lead to the complete collapse of the old institutions. Their positions as leaders, often full-time urban-dwelling officials of farmers' organizations, gave them a feeling of security and status which led them to depreciate the urgency of the problems of those still on the farm. Many of the early farm leaders were taken into the leadership of the Liberal Party and acquired an interest in preserving the political *status quo*.

The bureaucratic conservatism of the top officialdom was reflected in almost every advance of the farmers' movement. The S.G.G.A. first opposed Partridge's idea of a farmers' marketing company because of the fear that the failure of such a company would destroy the Association. Later, the leaders of the same organization fought against independent political action by farmers and had to be forced into it by rank-and-file pressure. The cleavage between the Farmers' Union and the S.G.G.A. was in part a result of the difference in attitude between the radicals who were ready to take on the job of organizing a Pool, and the overlapping officials of the S.G.G.A. and the Saskatchewan Co-operative Elevator Company who feared to endanger their organizations by new ventures.

This bureaucratization and growing conservatism of reform movements as they gain acceptance is found in every area of society. Trade-unions, coöperatives, and left-wing political parties have repeatedly become bulwarks of the *status quo*. In Saskatchewan, where continual adjustments to economic pressures and changes were necessary, the bureaucratic conservatism of top leaders resulted in agrarian distrust of all officialdom. Restrictions were placed on officials: they could not hold more than one position at a time or for longer than a certain term. Farm leaders were not to take part in politics while holding office in the coöperative or educational movement. The need for annual secret elections in the coöperative movement was recognized. Saskatchewan farmers repeatedly express their fear that farm leaders may be corrupted by the city and its influences. The "city" is the farmers' functional equivalent for bureaucracy.

To sum up, the first three decades of the twentieth century witnessed the creation of a powerful, organized, class-conscious agrarian movement in Saskatchewan. The wheat farmer, who was situated at the producing start and the consuming end of a highly organized and often monopolistic distribution system, became convinced that he, as the primary producer of wealth, was being exploited by "vested interests." He developed hostile class attitudes to big business, to the newspapers, which he believed served the "interests," and to merchants. As a result, a large proportion of the farming population supported an agrarian socialistic program designed to eliminate private profits by governmental or coöperative action before an explicitly socialist party appeared upon the scene.

Chapter IV

THE FARMERS' MOVEMENT
GOES SOCIALIST

THE SPLIT of the Farmer's Union from the S.G.G.A. in 1921 gave temporary formal recognition to a cleavage that had existed between radical and conservative members of the agrarian movement for a number of years. The successful joint struggle of the two rival educational organizations to build the Wheat Pool led to organizational unity in the United Farmers of Canada (Saskatchewan Section) in 1926, but it did not end the fundamental differences between those who saw the agrarian movement as a gradualist liberal development designed to solve specific problems, and the more class-conscious radicals who felt that the farmers would never be secure until the power of their economic enemies was broken. These radicals continued their fight in both the U.F.C. and the Wheat Pool during the prosperous 'twenties, when the combination of high prices and a Wheat Pool, which marketed the wheat of more than two-thirds of the farmers of the province, led the majority of farmers to lose interest in further reform.

A not inconsiderable sprinkling of pioneer settlers in the West had been active radicals in their earlier homes. In present-day

Saskatchewan the influence of these early socialists, many of them immigrants from England, is still apparent. In discussing with older members of the C.C.F. the causes of the development of socialism in the province, one may hear comments like the following:

> Like a great many others, I absorbed my socialist ideas and ideals from Robert Blatchford and his associates in the United Kingdom. On coming to Canada in 1902, I looked around for men of my understanding and found them in the old Grain Growers' Association. . . . From then on, through trial and error, we reached the Farmers' Union, the first lodge of which was organized at Ituna, my home town. . . . I was [then] in the delegate body of the Wheat Pool for sixteen years, from 1924 to 1942, with only two breaks in my term of office. In the early days a sprinkling of the delegates were socialist and near socialist in some of their statements. I saw the socialist sentiment grow from year to year in the organization, and many like myself who could hold the confidence of the farmers in our subdistrict were able to carry on socialist education at our meetings. This was a double-barreled gun, as we were paid for looking after the business of the Coöp and could through the meeting propagate the idea of a Coöperative Commonwealth.[1]

Similar work had been going on earlier. The first secretary of the S.G.G.A., Fred W. Green, had been a socialist in Lancashire, England. He often used his regular column in the *Grain Growers' Guide* to disseminate ideas on socialism without explicitly mentioning the word.[2] Under his secretaryship the S.G.G.A. distributed thousands of copies of Edward Bellamy's socialist classics, *Looking Backward* and *Equality*. Many C.C.F. farmers cite these books as their first contact with socialist ideas.

The left-wingers stressed the existence of a basic cleavage between the producers of wealth—the farmers and workers—and the "vested interests." In the *Western Producer*, the weekly organ of the Wheat Pool, which went to most of the farm homes in the province, the radicals repeatedly presented an extreme ideology of class conflict.

> The laboring people should unite and protect themselves against all idlers. You can divide mankind into two classes, the laborers and the idlers, the supporters and the supported, the honest and the dishonest. Every man is dishonest who lives on the unpaid labor of others no matter if he occupies a throne.[3]

---

[1] For notes to chapter iv see pages 294–295.

The workers know that capitalism is the cause of poverty, of unemployment, of mortgages and debts—and that the farmers will find no solution to their problem within the framework of the capitalist society. Something more do we know and it is this: that the ending of capitalist exploitation is the task of the industrial and agrarian workers.[4]

Politically, the leftists supported the activities in the House of Commons of J. S. Woodsworth, a Methodist minister, who was to become the first national leader of the C.C.F. Woodsworth was elected to Parliament continuously from 1921 as an Independent Labor Party member from the city of Winnipeg. He felt that the coöperative farmers of the West were a promising group for socialist propaganda and cultivated them.[5] The Farmers' Union convention of 1924 adopted a resolution endorsing Woodsworth's efforts to nationalize the banking system and calling upon "every citizen to vote only for those federal nominees who pledge themselves to support . . . the principles embodied in the Woodsworth motion [to nationalize the banks]."[6] From 1927 to 1929 the United Farmers of Canada also supported Woodsworth and sent him on frequent speaking tours throughout Saskatchewan to preach his socialist message.[7]

Having helped build the Wheat Pool, the left-wingers now began to argue that it was not enough. Partridge, now an elderly man, sounded a new battle cry. In 1926, noting the failure of "the great Raisin Growers' Coöperative Association of California [which] went broke a short time ago" as a result of opposition from "vested interests," he drove its moral home as an argument for an all-out coöperative commonwealth as the only safeguard for farmers.

Vocational coöperation is not the cure, as many think, for ills due to selfishness and to great inequality of wealth and opportunity from which we are suffering today. Canada is full of vocational coöperation. A trust, a merger, a manufacturer's association, a trade union, a grain-grower's selling or buying agency, a retail merchant's association, are all coöperatives for vocational advantage. When we have been convinced by actual trial that these partial coöperatives are weak and temporary remedies—just a replacing of the competitive struggles of individuals by the competitive struggles of groups—and not a cure of our ills, we will then seek in national coöperation an ending of the costly war of clashing vocational interests and the establishment of a single basic interest—the ample supplying of our physical needs. . . .

Take it or leave it—we must speedily establish a system of production for *Use* instead of for *Profit* or our present so-called civilization will perish.[8]

During the late 'twenties the left-wingers, consciously thinking of themselves as such, attempted to involve the organized farmers' movement in new struggles. In 1927 the left wing undertook a campaign that was to have significant results for the eventual emergence of the C.C.F. Seeking to extend economic coöperation, they proposed that the Wheat Pool secure 100 per cent control of wheat marketing in Canada instead of the 60 per cent control it then had. They urged that unless the Pool controlled the entire crop it would not be strong enough to resist a decline in the price of wheat; for as long as a minority of farmers stayed outside the Pool, it would be in a weak bargaining position on the world market. They suggested, therefore, that the Pool ask the provincial government to enact legislation requiring that all grain grown in Saskatchewan be marketed through one Pool, subject to the approval of two-thirds of the farmers in a special referendum.[9]

The more conservative leaders of the Wheat Pool, led by A. J. McPhail, its president, opposed the plan: first, because they thought that it was not necessary and would give the government control over the Pool; second, because it had undesirable features of compulsion that were contrary to coöperative principles.[10] The prosperity of the 'twenties, the fact that for the first time the price of Canadian wheat was "frequently higher by several cents a bushel than the corresponding price across the International Boundary,"[11] negated the pessimistic predictions of the radicals, and the 1929 convention of the Wheat Pool rejected a compulsory pool by a substantial majority. The U.F.C., which was a smaller organization composed of the more class-conscious farmers, passed a resolution favoring the 100 per cent pool in its 1928 convention.[12]

As a result of the controversy, George Williams, one of the left-wingers in the U.F.C., was elected president of that organization in 1928. A year later the left wing repeated its presidential victory, and for the first time won a clear majority of the executive board as well. The rift between the two groups became so bitter that the right-wing minority on the executive board and the entire administrative staff of the organization resigned, charging that the agitation for a 100 per cent pool was "destroying the foundation of the whole coöperative movement."[13]

The dispute may seem far removed from the emergent socialist ideology, but actually it contained the nucleus of all that was to follow. The right-wing officials of the coöperative movement were opposed to any reliance of the movement on the state, believing in gradual education and recruitment. The left-wingers feared that education would take too long and that the coöperative farmers, who were a majority of the total farming population, had to use the state to prevent the minority from weakening the movement. The U.F.C. convention of 1929 clearly indicated the long-range motives of the left wing when it established as a basic principle of the U.F.C. that "the farmers are in favor of the abolition of the present system of capitalistic robbery and the establishment of a real coöperative social system controlled by the producers."[14]

The year 1929 was decisive. Everywhere in the province the rift between the left and right wings over the plan for a 100 per cent pool continued in both the local committees of the Wheat Pool and the lodges of the U.F.C., with the U.F.C. pushing forward and consolidating its position favoring radical action and the Wheat Pool hanging back. Times were good and this played into the hands of the conservatives, who were able to retain the support of the majority of the 80,000 Pool members. Then came the financial crash in the autumn of 1929. Had this not happened, the Saskatchewan farmers probably would have oriented ideologically in a stable, conservative direction. The intruding variable of the world business depression gave a positive and final decision to the leftist side, for the economic collapse bankrupted the gigantic Canadian Wheat Pool.

In the fall of 1929 the Wheat Pool made an initial payment to the farmers of $1.00 a bushel. World prices at that time were about $1.50 a bushel, and there was ample reason to expect that the Pool would eventually add substantially to the original payment. The October stock-market crash brought prices down on the Grain Exchange as well. By the end of the crop year, July 31, 1930, the price of wheat on the Winnipeg Grain Exchange had fallen below the initial payment of $1.00 a bushel. The Pool was threatened by bankruptcy and the governments of the three Prairie Provinces agreed to guarantee the banks' advances in order to save the Pool. Conditions grew even worse in 1930, whereupon the Pool lowered its initial payment on No. 1 Northern wheat to 50 cents.[15]

In these two catastrophic years the wheat pools of the West lost about $25,000,000 because of overpayments to farmers. They were forced to give up their sidestepping of the Grain Exchange and to deal again on the Exchange.[16] Wheat prices had become too precarious to continue the system of initial payments, with final payments being made when the total crop was sold. By December, 1932, No. 1 Northern wheat had dropped further, to 38 cents a bushel.[17] At this point the pools were forced to stop their marketing operations and become primarily farmers' elevator companies.[18]

The alarmist prophecies of Partridge and other left-wingers had come true. The wheat pools, the pride of western agriculture, had collapsed. One can scarcely overemphasize the effect of this breakdown on the farmers of Saskatchewan. The left-wingers and socialists, who had made little headway in gaining the support of the Wheat Pool members for more radical measures before 1929, now saw the opposition to their proposals virtually disappear.

The convention of the Saskatchewan Wheat Pool in June, 1930, reversed its previous opposition to the 100 per cent pool. A referendum revealed 34,621 members voting in favor of a compulsory pool and 13,621 voting against it. Of the 48,000 farmers who voted, 71.3 per cent favored the left-wing proposal.[19] The provincial legislature passed the enabling legislation after a delegation of 1,500 farmers, the largest in the history of the province, descended on Regina to demand its passage.[20] The legislation, however, never went into effect, for the courts declared it unconstitutional.

The Saskatchewan farmers' movement had reached a turning point in its history. In their desire for security the farmers had tried various expedients of political and coöperative action, but each remedy in turn had failed to eliminate the hazards of the fluctuating wheat economy. After thirty years of hard work, individually and collectively, western farmers saw the fruits of all their labor destroyed. The depression forced the price of wheat down to its lowest level, increased the volume of farm debt to a new high, and destroyed the equity of thousands of farmers in their land. Because of the drought that began in 1930, many farmers could not even maintain a bare subsistence. (See chap. v.)

The left-wing leaders who dominated the U.F.C. decided that the time was ripe for an avowed socialist movement among the farmers. George Williams, left-wing president of the U.F.C., had attempted without success, in the middle 'twenties, to organize a

radical farmers' party. Efforts had been made at every convention from its founding one in 1926 to get the U.F.C. to support independent political action. But these were defeated in view of the apparent success of pure coöperation.[21]

The convention in February, 1930, met a few months after the disastrous fall in the price of wheat. Williams and his followers seized the strategic time to channel the U.F.C. in a socialist direction. E. A. Partridge, now honorary president of the U.F.C., told the delegates that "true coöperation has its final goal in socialism, which is the continual observance of the Golden Rule." In the discussion on the resolution in favor of political action, various delegates argued in the same vein. "It is a fight to the finish between capitalism and coöperation, and how can we support coöperation better than by putting farmer members in our Provincial and Federal Legislatures?"[22]

The majority of the delegates, 306, favored political action; 165 opposed it. But the resolution was defeated, because two-thirds of the votes (314) were needed for a constitutional amendment.[23] The depression was only five months old, and the effort to secure the 100 per cent pool had not yet been outlawed by the courts, so the opponents of political action could still argue that coöperative self-help had not failed.

At the convention of 1930 the left wing accepted a compromise resolution suggesting that "the farmers should set up an organization outside the United Farmers of Canada for the purpose of more directly selecting and electing representatives to the Legislature and the House of Commons pledged to support the demands of organized agriculture."[24] The U.F.C., accordingly, adopted a farmers' program that was recommended to all candidates who wanted farmers' support. Its principal planks were:

1. Abolition of the competitive system and substitution of a coöperative system of manufacturing, transportation, and distribution;
2. 100 per cent marketing pool by legislation;
3. Abolition of military training and removal of all war incentives from school books and moving pictures. Teaching of coöperative principles in public schools, colleges, and university;
4. State medicine and health insurance;
5. Free trade with the mother country.[25]

The convention also called for the nationalization of the Canadian Pacific Railway, public utilities, and natural resources.

A few months after the U.F.C. convention, the Farmers' Political Association (F.P.A.) was formed by the political activists of the farmers' movement to contest the Dominion election of 1930. The leaders of the new organization were active members of the U.F.C., though officials of the U.F.C. were forbidden by the constitution to participate. The new party called for the encouragement of "all coöperative enterprises as steps leading to the establishment of a coöperative commonwealth . . . public ownership of our public resources and lower tariffs."[26] It was backed by the remnants of the old Progressive Party, which had continued in a few constituencies, and by the newly formed urban Independent Labor Party.

The propaganda of the F.P.A. stressed the need for workers' and farmers' class representation in Parliament because "powerful capitalists by campaign fund contributions had made the political parties responsible to them instead of to the people."[27] Though the party did not mention socialism in speeches or printed propaganda, it stressed the need for a new system of production for use in a coöperative commonwealth. The basic rural bias against urban domination can be seen in the demand that "the country school house should be the basis of [political] organization, rather than city hall."[28]

In the Dominion election of that year the new farmers' organization succeeded in obtaining 40,000 votes.[29] Only thirteen constituencies out of a total of twenty-one in the province had farmers' candidates, as the organization had been initiated only a few months before the election. The party won 23.1 per cent of the vote in these thirteen predominantly rural constituencies. Actually, its rural vote was higher than the figure indicates, as the party had virtually no organization or support in the small urban centers. This seemed to be a significant indication of the desire of the agrarians for a new political movement, for the F.P.A. was able to get this vote with scanty funds and in spite of the fact that it was a small local party fighting in a national election.

The election was important from another point of view as well, for it resulted in a partial shift in Saskatchewan from its traditional Liberal allegiance to the Conservative Party. The latter, as the official opposition and the only other national political party, received the votes of many who blamed the depression on the incumbent Liberals. The Tories, while sweeping the rest of Canada, gained nine of the twenty-one seats in Saskatchewan, whereas in

the previous election they had not captured a single constituency. To vote Conservative represented a major shift in the electoral traditions of Saskatchewan, since the farmers had always favored a low tariff, associated with the Liberal or Progressive parties. Despite the growing radical declarations of farm leaders when meeting as an embattled bloc in conventions, the majority of the farmers were still careful men and, when faced with an election, tended to choose the lesser of two evils. They were learning—but the hard and slow way.

In the economic confusion and political fumbling of the first years of the depression, revolt was taking shape among the farmers. In the autumn of 1930 there was a movement for the secession of the Western Provinces. If the farmers could not live with the financial and industrial East, they would try living without it. The new movement believed that if the Western Provinces could secede from Canada they would cease subsidizing eastern manufacturers through high tariffs, and could establish a barter trade agreement with England, sending wheat in return for manufactured goods. The movement was backed by many prominent farm leaders, including A. J. Macauley, president of the U.F.C., and John Wesson, director and later president of the Wheat Pool.[30] This may seem a far cry from the emerging socialist movement, but in the minds of many radical farmers it was tied up with their traditional fight against the national economic structure controlled in Montreal and Toronto. As early as 1926, at the height of prosperity, E. A. Partridge had suggested that the progressive provinces of the West secede from the hopelessly reactionary and business-dominated provinces of the East and form a western coöperative commonwealth.[31]

Throughout the winter of 1930–1931, large meetings demanded secession. The reforms that were expected to result from secession included nationalization of banks, reduced interest rates, lower cost of farm implements, free tariff, and a moratorium on all debts. Newspapermen reported that the movement was most popular with the grain farmers, but was not popular with those who produced livestock.[32] As always, it was grain farmers who were most disastrously affected by the decline in prices.

Secession may now seem a wild idea, but the fact that it was seriously considered indicates the desperate condition of the grain growers. Their livelihood was being destroyed by forces beyond

their control. Meanwhile, the politically sophisticated leaders of the U.F.C., who in 1930 had persuaded that body to go on record in favor of independent political action, had not been idle. Some had gone along with the secession movement, but not as an alternative to forthright political action. There were rumblings of radical discontent in eastern centers like Toronto, and the extreme step of seceding did not seem the only choice.

In February, 1931, while the secession movement was still strong, the U.F.C. board of directors, composed of socialists, both old and newly converted, received overwhelming convention support for an economic and political program that stated an ultimate socialist objective: "That in the opinion of this convention the present economic crisis is due to the inherent unsoundness of the capitalistic control of production and distribution and involves the payment of rent, interest and profit, we recognize that social ownership and coöperative production for use is the only sound economic system."[33] The farmers were in a mood for desperate remedies. Delegates told of the intolerable nightmare of succeeding evictions in their neighborhoods, and demanded action: "We can fight against evictions, against foreclosures, directly, or we can fight through our legislatures, but if we urge the legislatures to fight the creditors, they fight the creditors with creditors, for the legislators are of the creditor class. We may get concessions for a short time if the farmers appear militant. The only way is to do the fighting ourselves."[34]

The provincial economic program adopted by the convention accordingly demanded a moratorium on "foreclosures, evictions or seizures, and exemption of the farmers home quarter-section [160 acres] from seizure, crop insurance, adjustment of farm debts," and that "no more homesteads be granted on farm lands sold," but that "*use leases [on all farms] be instituted and that all land and resources now privately owned be nationalized as rapidly as opportunity will permit.*"[35] The federal part of the program demanded a fixed price for grain above the costs of production, fixed prices for the goods farmers consumed, nationalization of railroads and lower freight rates, government control of currency and credit, the 100 per cent Wheat Pool, and the abolition of the Grain Exchange.

The opposition to radical proposals which had existed at earlier conventions had all but died out at this one. After two years of

depression, the Wheat Pool was bankrupt. The temper of the delegates can be seen from the fact that the only amendments to the program recommended by the executive were in a more radical direction. The proposal for land nationalization came from the floor of the convention. It was introduced by delegates who had been influenced by the British Labor Party, which had a similar rural program. During the depression the lessening of the sense of security on the part of landholding farmers taught many of them that the ownership of property was not the crucial factor; rather, it was the use of that property. They proposed to let the Commonwealth hold title and modify the risks of fluctuating values, provided the farmers could farm the land and concentrate on their proper business as wheat growers.

After agreement was reached on the economic policy, the leaders of the U.F.C. brought in a resolution on political action: "Should the Federal or Provincial Governments or either of them fail to accede to these demands . . . the U.F.C. [should] take political action as an organization which should seek the coöperation of all citizens in electing candidates pledged to these principles."[36] The provisional form of the resolution was adopted because the leaders sought to put the onus of responsibility on the governments of the day, stating that farmers would take political action only if their demands were refused. This time there was little opposition, and the resolution was overwhelmingly approved. Delegate after delegate demanded that the farmers take over the government themselves in statements such as the following:

You have been passing legislation here in your interests. We have done it for years at conventions similar to this, and after we did that, practically all the influence we had was to send a delegation to some political leader whether it be a provincial or federal one, and ask him, "Please, Mister, will you give us this?"[37]

We are fighting the capitalist party. Why is it that these members of two different political parties are really fighting for one group? The reason is that the majority of the members are engaged in callings that depend on profit, and are those who exploit the farmers.[38]

While the Saskatchewan farmers' movement was tending in a socialist direction, an urban socialist movement emerged in the cities of the province. In 1929 a small group of trade-unionists and teachers under the leadership of M. J. Coldwell, a former member of the English Fabians, who was then a school principal in Regina,

decided to form the Independent Labor Party (I.L.P.) of Saskatchewan. Most of the members were Englishmen who had belonged to, or had supported, the labor movement in the United Kingdom.[39] They had been inspired to organize by the success of the I.L.P. of Manitoba, which had elected a mayor, two members of Parliament, and several provincial legislators from Winnipeg. J. S. Woodsworth, then an I.L.P. member of Parliament for Winnipeg, and the recognized leader of the Ginger Group of left-wing farmer and labor members of Parliament, was instrumental in organizing the Saskatchewan group.

The depression began soon after the Saskatchewan I.L.P. was organized, and unemployment developed in the urban areas. The socialist I.L.P. spread until it had branches in all the cities and many of the larger towns of the province. It never, however, had more than 500 members.[40] The Party advocated increased relief to the unemployed. It also contested municipal election campaigns and succeeded in electing a few aldermen.

Realizing that it could not hope to become a major group without the support of the farmers in overwhelmingly rural Saskatchewan, the I.L.P. attempted to coöperate with the growing left-wing political-action movement among the farmers. In 1930 the Party supported the short-lived Farmers' Political Association in their election campaign. One year later, when the U.F.C. decided to enter politics on a socialist basis, the leaders of the U.F.C. and the I.L.P. agreed to work together to create a large farmer-labor party with a socialist program.

The leaders of the two organizations followed the tactics which had been mapped out by the U.F.C. leaders at their convention. Instead of launching a political movement at once, the executive of the U.F.C. organized a series of district conventions, ostensibly for the purpose of putting pressure on the provincial government to accede to the demands of organized farmers and workers. Large meetings were held to introduce a program of action designed to protect workers and farmers against creditors. Delegates were elected from each of the district conventions to go to Regina, the provincial capital, to ask the government to implement their demands. If the government failed to do so, the U.F.C. was authorized to enter political action.

The strategy worked well. The delegates met in Regina on June 26, 1931, with representatives of the I.L.P. led by Coldwell.[41] As

was expected, the Conservative government rejected their demands. The delegates were especially infuriated by the statement of Mr. Buckle, the Minister of Agriculture, that "the most hopeful development he had noted was the successful launching of a Colonization Company by an aggregation of Land and Mortgage Companies."[42] This approval by a cabinet minister of the growth of tenant farming under the ownership of the mortgage companies was anathema to the farmers. It provided further justification for the U.F.C. proposal that every farmer be given a use-lease title to his land instead of a private title that could be lost to a mortgage company.

The answer of the joint conference of U.F.C. and I.L.P. delegates to this rebuff was a decision to work together to "establish a coöperative commonwealth, and that in the event of an approaching election, municipal, provincial or federal, we will constitute ourselves as a committee ... with the view of gaining individual support for candidates pledged to our principles."[43]

The two organizations threw themselves into the work of building the new political movement. The U.F.C. had nominally over 20,000 members, though less than 10 per cent had been able to pay dues because of the depression.[44] The difficulty of organizing a new movement in a poverty-stricken province was tremendous. Tens of thousands were completely dependent on relief for food, clothing, and seed grain. The attitude of many of the impoverished farmers was similar to that of unemployed workers—apathetic rather than protesting.

Many in my district oppose the government but are afraid to attend, for this is an 100 per cent relief district and they are all afraid to compromise themselves until they know how their relief applications will be treated.[45]

I received a letter from the Chairman of the ———— Constituency in which he states that in his opinion, the constituency is not organized properly for an election and the farmers would support a Government candidate because they are all on relief and will be looking for assistance.[46]

In spite of the severity of the depression and drought and the consequent lack of finances, U.F.C. and I.L.P. organizers toured the province speaking to large meetings of farmers and workers. They were aided by the fact that the U.F.C., as the educational organization of farmers, received free space every week in the

Western Producer, the organ of the Wheat Pool, which went to the majority of farm homes in Saskatchewan.[47] The farmers' movement had started on a new path the end of which was now a socialist society rather than a series of immediate reforms. This was the beginning of a movement which within the next decade and a half was to sweep Saskatchewan and become a major threat to the old parties in most of the provinces of Canada.

Meanwhile, similar developments were occurring elsewhere in Canada. A national movement, the Coöperative Commonwealth Federation, was being born. The United Farmers' organizations in Alberta and Manitoba followed Saskatchewan in endorsing "the establishment of the coöperative commonwealth state."[48] In British Columbia the Socialist Party, which had existed in that province since the turn of the century, succeeded in electing its first member of Parliament from the city of Vancouver in 1930.[49]

Intellectual and religious Canada also began to stir in a socialist direction. In 1931 a large group of university professors and other intellectuals formed the League for Social Reconstruction, modeled on the English Fabian Society, to do educational and research work for Canadian socialism.[50] The Toronto conference of the United Church, Canada's leading Protestant group, unequivocally stated:

> First of all, it is our belief that the application of the principles of Jesus Christ to economic conditions would mean the end of the capitalist system. (By the capitalist system we mean that order of things under which capital, which is a vital factor in the economic field and represents the part of the economic product used as a means to further production, is owned and administered by individuals and special groups with a view to their own profits. Our contention is that capital, especially in those large-scale forms that are essential to the life of the whole people, should be owned and operated instead, not for private gain, but in the services of the general good.)[51]

As the Conservatives revealed their inability to cope with the deepening depression, which had started under the Liberals, socialists made headway in converting the Canadian people. It became clear that Canada was ready for a new radical third party. The direct impetus for organizing such a party came from Saskatchewan, where the socialist faction had complete control of a mass organization. The U.F.C. suggested to Woodsworth and other left-wing members of Parliament that a national conference

be held. All groups who believed that capitalism should be overthrown, and that a new social order based on production for use and not for profit was needed, were invited to Calgary, Alberta, in August, 1932. The conference was attended by the Ginger Group of members of Parliament, the representatives of the United Farmers' organizations of Manitoba, Alberta, and Saskatchewan, and delegates from the Labor and Socialist parties of the three Prairie Provinces and British Columbia.

The conference brought together, for the first time in Canadian history, Marxian socialists from British Columbia, men raised in the traditions of the British labor movement, and the agrarian radicals. The delegates decided to form a new national political party to be known as the Coöperative Commonwealth Federation (C.C.F.). Its first national convention, meeting in Regina in July, 1933, drew up a lengthy program that was a compromise between the Marxian socialists and the much more conservative farmers' representatives from eastern Canada.[52] Each provincial section of the party, however, was left free to interpret the program as it saw fit and to draw up its own provincial program.

The Regina convention marked a turning point in the history of the Saskatchewan farmers' movement as well as in the socialist movement across Canada. For the first time the agrarians had become part of a national radical movement allied with urban labor. Instead of attacking only the aspects of the economy that could be controlled by coöperative action within the province, the farmers were now engaged in a frontal attack on the total economic structure. The organized class consciousness that had developed to defend the farmers' economic position now assumed the offensive.

Chapter V

THE ECONOMIC CONSEQUENCES OF THE DEPRESSION

O NLY BY KEEPING in mind the background of the "terrible 'thirties" can one understand the rapid growth of the C.C.F. in Saskatchewan and the continued existence of protest movements in the West. Saskatchewan, a community that had enjoyed year after year of prosperity, was struck without warning by a misfortune that lasted for nine years and wiped out the source of income of well to do and poor alike—a combined catastrophe of drought and low prices. At the same time, a great economic depression hit the whole world, distracting outside attention from the crisis in Saskatchewan.

Before the depression this province was one of the most prosperous farming communities on the North American continent. Serious differences of income and size of farms had not yet developed. The rich soil produced a crop that was in great demand in the industrial nations of Europe.

In the four years 1925 to 1928, Saskatchewan agriculture flourished. Wheat crops averaging 260 million bushels sold at an average price of $1 at country delivery points during this period, and the returns were on the whole well distributed. Gross agricultural income was about $400

millions a year. . . . On the whole, the net cash income of the average citizen in Saskatchewan during this period probably exceeded that in any other economy in the world of about equal population, with the exception of certain areas in the middle west of the United States.[1]

From 1930, the farmers of Saskatchewan were destitute. They were affected not only by the decline in the price of wheat, which at one point reached a low of 19 cents a bushel, but by the longest and severest drought in the history of western settlement. Table 4 (p. 28) shows that the yield per acre fell as low as 2.7 bushels, while the average annual price fell as low as 35 cents. Conditions grew steadily worse. If the crops were good one year in certain parts of the province, the price of wheat was too low to enable farmers to make a profit or to build up reserves. Except for the poor-soil areas in the extreme north, almost every farm was completely dried out during some years. Many did not yield a decent crop for six or seven years. It is impossible to exaggerate the extent to which the social, economic, and political life of the province was affected by the depression in the 'thirties.

The blunt, dry language of economists who recorded the catastrophe tells the financial side of the story.

Gross cash income (the average for 1928–1930 compared with the average for 1930–1937) fell from 100 to 32, while cash operating expenses fell from 100 to 67. The result was that the net cash income fell from 198 million dollars to 20 million dollars, while in the year 1932 there was not sufficient net income to pay the mortgage interest and nothing for living expenses which had to be met out of borrowing, past savings, consumption of capital and government relief.[2]

The year-by-year reports of the University of Saskatchewan show clearly what crop failures and low prices meant to the farmers:

To pay interest on the present [1934] farm debt of Saskatchewan would have required about 4/5 of all wheat available for sale from the 1933 crop, and for payment of farm taxes two-thirds of this wheat.[3]

To pay interest on the present farm debt [1935] of Saskatchewan would have required about two-thirds of all the wheat available from the 1934 crop . . . , to pay the current [tax] levies would have required at least one fifth of the wheat for sale.[4]

---

[1] For notes to chapter v see pages 295–296.

It would require more than one half of all the wheat available for sale from the 1935 crop . . . to pay the interest on the present farm debt, and to meet the current tax levies at least one-sixth of the revenue would have been demanded.[5]

The disaster of the 1937 crop year is the worst of the series. . . . Since 1930 the average values of the wheat crops have been about one-quarter of those from 1924–1928, with that of 1937 being only one-eighth of the amount. The absence of receipts from other sources, the loss of feed crops, and the partial or complete failures of pastures and grazing areas accentuated the difficulties. . . . Only about 14 million bushels of wheat were available for sale from this crop, which is scarcely one tenth of the average for this ten year period.[6]

The 1938 crop year proved to be a very disappointing one for Saskatchewan farmers. The spring and early summer gave promise of a good harvest, but rust and grasshoppers, with scattered drought, seriously reduced yields and grades of all crops over most of the province. Added to this depressing production situation, prices for grain on the open market declined to very low levels.[7]

The 1939 crop proved to be one of the best in the history of the province. . . . From 1930 to 1938 the average gross value per acre of wheat for Saskatchewan was about $5.10; the extreme range was from $6.60 per acre in 1936 to $2.73 in 1937. In light of the facts 1939 may be considered a comparatively good year as the average gross value per acre of wheat is $9.00, the best since 1930. [The Dominion government regards a crop of less than $6.00 an acre as a crop failure.]

For the first time in 10 years, the average Saskatchewan farmer has been able to meet farm cash operating and living costs. However, a still higher income will be necessary to allow satisfactory servicing of the present indebtedness.[8]

The effects of the drought and depression were felt by every group in the rural population. In the early years of the decade, the larger, well-to-do farmers actually suffered more in straight monetary terms than the smaller farmers, as they required large amounts of working capital and did not earn enough to meet the year's expenses. They therefore went deeper into debt.

In the first period, 1929–31, the small farms had a small Net Cash Income but increases in size of the farm were accompanied by a declining income until at 500 acres no Net Cash Income was obtained. Farms larger than 500 acres experienced operating losses. For the period of the severe depression, 1932–34, the smallest sized farms had practically no Net Cash Income and increasingly larger operating losses resulted for larger farms.[9]

TABLE 8

RELATION OF SIZE OF FARM TO FARM INCOME, 1932–1934

Cultivated acres	Net cash income	Net farm income	Cash family living	Farm surplus
	Yield of 0–4 bushels per acre			
0–249..........	$ 28	−$ 102	$ 270	−$ 372
250–399..........	−150	− 552	360	− 912
400–549..........	−280	− 862	450	−1,312
550–699..........	−430	−1,220	552	−1,772
700–849..........	−530	−1,705	690	−2,395
	Yield of 5–8 bushels per acre			
0–249..........	$ 138	−$42	$ 283	−$ 325
250–399..........	138	−255	415	− 670
400–549..........	138	−405	522	− 927
550–699..........	123	−577	660	−1,237
700–849..........	149	−825	837	−1,662
	Yield of 9–12 bushels per acre			
0–249..........	$ 216	$ 35	$ 307	−$ 272
250–399..........	365	− 27	457	− 484
400–549..........	480	− 77	577	− 654
550–699..........	568	−130	722	− 852
700–849..........	725	−207	905	−1,112
	Yield of 13–16 bushels per acre			
0–249..........	$ 245	$ 80	$ 315	−$ 235
250–399..........	615	180	497	− 317
400–549..........	860	260	642	− 382
550–699..........	1,082	355	817	− 462
700–849..........	1,370	470	1,025	− 555
	Yield of 17–20 bushels per acre			
0–249..........	$ 408	$ 200	$ 330	−$ 130
250–399..........	858	410	565	− 155
400–549..........	1,202	590	715	− 125
550–699..........	1,532	785	917	− 132
700–849..........	1,928	1,020	1,170	− 150

SOURCE: University of Saskatchewan, College of Agriculture, "Changes in Farm Income and Indebtedness in Saskatchewan during the Period 1929 to 1940," Agricultural Extension *Bulletin* 105 (1940), p. 13.

Table 8 makes clear the relation between the size of farms and the loss of farm income.

No other province in Canada—and, for that matter, few other places in the entire world—suffered so sharp a decline in income and required so much government assistance in order to survive. Every available economic index points to this fact. The decline in provincial per capita income was greatest in Saskatchewan, as

TABLE 9

DECLINE IN PROVINCIAL INCOMES

Province	1928–1929 average per capita	1933 average per capita	Percentage decrease
Saskatchewan..............	$478	$135	72
Alberta...................	548	212	61
Manitoba.................	466	240	49
Canada, national average....	471	247	48
British Columbia...........	594	314	47
Prince Edward Island........	278	154	45
Ontario...................	549	310	44
Quebec...................	391	220	44
New Brunswick.............	292	180	39
Nova Scotia...............	322	207	36

SOURCE: *Report of the Royal Commission on Dominion-Provincial Relations: Canada, 1867–1939* (1940), Book I, p. 150.

table 9 indicates. It is worth noting that Alberta, the only province that is comparable to Saskatchewan, is the home of the successful Social Credit protest movement and, like Saskatchewan, is a wheat province.

A comparison of the relative economic decline by industries reveals similar results. Agriculture in the Prairie Provinces declined in monetary income by 92 per cent from 1928 to 1932. In the rest of Canada the agricultural decline was 68 per cent, while the loss in salaries and wages was appreciably less.

Table 10 helps in part to explain the reasons for the varying reactions of different classes and communities to the depression. Only the wheat farmers of the West and the rural community of Saskatchewan were adversely and uniformly affected by the economic decline. Some working-class groups improved their economic position in terms of their share of the national income. The

nonagricultural middle and upper classes likewise increased their proportionate share.

The extent of the depression in Saskatchewan forced hundreds of thousands of farmers and workers to go on government relief rolls. The drought, and the fact that many grain growers did not raise livestock, meant that government relief foodstuffs had to be

TABLE 10

DEPRESSION DECREASES IN NET MONEY INCOME
BY SOURCE OF INCOME

Source of income	Percentage change 1932–33 average income from 1928–29 average income
Agriculture, Prairie Provinces........................	−94
Fisheries..	−72
Salaries and wages in construction.....................	−68
Agriculture, other provinces..........................	−64
Salaries and wages in exporting industries..............	−50
Total national income................................	−41
Dividends received by stockholders....................	−40
Salaries and wages in protected manufacturing industries.	−37
Income of small businessmen and professionals..........	−36
Salaries and wages in sheltered occupations.............	−30
Miscellaneous income................................	−18
Bond interest, property income from life insurance, and interest on farm mortgages received by individuals.....	+13

SOURCE: *Report of the Royal Commission on Dominion-Provincial Relations: Canada, 1867–1939* (1940), Book I, p. 150.

brought into one of the most rural areas in the world in order to prevent starvation. In 1937 "the completeness of crop failure . . . had placed two-thirds of the rural population on the relief rolls, and 290 of the 302 rural municipalities of the province had sought assistance from the government."[10] Thousands of carloads of vegetables, fruits, clothing, and coal were brought in by voluntary relief agencies and the Red Cross. The total cost of relief from 1930 to 1937 amounted to almost two-thirds of the total local and provincial government revenues in the province.[11] The proportionate amount of government relief in Saskatchewan was far greater than that of any other province in Canada, as table 11 indicates.

The excessive costs of relief in Saskatchewan were not a result of any extravagance in the scale of allotments. The Saskatchewan Relief Commission in 1933–1934 set a maximum monthly food allowance for a family of five at $10 plus one 98-pound bag of flour. The Bureau of Public Welfare, which took over the relief work, set monthly relief limits for the same size of family at $13.15 in 1935, $16.50 in 1936, and $20.20 in 1937, with no separate allow-

TABLE 11

Disparities in Relief Burden of Various Provinces, 1930–1937

Province	Ratio of total relief costs to total provincial income	
	Relative severity of burden; index of ratios, national average = 100	Percentage of total relief expenditures to total provincial income
Saskatchewan............................	367	13.3
Manitoba...............................	115	4.2
British Columbia.......................	100	3.6
Alberta................................	100	3.6
Canada, national average...............	100	3.6
Quebec................................	90	3.2
Prince Edward Island..................	76	2.8
Ontario...............................	76	2.7
Nova Scotia...........................	70	2.5
New Brunswick........................	67	2.4

Source: *Report of the Royal Commission on Dominion-Provincial Relations: Canada, 1867–1939* (1940), Book I, p. 164.

ance for flour. "If the applicant had meat, 10 per cent was to be deducted from the allowance; if dairy products, a further 10 per cent; if potatoes, 5 per cent; where it is practicable for the relief recipient to have wheat gristed, no order for flour [was] issued."[12]

The Relief Commission permitted no purchases of fruit, and no vegetables except potatoes and dried beans. It is not surprising, therefore, that the federal Minister of Agriculture, James G. Gardiner, who had been Premier of Saskatchewan in 1935–1936, reported, in 1937, "There have been reports from prairie medical men that they have seen signs of scurvy for the first time. It is not on a widespread scale and the number of cases is not available.

TABLE 12

RETAIL MERCHANDISE TRADE BY PROVINCES

| Province | Total net sales | Index of retail sales (1930 = 100) | | | | | | | |
	1930	1930	1931	1932	1933	1934	1935	1936	1937
Prince Edward Island	$ 13,733,700	100.0	83.8	67.4	64.7	70.3	71.9	82.4	85.3
Nova Scotia	99,519,900	100.0	90.3	75.1	69.2	77.2	81.6	88.7	99.8
New Brunswick	84,371,900	100.0	85.0	67.6	62.1	69.1	73.1	79.4	90.9
Quebec	651,138,500	100.0	86.4	71.5	64.9	69.0	71.3	76.5	86.9
Ontario	1,099,990,200	100.0	86.6	71.8	67.4	74.9	78.0	83.0	92.9
Manitoba	189,243,900	100.0	81.3	69.6	64.5	69.4	73.4	78.5	85.2
Saskatchewan	189,181,100	100.0	70.8	59.2	54.5	59.4	63.2	69.2	68.3
Alberta	176,537,100	100.0	76.1	65.6	61.8	69.0	74.0	78.7	86.3
British Columbia	248,597,500	100.0	83.7	65.9	62.6	69.6	75.8	84.0	93.6
Canada, totals	$2,755,569,900	100.0	82.2	69.8	64.8	74.1	74.6	80.1	89.0

SOURCE: *Retail Merchandise Trade in Canada, 1937* (1938), quoted in G. E. Britnell, *The Wheat Economy* (1939), p. 198.

It is apparent, however, that there has been a shortage of vegetables and fruit in the diet of people on relief."[13]

A further index of the effect of the decline in income on living standards can be seen in the decline of the volume of retail trade in Saskatchewan compared to the rest of Canada. As table 12 indicates, no other province came close to Saskatchewan in this respect. Between 1930 and 1933, retail sales in the province fell more than 45 per cent.

The economic statistics give the objective picture of the effect of depression and drought on the economy, but leave out the complete destruction of the way of life, the hopes and aspirations, of hundreds of thousands of people. The depth of their misery and defeat is suggested by accounts of contemporary journalists:

There is virtually nothing in the rolling hills and valleys at Buffalo Gap and Big Beaver, which is near the U. S. border due south of Bengough. Gardens were a failure. Potatoes will have to be brought in. Clothes are worn thin. . . . One man told of children whom he knew, who had not tasted any other vegetables than potatoes for over two years. Meat, bread and potatoes form the diet of the majority, it was stated, but this year it was feared that the meat will often be lacking and the potatoes as well. Such is the progressive effect of years of drought.[14]

Many of the social necessities of rural life had to be discarded by Saskatchewan farmers. "Clothing has been reduced to a minimum and bed clothes are reported as a great necessity, being but a remnant of what they once were and worn thin with age. . . . One farmer described the situation as 'patching up old clothes with clothes already patched only to discover that the garment had given way somewhere else.' "[15]

The rural telephone system, which had been built up by the government and local farmers' companies, reached a total of 71,616 telephones in 1930. It declined to 39,488 by 1934.[16] One woman living in rural Saskatchewan commented on the significance of this fact.

Consider a farmer's financial straits when for $10.50 a year he will do without a telephone. Perhaps he is 10 or 15 miles from town, perhaps a mile from his nearest neighbor, yet for the sake of that paltry sum, he will face the hazards, the isolation, the social inconvenience of doing without his telephone. I think this more than anything else shows our western financial position.[17]

The automobile, which during the 'twenties replaced the horse and buggy on most Saskatchewan farms, also began to vanish. The number of cars registered in the province fell from 108,630 in 1929 to 69,040 in 1933. This represented a drop of 36 per cent, while for Canada as a whole cars declined only 13 per cent in the same period.[18] As the number of cars in operation decreased, the use made of the remaining ones declined; the average number of gallons of gasoline for each registered motor vehicle dropped from 366 in 1929 to 256 in 1933 in Saskatchewan, while the decline for Canada as a whole was from 404 to 395 gallons.[19]

Educational standards fell sharply. Schools shortened their academic year, and teachers' salaries were so small that many had to apply for relief. In 1930 the average salary of a male rural teacher with a first-class certificate was $1,159; in 1935 it was $523. Salaries of women teachers fell from $1,142 to $443.[20] Many local school boards could not pay even these small sums, and teachers were often forced to accept interest-bearing notes instead of salary. "Information was given of cases where one girl wore the 'dress' to school one day while a sister stayed at home. Next day they alternated, one staying home and one going to school."[21] The provincial government was forced to waive, temporarily, the requirement that school children pay $2 to take the annual provincial examinations, as many parents could not afford this petty sum.

The Ford car has become a horse-drawn vehicle. The rural telephone system is breaking down with the staggering losses in the number of subscribers every year. Farm products (where there have been crops) supply an ever larger part of the farm diet. Farm clothing constitutes a problem of the first magnitude; it has been estimated recently that it would take $30,000,000 to restore the clothing of the rural population of Saskatchewan to pre-depression standards. The unrepaired houses aggravate a fuel problem which has always been acute on the prairie plains where no wood is available. . . . The total arrears in rural taxes at the end of 1932 was almost equal to two years taxes on every acre of farm land in Saskatchewan. . . . Less than 40 per cent of rural schools were open for the full year in 1932. . . . A considerable number of rural schools close for some months during the winter because (*a*) the school district can not afford to buy coal; (*b*) children have not sufficient clothes to go to school.[22]

One Saskatchewan farm youth depicts the effects of the torturous drought years.

The first calamity which we suffered was drought. It was a long torturous summer. Our grain, grass, fruit trees, and garden were all
burned to the ground, leaving no feed for the horses, cows, and hogs,
plus the fact that it left no fruit or vegetables to provide us for the long
winter. We managed somehow for the first year, since it was the first
time we'd ever had such an experience. We mended our old clothes,
and resoled our shoes. We managed to buy food for ourselves and the
stock and to pay the doctor and the dentist and the veterinary bill. It
meant going without anything that wasn't absolutely necessary, and the
first year we felt like experts. We never doubted for a minute that when
next year came things would be better.

The following spring promised to be a good year, and optimists and
gamblers that all farmers must be, they got seed on credit, and everyone
worked hard and planted his crops. Things seemed to be working out
again for all of us. People became a little more dependent on each
other, using one plough because each couldn't afford repairs. People
became closer because they had common experiences. Again the summer months became intensely hot and people were fearing what might
happen. Then about noon one day everything became black. At first
we couldn't imagine what was happening. Dust was sifting through the
open doors and windows. Our priceless seeds were gradually being
blown from the soil. I shall never forget that night as we sat silently
eating our supper. It was happening to us again! Soon we would have
no garden left. By this time we really had no money. Our only thread
of life was our cows. There was enough grass and pasture that they
could eat, and we sold cream for almost nothing, and had those wonderful cream checks. . . .

We got through that winter somehow. We had to be on relief. I guess
lots of city people thought that we were a shiftless lot. . . .

In the spring the people again renewed their hope. We thought there
could never, never be another winter like that. Again the spring seemed
a bewitching promise. It was after this one that I came to loathe the
springs. They were so deceptive, and I became a realist about the seasons; preferring the harvest to all because then you knew if it was
good or bad, and whether or not you were going to eat and be warm
and have enough clothes to go to school.[23]

The complete breakdown of the provincial economy forced a
migration from the drought-devastated areas. Farms in southern
and central Saskatchewan were abandoned. Many families moved
to the northern fringe of the province where unbroken bushland
was available for homesteads. The soil was much poorer than in
the south, but at least it rained in the north. Between 1930 and
1938 over 45,000 persons moved to this northern frontier.[24] They

had given up their farms to move to a land where they had to clear much of the forest and build new homes, roads, hospitals, and schools. Until the war prosperity of the 'forties, many of the settlers were dependent on government relief, for it took years to clear the land and raise a paying crop.

The hardships they faced can be seen from the following extracts from the diary of the Rev. A. M. Nicholson, then a United Church minister in the north:

Thursday, March 28, 1935

Drove from Carragana to Bell's Hill. R—— offered to send one of the family to a neighbor's and let us have the bed. . . . They had no hay or oats for our team. . . . They apologized for their food—moose meat, white bread, tea without sugar or milk. They had no fruit, butter or potatoes.

Friday, March 29

. . . They had gone to the neighbors for additional food supplies and we had potatoes, butter and a pie as "extras" for breakfast. . . . Supper with S—— M——. Bread, butter, tea (cream and sugar); no meat, fruit or syrup. It is hard for bachelors to get adequate relief, he complained. . . . We went to J—— R——'s for the night. J—— and the man who is "batching" with him slept on the floor while F—— and I had the only bed in the shack. They had a cup of tea and bread without butter before we went to bed.

Saturday, March 30

. . . J—— had hot cakes for us for breakfast with syrup he made from white sugar and water. He had a drink made from roasted wheat which we called "Bennett Coffee." We had dinner at K——'s, tea, bread, and corn syrup. Relief allowances were always so low that food was very scarce at the end of the month, they complained. We went to E—— T——'s for the night. I had known E—— when I taught school at Davidson 15 years before. Dry years drove him north. He had a small 2-roomed log house.

Sunday, March 31

What poverty! Their tea kettle sprung a leak last Fall and the trouble with the relief system, said F——, was that it assumed that people never required a new lamp chimney, tea kettle or wash basin. For five years they had been seeing one utensil or implement after another wear out without being able to replace it.

Mr. and Mrs. J—— P—— kept us for the night. J—— homesteaded near Strasburg about 30 years ago. He put up good buildings—later bought another quarter on which he paid $2,000 cash. Finally he lost the

half [section—360 acres] because he could not meet his payments. Mrs. P——— in her early fifties is almost blind because she cannot get the necessary medical care for her eyes.[25]

Saskatchewan lost about 155,000 people to other parts of Canada and foreign countries.[26] While the population of Canada increased 1,140,000 from 1931 to 1941, that of Saskatchewan dropped from 921,785 to 895,992. The remainder of the decline is derived by adding the natural increase of births over deaths for that period. Within one decade, at least one-fifth of the people were forced to leave their homes in order to obtain a livelihood.

The drought cycle ended in Saskatchewan in 1939, coinciding with the end of the world-wide depression and the outbreak of the Second World War. The depression in wheat prices did not, however, end until 1943, as the war cut off some of Canada's export markets. The price of wheat per bushel was 54 cents in 1939, 53 cents in 1940, 53 cents in 1941, and 69 cents in 1942.[27] These were years of revival for the farmers, however, as they could at least eat well and begin to rehabilitate their farms.

The war years after 1942 brought abundant crops and higher prices for farmers. The year in which the C.C.F. took office, 1944, was also the year of the highest farm income in Saskatchewan history; the gross income per farm was $4,516. Much of the increased income of the 'forties has been used to rehabilitate the farms. Estimates of the effects of the depression on farm machinery alone indicate that there will be an annual expenditure of $25,000,000 for many years to replace worn-out machinery.[28] Payment of debts and taxes accumulated during the depression is only now ending.

Saskatchewan is riding the crest of the economic and climatic cycles, but it is still thinking in terms of the 'thirties. As one interviews the residents of rural Saskatchewan today, one cannot help being impressed by their ever-present fear that prosperity will not last, that a new drought or depression will set them back again. At farmers' conventions, at "bull sessions" in the local stores, the discussion always turns to the control of wheat prices, to crop insurance, and to the politicians who are believed to have power to prevent another catastrophe.

Chapter VI

THE MOVEMENT GROWS
TO POWER

T HE YEAR 1932 saw the Saskatchewan farmers and the socialist movement united in a national attempt to establish socialism in Canada. Joining with other groups in the rest of Canada did not greatly affect the Saskatchewan movement beyond giving it a base from which to take part in national elections. The Saskatchewan group called itself the Farmer-Labor Group, and did not officially adopt the name Coöperative Commonwealth Federation for provincial usage until 1935. The new C.C.F. was to remain essentially a federation of provincial parties, each of which had its own approach to socialism and politics and did not interfere with the activities of other provincial sections.

The creation of a mass socialist party in Saskatchewan was not, therefore, the local extension of a new national movement but, rather, an endemic movement having its roots in Saskatchewan. A small group of convinced socialists in key positions in the farmers' movement prompted action in the face of the double catastrophe of depression and drought. These socialists attempted to use this opportune moment to make a drastic change in the thinking and organized actions of farmers and workers. They hoped to build

a radical socialist party that would completely change the social and economic structure of Canada.

The early radical promotion group, many of whom had socialist ideas as a result of earlier experiences in other socialist movements or because of intellectual contact with socialist ideas, was only a small segment of the new party. These socialists, however, gained an influence that was out of proportion to their numerical strength in the new Farmer-Labor Group because of the obvious failure of other attempted solutions to the farmers' economic problems, especially the efforts at economic coöperation and political pressure on old party governments. This suggests that proposals for radical change tend to get a hearing only after the more moderate possibilities have been exhausted. Radical reformers who believe that they can get people "rationally" to reject efforts at moderate and ameliorative reform without trying them succeed only in isolating themselves from any influence in the later development of a movement, as the experience of American socialism well demonstrates. Men like E. A. Partridge, George Williams, and M. J. Coldwell were able to retain their influence with the agrarians because they had participated actively in the earlier nonsocialist efforts, even though they were confident that socialism was the long-term solution to the farmers' problems.

The willingness of agrarian activists in the U.F.C. to place themselves under the command of the socialists, who appeared to have a new and workable answer to their problems, can be seen in the selection, by the joint convention of the U.F.C. and the I.L.P. in 1932, of M. J. Coldwell, the leader of the urban socialists, as the provincial leader of the new Farmer-Labor Group. The socialist leaders of the new party also succeeded in getting the movement to accept their proposals on most questions of policy and ideology. The convention of 1932 instructed the Saskatchewan delegates to the "New Party" national conference in Calgary to vote for "Socialist Party of Canada" as the name of the national party. The predominantly rural delegates voted down all objections to the word "socialist."[1] The position of the socialist leaders was stated by George Williams, the foremost rural socialist in the party. "The history of socialist groups elsewhere showed that, where an effort was made to camouflage under a vote-catching label, disaster followed. The Labor Party [of England] had striven

---

[1] For notes to chapter vi see pages 296–298.

for power and neglected socialist education. They gained power, but when the crisis came, the people in their ignorance elected a Conservative government."²

The new party advocated socialization of all private industries in Canada. This applied to land as well, since the U.F.C., under the impact of the depression, advocated a form of land nationalization in which the state would hold title to the land and the farmers would be given a use-lease title. This appealed to many agrarians as a means of preventing foreclosures by banks and mortgage companies, and it satisfied the socialists' desire for government ownership.

The U.F.C. and the I.L.P., working together as the Farmer-Labor Group, began an intensive campaign to win the next election, which legally had to be called by 1934. The U.F.C. was in charge of the work in rural areas, while the I.L.P. campaigned in the towns and cities. The joint provincial organization was controlled by a board of seven representatives from each organization and seven elected at the annual joint conventions of the two groups. It was difficult to raise money for an active campaign in a province as poverty-stricken as Saskatchewan, but the party depended upon active support from local farm leaders who could campaign during the slack seasons. Speakers and organizers preached the gospel of a new social order. The opposition did not take the new party seriously at first; but as the party succeeded in holding large meetings and constituency nominating conventions, the old parties turned a large part of their fire against the socialists.

The most vulnerable plank in the program of the party was its sponsorship of socialization of land. Both Liberals and Conservatives concentrated on making farmers believe that the new party would take away their land and set up state farms similar to those in the Soviet Union. As a Liberal speaker declared, "The C.C.F. debt policy means surrender of the Torrens title ... and you are not going to get it back.... You will have your land only as long as you are a good socialist.... If you do not agree with the state you are in a position where the state will dictate to you. Once in power the C.C.F. will socialize everything and not wait for votes."³

The U.F.C. and the I.L.P. were repeatedly attacked as communistic and revolutionary and were forced to dissociate themselves from Russia and the Communists. They bitterly fought

this campaign of insinuation. Frank Eliason, the secretary of the U.F.C., wrote to the editor of the Regina *Leader-Post* in September, 1931.

> You, sir, either know or you do not know that there is no connection between the Soviet Union and the U.F.C. If you know there is no connection, the paragraph [in a previous issue] is not only a base insinuation, but is a deliberate untruth uttered in an effort to discredit the U.F.C. . . .
>
> So far from the U.F.C. being under the influence of Moscow, as you suggest, prior to the issue of your editorial we had prepared a severe criticism of Communism. . . . The only kind of revolution the U.F.C. stands for is a revolution by constitutional means, viz., the use of the ballot.[4]

The opposition used every available method to defeat the new party. The Regina public school board, controlled by local business and professional men, ordered M. J. Coldwell, who was then a principal of a Regina school, to withdraw from politics or be discharged. This was a serious threat, since Coldwell had an invalid wife. Coldwell refused to give up his political rights as a citizen and was discharged by the board.

The two old parties, all the daily newspapers of the province, and most of the weeklies circulating among farmers made repeated attacks on socialism and the new party. They tried continually to drive a wedge between the farmers' demands for economic changes and their desires to retain control of their farms.[5] The Liberal Party, which was the opposition party provincially and federally, campaigned as a progressive, nonsocialist reform party that would give farmers what they wanted—higher farm prices, increased relief, and protection against foreclosures—without threatening their position as landowners.

The Catholic Church joined in the attack. A letter read in all Catholic pulpits in the province just before the election of 1934 clearly repudiated socialism.

> Catholics will be guided by the words of Pius XI, "Whether Socialism be considered a doctrine, or as a historical movement, if it really remains socialism, it can not be brought into harmony with the dogmas of the Catholic Church . . . the reason being that it conceives human society in a way utterly alien to Christian truth . . . the hierarchy of Canada has recently issued a collective warning that Catholics of this country be ever on their guard."[6]

Various Catholic priests throughout the province publicly attacked the C.C.F. both inside and outside their pulpits.[7] Members of the party among students at Notre Dame College at Wilcox, Saskatchewan, were told they must resign either from the school or from the C.C.F.[8]

Though opposition to the C.C.F. was great, the leaders of the party firmly believed that they would win the election and convert the province to socialism. They were convinced that the desperate economic conditions in the province had destroyed all faith in the old order. On election day, in June, 1934, the C.C.F. received 103,582 votes, almost 25 per cent of the total. The triumphant Liberals obtained 206,191; the Conservatives, who had previously formed the government, fell to 114,973. In spite of finishing third in the popular vote, the C.C.F. became the official opposition in the legislature, because the Tories failed to win a single constituency, whereas the C.C.F. won five.[9]

In rural districts the C.C.F. won almost 30 per cent of the vote, and was a close second to the victorious Liberals.[10] Many predominantly rural constituencies were lost because of the overwhelming vote for the old parties in small towns and villages. The large rural vote polled by a new party advocating socialism and state ownership of land is an indication of the effect of the depression and drought on the farmers of Saskatchewan. This vote was achieved by a party that had little funds, no regular press, no representatives in the legislature, and the opposition of two powerful and experienced party machines, as well as the Catholic Church, all the daily newspapers, and almost the entire urban middle class.

To the C.C.F. leaders, however, both agrarian and socialist alike, the election was a great defeat. They had been sure that they would win and form the first socialist government in Canada. Some of the leaders were so overwhelmed by what they considered a repudiation by the electorate that they seriously thought of abandoning politics. The agrarian leaders in the executive of the U.F.C. began to consider withdrawing from the C.C.F. and resuming their original role of a farmers' pressure group which attempted to influence all parties on the farmers' behalf.

Before the Saskatchewan C.C.F. could assess its position, it was thrown into the federal elections of 1935, the first national election that it contested. The national party was much weaker than the

Saskatchewan organization. With the exception of British Columbia and Alberta, the new party had little strength in the rest of Canada. The Trades and Labor Congress (A. F. of L.) opposed it, and it therefore had little urban support outside the old socialist strongholds of Winnipeg and Vancouver. The party was obviously not a realistic alternative to the incumbent Conservatives, and faced the traditional danger to third-party movements on this continent—the fear of would-be supporters of wasting their vote by voting for a hopeless candidate.

The situation was further complicated on the prairies by the appearance of the Social Credit Party. The Social Crediters, under William Aberhart, swept the Alberta provincial elections early in 1935 and then proceeded to organize in other provinces.[11] They had been able to make more headway than the C.C.F. because their reform program did not involve socialization. The Social Credit promise of $25 a month to every person and the abolition of interest on debts appealed to many impoverished farmers, and the threat of losing their land was not involved.

In Saskatchewan as well as in Alberta, many C.C.F. agrarian supporters and some party leaders were attracted to the electorally more successful Social Credit movement. Like the C.C.F., the Social Credit Party was opposed to eastern financial control and favored immediate action to save farms from foreclosures. Local Social Credit associations were formed throughout Saskatchewan, and in many areas, especially those close to Alberta, C.C.F. organizations joined the Social Credit movement.

A movement developed, both within and without the C.C.F., for unity between the two third-party western protest groups. The nonsocialist agrarian leaders in the C.C.F., who had accepted the leadership of the socialists in 1931 and 1932, did not recognize the existence of any important differences between the two movements. They viewed both as fighting the "interests," as being against the Grain Exchange and other traditional enemies of the farmers. In two Saskatchewan federal constituency organizations the unity movement resulted in the nomination of joint candidates by the C.C.F. and Social Credit parties.

A rift developed within the party as the socialists in the C.C.F. bitterly opposed the movement to merge with Social Credit. They believed that Social Credit was a "reformist capitalist" party, and that more far-reaching changes were necessary to create a stable

society. Various leaders of the party, such as "Jake" Benson, an agrarian progressive who had never accepted socialism, were expelled for coöperating with the Social Credit Party. The point of view of the socialists is expressed in an extract from a letter by Tom Johnson, a party leader, to the C.C.F. executive.

I am firmly convinced that our future strength depends upon the organization repudiating any candidate that departs from our principles in the hope that by doing so he may get elected at this time. Compromise will mean ultimate defeat. We have told the people that socialism is the only way out. Any departure from that position would brand us as a party that wants to get office and will grasp at any straw.[12]

The 1935 election in Saskatchewan resulted in a greater defeat for the C.C.F. than that of 1934. The party elected only two members of Parliament from the twenty-one seats in the province. One of the victorious C.C.F. candidates had been endorsed also by Social Credit. The total strength of the C.C.F. declined from 25 per cent in the provincial election of 1934 to 19 per cent in 1935. Social Credit took away much of the socialist support in western Saskatchewan, and received a slightly higher provincial vote than the C.C.F. The total vote of the two third parties was, however, 39 per cent—larger than that of either of the old parties.[13]

Rural Saskatchewan was beginning to make a definite break with the two old parties. In the rural areas close to half of the total vote went to parties favoring economic change beyond the program of the Liberals and the Conservatives. The 1935 vote and the unity movement within the C.C.F. indicate that the protesting farmers had not become socialists. They were ready, however, to support radical economic innovations. Some of them wanted to try the solution of Social Credit, as they earlier had tried coöperation and the Progressive Party. Here again is evident the characteristic fumbling of the western farmers as they turn to different ways of solving their economic problems.

The defeat of 1935, coming on the heels of that of the year before, had a drastic effect on both agrarian and socialist leaders of the Saskatchewan C.C.F. True to the traditional reformer's weakness, they had been counting too heavily on the rational persuasiveness of their cause. They believed that socialism was the correct solution to the social and economic problems of the day and that, if it were honestly presented to the people, it would be accepted. Previous Saskatchewan reform movements, such as the

Progressive Party and the Wheat Pool, had succeeded in winning majority support in a few years. It galled the C.C.F. leaders that the "opportunistic, reformist" Social Credit Party could so easily upset the young socialist movement. They had been psychologically unprepared for rejection by the people whom they were trying to help.

The party leaders concluded from the setback that they were overvaluing the political realism of the common man. Since the farmers were apparently not yet ready to support a complete socialist program, a definite choice had to be made: Should the C.C.F. continue as an independent socialist party preaching that socialism is the only hope for a decent society, until the pressure of events brought the majority over to them? Or should the party compromise its program by modifying its radicalism in order to win an electoral majority for a program of immediate reforms that would put the party in power?

Faced with these alternatives, even the veteran socialist leaders of the Saskatchewan C.C.F. chose the path of compromise. Accordingly, the 1936 convention adopted a new provincial program that contained no mention of socialism and dropped completely the plank calling for nationalization of land.[14] It also reversed its previous policy on coöperation with other political groups by adopting the following resolution:

Whereas we believe that a victory for democracy and progress can only be won by the coöperation of the various progressive political organizations of Saskatchewan, and

Whereas it is most desirable that the initiative to secure this unity should be taken by the C.C.F.,

Be it resolved that this convention urge upon the Provincial Council the advisability of issuing a call to all progressive organizations, political, cultural and economic to meet in convention to seek to discover common ground upon which we may unite for action and a common goal to which we may unitedly move.[15]

The earlier agrarian emphasis on immediate reforms to alleviate the consequences of the economic constraints on farmers had again won out. George Williams, former U.F.C. president, who had become provincial leader of the party in 1935 after M. J. Coldwell was elected to the federal House of Commons at Ottawa, together with the other agrarian and socialist leaders of the party, drastically changed their policy to one of uniting with Social Credit

and "progressive" Conservatives against the incumbent Liberals and "eastern interests," even if it meant dropping socialism temporarily.

M. J. Coldwell was the only prominent Saskatchewan leader who vigorously opposed the swing in policy. He was joined in his opposition by J. S. Woodsworth, the national leader of the C.C.F., the foremost socialist in Canada. Woodsworth told the Saskatchewan convention in July, 1936, in no uncertain terms, that his socialism and Social Credit did not mix: "Social Credit stands for capitalism. I am a socialist and I'm not going to enter into political alliances with those who uphold capitalism."[16]

It is highly significant, therefore, that the proposal to reverse C.C.F. policy and unite with other "progressive" parties met very little opposition from the convention delegates. Only 8 votes out of a total of 312 were cast against the unity resolution.[17] The agrarian reform tendencies in the Saskatchewan farmers' movement had overwhelmed the original hopes of the small socialist promotion group. The farm leaders wanted immediate economic action and political power, and did not care whether or not the goal was socialism.

The Saskatchewan C.C.F. was the only provincial section of the national party to modify its socialist policies significantly at this time and to favor political alignments with other parties.[18] This was a consequence of two factors. (1) With the exception of the old Marxian British Columbia section, the Saskatchewan party was the only division of the C.C.F. that had hopes of gaining political power within a short period of time. The other sections were small minority parties with little mass support. There was, therefore, very little pressure on these organizations to engage in practical politics. They could afford to be "pure," as they had no vested political position to lose. (2) The Saskatchewan C.C.F. had fewer doctrinaire old socialists in proportion to its total membership than other sections of the party. In every other province the party was led by men who had been in small, isolated socialist parties for years before the C.C.F. was organized and who were, therefore, comparatively unaffected by a new defeat. In fact, for those old socialists, such as Woodsworth, the establishment of a national party, which received 10 per cent of the national vote, was a major socialist victory, not a defeat, and did not necessitate political compromise.

The subsequent national convention of the C.C.F. in 1937 defeated efforts to get the party to form alliances with other groups. Saskatchewan, however, was permitted to continue its independent course of favoring coalitions, because of the C.C.F. principle of provincial autonomy. Between 1936 and 1938 the Saskatchewan C.C.F. entered into repeated negotiations with all the provincial parties opposed to the Liberals, that is, Social Credit, Communist, and Conservative. Repeated efforts were made to secure a real coalition that would sweep the Liberal government out of power and replace it by a "progressive" administration pledged to help the farmers.

In 1937 the C.C.F. provincial executive sent greetings to the Social Credit convention: "Through the medium of this message of greetings, the Saskatchewan C.C.F. desires to extend to your organization an invitation to meet a committee from the Saskatchewan C.C.F. to canvass the possibility of coöperation, in order to prevent the forces of reaction again sweeping Saskatchewan by splitting the reform vote."[19] The Social Credit organization, which was under the influence of Premier William Aberhart of Alberta, refused to consider a coalition because of the bitter attacks on the Alberta government which the Alberta C.C.F. was continually making.

The C.C.F. also attempted to secure an alliance with the provincial Conservative Party, which as an opposition party had adopted a reform program. The *New Era,* the organ of the Saskatchewan C.C.F., in defending such an alliance even went so far as to comment:

But, says the *Leader-Post* [leading Liberal daily], the mixture is a little strange. What of those Conservatives who denounce the C.C.F. and all its policies!

We might say in reply that there are no such Conservatives. The western Conservatives who are opposed to a farmers' wheat board and a marketing act are very scarce. The Conservatives who oppose electoral reform as embodied in proportional representation and the single transferable ballot are scarcer still. The Conservatives who would sooner see our present reactionary government retain power than the election of one of a more progressive nature are non-existent. . . . Our Liberal Government has become a reactionary Tory organization and most of the Conservatives have gone far to the Left.

. . . It is quite clear that consideration of ways and means to split the progressive vote has occupied the attention of the Liberal Board of

Strategy. Perhaps the Weyburn nomination [a joint C.C.F.–Conservative candidate] is an indication of the reply that can be expected to the forces of reaction.[20]

These statements indicate the effect of coalition tactics on a radical party. The participants in any coalition are obliged to defend one another. The Saskatchewan C.C.F., which was organized under the Conservative government of J. T. M. Anderson, was now forced to say that Anderson and his party, which the C.C.F. had castigated as a business-controlled party, were progressives. The Alberta C.C.F., which was attacking the Social Credit government in that province as a fraudulent reform administration that did not actually fight big business, found the ground removed from beneath it by the alliances of the Saskatchewan party.[21] The whole purpose and program of the C.C.F. had therefore changed. It could no longer carry on a systematic attack on capitalism and all its institutions. The party had become a farmers' pressure group seeking to win agrarian reforms.

C.C.F. efforts to secure coöperation among the opposition parties floundered in the sea of competitive politics. The local organizations of the opposition parties found it difficult to agree on which party should get the nomination. Actually, no over-all agreement was reached with any other party. However, in a large number of constituencies one or another of the parties made no nomination, but simply supported the group that did. The C.C.F. contested only 30 seats out of the 52 in the province, the Social Crediters ran candidates in 41 constituencies, and the Conservatives nominated 25. In six districts, unity candidates backed by two or more parties ran.

As the C.C.F. moved away from orthodox socialist principles and tactics, it ceased being the butt of vigorous attack from all sides. The opposition forces concentrated their main fire on the Liberal government. The former Conservative Premier of the province, J. T. M. Anderson, in an appeal for C.C.F. support in areas where it was not running its own candidates, went so far in 1938 as to repeat the contention of the C.C.F. *New Era,* that the C.C.F. program and the Tory one were similar. Appealing to the supporters of the C.C.F., he stated, "Every plank in the C.C.F. platform is ours and there is no reason why the members of the [C.C.F.] party can not conscientiously support us in this effort to rid the province of a discredited administration."[22]

The Liberals, on the other hand, concentrated their fire on the Social Crediters, who had polled the largest vote of the opposition parties in 1935 and were contesting the most seats. Of the Liberal propaganda attacking the other parties in the election of 1938, ten pamphlets were directed against the Social Credit Party, two against the C.C.F., and none against the Conservatives.[23] The Catholic Church had apparently lost its fear of the consequences of C.C.F. victory, for there is little evidence of continued overt opposition to the C.C.F. from the Saskatchewan hierarchy.[24]

The election results gratified the C.C.F. as much as the earlier ones had depressed it. The party won eleven out of the thirty seats which it contested, and received 11,000 more votes than Social Credit, though it ran in eleven fewer constituencies. In fact, Social Credit succeeded in electing only two candidates, while two unity candidates supported by all three opposition parties were also elected.[25]

Again, the C.C.F. leaders had guessed wrong. They had feared that the Social Crediters, supported by their Alberta party, would become the largest opposition party in the legislature. The Social Crediters apparently lost their appeal to the Saskatchewan agrarians as a result of the failures of the Alberta government to fulfill its original promises of $25 a month and the cancellation of all interest. Social Credit had had three years of power in Alberta and had done little in the way of reform.[26] The continuing depression and drought, the weakness of the Social Credit government, and the fact that the scare propaganda against the C.C.F. disappeared, all enabled the C.C.F. to grow, in spite of the pessimism of its leaders.

The C.C.F. was now the leading opposition party in Saskatchewan. The Conservatives for the second time had failed to elect a single representative and could therefore be ruled out as a major factor in Saskatchewan politics. Social Credit had finished a bad third in the election and its provincial organization soon disintegrated, with many of its supporters going over to the more successful C.C.F.

The C.C.F. strength in 1938 brought about almost as complete a reversal in policy and tactics as had resulted from C.C.F. weakness in the elections of 1934 and 1935. Many leaders of the party felt that they had made a mistake in compromising with the other opposition parties. Actually, the period before the election, 1937–

1938, had been the worst years of the 'thirties, as virtually the entire province suffered from drought in 1937. The average crop yield was under three bushels an acre, and two-thirds of the farm population received relief during this period. (See chap. v, p. 94.) The farmers were restless and bitter over the low relief allotments and, as the 1938 election revealed, actually moved left again. But so preoccupied were the C.C.F. leaders with efforts at unity and removal of the stigma of radicalism that they failed to sense the renewed readiness for a more radical program.

But immediately after the elections of 1938, the party plunged into an organizing drive, looking forward to the 1940 federal elections. They refused all offers of unity with other "progressive" opposition groups. The party leaders had learned their lesson. This time it was to be a C.C.F. government or nothing. The basis for this policy was made clear in a letter of May 29, 1939, from George Williams, the provincial leader, to a member who had urged continuation of the unity program.

. . . a few years ago we had a Saskatchewan Provincial Convention mandate to coöperate with other Progressive groups. We tried that and no one can say that we did not sincerely do our best to make it work. The results were not only disappointing but even possibly disastrous. It being now admitted that had we gone our own way with a full slate, . . . we might now be the government.

The 1939 provincial convention ratified with little opposition the new change in policy, as set forth in the following resolution:

Resolved that this Convention reiterates its faith in the C.C.F. platform, the C.C.F. organization and in the ultimate victory of the C.C.F., and instructs its officers and members to do everything within their power to ensure that C.C.F. candidates contest every election and by-election in order to elect a C.C.F. government for Saskatchewan and a C.C.F. government for Canada.[27]

This reaffirmation of independent action did not include a revival of the earlier doctrinaire socialism in the C.C.F. platform. Rather, it represented the recognition by its leaders that the party had become the sole voice of agrarian protest in the province and therefore did not have to compromise with other opposition groups. C.C.F. leaders adhered to the views, formed after the election defeats of 1934 and 1935, that emphasis on socialist principles does not win elections. In the sober light of experience it

seemed wiser to eliminate issues and symbols likely to antagonize the voters. As George Williams stated this conclusion, "I believe the growing popularity [of the Saskatchewan C.C.F.] . . . is caused by the policy we have adopted. We have purposely and painstakingly avoided theoretical discussion and we have addressed ourselves to the task of offering worthwhile and practical suggestions as to the solution or alleviation of current problems."[28]

Before the Saskatchewan C.C.F. could reorganize to take advantage of its new, powerful position, the outbreak of the Second World War disrupted the unity of the party. Nationally, the C.C.F. had from the beginning favored an antiwar, neutral policy for Canada. The national leader, J. S. Woodsworth, was a convinced pacifist who had vigorously opposed the First World War. Upon the outbreak of war in 1939 the C.C.F. movement split into three groups on the war question: one minority, following Woodsworth, was opposed to Canadian entry into what it considered to be an imperialist war; a second even smaller minority favored all-out support of the war; the majority of the party's national leaders backed the position of M. J. Coldwell in supporting Canada's declaration of war but opposing the sending of troops overseas.[29]

The National Council of the C.C.F. voted in September, 1939, to support Coldwell's position. All the C.C.F. members of the federal House of Commons, except J. S. Woodsworth, voted for war. Woodsworth, though the national leader, received the permission of the party to cast a personal vote against the war.[30]

In Saskatchewan the same three-way split occurred. The majority of the Provincial Council voted in favor of the Coldwell middle-of-the-road position. It adopted a compromise program of immediate domestic demands, which neither supported nor opposed the war. Members of the party were left free to take any position they desired.[31]

A federal election was called early in 1940. The strength of the C.C.F. appeared at a low ebb because of its dissension over the war question. During the campaign, some members of the Saskatchewan C.C.F. ran on an antiwar platform, some on an all-out support of the war, and still others on the party program of economic but not military aid to the Allies.

The election results were surprisingly favorable to the Saskatchewan C.C.F., for it elected five members of Parliament out of a possible twenty-one members in the province. This represented a

gain of three seats from the previous election in 1935. Outside Saskatchewan the C.C.F. succeeded in winning only two constituencies. In the fifteen Saskatchewan seats, which were predominantly rural, the party received 101,450 votes, compared with 104,441 votes for the Liberals.[32] This meant that the C.C.F. was the first party among the agrarians, as the vote included small towns and villages that were overwhelmingly opposed to the C.C.F.

The C.C.F. was again definitely on the upswing as the party of rural Saskatchewan. Economic conditions in the province were beginning to improve, as the disastrous drought of 1930–1939 had ended, but the price of wheat remained very low, being 54 cents a bushel in 1939, and 53 cents in 1940.[33] The C.C.F. was the major Saskatchewan opposition party fighting for higher wheat prices, while the incumbent Liberals were blamed for the continuation of low prices. The farmers were being squeezed by the rising costs of manufactured products. To them, the fact that the C.C.F. was fighting the economic battle of agriculture in Parliament and in the legislature was evidently more important than the party's confusion on the war question.

The years 1940–1941 proved to be a turning point in the fortunes of the C.C.F. Again, the fight for higher wheat prices was responsible. Economic conditions were continuing on a depression level in Saskatchewan, although prosperity was returning to the rest of Canada. The fall of western Europe to the Germans had destroyed the European wheat market and resulted in a continuation of low wheat prices. In response to these conditions, the Wheat Pool committees demanded that a Saskatchewan delegation be sent to Ottawa to seek higher prices; 185,000 signatures and $40,000 were collected to support the delegation. Many farmers who had previously supported the Liberal Party took part in the campaign, including old W. R. Motherwell, the first president of the Saskatchewan Grain Growers' Association and a former Liberal Minister of Agriculture in the national government.[34] The C.C.F. was, however, the only political party to give all-out support to the farmers' demands. As a result of the campaign, the federal Liberal government agreed to raise the price of wheat to 90 cents a bushel— as against $1 a bushel, which was demanded by the Wheat Pool and the C.C.F.[35] In the course of the struggle the C.C.F. actually doubled its membership, although, with no election pending, membership figures could normally be expected to decline.[36]

The year 1941 also witnessed change in the leadership of the provincial party—the third since 1932. Increasing resentment had developed within the party against George Williams, who had led it since 1935. Williams had antagonized many in the party by his attempts to extend his control over all facets of party activity.[37] He had assumed the positions of party legislative leader, president of the provincial organization, director of the party newspaper, and head of the party's organizational and office staff. Many felt that Williams was ambitious for power, and that he had deliberately attempted to eliminate prospective rivals from influence in the party. An attempt was made in 1940 to defeat him as provincial president, but it failed. Shortly thereafter, Williams enlisted in the army. At the 1941 convention, T. C. Douglas, a C.C.F. member of Parliament, was elected provincial president over a candidate endorsed by Williams.

Douglas was a Baptist minister, who had first been elected to Parliament in 1935 from Weyburn. He had been one of the early members of the Saskatchewan I.L.P. He was by far the best and most popular orator in the party. Many of the provincial leaders who sponsored his election believed that Douglas' popularity and oratorical ability could unify the party and give it a leader acceptable to all groups in the province. His skill as a public speaker was no small advantage in an agricultural community where public debate is popular and campaign meetings are well attended.

The C.C.F. was now firmly convinced that it was on the road to power. In 1942 Saskatchewan had the largest wheat crop in history. Prices, though still considered low by the farmers, were higher than in previous years as a result of the Wheat Pool campaign. The farmers strongly resented the provincial and federal Liberal governments, which held down the price of wheat and symbolized the terrible depression years. Money began to pour into the C.C.F. treasury, and the party was able to put paid organizers into almost every constituency in the province and to start a weekly newspaper. The membership grew rapidly. Many prominent individuals in the farm and labor government who had shied away from identification with the C.C.F. when it was a struggling young radical movement now climbed on the band wagon, seeking party nominations. Local politicians, officials of the Teachers' Federation, Wheat Pool employees, and trade-union leaders openly identified themselves with the party; and some became candidates.[38]

Nationally, the C.C.F. had lagged behind its Saskatchewan Section. In the federal election of 1940 it had elected only two members of Parliament outside Saskatchewan and received about 9 per cent of the popular vote. The Canadian Gallup Poll indicated that national party support remained constant for the first three years of the war, until 1942.[89] Outside Saskatchewan, the party had stagnated in terms of popular vote from 1932 to 1942.

Suddenly, in 1942, the C.C.F. began to grow rapidly in all parts of the country. It won a series of federal and provincial by-elections, and in August, 1943, won a major triumph in Ontario, gaining 34 of the 90 seats in the legislature, compared to none in the previous election. The Gallup Poll indicated that C.C.F. support rose from 8 per cent in the beginning of 1942 to 29 per cent in September, 1943.[40] Party membership also increased greatly, from less than 20,000 in 1942 to about 100,000 in 1944.[41]

It is difficult to explain this dramatic rise in the fortunes of the national party. The factors involved relate mainly to the end of the depression and the war. (1) Canadian unions doubled in membership from 1939 to 1943. The Canadian Congress of Labor (C.I.O. in Canada) was founded in 1940, and many of its new unions were led by members of the C.C.F. The Ontario victory in 1943 was in large degree a result of trade-union leadership. (2) The end of the depression gave many workers and farmers the economic and psychological security to begin to think in long-range terms rather than in immediate, personal ones, and therefore the C.C.F. program of postwar reforms to prevent a new depression could receive support. (3) The rising cost of living and increased taxation created resentment against "war profiteers" and the government, which benefited the C.C.F. since it called for increased controls of profits and prices. (4) Canada had not had any middle way or New Deal reforms during the depression. Because it was dependent on foreign trade, it suffered more from the depression than had countries of greater self-sufficiency. Relief standards were lower than in the United States. The incumbent Liberal government symbolized the deprivations of the 'thirties, and the opposition Tories were a right-wing party. The C.C.F., as the party of reform, was the logical instrument of the desire of many Canadians to obtain the benefits of social security legislation, economic planning, labor legislation, and guaranteed minimum prices for farm products.

The effect of the absence of a reform administration in Canada during the depression can be seen in the significant differences between the responses of Canadians and Americans to the following Gallup Poll question: "After the war, would you like to see many changes or reforms in Canada (the United States), or would you rather have this country remain pretty much the way it was before the war?" In September, 1943, 71 per cent of the Canadians polled favored changes or reforms. The majority specified better employment and working conditions, social security, and "more even distribution of wealth." In the same month, only 32 per cent of the Americans polled favored postwar reforms, and about half of these suggested a return to the era before the New Deal, with tighter controls over trade-unions, less government bureaucracy, reduced taxes, and a free hand for business enterprise."[42] Apparently, the "go slow and muddle through" policy of Mackenzie King resulted in greater support for far-reaching social reform than did the liberal reform program of Roosevelt, which was bitterly opposed by American businessmen and supported by many American socialists and liberals.

The growth of the C.C.F. nationally strengthened the Saskatchewan movement and gave it greater assurance that it was on the eve of forming a provincial government. This point of view was shared by the incumbent Liberals. Under Saskatchewan law, a provincial government has to call an election at least once every five years. An election was due in 1943. The Liberals, fearing defeat, passed a law extending the life of the legislature to 1944, arguing that the war made it inadvisable to hold an election. This excuse only increased the opposition to the government among many nonpartisan people, and strengthened the morale of the C.C.F.

The party leaders tried to make the C.C.F. a broadly based farmer-labor opposition to the government. While maintaining C.C.F. independence of other political groups, they welcomed the adherence to the party of many prominent persons who had not previously supported the movement, and even gave some of them nominations. The weakened Conservatives, who nominated in only half the constituencies in the province, were urged to vote C.C.F. to get rid of the Liberal "machine."[43]

The party realized that its program for the elections would probably be a program of a government, not of an opposition, party.

They therefore appointed research committees to examine realistically the potentialities of the provincial government. The eventual program was based on the need for extended social security and welfare work, educational facilities, farm security legislation, trade-union rights, and minor experiments in socialization. Though still mentioning the goal of socialism or a coöperative commonwealth, the party campaigned primarily as a social reform movement.

As the 1944 elections drew near, it became increasingly clear that the C.C.F. would win the province. Its meetings were large and enthusiastic. The party membership grew to include one out of every twelve voters in the province.⁴⁴ On election day, June 3, 1944, the C.C.F. carried 53 per cent of the voters of Saskatchewan.⁴⁵ After thirteen years of organization, the Saskatchewan C.C.F. took power as the first "socialist" government in the United States or Canada.

The development of a mass socialist movement in Saskatchewan seems to follow more or less logically from previous socioeconomic conditions and a history of agrarian protest. The question may be raised, however, why Alberta and North Dakota—Saskatchewan's neighbors, which have a similar history and social and economic structure—did not develop the same response to the severe predicament of the 'thirties. It is necessary to isolate the significant differences among these three wheat areas which resulted in different patterns of behavior. However, in comparing the political scenes in the three areas, one is struck less with the differences than with the similarities. Each of these governmental units elected agrarian radical governments as a result of the depression. Alberta, in 1935, replaced the old United Farmers of Alberta government, which had been in power since 1921 and proved inept at coping with the depression, by the monetary reform government of the Social Credit Party; while North Dakota returned the agrarian, semisocialist Non-Partisan League to power in 1932.

Social Credit, the N.P.L., and the C.C.F. were like responses to very similar conditions. Each movement represented an attack by western farmers on the economic power of eastern big business and sought to preserve their economic and social status by preventing the foreclosures of farm mortgages. The movements offered the farmers a scapegoat, in the form of external economic constraints, on which to blame their difficulties, and at the same time presented a solution that was "logical" in terms of the historical

experiences of the organized farmers' movement. Nevertheless, there were important differences among them, differences of ideology, tactics, and objectives, which were largely a result of the variations in the historical backgrounds of the areas, and in the men who commanded community leadership.

In Alberta the political option of forming a class-conscious agrarian party out of organized farmers' movements, as the U.F.C. did in Saskatchewan, was almost impossible, since the Alberta equivalent of the U.F.C., the United Farmers of Alberta (U.F.A.), was in power when the depression began. Though the U.F.A. adopted a socialist program in 1933 and affiliated to the C.C.F. nationally, the option of a U.F.A.-C.C.F. government did not represent a new and radical alternative to the people of Alberta. The radical new choice was presented by William Aberhart, a radio evangelist, who became an advocate of the Social Credit doctrine and succeeded in winning the support of the majority of the rural electorate by a combination of religious fervor and economic radicalism.

In North Dakota the radical Non-Partisan League had been out of power during the middle and late 'twenties. It was, therefore, able to make a political comeback as the expression of the discontent of the 'thirties. A description of the political situation in 1934 indicates the political temper of the state during the depression.

Farmer loyalty to William Langer [N.P.L. Governor] . . . is explained by Langer's proclamation, in April, 1933 of a moratorium on the foreclosures of farm and home mortgages . . . the farmers regard it as a *coup d'etat* against Money. The banks, insurance companies, and all other out-of-state creditors are naturally horrified at North Dakota's official attitude toward sanctity of contract. Everyone—borrowers and lenders alike—accepts moratorium as a breach in the walls of capitalism. And the farmers are not disturbed.

Why should we worry about property rights, the farmers ask when you suggest that they are striking at the fundamental economic structure. . . . When your farm is covered with mortgages, your cattle tied up with a barnyard load, your machinery attached by a chattel mortgage, your previous year's taxes unpaid, and your coming crop covered by a seed lien—and then you get no crop—you fail to see just what it is you may lose with the collapse of capitalism.[46]

The Social Credit Party, while attacking the Grain Exchange and eastern financiers, did not propose a fundamental change in

the going capitalist system. It hoped to make capitalism work by nationalizing the banks and pumping new currency into circulation whenever prices fell. The N.P.L. was prepared to socialize much of the industry within North Dakota and to support nationalization of large-scale industry, but its leaders, for electoral reasons, refused to break with the Republican Party. The Saskatchewan C.C.F., therefore, was the only one of the three movements that sought to make fundamental changes in the political and economic structure of the country.

Many of the farmers, however, did not see vital differences in the program and tactics of these movements. In Saskatchewan, farmers, inside and outside the C.C.F., sought to force the party to unite with Social Credit, and it actually did so for two years. In the federal elections of 1935, Social Credit received more votes than did the C.C.F. in Saskatchewan, and carried many districts that had voted C.C.F. the year before. The existence of a strong Social Credit movement in Alberta has completely blocked the growth of the C.C.F. in that province. It has still to carry a single rural constituency in Alberta.

In North Dakota the same confusion of agrarian ideology exists. Norman Thomas, running as the Socialist candidate for president in 1932, received an insignificant number of votes, while the then extremely radical N.P.L. was sweeping the state. Though N.P.L. leadership was aggressively socialist in 1932 and 1934, proposing government ownership of many industries within the state, a N.P.L. congressman, William Lemke, won 13 per cent of the state vote as the Union Party's candidate for president in 1936.[47] The Union Party, which was founded by Father Charles Coughlin, was in many ways the American equivalent of Social Credit, and, like it, was antisocialist and opposed to government planning, but was also against the eastern "financial interests."

Each movement—the Social Credit Party, the C.C.F., the N.P.L., and the Union Party—provided a functional definition of the situation within the cultural framework of the wheat belt. Each interpreted the depression as being caused by eastern "capitalism," "vested interests," or "financiers." Within that framework, however, one could apparently build either a leftist or a rightist ideology. The radicalism and strength of the N.P.L., which remained a faction of the Republican Party, waned after economic prosperity began to return and the farmers received their immedi-

ate economic objectives of a guaranteed parity price and crop insurance from the federal government.⁴⁸ No real basis for a permanent radical movement was created, since the specific socialistic program of the N.P.L. was never integrated into a philosophy that required a new social order and permanent political action. Social Credit became the conservative and antisocialist party, and large sections of it accepted many of the anti-Semitic and semi-Fascist ideas of Major Douglas, the founder of the international movement.⁴⁹ Anti-Semitism—specifically, opposition to Jewish financial interests—could be linked to the opposition of western agrarians to eastern bankers. The myth of the powerful Jewish financiers has also received strong support in North Dakota, where it was propagated by the Coughlinites.⁵⁰ In Saskatchewan, however, the fact that socialists obtained control of the agrarian protest and directed it into a new national socialist party gave farmers a different interpretation of the nucleus of external economic power, though essentially it played the same role of providing an external scapegoat for the personal misfortunes of farmers.

The situation of different ideologies playing the same functional role is not peculiar to the western wheat belt. In Latin America, various ideologies—Peronism, Apristaism, socialism, communism, and old-fashioned military nationalism—win support from the miserably exploited peons. Each of these movements has a different economic and social program, but concentrates its propaganda on attacking external imperialist control as the cause of the poverty of South America. Like the western farmers, the lower classes south of the Rio Grande follow different variants of anti-imperialism as a purported solution of their ills.

Economic determinists may still insist that there is some variable peculiar to the economic structure that creates the variations in the ideological superstructure. This is not so in western Canada, unless one includes chance factors such as the tactics pursued by different persons in comparable situations within a deterministic theory. For example, the reason that Alberta elected a farmers' government in 1921, whereas Saskatchewan did not, appears to lie in the fact that the Alberta provincial election of that year was called after the United Farmers of Alberta had decided in favor of independent political action in the province.

In Saskatchewan the incumbent Liberal government realized that a farmers' party could defeat it, and called the provincial elec-

tion before the Saskatchewan Grain Growers' Association could meet in convention to launch a provincial party. That strength for a farmers' government existed in Saskatchewan as well as in Alberta is indicated by the fact that independent farmers' candidates carried twelve of the thirteen seats for which they ran. This occurred in spite of the fact that each candidate was running independently of any party organization. It seems likely, therefore, that, had the election been held a short time later, Saskatchewan, like Alberta, would have had a farmers' government in the 'twenties. A Saskatchewan farmers' government would have been as helpless before the onslaught of the depression as the Alberta government, and would probably have gone down to a similar disastrous defeat before Social Credit or some comparable new variant of agrarian protest.

Chapter VII

IDEOLOGY AND PROGRAM

T HE IDEAS that guide a new political movement like the C.C.F. are a combination of primitive doctrine, promotional slogans aimed at holding and recruiting members, and the general values of the culture in which it has arisen. These ideas had been accumulated, in part by trial and error, over the thirteen years in which the party emerged into power. The meaning of this C.C.F. socialism can be appraised by studying the changes through which the party ideology passed.

The collectivist reform program of the organized farm movement of Saskatchewan was unified after 1931 under the general heading of "socialism." This did not mean that the agrarian leaders who accepted the term as a description of the kind of economic society for which they were fighting had suddenly adopted a new economic or philosophical doctrine. To many of them the socialist proposals seemed the same as the program that the organized farm movement, especially the U.F.C., had worked out from 1902 to 1930.

In reply to the question "When did you become a socialist?" one old farmer answered:

Why, I've been a socialist all my life, and so were most of the farmers around here. Of course, I didn't know it until after the C.C.F. was

started, and the Liberals began telling us that government marketing of wheat and ownership of the banks and railroads was socialism. Don't let anyone tell you that the farmers aren't socialists. They all are, even those who still vote Liberal. The trouble is that all the propaganda around gives them a wrong idea of what socialism is.[1]

The socialists in the farm movement and the urban Independent Labor Party were able to capture the ideological control of the new Farmer-Labor political movement as a result of the catastrophic depression and drought and the obvious inadequacy of the accepted rural institutions to cope with them. Economic conditions in 1931 and 1932 were desperate, and the militant agrarians of the U.F.C. were not in a mood to quibble over a program or a specific statement as being too radical. They were even willing to call the new party the "Socialist Party of Canada." (See chap. vi, p. 104.) The period up to the elections of 1934 and 1935 was distinctly a radical, agitational stage. The old socialists would brook little compromise and secured the acceptance of a program calling for a completely socialized society, including the ownership of land.

When campaigning for the new party in 1933–1934, however, the leaders soon found that to many people the word "socialism" had unfortunate connotations of atheism, confiscation of land, and dictatorship. Some of the agrarian C.C.F. candidates realized that greater strength could be achieved for an independent farmers' party that opposed the eastern capitalists than for a socialist party. Even before the first election in 1934, party leaders began to omit all reference to socialism in their propaganda. Some rural leaders tried to discourage urban socialist speakers from mentioning socialism, Russia, and other tabooed topics when they visited rural areas. One very successful C.C.F. candidate admonished such campaigners: "You can say anything you want about capitalism, the banks, and so forth. Be as radical as you want. But you can't speak here if you are going to talk about socialism. The farmers here hate the C.P.R. and the Grain Exchange and will fight like hell for the coöps. . . . Socialism to them means Russia and anti-religion."[2]

Propaganda in a rural constituency in 1934 reveals the conscious attempt to avoid using socialist terms that might lose votes.

---

[1] For notes to chapter vii see pages 298–299.

Do not be misled by false and malicious propaganda spread at your expense by the Liberal and Conservative parties about the Farmer-Labor (C.C.F.) movement.

There is no difference between the Liberal and Conservative parties. They are nothing but servants of the money lord–bankers and the financial magnates. They want power to carry on the collecting of money for their masters and thereby further impoverish you. They have exploited the people of Canada and its resources. They have forever mortgaged your homes, your farms, and your future to the financiers and the capitalists.

VOTE FOR A NEW DEAL

Canada is on the verge of total collapse. Save Saskatchewan from the curse of either Fascism or Communism.[3]

This was typical of C.C.F. campaign leaflets in many rural districts. The provincial organization of the party, however, which was controlled by convinced socialists, such as M. J. Coldwell and George Williams, continued to emphasize socialism, the overthrowal of the capitalist system, and the socialization of all industry.

The electoral defeats of 1934 and 1935 and the rise of Social Credit as an opposition reform movement destroyed the confidence of many of the socialists in their program. Actually, the theoretical socialists in the top leadership of the provincial party now felt that they were wrong in attempting to force their program and terminology on the farmers. They accepted the arguments of agrarian leaders that converting farmers to complete socialism was a task of many decades and that a successful political movement must concentrate on immediate demands.

How pointedly all reference to socialism was removed from C.C.F. propaganda appears in the following paragraph from a leaflet published in 1936. It is identical with a party pamphlet of 1934, except that the 1936 version substitutes "C.C.F." for each mention of the word "socialism."

[The opposition claims] That the *C.C.F.* Will Destroy the Home and Substitute Free Love for Marriage.—This is the last argument of a dishonest person. Many honest people do not at first understand *C.C.F.* ideas, but no honest person has ever charged the *C.C.F.* with a desire to abolish marriage and return to a state of barbarism; nowhere in the literature of the *C.C.F.* is such an absurd thing even hinted at. The *C.C.F.* believes that women are not now possessed of all the rights to

which they as human beings are entitled. We propose that when it is possible for all men to have employment, as it will be under the C.C.F., that the same opportunity shall be open to women. She will be an equal and a partner.[4]

The campaign literature of the C.C.F. between 1936 and 1938 avoided the word "socialism." The party leaders were trying to popularize the C.C.F. by speaking in the traditional language of agrarian radicalism, as in a radio speech by George Williams, the then provincial leader.

My friends, is it not fairly obvious that the only way to get people into office who will do something for the *west* is to elect men and women of a *western* party, such as the C.C.F., who are not continually looking for a cabinet position in Ottawa and willing to sell out their *western* principles in order to get it. . . . Elect a truly *western* government that will really fight for Saskatchewan and it will be done.[5]

The implications of the C.C.F.'s shift from being a socialist to a social reform party can be seen most directly in the crucial area of nationalization of industry. In Western democratic society, the foremost difference between socialist movements and progressive nonsocialist movements is their attitude toward changing the power structure of society by government ownership of industry. The original objective of the Saskatchewan C.C.F. in the early 'thirties made it clear that the party believed in a completely socialized economy.

Objective:
The social ownership of all resources and the machinery of wealth production to the end that we may establish a Coöperative Commonwealth in which the basic principle regulating production, distribution, and exchange will be the supplying of human needs instead of the making of profits.[6]

In explaining this clause the C.C.F. provincial leadership made it clear that they were not prepared to compromise on the issue.

The wording of the objective is "Social Ownership of all resources and the machinery of wealth production." This, therefore, includes all industries. We recognize the rights of the individual to own personal property which he can use for his comfort and well-being. Personal property is inclusive of home, clothing, furniture, etc.
. . . in compensating industries taken over, we will have due regard to the interests of society as a whole, and at the same time protect the

individual in society. We will compensate small bond-holders in full in order to give them a reasonable purchasing power. And in compensating large holders of capital or bonds, our discount will be continuously heavier in order that we will not build up capital in the hands of one to the detriment of the whole.[7]

This forthright objective had been inserted in the program by the more socialist elements in the party; but this extreme statement on complete nationalization and the manner of compensation was not part of the traditional agrarian ideology favoring public ownership of only the more important industries, especially those that affected agriculture. Gradually, under the pressure of opposition criticism and electoral defeat, the socialists dropped the insistence on a totally socialized society. By the election year 1938, the C.C.F. policy emphasized government planning more than ownership. It no longer directly attacked private ownership and profit, as the rewording of the party objective indicates.

The purpose of the C.C.F. is the establishment in Canada of a Coöperative Commonwealth in which the principle regulating production, distribution, and exchange will be the supplying of human needs.
To this end a C.C.F. government in power in Saskatchewan would substitute social planning in the place of the ruthless competition now practiced under capitalism.[8]

Instead of "all industries" under public ownership, the party now proposed a "sane policy of Public Ownership, of governmental assistance to the needy, governmental regulation of Big Business, and governmental assistance in creating publicly owned Coöperative Institutions."[9] A later publication by the leader of the Saskatchewan C.C.F. in 1938 made it clear that the party was interested primarily in regulating industry and in preventing undue exploitation rather than in widespread government ownership.

A C.C.F. government will say to timber operators, "We are not interested in the title to the mills, but we are interested in the price at which you sell your timber, because we want it to be produced for use, and we are interested in the wages you pay, because we want these men to be able to buy goods, and we are interested in the preservation of our Timber Resources; therefore, although we are not taking the title to the mill, we are going to insist that you plant two trees to take the place of every one you cut, and we are going to set your wage scale for your workers in order to prevent exploitation, and we are going to develop some Coöperatives and State Mills in order that, by competition,

we may fix prices where they ought to be, by creating some non-profit institutions." . . . In that case *the Government would have brought about Socialism, although they did not touch the title,* because they would have forced these people to sell their products at a reasonable price and pay wages high enough to enable the workers to buy the goods.[10]

The C.C.F. did not return to its advocacy of widespread public ownership after the 1938 elections. The provincial platform of 1944, the one upon which the party won power, urged government ownership only for natural resources and public utilities. In analyzing Saskatchewan C.C.F. propaganda for socialization from 1936 to the present, it is significant to note the nature of the industries concretely marked for socialization, as contained in extracts from various party publications.

Socialization of the banking, credit, and financial system of the country together with the social ownership, development, operation, and control of utilities and natural resources.[11]

. . . the national issue and control of currency and credit.[12]

. . . [public ownership of] coal, clay, mineral, water-power, oil, and timber resources.[13]

Public property will consist of the Natural Resources, the Timber Lands, the Mines, the Oil Fields, Public Utilities such as the banking system, transportation systems, Power Plants, etc.[14]

The Social Ownership of public utilities such as transportation. . . . The Public Ownership and development of certain of our Natural Resources—mines, electric energy, waterways, large-scale lumbering.[15]

We believe, for instance, that the banking system ought to be owned and operated by the people of Canada through their federal government. . . . There are other great monopolies such as our railways, packing plants, milling concerns, the tobacco and farm implement industries, which have become so powerful that they can now set the price for both the producer and consumer and, consequently, exploit both of them. The C.C.F. contends that such monopolies should be owned by the people through the federal government.

In the same manner there are economic activities which ought to be owned by the people through their provincial governments. Already hydro-electric power has been taken over by the government in some provinces—we think that this should be extended. We believe that other forms of power such as natural gas, coal and oil wells should belong to the people of a province rather than to a privileged few.[16]

Proposals to place almost all the foregoing industries under public ownership appeared repeatedly in the program of the Saskatchewan farmers' movement long before the C.C.F. was formed. The
Saskatchewan Grain Growers' Association, the Farmers' Union,
the United Farmers of Canada (Saskatchewan Section), and the
Progressive Party, all urged the nationalization of banking, transportation, and public utilities. (See chap. iii.) Oil wells, mines,
timber resources, and packing plants were added to the list of
industries to be nationalized. Nonprofit government operation of
these industries would reduce production costs for the farmer and
make him less subject to external economic control. In continuing
to advocate the nationalization of such industries, the C.C.F. was
not clashing with any of the private property values of the agrarians, but rather had become the political voice of the traditional
agrarian economic protest movement.

While modifying its goal of total socialization, the C.C.F. has
continued its emphasis on the extension of the social services rendered by the state, such as social security, health, and education.
These services assume major importance in a province like Saskatchewan, where health and educational facilities tend to be poor
because of the sparseness of the population. The farm movements
of the province have always demanded more government aid for
such services. All C.C.F. literature and programs since the start
of the party have urged government protection against illness,
accident, old age, and unemployment, increased funds for education, and socialized medicine. These social security aspects of the
party's program gradually assumed greater importance in its propaganda as the stress on socialism declined, until today it is the
most important part of the provincial program.

Both program and propaganda for social services have remained
fairly constant. Party policy on education, however, changed drastically with the other shifts designed to accommodate to existing
values. Many socialists in the party believed that the educational
system was biased in favor of capitalist social and economic values.
Under their influence, the party in its 1933–1934 program advocated not only increased expenditures for education but also basic
changes in curriculum.

Education Program . . .
d) The teaching of the principles of coöperation.

e) The teaching of the origin of money and its function as a medium of exchange.

f) Elimination of all glorification of war, and to substitute calisthenic drill in place of cadet training.[17]

This plank was not a minor part of the early program. The *Handbook for Speakers*, put out by the party in 1933, laid especial emphasis on it.

This is one of the most important planks in this particular program. If we are going to establish a Coöperative Commonwealth, we must have coöperation definitely taught. If a Farmer-Labor Government is returned to power in the Province of Saskatchewan, one of the first things that the Head of the Department of Education would have to do would be to call together the teachers of the various points in the Province, explain coöperation to them, and then tell them to go into the schools and teach coöperation.[18]

M. J. Coldwell, the provincial leader, reiterated this point in a campaign speech: "We propose to stop teaching capitalism in the schools. We will substitute teaching coöperation for competition."[19]

The proposal to change the school curriculum met vigorous criticism from opponents of the C.C.F., who charged that it meant introducing politics into the classroom. The socialists answered that politics already existed in the classroom in the form of a pro-capitalist history and economics. After the disastrous defeats of 1934 and 1935, the educational proposal was dropped. No mention of curriculum revision was made in the election programs of 1936 to 1938. The 1944 program suggested some general curriculum changes, but did not revert to the original platform.

Curriculum Revision: The C.C.F. proposes to revise the school curriculum so that the material of school studies may prepare students adequately for intelligent participation in the life of their community and not, as now, inadequately for a University to which the majority will never go.[20]

The basic cultural conservatism of the Saskatchewan C.C.F., the fact that it was an outgrowth of significant permanent forces within western Canada rather than a new radical movement seeking to make far-reaching changes, can best be seen through analysis of the impact of religious beliefs on the party. Socialism has traditionally been identified as basically materialist and anti-religious. Marx's classic statement, "Religion is the opiate of the

people," has been reiterated by European socialist parties; for the tenser political situation in Europe showed the fundamental opposition of authoritarian religions and socialism more clearly than it has in Canada and the countries of the British Commonwealth. European socialism, accordingly, has been able to win its way in spite of its antireligious stand, because in many of these countries the church was identified in the minds of the lower economic groups with the upper class or with the state. In Germany the Lutheran Church was a state church; in Russia the same was true of the Greek Orthodox Church; in southern Europe the Roman Catholic Church possessed tremendous wealth and political power; in France anticlericalism was a deep and bitter heritage from the French Revolution, which had fought the clergy as a part of the privileged class.

The socialist and working-class movements of the self-governed countries of the British Commonwealth have, on the other hand, been unique in their ability to gain the support, or at least the real neutrality, of the churches toward their political efforts. This happened for three main reasons: (1) the Anglo-Saxon left-wing movements never accepted a Marxist theoretical approach to socialism with its initial antagonism to organized religion; (2) the strong nonconformist churches in the British countries were primarily poor men's churches, whose ministers often took part in the organization of workers' parties; and (3) the Catholic Church has been relatively weak in the British Commonwealth.[21]

The same factors have operated in Canada—outside French Quebec—and in Saskatchewan in particular. The largest Protestant church in western Canada, the United Church of Canada, resulted from an amalgamation of Presbyterians, Methodists, and Congregationalists because of the thinly scattered population of the frontier provinces. Coming out of the nonconformist British tradition, many of the United Church ministers stressed the social gospel rather than a fundamentalist view of salvation, and were sympathetic to the social and economic strivings of their rural members. The ministers lived close to their parishioners and shared their fortunes and misfortunes. In May, 1931, after depression and drought had hit the province, the Saskatchewan conference of the United Church adopted this resolution: "We believe that the competitive system must be transformed into a coöperative system and that production and distribution, together with the whole

fiscal system, must be democratically controlled in the interests of human needs, rather than for private profit."[22]

As had been true in nineteenth-century England, many of the leaders of the C.C.F. were former ministers. J. S. Woodsworth, the first national leader of the C.C.F. and the foremost socialist of western Canada, was a Methodist minister who had been engaged in missionary and social welfare work among poor immigrants. His socialism was based on a conviction that there was a contradiction between the ideals of Christianity and the poverty and insecurity in contemporary society. Woodsworth preached the message of an idealistic Christian socialism at hundreds of farmers' meetings and conventions. Both the Farmers' Union and, later, the United Farmers of Canada arranged lecture tours for him in Saskatchewan during the 'twenties.

Two of the five members of Parliament elected by the Saskatchewan C.C.F. in the 1940 elections were ministers. One of them, T. C. Douglas, who was first elected in 1935 and later became the leader of the Saskatchewan party and Premier of the province, expressed a point of view that appealed to many Saskatchewan ministers who became active members of the C.C.F.

The religion of tomorrow will be less concerned with the dogmas of theology and more concerned with the social welfare of humanity. . . . When one sees the church spending its energies on the assertion of antiquated dogmas . . . but dumb as an oyster to the poverty and misery all around, we cannot help recognize the need for a new interpretation of Christianity. . . .

[We have] come to see that the Kingdom of God is in our midst if we have the vision to build it. The rising generation will tend to build a heaven on earth rather than live in misery in the hope of gaining some uncertain reward in the dim distant future.[23]

It is not surprising, therefore, that, like British socialism, the Saskatchewan C.C.F., from the time of its formation and right down to the present, has had a moralistic and religious emphasis. The C.C.F. stresses its support of Christianity and the fact that many of its leaders are religious; and it makes political capital of the fact that some churches are anticapitalist. Since the C.C.F. is dominated by those who think that socialism and Christianity are but secular and sacred versions of the same philosophy, the few in the party who hold Marxist materialist views have kept these in the background. The majority of the party agrees on the neces-

sity of winning the religious people, and the British tradition has made it both easy and logical to abolish the antireligious connotation of socialism.

In fact, the Saskatchewan C.C.F. has consciously suppressed any expressions of irreligious attitudes by its members. In January, 1936, the *Research Review,* a magazine published by a group of young C.C.F. members in Regina, published an article, "Socialism and the Church," by George Webster, a Marxist socialist who belonged to the more radical British Columbia party. The article criticized the clergy for having a conservative outlook resulting from their social position, and contended that "they may tend to be too readily satisfied with reformist half-measures." This statement brought prompt, open repudiation in the legislature from George Williams, the leader of the party. The provincial executive of the C.C.F. urged its leading members on the *Review* to resign.

The following extract from a C.C.F. leaflet is typical of the C.C.F. attempt to identify its teachings with those of the Christian churches:

The question is not so much whether the C.C.F. is opposed to Religion as to whether Capitalism is opposed to Christianity. The Anglican, Roman Catholic, and United Churches have declared that the Capitalist system is opposed to Christianity. On one side of the fence— Christianity; on the other—the social system under which we live. . . .

If the Anglican, Roman Catholic, and United Churches are right, then those who are fighting Capitalism's battle are fighting against Religion and Christianity.[24]

Such statements gave support to the C.C.F. contention that it was "the true Christian party," and allayed the apprehensions of many religious people. But although the C.C.F. was successful in identifying itself with the Christian social gospel, it met the active resistance of the Catholic hierarchy. Cardinal Villeneuve of Quebec, the leading Catholic dignitary in Canada, stated in 1934 that a good Catholic could not support the C.C.F. This was followed up in Saskatchewan by a pastoral letter, issued just before the elections, warning Catholics against socialism, and pressure was placed on Catholics in the C.C.F. to leave the party. The C.C.F. leaders did not react to this opposition by becoming anticlerical, though some of its members did. Rather, they sought to convince both the members of the hierarchy and lay Catholics that the C.C.F. was not the type of socialist party condemned in the papal

encyclicals. M. J. Coldwell, as leader of the Saskatchewan party, made this clear in answering Cardinal Villeneuve in 1934.

The C.C.F. was socialist in the sense that the British Labor and So-cialist Party and the New Zealand Labor Party are socialist parties, for we share their philosophy and have a similar program.

Yet the Prime Minister of New Zealand and four members of his cabinet are devout Roman Catholics, and the late Cardinal Bourne of England stated explicitly that the British Labor Party, though a So-cialist Party, did not fall within the category of those movements con-demned by the Pope. Why, therefore, should the C.C.F. receive condemnation from Cardinal Villeneuve?[25]

Following the C.C.F's ideological shift to the right in 1936, the Catholic Church dropped its overt hostility to the party. In private, however, members of the Saskatchewan hierarchy have continued to put pressure on leading Catholics not to support the C.C.F. A few devout Catholic members of the C.C.F. have made significant gains in campaigning in Catholic districts by completely eliminat-ing the scare word "socialist" in their party propaganda. One such Catholic, Joseph W. Burton, formerly member of Parliament from the predominantly Catholic district of Humboldt, succeeded in winning the constituency by presenting the terms "coöperative order" and "new social order" as objectives of the C.C.F.

The founders of the C.C.F. were moved by the thought that there could be an abundant life for all. . . . Fundamental to this is the Chris-tian idea of mankind. Has he not been created by almighty God as His masterpiece, made to His image and likeness? Was he not to be crowned with glory and honor and placed over the works of the Maker's hands? What of the fulfillment of the Divine destiny, what did they find? They found that for the past hundred years the homes men lived in, the nutrition they had, the clothing they wore, the wages they received, the education and security they enjoyed were far from being commen-surate with their dignity and honor. It was such conditions that made men like J. S. Woodsworth think of a new order to supersede the old.

You and I have the responsibility of laying the foundation for the new structure and that foundation must be social justice, because only in social justice can social security be built. That will be the new order.[26]

Besides its socialist and social reform propaganda, the C.C.F. concentrated on demonstrating that it was the only party that fought for the immediate economic interests of the people. To do so, it evolved a program supporting the economic demands of the

three class groups to whom it directed its electoral appeal: farmers, urban workers, and small businessmen. The socialists drew up programs designed to convince each of these groups of their place in a completely socialized society. Such proposals were dropped after the election defeats. An analysis of the propaganda addressed to these groups is further confirmation of the thesis that the C.C.F. grew culturally conservative as it moved toward power.

Historically, security of landownership is the farmer's deepest demand. The fact that he puts his own work into improving his land makes the tract on which his life depends more than a job. But single-crop farming makes the dependence of the Saskatchewan farmer on the price of wheat a more prominent factor in his political thinking than are prices in diversified farming areas: the whole life of the community depends perilously and visibly on a single price which the farmer is powerless to influence. This has meant that C.C.F. ideology in Saskatchewan has to be based on two principles: long-run tenacity of landownership and the short-run, perennially fresh fighting issue of the price of "this year's" wheat.

The depression and drought of the 'thirties demonstrated to many farmers the comparative worthlessness of owning land if it would not produce an income. As tens of thousands of farm families were forced to leave the province or to trek to the northern bush frontier to earn a living, fear spread throughout the province. It is impossible to overemphasize the farmer's continuing fear of losing his entire means of livelihood. He was unable to pay the accumulated interest on his debts and taxes. The number of actual foreclosures and tax sales was, however, very small. The economic disaster was so overwhelming and universal that mortgage companies and banks could gain nothing by foreclosing, as a forced sale would bring little in return. The provincial government would have had to stop any mass wave of foreclosures, for no government could have remained in office if it permitted its citizens to lose all they had.

Debt-ridden farmers did not, however, stop to think logically. The threat of foreclosure was very real to each farmer who could not pay his debts. Between 1928 and 1932 the interest owed on debts in rural Saskatchewan rose from one-tenth to nearly three-quarters of the net cash operating income of the farmers. The threat to the farmers' ownership of land seemed to come from

the mortgage companies. Many Saskatchewan farmers literally had "little to lose but their mortgages."

The militant agrarians' party, the C.C.F., concentrated on an effort to convince the farmers that it was the only party that could protect them—provincially, through government action to stop foreclosures, and federally, by government marketing of farm products, a guaranteed minimum price, and crop insurance. The C.C.F. endeavored to identify the old parties with the banks, the Grain Exchange, the railroads, and eastern manufacturing interests. It contended that only a people's party, like the C.C.F., which was not dependent on campaign contributions from large corporations, could be expected to help the farmers. "He who pays the piper calls the tune" became the favorite propaganda attack on the old parties by the C.C.F.

It would be impossible without interviewing a large sample of the Saskatchewan farming population to discover what the C.C.F. meant to the people who supported it. The C.C.F. leaders were sure that land security and prices were the two most significant problems, and their propaganda concentrated on these issues. Though there were many changes in program and ideological appeal in the thirteen years between the time the C.C.F. was organized and the time it was elected, there was no slackening of emphasis on these basic farm issues. The C.C.F. was a farmers' party and reflected the primary concerns of its members.

The socialists in the party succeeded, in the early period of the movement, in getting the farmers in the U.F.C. to accept the principle of nationalization of land. This proposal, however, was never suggested as a means of making farmers employees of the state or even members of coöperative farms. The C.C.F. farmers accepted it as a means of guaranteeing permanent land tenure to working farmers. This can be seen clearly in the wording of the plank on use-lease titles in the 1933–1934 program.

Security of tenure to be obtained by institution of perpetual "use-hold" on homes and lands instead of patents or Torrens' title. Substitution of perpetual "use-hold" for home and land titles when and if requested by the present registered owner, or dispossessed owner who now occupies under a lease. The prevention of immediate foreclosures, due to arrears of mortgage installments or purchase agreements with mortgage, land and investment companies and private individuals, by an exchange of provincial non-interest-bearing bonds for equity based on actual economic value of the land and homes.[27]

Though C.C.F. leaders presented the program as one designed to protect the agrarian's control of his farm, the sheer suggestion of nationalization of land was the most controversial aspect of the program. The party leaders, therefore, dropped it in 1936, and concentrated on protection of the farmer's equity in his land. The C.C.F. sought to appeal to the farmer in terms of his basic desire to become or to remain a property holder. Socialism for the farmer was henceforth to mean the protection of his property by control of the rest of the economy, and especially big business. This goal was clearly stated in all party literature after 1936. "The C.C.F. believes in the family farm as the basis of rural life. Living standards for farmers must rise with those in the rest of the community."[28]

T. C. Douglas, the provincial leader after 1941, often promised that a C.C.F. government would resign if a single farmer was evicted from his farm. The first and major plank in the party platform in 1944 was security of landownership.

Insecurity for farmers in Saskatchewan may be summed up in two words, *debt* and *eviction*. That this is true, is shown by the fact that in 1940 the Saskatchewan Debt Adjustment Board permitted 1,753 foreclosures; in 1941 it permitted 830 foreclosures; in 1942 it permitted 741. The fact is that the farms of Saskatchewan are passing into the hands of mortgage and loan companies, and farmers are becoming tenants rather than owners. The C.C.F. is determined that this policy of making a farmer a tenant on his own land must cease.

To provide protection and security for farmers on their land, a C.C.F. Government in Saskatchewan will take the following steps:

1. It will stop foreclosures and evictions from the farm home.

One of the first acts of the C.C.F. Government will be to use its legislative power to prevent the eviction of Saskatchewan farmers and thereby give them security on their farms.

2. It will introduce legislation to protect them from seizure of that portion of a farmer's crop that is needed to provide for his family.

A C.C.F. Government will consider it a first duty to pass legislation to provide that the farmer shall have enough of his crop to buy necessities for his family and pay his bills to his local merchant.

3. It will use the power of debt moratorium (that is, of suspension or postponement) to force the loan and mortgage companies to reduce debts and mortgages to a figure at which they can reasonably be paid at prevailing prices for farm products.

The C.C.F. believes that every settlement of farm debt should take into account the years of toil that a farmer has put into his farm, and

that this equity should be protected. A C.C.F. Government will call a halt to foreclosures while the settlements are being worked out.

4. It will prevent the accumulation of new debt.

A C.C.F. Government will pass legislation to provide that all existing and new land contracts shall contain a crop failure clause stating that in any year in which the farm income falls below six dollars an acre (*a*) there shall be no interest chargeable; (*b*) there shall be no instalment of interest payable; and (*c*) the length of the contract shall be extended one year. In this way both debtor and creditor will share the burden of crop failure and loss, and the crushing weight of accumulating interest debt will be lifted from Saskatchewan farm homes.[29]

Sheer ownership of land meant little, however, in a commercially oriented farm economy without decent prices and crop insurance. The farmers' movement had been fighting for three decades to eliminate fluctuations in income, and the C.C.F. as its new political voice took over the battle. C.C.F. members of the federal Parliament from Saskatchewan have consistently fought for higher guaranteed prices to agriculture through government marketing boards.[30] The following statements are typical of provincial programs and literature.

It [a C.C.F. government in Saskatchewan] will press for the closing of the Winnipeg Grain Exchange and the setting of Parity Prices for agricultural products. The C.C.F. believes that there should be no speculation in food, and for that reason it has consistently urged that the Winnipeg Grain Exchange be permanently closed. In its place, the C.C.F. advocates the setting up of appropriate Marketing Boards upon which the producers should have majority representation. Parity Prices will assure that the farmers receive their just share of the national income.[31]

The significance of the fact that the C.C.F. was the only party that uninterruptedly concentrated on increasing farm prices through government action can be seen in the growth of the party in 1941–1942. Once the drought and its immediate threat to the farmers' basic livelihood had ended, Saskatchewan farmers became concerned with increasing their income. The C.C.F. was able to double its membership and proceed to power as a result of its coöperation with the Wheat Pool's "March on Ottawa" campaign. (See chap. vi, p. 117.) Here was concrete evidence that the agrarian protest aspect of the C.C.F. program was more significant in the minds of farmers than its general program of total social reform.

The second element to which the C.C.F. has appealed is the urban working class, 20 per cent of the population of the province if one includes all employees. The original (1932) name of the party, Farmer-Labor Group, indicates the basic concept of the unity of the producing classes, farmers and workers, against their common economic enemies. Despite these gestures toward urban workers, however, the party was basically agrarian from the start. Success or failure for the new movement depended mainly on winning a majority in the rural districts. It is characteristic that the only appeal to workers in the first program of the provincial party for the 1934 campaign barely mentions labor in the course of a 1,500-word statement.

Social Legislation to secure to the worker and the farmer:—

(*a*) An adequate income and leisure, with an effective voice in the management of his industry.

(*b*) Freedom of speech and the right of assembly.[32]

Specific labor planks such as an eight-hour day or a minimum wage were lacking. The speaker's handbooks and propaganda leaflets rarely mentioned labor, and then only incidentally.

The party was badly beaten in the cities and towns of Saskatchewan in the 1934 and 1935 campaigns; this led it to abandon the urban field in the 1938 election. No C.C.F. candidates ran for the six seats in Regina, Moose Jaw, and Saskatoon. The revised program of 1936 contained only one three-word plank for labor—"Work with Wages." The basically rural orientation of the C.C.F. can be seen from this statement in a pamphlet explaining the party platform. *"Work and wages is generally considered to be an urban problem. Possibly we think of it in that light because the farmer has plenty of work.* We suggest, that he should have some wages along with his work. Primarily this plank is a labor plank."[33]

Obviously, labor was not conceived as basically part of the core of the movement. The attitude toward this outsider whom "we" were trying to convert was characteristically expressed in an interview by a leading agrarian in the C.C.F.

Do you think that the workers will ever become socialists? It's easy to convince farmers of the value of socialism. They can see that, if the state takes over the monopolies, farm-implement industries, and railroads, and markets wheat without a profit, their income will be much higher. But how can we get the workers to recognize that the C.C.F. will benefit them also? All they care about is higher wages and they

think that they can get them through their unions. Personally, I doubt if we'll ever win the government at Ottawa, for the workers just won't vote for us in the big eastern cities.

After its victories in the 1938 elections, the C.C.F. began to gain working-class support. The leaders of the small trade-union movement in the province became interested in a party that professed to be more prolabor than the two old parties and now appeared to be capable of forming the next provincial government. As a result, the enlarged trade-union wing of the party drew up a complete labor program setting forth the traditional demands of organized labor, with the addition of certain social services.

1. The Right to Organize:
The C.C.F. will make it compulsory for employers to enter into collective bargaining with the labor union selected by the majority of their employees.

2. Minimum Wage Act:
The C.C.F. will increase the rates of wages established by the Minimum Wage Board and will take action to enforce their payment and to extend the act to protect the employees in other low-paid industries.

3. Workmen's Compensation Act:
The C.C.F. will eliminate the three-day waiting period before benefits are paid, and will raise the compensation to a higher percentage of regular wage paid.

4. Labor Representation on Boards and Commissions:
The C.C.F. will appoint Labor representatives to all boards, commissions or other bodies dealing with Labor matters, and will consult with the official organizations of the Trade-Union movement before making such appointments.

5. Department of Labor:
The C.C.F. will set up a Department of Labor with a Minister of Labor in charge.

6. Socialized Health Services:
The C.C.F. will provide a complete system of socialized health services so that all will receive adequate medical, surgical, dental, nursing, and hospital care without charge.

7. Old-Age Pension:
The C.C.F. will raise the amount of the Old-Age Pension and will bring pressure to bear on the Federal Government to reduce the age to 65 years.

8. Housing Program:
The C.C.F. will press the Federal Government to institute a National Housing Plan to provide low-cost and low rental homes.

9. Security:

The C.C.F. will provide for the workers security of tenure in their homes, and will bring about adjustment of debts for urban dwellers as well as for the farmers.

10. Unemployment and Postwar Reconstruction:

Mass unemployment in wartime is not tolerated. In peacetime it should be equally intolerable. The C.C.F. demands that our natural resources, now being used to bring about Victory, shall be used in peacetime to bring about security and a higher standard of living. The C.C.F. is determined that we shall not drift back into the chaos of unemployment and depression which preceded the war; and therefore will formulate definite practical plans for postwar reconstruction and adjustment of our social and economic life.[34]

It is significant to note that this is basically a trade-union program, not a socialist one. There is no mention of the advantages to labor under socialized industry, nor of the possibilities of labor representation in the management of industry. Labor leaders, like the farmers, were primarily interested in the party as a means of advancing their own economic objectives.

The coöperation of organized labor and farmers may appear strange in terms of the popular stereotype of rural antagonism to labor. Actually, this stereotype, like many others, includes diverse groups and patterns of behavior. There are numerous farm groups on this continent, each with separate economic interests and social values. In Ontario and in the eastern part of the United States, the economically stable farmers are usually associated with the economic and social middle class of the neighboring towns, and they tend to accept the urban middle-class fear of a powerful labor movement. The economic power of big business is not so apparent to the eastern farmer, and the efforts of unions to secure a larger share of the national income seem a threat to him.

In the western wheat belt, however, farmers have often been involved in economic and political struggles with eastern big business. Organized labor has been a small group, which does not constitute a visible threat to farmers. The railroads, banks, grain exchanges, and manufacturers who increased prices, on the other hand, have been highly visible exploiters of agrarians. Grain growers, therefore, having identified their enemy as "the interests," have tended, when organized in class-struggle groups, to view labor as a potential ally rather than as an opponent. This fact is borne out by the history of the Greenbackers, the Populists, and

the Non-Partisans in the United States, and of the Progressives and the C.C.F. in Canada. (See also chap. i.) The Non-Partisan League, representing the overwhelming majority of North Dakota farmers, actually signed a closed-shop agreement with the revolutionary I.W.W. in 1917, in which the N.P.L. agreed that its supporters would hire only "wobblies" as harvest hands, while the I.W.W. pledged that its members would work only for N.P.L. farmers.[35] In the United States today the Farmers' Union, which is largely a grain-growers' movement, has been continuously pro-labor and works with the C.I.O. on political issues.

In Saskatchewan the farmers' movement frequently coöperated with labor before the C.C.F. was organized. The Farmers' Union passed resolutions supporting various strikes, and even contributed to the strike funds of the Nova Scotia coal miners in 1923.[36] During the Wheat Pool campaign, the unions reciprocated by permitting the farmers to use the office facilities and staff of the local Trades and Labor Councils (A. F. of L.).[37] Although sources of friction have existed and still do exist within the Saskatchewan C.C.F., there has rarely been a significant objection from either group to the demands of the other. The unionists recognize that unless they have the backing of the farmers they cannot receive state help from the province, which controls all labor legislation; while farm leaders know that without trade-union support nationally they cannot hope to gain federal power, which they need to secure higher prices. It has, therefore, been in the interest of the organized groups on both sides to dissuade any latent rank-and-file hostility.

Farmer-labor coöperation is further strengthened by the fact that many of the older rural settlers are former workers with trade-union experience; while many of the younger workers are migrants from farms and have relatives who are still engaged in farming. This has made both groups more receptive toward supporting each other than would be true in older and more industrialized areas.

Though coöperating with urban labor, Saskatchewan farmers have a tradition of antagonism to all middlemen, including small businessmen. The consumers' coöperative movement, which first appeared early in the present century, is designed to eliminate the profits of retailers. In its early radical period the C.C.F. advocated the complete elimination of private business. A pamphlet issued in 1933 made this explicit:

Our coöperative organizations in Canada are far too insufficient to allow us to have much hope of setting up distribution on a coöperative basis with the coöperative system we now have. We might have a State distributing agency, for instance, in which the present storekeeper would become a civil servant and have his salary paid by the State, and the prices governed by the State to give people a decent standard of living.[38]

Propaganda issued before the 1934 elections reëmphasized state distribution and the employment of retailers as civil servants:

Business Men
You have always voted Grit and Tory
Because
You thought you were in business for Profits
You Never Made Any
The postmaster is sure of his income
Why not be sure of yours, under a planned economy,
in which you will be guaranteed an income
as a distributor.
Vote C.C.F.[39]

There were few small merchants in the new party, and there was no vocal opposition to the desire to eliminate their businesses. But in the 1934 and 1935 elections, merchants voted overwhelmingly against the C.C.F. (See chap. viii, pp. 161–162.) Many constituencies were lost to the party because the old-party plurality in the small urban areas outweighed the C.C.F. lead in the country. Moreover, Social Credit was able to secure the support of many businessmen who were attracted to its policy of increasing purchasing power by distributing money.

The Social Credit gains among small merchants and professional men showed that these people could be won away from the old parties. The C.C.F. leaders, seeking votes, decided to attempt to win over small business to their own ranks. This necessarily involved the adoption of a policy designed to protect small business against the monopolies. The economic goal of the C.C.F., "Production for Use and Not for Profit," was changed by dropping out the last four words. George Williams, the provincial leader, clearly stated the reasons for the change: "The farmer and the small businessman in Saskatchewan have difficulty in understanding the C.C.F. manifesto when they come to the section which sets out that production under socialistic policies can only be carried on when it is 'not for profit.' "[40]

This new appeal of the C.C.F. to small business has never been dropped. The party conceives of the people for whom it speaks as farmers, laborers, and small businessmen. The following are typical of the efforts to attract small business.

The C.C.F. intends to break the power of the Canadian monopolies which are exploiting our people—but has no intention of interfering with the retail merchant in the conduct of his business. The C.C.F. has no desire to curtail the wages he receives as a distributor—but rather—C.C.F. policies will increase his sales. . . .

What does this [the C.C.F. program] do for the retail merchant? It does not interfere with his legitimate income as a merchant, but it does increase his income—for is it not obvious that every government development which pays out wages to workers, every pension paid out of new wealth created increases the amount of business done in our stores, and it does it without resorting to a taxation of Peter to clothe Paul, and without increasing the Public Debt."

Though C.C.F. leaders seek the support of the urban middle classes, the latter make little response. There is an essential conflict between the party's support of the large consumers' coöperative movement and its appeal to small merchants. In Saskatchewan, coöperative stores are as great a menace to private country stores as are chain stores. The overwhelming majority of rural members of the C.C.F. are coöperators; as such, they are not very friendly to businessmen. This cleavage between the two groups is minimized, however, in party ideology. Here, then, is another example of ideological compromise to gain an electoral majority. In practice, most of the agrarian members ignore the party's appeals to small business and remain critical of private enterprise while working to build the coöperatives.

In spite of its programmatic appeals to small business, the C.C.F., after 1936, laid increasing stress on its identification with the coöperative movement. Organized by people active in the coöperatives, the party was able to capitalize on the previous acceptance by a large proportion of Saskatchewan farmers of non-profit enterprise as superior to private capitalism. The very name of the party, the Coöperative Commonwealth Federation, meant to many that it was the political arm of the coöperatives, an idea which the C.C.F. did not try to dispel. The *Saskatchewan Commonwealth*, the party newspaper, stated this explicitly in 1944.

The growth of the coöperative movement in Saskatchewan during the past few years as shown by articles in this and the last issue of the

Saskatchewan Commonwealth is a most inspiring picture for those who believe in the necessity for extending the coöperative movement from the political as well as from the economic or commercial angle.

We cannot urge too strongly upon our readers that they should continue to organize what might be called the two great departments of the coöperative movement, and to express the hope that neither department will be neglected, but that the two will go forward hand in hand until the economic security which is possible through the further development of both departments of this great movement is within the reach of all.[42]

Every election program of the C.C.F. and most of the speeches by party leaders stressed this relationship between the C.C.F. and the coöperatives. Anyone listening to C.C.F. speeches or reading C.C.F. literature by 1944 would think that he was asked to vote for the coöperatives' party, as an excerpt from an article in the *Commonwealth* makes clear.

This movement [the C.C.F.], founded by the people, has also grown by leaps and bounds, just as did the original coöperative movement, and it is now being viciously opposed by the same vested interests which oppose coöperation of any sort. The issue is, however, clear cut. The people are being asked to make their choice between coöperation and competition and the majority are choosing the former.

That which is founded on a just principle can not be stifled and so the coöperative movement—commercial and political—marches on.[43]

There can be little doubt that this propaganda has been effective in overcoming the prejudices against the C.C.F. as a socialist party. Some C.C.F. leaders publicly assert that they are coöperators and not socialists. In most places in the province there is a strong interrelationship on the local level between C.C.F. leaders and the coöperatives. The same men often lead both.

Though the C.C.F. leaders tried to eliminate discussions of socialism and to drop ultraradical aspects of their program, the opposition groups would not let them do so. Socialism and the C.C.F. platform before 1936 formed the major core of the Liberals' attack. Reporters on the Regina *Leader-Post*, the leading Liberal daily in the province, were ordered to play up stories in which members of the C.C.F. anywhere in Canada were reported to have talked about socialism or the nationalization of industries.[44] In 1944 the Liberals reprinted the twenty-four-page *Handbook for Speakers* issued by the C.C.F. in 1933; these booklets were dis-

tributed in the thousands to remind farmers that the C.C.F. had once stood for total socialization.

It is ironical that one of the major factors in popularizing the concept of socialism in rural Saskatchewan was the attacks made on it by the daily press and the old parties. Liberal propaganda continually attempted to associate the C.C.F. with red radicalism, as in the heading of a party leaflet in the 1944 campaign:

THE C.C.F. PLATFORM

MEANS THE SAME TODAY AS IN 1934

SOCIALISM AND DICTATORSHIP

These attacks were not very successful among the farmers by 1944. The daily papers were distrusted because of their earlier opposition to farmers' movements such as the Progressive Party and the Wheat Pool in the 'twenties. The Regina *Leader-Post* was known in many areas as "the Misleader" from Wheat Pool days. (See chap. iii, p. 63.) Invectives against the C.C.F., while the party fought in the legislature and the House of Commons for higher prices for wheat, debt reduction, and increased social services, only served to make socialism palatable to the farmers. If socialism meant $1 a bushel wheat as it did in 1941, while Liberalism meant 70 cent wheat, then socialism was not so bad. Many farmers explicitly reported that they began to think of themselves as socialists as a result of the attacks on socialism by groups whom they considered enemies of the farmers.

As the C.C.F. moved toward power in the 1940's, some of its leaders again began to speak of socialism as the ultimate objective of the party. The opposition's attacks on socialism forced the C.C.F. to defend it on the public platform. The increasing strength of the party in spite of the strenuous redbaiting by the Liberals convinced party leaders that socialism was no longer the handicap they had imagined it to be in the 1930's. Party propaganda, however, consisted mainly of a series of specific reforms to which the C.C.F. committed itself when it should become the government of Saskatchewan. The new socialist order, though it was mentioned, remained in the background. The electors were asked to vote for security and reform, not for a socialist society. In 1944 the C.C.F. still found it possible to appeal to the supporters of the Conservative Party as follows: "The problems which face us all, both now and in the postwar period, are too vital and important to become the football of ambitious party leaders. If the Conservatives are

desirous of ridding themselves of the yoke of Liberalism, then there is only one sure way of doing it, and that is by supporting the C.C.F. candidate in their riding."[45]

The C.C.F. movement in Saskatchewan won majority power after thirteen years of organization and propaganda. During that period the ideology of the movement was in a state of continuous adjustment. Aspects of the original program that were risking popular support by challenging basic social values were eliminated. In summary, the significant changes in the C.C.F. program and ideology were as follows:

1. The virtual dropping of the explicitly socialist goal and its replacement by phrases such as "a new social order" or the "coöperative commonwealth."

2. The elimination of any suggestion of land nationalization, succeeded by emphasis on protecting the owner's title.

3. The withdrawal of plans to socialize all, or even the majority, of private industry. This was replaced by a stress on state economic planning and the socialization of public utilities and industries directly infringing on the rural economy.

4. An increased emphasis from 1936 through 1944 on social security.

5. The inclusion of small businessmen as a group whose status would be preserved and strengthened under a C.C.F. government.

6. The elimination of plans to change class biases in the educational system.

7. The development in the 1940's of a complete labor and trade-union policy as a consequence of the increase in urban C.C.F. organization.

The formal aims of the party in 1944 were a compromise between the original goals of the small nucleus of socialists in the leadership of the U.F.C. and I.L.P. in 1932, and the basic political, social, and economic values of the farmers. The socialists had attempted to convert the people of the province to the necessity of a fundamental societal change that would affect the entire economic structure of the country. They soon learned, however, that the majority of farmers and many of their original followers were more interested in immediate reforms that would improve their economic position than in a new social order. The strong appeal in the middle 'thirties of the Social Credit and progressive coalition movements was clear evidence that the particular ideology of socialism was

not important to farmers. If Social Credit would fight "the interests" and give security to the farmers, they would become Social Crediters like the farmers of Alberta.

When one considers the changes in C.C.F. policy, together with the constant emphasis of the Saskatchewan C.C.F. members of the House of Commons on raising the price of wheat, it becomes clear that the C.C.F. has gradually changed, under external and internal pressure, from an agrarian socialist party to a liberal agrarian protest movement, following in the direct tradition of the Populists, the Non-Partisan League, and the Progressives. No single modification of party policy and emphasis was sufficient to change the character of the movement, but taken together they constitute a qualitative change. The socialists had won power, but the method and conditions under which they succeeded had in large measure adversely affected their socialism.

This process was not confined to the Saskatchewan Section of the C.C.F., though it initiated some programmatic changes before other sections. This resulted mainly from the fact that the Saskatchewan C.C.F. was closer to power and had a smaller proportion of doctrinaire and intellectual socialists. Actually, many in the C.C.F. outside Saskatchewan reprimanded the provincial party for its "opportunism" during the 1936–1939 period. The national C.C.F. and its provincial sections began, however, to change their orientation during the war, when the party gained electoral strength throughout the country.

It is not part of this study to analyze the national party, but its programs and propaganda literature issued from 1933 to 1948 clearly reveal the attempts to win majority power by eliminating aspects of socialist ideology that might antagonize significant sections of the electorate. The turning point in the development of the national party can probably be centered in the withdrawal from politics and subsequent early death of J. S. Woodsworth, the leader of Canadian socialism from 1921 to 1940. Woodsworth, who had spent a large part of his life in political isolation trying to build a socialist party, resisted all efforts to achieve rapid party growth through ideological compromise. The newer and younger socialists who joined a going movement wanted power and proceeded to try to gain it.

Karl Mannheim has pointed out that a new doctrine can succeed only if it is based on attitudes already present in a society.

Only when the utopian conception . . . seizes upon currents already present in society and gives expression to them, when in this form it flows back into the outlook of the whole group, and is translated into action by it, only then can the existing order be challenged by the striving for another order of existence. Indeed, it may be stated further that it is a very essential feature of modern history that in the gradual organization for collective action social classes become effective in translating historical reality only when their aspirations are embodied in utopias appropriate to the changing situation.[46]

The C.C.F. in Saskatchewan is a "class" party in the objective sense, since its program reflects the aspirations of a class created by constraining economic forces. As a result of the depression, it became the political voice of angry, exploited, rural Saskatchewan. Like the Russian Bolsheviks in 1917, the C.C.F. adapted socialism to "currents already present" in agrarian society. This generalization still leaves the problem of deciding how far such present "currents" can be extended. There were plenty of currents in Saskatchewan that a socialist utopia could use—and the Social Credit movement shows how easy it is to hitch different utopias to existing needs. It is one thing, however, to attach the provocative title of "socialism" to a movement, and another to create the ideological structure capable of sustaining far-reaching social changes. It may be said of most political innovators not content with the role of a permanent minority that they err on the side of underplaying the potentialities of "currents already present." The problem of major social and political change balances between what one can surely get as a short-run objective and what one dares hope to gain by boldness. To choose the former, as democratic socialists traditionally have done, may mean to forego the possibilities of realizing the latter.

From the short-range point of view, it was the particular good fortune of the Saskatchewan C.C.F. that, unlike other socialist parties on this continent, it did not have a powerful core of doctrinaire leaders who forced the movement to adopt an ideology that did not grow out of "currents already present in the society." Most of the earlier socialist parties in Canada and the United States—the Socialist Labor Party, the Socialist Party, and the Communist Party—were movements that sought to transfer to the North American environment the ideology of European socialism.

These movements failed to win significant national support for a variety of reasons that would take another series of studies to

elaborate. It is significant, however, that the most successful social-ist or semisocialist parties in the United States—the Socialist Party of Oklahoma, the Non-Partisan League, the Farmer-Labor Party of Minnesota—based their attack on the capitalist economic structure, not in terms of a Marxian doctrine of class struggle, but as a con-tinuation of the traditional struggle of farmers and workers, the common people, against "the vested interests" of eastern bankers and Wall Street, the symbol of concentrated wealth. North Ameri-cans have shown their willingness to organize against capitalist power in order to protect their opportunities to have a good job or to run their own farm or small business; but propaganda de-signed to appeal to a permanently exploited proletariat of workers and landless or mortgaged farmers has made little impression.

Myrdal has pointed out the extent to which the values of the American creed of equality, of freedom of opportunity, of demo-cratic classlessness have permeated every aspect of the culture. One would expect, therefore, that a successful socialist movement on this continent must basically be one that does not attempt to destroy the American creed, but presents its program for change in terms of amplifying and extending American values to all parts of society.

In Europe, where social and economic class lines were more firmly drawn as a result of a feudal past, labor and socialist parties basing their doctrines on a fundamental conflict of interests were successful in appealing to the proletariat. In most of the European countries the upper classes never accepted freedom of social mo-bility as part of their publicly proclaimed values. Class differences were openly recognized by all groups. Socialist and Labor parties were able, therefore, to be radical in both economic and cultural spheres. As class-conscious Marxists they rejected the capitalist or ruling-class culture around them. They built their own culture, with their own flag, songs, plays, and educational program, and rejected the traditional values of religion and patriotism.

While still in the early agitational stage, these movements de-manded total revolutionary change. But this stage could last only so long as the movements were illegal or comparatively small radical sects. Once a movement achieves legality and wins broad lower-class support, it finds that an ultrarevolutionary, antisocietal approach tends to repel groups who want a change but are not completely dissatisfied with the *status quo*. At this stage, radical

parties must make a choice: either continue to try to win majority support for an all-out radical socialist program, without compromising the original revolutionary doctrine, or seek to win votes for a limited set of objectives by compromising and modifying the parts of the program that challenge the basic values of the more stable groups.

This choice cuts across the traditional division of the socialist movement into revolutionary and democratic socialists. Revolutionaries such as Rosa Luxemburg in Germany and Bela Kun in Hungary would stand for no compromise; Lenin and the Russian Bolsheviks are examples of a revolutionary group that concentrated on power rather than program. Lenin, realizing that the Russian peasants would not support the Marxist program of nationalization of land, changed it to "Land to the Peasants," whereas Luxemburg and Kun continued to advocate the nationalization of land.[47]

On the other hand, the Austrian Social Democrats and the Socialist Party in the United States, though they were democratic socialists in philosophy, adhered in large measure to the uncompromising school of socialism.[48] The American Socialists before the First World War had many leaders who were suspicious of the support which the party received from Midwestern farmers, and these leaders prevented the party from appealing to the farmer on the basis of his interest in keeping his land. The Socialist Party also opposed the First World War, and this action was contrary to the patriotic principles of many potential supporters.

These two types of radical parties never exist in a pure form, except for a few doctrinaire socialist sects such as the Socialist Labor Party. The distinction between the two is useful, however, in partially explaining the development and the success or failure of left-wing movements. No uncompromising Marxian group has ever won majority power in any country in the world. Every nominally "socialist" governing group—Russia, Britain, China, Yugoslavia, Sweden, New Zealand, Australia, Saskatchewan—immediately before they won power had programs appealing to most sections of the population in terms of the latter's own immediate values. The Communist Party of France, which is the largest electoral Communist Party in a democratic country, dropped many parts of its original internationalist and leftist program during its election campaigns in 1945–1947. It appealed to the peasants as the party

that desired to protect private landownership, and to the middle class as the party that wanted to protect small business from the trusts.[49]

The history of most leftist parties has been largely an evolution from the class-conscious internationalist Marxist position to an "opportunistic" national appeal in which large segments of the population are wooed with specific planks directed to their own interests. Socialist parties originally envisaged socialism as a society in which there would be some form of social ownership of all industry, business, and land. This concept has gradually been modified until today many socialist movements stand for national economic planning, state ownership of certain large-scale monopolies, private ownership of most of industry and the distribution system, and the maintenance and extension of family-owned farms.[50]

With this change in economic doctrine has come a shift in the cultural and philosophic phases of socialism. Antagonism to religion has died away, and efforts have been made to link socialism and religion. Opposition to patriotism and symbols of nationalism has also disappeared. Antagonism to the monarchy has died among the socialists of the British Commonwealth and Scandinavia and, until they consolidated power, among the Communists of Rumania.

Official contempt for "bourgeois" sex mores and family system vanished long ago among leftist movements. In Italy the Communists opposed the establishment of divorce laws. The press description of the inauguration of a Communist, Klement Gottwald, as "president" of Czechoslovakia, indicates clearly the conscious recognition by the leaders of the Cominform that, while they are in the process of securing power, they must compromise with institutions they oppose.

The new president [Gottwald] swore allegiance to the Peoples' Democracy constitution, . . . crossed back into the courtyard where Catholic Archbishop Josef Beran greeted him and Mrs. Gottwald at the door of St. Vitus cathedral.

The archbishop shook hands heartily with the presidential couple and then escorted them into the church for a Te Deum (thanksgiving) mass. . . .

The government-controlled Catholic People's party commented that the cathedral service "was an extraordinary novelty in the history of presidential elections and the faithful will receive it with great satisfaction."[51]

The social changes introduced by *democratic* radical movements appear to result more from objective pressures in the society for such changes than from a small doctrinaire minority converting the majority of the population. The stronger a radical social movement becomes in a democracy, the less radical it appears in terms of the general cultural values. As it captures society, society captures it. The amount of change that the movement introduces into the culture as a result of assuming power appears relatively slight compared to the original goals.

This may not hold true, however, for totalitarian groups such as the Communists, who set up a dictatorship after taking power. These groups have two programs—one with which to win power and the other to go into effect while in power. In order to win power, the Communists (and the Fascists as well) publicly modify their goals in the direction of culturally approved objectives. Once having gained power and no longer subject to public opinion, they introduce changes which the electorate has never approved. The Russian Bolsheviks, for example, proceeded to nationalize land in 1929, though Stalin stated as late as 1928 that private agriculture would be desirable for at least another fifty years.[52] In order to force changes against the will of large sections of the population, however, the dictatorial "reformers" must use police measures continually against discontented elements. This strengthens the totalitarian nature of the state and destroys the original goal of an ultimate total democracy.

The democratic socialist party bidding for actual power or newly come to power is also placed in a difficult position, which is well illustrated by the British Labor government as this is written (1949). The winning of votes, particularly the decisive marginal votes of the middle class, calls for a policy of ideological opportunism and gradualism. But the preëlection period, which presents the threat of socialism during the continued operation of capitalism, invites loss of confidence by businessmen and, more dangerous, active sabotage of the socialist program. Thus the means employed by democratic radicals to secure power are as likely as are those of dictatorial "reformers" to endanger their original objective.

Chapter VIII

C.C.F. SUPPORT

HE ANALYSIS and understanding of a social movement necessarily involve a discussion of the support the party receives as well as the nature of the opposition it meets. The C.C.F. is ideologically a farmer and labor party attempting to replace the political and economic hegemony of big business by "the rule of the people." The movement has three important aspects: primarily, it represents the latest historical phase of the almost continuous struggle of western grain farmers with eastern business interests; second, within the Saskatchewan setting the movement is an outgrowth of the conflict between farmers, as consumers and producers, and middlemen who derive profits from them; and lastly, within the larger urban centers, it reflects the hostility between employers and workers.

The class-struggle aspects of the C.C.F. are brought out clearly by the results of the three provincial elections contested by the party before it took office in 1944. The difference between the vote received by political parties in rural areas and that received in the small trading villages and towns reflects the fact that the urban middle class and the farmers divided sharply in their reaction to the C.C.F.

The majority of the urban middle classes in the trading enclaves in Saskatchewan remained hostile to the C.C.F. in every election, in spite of the fervent overtures of the party leaders. It is significant to note that this cleavage in voting behavior between town and countryside occurred in other agrarian movements, as in the Non-Partisan League.

The urban gains of the C.C.F. in the elections of 1938 and 1944 are in part a result of its changed ideological position. As we have seen, the party in 1938 entered into formal and informal coalition

TABLE 13

PERCENTAGE OF VOTES RECEIVED BY C.C.F.

Elections	Rural areas	Small urban districts*
1934.................	29.8	12.9
1938.................	36.3	26.8
1944.................	58.1	38.8

Raw data in *Official Election Results*, Secretary of Executive Council, Province of Saskatchewan.
* Population less than 1,000.

agreements with the Social Crediters and the Conservatives against the Liberals who were in office. This led many supporters of the other parties to vote C.C.F. in constituencies where their own candidates were not running. As table 14 makes clear, the C.C.F. received a large portion of the Conservative and Social Credit vote.

The urban support of the C.C.F. was still very low where it did not receive the support of members of other opposition parties. In constituencies where all four parties ran, the C.C.F. received 17.5 per cent in small urban centers, as compared to 31.7 per cent in rural areas. The Social Credit Party, which promised to end the depression by issuing monetary dividends to all, became the party of the urban middle-class group that wanted reforms in the economic structure.

By the election year 1944, it was clear to everyone in Saskatchewan that the C.C.F. was the only opposition party that could succeed the Liberals. The Conservatives nominated candidates in only half of the constituencies in the province, while the Social Crediters withdrew from the provincial field. The C.C.F. was able, therefore, to win the votes of many people who wanted to get rid

---

[1] For notes to chapter viii see pages 299–301.

of the incumbent Liberals and could do so only by voting C.C.F. This accounts in part for the growth of the C.C.F. among middle-class groups.

The gain of the C.C.F. in the small towns probably does not indicate any significant lessening of the cleavage between country-side and trading center. The election statistics for small towns and villages conceal a conflict within the urban areas, for the C.C.F. received a higher vote from small-town workers and farmers than from business and professional people. This is indicated by the

TABLE 14

PERCENTAGE OF VOTES IN SMALL URBAN DISTRICTS,* 1938

Party	All parties running	Three parties running	Two parties running
C.C.F.	17.5	23.2	43.0
Liberal	45.9	51.7	57.0
Conservative	14.9		
Social Credit	21.7	25.1	

Raw data in *Official Election Results*, Secretary of Executive Council, Province of Saskatchewan.
* Population less than 1,000.

electoral data in towns that are large enough to have separate polling centers for different districts. The C.C.F. was appreciably stronger in working-class sections than in districts inhabited by business and professional men.[2] C.C.F. organizers report that their strength in the villages of Saskatchewan comes from workers and farmers who live in the towns.

The same internal class cleavage existed in the larger urban centers. In every city of the province, C.C.F. strength was considerably higher in working-class districts than in middle-class areas. The election results for the city of Regina indicate this clearly.

The attempt of various C.C.F. leaders to unite small business-men, farmers, and workers in one party was foredoomed to failure, for it ignored the fact that in Saskatchewan small businessmen are the only immediate representatives of the "profit" system and, therefore, are resented by the farmers, who desire to eliminate them rather than to win their support. The coöperative store and the Wheat Pool elevator are the core of emotional loyalty for the C.C.F. farmers. The general store, the bank, and the insurance office are symbols of economic oppression.

Business and professional men, on the other hand, tend to identify themselves with large capital rather than with workers and farmers. Objectively, the urban middle classes may have, in the monopolists, a common enemy with other groups, but, in fact, local merchants, doctors, bank managers, and lawyers regard themselves as superior to both farmers and workers, and aspire to the status of the upper classes in the large cities. The country grocer or butcher in the small villages of the wheat belt is in the highest social class in his community, even though his economic compeers

TABLE 15

PERCENTAGE DISTRIBUTION OF VOTES IN REGINA

Party	Working-class polls*		Middle-class polls*	
	1934	1944	1934	1944
C.C.F.	25.5	61.6	19.4	32.2
Liberal	44.0	29.7	45.5	52.3
Conservative	30.4	8.7	35.1	15.5

Raw data in *Official Election Results*, Secretary of Executive Council, Province of Saskatchewan.
* The difference between the polls was based on information obtained from interviews with officials of the city of Regina and from local politicians and old residents.

in the large cities are probably in the lower middle class.[3] This tends to give the small-town merchant a greater social stake in preserving the *status quo* than his big-city brother, and it is more difficult to recruit him to a radical social movement. Furthermore, the program of the C.C.F. to take over retail distribution, medicine, banking, and insurance, under coöperative or government ownership, seemed to adversely affect a large group of the small-town middle class. They therefore remained actively hostile to the new party.

Before the C.C.F. was organized, the urban middle classes dominated the political life of the province. They were and still are the leaders of the Liberal and Conservative parties. The political machines of the old parties were centered in the towns and cities, and were operated by lawyers, insurance men, and other members of the middle class. (See chap. ix, p. 193.) The C.C.F. represented a threat to the political control and influence of the urban middle classes, as well as a challenge to their economic interests. The change in the class base of political control in Saskatchewan which the C.C.F. introduced is clearly indicated in table 37 (p. 194).

The election statistics cited tend to confirm the interpretation that the C.C.F. has been primarily a farmer-labor party. In every election that it has contested, the party received more support from these two groups than it did from the urban middle classes. These data, however, reveal little of the dynamics of the growth of the C.C.F. An analysis of the shifts in electoral behavior within the working class and the farm population is necessary in order to understand the real significance of Saskatchewan radicalism. Fortunately, the Canadian census makes such an analysis possible, as it supplies social and economic data for rural municipalities, which do not include organized urban communities.[4]

C.C.F. rural support doubled between 1934 and 1944. The party received 29 per cent of the farm vote in 1934, and 58 per cent in the election that swept it to power. One possible interpretation is that these gains reflect the changes in the party program between 1934 and 1944, that the party won the support of the extremely poor farmers to whom it addressed its propaganda in the early radical period, and later gained the more substantial middle-class agrarians by modifying its radicalism to win the support of the conservative and well-to-do elements. Many political observers, including some C.C.F. leaders, made this interpretation of C.C.F. growth.

Actually, the exact opposite occurred. C.C.F. supporters in 1934 came from the groups in the rural population which had the highest social and economic status. The party's vote was highest in prosperous farm areas where land-tax assessment was high and tenancy was low. Strong C.C.F. districts were also characterized by being predominantly Anglo-Saxon and Protestant. Though the correlations between the various ecological factors and the C.C.F. votes are not very great, as can be seen from table 16, an analysis of these factors by the Lazarsfeld latent-attribute method reveals that the cluster of factors that make for high status in Saskatchewan was highly interrelated with the C.C.F. vote in 1934.[5]

The differences between the support of the C.C.F. and of the Liberal Party may be explained on the basis of cultural attributes: the Liberals derived more of their support from the poor non-Anglo-Saxon and Roman Catholic elements than did the C.C.F. The Conservatives, who were traditionally the party of the Anglo-Saxon Protestants, continued to receive most of their backing from that part of the population. The C.C.F., however, was supported

TABLE 16

CORRELATIONS OF CENSUS DATA FOR RURAL AREAS OF SASKATCHEWAN WITH POLITICAL PARTY VOTE, 1934

Group	C.C.F.	Conservative	Liberal	Assessment of Land	Tenancy	United Church	Roman Catholic	Anglo-Saxon
C.C.F.	x	−.23	−.65	.25	−.11	.40	−.29	.44
Conservative	−.23	x	—	−.04	.20	.33	−.37	.35
Liberal	−.65	—	x	—	.03	−.43	.25	−.40
Assessment of Land	.25	−.40	−.20	x	.18	.57	−.27	.51
Tenancy	−.11	.20	.03	.18	x	.19	.14	.08
United Church	.40	.33	−.43	.57	.19	x	−.45	.85
Roman Catholic	.29	−.37	.25	−.27	.14	−.45	x	−.50
Anglo-Saxon	.44	.35	−.40	.51	.08	.85	−.50	x

by the well-to-do, Anglo-Saxon Protestant areas, while the Tories were found in the poorer districts.

The shifts in the electoral strength of the political parties between the elections of 1934 and 1938 are difficult to analyze because of the multiplicity of parties and the coalitions among them. In some constituencies in 1938, the C.C.F. ran against three other parties—Liberals, Conservatives, and Social Crediters; in others it received the support of Social Crediters or Conservatives against Liberals. The C.C.F., in turn, did not contest 22 out of the 52 seats in the province and supported, formally or informally, one or the other of the opposition parties. The entry of Social Credit as an alternative protest party greatly complicated the picture, for in areas where the Social Crediters ran against the C.C.F., the party's vote declined below that received in 1934, while in constituencies where the C.C.F. alone opposed the old parties, its vote went up.

The principal change in C.C.F. support in the 1938 election from that of 1934 was that it tended to receive the support of many poorer Anglo-Saxon Protestants who had previously voted Conservative. This was probably a result of the fact that the Conservative Party did not contest half the seats in the election, and its rural supporters tended to vote C.C.F. where their party did not run. As in 1934, the C.C.F. was opposed by the poorer non-Anglo-Saxon and Catholic areas. Catholic farmers either continued to vote for the Liberal Party or backed the Social Credit movement, which had more appeal to dissatisfied Catholics than did the socialist C.C.F.

As the depression came to an end, the C.C.F. recruited many more supporters from the socially and economically depressed part of the rural population that had previously supported the old parties. In the election of 1944 the party made most of its electoral gains from the low-status groups, the poorer and non-Anglo-Saxon farmers, as table 17 indicates.

The inconclusive correlations between the C.C.F. vote and the ecological variables resulting from the 1944 election returns are due to the fact that C.C.F. gains canceled out the effect of the original (1934) C.C.F. support. The party made its greatest gains in the areas where it had been weakest in 1934, and the ecological analysis of the 1944 vote does not reveal significant differences between C.C.F. and anti-C.C.F. areas.

The data cited above raise some interesting questions about the nature of radical political activity. It is popularly assumed that radical political action in a crisis is related to poverty and low social status. Marxists have traditionally believed that revolutionary action would be brought about by increasing economic misery. The Saskatchewan situation suggests, however, that within an exploited economic group, such as the prairie wheat farmers, those who possess economic and social status within the class are most resentful of a threat to their security. The poorer, socially outcast

TABLE 17

CORRELATIONS BETWEEN C.C.F. VOTES IN 1934 AND 1944,
AND C.C.F. GAINS

Group	C.C.F. votes		C.C.F. gains between 1934 and 1944
	1934	1944	
Assessment of Land............	.25	− .08	− .26
United Church................	.40	.10	− .27
Roman Catholic...............	− .29	− .10	.06
Anglo-Saxon..................	.44	.04	− .42

groups, when they are seriously affected by economic reverses, are likely to be politically apathetic rather than rebellious. In Saskatchewan this group did not organize for remedial action but had to be organized from the outside by leaders of the more prosperous farmers. In 1934, in the depths of the depression, low-status farmers—the poor, non-Anglo-Saxon, and Catholics—tended to remain loyal to the Liberal Party.

There is a second related explanation of the differences in 1934 between supporters of the C.C.F. and of the old party. The C.C.F. was organized mainly by men who had been active in farmers' movements: the Wheat Pool, the Saskatchewan Grain Growers' Association, the Farmers' Union, and the United Farmers of Canada. Studies of rural coöperative and economic class organizations in the United States have indicated that such organizations are composed primarily of well-to-do farmers of Anglo-Saxon or northern European extraction. Poorer agrarians and those belonging to low-status ethnic groups have not generally participated in organized farmers' movements.[6] The battle for higher prices and a better economic return for their labor has been conducted by the farmers who need it least.

This is true of Saskatchewan as well. An unpublished study, the source of which is confidential, has shown that members of the Wheat Pool and consumers' coöperatives in the province are predominantly well-to-do farmers. The ethnic settlements have long been obstacles in the path of the coöperative movement. The comparatively wealthy Anglo-Saxon farmers had learned, before the C.C.F. was organized, to react through class organizations to economic problems. The C.C.F. was founded in 1931 as the newest in the long chain of such protest movements, and as such it received the support of the more economically and politically class-conscious agrarians.

The less prosperous Saskatchewan farmers began to support the C.C.F. only after the depression had ended and economic conditions had improved. The combination of a long economic depression that had deprived them of all material rewards and a subsequent economic boom was necessary before they could turn to political action on their own behalf. These developments challenge the assumption that radicalism necessarily wanes during economic prosperity. Often, as in Saskatchewan, an upswing in the business cycle may prove to be the stimulus that gives the depressed members of society enough personal security to engage in politics.

Farmers in the lower stratum, once aroused, however, seem to become stronger supporters of the radical movement than well-to-do farmers. C.C.F. field organizers confirm from their campaign experiences the indications of the election results. Those interviewed almost invariably reported that it was difficult to organize the poorer farmers during the 'thirties, but that during the war they became stronger supporters of the party than many of the wealthy grain growers.

The implications of these data for theories of radical political behavior are not limited to farmers. A similar pattern exists among urban workers. The data were obtained by dividing the city of Regina, the largest urban area in the province, into three sections: the East End, composed mainly of foreign-born, unskilled workers; the North End, inhabited by better-paid, skilled Anglo-Saxon workers; and the West End, a middle- and upper-class section. The differences in the electoral behavior of the two working-class sections are similar to those found in rural areas.

In 1934 the C.C.F.'s greatest support in Regina came from the upper strata of the working class, while the poorer, the unskilled, and the unemployed workers in the East End remained as loyal to the old parties as did the business-class district. It was only when the depression ended that the lower strata turned to the C.C.F.

Ethnic and religious factors appear to play an important role in distinguishing C.C.F. support and its opposition. It is impos-

TABLE 18

PERCENTAGE DISTRIBUTION OF VOTES IN REGINA

Party	West End* middle class	Per cent gain or loss	N. End* skilled workers	Per cent gain or loss	East End* unskilled workers	Per cent gain or loss
			1934 Election			
C.C.F..............	19.4	....	33.2	....	19.5	....
Liberal.............	45.5	....	32.9	....	52.8	....
Conservative........	35.1	....	33.9	....	27.7	....
			1944 Election			
C.C.F..............	32.2	64.9	60.8	83.1	62.1	218.5
Liberal.............	52.3	14.9	26.9	−18.2	31.5	−40.3
Conservative........	15.5	−55.8	12.2	−64.0	6.4	−76.9

*Raw data in *Official Election Results*, Secretary of Executive Council, Province of Saskatchewan.

sible, however, to obtain correlations with which to analyze the effect of these factors because the different cultural groups are concentrated in a few areas. The 58 per cent of the rural population who are non-Anglo-Saxon live in ethnic enclaves, and most census areas (rural municipalities) do not contain more than one or two ethnic groups in significant numbers. It has been necessary, therefore, to examine the municipalities that have a large proportion of cultural subgroups, and compare them with the general population in order to estimate the role played by cultural background in C.C.F. support.

The ecological data indicate that the Anglo-Saxons and the Scandinavians of the province have tended to be members of the C.C.F. This is probably because supporters of the coöperatives and the farm movement are generally C.C.F. voters. The Anglo-Saxons tend to be coöperators because of their superior economic

position, which enables them to invest in coöperatives. Many of the Scandinavians have had favorable experiences with the coöperative and socialist movements in their home countries and consequently joined these movements in Saskatchewan. C.C.F.

TABLE 19

C.C.F. SUPPORT IN RURAL SASKATCHEWAN MUNICIPALITIES WITH HIGH PROPORTION OF SCANDINAVIANS

(Percentages)

	Scandinavians*	C.C.F. votes†		
		1934	1938	1944
All rural areas in province......	10.1	29.6	36.3	58.1
Scandinavian rural municipalities........................	31.9	40.0	45.0	58.6

* *Farms and Farmers in Canada: Facts from the Census, 1941 and 1931* (1944), p. 10.
† Raw data in *Official Election Results*, Secretary of Executive Council, Province of Saskatchewan.

TABLE 20

C.C.F. SUPPORT IN RURAL SASKATCHEWAN MUNICIPALITIES WITH HIGH PROPORTION OF FRENCH CANADIANS

(Percentages)

	French Canadians*	C.C.F. votes†		
		1934	1938	1944
All rural areas in province......	5.0	29.6	36.3	58.1
French-Canadian rural municipalities....................	29.5	24.2	31.7	49.6

* *Farms and Farmers in Canada: Facts from the Census, 1941 and 1931* (1944), p. 10.
† Raw data in *Official Election Results*, Secretary of Executive Council, Province of Saskatchewan.

organizers report that the Scandinavians were the easiest group to organize into the party.

Other non-Anglo-Saxon ethnic groups have been more difficult to organize. Many have remained loyal to the Liberal Party, the traditional party of the minority ethnic groups in Canada, as contrasted with the Protestant Anglo-Saxon Tories. The French Canadians of the province, who come from traditionally Liberal Quebec and live in French-speaking enclaves, have remained more strongly opposed to the C.C.F. than the rest of the population.

The Mennonites, who comprise 4.6 per cent of Saskatchewan's population, are also strongly opposed to the C.C.F. Many of them are refugees from the Russian Revolution and identify the C.C.F. with the hated communism of Russia from which they escaped. The largely Mennonite constituency of Rosthern is the strongest anti-C.C.F. seat in the province.

The vote of the Ukrainians is the most difficult to explain. Though the majority are Roman Catholic by birth, they tend to be less influenced by the Church than other Catholic groups. The

TABLE 21

C.C.F. Support in Rural Saskatchewan Municipalities
with High Proportion of Mennonites

(Percentages)

	Mennonites*	C.C.F. votes†		
		1934	1938	1944
All rural areas in province......	4.6	29.6	36.3	58.1
Mennonite rural municipalities.	46.7	19.4	31.9	45.0

* *Eighth Census of Canada, 1941*, Bulletin A-5, pp. 2-3.
† Raw data in *Official Election Results*, Secretary of Executive Council, Province of Saskatchewan.

Ukrainians, in fact, are the only predominantly Roman Catholic national group whose support of the C.C.F. is commensurate with that of the general population. The strong C.C.F. vote may be an indication of the weakened position of the Catholic Church among the Ukrainians, rather than of Catholic support for the C.C.F. A large minority of Ukrainians belong to the Greek Orthodox Church and therefore are exposed to different religious pressures. The so-called "Red" Ukrainians, who ideologically support the Soviet Union, are mostly agnostics and atheists.

The Ukrainians live in the poorer northern and central districts, since they were comparatively late settlers. They were not among the early strong supporters of the coöperative and farmers' movements, as can be seen from their voting behavior in 1934. In succeeding elections, however, the C.C.F. was able to make great gains among the poorer Ukrainians after concentrated organizational work in these districts. Today the Ukrainians are among the strongest supporters of the C.C.F.

Persons of German extraction constitute the largest non-Anglo-Saxon ethnic minority in Saskatchewan. They are divided between the Roman Catholic and the Lutheran churches. It is difficult to ascribe any significance to the voting data for the German areas. Like most of the other ethnic minorities, the Germans tend to be

TABLE 22

C.C.F. Support in Rural Saskatchewan Municipalities
with High Proportion of Ukrainians

(Percentages)

	Ukrainians*	C.C.F. votes†		
		1934	1938	1944
All rural areas in province......	10.3	29.6	36.3	58.1
Ukrainian rural municipalities.	59.6	21.1	42.7	59.6

* *Farms and Farmers in Canada: Facts from the Census, 1941 and 1931* (1944), p. 10.
† Raw data in *Official Election Results*, Secretary of Executive Council, Province of Saskatchewan.

TABLE 23

C.C.F. Support in Rural Saskatchewan Municipalities
with High Proportion of Germans

(Percentages)

	Germans*	C.C.F. votes†		
		1934	1938	1944
All rural areas in province......	15.1	29.6	36.3	58.1
German rural municipalities....	57.7	24.0	34.5	54.0

* *Farms and Farmers in Canada: Facts from the Census, 1941 and 1931* (1944), p. 10.
† Raw data in *Official Election Results*, Secretary of Executive Council, Province of Saskatchewan.

more opposed to the C.C.F. than those of Anglo-Saxon extraction. German Catholics are reputed to be highly resistant to the party's appeal.

The evidence indicates that Roman Catholic opposition to socialism is the most significant of the ethnic and religious factors involved in the Saskatchewan vote. Catholics have been and remain the backbone of the Liberal Party's support in the province. In every election they give less support to the C.C.F. than do the Protestants. A Saskatchewan Catholic priest who is engaged in a

study of the C.C.F. and has studied the attitudes of both lay and clerical Catholics indicates the causes of their hostility to the party.

The mentality of most Catholics I have met across Canada, including the clergy, is infected with a terribly distorted view of the C.C.F. *reality*. The result is that Catholics generally are afflicted with a deep-rooted, though unconscious, prejudice against the C.C.F. It is virtually identical with the kind of prejudice against Catholics found in the typical Ontario Protestant of twenty years ago. Catholics by and large condemn the C.C.F. for something it is not; they are enslaved by the tyranny of a single word—"socialism." If I may generalize on the fairly large sample I have interviewed across the continent, then the overwhelming majority of Catholics are unconsciously banded together in a compact political unity based on an illusion. (I suspect that this is not true of Nova Scotia, due mainly to the enlightened leadership given the people by the priests of Saint Francis Xavier.) The result is that Catholics tend to fall into a mould of political and economic thought quite out of line with that of the encyclicals. Enslaved mentally by the tyranny of that awful word, they are virtually forced to devour with avidity all the "anti-socialist" propaganda dispensed so generously and freely by the forces of reaction. And we come to the sad and tragic paradox where we find that Canadian Catholics, by and large, have divorced themselves from those constructive and creative forces about which Maritain has written so well, and which are the only hope we have of winning the peace. Outside of Joe Burton of Humboldt, there is not a single Catholic in a place of influence or leadership in the Saskatchewan C.C.F. movement. With rare exceptions the same is true all across Canada. The influence of Catholic leadership, both clerical and lay, and a considerable portion of the Catholic vote is thus spent in prolonging what Maritain has called the agony of the modern world.'

The decline in overt clerical hostility to the C.C.F. in recent years has been associated with C.C.F. gains in Catholic areas. It is questionable, however, whether the change in the official attitude of the Church is a cause of the increased Catholic support of the party. The hierarchy in Saskatchewan still believes, as Father Cullinane has indicated, that C.C.F. socialism is evil and represents a threat to the Church.

The increasing support of the C.C.F., both Catholic and non-Catholic, has led Catholic leaders to recognize that the C.C.F. has become a permanent factor in Saskatchewan and Canadian politics and that the Church cannot afford to antagonize a prospective governmental party. The Church also has been under

pressure from lay Catholics, who joined the C.C.F., to cease her opposition to the party. The decline in the C.C.F.'s aggressive radicalism both in Saskatchewan and across Canada has reassured Catholic leaders that the C.C.F. does not necessarily represent a threat to the Church. At present, however, there can be little doubt that members of the Canadian hierarchy prefer a non-C.C.F. government and that this feeling is reflected in Catholic voting.

The influence of the Protestant churches on Saskatchewan political behavior is more difficult to analyze; with the exception of the United Church, no one Protestant sect has a sufficiently large proportion of the population to lend itself to a statistical analysis from census data. Two factors do stand out, however: membership in the United Church tends to be consistently and positively associated with C.C.F. support, and there is some evidence that Anglicans are opposed to the movement.

The United Church of Canada is comparable to the nonconformist workingmen's churches of Great Britain. It has stressed the social-gospel aspect of Christianity. Many of its leaders have been active in secular reform activities.[8] A number of church conferences have officially attacked private capitalism as "unChristian." Since it has the least fundamentalist and conservative creed, the United Church tends to attract and influence those who believe in a liberal Christianity that is concerned with establishing "the good life" on earth. Many C.C.F. members of the United Church explicitly state their belief that a good Christian must be a socialist.

The Anglican Church has remained "essentially an English institution, maintaining English traditions and a close relationship with England."[9] It is more of an urban, middle-class church than is the United Church. Its adherents tend to be more conservative and traditionalist than do those of other denominations. They are prone, therefore, to be found in the ranks of the Conservative Party, which is associated in the minds of many people with strong Empire ties. A Gallup Poll sample (see p. 301) indicates that Anglicans constitute the largest group of Tory supporters in the province, and that they are overwhelmingly opposed to the C.C.F.

Veblen has suggested that the capacity of a society for change "depends in large measure on the degree . . . of exposure of the individual members to the constraining forces of the environment." The process of social transformation will be retarded, however, "if

any portion or class of society is sheltered from the environment in any essential respect, [for] that portion of the community or that class will adapt its views and its scheme of life more tardily to the altered general situation."[10]

The western rural community possesses Veblen's prerequisites for social change more than any other group in the United States or Canada. Saskatchewan comes closer to being an economically undifferentiated society than most rural or urban areas, for almost every farmer is dependent on wheat for his basic source of income. When, in the price decline of the early 'thirties, the cost of the production of a bushel of wheat came to exceed its sales value, the deficit of larger and more prosperous farmers was greater than that of small farmers. (See table 8, p. 92.) Some of the wealthiest rural districts in the province were among the worst afflicted by hard times. Nearly every farmer was forced to accept some form of government relief.

This situation meant that the threat to the basic social and economic values of rural Saskatchewan was experienced more or less equally by all sections of the population, for climatic and economic forces played few favorites. A unity of suffering and interest existed despite differences in economic status. As in most wheat areas during crises, there was no "sheltered" group in rural Saskatchewan in the 'thirties. Most of the rural community, therefore, supported the movement for change.

In urban areas, in contrast, the population is unequally affected by economic depression. The upper and middle classes retain their relative social and economic position, though their total income may decline. Sections of the middle class and working class may actually experience an increase in real income as a result of the decline in prices. Only a minority of workers are ever unemployed. Thus a new movement for social change cannot appeal equally to all classes or even to all sections of the working class.[11] The fact that economic crises have given rise to successful agrarian parties more often than to workers' protest parties is partially a result of this difference between the rural and the urban community.

The effect of a depression on the farmer, especially in Saskatchewan, and on the urban worker differs also in another important respect. The relations between the "uncontrollable" external forces and the farmer's plight are more directly visible than they are in an urban economy. The worker who cannot get a job has been

taught to blame his own ineptitude for his failure.[12] As a result of economic crisis, many of the unemployed lose confidence in themselves and become apathetic. Farmers, however, are more apt to lose confidence in the traditional values of society under extreme economic conditions. The farmers of Saskatchewan could not be blamed for the economic problems that threatened them. It was not their fault that they could not raise crops because of the drought or the decline in the price of wheat.

Saskatchewan differed also from rural areas where large variations in types of farming exist. Such variations usually create differences in economic and political interests and behavior. Ecological studies of agrarian voting behavior in the United States indicate that the most important factor differentiating rural districts supporting protest movements from those opposing them has been the type of crop: there has often been a significant difference between the vote in wheat areas and in corn or mixed-farming regions.[13] The last large agrarian party in the United States, the Non-Partisan League, was able to win majority support only in North Dakota, a state that is similar to Saskatchewan in having a one-crop wheat economy, and it secured only minority support in states where farming was more diversified. Fluctuations in economic conditions affect different farming regions unequally, and are reflected in the voting and organizational behavior of the population.

The most significant feature of the growth of the C.C.F. has been the apparent contradiction between the pattern of C.C.F. growth and the belief that radical movements are based on the poorest segment of the population and grow best during economic depressions. The earliest support of the party came from the upper layer of farmers' and workers' groups. Among the more depressed strata its greatest growth came in a period of rising prosperity. The phenomenon of intensified radical behavior in a period of prosperity following a depression has been paralleled in other parts of Canada. Nationally, the C.C.F. did not gain much between 1935, the year of the first federal election which it contested, and 1940, when the depression receded. It had about 10 per cent of the vote on both occasions. The party began its rapid national growth in the latter part of 1942. It won a series of by-elections all across Canada and increased its representation in the Ontario legislature from no seats in 1937 to 34 seats in 1943.

Canadian workers and farmers apparently learned the economic lessons of the depression only after the event. During the depression, poverty, insecurity, and unemployment did not stimulate mass upheaval. A research study on the effect of unemployment in Marienthal, Austria, throws some light on this problem. The workers, instead of becoming more radical when the town's leading factory closed, became politically apathetic. They tended to withdraw into the family circle and lose interest in the outside world.

Those who are on the bottom of the economic scale will not revolt if they are pushed down further. A person must have a certain amount of security to fight for a larger share. Those who have nothing to lose but their chains are too closely chained, psychologically, to the desperation of their lot to generalize their predicament, face the consequences of a malcontent position, or otherwise add to their suffering by striving for social change. They are too deeply concerned with the all-absorbing, time-consuming, dismaying problem of getting by on "handouts" to afford the luxury of thought and effort for a distant eventuality, however promising. The authors of the Marienthal study point out that

[unemployment in Marienthal resulted in a] drop from the higher cultural level of political struggle to the more primitive level of mutual individual animosity . . . the few who are politically active, especially among the young people, are still at work. The group of Socialist Working Youth has 37 members; of these only 7 are unemployed. As soon as an official of this group becomes unemployed he gives up all his duties and, tired of politics, withdraws. . . .

It is typical of the whole situation when a leading political functionary of the place reports:

"Previously I used to know the *Arbeiterzeitung* [the Socialist Party newspaper] by heart; now I look at it just a bit and then throw it away, in spite of the fact that I have more time."

As a matter of fact, from 1927 to 1930 the subscriptions to the *Arbeiterzeitung* have dropped about 60 per cent. This is not, as one might suppose, to be interpreted as a mere economical counting of pennies, for the *Arbeiterzeitung* issues an unemployed subscription that costs only four groschen per copy; it is the interest in politics that has lessened. The subscription to the *Kleinen Blatts*, which has the same political direction, only in general is more concerned with entertainment than politics, has declined only by about 27 per cent in spite of its higher price—10 groschen per copy.[14]

It is the people who have something to lose in the form of economic and social status who fight back. Well-to-do farmers and skilled workers will resist economic adversity. They know that loss of farm income or reduced wages are not their fault. They are more likely to join or support a new radical movement than are the poor farmers or unemployed workers.

Emile Durkheim has pointed out that sheer poverty does not lead to lack of adjustment with society.

> ... poverty ... by its very nature ... acts as a restraint. Whatever one may do, one's desires are obliged, in some measure, to reckon with the available resources; what one has acts in part as a guide in determining what one would like to have. Consequently, the less one possesses, the less he is inclined to extend endlessly the range of his wants. By subjecting us forcibly to moderation, poverty habituates us to it, and besides, where mediocrity is a general condition, nothing occurs to excite envy. Wealth, on the other hand, by virtue of the power which it confers upon its possessor, creates the illusion that we can rise simply by our own efforts. By reducing the obstacles which are placed in our way, riches lead us to believe that such obstacles can be mastered indefinitely. Now the less a man feels himself restrained, the more intolerable any actual restraint seems to him. It is not without reason, then, that so many religions have glorified the benefits and the moral worth of poverty. Poverty is, indeed, the best school for teaching a man self-restraint.[15]

The return of prosperity removes the main cause of political apathy among the poorer farmers and workers. The radical movement is able to capitalize on the adverse experiences of the poorer classes during the depression. The C.C.F. in Canada was able to convince many workers and farmers that a change in the economic system would prevent a new depression. The resentment of the lower strata of the population over their treatment during the depression was therefore channeled during prosperity.

The effects of the depression on political behavior in other countries would seem to contradict this general theory. Radical parties made headway in many European countries, in New Zealand, and in North Dakota and Minnesota during the 'thirties. It must be remembered, however, that the Labor Party in New Zealand, the Social Democratic Party of Sweden, the Farmer-Labor Party in Minnesota, and the Non-Partisan League in North Dakota, which achieved power in the depression period, were not depression-born movements. Each was the largest opposition group in its

country or state before the depression. As the alternative government, it capitalized on the discontent with the government in power. Leftist governments that were in power when the depression started, as in Australia and England, also lost office because the government in power was blamed for troubles that began while it held office.

The development of political class consciousness is similar to the emergence of economic class consciousness, or trade-unionism. The greatest growth of the latter usually occurs during an economic upswing following a depression. A depression weakens working-class morale and makes it almost impossible to recruit workers into unions. The immediate objective of workers becomes simply to have and hold a job. The worker is not open to new ideas, such as those of trade-unionism or a radical political party.[16] Only after the worker's economic position has been fortified by some degree of security is he free to consider ways and means of improving his position or of preventing a recurrence of past evils.

Once the process of radicalization develops—a conscious discontent with one's lot and a conviction that economic and social conditions can be improved through collective class action—the poorer section of the working and farming classes appears to become the firmest base of the class movement. Additional moves in a leftist direction may now come from the more depressed elements. This can be seen in Saskatchewan, where the Labor Progressive Party (Communist) gained what little strength it has in the poor sections on the northern frontier and in the East End in Regina.[17] A farmers' strike in the autumn of 1946 in Saskatchewan and Alberta was, for the most part, a movement of the smaller and poorer farmers who were dissatisfied with the price of wheat and supported strike action to gain immediate economic benefits.[18]

Chapter IX

C.C.F. LEADERS

THE ELECTION data presented in chapter viii contradict theories which assume that radical parties are movements of the "down-and-outers," the bottom level of society. To what extent are similar stereotypes about radical leaders correct? It has been suggested that the nucleus of leadership in a social movement comes from marginal groups, with their concomitant of economic, social, or personal maladjustments.[1] These groups should be most likely to accept a new radical program for social change in a period of social disequilibrium such as depression or drought, while the old community and class leaders attempt to maintain the *status quo*.[2] Actually, however, research data on the nature of leadership in new social movements are scanty and inconclusive.

In Saskatchewan it has been possible to trace the social and economic backgrounds of leaders of an organized protest movement. Information was obtained about the social, economic, and political backgrounds of delegates attending C.C.F. provincial conventions in 1945 and 1946. These delegates, who were elected from forty-five constituency conventions held throughout the province, represented the best large-scale cross section of secondary party leaders. Of the 800 delegates who attended these conven-

---

[1] For notes to chapter ix see pages 301–302.

tions, 628 filled out questionnaires. Of these, 71.8 per cent were farmers or farmers' wives; 11.0 per cent, workers; 10.5 per cent, business or professional men; 2.7 per cent, teachers; 4.0 per cent, miscellaneous or unknown.

The backgrounds of the 431 rural C.C.F. convention delegates explain in large measure the reasons for the comparatively rapid growth of the C.C.F. in rural Saskatchewan. These active secondary leaders of the party were also the rural community leaders.

TABLE 24

431 RURAL DELEGATES TO C.C.F. CONVENTION HOLDING POSTS IN
COÖPERATIVE MOVEMENT, 1946

(Percentages)

Post	All delegates	Delegates over 45 years old	Delegates under 45 years old
Any in a coöperative..............	73.6	77.9	66.1
Wheat Pool committee............	60.4	64.8	54.4
Chairman or secretary, Wheat Pool committee.....................	34.1	39.2	25.0
Wheat Pool delegate..............	10.4	13.7	3.6
Director consumers' coöperative....	39.2	39.2	39.2
Director provincial coöperative.....	10.0	13.7	3.6
Director Credit Union............	5.7	5.9	5.4

Three-quarters of them held some position in a local or provincial coöperative. Official positions in the coöperative movement are a good index of community leadership, as the coöperatives are the major rural organizations in Saskatchewan. At the end of 1944, the year in which the C.C.F. came to power, the coöperatives had 299,686 members. This meant that there were approximately two coöperative members for every farmer in the province.

The interrelations between C.C.F. and coöperative leaders suggest that the coöperative leaders started the C.C.F. or that C.C.F. supporters succeeded in replacing the old coöperative leadership as radicals achieved wider influence in the rural community. From the fact that 58.9 per cent of those C.C.F. delegates more than 45 years of age in 1945 held posts in coöperatives *before* the C.C.F. was organized, it is clear that the C.C.F. did not win control of the coöperative movement from the outside, but rather that the existing coöperative leaders organized the C.C.F. Further evi-

dence in support of this conclusion can be found in the fact that the average number of years of membership of the older C.C.F. delegates in the Wheat Pool, the largest coöperative in the province, was 20.4 years, and the median period was 21.7 years. The majority of them joined the Pool in 1923 and 1924, when it was first organized and was the major agrarian protest movement.

Another index of the leadership of C.C.F. men in the community is their participation in farmers' educational organizations: the Saskatchewan Grain Growers' Association, the Farmers' Union,

TABLE 25

FARMERS' EDUCATIONAL ORGANIZATIONS OF 1945 AND 1946
C.C.F. DELEGATES OVER FORTY-FIVE YEARS OLD

(Percentages)

Organization	Members	Officials
Saskatchewan Grain Growers...................	56.4	19.4
Farmers' Union..............................	33.7	11.8
United Farmers of Canada....................	78.9	30.5
None.......................................	18.8	59.1

and the United Farmers of Canada (Saskatchewan Section). These organizations have been in the forefront of all the struggles of the farmers since 1901. They supported the formation of most of the coöperative ventures and independent political efforts in the province. Since the organization of the C.C.F., the present farmers' educational organization, the U.F.C., has declined greatly in membership and influence because most of its supporters have become active in the C.C.F. This transfer of participation from the educational organization to the political party is clearly shown by the organizational backgrounds of the C.C.F. leaders who are old enough to have taken an active part in these educational associations before the organization of the C.C.F.

C.C.F. leaders were active in farmers' educational organizations before the formation of the C.C.F. Of the older group of C.C.F. delegates, 70.1 per cent were in one or more of these organizations before 1931, when the C.C.F. was formed in Saskatchewan, and 55.1 per cent of those who belonged to these organizations before the formation of the C.C.F. held official positions in them.

The rural areas of Saskatchewan have their own separate non-

partisan governmental institutions. The C.C.F. delegates, as table 26 indicates, are also leaders in this form of community activity. The overwhelming majority of rural C.C.F. officials are community leaders, but it could not be concluded from this information alone that the C.C.F. rural leaders and the community leaders are the same. It is conceivable that those who are active in all three provincial political parties are community leaders. To examine this possibility, information was gathered about the political backgrounds of officials of the coöperatives. Two sets of data were

TABLE 26

Public Posts Held by Rural Delegates to 1945 and 1946
C.C.F. Conventions

Public post	Percentage of all delegates	Percentage of delegates over 45 years old	Percentage of delegates under 45 years old
Reeve (mayor)....................	10.5	17.8	3.5
Rural municipal councilor..........	19.5	33.9	5.3
Hospital board....................	9.5	9.9	7.0
School board................·............	55.8	73.3	35.1
Telephone board..................	34.2	39.6	17.5
Any public post..................	67.4	84.2	51.8

obtained. From persons active in the coöperative movement of the province, information was obtained about the political affiliations of 113 out of 165 subdirectors or delegates of the Saskatchewan Wheat Pool, the largest and most important coöperative. Moreover, questionnaires similar to those given to the C.C.F. delegates were filled out by 122 delegates to the conventions of two of the more important coöperative organizations. The two sets of data, presented in table 27, are strikingly similar.

Though the coöperative movement is officially neutral in politics, there can be no doubt that its leaders are largely supporters of only one party, the C.C.F. These coöperative supporters are not recent adherents of the party. Of the 122 delegates who filled out questionnaires and indicated their support of the C.C.F., 87.8 per cent had backed the movement before 1936, and 64.6 per cent in 1933 or earlier. The close ties between C.C.F. and coöperative leaders are further indicated by the fact that most coöperative leaders have held some post in the C.C.F. party. These C.C.F.

coöperative leaders, like the delegates to the C.C.F. convention, were active also in the three farmers' educational organizations; 75.3 per cent of them belonged to, and 52.0 per cent have held official positions in, one or more of these organizations.

TABLE 27

PARTY AFFILIATION OF DELEGATES TO WHEAT
POOL AND TWO OTHER COÖPERATIVE
CONVENTIONS, 1946

(Percentages)

Party	Wheat Pool delegates	Coöperative convention delegates
C.C.F.	84.9	82.9
Liberal	10.6	10.6
Conservative	1.8	1.6
Social Credit	1.8	0.8
Labor Progressive	0.9	0.0

TABLE 28

C.C.F. PARTY POSITIONS HELD BY RURAL
DELEGATES TO TWO COÖPERATIVE
CONVENTIONS, 1946

(Percentages)

C.C.F. position	Coöperative delegates
Any C.C.F. post	69.1
Poll committee member	56.7
Secretary, poll committee	14.4
Chairman, poll committee	7.2
Zone organizer	14.4
Constituency committee member	38.1
President of constituency	7.2
Provincial Council member	7.2

That the C.C.F.'s earliest electoral support came from the more prosperous farmers is clearly reflected in the economic background of the party's local officials.

More than 50 per cent of Saskatchewan farmers are members of minority ethnic groups. Studies of radical movements have indicated that a disproportionate number of leaders come from such

groups. In terms of the earlier data concerning the C.C.F., one would expect to find, however, that C.C.F. rural leaders come from groups that have superior status in the community. This expectation is confirmed by the data in table 30.

TABLE 29

Economic Status of Rural Delegates to C.C.F. Conventions and to Two Coöperative Conventions

	Total population, Saskatchewan, 1941*	C.C.F. delegates	Coöperative delegates
Size of farm (acres)...............	433.2	673.7	689.4
Value of farm.....................	$6,435.0	$12,983.4	$14,189.9

* *Farms and Farmers in Canada: Facts from the Census, 1941 and 1931* (1944), pp. 3, 10.

TABLE 30

Ethnic Origin of Rural Delegates to C.C.F. Conventions and to Two Coöperative Conventions

(Percentages)

Nationality	Rural population 1941*	C.C.F. delegates			Coöperative delegates
		All	Over 45 years old	Under 45 years old	
Anglo-Saxon........	41.9	59.8	63.0	52.8	75.3
German............	15.1	10.3	9.6	11.1	5.6
Ukrainian..........	10.3	2.5	0.9	4.4	0.0
Scandinavian.......	10.1	16.3	16.4	16.1	11.2
French............	5.0	2.0	1.8	2.2	1.1
Dutch.............	3.8	1.8	2.2	1.1	3.3
Polish.............	3.2	0.5	0.0	1.1	0.0
Others.............	10.6	6.8	6.0	8.3	3.5

* *Farms and Farmers in Canada: Facts from the Census, 1941 and 1931* (1944), p. 10.

Scandinavians, who are the social equals of Britishers in the West, and Anglo-Saxons are disproportionately represented in the C.C.F. rural leadership. In a culture dominated by Anglo-Saxons, persons of British descent tend to be chosen for leadership. Prejudice against "foreigners" makes those of other origins shy away from exposing themselves to criticism by becoming leaders. The same trend holds true if country of birth is considered. Although, according to the census of 1941, 36.0 per cent of Saskatchewan

farmers of forty years and over were born in non-English-speaking countries, this was true of only 17.8 per cent of the C.C.F. delegates forty-five years of age or over in 1945.

It is interesting to note that ethnic cleavages seem to be disappearing among the younger generation of C.C.F. leaders. There are 10.2 per cent more non-Anglo-Saxons among the group under forty-five years than among those above that age. The younger members of ethnic groups, who were born in Canada and speak English well, are beginning to assume their proportionate place

TABLE 31

RELIGIOUS AFFILIATION OF RURAL DELEGATES TO C.C.F. CONVENTIONS
AND TO TWO COÖPERATIVE CONVENTIONS

(Percentages)

Religion	Total rural population, 1941*	C.C.F. delegates			Coöperative delegates
		All	Over 45 years old	Under 45 years old	
Protestant.........	64.2	86.8	90.2	78.9	90.8
Roman Catholic....	30.3	11.7	7.9	17.7	9.2
Greek Orthodox....	5.0	2.3	1.5	3.4	1.1

* *Eighth Census of Canada, 1941*, Bulletin A-5.

in rural society. The increase in non-Anglo-Saxons among the younger and more recent C.C.F. leaders may also reflect the increased electoral support for the C.C.F. among minority ethnic groups.

C.C.F. leaders, as a group, differ significantly from the general rural population in religious affiliation. Here again the minority groups are underrepresented. The relative absence of Catholics among C.C.F. leaders is due to a number of factors, some of which were cited earlier. In the early period of the movement the traditional hostility of the Church toward socialism was directed against the C.C.F. in Saskatchewan. This undoubtedly prevented many Catholic supporters from aligning themselves with the party. Another reason is that most of the Saskatchewan Catholics come from minority ethnic groups—Ukrainians, French, Polish—and therefore are likely to be underrepresented in rural leadership. Protestant prejudice against Catholics is another factor in accounting for the lack of Catholic C.C.F. leaders. The C.C.F. as a movement is not anti-Catholic, but anti-Catholicism has deep roots among many

Protestants in Saskatchewan. This religious prejudice has served to keep Catholics out of leading positions in many community institutions. But resistance to the participation of Catholics in the C.C.F. and in community institutions may be decreasing. There are more than twice as many Catholics in the group of C.C.F. leaders below forty-five years of age as in the older group.

The influence of religious affiliation on political behavior becomes even clearer if the denominational differences among Prot-

TABLE 32

PROTESTANT DENOMINATIONS OF C.C.F.
RURAL DELEGATES

(Percentages)

Denomination	Protestant rural population*	Protestant C.C.F. delegates
United Church.........	34.8	54.5
Lutheran..............	21.8	20.4
Anglican..............	16.4	11.5
Mennonite............	7.3	0.0
Presbyterian..........	8.1	6.4
Baptist...............	3.1	3.0
Total Protestants....	100.0	100.0

* *Eighth Census of Canada, 1941,* Bulletin A-5.

estants in the C.C.F. are examined. The data in table 32 reinforce the interpretation of the election results, that membership in the United Church is conducive to support of the C.C.F., while Anglicans tend to be opposed to the party.

It is significant that the social and economic characteristics of coöperative leaders differ from those of the general rural population in the same way as do those of C.C.F. officials. (See tables 29 and 30.) The coöperative officials and the C.C.F. party leaders are predominantly well to do, Anglo-Saxon, and Protestant. Wealth, Anglo-Saxon origin, and Protestantism are the main objective social factors that one would expect to be associated with status in our culture.[3]

The sample of non-C.C.F. coöperative officials was not large enough to justify any conclusions about the backgrounds of farm leaders who do not support the C.C.F. Only twenty-one, or 17.7 per cent, of the coöperative delegates who filled out questionnaires

were not C.C.F. supporters. One difference between them and the backers of the C.C.F. does stand out, however: 38.1 per cent of those who did not support the C.C.F. were Roman Catholics, gests anew that the opposition of the Church to socialism has been a major factor in deterring Catholic farmers from backing the C.C.F.

These facts tend to confirm the earlier interpretation that the C.C.F. is not a radical movement for change within the rural social

TABLE 33

OCCUPATIONAL BACKGROUND OF 230 URBAN C.C.F. LEADERS

(Percentages)

Occupation	Convention delegates	Constituency executives	Provincial Council and constituency presidents	Total (230)
Workers..............	45.9	63.6	52.2	50.0
Business and profes- sional men.........	43.4	24.7	38.1	34.3
Teachers.............	11.2	11.7	9.6	11.3

structure, but the spokesman of the rural community organized on a class basis to preserve itself by changing the larger social order of which it is a part. The C.C.F. movement is a direct continuation of the earlier efforts of the Saskatchewan rural community to create a stabilized rural economy. It is the political voice of the rural community, and is led by the "normal" community leaders.

C.C.F. support in the urban districts of Saskatchewan is largely from the working class. This urban base is reflected in the backgrounds of the party's nonfarmer leaders. Most of the working-class leaders of the C.C.F. are skilled workers: 84.0 per cent of the worker delegates to the 1945 and 1946 conventions were members of skilled trades, as were 89.5 per cent of the working-class members of the constituency executives and the Provincial Council. These leaders of the C.C.F. were among the higher-paid labor groups in the province, earning an average of $2,454 a year in 1945.

Of all the C.C.F. labor leaders about whom there are data, 51.3 per cent were railroad workers. The six C.C.F. labor members of the 1944 legislature were all railroad employees. Skilled rail-

roaders in western Canada have a special status. They are among the highest-paid workers, often earning as much as many small businessmen. Their trade-unions are the oldest and strongest in the nonindustrial, agricultural West. For a long time the westerners' only direct contact with organized labor was through the unions of railroad workers. When the C.C.F. was first organized, the railroaders virtually symbolized "Labor" to the farmers. They were the "Labor men" whom the agrarians in the C.C.F. sought out to form joint Farmer-Labor committees, as the following statements from a C.C.F. leader indicate.

I had an opportunity to confer with one of the leading *Railway* men at Wynyard regarding the political situation and I am told that the matter of political action has been discussed and that almost everyone of the *Railway employees* has stated at one time or another during the past six months that they will never again vote for the two existing political parties.

In my opinion the Wynyard Constituency Committee should appoint a delegation to call upon Mr. Elliott Sherman, who is Mayor of the town of Wynyard, and suggest to him that the *Labor men* be called together for a conference and appoint a representative of *Labor* on your Constituency Committee. I trust that you will take immediate action in this matter because although some of the *Railway men* at Wynyard have been known to be closely allied with the Liberals and Conservatives, it is very apparent to me that they have now changed their mind, and in a political fight every vote counts.

I may say for your information that I have had a number of meetings with *Labor people* here, and we are forming a branch of the Independent Labor Party in Saskatoon. We have been working at night and have drafted a Federal and Provincial Policy. We are meeting again on Friday night to draft a Civic policy. After the Organization Committee have drafted a full program, we will call the members together and complete the organization. I am in hopes that when the party is formed, they will advise the *Labor people* at points such as Wynyard to lend their support to the Farmers' candidate, and we in turn will advise farmers in City Constituencies to join with the *Labor people*.[4]

Many of the railroad workers entered the C.C.F. at a fairly early date as representatives of Labor. The depression had reduced their income greatly, and the new Farmer-Labor Party gave them an opportunity to join the organized agrarians in a political bloc that would give them added strength. The urban areas were, therefore, won to the C.C.F. in the same way as were the rural dis-

tricts. The upper strata of the working class, the organized skilled workers, joined the movement first and became its leaders. This is confirmed by the organizational affiliations of the group. Of working-class leaders of the C.C.F., 60 per cent were members of trade-unions, and 40.0 per cent have held official posts in union locals.

C.C.F. working-class leaders are similar to rural leaders in their personal background also. Working-class leaders belong to the culturally dominant group of Anglo-Saxon Protestants. Their re-

TABLE 34

Ethnic Origin and Religious Affiliation of Working-Class C.C.F. Leaders

Ethnic origin	Percentage	Religious affiliation	Percentage
Anglo-Saxon............	77.8	United Church..........	53.8
Scandinavian..........	11.1	Anglican...............	15.4
French Canadian......	2.2	Lutheran...............	11.5
German..............	4.4	Baptist................	3.8
Ukrainian............	3.3	Presbyterian...........	3.8
		Roman Catholic........	3.8
		Greek Orthodox........	7.7

ligious affiliations indicate the positive relationship between United Church membership and C.C.F. support as well as the negative influence of the Catholic Church on the movement.

The urban business and professional groups overwhelmingly support the Liberal and Conservative parties, though a growing number of them have been voting C.C.F. in recent years. The contrast in the class electoral support of the three main parties is reflected in the economic backgrounds of their leaders, as indicated in table 37. The majority of leaders of the old parties belong to the urban middle class, while C.C.F. leaders are predominantly farmers, and to a lesser extent workers.

The C.C.F. has made overtures in recent years to small businessmen, urging them to support the new party to protect themselves from the monopolists. This appeal has not been very successful. The rural members of the C.C.F. regard the small merchants as part of the exploitative profit system which they would like to eliminate through coöperatives. The small-town merchant, in turn, looks upon the coöperatives as a major threat to his security, at

least as great a threat as chain stores and mail-order houses. This identification of the C.C.F. with the coöperative movement prevents the party from appealing successfully to small businessmen.

The fact remains, however, that a minority of the business and professional groups do actively support the C.C.F. The data available about the backgrounds of these people are scanty, but they suggest certain interesting hypotheses about the causes of this deviant class behavior. Urban middle-class leaders of the C.C.F.

TABLE 35

ETHNIC ORIGIN OF C.C.F. LEADERS

(Percentages)

Nationality	Farmers	Workers	Business and professional men
Anglo-Saxon..........................	59.8	77.8	36.7
German............................	10.3	4.4	10.0
Ukrainian..........................	2.5	3.3	20.0
Scandinavian.......................	16.3	11.1	13.3
French............................	2.0	2.2	3.3
Dutch..............................	1.8	....	6.7
Polish............................	0.5	....	3.3
Others............................	6.8	....	6.7

differ significantly from farming and working-class leaders in one essential respect—ethnic origins.

The data are suggestive of the relationship between a marginal social position and radical political behavior in members of an upper economic class. The C.C.F. in Saskatchewan is the party of workers and farmers. Economic constraints on these two groups led them to accept the need for widespread social reform designed to better their economic condition. They were led into the new social movement by men of their own class who had both status and organizational experience.

The business and professional groups, on the contrary, decisively rejected the new party, which was directed against them as the local representatives of the capitalist system. To support the C.C.F., therefore, would be abnormal class behavior for a member of the urban middle class. The few who did so were regarded as "crackpots" by other businessmen. Most of the social and economic coercions on middle-class individuals tended to keep them sup-

porting the old parties, which were controlled by men having the same class background.

The middle-class people who joined the C.C.F. were, however, precisely those who were not accepted socially in the urban business community. They belonged, predominantly, to minority ethnic groups; these groups were not part of the urban "upper class," which in Saskatchewan is largely Anglo-Saxon. This is true even in areas where the population of the surrounding countryside is composed overwhelmingly of members of minority ethnic groups.[5] The non-Anglo-Saxon businessmen are often newcomers to the business life of the towns, being former farmers or children of farmers. They tend to retain their ties with the minority ethnic group of the surrounding countryside, and remain socially marginal to the business community. This was clearly brought out in a study of a small, predominantly Anglo-Saxon town in a Ukrainian farming district. According to one young Ukrainian merchant, "The Anglo-Saxons made it plain that they were better than the Ukrainians and didn't want us, so the Ukrainians said, 'To hell with you, we can get along by ourselves.' "[6] The two C.C.F. Ukrainian members of the Saskatchewan legislature in 1944 were small-town merchants who came from farm families. Both reported close ties with the Ukrainian rural community.

The data suggest that "deviant" class political behavior can be explained partially by other "deviant" sociological characteristics. Socially, the businessmen of the ethnic minority are part of the lower-class group of the Saskatchewan population. They are not exploited economically, but they are deprived socially of many of the privileges that usually go with business status. The cleavage between them and the Anglo-Saxon "upper class" is often as great as the split between the farmers and the business community. Subject to the cross pressures of contradictory statuses, many members of the minority groups have seen fit to identify themselves with the political party which is opposed by the "upper class" and which promises to strike at the community power of these dominant groups.

The acceptance by some C.C.F. agrarians of the minority ethnic members of the business community as party leaders is probably related to the fact that in Saskatchewan ethnic ties within groups which are rejected by the majority of the community outweigh economic class cleavages. The C.C.F. Ukrainian farmer will accept

the guidance of a Ukrainian merchant, whereas the Anglo-Saxon farmer will not follow a businessman from his own national group.

Members of a dominant economic class who belong to a minority cultural group and are not socially accepted by the rest of their class tend to participate disproportionately in political movements whose programs appear to be inconsistent with upper-class eco-

TABLE 36

ETHNIC AFFILIATION OF BUSINESS AND PROFESSIONAL MEN WHO
ARE LEADERS OF SASKATCHEWAN POLITICAL PARTIES

(Percentages)

Nationality	C.C.F. leaders*	Liberal leaders†	Conservative leaders‡
Anglo-Saxon....................	36.7	84.7	96.4
Ukrainian.......................	20.0	1.7	0.0
French Canadian................	3.3	10.2	0.0
Scandinavian....................	13.3	1.7	1.2
German.........................	10.0	0.0	2.4
Mennonite......................	6.7	1.7	0.0
Polish..........................	3.3	0.0	0.0
Others..........................	6.7	0.0	0.0

SOURCE: *Canadian Parliamentary Guide*, 1935, 1939, 1945; and interviews with leaders of the three political parties.
* 68 convention delegates, 1945 and 1946; constituency officials, 1946.
† 83 members of the legislature and candidates in 1938 and 1944, and 1946 constituency officials.
‡ 59 members of the legislature in 1934, candidates in 1944, and constituency officials in 1946.

nomic interests, but which give minority-group members of the upper class the possibility of assuming higher social status, or of striking at those who deny them the status that should be a concomitant of their economic position. The contrast between the ethnic backgrounds of C.C.F. and old-party urban middle-class leaders leaves little room for doubt that this is true in the province of Saskatchewan.

The Saskatchewan C.C.F. data on the backgrounds of "upper-class" radical leaders are similar to those found in European socialist movements. Robert Michels, the foremost analyst of Social Democracy before the First World War, reported that the Jews, who constituted the principal minority group in the ethnically more homogeneous European countries, played a disproportionate role in the socialist movement. Middle-class and upper-class Jews, who had an inferior social status, were attracted to a movement that promised to eliminate the causes of Jewish inferior status. Michels'

explanation of the position of the Jew in the socialist movement also suggests that deviant economic class behavior is related to marginal social status.

The origin of this predominant position [of the Jews in the European socialist movement] is to be found, as far at least as concerns Germany and the countries of Eastern Europe, in the peculiar position which the Jews have occupied and in many respects still occupy. The legal emancipation of the Jews has not been followed by their social and moral emancipation. In large sections of the German people a hatred of the Jews and the spirit of the Jew-baiter still prevail, and contempt for the Jew is a permanent feeling. The Jew's chances in public life are adversely affected; he is practically excluded from the judicial profession, from a military career, and from official employment. . . .

Even when they are rich, the Jews constitute, at least in eastern Europe, a category of persons who are excluded from the social advantages which the prevailing political, economic, and intellectual system ensures for the corresponding portion of the Gentile population: Society in the narrower sense of the term is distrustful of them, and public opinion is unfavorable to them.[7]

The question will naturally be raised, If the C.C.F. is the party of the leaders of the Saskatchewan rural community, where do the two old parties get their leaders? Unfortunately, no data comparable to the material on the C.C.F. could be obtained, as neither of the old parties held a convention during the course of the field work. A statistical breakdown of biographical material in the *Canadian Parliamentary Guide* and of data obtained in interviews with Liberal and Conservative leaders suggests that in the older parties the leaders come from the business and professional groups, even though Saskatchewan is preponderantly a rural area. The data in table 37 help confirm the interpretation that the political cleavages in Saskatchewan life are closely related to economic class cleavages.

There are, however, large numbers of Saskatchewan farmers who did not support the C.C.F. in 1944. Obviously, this large anti-C.C.F. rural minority must have a leadership structure. One can, however, do little more than suggest tentative hypotheses as to its nature. Many of the non-C.C.F. rural leaders may be comparable to the C.C.F. urban middle-class leaders; that is, they are not so well integrated in the rural community as their C.C.F. neighbors and are therefore exposed to a larger number of non-

economic cross pressures. Since the old parties are predominantly urban middle-class organizations, the farmers who are active in those parties may have stronger social or economic ties with urban life than do the members of the C.C.F. This may come about

TABLE 37

Distribution of Occupations of Leaders of
Saskatchewan Political Parties

(Percentages)

Party	Business and pro-fessional men	Farmers	Workers	Teachers
Liberal:				
Executive, 1946....................	65.0	20.0	5.0	0.0
Constituency presidents, 1946........	41.0	41.0	6.0	2.4
Members of legislature, 1934.........	46.5	46.5	2.3	2.3
Members of legislature, 1938.........	56.2	34.4	3.1	3.1
Conservative:				
Provincial Council, 1946.............	63.9	26.7	5.3	2.7
Members of legislature, 1929.........	58.4	20.8	4.2	4.2
Candidates, 1938....................	54.2	20.8	4.2	16.7
Candidates, 1944....................	30.0	45.0	5.0	7.5
Social Credit:				
Candidates, 1938....................	45.0	20.0	10.0	10.0
C.C.F.				
Constituency Executive, 1946........	5.1	75.1	13.1	2.4
Provincial Council and constituency presidents, 1946..................	13.1	65.6	17.9	3.3
Members of legislature, 1944.........	6.4	59.6	12.8	14.9

Source: *Canadian Parliamentary Guide*, 1930, 1935, 1939, 1945; and interviews with leaders of the Liberal, Conservative, and C.C.F. parties.

through active membership in a church such as the Anglican or Catholic churches, where religious ties outweigh class cleavages, or through membership in lodges and fraternal orders such as the Orange Order.

Second, there are a large number of cultural subgroups within the Saskatchewan rural community that are not supporters of the C.C.F. The Mennonites, the French Canadians, the Catholic population as a whole, and other minority groups have never been completely integrated into the general rural community. They

therefore have an independent leadership structure, which differs from the dominant cultural group in its reactions to external social and economic pressures.

A third possible source of anti-C.C.F. rural leadership may come from the large group of farmers who have had personal ties with, or received favors from, the Liberal Party, which dominated the political life of the province and of the nation during most of the twentieth century. The well-organized provincial Liberal machine placed many farmers under personal obligation as a result of its effective distribution of patronage and Tammany Hall type of service.[8] Until the C.C.F. came on the scene in the 'thirties, most of the officials of the rural municipalities were connected with the Liberal Party, and many of them probably remained loyal to the Party. These personal relations with the Liberals undoubtedly constituted one of the effective cross pressures working against the C.C.F. in the rural community.

The suggestions about the sources of Liberal leadership, however, must remain in the category of unproved hypotheses until further research is done on the Saskatchewan political scene in particular and on the effect of cross pressures on political behavior generally. We know that group affiliations determine the social behavior of individuals, but we know little about the strength of group affiliations, especially those related to class actions in cross-pressure situations. Marxists assume that class position always takes priority. This may be true in terms of long-run historical analysis, but we have no systematic information on what happens in concrete situations in different societies.

The growth of the C.C.F. was a result of a drastic shift in the political loyalties and attitudes of two economic classes, farmers and workers. This change may be related to the economic constraints on these classes.

Anyone who is required to change his habits of life and his habitual relations to his fellow-men will feel the discrepancy between the method of life required of him by the newly arisen exigencies and the traditional scheme of life to which he is accustomed. It is the individuals placed in this position who have the liveliest incentive to reconstruct the received scheme of life and are most readily persuaded to accept new standards; and it is through the need of the means of livelihood that men are placed in such a position. The pressure exerted by the environment upon the group, and making for a readjustment of the group's scheme of life, impinges upon the members of the group in the form

of pecuniary exigencies; and it is owing to this fact—that external forces are in great part translated into the form of pecuniary or economic exigencies— . . . that we can say that the forces which count toward a readjustment of institutions in any modern industrial community are chiefly economic forces; or more specifically, these forces take the form of pecuniary pressure.[9]

It is obvious that social change is not a simple reflex action. Economic pressures, like all other social forces, operate through individuals. The degree to which an individual or group is affected by such pressures varies according to position in the social structure. The question of who is most affected by changing social pressures, who leads the members of a group or class to accept a change, has never been answered satisfactorily. Various theorists have suggested that receptivity to new ideas is related to marginal social status. Such an acute observer as Karl Mannheim has stated that psychopathological types are the innovators, the leaders of change.

There can be little doubt that maladjusted persons are prone to accept the need for change before the rest of society. It is highly dubious, however, whether they are actually the informal molders of new opinions at the "grass-roots" level. The statistical data on the backgrounds of C.C.F. leaders demonstrate that in Saskatchewan a radical movement for economic reform was led at the grass-roots level by those possessing status within the farming and working classes. The local leaders of the party were not the marginal or deviant members of the society, but rather the old class leaders. This process was very apparent in the rural communities of Saskatchewan, since class and community leaders were largely the same people. A class or a community will not usually accept the leadership of its deviant members. The C.C.F. was able to grow rapidly in Saskatchewan because the "normal" class leaders were the first to become members of the party.

Recent sociological researches have cast some light on the social forces that determine public opinion. Studies of voting behavior indicate that group membership is the foremost factor in affecting vote decision; that is, persons in the same religious group or social class tend to vote similarly. Paul Lazarsfeld suggests that individuals who belong to formal organizations composed of persons with the same social and economic background as themselves are more likely to vote with the majority of their socioeconomic group

than are individuals who are not integrated into their class through formal organizational affiliations.[10]

Concretely, this meant, in the United States, that the proportion of Republicans was larger among those with high socioeconomic status, who belonged to various high-status organizations, than it was among those with the same class background who were not members of such associations. Among the working class, those who belonged to trade unions were more likely to be Democrats than were the nonjoiners. These facts are explained by Lazarsfeld as follows:

... people who live together under similar external conditions are likely to develop similar needs and interests. They tend to see the world through the same colored glasses; they tend to apply to common experiences common interpretations. They will approve of a political candidate who has achieved success in their own walk of life; they will approve of programs which are couched in terms taken from their own occupations and adapted to the moral standards of the groups in which they have a common "belonging."[11]

The research findings on the effect of group structure in reinforcing the political attitudes of members are based on analyses of comparatively static electoral situations in the United States. The basic core of Democratic and Republican strength has not changed since it has been under the observation of social scientists. In Saskatchewan, however, where fundamental shifts have taken place within a comparatively brief period, the data on C.C.F. electoral support and leaders would appear to contradict the findings reported in *The People's Choice*. In 1934, in Saskatchewan, the C.C.F. was a minority party among all social classes. On the basis of Lazarsfeld's analysis of a comparatively static situation, those who belonged to class organizations, such as coöperatives and trade-unions, should have voted for the old parties, as did the majority of the class. In fact, however, the members of class organizations were the leaders and first supporters of the C.C.F.

The data indicate that when the attitudes of a class are in flux, because of changing social and economic pressures, those who are most thoroughly integrated in the class through formal organizations are the first to change. In Saskatchewan it was the local leaders of the Wheat Pool, of the trade-unions, who were the first to join the C.C.F., the first to become cognizant of the need for change. Their position made it incumbent on them to

make decisions and set new patterns of behavior when traditional methods were no longer adequate. These leaders were in the best position to realize the long-range implications for people in their economic position. The unorganized mass became C.C.F. supporters only gradually, following the organizationally active members of their class.

A study of Saskatchewan voting behavior today would, however, probably result in findings similar to those obtained by Lazarsfeld from the 1940 elections in the United States. The political situation in Saskatchewan is now relatively static. The "normal" class behavior for workers and farmers is to vote C.C.F. An unpublished study of coöperative members in Saskatchewan indicates that about 75 per cent of the members of the Wheat Pool and other coöperatives voted C.C.F. in 1944, though only about 58 per cent of the total farming population did so.[12] Those who now belong to formal organizations among the farmers are more prone to vote with the majority of the class than are those who are isolated. Among urban middle-class groups, however, isolated individuals are more likely to be members of the C.C.F. than those who are integrated in organized group activity.

It is necessary, therefore, to modify the assumptions about the marginality of leaders of new social movements. When a large social class or group is changing its attitudes, the normal integrated leaders of the class are the first to change. They are more exposed to the social pressures on the class than are marginal, deviant, or apathetic members. The relationship between marginal social position and radical political behavior holds true only for radicals who come from the upper classes.

In small, isolated political parties such as the Communist parties of the United States and Canada and the Socialist Party in the United States, one would probably find, as Harold Lasswell did in his study of the Communist Party of Chicago, that the members and the leaders of these groups are disproportionately maladjusted socially. This is true, however, only of small parties, which are not genuine expressions of large-scale social pressures. These small parties are themselves marginal to the total society. If a small radical party succeeds in becoming the political voice of a large group, it will necessarily attract the normal, integrated members of the class. The C.C.F., starting as a large movement, was therefore led from the beginning by the normal class leaders.

Chapter X

SOCIAL STRUCTURE
AND POLITICAL ACTIVITY

VARIOUS OBSERVERS of the North American scene have called attention to the problem of mass passivity and political apathy in our culture. Myrdal has pointed out that the masses in America "are accustomed to being static and receptive. They are not daring, but long for security. They do not know how to coöperate and how to pool risks and sacrifices for a common goal. They do not meet much. They do not organize. They do not speak for themselves: they are the listeners in America. They seldom elect representatives from their own midst to Congress, to state legislatures or to city councils. They rather support friendly leaders from the upper strata, particularly lawyers."[1]

Myrdal's description is accurate for most parts of the United States and Canada. It does not, however, give a picture of Saskatchewan political activity. The Saskatchewan C.C.F. has succeeded in involving more people in direct political activity than any other party in American or Canadian history, with the possible exception of certain similar farmers' parties.[2] In 1945 the party had a dues-paying membership of 31,858, or approximately 4 per cent

[1] For notes to chapter x see pages 302–304.

of the total population and 8 per cent of the 1944 electorate. C.C.F. membership in the province has reached the equivalent of a national dues-paying membership of about 500,000 in Canada and 6,000,000 in the United States. One can hardly speak here of mass passivity. An examination of the factors related to the attainment of so large a membership should throw light on some of the reasons for political apathy in other areas of the continent.

TABLE 38

ELECTIVE POSITIONS, RURAL SASKATCHEWAN

Position	No. of local groups	No. of officials in each	Total
Municipal council.................	304	7	2,128
School-board member..............	5,184	3	15,552
Hospital-board official.............	79	6	474
Telephone-board director..........	1,127	5	5,635
Wheat Pool and other marketing coöperatives...................	1,257	10	12,570
Coöperative store.................	519	8	4,152
Community hall..................	203	5	1,015
Miscellaneous coöperatives.......;..	48	5	240
United Farmers, etc.*.............	....	..	......
Lodge*...........................	....	..	......
Church group*...................	....	..	......
Political party*..................	....	..	......
Minimum total.................			41,766

* Figures not available.

The most important single factor differentiating the Saskatchewan social scene from other regions is the high degree of individual participation in community organizations in rural districts. There are from 40,000 to 60,000 different elective rural posts that must be filled by the 125,000 farmers. There is, then, approximately one position available for every two or three farmers. Table 38 indicates the nature of these posts.

The large number of positions in rural Saskatchewan does not mean that one out of every two or three farmers is a community official, for many rural leaders are active in a number of organizations. In most communities the same people are on the rural municipal councils, the boards of directors of local coöperative stores, and the executive of the United Farmers of Canada (Sas-

katchewan Section). A rough estimate, drawn from many interviews and more than 800 questionnaires filled out by Saskatchewan rural leaders, indicates, however, that at least 15 per cent of the farmers hold community posts to which they have been elected by their neighbors. This proportion of formal community leaders to total population is much larger than has been attained in any urban area. It is probably also greater than that found in other rural areas, for Saskatchewan has the largest coöperative movement on the continent and more local governmental units than any other American rural state.[3]

This situation is a result of an almost unique combination of factors that have created the formal structural conditions for widespread individual participation in community affairs. The farmers have been faced, in the forty years since the province was created, with a series of major social and economic challenges requiring the establishment of a large number of community institutions to meet them. Pioneering on the unsettled prairie in the two decades before the First World War, farmers had to establish local rural governments, hospitals, schools, and a telephone system. They were faced with the hazards of a one-crop wheat economy that was subject to extreme fluctuations in income because of variability in grain prices and climatic conditions. Their position as isolated individual producers and consumers at the end of the distribution system left them exposed to monopolistic exploitation by the railroads, the grain companies, and the retailers. Through the formation of coöperatives and political pressure groups, Saskatchewan farmers sought to improve their competitive position in the fluctuating price economy and to reduce the cost of the articles they bought. All these community and economic associations had to be organized by a handful of people.

The area of effective community action in the wheat economy of Saskatchewan is necessarily limited by distance. Wheat farms are large, and wheat regions are consequently sparsely settled. The rural municipalities, the local governmental units, contain less than 400 families, and each municipality (about eighteen square miles in area) contains a number of distinct communities. There are about 1,500 railroad stops, over 1,100 rural telephone companies, and more than 5,000 local school districts in Saskatchewan.[4]

The sheer need for extensive community organization would not necessarily result in widespread participation in community affairs

by farmers. In many rural areas on this continent, the community institutions serving farmers are controlled by members of urban business and professional groups of the neighboring towns. County government positions and consolidated school-district posts are open to nonfarmers in many agricultural districts. Within the rural areas of the Southern States or in parts of California, where significant social and economic cleavage exists within the rural community, the wealthier and upper-class farmers are the formal community leaders, and the bulk of the poorer farmers are politically apathetic.

Rural Saskatchewan, however, is socially a "one-class" community. Differences in income and status do exist within individual rural communities, but they are not large enough to bring about the emergence of distinct social classes. The wheat farmers have more in common with each other economically and socially than with any other group. The organized community life of the agrarian population is conducted independently of the activities of neighboring towns and cities. Very little intermingling takes place between the cliques of the town and those of the countryside.[5] Almost all the formal community positions must be held by farmers. Neither the rural municipal councils nor the rural school boards are legally open to town lawyers or other members of the urban middle class. The coöperatives are almost completely rural organizations.

Under these conditions, any farmer who has executive ability is forced to accept community responsibility. A large portion of the population has become accustomed to playing an active role in different organizations. Rural leaders must conduct meetings, write reports, make speeches, and recruit members. One informant described the effect on his father of being in a leading position:

My father was elected vice-president of the S.G.G.A. local early in the 'twenties. He hadn't wanted the job, but he was a leading farmer in the district and had been a member for a long time, so some of the other officials prevailed on him to take the post.

Shortly after he was elected, the local sponsored a meeting by a Progressive M.P. The chairman of the lodge took sick and my father was told that he would have to preside over the meeting. He tried to get out of it, for he had never made a speech in his life. He couldn't, however, and had to preside. For days before the meeting he stopped all work and went around the house reciting a five-minute speech which he had memorized. The family almost went crazy listening to it.

On the day of the meeting, he delivered the speech and afterward was complimented on his ability by the M.P. After that he lost his fear. He would chair meetings and gradually began to make speeches for the organization. By the time the C.C.F. was organized he had no fear in facing a meeting of hundreds and speaking for hours. Before he died he must have delivered hundreds of speeches at C.C.F. meetings, coöperative meetings, and other farmers' gatherings.

As officials in coöperative and governmental units, local farm leaders study and make decisions on the policies of larger organizations and governments. The members of school boards, hospital boards, and rural municipal councils become acquainted with the problems of taxation and administration, and with the policies of provincial and federal governments. The leaders in farmers' coöperatives and educational organizations must act on the policies of governments that affect them. The 11,000 or more Wheat Pool committeemen are kept up to date by the Pool's educational department on all national and international aspects of the wheat problem. They learn at once of government decisions that may affect their economic position. The Pool has sixteen field men who visit the committees periodically to keep them informed of problems of the coöperative movement.[6]

This structure of grass-roots participation provides direct channels of communication between the mass of farmers and their leaders. The Saskatchewan rural community is highly receptive to outside pressures and can be quickly mobilized by its leaders. A striking example of this mobilization took place in 1941–1942. Wheat prices were fixed by the Canadian federal government at 70 cents a bushel in 1941. The Wheat Pool had demanded a higher price, but the government refused because the Nazi conquest of Europe had closed many Canadian markets. Crop conditions were bad and the farmers who had anticipated a period of war prosperity began to fear that 1941 would be another depression year for them, though the prices of goods they bought were rising. Wheat Pool committees passed resolutions demanding that the provincial organization take action to gain a higher price and crop insurance. The Pool leaders organized meetings throughout the province to discuss the problem. "Farmers by the thousands flocked to these meetings, leaving their threshing machine standing idle in many instances, in order to raise their voices in the interests of a better deal in agriculture."[7]

The Wheat Pool officials, who are relatively conservative, desired to limit the farmers' protest to resolutions and to personal pressure on members of Parliament. This, however, did not satisfy the farmers of Saskatchewan. A grass-roots demand for action swept the province. One militant old farmer described what happened at one Pool meeting.

When in 1941 things got intolerable and we resorted to mass meetings I was at the one in Swift Current. I was never at a meeting where the audience was so hostile to the platform. You could feel it like a chill through the church and there were noted men on it too.

A little old fellow got up and moved that we send two men from each sub-district to Ottawa and demand dollar wheat. There was a loud guffaw, but he soon got a seconder and it carried unanimously. The point I want to make is this: it was right from the grass roots, there were no paid officials on this, though there was one on the platform. The idea went through the Province like a prairie fire. Forty thousand dollars were collected in spite of the determined opposition of the Liberal machine. Four hundred men were sent to Ottawa; preachers, sinners, and lawyers. Twenty cents more per bushel was eventually secured.[8]

The "March on Ottawa" is but one of a number of movements which the dirt farmers began and carried through against the opposition of the bureaucracy of farmers' organizations and of the government.[9] Though the forces making for bureaucratic control of the farmers' movement exist in Saskatchewan as they do elsewhere, the structural conditions for rank-and-file participation and for resistance to such control are stronger there than in most other areas. There are comparatively few paid positions in the farmers' coöperative and educational movements. The secondary leaders of all the farm groups are working farmers who are just as much affected by economic pressures and general currents of opinion as are the rank and file. Unless these leaders express the feelings of their neighbors, who have chosen them, they will be replaced by others who do. The extent of direct participation means that the farmers' movement must always be receptive to the needs of the members. Further, it results in heightened awareness by the farmers of large-scale political and economic events.

This widespread activity makes for rapid political changes. Its effects can be seen in the influence of the "March on Ottawa" movement on the growth of the C.C.F. In 1941 the C.C.F. was the only party to support fully the demands of the organized farmers. The

federal Liberal government refused to meet some of them. This fact was known to the rural leaders and, through them, the knowledge spread to most of the farmers of the province. Between August 31, 1941, and July 31, 1942, the period of the agitation resulting in the "March on Ottawa," C.C.F. membership rose from 4,460 to 9,813.[10] This increase is highly significant, for it occurred between elections at a time when there was no prospect of another election and party membership normally could be expected to decline.

In the past the social organization of the economy—the fact that almost all the farmers were wheat farmers and therefore had common interests and problems—meant that "solutions" to problems in one area were rapidly accepted in others. Each rural community in Saskatchewan is a replica of every other. An example of rural flexibility in adopting a common solution to a community problem can be seen in the rapid spread of the municipal doctor scheme, which began in the early 'twenties. Saskatchewan farmers have always found it difficult to secure adequate medical care at a reasonable cost. There was often a rapid turnover in physicians and it was difficult to get good ones. In 1921 the rural municipality of Sarnia decided to hire a doctor on salary, so that farmers could be assured of medical services and the physician would be guaranteed his salary.[11] This plan proved successful, and gradually spread until, by 1944, in spite of opposition from the organized medical profession, one-third of the rural municipalities of Saskatchewan had doctors on salary. Once it had proved itself in a few areas, the system was accepted and advertised throughout the province by the organized farmers' movement. The United Farmers of Canada (Saskatchewan Section) spread circulars and other propaganda materials, such as the following:

At present we are committed to pooling our wheat and other farm products. The municipal doctor scheme is in reality a pooling of our doctor bills. Or we might look on it as an insurance against unduly high doctor bills in any one year—an equalization scheme. . . .

In no case where the municipal doctor scheme has been tried has there been any complaint from either ratepayers or doctors. In —— Municipality during eight years under this scheme their death rate is much below the average for the province and they have had no maternal deaths during this time. . . .

For additional information before voting on this important question, attend a meeting to be held in the Orange Hall on Friday, December 7, at 3 P.M. sharp. The meeting will be addressed by Mr. —— of the

Research Department of the United Farmers of Canada. Mr. —— and Mr. ——, Secretary-Treasurer and Reeve, respectively, of the Municipality.[13]

The rapid acceptance of new ideas and movements in Saskatchewan can be attributed mainly to the high degree of organization. The small rural communities are forced to adjust to changing economic and social situations. Interest in political and economic matters is continually being stimulated. Farmers derive most of their ideas and knowledge of larger problems and policies from well-informed neighbors who hold community posts.

The Wheat Pool, the coöperatives, the agrarian Progressive Party of the 1920's, and the C.C.F. were all built rapidly through this structure of organized farmer opinion. The role of the social structure of the western wheat belt in facilitating the rise of new movements has never been sufficiently appreciated by historians and sociologists. To the economic and cultural factors usually associated with the development of these movements should be added the variable of social structure. Repeated challenges and crises forced the western farmers to create many more community institutions (especially coöperatives and economic pressure groups) than are necessary in a more stable area. These groups in turn provided a structural basis for immediate action in critical situations.

Though it was a new radical party, the C.C.F. did not have to build up an organization from scratch. It was organized from the start by the local "class" and community leaders of rural Saskatchewan. The fact that the province was so well organized on an occupational basis enabled the new party to obtain the support of the politically conscious community leaders. By the early 1940's, C.C.F. committees, composed in the main of the same people who were the officials of the other rural organizations, were operating in almost every district in the province. It was this "machine" that brought the C.C.F. to power.

Today the C.C.F. has become the political voice of the organized agrarian community. The organized farmers are brought into direct contact with "their" government by active participation in a class political party that controls the state.

The basic unit of political organization in rural Saskatchewan is the poll, the smallest voting district. Each provincial constituency is divided into from one hundred to two hundred polls. The C.C.F. has attempted to build up in each district a working committee of

two or three people who will take charge of C.C.F. educational work among the one hundred to two hundred voters in the poll. Above the local organizations is the constituency. A C.C.F. constituency has a committee of twelve to twenty-five members and an executive committee of seven to twelve members. The committees are elected at annual conventions, which are attended by three delegates from each poll. The leading body of the entire party is the Provincial Council, which has representatives from each constituency and meets several times a year. The provincial party organization supervises the work of each constituency body. Between Council meetings, the party is governed by an executive body of nine. This provincial organization is controlled by the annual provincial convention. Each constituency convention elects ten delegates to the provincial convention. The convention elects top party officers and determines policy.[13]

If the formal pattern of the C.C.F. party organization were actually followed, about 24,000 people would be active party members, either as members of poll committees or as delegates to the party conventions and committees. Actually, this optimum figure is never reached, for many districts have no active poll committees. In recent years the average attendance at the fifty annual C.C.F. constituency conventions has been about 100 delegates, 5,000 people in all. Many more electors, however, are active in the local organizations than attend as convention delegates. One could safely estimate that between 10,000 and 15,000 people take part in the actual operation of the party.

Between elections, this activity does not include much formal party work. Poll committees usually meet once or twice a year to discuss the work of the local and larger party bodies. They arrange public meetings for party leaders and enroll new members. In some areas, committees meet regularly to discuss party policy and to analyze books and outlines suggested by the provincial office. The constituency committees, which have about 1,000 members, have much greater responsibilities and consequently meet from six to twelve times a year. These committees are the grass-roots bodies which influence the work of the C.C.F. members of the legislature and the provincial party.

The fact that the majority of C.C.F. members and officials are not continuously active in party work does not mean that they are not acting politically in other community roles. Most of the

active C.C.F. members have administrative tasks in rural organizations. They are members of local coöperative store boards, Wheat Pool committees, and U.F.C. executive bodies, and do not differentiate between their activities in these organizations and in the C.C.F. One informant expressed this feeling clearly.

It's really all one movement that we have here. We are building socialism through the Wheat Pool, through our coöp store, through our U.F.C. local, as well as through the C.C.F. They are all part of one movement, the "people's movement." Sometimes one organization or fight is more important than the other, but we need them all. The fact that our poll committee doesn't meet except before conventions doesn't mean the C.C.F.'ers here don't care about the party. We feel that we are building the C.C.F. when we build our coöp store, and we are building coöperation and destroying the profit system when we build the C.C.F.

At first glance the relationship between the C.C.F. and other rural community organizations appears similar to the pattern of party-society relations advocated by the Communist Party. Communists want to be the vanguard of the working class, the class leaders. To accomplish this, they attempt to permeate working-class organizations and become their officials. In the Soviet Union, Communists are placed in key positions in trade-unions, coöperatives, and local governments. In democratic countries they use the tactics of "boring from within" to achieve positions of leadership.[14]

In Saskatchewan, however, the "vanguard," the leaders of the farming community, started the C.C.F. As a result, C.C.F. activity and community activity are closely interrelated. This situation is not a result of any planned action, but is, rather, a consequence of the tight organization of the farming community on an occupational basis. The C.C.F. is the class party, the farmers' party, and thus controls the farmers' organizations. Many leaders of the C.C.F. and of rural organizations are not aware of this close interrelationship. The party makes no direct efforts to influence other institutions and has no explicit policy for its members to follow in them. There are no C.C.F. caucuses in the coöperatives or other rural groups. In practice, however, most of the secondary leaders are C.C.F. members and therefore support the policy of the party and the C.C.F. government. The leaders are, in fact, continually engaged in political activity.

The relationship between the C.C.F. and rural community or-

ganizations is a two-way affair. C.C.F. leaders in their capacity as local government officials and coöperative leaders know the needs of the community and the effect of government policies on the rural community. They use the party organization as a direct channel of communication to the legislature and the cabinet. A stream of resolutions moves constantly from local and constituency committees to the Provincial Council and the government.

Since the election of 1944, interest in C.C.F. conventions and governing committees has grown greatly. Through participation in this organization at least 10,000 people are led to feel that they are taking a direct part in the establishment of government policy. The vitality of grass-roots participation in rural Saskatchewan leads to vigorous criticism of the activities of the government and the party. The active members in the C.C.F. are mainly experienced local leaders, who represent the grass-roots, not the summits, of the rural community. The C.C.F. differs from many European socialist parties and the nonsocialist parties in the United States and Canada in that its secondary leaders are unpaid and receive little additional status from their party position. The party officials had status in the community before they became C.C.F. leaders, and therefore are relatively independent of top control. This pattern of grass-roots democracy runs through all the farmers' movements in Saskatchewan, and the C.C.F is only continuing it. In order to perpetuate interest and loyalty to the party, C.C.F. leaders are almost forced to encourage criticism and suggestions from the rank and file. Many C.C.F. leaders, from Premier Douglas down, reiterate that they are only the servants of the majority of the party. Theoretically, the party leadership and the government must accept any policy adopted by the provincial convention.

Many members of the C.C.F. now conceive of government as a tool to be manipulated by the people. They come to constituency conventions fully prepared to let the government know their opinions. The resolutions adopted at conventions reveal the operation of this conception of direct democracy:

That the Government investigate and pass legislation which will stop completely the overloading and crowding of live stock in stock cars, trucks or any other vehicle.

That a stop be made to the shipping of live stock unfit for human consumption to packing houses or stock yards. The only exception being stock clearly designated for purposes other than human consumption.[15]

Whereas the Department of Health is prepared to go to considerable work and expense to have all citizens tested for T.B. to have the disease controlled and

Whereas after the test has been taken and even if your family shows no signs of the disease they may go home and drink milk from a diseased cow

Therefore be it resolved that the Government make an extensive test of all cattle as soon as possible regardless of whether the present veterinary profession have time to do it all or not.[16]

That we the delegates of Saltcoats Convention, especially the women members, desire the Government to investigate the possibility of the Woolen Mill handling woven materials, as blankets from this class of goods fulfill many useful purposes on the farm.[17]

The lack of inhibitions in criticizing government policy can be seen in a number of resolutions.

Be it resolved that we consider the five C.C.F. Cabinet Ministers who talked and voted against the resolution to exempt single men up to $1,200 and married men up to $2,500 on the Federal Income Tax, were badly out of line, . . . especially Mr. Fines, who actually implied that he would tax the lower paid classes exactly as the Capitalist King Government is doing.[18]

Whereas the existence of natural gas and oil in commercial quantities in the Province of Saskatchewan has been proven conclusively;

And whereas the C.C.F. as a Socialist Party believes in and advocates the public ownership of the natural resources of this Province for the benefit of the people of Saskatchewan;

And whereas a resolution was passed at the 1945 Provincial Convention urging the Government of Saskatchewan to undertake the development and distribution of natural gas and oil in this Province;

And whereas natural gas and oil in the Province of Saskatchewan continues to be extensively exploited by private persons and concerns;

Therefore be it resolved that the Government of Saskatchewan be called upon to show cause why the exploitation of these resources has been allowed to fall into private hands.

And be it further resolved that the Government of Saskatchewan be immediately called upon to place these resources under social ownership, control and operation for the immense benefit of the people of Saskatchewan.[19]

Free forums, such as the constituency conventions provide, strengthen the C.C.F. in innumerable ways. The top leaders can never depart far from the thinking of the rank and file without

being made aware of it. The conventions serve, also, to preserve the vitality and support of the party. In interviews many C.C.F. members stressed this existence of direct democracy through the party.

Well, what did you think of that speech? I really made B. [a Cabinet minister] squirm. Don't misunderstand it though. I think B. is doing a good job, but like all men, he makes mistakes and he has to be told about them. That's the wonderful thing about this party. The members really run it. No one in this room would have the least hesitation about telling anyone from Coldwell or Douglas down that he is wrong if he thinks so. Can you see any Liberal supporter doing that to old Gardiner? Why, did you know the Liberals haven't had a convention since 1933?[20]

To what degree can the formal structure and appearance of grass-roots democracy in the C.C.F. be said to be real? Do the people really govern? One cabinet minister, in discussing the role of conventions, said:

They are today the most important part of the C.C.F. organization. I think we are doing good work and that the majority of the people approve our policies. However this will not keep us in power. A lot of good governments have been defeated and lost power. Our people will not actively support and work for the C.C.F. once their feeling of "Get the Rascals out" is over. . . .

The one thing that maintains our active support is the feeling that the people run the government, that we are only their servants. The conventions reinforce that feeling every year. It is therefore important that we never refuse to carry out anything demanded at the Provincial Convention unless we have a darn good explanation. Our supporters will put up with mistakes or with inefficiency, but they won't stand for dictation. The one thing that can kill the C.C.F. is the idea that we are another party like the Liberals and Conservatives, that the government is composed of another group of politicians and "heelers" who come around every four years for votes.

Cabinet ministers and party leaders appear to act on these principles. *This does not mean that they do not make policy.* In fact, almost all important provincial policies are set by the cabinet and the members of the legislature. At provincial conventions the final form of resolutions, suggesting changes in policy, is usually determined by top leaders. This control, however, is exercised by men who combine superior oratorical ability, status, and information. When the leaders oppose a resolution they are able to control the overwhelming majority of delegates.

In the 1946 convention a resolution proposing government ownership of gas and oil appeared to be favored by the majority of the delegates, for it had been a traditional demand of the farmers' movement and of the C.C.F. Two cabinet ministers armed with statistical data were able to convince the convention that the oil and gas fields were not yet proved commercial fields and that the cost of developing them as a risk investment was beyond the financial ability of the province.

On certain issues, however, government and party leaders have been voted down and accepted their defeat. The 1946 provincial convention adopted two resolutions recommending changes in government policy that had previously been rejected by the cabinet and the C.C.F. legislative caucus: one supported the right of married women to work for the government, and the other urged the forty-four-hour week for labor with no reduction in pay. At the following session of the legislature both proposals of the convention were adopted.

There has been, however, one major issue in which the government has not completely followed convention instructions. The 1945 and 1946 conventions urged the government to fill all policy-making positions in the civil service with persons who support C.C.F. ideals. The cabinet at first refused, but gradually has been making concessions to the pressure from the conventions.

Direct democracy in the C.C.F. and other Saskatchewan farm organizations is limited by the extent of the knowledge, experience, and interests of the secondary leaders. C.C.F. conventions fail to pass resolutions on a multitude of important problems because the delegates lack opinions about, or knowledge of, these problems. The conventions rarely bother with the details of a government health scheme, the methods of operation of government industry, the problems of debt refunding or repayment, priorities in economic planning, or provincial proposals to Dominion-provincial conferences, though these administrative details may be more important than the broad over-all policies with which the resolutions deal. Other important issues neglected by the conventions are foreign policy and other aspects of national affairs that do not affect agriculture. The overwhelming majority of resolutions reflect the day-to-day economic and social concerns of farmers and workers: farm regulations, provincial tax legislation, roads, liquor laws, and social services [21]

The extensive grass-roots discussion of governmental problems is not new in the history of the province. Long before the C.C.F. was formed, the Saskatchewan Grain Growers' Association met in annual district and provincial conventions to adopt policies to be urged on governments. The annual meeting of the S.G.G.A. was known as the "Farmers' Parliament" and was well attended. The Liberal Party, which then controlled the province, paid close attention to the actions of these conventions and wherever possible implemented the recommendations of the S.G.G.A. In order to maintain the support of the organized farmers, it offered cabinet posts to Grain Growers' officials.[22] The provincial Liberals lost their hold on the farmers' movement when the Progressives were formed in 1920, because the federal Liberal Party would not meet many of the agrarian demands.

The fact that extensive participation in the Saskatchewan C.C.F. is not a result of the growth of a new political movement or of some characteristic inherent in the C.C.F. becomes clear if the organization is compared with the party elsewhere in Canada where it has been successful. Of those voting for the C.C.F. in Saskatchewan, 15 per cent were party members. The British Columbia C.C.F., which is largely an urban working-class movement, won 39 per cent of the total vote in the 1946 provincial election, but less than 5 per cent of its supporters are members of the party. In one Vancouver constituency that has elected socialist or C.C.F. candidates since 1930, party leaders do not know who their supporters are, and only a handful of them are in the party.[23] In Toronto the C.C.F. received 133,443 votes in 1945, but has never enlisted more than 3.8 per cent of this figure in the movement. Actually, the Toronto C.C.F. has considerably less than 1,000 active members. The growth of the C.C.F. movement in Toronto and Vancouver has not been the result of, nor has it resulted in, an increase in direct political participation by the masses. The party in these cities resembles the traditional North American parties, with little direct contact between the organization and the major part of the electorate.

If one notes the differences between the community structure of Saskatchewan and that of cities such as Toronto and Vancouver, the relationship between structure and the extent of political activity becomes clear. The 600,000 rural residents of Saskatchewan elect 2,100 members of municipal councils and 15,000 members

of school boards. Large cities, however, have an insignificant number of community positions compared to their total population. The 800,000 citizens of Toronto elect only 24 members of a council and 18 members of the school board.

In most North American cities the majority of political and community posts are held by members of the middle and upper classes.²⁴ The city councils are filled with lawyers and other business or professional people. Many community organizations such as hospital boards, Y.M.C.A. boards, and community chests are dominated by members of the upper classes. This again is in striking contrast to rural Saskatchewan, where farmers must fill these posts themselves.

Trade-unionism is the major institutional exception in urban life in which workers are given an opportunity to hold office and take responsibility. The ratio of officials to total union membership, however, is often very low. There are many union locals with thousands of members and two to twenty officials. In Saskatchewan the ratio of members to officials in the coöperatives and educational organizations ranges from five to one to twenty to one. The Saskatchewan Wheat Pool, the largest farm organization, has a total membership of 60,000 to 70,000. About 11,000 farmers are elected members of Wheat Pool committees in their localities. One out of every six members of this organization, which most closely approximates a trade-union in rural Saskatchewan, is a local official who meets regularly with others from six to twelve times a year to discuss and act on local, provincial, and national matters. Local members usually attend meetings twice a year. The average local Pool organization has about sixty members.

The coöperative movement is extremely weak in the urban areas of Canada and the United States. In contrast with Europe, coöperatives in America have not succeeded in interesting many workers. The coöperatives, therefore, do not serve as a basis for training leaders and creating channels of communication between workers and larger institutions. The few urban coöperatives that do exist tend to be led by members of the middle class. The breakdown or absence of real neighborhoods in urban centers has also served to prevent the formation of a local corps of leaders. The political machine has provided the only effective urban leadership group, and it could hardly be expected to be a vehicle for new ideas and

for social change. Outside the factory, the urban working class is dispersed. There are few channels for genuine intraclass communication.

The building of a new mass political organization is, therefore, much more difficult in a city than in a rural community or small town. It is almost impossible to locate the informal leaders of the lower classes. The people are not accustomed to making political decisions. In the anonymity of city living, organized person-to-person political contact is difficult.

If it is true that popular interest and participation in political activity are facilitated by the wheat economy of Saskatchewan, one should expect similar patterns of behavior in comparable areas. Saskatchewan's neighbors permit such comparisons. The state of North Dakota, economically and geographically, is almost a replica of Saskatchewan. It is sparsely settled, has a one-crop wheat economy, and is rural for the most part. The environmental and economic challenges which forced the farmers of Saskatchewan to establish many different organizational structures were similar in North Dakota. This state should therefore be expected to have a high degree of political activity.

The historical facts tend to confirm this expectation. In that state the Non-Partisan League secured its greatest strength and membership. At its height, in 1920, it had 50,000 members, which was 7.7 per cent of the total population. The League won more than 1,000,000 votes in various states and had 300,000 members, but in no other state was the ratio of its membership to population or to its electoral support so high as in North Dakota.[25] Today the Farmers' Union, which is politically the most active of the major farmers' organizations, is strongest in North Dakota.

The Farmers' Union is by far the biggest single force in the state, and its North Dakota unit is probably the strongest farmers' organization in the whole country on a state level. . . . Of the 57,000 farmers in North Dakota, more than 30,000 are members, which must be something of a record for saturation in any movement.[26]

Fifteen hundred local groups of the National Farmers' Union [of North Dakota] meet with staff organizers once or twice a month for discussions on local, national and world problems. . . . Each year with wives and children over sixteen voting in addition to the farmers themselves, the locals elect their officers and their delegates to the state convention where the next year's program is planned.[27]

In Canada, Saskatchewan's neighbor on the west, Alberta, is somewhat similar in economic and social structure. It too has widespread community participation through local governments and coöperatives. Politically, also, Alberta tends to resemble Saskatchewan. The last thirty years have seen the growth of three large social movements: the Progressives and the United Farmers of Alberta in the 'twenties, the Social Credit Party in the last decade, and a growing C.C.F. movement today. Alberta farmers, like those of Saskatchewan and North Dakota, are quick to react politically when a threat to their society or economy arises.

Manitoba, Saskatchewan's eastern neighbor, however, has had much less community and political activity. Its coöperative movement is considerably weaker than those of the other provinces. There has not been a significant farmers' political movement in Manitoba since the early 'twenties. It is the only one of the three Prairie Provinces that does not have a farmers' educational and political pressure organization such as the U.F.C. (Saskatchewan Section) or the United Farmers of Alberta. The differences between Manitoba and the rest of the Prairie Provinces help to confirm our hypothesis as to the causes of political apathy.

Manitoba has been less exposed to the vagaries of weather and price fluctuations than the rest of the northern prairie region. Only a small part of Manitoba is in the drought belt. The province is no longer a one-crop wheat region. Many of its rural residents practice mixed farming and have a large immediate market in Winnipeg. This tends to reduce economic hazards. The economic need for a large coöperative movement is not so great.

A second reason for the smaller degree of political participation is the strength of urban influence in rural Manitoba. The inhabited portion of Manitoba is a much smaller area than that of either Alberta or Saskatchewan. Much of the rural part of the province is close to the large city of Winnipeg. The important community and provincial institutions are concentrated in the one city that is accessible to most farmers. The need for duplicating the community services that exist in urban areas is not so great in rural Manitoba as it is in Saskatchewan and, consequently, local activity is weak. The Manitoba Wheat Pool has only two districts as compared with Saskatchewan's sixteen.

Manitoba is the oldest of the Prairie Provinces. Its pioneer days are almost a generation behind those of Saskatchewan. The striv-

ing to create and maintain basic community institutions ended long ago. Other things being equal, older organizations tend to enlist less participation and interest than new ones. It is significant that during the period between the 1890's and the early twentieth century, when economic and ecological conditions in Manitoba approximated those of Saskatchewan and Alberta today, the Manitoba agrarian political movement was strong. In the 'nineties the wheat farmers organized a strong third party. The Manitoba Grain Growers' Association and later the United Farmers of Manitoba were large and powerful pressure groups which made and unmade governments and built the first large coöperative movement in western Canada.

A Saskatchewan informant who took part in a recent C.C.F. election campaign in Manitoba indicated clearly the effect on political life of the lack of community participation.

I was in Manitoba at the last Federal election in Russell, the home of Hon. J. A. Glen, and was able to see the C.C.F. in operation. Many of the conditions were akin to Saskatchewan, but the ground work was missing. No trained speakers were at hand. Many were poorly equipped to conduct a meeting. No experience had been gained like Saskatchewan's Wheat Pool Delegates and field men had gained in meeting the exacting demands of the farmers under contract to the Pool. If Glen had been running in a Saskatchewan riding he wouldn't have lasted as long as a snowball in hell.

They have no system of carrying on coöperative education in Manitoba like in Saskatchewan. The farmers just aren't used to attending meetings and discussing their problems.

Myrdal has described the relationship between political apathy and the lack of community organization in America.

In local politics, America has, on the whole, not spread political responsibility upon countless citizens' boards, as have, for example, the Northern European countries (including England), thereby widening political participation and making politics more anonymous and less dependent on outstanding leadership. Much more, not only of broad policy making, but also of detailed decisions are, in America, centralized in the offices of salaried functionaries. *Political participation of the ordinary citizen in America is pretty much restricted to the intermittently recurring elections. Politics is not organized to be a daily concern and responsibility of the common citizen.* The relative paucity of trade unions, coöperatives, and other civic interest organizations tends to

accentuate this abstention on the part of the common citizens from sharing in the government of their communities as a normal routine of life. In this essential sense American politics is centralized.[28]

A description of the Saskatchewan scene is the inverse of Myrdal's description of the American scene. The tendency in local politics has been to spread political responsibility among countless citizens' boards; this has brought about wider political participation and has made politics more anonymous and less dependent on outstanding leadership. *Political participation of the ordinary citizen in Saskatchewan is not restricted to the intermittently recurring elections. Politics is organized to be a daily concern and responsibility of the common citizen.* The relatively large number of farmers' organizations, coöperatives, and other civic-interest organizations encourages common citizens to share in the government of their communities as a normal routine of life. In this essential sense, Saskatchewan politics is decentralized.

Widespread community participation and political interest have developed in Saskatchewan in response to the environmental and economic problems involved in creating a stable community. No one factor—the small units of government, the vulnerable one-crop economy, the "one-class" society, the sparse settlement of the area, the continual economic and climatic hazards—developed because of an interest in maintaining an active grass-roots democracy or a concern for politics. The combination of all these factors, however, has made for a healthy and active democracy. Unplanned structural conditions have facilitated rapid popular response to economic and social challenges and the acceptance of new methods and ideas.[29]

The Saskatchewan pattern, while offering confirmation of the "small democracy" theories, provides no panacea for those who would plan society so as to create the basis for popular community activity. Early in the nineteenth century Thomas Jefferson advocated "general political organization on the basis of small units, small enough so that all its members could have direct communication with one another and take care of all community affairs."[30] This and similar proposals have been ignored, for small communities were not functional in the development of a great industrial nation. In the nineteenth century, anyone who objected to the growth of large cities was called a "reactionary" or a "utopian" trying to block the march of civilization.

The small agrarian community in Saskatchewan has been pre- served only because this pattern was functional in the wheat economy. The grain companies, the coöperatives, the political parties, and the farmers, all would have preferred larger com- munities and more centralization. They would laugh at the rational democrat's argument for their type of living and their type of economy. To the people of the West, decentralization has meant poor community services and little access to many material and cultural values. They welcomed the automobile and better roads, which are resulting in the breakdown of the smaller communities and the growth of large towns and cities. It remains true, however, that the smaller the community and organizational unit, and the less economically and socially stratified the society, the better are the possibilities for grass-roots political activity. Saskatchewan demonstrates that widespread and continuous political interest is not incompatible with efficient, large-scale organization.

Chapter XI

POLITICS AND SOCIAL CHANGE

THE C.C.F. has held office in Saskatchewan for six years, from 1944 to 1950. It has had the opportunity of demonstrating to the people of the province as well as to the rest of Canada how successful a new party based on the support of the farmers and workers can be in carrying out its goals of a more democratic society. Its overwhelming parliamentary majority has meant that there were few formal restraints in the path of enacting and administering its program.

It is obvious that democratic reform governments are more a result than a cause of social change. As a result of breakdowns in the integration of existing value structures, community mores gradually change. The need for explicit formal institutional changes gradually becomes recognized by different strata of the population who are adversely affected by the breakdown in the old community integration. The organizations or persons who propose reforms that appear to fill the needs of maladjusted groups win influence and, if the crisis is widespread, power. In a stable democracy, however, the reformer will gain power usually after all elements, even the more conservative ones, recognize the need for change.

Many societies, of course, become so unstable in their structure that agreement on widespread reforms is impossible. This is es-

pecially true when the socially defined "needs" of one class necessitate the elimination of the power, wealth, and influence of another class. This was true in China and much of eastern Europe during the past thirty years, and in pre-Hitler Germany. In more stable societies, however, where no class has to make far-reaching changes in the position of another group to accomplish its aims, compromise on objectives is usually reached. The situation that leads workers or farmers to demand new forms of economic security also changes the values of the dominant groups. This shift in the publicly proclaimed values of the upper strata is made grudgingly in order to maintain power and influence, as in Great Britain today. This fact, however, does not change the significance of the basic agreement on objectives by rival democratic political movements.

The radical party in a stable society, therefore, is not on the left side of a fundamental cleavage, but is on a point in a continuum. Where real cleavage as to aims occurs, the revolutionary situation makes the continuance of democracy difficult. The actions of most electorally successful radical parties have, therefore, not differed greatly from the policies that were acceptable to their conservative oppositions. History has shown that socialists come to power democratically only when their opposition is almost "socialist." Conservative parties in Norway, Sweden, England, New Zealand, and France, in the years after the Second World War, accepted the nationalization of various major industries and the extension of social welfare. The attitude of English Conservatives to the policies of the Labor government is a good example.

In Britain's hour of need for leadership, the loyal Opposition does not want to take power. . . . the Tory futility is rooted in something far more significant for Britain's future than the political manoeuvres of the moment. The hard truth is that Big-C Conservatives have lost their faith in small-c conservatism. They are now economic and political agnostics, with no new belief to replace their lost faith in free enterprise.

British Tories agree almost unanimously on the necessity of thorough public controls. They quarrel mostly with the degree and not the principle of public ownership. They believe that free enterprise has gone out of their lives; and a sizeable minority believes that it is a good thing. . . .

The Conservative Party may continue for a while to be an alternative to a Labor Party. But it is now clear that it will be conservative in name only. Said one grim Tory M.P. last week: "When we get back into power, we'll show them how to run Socialism properly."[1]

---

[1] For notes to chapter xi see pages 304–306.

Henry Wallace, who is considered to be on the left side of the American political spectrum, found himself on the right in many European countries when discussing economic policies. In England he described himself as a "Progressive Conservative," and in Norway he spoke at a meeting "whose chairman explained that he was a Conservative.... But labels mean little; in many ways, the student [chairman] was politically to the Left of myself [Wallace]."[2]

Many European governments that do not have a "socialist" majority have nationalized part of their economy. The breakdown of the European economy and the loss of overseas investments have apparently caused many groups in countries like England and France to recognize the need for state planning and government ownership. "Socialist planning" has been instituted only when all parts of the community accept it. This is not to imply that there are no serious political and class cleavages in European countries. The conservatives and the old ruling classes are struggling, often successfully, to maintain much of their old power and privileges in the new planning state by retaining control of important positions in the new government industries and power structure.

The general climate of opinion determines what is radical or conservative at a given time and place. The introduction of major changes in the economy may not necessarily be radical for one community, though similar reforms would outrage the sentiments of other regions. With few exceptions, democratic leftist parties have implemented only those aspects of their program which met little popular resistance. The radical party, however, does a more thoroughgoing job of introducing change than would its conservative opposition, because the radicals believe in the changes.

In Saskatchewan and other Prairie Provinces, political climates of opinion have usually been to the left of the rest of the country. Before the First World War, the old party governments of the Prairie Provinces engaged in experiments in government ownership and supported the growing coöperative movement. In Saskatchewan, following the Progressive upswing after the First World War, the Liberals and the Conservatives attempted to regain their influence with the farmers by becoming markedly more radical than their fellow party members in eastern Canada.[3]

Saskatchewan representatives of both old parties supported, at least verbally, government-guaranteed higher farm prices (parity),

government crop insurance, debt reduction and moratoriums on farm debts during crises, lower tariffs, government loan agencies, public ownership of power and other public utilities, state or socialized medicine, increased social welfare and pension benefits, and the expansion of the coöperative movement.

The only parts of the C.C.F. program that were not duplicated in old-party platforms were the proposals for government ownership. This difference is not so great as it appears, however, for many old-party Saskatchewan leaders supported government ownership of organizations that affected farmers, such as banking, transportation, and marketing. During the depression the former Conservative Premier of Saskatchewan, Dr. J. T. M. Anderson, put forth the following program for his party in order to win left-wing support:

1. Work and wages. . . . If industry will not absorb them [the unemployed] the Government must in a definite way do so, even if it means the *Government itself establishing new industries.* . . .
3. Drastic reduction in urban as well as rural indebtedness.
4. State medicine made available to all.
5. Equal educational opportunities. . . .
6. Increased social services. . . .
7. Support of coöperative marketing. . . .
12. Development of our natural resources in the interests of the province rather than in the interests of a few favored individuals.[4]

We believe in the policy of public ownership as shown in the matter of the power commission. Over 11,000 were built during the first year of [the Anderson Conservative] government and more would have been done had not some of the present private companies got so deep-rooted before we took office.

Nothing would please us more than for the government to be able to put $10,000,000 in the hands of the power commission.[5]

The linkage between the Saskatchewan Liberal and Conservative parties and their more conservative national organizations tended to discredit their efforts in the province. There is no doubt, however, that the provincial old parties are to the left within their national parties. Reforms that are still "radical" in Ontario or Quebec are well established on the prairies.[6]

The social and economic conditions of the wheat-growing areas of the Great Plains of North America have produced a self-interest economic radicalism that has resulted in different types of semi-

socialist experimentation by such movements as the Non-Partisan League, the Farmer-Labor Party, the United Farmers, Social Credit, the C.C.F., certain old party governments, and the great coöperative movement.[7] How radical has the work of the C.C.F. government in Saskatchewan been? The question must be raised in the context of the society within which it developed. What were the social and economic options for the C.C.F.? Has the government attempted to use social reforms to create the basis for a new socialist society with a new value orientation, or is it simply innovating in areas where there is specific public demand for change? For the purposes of this discussion, the ideal socialist society is defined as an economically equal one, with socially coöperative instead of competitive values. It is not maintained that such a society is necessarily possible or that the C.C.F. has the power to create it, but rather that a socialist movement can and should be evaluated on the degree to which its reforms lead to such a society.

Agriculture is by far the most important element in Saskatchewan society. Growing out of the farmers' movement, the C.C.F. has attempted to carry out in legislation and administration those aspects of the program of the farmers' organization that lay within provincial power. Immediately upon taking office, therefore, the C.C.F. legislature enacted farm security legislation providing that no farmer could lose the basic 160 acres on which he lived because of nonpayment of debt. It also stated that in any year in which the total income of a farmer's land fell below $6 an acre, he should not have to pay the interest owing on any mortgage for that year.[8] The purpose of this legislation was to make the mortgage company share the economic and climatic risks of farmers. The Provincial Debt Mediation Board, by using its power to recommend debt moratoriums, forced many mortgage holders to reduce debts, which had mounted during the depression.[9] The entire force of the government was put behind the pledge of Premier Douglas that "no farmer shall be evicted from his farm under a C.C.F. government."[10]

The government is further aiding the security of farmers by establishing seed and fodder banks in which supplies can be stored from good crop years, so that drought will not ravage the province. It has greatly raised appropriations for scientific farming and has increased the number of agricultural field representatives.[11] The provincial government and the C.C.F. members of the federal

Parliament have continually put pressure on the federal government to retain government marketing of wheat, which was established during the war.

Two aspects of the Saskatchewan C.C.F. policy—security of tenure and stability of farm income—have been part of the western agrarian program for decades. In themselves they are not radical, except as they involve decreasing the income of other hitherto more powerful groups for the benefit of farmers. All farmers' governments in the grain belt have attempted to effect similar policies. It should be noted, therefore, that the program of the Saskatchewan C.C.F. is designed to maintain the social and economic structure of the rural area, not to change it. In fact, the C.C.F. program is *conservative* within the rural economy. The party has done nothing to change the comparative position of tenant farmers or to equalize the economic status of the poorer and smaller farmers. Indirectly, farm security legislation makes it more difficult for the poor farmer to buy new land than for the well-to-do farmer, since the latter has more cash to pay for new land. An owner of farm land, to defend his own interests, will prefer to sell to those with greater assets, since the government is protecting farmers who cannot pay their mortgage debts.

Second, the C.C.F. policy of a guaranteed profitable price benefits the large farmer more than the small one, as the former's production costs per bushel of wheat are lower and his profit therefore greater. This enables the wealthy farmer to increase the size of his holdings and the amount of his equipment. These policies of the C.C.F. may, therefore, eventually lead to the creation of a class of large wealthy farmers and the elimination of the small farmer.

No one who knows the Saskatchewan farmer could realistically suggest the socialization of land as an alternative to C.C.F. agricultural policy. The Communist dictatorships of eastern Europe could enforce land nationalization only because they could ignore the sentiments of their disenfranchised electorate. A democratic socialist government must accept the desire of farmers to retain title in their farms. There are, however, two ways by which a radical government can prevent increased rural stratification: restriction of the size of farms, and experiments in voluntary coöperative farms.

Some of the more radical C.C.F. leaders have suggested legislation restricting the size of individually owned farms and placing

discriminatory taxes on absentee-owned farms.[12] The government and the majority of the legislative caucus have voted down such equalitarian proposals for two reasons: first, the party leaders fear that any proposals that affect land tenures will be regarded by many farmers as steps leading to nationalization of land; and second, most of the C.C.F. rural leaders belong to the more prosperous group who own large farms. They are as much concerned with mortgages, interest rates, reducing the cost of manufactured goods, and raising wheat prices as are the poorer farmers. The wealthy farmers, however, do not desire to equalize the position of all farmers at their own expense. The party, therefore, is under no pressure from its active members to become an equalitarian agricultural party.[13]

The same internal antiequalitarian bias of the Saskatchewan farmers' movement and the C.C.F. can be seen in the operation of the coöperative movement, which the government supports. The Saskatchewan government has given enthusiastic support to the growth of the large coöperative movement of the province.

Since the party took office, coöperative organization has increased greatly.[14] The major reason is the general prosperity of the rural areas, which enabled farmers to raise share capital for initial investments. There can be little doubt, however, that the C.C.F. government of Saskatchewan, by its enthusiastic support of coöperatives, has played an important part in the growth of the movement. It established a separate Department of Coöperatives with its own cabinet minister. Almost every new coöperative that I visited during my stay in Saskatchewan had been organized by members or supporters of the C.C.F. There are now about 500,000 members of coöperatives, an average of four memberships per farmer.

The growth of coöperatives creates the same dilemma for the development of rural society as do the C.C.F. agricultural policies. Coöperatives have been organized mainly by the upper strata of the farming population.[15] The poorer farmers either do not have the necessary share capital to start their own coöperatives or do not have the cash reserves to use them. They patronize the private companies, which give higher immediate benefits, rather than wait for an annual patronage refund. This has meant, in practice, that the larger farmers receive a higher price for their wheat and pay less for the goods they buy. Like the farm security legislation,

the coöperatives aid the farming community against outside exploiters, but *within* the rural community they help well-to-do farmers more than poorer ones.

Recognition of the fact that coöperatives unduly aid one section of the rural community has led some in the C.C.F. to advocate that the government take over certain functions of coöperatives. They argue that the C.C.F. position that coöperatives and government developments are both forms of "nonprofit" ownership is not true, for the question remains unanswered: Who is to obtain the profit from the "nonprofit" organizations? These radical members of the C.C.F. suggest that profits from socially owned institutions should go to the government and be used for increased social services to benefit the neediest elements of the population. Ardent coöperators in and out of the C.C.F., however, state that those who produce the wealth deserve the benefits, and therefore the profit should be returned in the form of patronage dividends. This problem has never been formally resolved by the C.C.F., but in practice the party is committed to giving coöperative principles a free hand in marketing and distribution, and in whatever other fields coöperatives had preëmpted before the C.C.F. was elected.

The C.C.F. government has advanced only one agricultural equalitarian proposal—voluntary coöperative farming. A small minority in the party have suggested that the coöperative farm is the real form of socialism in agriculture, since it lessens the individualistic work of the farmer and necessitates a more coöperative value system. The government, through the Department of Coöperatives, has given financial and research assistance to a few experimental farms. Neither the party nor the government nor the coöperatives, however, are engaged in any widespread program to educate farmers on the advantages of coöperative living on the sparsely settled prairies. Several cabinet ministers believe that coöperative farms are not feasible in the provinces. One of them stated in an interview: "Our farmers are too individualistic. They couldn't work together on a farm under a manager. There is no sense in antagonizing them by trying to get them into it."

The members of the Economic Planning Board of the government are also opposed to coöperative farms, because they cannot see how such farms could create more goods. They feel that government funds should be used in measures to increase economic security, as in irrigation and in seed and fodder banks.[16]

Most C.C.F. leaders assume that if farmers are given economic security and increased social services they will continue to support the movement in its efforts to socialize the rest of the economy. Experiences in other countries do not lend weight to this assumption. In fact, the contrary seems to be true—farmers tend to become conservative when they achieve their economic goals. The farmer is radical vis-à-vis the larger society when his economic security and land tenure are threatened. He may join other exploited groups, such as the workers, to win his own economic demands. However, once the farmer achieves these immediate goals and becomes a member of the secure property holders of society, he resents government controls and labor or tax legislation that interfere with the expansion of his business.

New Zealand farmers supported the guaranteed price policy of the Labor Party in the depths of the depression in 1935, when low prices threatened their security. When the depression ended, however, the rural districts turned against Labor's planning program, which called for maximum farm prices as well as minimum ones, and increased incomes of the poorer groups.[17] In the United States, President Roosevelt established the guaranteed parity prices and crop insurance demanded by organized farmers. In so doing, however, he lost the support of the rural areas, including the once-radical wheat belt.[18] In Russia the Bolsheviks lost the support of the peasants after they gave them title to the land. The well-to-do peasants (*kulaks*) sought to increase the size of their holdings and to restore capitalist labor relations; they objected to controlled prices.[19]

In Saskatchewan a rift of interests may be developing between small and large farmers. The large farmers, who have highly mechanized and economically efficient farms, can operate with a profit at a lower wheat price than the small farmers. The well-to-do farmers, therefore, can afford to buy more and more land, aided by the provincial government's farm security legislation. This is creating a potentially serious cleavage between big farmers and small and tenant farmers. At present the United Farmers of Canada (Saskatchewan Section) is reviving as an organization representing small farmers. The U.F.C. sponsored a farm strike for higher prices in 1947. This farm strike was opposed in the wealthier farm areas and supported in the poorer ones.[20] The organization differs from the C.C.F. in its belief in rural strikes.

This growing cleavage can result in one of two possibilities: the C.C.F., under pressure from the small farmers, will turn to the left; or the party will continue to aid the farming community vis-à-vis the larger society, but thereby strengthening the middle and wealthy section of the rural population. Another serious depression or drought, however, would probably re-create the unity of action of the Saskatchewan grain growers. The possibility still remains, nevertheless, that, like the Russian Bolsheviks during the N.E.P., the New Zealand Laborites, and the Roosevelt New Deal, the Saskatchewan C.C.F. is sowing the seeds of opposition to socialist change.[21]

Though labor's electoral power in Saskatchewan is comparatively slight, the C.C.F.'s hope of gaining national power rests on the support of the labor movement outside the province. Organized labor, therefore, has had an appreciable influence in determining government policy. At the first session of the legislature after the electoral victory in 1944, the government enacted a Trade Union Act, which was drawn up by the unions and is probably the most pro-union legislation in the democratic capitalist world. The whole trend of government labor action is biased in the direction of supporting trade-union organization and demands.

The Trade Union Act makes collective bargaining mandatory on the part of the employer. It gives maintenance of membership and the compulsory check-off to any union which is the bargaining agent of the majority of the workers voting in a Labor Relations Board election. It outlaws various antilabor practices by employers, and requires them to prove that they did not discharge an employee for union activity, thus placing the burden of proof on the employer rather than on the union.[22] An employer who consistently violates the orders of the Saskatchewan Labor Relations Board may have his plant expropriated by the government. This actually occurred in 1946, when the government took over the Prince Albert Box Factory after the owner had persistently refused to abide by the decisions of the Labor Board and had discharged his entire force in order to by-pass the Board's decision.[23]

The effect of Saskatchewan's labor legislation on trade-union organization is strikingly demonstrated in table 39. In the four years of C.C.F. government, trade-union membership increased by 118.5 per cent. In the same period the unions of the entire country increased their membership by only 25 per cent.

Besides aiding trade-union organization, the C.C.F. government has passed laws to strengthen the economic position of workers. The minimum weekly wage was raised to $18.50, one of the highest in Canada. Workmen's compensation payments were increased to 75 per cent of the worker's salary, given without a waiting period. This is the highest compensation rate on the continent. Two weeks' vacation with pay is now required by law, as well as a forty-four-hour week with no reduction in weekly pay.[24]

Most of the legislation benefiting workers was passed during the first year of the government, in the "honeymoon" period following the C.C.F.'s tremendous election victory. Since then, however, party support of labor's demands has been waning. Many of the rural leaders of the government feel that they have done more than enough for labor. Electorally, they feel that the legislation has injured the party with small businessmen and many of the farmers. The rural leaders argue that a provincial government has little or no power to increase the income of farmers, since that is a federal matter, and therefore it is unfair to farmers to continually better the economic position of urban labor. They suggest also that Saskatchewan, as a province surrounded by governments with "bad" labor practices, will not be able to maintain industries that must compete with the rest of the country. The C.C.F. legislative caucus in 1946 refused the request of the unions for a forty-hour week, and enacted a forty-four-hour week only after the trade-union delegates to the C.C.F. provincial convention of that year insisted on the compromise.[25] Under pressure from businessmen and members of the legislative caucus, enforcement of labor legislation has somewhat weakened, the longer the government remains in office.[26] The trade-union members of the provincial party have been fighting this trend away from support of labor, but it is very doubtful whether the Saskatchewan C.C.F., as a farmer's government, is free to enact further legislation helping labor.

The one area in labor relations in which the government is comparatively free from public opinion is in its internal administrative policy in the civil service and the government-owned Crown corporations. The policy of the government is to be a model employer, encouraging workers to join unions and giving the unions a closed shop and higher wages. In spite of this policy there have been a number of labor disputes in the Crown companies. Two groups of workers, those at the Prince Albert Box Factory and at the Govern-

TABLE 39

DISTRIBUTION OF TRADE-UNION MEMBERSHIP, DECEMBER 31, 1943–1947

Province	1943	1944	1945	1946	1947	Per cent gain 1943–1947
Nova Scotia	41,982	35,095	31,982	33,233	36,575	−12.9
New Brunswick	18,232	17,980	18,238	18,659	22,295	22.3
Prince Edward Island	383	925	721	823	714	86.4
Quebec	188,714	175,093	171,203	208,546	210,260	11.4
Ontario	211,970	210,952	204,399	236,729	286,981	35.4
Manitoba	29,664	33,100	34,106	38,681	40,327	35.9
Saskatchewan	11,124	16,557	19,290	21,756	24,306	118.5
Alberta	28,975	28,504	28,578	33,662	38,202	31.8
British Columbia	87,485	90,702	83,823	99,466	115,230	31.7
Yukon	116	295	157	249	200	72.4
Unspecified	10,019	9,510	10,092	9,401	10,479	4.6
Totals	628,664	619,613	602,589	701,570	785,569	25.0

SOURCE: Department of Labour, *Annual Report on Labour Organization in Canada*, 1945–1949.

ment Insurance Office, actually went on strike against the government, and employees of other Crown corporations have threatened to do the same in the past four years.

A basic conflict exists in the interpretation of the essential purposes of socialized industry from the managerial and employee standpoints. The government and its managerial personnel are primarily concerned with the financial success of their industries and thereby hope to demonstrate to the rural electorate that government-owned industries can operate as efficiently as private enterprise. As a result, government officials fear to inaugurate any experiments in labor relations that might injure the financial success of the Crown companies. They do not want to yield any aspect of control into the hands of potentially "irresponsible" workers' representatives. The government, believing that nationalization is benefiting the workers economically, expects them to work hard and coöperate with management.

The workers, however, have different criteria of success for socialized industry. Many of them, especially those who were socialists before the C.C.F. victory, expected a change in their status as workers, in their interpersonal relations with their superiors. They felt that social ownership implied that workers would be consulted on industrial policies. As one worker in a Crown corporation expressed it,

We have been working here for a long time. Why —— knows more about the operation of this plant than anyone in the office. Before the government took over no one cared whether the plant was operating efficiently or not. Afterwards we thought a labor-management committee would be set up. No one, however, asked us our opinion about anything. . . .

As far as the people in the office are concerned, we are just so many machines who must produce. ——, the Minister, came down once and gave us a pep talk on the necessity to prove social ownership can work. That's just a lot of talk so far as we are concerned. Why should we kill ourselves so —— [the manager] can get all the credit.

J., an official in the same Crown corporation, expressed his view on the effect of government ownership on labor.

The men have become impossible since the government took over the plant. The union is always demanding higher wages, shorter hours, rest periods, and extra overtime. Their demands are ridiculous.

There is sure to be a clash between the union's desires and the

government's demands that we show a profit. The government must show a profit to satisfy the voters. Unless we crack down on the union now, the government is going to be in trouble later on.

If Saskatchewan gets another drought or the wheat market drops, we will have a hard job making revenues meet expenditures. The workers don't realize this. They think because revenues are high now we can give them anything.

This executive was unaware of any desire on the part of his workers for participation in management. It is interesting to note that the employees in this plant complained that the management did not consider their feelings, but interpreted their grievances purely on an economic, dollars-and-cents level. The same pattern recurred in other government factories.

Virtually all the managerial personnel in Saskatchewan Crown corporations had previously been employed in private enterprise. Though most of them think of themselves as being friendly to labor, they cannot conceive of sharing authority with the worker. The worker is someone to be helped rather than consulted. Experience with trade-unions has tended only to make government managers fearful of yielding authority. Relations between unions and management have been concerned primarily with wages, hours, and working conditions, and the unions have necessarily taken a "hard-boiled" bargaining position in such negotiations. The managers, in turn, are convinced that the unions are not interested in the success of social ownership, for they appear willing to endanger it by insisting on uneconomic wages.

This situation has created a conflict in the minds of many government workers who belong to the C.C.F. Socialism to them meant a change in the status of labor in the factory. Since this has not happened, they either had to change their conception of socialism or refuse to accept their particular experience as an example of socialism in practice. A small proportion of the workers in the Crown companies have begun to believe the Communist arguments that the C.C.F. is not a truly socialist party. The majority of vocal, active unionists felt certain, however, that the managers were "reactionaries" who were sabotaging the C.C.F. government and should be removed from their jobs. In at least two government-owned plants, a committee of workers attempted to convince the cabinet minister in charge of their industry that the manager was a saboteur. When a minister supported the manager, many workers

argued that the minister was not a "real socialist." Others believed that he was surrounded with reactionary advisers who were giving him false information. During my stay in Saskatchewan almost every manager, regardless of political affiliation, was charged by the workers in his plant with being "reactionary and antisocialist." Managers who had been active socialists for years before they were employed by the Saskatchewan government were criticized just as vigorously as nonsocialist managers, indicating that the cleavage between workers in the Crown corporations and the managerial staff was a result of structural rather than ideological differences.

Both top management and the workers' representatives have stated their belief in a new pattern of social ownership that will benefit both workers and the community. In practice, the managers, who remained under government ownership at the top of the industrial structure, define their day-to-day goals as making a profit, demonstrating to their immediate political supervisor that they are doing a good managerial job, and, if they are socialists, convincing the public that social ownership helps everyone. The workers, viewing "socialism" or government ownership from the bottom of the industrial structure, define their goals in terms of "personal dignity," "equality," "not being shoved around," and "the right to make suggestions," as well as higher income.

Conflicts in the attitudes of workers and management in government industry have not been peculiar to Saskatchewan. In England there is increasing recognition of this problem as one of the most crucial which the Labor government faces. The *Economist* pointed out this difficulty in discussing a coal miners' strike.

The real issues which are being fought out at Grimthorpe, where the miners have now been on strike for more than three weeks, can be summed up as a struggle between rationalization and syndicalism. The argument over the extra working at the coal face appears to be merely the pretext for a showdown on whether control is to be exercised by an all-powerful Board, or whether the workers are to be given a measure of influence in the management of their own pits. Many miners expected nationalization to result in workers' control; instead it has resulted in a large bureaucratic machine leaving the individual miner face to face with the same managers with whom he has been wrangling over the past twenty years.[27]

Many workers in Saskatchewan government industries had never been part of the organized labor movement before the C.C.F. was

elected, and had little conception of the procedures for labor-management coöperation. Even the comparatively few workers who were old socialists had no definite idea of what they meant by "workers' control of industry." Both groups, however, did expect a greater sense of personal significance in the industrial structure under a socialist government. Some developed grievances against the C.C.F. management of their plant, which they probably would never have voiced against private owners.

Workers felt that arbitrary management decisions on overtime work versus Saturday work, sick leave, and similar problems contravened the fundamental principles of the government. The first major strike in government industry occurred primarily because, in the words of some of the workers, the manager was "shoving his weight around too much." Attempts by workers in one factory to abolish various practices of restricting output, after the C.C.F. government bought the plant, broke down completely because the active C.C.F. members in the factory were not able to discuss changes in work procedure with the management.

The failure of the C.C.F. to make innovations in the social structure of the factory has caused resentment. A change in the formal ownership of industry does not end the basic social frustration of the industrial worker if he feels he is merely a puppet in a dictatorially controlled industry. Unless socialist governments adopt methods that give workers a sense of democratic participation in the life of the factory, they may find, as the British and Saskatchewan governments have, that they will be faced with as much "sabotage" and "restriction of output" in socially owned industry as in private, capitalist enterprise. In fact, the sense of grievance of the worker in a plant owned by a socialist government may be greater than his grievance against management in a capitalist concern, since the worker's expectations are higher where "my government" owns the factory. Such working-class grievances may be of greater danger to the professed goals of a socialist government than the disturbances that result from changing managerial functions and status.

The basis of the educational program of the C.C.F. government is similar to that of its labor and farm policies. The government is, in effect, carrying out the policies advocated by the *organized* teachers of the province, just as it has enacted the programs of the *organized* farmers and workers. The Minister of Education

was president of the Saskatchewan Teachers' Federation for the three years immediately preceding his appointment. The policies and some of the personnel of the Federation were transferred to the Department of Education.

The new minister introduced changes in technical administration and in the curriculum. The first included raising the minimum salary of teachers from $700 to $1,200, providing free textbooks for students, setting up large school districts so that the cost of education should be more evenly spread between wealthy and poorer districts, establishing vocational high schools, and increasing scholarship funds for the provincial university. Most of these reforms were part of the program of the organized teachers and were advocated by farmers' groups as well. They were introduced soon after the C.C.F. took office, and were pressed with vigor, so that today the educational facilities in Saskatchewan compare favorably with those in any rural area on the continent.[28]

The second aspect of the education program goes beyond the reforms demanded by clients of the department, and involves the ideology of the C.C.F. movement. Many in the C.C.F. believe that the present educational system is geared to uphold the existing social order, and that the social sciences, especially, are biased in favor of the capitalist system. They argue that the "real causes of wars" are not taught in the schools, that students do not learn of the power position of monopoly capital in an erstwhile democracy, and that the achievements of the coöperative movement and of socialist governments in other countries are played down in the textbooks. The party and the government, however, have long tended to avoid anything that might be construed as bringing politics into the school. Here again, fear of antagonizing sections of the electorate has limited the actions of the government.

The Minister of Education, Woodrow Lloyd, has shown, however, that such sentiments are not completely dead in the C.C.F.

I suggest that in the past, education has been neutral. . . . On the great issues facing the people, peace, prosperity, social justice, education cannot be neutral. Surely history has illustrated the fallaciousness of neutrality. Generally speaking, public opinion was neutral as it watched the degradation of China, Ethiopia, and Spain. While it is not suggested that education should accept all the responsibility for this neutrality of feeling, it must be admitted that neutrality could not have existed had education been more inclusive, more adequate, vital, and vigorous in outlook.[29]

The Department of Education has been acting to a limited extent on the principles laid down by the Minister. The high-school curriculum has been revised to include a positive orientation toward international coöperation, national planning, and the coöperative movement. The Department has organized an Adult Education Division "to help clarify the thinking of citizens on the fundamental issues confronting modern society." This division has sponsored conferences on coöperative farming, government health plans, and farmer-labor institutes designed to bring urban workers and farmers together.

The most important single social reform of the government is socialized medicine. The C.C.F. has been committed to state medicine since its origin. Immediately after taking office, the government proceeded to initiate a state medical plan, which was later to become a most completely socialized system. All pensioners—the aged, the blind, and those receiving mothers' allowances—are now entitled to receive free medical, hospital, and dental services. Certain diseases, either costly tó treat or a community danger, are treated free. These include cancer, tuberculosis, mental illness, and venereal disease. On January 1, 1947, a free hospitalization plan was inaugurated through which all residents of the province receive hospital services in return for the payment of a per capita tax of $10.

The C.C.F.'s long-term health policies are the only ones that involve a direct clash with powerful "vested interests." The party leaders originally envisaged a medical system in which all doctors would work on a salaried basis, and in which the emphasis would be changed from curative to preventive measures. Under such a system, many physicians, besides suffering a loss of income, would be forced to readjust their methods completely. They would be paid to keep people well rather than to treat their ailments. The members of the medical profession who treasure their incomes, traditions of practice, and personal independence have uncompromisingly opposed the implementation of any government scheme that would fundamentally alter their status.

In most parts of North America the organized medical profession has resisted any form of state medicine. In Saskatchewan, however, doctors have been forced to accept the basic premise of the need for state provision of medical care, since almost every section of public opinion favored it. The lack of decent health facilities in

the sparsely settled rural regions made farmers acutely conscious of the need for government provision of such services, and the conventions of farmers' organizations since the First World War have requested state medicine. The Liberal and Conservative parties of the province also have repeatedly gone on record as favoring the change.[30]

The extent to which the public has accepted the necessity for socialized medicine is best illustrated by the municipal-doctor scheme, which began in 1921. By 1944, in 101 out of 303 rural municipalities, as well as 60 villages and 11 towns, having a total population of 200,000, doctors were working on a salary basis, treating all residents free of charge.[31] In effect, then, one-third of the rural municipal governments in Saskatchewan had a local version of socialized medicine. Research studies revealed that morbidity rates in municipal-doctor areas were lower than in comparable private-practice districts.

In view of the public support of state medicine, the Saskatchewan College of Physicians and Surgeons, the local medical body, has given support to the principle of government payment for medical care. The major conflict in Saskatchewan when the C.C.F. took office was not, therefore, whether there should be state medicine or private medicine, but what kind of state medicine there should be. The physicians favored health insurance under which they would continue to practice exactly as they did under private medicine, except that they would send their bills to the state instead of to the patients.[32] The C.C.F., however, has long maintained that health insurance was no solution to the problem of adequate medical care. A pamphlet issued by the party in 1937 makes this position clear.

The matter of payment or non-payment for medical services is probably not the most pernicious evil. With all the advances of medical services we cannot make them available to a very large number. In our present system of practice, preventive medicine is largely neglected because the members of the [medical] profession are almost wholly engaged in the curative end of practice, so that preventable deaths are not being prevented and correctable conditions are not being corrected. . . .

If we are to have an all-inclusive system the state must necessarily assume control. In this Province much has been done. The direct control by the state of Tuberculosis has resulted in such advance in the treatment and prevention of Tuberculosis that it is amazing. . . . In the

municipal doctor scheme much good has resulted, but there is no coördination in the scope of the work or the salary paid the doctor or in many other features. . . . The fact that the Governments of this Province have felt it necessary to undertake such schemes now mentioned, and many others to which reference might be made, indicates the great need of state or socialized medicine to provide for all the individuals in the state, an all-inclusive, coördinated, well functioning system of medical services.

The objective of a State Medical system should be to prevent disease and promote physical and mental health, and thus increase human efficiency, effectiveness and happiness. Prevention should be the foremost endeavor of any system because by it there will ultimately be a limitation of disease and its severity. . . . Disease or proneness to disease could be discovered at its source and measures undertaken before any advancement of ill-health began. . . . The doctor could then do the work for which he is best suited and especially trained and then he could devote his energies not to the competition of securing a living, but to the striving after better results in his work. The nurse could also be employed, when the necessity of the patient requiring special attention is the reason for her employment and not the financial position of the patient, irrespective of need.[33]

Soon after the C.C.F. took office in 1944, the conflict between the government and the medical profession began to take shape. The government appointed a Health Services Planning Commission to draw up a detailed program of socialized medicine. The Commission, composed mainly of C.C.F. experts, made two basic recommendations, which it considered essential to the success of the project, but which were in fundamental conflict with the policies of the organized medical profession. These were, first, that the program should be under the direct control of the government, and second, that the physicians should be paid by salary. The Commission explained its recommendations as follows:

The formulation of any policy that might be termed *"state medicine"* must be the duty of the Department of Public Health. Of all agencies interested in matters pertaining to the health and the medical care of the people of the province, it alone is responsible to the people, and it alone has the sanction of the law to make its policies effective.

Much has been said about the desirability of creating an independent non-government body to develop a province-wide health scheme. While such an organization has proven satisfactory in the case of the Anti-Tuberculosis League, there are certain features of it that make the extension to include all health services inadvisable:

a) The powers of policy making with regard to matters pertaining to the health of the people of the province are delegated by the constitution to the Provincial Government. It is true that these powers may be delegated to other agencies, but it would seem to be a most doubtful practice to delegate a matter of such importance to any group other than the elected representatives or those immediately responsible to them;

b) In so far as such an agency served any administrative function, it would be empowered to dispose . . . public funds. Again, it is doubtful if it is the best practice of representative government to permit any agency not directly responsible to the people or their representatives to control the spending of public revenues.[34]

One of the essential reasons for the Commission's insistence on direct provincial control of the scheme was omitted from the report for political reasons. The organized medical profession insisted that any state medical scheme should be controlled by an independent nonpolitical commission staffed largely by the profession. The Planning Commission, however, feared that such an "independent" body would be dominated by physicians who were hostile to the objectives of the plan and would therefore oppose measures that might jeopardize their own interests.

The second major recommendation that was opposed by the organized medical profession concerned the basis of remuneration.

The general practitioner service should be a salaried service. The municipal doctor system now in operation, despite its shortcomings has proven to be, on the whole, satisfactory. In support of a salaried service we may mention:

1. It has proven itself in Saskatchewan as a satisfactory method of providing medical care in small urban centers and rural areas.

2. It is an incentive to the physician to do preventive work, since he gains from health, rather than from illness. Surveys have shown that municipal doctors do relatively more preventive work than other rural physicians.

3. It removes the possible temptation for the physician to do unnecessary work, or work for which he is not well qualified.

4. It does not necessitate the constant supervision and red-tape which would be necessary under a fee-for-service payment. . . .

9. When graded salaries are possible, the incentive to do good work will be furnished not only by pride in good results but by the increased salaries which may be earned on the completion of a post-graduate course, the obtaining of a more responsible position, or a specialist's qualifications.[35]

After the publication of the report of the Health Services Planning Commission, the Minister of Health was under continual pressure from the organized medical profession to modify the plan. The Saskatchewan College of Physicians and Surgeons objected to these two recommendations. They insisted that a state medical scheme could operate successfully only if doctors who understood the problems of medical care controlled the scheme, and argued further that a state-controlled system would fail because of political interference. The physicians also insisted that remuneration be on the basis of a fee for service rather than a salary.

What incentives are there under a salaried scheme? It is only human nature not to do as well if one is not paid for it. An adequate financial reward for doctors is necessary if good medical services are to be provided. Competition between doctors is ·healthy.[36]

. . . the College of Physicians and Surgeons have made a very intensive study of the problem of socialized medicine and have for some time advocated a form of state aided health insurance, administered by a politically independent commission with representation on it from the public, the government, and those providing the service.

The College has opposed any system of state medicine whereby the doctors all become servants of the government on a salary. They have constantly advocated that the patient should have the privilege of choosing his own doctor.[37]

The spokesmen for the medical profession warned the government that the plan would fail unless it were modified. Some doctors even threatened that they would not coöperate or would leave the province to practice elsewhere.[38]

The impetus for implementing the scheme, as originally drawn up, came from within the government itself, from the small group connected with the Health Services Planning Commission. These medical experts, who were newly appointed by the C.C.F. government, and who were thoroughly in favor of a socialized medical system, warned the Minister of Health that health insurance requiring a fee for service would continue the worst features of private medical practice, with its emphasis on curative rather than preventive medicine; and that doctors might overcharge the government through unnecessary surgical operations. They pointed to the failure of the fee-for-service plan in New Zealand, where "numerous abuses [exist], including 'over-consultation,' the speedy examination of patients, some at rates of twelve patients an hour,

payment of $6,000 a year for one afternoon's work [during the week], and the charging of a fee for each patient seen on visits to institutions for the aged and invalid."[39]

These cross pressures on the government resulted in a modification of the original proposals of the Health Services Planning Commission. The Minister of Health proposed, instead of the original plan of direct government control, "to have a representative administrative body of all classes of the people . . . set up as a governing body with a small executive body on which the medical profession would be well represented."[40]

The medical profession regarded this concession as a major victory. One doctor suggested that the new plan meant that the government now stood for "health insurance rather than state medicine," and that discussions with the Minister reflected this shift in the government's opinion.[41] The doctors felt that, as experts on a commission meeting with laymen, they would have veto power and could forestall undesirable actions.

The second major compromise from the original proposals of the Planning Commission lay in the crucial area of payment to the doctors. In 1946 an experimental health region was set up in southwestern Saskatchewan, in the Swift Current district, to give complete medical and hospital care. The government agreed to pay the physicians on a fee-for-service basis, paying them 75 per cent of the existing standard rates. The local doctors and the College of Physicians and Surgeons accepted this proposal, which, in effect, gave them most of what they had originally asked for.

A third major government compromise lay in the policy of recruitment and licensing of physicians from outside the province and the country. Saskatchewan has the lowest ratio of doctors to population of any province in Canada except New Brunswick, and one-third of the physicians in the province were more than sixty years old at the end of the war. This fact naturally strengthened the position of the organized doctors. The Planning Commission felt that an organized campaign of recruiting doctors to the province was necessary if any state medical scheme were to succeed. Some government officials suggested that the College of Physicians and Surgeons was discouraging doctors from coming to Saskatchewan by warning them that the future of medicine was dark in the province. Moreover, government medical experts felt that the College was deliberately excluding refugee European physicians by imposing unduly difficult requirements.

A subcommittee of the provincial legislature was appointed to investigate the licensing power of professional groups such as the College of Physicians and Surgeons. Supporters of state and coöperative medicine testified that the College had used its power and influence to prevent doctors from coöperating with state and coöperative medical plans, as well as to keep doctors out of the province.

The legislative committee, which was controlled by a large C.C.F. majority, favored legislation that would take the licensing power away from professional groups and give it to a government board. This suggestion was greeted with widespread protests by various professional groups. Some of the medical leaders again raised the threat of leaving the province. The government, once more, agreed to a compromise that left the professional associations in control of licensing, but required that the profession inform the government of the reason for failing to grant a license.

The medical profession, therefore, still retains most of the legal base of its power to discipline dissident members and its influence over recruitment of physicians. There is little formal evidence that it is abusing that power, but obviously it is not doing its utmost to coöperate with the government in the vital campaign to secure new doctors. Efforts to reduce the shortage of physicians can be effected in four ways: by making conditions of practice attractive to young physicians, by encouraging doctors who believe in socialized medicine to come to Saskatchewan, by admitting refugee physicians, and by stepping up medical training at the University of Saskatchewan.

Instead of encouraging young doctors, such statements as the following are made by reputable physicians: "Saskatchewan's flair for political experimentation leaves the prospective doctor uncertain as to the security of his medical future in this province."[42] Enthusiastic believers in socialized medicine who have expressed their willingness to come to the province have received cold, formal replies from the College, which have discouraged some of them. The leaders of the organized medical profession are still hostile to the idea of bringing in refugee physicians, and require that they undergo prolonged additional training before they are permitted to practice. All these actions must be viewed in the light of the fact that there are not enough doctors in rural areas.

The conflict between the Saskatchewan government and the organized medical profession is the only major clash between the

government and a powerfully entrenched and socially necessary "vested interest" group. There are no major industries in the province, and the government, therefore, is not faced with the internal opposition of powerful industrial and financial interests. In embryonic form, however, the struggle with the medical profession is comparable to the problems faced by other socialist governments. The socialization of the medical profession in Saskatchewan is a small-scale equivalent of the problem of the socialization of a key sector of an economy which a controlling group is determined not to yield.

Like all other governments, one of the prime goals of a radical reform government in a political democracy is to be reëlected. Any plan of the government will come to naught if it is defeated after one term in office. The elected reformer must, therefore, hold two considerations in mind if he is to achieve the social reforms which his party proposes: first, he must make the changes that are necessary to secure the reforms; and second, he must not antagonize the majority of the electorate. To threaten the power, privileges, or beliefs of any socially necessary key group may lead that group to refuse to continue its work efficiently. Such "sabotage" could temporarily deprive the general public of the services it had previously received.

The Saskatchewan government was faced with the possibility that the socialization of medicine would cause a large number of doctors to leave the province. Members of the government feared that they would then be blamed for the consequent decline in medical standards and services. Similarly, if the British government were to socialize an industry in which the managers were strongly opposed to the plans of the government, the resultant decline in productivity could bring down the government at the next election.

This dilemma has been faced repeatedly by democratic reform governments. The Labor and Social Democratic governments of Sweden, Norway, New Zealand, and Australia have held political power for long periods without making significant inroads on "vested" property and managerial interests. Few industries have been nationalized by these governments, though they all profess socialist objectives. Each of these governments has increased its social services, as Saskatchewan has. Increased social services are an easy solution to the dilemma of the democratic socialist in office,

for they improve living standards but do not upset the *status quo* and are not violently opposed by the people with economic power or skill. Thus the medical profession had no serious objection to the establishment of free hospitalization in the province in 1947, for this measure satisfied the popular desire for increased state provision of medical care, but did not affect the position of the physicians.

The problem suggested is a major one in any attempt to secure important social change through democratic channels. Can the state make significant inroads on the power of entrenched groups which are economically or socially necessary without, in the process, giving up democracy? The degree to which a democratically elected government can successfully install far-reaching changes in the face of powerful opposition would seem to depend on the organized popular demand for its program. The British Labor government could not have refused to nationalize the coal mines without suffering a loss of many of its supporters. In Australia the recently defeated Labor government embarked on a campaign to socialize all banks, after being criticized by many of its more left-wing supporters.

The Saskatchewan government, however, is not backed by an electorate that understands or demands qualitative changes in medical care. The people wanted greater and cheaper quantities of the kind of service they already had. The farmers supported "state" medicine, but to them the term meant state payment for medical care, free medicines, free hospitalization, prepayment of medical costs, and medical care of pensioners and indigents. The public, including most of the members and leaders of the C.C.F., are not and were not aware of the dangerous implications of the professional control of licensing or of the fee-for-service plan for the program of the C.C.F.

There has been little criticism from members of the C.C.F. of the government's compromises with the medical profession. Party members and supporters enthusiastically approve every step toward the goal of a complete plan of medical coverage. Thus, government officials are faced on one hand with the popular demand for any kind of state medicine, and, on the other, with the threat of sabotage by physicians unless the plan of their organized profession is put into practice. The compromise of the basic goals of reform of medical practice naturally followed.

The dilemma of the reform politician can be lessened only if he wins an enlightened electorate before he assumes office. The pressures of groups opposing social change must be counterbalanced by other powerful groups. The lack of major groups in Saskatchewan opposing the well-organized medical profession has been a large factor in the success of that group. The experiences of the Saskatchewan government indicate that a socialist party may win power by playing down the radical elements of its own program. Many sincere reformers have done this with the intention of educating the electorate and carrying out radical reforms after they took office. Once in office, however, the party learns that it is too late for education, that it must back down before hostile power groups. It then becomes politically necessary to educate the public about the advantages of the compromise, not of further reform.

Like other socialist governments, the Saskatchewan C.C.F. has extended its social welfare work greatly. There has been little or no opposition to such efforts. The government set up a separate Department of Social Welfare for the first time in the history of the province, and has increased the amount of money spent for this purpose to the highest proportion of the total budget of any province in Canada.

The Department increased old-age pensions $5 a month above those paid by the federal government and granted free medical care to all recipients of government pensions. Mothers' allowances were greatly increased, and the province took over direct responsibility for all unplaced orphan children. A rehabilitation program has been started for the métis (half-breeds), and they are being trained for useful occupations. Old-age homes and the penal system are being modernized. For the first time, trained workers have been hired to staff the Department of Social Welfare.[48]

The only limitation placed on the social welfare work of the government has been financial. The government is afraid to increase taxes sharply for the benefit of social services, since the tax-conscious farmers would resent new direct taxes on land. So far as financial resources permit, however, the humanitarian goals of the C.C.F. movement have been carried out, and have resulted in one of the best social service programs in Canada. These developments confirm the pattern, suggested earlier, of reformers moving farthest in areas of least social resistance.

In explaining the significant difference between the reforms of the C.C.F. and those of various "progressive" nonsocialist governments, C.C.F. leaders point to the socialization of industry. Today the Saskatchewan government owns and operates a large number of enterprises, including electric power, telephones, bus lines, insurance, a printing company, a woolen mill, a fur-marketing service, a shoe factory, a tannery, a sodium sulphate plant, a seed-cleaning plant, liquor stores, two fish-filleting plants, a fish-marketing board, a lumber-marketing board, a box factory, and a brickyard. All except the telephones, liquor stores, and part of the electric power system were acquired since the C.C.F. took office.

The reasons given for government ownership of the different industries vary. The overriding consideration on a provincial level is the desire to obtain funds for extra social services. The C.C.F. looks upon government businesses as one of the best means of increasing the general revenues of the government without raising taxes. Second, the farmers' movement and the C.C.F. have long argued that natural resources and public utilities should belong to the people. The extension of government electric power lies in this category. A third motive given for government ownership has been the desire to keep money inside the province. The establishment of the Government Insurance Office and the replacement of the Greyhound Bus Lines by a Government Bus Company has been defended on the ground that Saskatchewan is keeping its money at home. The government has pointed out that residents of Saskatchewan paid over $50,000,000 in insurance premiums during the depression to non-Saskatchewan insurance firms and received only $19,000,000 in return for losses.[4] A fourth group of industries to be owned by the government are the small-scale enterprises that process Saskatchewan resources: the woolen mill, the shoe factory, and the brickyard.

The government has also set up a number of corporations that could best be described as service companies. These companies were organized to render a nonprofit service to groups that could not obtain the service elsewhere or that were, in the opinion of the government, being exploited by private interests. The fish-filleting plants, the fish-marketing board, the lumber board, the seed-cleaning plant, and the fur-marketing service fall in this category. There is also the Prince Albert Box Factory, which was expropriated as a result of a labor dispute.

There can be little doubt that the government's socialization program does establish a qualitative difference between the C.C.F. and other agrarian reform parties. The socialist ideology and beliefs of the C.C.F. have played a major role in the extent and vigor of the program. After the 1944 victory, party and government leaders indicated a real desire to socialize industry, in spite of the fact that this was played down in the election campaign.

Saskatchewan, however, has no large-scale industry. It has less than 2 per cent of the total industrial production of Canada.[45] Outside of public utilities, therefore, the only areas for potential government investment are businesses that would be considered small in the country as a whole. The Saskatchewan C.C.F. was therefore faced with the choice of leaving the nationalization aspects of the party to a future federal C.C.F. government, which could socialize big business in harmony with the party platform, or of sidestepping that platform and establishing state-owned small businesses. The government chose the latter course, because large sections of the party and its leadership were eager to demonstrate the value of government ownership.

In explaining the program to the people, however, the C.C.F. leaders have defended their activities more in terms of provincial sectionalism, that is, resistance to the industrially dominant East, than in socialist terms of eventual replacement of private ownership by social ownership. It is interesting to note that the Non-Partisan League in North Dakota also embarked on a program of state-owned industry that was defended in similar nonsocialist terms. Many western farmers have considered the lack of industry in the wheat-growing areas of the United States and Canada to be part of the exploitation of the West practiced by "eastern interests."

At the same time that the Saskatchewan government was starting on a program of government industry, it had to continue to support private industry, as the overwhelming majority of industry and future investment would necessarily remain in private hands for many years, and the party desired to win the support of small business. Cabinet members attempted to resolve the apparent contradiction between their promises and their actions by saying that the government would enter only the industrial fields that private enterprise refused to develop, and that where private business would develop an industry, the government would help them to

do so.⁴⁶ The government set up a fund from which private investors could borrow to start new industries.

This policy of government ownership of small industry was economically dangerous for the government. A number of the small industries that it started, especially shoes and woolen goods, were risky ventures in which private businessmen were afraid to invest. The government has been taking the risks of the marginal producer and has encountered difficulties in competing profitably with older private companies in other parts of Canada, where labor standards are lower than those set by the C.C.F. Some of these industries have either lost money or are making only a small profit, which will probably disappear with the end of a seller's market.⁴⁷

Faced by these coercions of the market economy, which many of the C.C.F. leaders did not envisage in their early socialist enthusiasm, a number of the government officials have become wary about engaging in further public enterprise. They fear that government industry operating at a loss will lead to a serious decrease in rural support. The government has therefore modified its original intention of socializing the oil fields, for they are still in the category of a risk investment, and private companies are being encouraged to come into the province on long-term leases.

These experiences point up the dangers facing socialist governments that do not have or do not take complete control over the economy. Government enterprise operating in a capitalist market is naturally subject to the same external constraints as private enterprise and reacts in the same way. The attempt to jump into this uncontrolled situation has made many C.C.F.'ers much more conservative in their attitude toward socialization of industry, and may seriously affect the party's action in the federal field. Industrial experience in the province of Saskatchewan seems to confirm the warnings of socialist economists who challenge the possibility of socialists successfully maintaining a mixed economy.⁴⁸ It is significant to note that the governments of various Australian states had similar experiences in the 1920's when they established state-owned small industries.⁴⁹ Many of these industries had to be sold in the 'thirties because they were losing money.

The experiences of the C.C.F. in power yield significant insights into the processes of social change in a democracy. The types of reform introduced by a political party include three main

factors: the ideology of the movement, the power of the forces that benefit from change, and the strength of the opposition. The extent of change in any area under Saskatchewan government control depends primarily on the degree of organized support for reform in comparison with the economic, political, or technical strength of the opposition. The socialist and progressive ideology of the C.C.F. has strengthened the left-wing forces, but it has not changed the usual role of pressure groups in a democratic society.

C.C.F. reforms in education, soon after the government was elected, reflected the strength and pressure of the organized teaching profession. The teachers and the farmers' organizations favored basic quantitative reforms in the educational system. These reforms were brought in quickly and vigorously because there was no organized opposition. Curricular changes did meet opposition and hence such changes have been comparatively minor. The powerful coöperative movement received a government Department of Coöperatives. The organized farmers' movement secured government protection for landownership and support in gaining higher prices. The trade-unions were given what they consider to be "the best labor legislation on the North American continent." The rural demand for state medicine is being fulfilled in a way that meets with the approval of the medical profession.

Earlier in this chapter, the question of the freedom of a radical government in a democracy to innovate beyond the popularly demanded reforms was raised. The experience of Saskatchewan would seem to repeat the pattern followed by other democratic socialist governments. The need of a democratic government to retain the support of a majority of the electorate is a powerful weapon in the hands of groups that wish to prevent social change. Any drastic change in basic institutions may endanger the popular support of the government. Socialist governments, therefore, have followed the path of least resistance, instituting reforms that meet the least opposition from entrenched interests.

Basic institutions are modified only when they have broken down completely. The extensive socialization of industry in Spain in 1936 took place only after the owners of the factories fled Loyalist Spain.[50] The government, however, later returned many of the confiscated industries in order to retain the support of the middle classes. The past or present majority socialist governments of Sweden, Norway, New Zealand, and Australia have not socialized

many industries, though they have held power for long periods of time.[51] Socialization has often taken place in these countries as a result of a loss of support to more radical parties demanding the changes. Only those parties that placed the achievement of their "reform" objectives above the maintenance of democracy, such as Communist Russia and Nazi Germany, have succeeded in fundamentally changing the social and economic structure.

A reformer who desires to make drastic innovations must be prepared to face resistance and sabotage from the groups whose power, status, privileges, or traditions he threatens. The democratic radical in opposition will suggest many reforms that appear logical and necessary to him. Once in office he finds that his goal must shift from reform to the maintenance of the equilibrium of the institutional order, unless he is prepared to place the success of his original goals over the possibility of losing power. To explain his refusal to carry out his program on the ground that it is opposed by various groups that make its success impossible is to admit that the proposed reform is utopian, that it never could have been carried out. Few politicians in office will face up to this problem. The result is that their over-all reform program often falls by the wayside.

It is not suggested that the reforms of the C.C.F. in Saskatchewan are not important. The sincere reformist beliefs of C.C.F. leaders have resulted in many actions that would not have been established by the old parties, whose loyalties are to the existing order. No one can challenge the fact that the C.C.F. has made trade-union organization easier, that it is protecting farmers against foreclosure and debt, that it has improved the lot of indigents in Saskatchewan, that it has reduced some of the serious financial burdens that result from illness, automobile accidents, or injuries at work. Actually, the Saskatchewan government has probably done as much to reduce economic hazards as a provincial government with limited powers can do.

The fact remains, however, that with few exceptions the C.C.F., like many other reform governments, has not innovated where the consequences would endanger its electoral support, because the transition period between the old reform and the smooth operation of a new pattern is, in a democracy, also an electoral period. Left-wing critics of the government, both within and outside the C.C.F., suggest that the government has been too conservative and cau-

tious in its policies, that it has been afraid to take risks or that it sees risks where none are present. However, even if the government had been more venturesome, the broad, over-all problem would still exist—the problem of maintaining sufficient equilibrium between elections to retain office. The question of how to reconcile the need for change and still keep a basically democratic structure seems to be one of the most crucial issues of our age.

Chapter XII

BUREAUCRACY
AND SOCIAL CHANGE

A͟ᴛ ᴀʟᴍᴏsᴛ every C.C.F. provincial convention and Council meeting, the problem of the relationship between the government and the civil service has been raised by party members.[1] Many in the C.C.F. believe that the retention in office of key civil servants appointed by Liberal governments is hampering the work of the government. This conviction is evident in the resolutions they have submitted to various constituencies between 1945 and 1947.

Whereas most of the Civil Service have been supporters of old line parties and most still remain sympathizers of said parties, and

Whereas in the last year under C.C.F. Government, new appointments or promotions to higher positions have been made mostly from supporters of the old line parties because recommendations on a possible new appointment or promotion are being requested from senior officers of said Departments who again are old line party supporters and only naturally recommend their own kind.

Therefore be it resolved that members of the Government in engaging Civil Servants, make appointments, wherever possible, from C.C.F. supporters to at least even up an equal proportion of Civil Servants as between the old line parties and C.C.F. supporters.[2]

[1] For notes to chapter xii see pages 306–308.

Whereas it is quite obvious that certain partisan Liberal employees in the Civil Service are using their inside position to belittle, entangle and obstruct the good work of our C.C.F. Government and

Whereas this can bring about lack of confidence in and place at a great disadvantage our C.C.F. party at the next Provincial election.

Therefore be it resolved that this C.C.F. Convention of the Qu'Appelle-Wolseley constituency do request our Government to be consistently on the lookout for these partisan Civil Servants and have them removed from positions of trust.[3]

Whereas certain recent appointments made by the Provincial Government have brought considerable criticism from the membership, and whereas personnel selected for certain vital positions have not in the past upheld the philosophy of the C.C.F. and are considered doubtful of doing so in the future, and whereas this type of appointment may develop serious opposition in the near future,

Therefore be it resolved that we request the Saskatchewan C.C.F. Provincial Government to be very careful in its appointments in the future, and suggest that socialist minded persons be appointed wherever possible.[4]

Be it resolved that the Government exercise extreme caution in the selection of members to various boards and other appointees holding responsible positions to forestall any sabotage, whether premeditated or because the proposed appointee lacks sufficient grounding in the fundamentals and principles of the Government.[5]

Resolved that the Convention go on record to ask the provincial Government to fill the key positions in the Civil Service with younger people, who are sincere and honest for the cause and principles of the Movement as laid down by our C.C.F. Party Convention.[6]

Whereas our original program for the C.C.F. stated that when elected to power persons holding key positions should be sympathetic to the C.C.F. cause;

And whereas two Provincial Conventions have passed resolutions asking that this be done;

Therefore be it resolved that the Government remove reactionary departmental heads and put in their places persons who are sympathetic to the C.C.F.[7]

That there should be special attention taken in respect to our public services, which we feel quite sure are being sabotaged in a good many ways by some of the personnel in the different services, which are undermining the interest of the public in a very serious manner;

Therefore we recommend that special investigations be made in these different departments, with special authority to deal with these matters and then clear up.[8]

Whereas the Provincial Government has given all its civil servants, regardless of political affiliations, every consideration, and has taken on new personnel without consideration of their political affiliations, which confirms the original C.C.F. policy;

And whereas it has been found that several of these appointees have been sabotaging the C.C.F. Government in an underhand manner, by giving out incorrect information, which has a mischievous effect in the country, which must be counteracted by local people, and the executive;

Be it resolved that the Government discharge all such officials coming under this class and replace them with loyal coöperators and efficient personnel.[9]

The discussion of the role of the civil servant raises again, this time on the level of the problem of government bureaucracy, the question of how free reform governments are to innovate. Writers and social scientists have long called attention to the fact that in the state and other large social organizations, administrative functions cannot be separated from policy-making power.[10] It is impossible to understand the operation of a government simply by analyzing the goals of the politicians in power and the nongovernmental pressures on them. The members of the civil service constitute one of the major houses of government, with the power to initiate, amend, and veto actions proposed by other branches. The goals and values of the civil service are often as important a part of the total complex of forces responsible for state policy as those of the ruling political party.

The political problem of the power and influence of a permanent civil service with its own goals and traditions was not important so long as the social and economic values of the bureaucracy and the governing politicians did not seriously conflict. The problem becomes crucial, however, when a new political movement takes office and proposes to enact reforms that go beyond the traditional frame of reference of previous governmental activity or which upset the existing set of relations within the bureaucracy. It is especially important today, when the explicit formal goals of many democratic states are changing from the laissez-faire police regulation of society to those of a social-welfare planning state.[11]

The tradition and concept of a merit nonpatronage civil service was related in many countries to the needs of the dominant business groups, who demanded cheap and efficient service from the state. J. Donald Kingsley has shown how in England the policy of a merit civil service grew with the increase in political power of

the business class.[12] The business groups desired an efficient state that would facilitate and protect the development of commerce. Permanent, nonpolitical officials insured continuity of government regulations and practices, and made for stable relations with the state, regardless of shifts in party fortunes. This idea of a merit civil service was not challenged as long as party politics remained contests between groups who accepted the basic orientation and activities of the state and the society. The establishment of reform and socialist governments, which propose radical changes in the functions of the state, raises the problem of whether such reforms can be successfully initiated and administered by a bureaucratic structure that is organized to regulate different norms, and whose members possess values that do not correspond with those of the "radical" politicians.

Since the days of Karl Marx, some socialists have maintained that a successful socialist state must destroy the old state apparatus and erect a new administrative organization.[13] In recent times, persons who have served in, or studied, socialist governments have suggested that one crucial reason for their failure to proceed more vigorously toward the attainment of their goals has been the "bureaucratic conservatism" of old civil servants.

In Weimar, Germany, the Social Democratic Party, which held majority power from 1918 to 1920, was not able to make fundamental changes in the power and economic structures. Participants in that government report that the bureaucracy played a major role in obstructing changes, as the following statement by Arnold Brecht, a former important Social Democratic government official, suggests:

One of the finest Labor Ministers in post-war Germany, a great authority in law philosophy, liked to mock himself in relating how the scientific atmosphere of the Ministry of Justice lulled his activity. There were the most admirable experts, modest and seriously prepared to submit to any better argument, intent upon justice and truth, upon science and social achievements, ready to do what they were ordered to do when the arguing stopped. . . . While the political heads changed frequently, the officials as a whole stayed, willing to do anything they were ordered to do. . . . Why not hear them. . . . They would not just say no to new proposals. . . . But they would adjust the political plans to expediency, and would take the fundamentals of the radical proposals and reduce them to cautious experiments in various directions, preserving a conservative trend.[14]

George Lansbury, who was a member of the second Labor government in Great Britain, and subsequently became leader of the Party, unequivocally declared, "All through the life of the late [1929–1931 Labor] Government, Treasury officials obstructed and hindered the Ministers in their work. No one can deny this."[15] A study by a political scientist of the work of this government bears Lansbury out.

Philip Snowden's sympathies were with the socialists when he headed the Treasury in a Labor Cabinet, but his budgets might well have been drawn up by Conservatives. . . . the influence of his permanent officials, and of outstanding persons of the City, outweighed that of his cabinet colleagues; and before many months of service, the radical became proud of his conservatism.

George Lansbury, First Commissioner of Works in the second Labor Government, strove for many reforms, particularly in the fields of unemployment, old age pensions, and education. As one of a group of officials called upon to solve these problems, he found the road to reform blocked at every turn by the civil servants. These officials, he said, acted quite constitutionally, refusing to comment on policy, only questioning whether or not a proposed policy would work. But Treasury representatives always found reasons why ministerial proposals could not be carried out. Lansbury soon came to feel the futility of his position and concluded that if a Socialist Government was to succeed, dependence could not be placed on civil servants who were not Socialist.[16]

An Australian participant in a Labor government, V. G. Childe, former secretary to the Premier of New South Wales, pointed to the role of "outwardly obsequious civil servants" in helping to transform the attitudes of Labor ministers.[17] "In France, too, reactionary officials successfully sabotaged the efforts of the Blum government in finance and foreign affairs."[18]

Saskatchewan is the latest in the series of examples of radical governments attempting to make drastic changes in the direction and functions of government while retaining permanent civil servants in key administrative policy-making posts. There are, however, major differences between Saskatchewan and most other countries in which radical parties have come to power. Civil-service traditions are very different from those prevailing in England and other British Commonwealth countries; they are, in fact, more similar to those of nineteenth-century United States than to those of England. Party loyalty and obligations determine the choice of civil servants, as the following report makes clear.

It is possible to find four main corrupt features in the Saskatchewan Liberal organization, features which are common to most party organizations in Canada, whether Liberal or Conservative: the use of the civil servants as party workers; the patronage system by which party supporters were appointed to the civil service; the use of public works appropriations, particularly the road money, for pork barrel purposes; and the granting of contracts, especially in public works and printing, in return for financial or press support. . . .

The patronage system gave the party the votes of practically all the provincial civil service. Whenever the votes of the civil service can be separated, they appear to have voted en bloc for the Liberals, even in federal elections. For example, one provincial institution, the Weyburn Mental Hospital, cast in the federal general election of 1925, 135 votes for the Liberal candidate, 5 for the Conservative, and 1 for the Progressive. In the rest of the constituency the Liberals received about 4,800 votes, and the other two candidates about 2,000 each. In the federal election of 1921, the Provincial Hospital at North Battleford cast 141 votes for the Liberal, 5 for the Conservative, and 16 for the Progressive. The vote . . . in the rest of the constituency was: Liberal, 4,500; Conservative, 700; Progressive, 8,800.[19]

During the 1930's, administration of relief and awarding of government jobs were more directly partisan than ever before. Many C.C.F. supporters assert that they were warned by relief inspectors to cease working for the C.C.F. As a result, the attitude of the C.C.F. toward the civil service differed from that of many European socialist parties. The dislike of the blatant excesses of patronage government led the party, while in opposition, to oppose partisan appointments; but the recognition that the civil service was honeycombed with Liberal politicians made C.C.F. leaders specifically exempt deputy ministers and other major policy posts from civil-service protection. Unlike socialist parties in Europe and Great Britain, which were prevented from advocating changes in the civil service because of the popular acceptance of a politically neutral bureaucracy, the C.C.F. was free, in terms of the political values of Saskatchewan, to advocate the replacement of top-ranking conservative civil servants by C.C.F. experts, and did so in its 1944 program.

The C.C.F. pledges itself to remove party patronage from the public services of Canada. While recognizing that heads of commissions, Deputy-Ministers, etc., *must be in agreement with the policy of the*

government and should therefore be government appointments, all other Civil Service appointments should be, and under a C.C.F. government, will be, placed under the control of a nonpolitical commission.[20]

The leader of the party, and later the Premier, T. C. Douglas, in a preëlection speech made clear his insistence on having sympathetic experts. "It is most necessary for any government that those in charge of various departments shall be competent and capable of absorbing new ideas and techniques. No matter how good legislation is, if those in charge of administering it are unsympathetic or incapable of a new approach, little good will come of it."[21] Judging by the preëlection attitudes of C.C.F. leaders, Saskatchewan should have been a good example of an attempt to institute reforms with a new administrative apparatus. After the election in 1944, both opponents and supporters of the party expected that key posts in the civil service would be filled from the ranks of experts sympathetic to socialist objectives.[22] Some of the new cabinet ministers told party intimates, before the election, that the incumbent deputy ministers were "reactionaries" who could never be expected to carry out C.C.F. policies.

Once in office, however, the new C.C.F. cabinet ministers changed their views. Instead of the expected housecleaning, most of the key civil servants were retained. Few changes in the top administration were made during the first two years of the C.C.F. government. Men who had served under the Liberals were promoted to fill vacancies in the upper levels of the civil service.

Every group of responsible C.C.F. leaders except the cabinet ministers, however, continued to believe that extensive changes in the top-level personnel of the government were necessary if the movement was to carry out its objectives of social reform. This attitude was expressed by members of the Provincial Council, C.C.F. members of the legislature, Saskatchewan members of the federal House of Commons, and every provincial convention since the party took office.[23] The party leaders who formed the government were no less committed to the goals and program of the party. The changes in the objectives of C.C.F. cabinet ministers must, therefore, be dealt with on the structural, rather than the ideological or personal, level.

The difference between the cabinet and the rest of the party hierarchy lay in the fact that the new ministers were exposed to unanticipated pressures. They were faced with the immediate

problem of assuming responsibility for departments that had to deal with a multitude of day-to-day problems. No department could stop operating until the new administration rebuilt its working apparatus. The new ministers, like most politicians, were amateurs in their respective departments. None of them had ever had administrative experience in a large organization.

The members of the cabinet were under pressure to implement the legislative and administrative reforms promised by the party platform. This platform, like that of most political parties, was necessarily general, lacking concrete steps to be taken after election. Beside drawing up new legislation, changing administrative regulations of their departments, and taking part in cabinet meetings, the ministers had to continue being active politicians, making speeches and caring for the needs of their constituents.

In any government, such pressures force the cabinet ministers to lean heavily on their civil service.[24] In Saskatchewan, however, many of the cabinet ministers had anticipated deliberate "sabotage" or resistance to their plans by the Liberal civil service. They entered office ready to remove the deputy ministers as soon as they showed signs of opposition to government plans. The key civil servants, on the other hand, expected to be discharged soon after the C.C.F. took office.[25] They knew that the C.C.F. was aware of the partisan nature of their appointments. Some of them had begun to look for other jobs, or planned to retire. The majority, however, in the hope of maintaining their positions, tried to ingratiate themselves with their ministers.

A——, a deputy minister, went to his Minister shortly after the election, and told him that he had been a member of the British Labor Party, thirty years ago, and that he was pleased at the opportunity of working for a socialist government.

B——, who had been an active Liberal, and had been engaged in relief work in the 'thirties, told his minister that he had been unhappy in his job under the old government, because all members of the department had been forced to engage in partisan work. Now that the C.C.F. was in office, he hoped to be really free to do his work. He told the minister stories of the inefficiency of certain parts of the department.

The wives of two deputy ministers began a campaign of wooing the wives of their respective ministers, who were new to Regina. They entertained them and introduced them to various people in the city. The deputies, themselves, offered to assist their ministers in various reforms.

C——, another deputy, came to his minister and offered to draw up the working plans of a major C.C.F. reform.[26]

The leading civil servants did their utmost to convince the cabinet that they were coöperative. In many departments, during the early period of the C.C.F. government, the best "socialists" in Saskatchewan were in the top ranks of the governmental bureaucracy. The administratively insecure cabinet ministers were overjoyed at the friendly response they obtained from the civil servants. To avoid making administrative blunders that would injure them in the eyes of the public and the party, the ministers began to depend on the civil servants. As one cabinet minister stated in an interview, "I would have been lost if not for the old members of my staff. I'm only a beginner in this work. B—— has been at it for twenty years. If I couldn't go to him for advice, I couldn't have done a thing. Why, now [after two years in office] I am only beginning to find my legs and make my own decisions. . . . I have not done a thing for two years without advice."

The failure to change key members of the civil service had important consequences for the future work of the government. Some of the civil servants interpreted it as revealing personal weakness on the part of their ministers and political weakness on the part of the C.C.F. The deputy ministers, realizing that there was no danger of being discharged, fell back into the traditional bureaucratic pattern. A number of civil servants were able to convince their ministers that certain changes were not administratively feasible or that they would incur too much opposition. Some deputy ministers exchanged information with other deputies on their technique of controlling their ministers. It is difficult to demonstrate concretely—without certain breaches of confidence—which policies were drastically affected by civil-service action, but it is a fact that some key officials boasted of "running my department completely," and of "stopping harebrained radical schemes."

The resistance of top-line civil servants to C.C.F. measures was not necessarily a result of conscious opposition to the party. The most important bureaucratic conservative influence on the government does not seem to be a result of attempts to injure the government in the eyes of the electorate. Many top-ranking civil servants, even though appointed as political partisans, appeared to be honestly concerned with doing their jobs. Their objections to C.C.F. proposals were based on a desire to maintain the stability

of their departments and their own positions. These civil servants would probably have attempted to modify Liberal or Conservative schemes which they considered to be unworkable. The bureaucracy, however, had become institutionalized under old party governments. It had a set pattern of reacting to problems. New methods of administration were often designated "difficult" or "impossible" because they had never been tried before or would require revamping the work of a department. In opposing such changes, the civil servant was only taking the easy way out of preserving the *status quo* of his own area of working and living. Harold Laski has pointed this out as a characteristic of bureaucracy in general.

> In all large-scale enterprises men who are desirous of avoiding great responsibility (and the majority of men is so desirous) are necessarily tempted to avoid great experiments. In a political democracy this obviously becomes an official habit where there is a . . . bureaucratic system. . . .
>
> The tendency accordingly has been a certain suspicion of experimentalism, a benevolence toward the "safe" man. . . . Administrative codes . . . are applied simply from the conservatism of habit.[27]

Civil-service modification of C.C.F. goals took three major forms: (1) the continuation of traditional and, from the C.C.F. point of view, reactionary procedure in government departments; (2) changes in the intent of new laws and regulations through administrative practices; (3) influence on cabinet ministers to adopt policies advocated by top-level civil servants. Information on the role of the civil service in modifying government activities was difficult to obtain, but, in discussing the work of the government, C.C.F. leaders, cabinet ministers, and civil servants provided significant glimpses into the operation of government policy.

Many local C.C.F. leaders expressed public resentment against the continuation of undesirable practices by local representatives of the government. Informants reported that before the C.C.F. was elected it was common practice in two departments to discriminate against non-Anglo-Saxon groups. These practices continued after the C.C.F. took office, for no one gave explicit orders to the contrary. The ministers were not aware of the fact that discrimination was the informal policy of the department. One cabinet minister changed the procedures in his department when he learned about these practices from local C.C.F. leaders, who had

received complaints from people who had been discriminated against. The discrimination practiced by the second department was known only to persons within the department; as no public complaint was ever made, no changes occurred.

Similar charges about the continuation of "reactionary" practices were reported about the work of local field men in government departments. These men had built up a local network of informants over a period of years. Many of the informants were active Liberals or local businessmen. The civil servants continued to rely on them for information after the C.C.F. took office. This sometimes resulted in government actions favoring the preservation of the partisan *status quo* in local administration. One cabinet minister, who has since discharged a large part of his field staff, found as a result of complaints from local members of the C.C.F. that members of his staff continued to grant leases and farming privileges to well-to-do persons who had secured them under previous governments, though it was now government policy to give them to poorer farmers and landless veterans.

The Deputy Minister of Labor was demoted in 1946, after repeated complaints from trade-union and C.C.F. labor leaders, who felt that the Deputy did not understand trade-union objectives, and was hostile to many of them. These labor leaders maintained that the Deputy insisted on carrying out the letter of all regulations, even when the resultant action was contrary to the over-all policy of the government. The unionists, who had expected and had been promised sympathetic and immediate action on their behalf, found themselves frustrated by the slowness of civil-service procedure, and were forced repeatedly to appeal to the Minister and the Premier.

An investigation by the Premier's office in 1946 revealed that patients in government mental hospitals were being neglected by attendants. Facilities that had been erected for patients were forbidden to them and were used by the staff. These practices continued for two years after the C.C.F. took office. The administrators of the mental hospitals, who were responsible for staff appointments, could not be expected to report the need for drastic changes. The defects were remedied only after complaints from C.C.F. supporters who lived near the hospital.

Some time after the government took office, a cabinet minister discovered, during a visit to one of the provincial institutions, that

inmates were being fitted with eyeglasses chosen from a large collection gathered from dead inmates. No one had thought it necessary to bring to his attention the fact that money was being saved by depriving people of optometrical services.

Civil-service activities that ran counter to over-all government policy could be checked only when the portion of the public served by the departments could observe what was being done. The permanent civil servant at the top of the administrative hierarchy was too deeply involved in the structure of mutual informal obligations and personal relations that exist in any long-established institution to call to his minister's attention practices that were contrary to C.C.F. objectives. The older civil servants did not realize that many of the practices of previous governments were repugnant to people who believed in the social reform philosophy of the C.C.F. movement, and thus were often not aware of any conflict between practices and objectives.

Cabinet ministers can hope to control the activities of their bureaucracy through reports from clients of government departments or sympathetic party followers. The minister, however, is at the mercy of his subordinates in situations in which the public at large is not aware of government activity. In such situations, civil servants who do not agree with, or do not understand the purposes of, the government are able to modify policy without much fear of detection. Max Weber has pointed out that the absolute dictator is often completely in the power of his bureaucracy, since, unlike the democratic ruler, he has no means of discovering whether his policies are being enforced.[28] Weber suggested that the bureaucracy is less powerful in a democracy, for the governing politicians will be kept informed by the public. This suggestion is only a half-truth, however, for the public can be aware of only a part of the government's activities. The areas of government work that are hidden from the eyes of the public are often closed to the cabinet minister as well. When the clients and the civil servants of a government department both disagree with the minister's policies, there is a great possibility that government policies will not be enforced. Both the clients and the bureaucracy will attempt to convince the minister that his policy is wrong, or they may simply ignore it.

One cabinet minister decided that certain government work that had previously been contracted out to private concerns should

be done by government employees whenever possible. His deputy minister, however, continued sending the work out to private concerns. This deputy told confidants that he considered government employees less competent than employees of private firms. Jobs were sometimes done twice, first by civil servants and later by private firms.

It is much more difficult to gather evidence about practices that take place behind closed doors. Members of the civil service have reported numerous examples of the modification of policies by civil servants—in confidence, however, which indicates that those coming to public or ministerial attention are only a small part of the actual efforts to change government policy at the administrative or enforcement level.

The modification of goals through administrative decisions represents only one aspect of the power of the civil service "House" to influence policy. Direct influence over the making of final policy, however, constitutes an aspect of the power of the permanent civil service which is as important as its ability to modify accepted policy through administrative procedure. An outsider cannot scientifically analyze the component elements entering into the decisions of a government department. Both permanent civil servants and new appointees of the C.C.F. report, however, that a number of top-ranking civil servants were able to convince cabinet members that some aspects of the C.C.F. program were impractical to administer. It is impossible to demonstrate that these civil servants were objectively wrong or insincere in opposing specific changes. Their objections to C.C.F. policy were usually based on the honest belief that the changes would not work.[29]

Civil servants, of course, do not operate in a social vacuum. Their opinions about relative "right" and "wrong" are determined, like those of all persons, by pressures existing in their social milieu. A department official is interested not only in whether a minister's proposals can be put into practice, but with the effect of such policies on the traditional practices of the department and on its long-term relations with other groups. A reform which may be socially desirable, but which disrupts the continuity of practices and interpersonal relations within the department, will often be resisted by a top-ranking civil servant. He is obligated to protect those beneath him in the administrative hierarchy from the consequences of a change in policy.

Second, and equally important, the opinion of government officials on the feasibility of any proposal is necessarily colored by their political outlook and by the climate of opinion in their social group. Many top-ranking civil servants in Saskatchewan are members of the upper social class of Regina. Most of their social contacts are with people who believe that they will be adversely affected by many C.C.F. policies. Government officials who belong to professional or economic groups whose position or privileges are threatened by government policies tend to accept the opinion of their own group that reforms which adversely affect the group are wrong and will not work. Cabinet ministers who desire to make social reforms may therefore be dependent for advice on permanent civil servants who, in part, are members of the special-interest group which the ministers oppose. In Saskatchewan, as in other places, civil servants have been known to reduce the significance of reforms directed against their own group. They could hardly have been expected to draw up effective safeguards against "evils" the very existence of which they denied.

The long-term effects of retaining a permanent civil service, when a government attempts to enact a fundamental change in policy, vary. In Saskatchewan, because of the partisan nature of earlier civil-service recruitment, far more of conscious political obstructionism has probably occurred than in a nonpartisan merit civil service such as that of Great Britain. On the other hand, the small size of the bureaucracy in Saskatchewan makes it difficult for civil servants to conceal their obstructionist activities. C.C.F. party leaders and members of the legislature have been able to uncover numerous examples of bureaucratic resistance to government policy that would probably have gone unnoticed in a larger structure.

The failure of the government to discharge old top-level civil servants has precipitated a major conflict within the C.C.F. movement between the cabinet ministers and many of the party leaders who do not hold office. The majority of the C.C. F. members of the legislature, of the party Provincial Council, and of delegates to provincial conventions have repeatedly demanded that the government "carry out C.C.F. policy" by replacing old administrators with more sympathetic personnel. The members of these groups cite many examples of actions that they consider to be administrative sabotage on a local or provincial level.

For a long while after taking office, most C.C.F. cabinet ministers refused to admit that they were unduly dependent on the civil service or that they were being deflected from carrying out party policy. They defended the retention of old civil servants on a number of grounds:

1. "It is easier to teach an engineer to be a socialist than a socialist to be an engineer."

2. The C.C.F. stands for a nonpartisan civil service, and to discharge or demote civil servants for their opinions would continue the worst evils of patronage politics.

3. Civil servants only carry out policy, they do not set it. The background of the government official does not matter, therefore, so long as he carries out government policy.

The attacks on the cabinet by the rest of the party and the passing of resolutions demanding action by every provincial convention since 1945 have gradually forced the cabinet to modify its public position and to accept the principle of a partially politicized bureaucracy. Premier T. C. Douglas stated, at the 1946 convention, "We know that people can't carry out a socialist program unless they believe in socialism. We want more socialists in the government service, but they must be trained and efficient. Until we have enough socialists trained for expert jobs, we must use our discretion in using civil servants who are not socialists but who are competent and are only trying to do a job."[30]

The cross pressures of the needs for administrative stability and for party harmony have resulted in a number of concessions to the demand for changes in top-level personnel, while retaining most of the old key officials. At least two deputy ministers and a number of division heads have been removed or demoted because party members disapprove of their activities. Certain of the new agencies created by the C.C.F. government—the Economic Planning Board, the Health Services Planning Commission, and the Division of Adult Education—have been staffed mainly by persons selected because of their sympathies with the objectives of the C.C.F. as well as their technical abilities. As vacancies appear in major posts, the tendency to appoint members of the C.C.F. has increased. These appointments cannot be regarded as the return of patronage politics, since many of the new appointees had not been active in the Saskatchewan party. The head of the Economic Planning Board is an Englishman who belonged to the British

Labor Party; two major appointments in public health went to Americans who were supporters of socialized medicine. Many other government appointees are members of the C.C.F. from other provinces.

An unplanned consequence of the struggle in the C.C.F. over civil-service reform has been an experimental test of the theories of those who urge that a radical reform government must have a sympathetic bureaucracy to carry out its program successfully. The Saskatchewan civil service today is a compromise between two approaches to the problem of bureaucracy; the larger part of it is a carry-over from previous governments, but a large minority of top-level positions are held by socialist experts. Many of the older civil servants had resisted changes which the C.C.F. ministers wanted. Some refused to serve on top-level committees where they would be personally responsible for government policies.

Many of the new C.C.F. civil servants, on the other hand, have suggested new policies that would probably never have been proposed if policy formation had been left to the cabinet and the permanent civil service. The ministers did not have the technical knowledge to suggest needed changes, and the old civil servants were not imbued with the C.C.F. values of finding means to reduce the wealth and power of private-interest groups and of using every agency of government to raise living standards. In at least two departments, the differences in orientation of the new and the old civil service resulted in a covert struggle to determine department policy. The permanent civil servants in two departments repeatedly brought their ministers in contact with representatives of the more conservative groups, while the C.C.F. civil servants encouraged supporters of reform to visit the ministers and impress them with the widespread public support for changes.

To specify the innovations initiated as a result of the activities of party experts would compromise the position of informants now working for the government. It is apparent, however, that there is a direct relation between the extent and vigor of reform and the degree to which key administrative positions are staffed by persons who believe in the formal goals of the C.C.F. If the government had followed its original intention of completely separating the civil service from politics, many of the changes that have been accomplished, both on the administrative and the legislative level, would not, in all probability, have taken place.

In recent years many have become concerned with the problem of bureaucracy in a large-scale society. The sheer size and complexity of social organizations, whether private or public, have created the need for a new "class" of administrators or bureaucrats to operate them efficiently. This new administrative group, necessarily, has been given a large amount of discretionary power. Once entrenched in corporations, trade-unions, political parties, and governments, the administrators develop "vested interests" of their own which may conflict with the interests of those who placed them in office. It seems to be universally true in social organization that men in power seek to maintain and extend their power, status, and privileges. Modern democratic society, therefore, faces the dilemma of making extensive grants of power without at the same time abdicating the right of the democratic constituency to change the policies and the personnel of the bureaucracy.

The justified concern with the dangers of oligarchic or bureaucratic domination has, however, led many persons to ignore the fact that it does make a difference to society which set of bureaucrats controls its destiny. There are bureaucracies and bureaucracies. To suggest, as many social scientists have done, that trade-unions, coöperatives, corporations, political parties, and states must develop a bureaucratic social structure in order to operate efficiently still leaves a large area of indeterminate social action for a bureaucratically organized society. Bureaucrats are human beings, not automatons. The desire to maintain a given bureaucratic organization is only one of the complex series of factors determining their actions. In a given situation, each group acts somewhat differently, according to its background. The reactions of the Russian "socialist" bureaucrats to problems of power were very different from those of the English socialist bureaucrats. A deterministic theory of bureaucratic behavior, such as that advanced by Robert Michels or James Burnham, neglects the implications of an alternative pattern of bureaucratic response.[31]

The focus on a single theory of bureaucracy has been encouraged by the lack of a sociological approach among political scientists. For the most part they have not raised questions about the social origins and values of government administrators and the relationship of such factors to government policy.[32] It is possible that the political scientists' blindness to the sources of civil-service

"biases" may be related to their own identification with the government administrator, and their disinclination to accept the fact that the behavior of their own group is determined by personal "prejudice-creating" factors. Political scientists accepted the value of an unbiased civil servant who makes his decisions after analyzing the facts, presents the data to his minister, carries out the policy of the government in power, and then reverses his policy when a new government comes into office. Political history has been analyzed mainly in terms of struggles among interest groups and political parties. The civil service, like the political scientists, was simply a passive, neutral factor.

In recent years, however, political scientists have become aware of the fact that the government bureaucracy does play a significant role in determining policy. They still, however, leave the bureaucrat in a social vacuum. They now recognize that he plays an active role, but the determinants of that role are analyzed purely on the bureaucratic level. The bureaucrat's actions are analyzed on the basis of the goals of the civil service—self-preservation and efficiency. These interests may be defined in terms of prestige and privilege, preservation of patterns of organization or relationships within a department, or maintenance of department traditions and policies. There is little recognition that the behavior of government bureaucrats varies with the nongovernmental social background and interests of those controlling the bureaucratic structure. Members of a civil service are also members of other nongovernmental social groups and classes. Social pressures from many different group affiliations and loyalties determine individual behavior in most situations. The behavior of an individual or group in a given situation cannot be considered as if the individual or group members had no other life outside the given situation one is analyzing.

The direct relationship between class affiliations of members of a bureaucracy and the policies of the government has been demonstrated in the English civil service. J. Donald Kingsley has shown that as England changed from an aristocratically controlled nation to a capitalist state its civil service changed correspondingly.[33] The aristocrats who once dominated the British civil service gradually gave way to members of the middle class.

The experiences in Saskatchewan also indicate the relationship between the background and the actions of the civil service. Trained in the traditions of a laissez-faire government and belong-

ing to conservative social groups, the civil service contributes significantly to the social inertia which blunts the changes a new radical government can make. Delay in initiating reforms means that the new government becomes absorbed in the process of operating the old institutions. The longer a new government delays in making changes, the more responsible it becomes for the old practices and the harder it is to make the changes it originally desired to institute. The problem has not been crucial in Saskatchewan because of the small size of the government and its fairly limited powers. On a larger scale, however, as in Great Britain today, dependence on a conservative bureaucracy may prove to be significant in the success or failure of the Labor Government.

The suggestion that shake-ups in the civil service on the expert policy-making level may be necessary at times for the adequate functioning of democratic government has rarely been considered by North American political scientists. On this continent, the problem of the civil service has traditionally been that of patronage appointment with its resultant inefficiency and malpractice. European social theorists, on the contrary, have been concerned with the implications for social change of a permanent governmental bureaucracy with its own vested interests and social values.

The necessity to face up to the problem of bureaucratic resistance to change becomes urgent only when a "radical" party comes to office. The theory of civil-service neutrality breaks down when the total goals of the state change. A change from the Liberal to the Conservative Party or from the Democratic to the Republican Party does not usually require a civil servant to make any major adjustments.[34] The functions of the department and of the government as a whole remain fairly constant.

The socialist state, however, which has as its goal a reintegration of societal values, giving priority of government services to groups that had been neglected and securing a large measure of government control, may fail in its objectives if it leaves administrative power in the hands of men whose social background and previous training prevent a sympathetic appreciation of the objectives of the new government. "The planning state . . . will require men wholly committed to the purpose the State is undertaking to serve . . . men of 'push and go,' energetic innovators and hard-driving managers."[35]

In American history, the two most significant departures from a merit civil service came during administrations which proposed shifts from the values and purposes of the previous government. Andrew Jackson felt it necessary, as the spokesman of the eastern workers and the western farmers, to break up the old permanent staff of the government in order to effect his program. His actions were based in part on a reasoned criticism of the actions of the civil service of his day, expressed in his Message to Congress in December, 1829.

There are, perhaps, few men who can for any great length of time enjoy office and power without being more or less under the influence of feelings unfavorable to the faithful discharge of their public duties. Their integrity may be proof against improper considerations immediately addressed to themselves, but they are apt to acquire a habit of looking with indifference upon the public interests and of tolerating conduct from which an unpracticed man would revolt.[36]

During the period of the American New Deal in the 1930's, "leaders of the Roosevelt administration privately complained of the difficulty of deflecting the bureaucracy from its ancient ways. The public service machine tended to continue in a straight line in disregard of the deviating influences of different public policy."[37] According to James A. Farley, "Some of the greatest troubles the President had were caused by subordinate officials who were in sharp disagreement with his policies and, rightly or wrongly, were sabotaging the job he was trying to accomplish."[38]

"The Roosevelt Administration was forced to assemble almost a whole new set of officials to carry out the New Deal reforms."[39] Roosevelt felt that these reforms would fail if they were left in the hands of the traditional departments. In 1933, 80 per cent of federal employees were under merit civil service, but by July 1, 1937, the proportion of merit positions had fallen to 63 per cent because of the establishment of over 200,000 new positions in New Deal agencies, many of which were exempt from the rule of merit.[40]

When the Tennessee Valley Authority was set up, its chief exponent, Senator Norris, urged that it be free from civil-service control. He argued that only people who believed in the purposes of the new agency could make it a success. The oath which a T.V.A. employee must take on entering office pledges him to uphold not only the Constitution of the United States but also the ideals of the T.V.A.

There is no simple solution to the dilemma of keeping government administration efficient as well as responsive to the will of the electorate. The increase in the power, functions, and sheer size of modern government necessitates the search for some means of controlling the bureaucracy. It is utopian to think that the electorate's dismissal of the inexpert politician, who formally heads the bureaucracy, will by itself change the course of bureaucratic activities. As Max Weber stated: "The question is always who controls the existing bureaucratic machinery. And such control is possible only in a very limited degree to persons who are not technical specialists. Generally speaking, the trained permanent official is more likely to get his way in the long run than his nominal supervisor, the Cabinet Minister, who is not a specialist."[41]

Government today is a large-scale administrative job requiring experts to operate it. Unless the electorate is given the opportunity to change the key experts as well as the politicians, elections will lose much of their significance. This problem will become more and more significant as efforts are made to increase the economic and social welfare role of the state.

Chapter XIII

EPILOGUE

THE C.C.F. today represents the culmination of a half-century of political and economic efforts by western grain growers to establish a stable economy. It is the apex of a movement that started with the Territorial Grain Growers' Association in 1902, and continued with the Grain Growers' Grain Company, the Saskatchewan Coöperative Elevator Company, the Progressive Party, the Farmers' Union, the Wheat Pool, and the United Farmers of Canada (Saskatchewan Section). After almost fifty years of organization, the Saskatchewan farmers today have the largest coöperative movement on the continent and the only independent agrarian government. They have probably gone as far as a sectional agrarian group can go within geographic, economic, and constitutional limits to establish direct producers' control over their economy.

No complex society, however, has yet discovered the secret of harmony or equilibrium. Social movements are faced with the dilemma of maintaining their stability and social gains, and at the same time sustaining the base for a continued effort to reach their long-term objectives. The history of the Saskatchewan farmers' movement indicates anew the inherent difficulty involved when a reform organization attempts both to maintain organizational stability and to change the larger society. Each successful

social organization creates a new "vested-interest" group, and consequently a new opponent of further change. The leaders of the Saskatchewan Grain Growers' Association feared that the organization of a farmers' marketing company would endanger the survival of their own group. The Coöperative Elevator Company objected to a merger with the Wheat Pool. The S.G.G.A., in turn, feared to launch a new political movement after the First World War, and the leaders of the U.F.C. (Saskatchewan Section) had to be changed in an internal struggle before that organization would support the compulsory Wheat Pool and independent political action in the 'thirties. (See chaps. iii and iv.)

The combination of an extremely unstable economic structure and the widespread distribution of secondary local leadership prevented the Saskatchewan rural community from establishing a stable traditional order. The bureaucratic conservatism of the leading agrarian officials rarely succeeded in preventing the farmers of the province from creating new institutional means to attain their economic ends.

The agrarian community now stands in a position similar to its situation in the late 1920's. It is experiencing a period of high prices and good crops. In June, 1948, it gave the C.C.F. a new vote of confidence by reëlecting it with a secure parliamentary majority of 31 out of 52 legislative seats. (The drop in C.C.F. support from 1944 was primarily a result of a coalition between the Liberals and the Conservatives and the reappearance of the Social Credit Party as an alternative "reform" movement.)

Ostensibly, therefore, Saskatchewan seems to have remained near the radical peak that it reached in 1944. The government remains socialist. The coöperative movement is larger and stronger than at any time in the history of the province.[1] The actions of the agrarians in continued support of economic and political reform would seem to challenge the generalizations made earlier in this study that farmers (and other groups as well) become conservative after they achieve their immediate economic reforms, as in New Zealand, Russia, and the United States. (See chap. xi, p. 229.)

A shift in the direction of conservatism and traditionalism may, however, take two forms. Politically, it may be reflected in a change of support from a radical to a conservative party, as in New Zealand, where the farmers who supported the Labor Party in 1935

were voting for the Conservatives in 1948. (See note 17, p. 304.) More frequently, however, conservatism may increase through the institutionalization of a once-radical organization. The new political movement, as it becomes organizationally stable and achieves some of the goals of its followers, may become a normal integrated part of society. This process has often occurred, as in the shift from sect to church in religious movements and in institutionalization and "bureaucratic conservatism" in organizations like coöperatives, trade-unions, and political parties.

The Social Credit movement in Alberta is probably the most recent example of such a change. It started out only seventeen years ago as the foremost opponent of the "eastern banks" and "vested interests"; today it is commonly recognized as one of the conservative parties of Canada, receiving the open support of the conservative business groups that once opposed it.[2]

The metamorphosis of the Social Credit movement in Alberta from a radical to a conservative movement raises the question of the possibility of the same phenomenon in Saskatchewan. A comparison of the two movements is difficult: the Social Credit Party has been in power for sixteen years, whereas the C.C.F. has held office for only six years. Recent events suggest, however, that conservative forces are gradually changing the character of the Saskatchewan C.C.F. This generalization can be supported in the areas of social welfare and health, labor, and government ownership.

The government attempted early in 1948 to reduce its contributions to old-age pensioners by $5 a month after the federal government had raised its contribution by a similar amount. This action was reversed just before the election in June, 1948, because of the protest of the politically powerful Old-Age Pensioners' Association. Since the election, the government, instead of giving pensioners free drugs, requires them to pay 20 per cent of the cost. Work on a university hospital in Saskatoon, which would have been the base of a provincial medical school, was stopped in 1948 in order to save funds. No major steps have been taken for two years to implement the original plan of socialized medicine. The government has refused to expand any social services that would require increased taxes.

The C.C.F. government has gradually ended its liberal wage policy in negotiating with unions in government-owned industries.

A three-week strike occurred in the Government Insurance Office in November, 1948, when the government refused to increase wages. According to the union, the government would not even negotiate the union's demands until the strike took place. The Insurance Office is one of the best profit makers of the government. Union leaders have stated that resistance to union demands is present in other Crown companies and in the civil service.

The extent to which leaders of the C.C.F. have modified their earlier prolabor attitude can be seen in a press report of the 1948 convention:

Resources Minister J. L. Phelps told the provincial C.C.F. convention Friday, "We appreciate support we received from labor but we must impress upon labor that there are two sides to every question.

"We have sought to drive employers and employees apart. It should be our effort to bring labor and management close together."

Mr. Phelps made his observations when a resolution dealing with labor matters was before the convention.

It called upon the labor department to investigate further ways and means whereby its field staff and inspectors "convey the true intent and meaning of laws and regulations under its jurisdiction to employees in Saskatchewan."

At Mr. Phelps' suggestion, the convention approved the addition of the words "and employers."

The Minister said the C.C.F. on too many occasions had taken the stand labor was always right.

"Perhaps it is not always right," he said.

It was his opinion the C.C.F. should encourage labor to take upon itself more responsibility, because nowadays the employer was not always "the big bad wolf" he was in the past.

Mr. Phelps suggested the reason the C.C.F. may have lost support in rural areas was that the party had moved too fast in its labor legislation to the detriment of those living there.

As long as people lived under a capitalist system, there would continue to be a degree of exploitation by employers, but not all of them were offending, he said.[3]

The government has proposed no new provincially owned industries for its second term in office. Actually, it closed down one of the old ones, the tannery and shoe factory. Since the election in June, 1948, Premier Douglas has made trips to England, eastern Canada, and New York, "to talk to industrialists and heads of mining companies who might be interested in investing some capital

in Saskatchewan's development. . . . On his return from Britain, Mr. Douglas announced that British and Swedish capital might be invested in the province and that representatives of these two countries may come to Saskatchewan to investigate the possibilities. On his return from New York he said financial discussions were of an exploratory nature."[4]

The farmers' movements and the C.C.F. once stood for the socialization of oil, but the Saskatchewan government is now encouraging private oil companies to prospect in the province, guaranteeing them long-term leases. The shift in the thinking of C.C.F. leaders is, however, most evident in the fight that Premier Douglas made at the 1948 national convention against the proposal to nationalize the banks.

He [Douglas] believed in ultimate socialization of banks . . . , but he believed the amendment [to obtain control over rather than nationalize the banks] should go through and a C.C.F. government should first try to control the policy of the banks.

Socialization was not an end in itself, according to the Premier, and sometimes the desired results could be obtained without the government taking over a business.

For example, the Premier revealed when the C.C.F. came to power in Saskatchewan, it gave serious consideration to socializing breweries in the province. But they found that as they had the power to set beer prices, license brewers, and otherwise control them, socialization of the industry was unnecessary. He felt the same principle might well work in the case of the banks.[5]

Douglas found, however, that he was in a minority in the national convention. The proposal that a federal C.C.F. government should nationalize the banks passed by 94 votes to 56. If the attitude toward nationalization of banks is to be used as an index of radicalism, the leader of Saskatchewan socialism now stands to the right of the majority of his national party, and opposes a demand made by Saskatchewan farmers' organizations years before the C.C.F. was organized. (See chap. iv, p. 75.)

These changes in the policies of leaders of the C.C.F. in the last few years suggest anew that any evaluation of the present "radicalism" of Saskatchewan must consider not only election results but the changing content of party actions. The socialism of the 1949 Saskatchewan C.C.F. is a far cry from the first years of the movement when the party proposed the complete elimination of private enterprise as its goal.

It is again a question of how much reform can be expected from a "radical" politician in a democracy. (See chap. xi.) The social reforms to which he is committed before taking office often become apparent hindrances in maintaining power. Innovations usually turn out to be more difficult in operation than they seemed in the planning or propaganda stage. In a stable prosperous situation, such as Saskatchewan is now experiencing, stability may seem preferable to innovation. The continued prosperity of the farmers has sharply reduced the popular demand for reform, and adherence to ideological principles may not appear to be worth the danger of losing support if the reform fails. The C.C.F., which in opposition ridiculed the Liberals' question about the source of the money to pay for increased social services, is now itself engaged in curtailing social services rather than risk the wrath of tax-conscious farmers.

The C.C.F. leaders also face the problems inherent in operating what Premier Douglas once called "a beachhead of socialism on a continent of capitalism." Like the earlier North Dakota Non-Partisan League, it has attempted to try certain socialist experiments with little or no control over the economic structure. A provincial or economically weak national socialist government remains subject to many of the coercions of the old economic system, in much the same manner as a private businessman. Its industries must compete on the free market with other private concerns. It must sell its bonds through regular banking channels. As a thinly populated province, Saskatchewan does not have enough government capital to develop its own resources, such as oil. Such weaknesses force the government to adhere to the regulations of the larger economy.

As politicians, however, C.C.F. leaders cannot afford to admit that they are making "nonsocialist" concessions and that they are not able to carry out their original program. They are, therefore, forced to defend compromises and capitulations as positive goods. They must praise certain segments of private industry, and thereby weaken the force of their long-term socialist arguments. It is difficult for C.C.F. leaders to invite private industry into the province—even subsidize it—and, at the same time, to denounce as exploiters the industrialists or bankers whose money they need.

Dealing with economic problems within the framework of capitalism, the C.C.F. administrator must view many of them as a

private businessman does. He, too, must show a profit to his stock-holders (the tax-conscious farmers), avoid wage increases if possible, and raise prices. As a result, he sees the businessman's point of view in a new light. J. L. Phelps, who was quoted above as a critic of labor, entered the government as its most radical member. After being placed in charge of most of the new government industries, he gradually became more and more critical of trade-unions. Another high C.C.F. official, who has had many dealings with bankers, stated in an interview that the C.C.F. attitude toward bankers was unrealistic, as they were "only honest men doing a job and did not care what kind of government held power."

These changes in policy do not mean that the party and the government have ceased responding to the needs and demands of its farmer and labor supporters. Compared to the other three provincial political parties, it is still the most "radical" party. The C.C.F. retains a large part of its agrarian and socialist ideology of opposition to big business, and supports organized agriculture and labor in their efforts to secure a higher standard of living in conflicts with private business groups. There can be little doubt, however, that its years in office have tempered the party's radicalism.

The fact that social reform movements rarely succeed in reaching the goals they were ostensibly organized to achieve has long concerned persons interested in the problems of social change. Conservatives have used such facts to demonstrate that radical social movements are utopian, and therefore are not worth the trouble they cause. This thesis has been argued in relation to the French Revolution, the American Civil War, and the Russian Revolution. Radical social thinkers, on the other hand, have cited the negative results of other social movements as evidence for the fact that the leaders of all other movements but their own made serious blunders in strategy. Socialist literature, especially, includes innumerable books and articles explaining the failure of various socialist parties.[6]

The decision on whether a given social movement was worth while is largely a value judgment which no one has the right to make under the guise of scientific or historical objectivity. It is my own belief that, in general, the democratic movements of the left since the American Revoution were and are historically justifiable and necessary to attain the values of an economic and political

and social democracy. In spite of their many and obvious failings in terms of democratic values, the alternative to them was a more rigidly stratified and sometimes a dictatorial society.

It is impossible to agree with the efforts of those who would attempt to deal rationally with the problem of the "bureaucratic conservatism" or "institutionalization" of social movements by proposing "logical" solutions to make these movements more democratic or more militant. Socialists, though materialists in their philosophy, become idealists as political citizens, arguing that the movement should do this or that, or avoid doing something else. These solutions are similar to attempts to cure the ills of the present economic system by calling upon all capitalists to be responsible economic statesmen, to collaborate with unions, to pay high wages, and not to discharge employees. Most socialists recognize that the private businessman must act within the coercions of the economic structure. He must make a profit, and therefore treats his employees as impersonal economic commodities. He must buy as cheaply as he can, and sell as dearly as he is able.

The radical politician is in a position similar to that of the private businessman. He cannot change the institutional forces within a few months or even years. Large portions of the provincial, national, and international power structure are retained by nonsocialist or antisocialist groups. The socialist in office is not free, is not all-powerful. Once he accepts the rules of the society, even as a temporary compromise (until the millennial day when he will be free to act), he is caught in a vicious cycle. To stay in power, he must make repeated compromises. Each compromise is in itself unimportant, but eventually he departs so far from his original aims that they cease to be real ends and become only rituals to be observed during election campaigns. The ideals of democracy and a classless society would appear to have become such rituals in the Soviet Union, while the goal of a socialist society in which capitalism is eliminated has now only ritual significance for most of the socialist parties of Europe and the British Commonwealth.

Leon Blum, the former Socialist Premier of France, pointed to the problem of carrying through a program of far-reaching social change in evaluating the work of his Popular Front government:

The Socialist Party was called upon to take its share of the task of government, but it knew perfectly well that it could exercise power only within the framework of bourgeois society. It was, indeed, for

this reason that it had avoided power as long as circumstances made this possible. Even when the elected Chamber seemed to be held by a working-class majority, the bourgeoisie kept in its hands methods of resistance which yielded only temporarily to fear, and became effective again as soon as the fears were stilled. It kept its grip on the local Councils, *the Civil Service, the Press, finance, big business.*[7]

The same problem in a German setting was summed up by Fritz Tarnow, a German labor leader, at the German Social Democratic Party congress in 1931:

Are we sitting at the sickbed of capitalism, not only as doctors who want to cure the patient, but as prospective heirs who cannot wait for the end and would like to hasten it by administering poison? We are condemned, I think, to be doctors who seriously wish to cure, and yet we have to maintain the feeling that we are heirs who wish to receive the entire legacy of the capitalist system today rather than tomorrow. This double role, doctor and heir, is a damned difficult task.[8]

The "damned difficult task" is made even more difficult by the fact that the leaders of any organized reform movement have a stake in the existing situation. The organization itself, rather than its formal goal, becomes the ends of men involved in a bureaucratic apparatus. The leaders of the international socialist movement have shown time and time again that, when faced with a choice between fundamental principles or organizational survival, they choose the path that appears to lead to immediate preservation of the strength of the organization. The reversal of the Socialist antiwar attitude immediately upon the declaration of war in 1914 is well known. The policy of Social Democratic trade-union leaders in attempting to come to terms with the Fascists and Nazis in Italy and Germany is an even more convincing and clear-cut demonstration of the way in which the goal of organizational survival can lead men step by step into supporting everything they personally oppose.[9]

These examples of Social Democratic and trade-union "betrayal" of principles are not cited to suggest that there is some special weakness in these movements. Similar examples can be found in the records of the anarchist and Communist movements, as well as in Liberal and Conservative groups. The history of most of the religious sects of the world also bears witness to the power of organization over ideology or theology.

Organizations are always started as means of attaining certain value ends. However, organizations become ends in themselves, which often are obstacles in the achievement of the original goals. This does not mean that organized social effort does not secure many of the value ends that it was set up to achieve. The farm organizations of Saskatchewan have helped to better the economic lot of the agrarians of the province. The trade-unions have increased the living standards of their members. Gradually, however, every large-scale social organization falls victim to the virus of bureaucratic conservatism, and to the fear that a further challenge to the *status quo* will injure its power and status; or the organization may become, as the German labor leaders suggested when proposing collaboration with the Nazis in 1933, "an indispensable part of the very social order ... increasingly integrated into the state [society],"[10] and as such will be one of the forces resisting further change.

In a world in which the rate of growth of social and economic problems is apparently faster than the increase in our ability to cope with them, conclusions such as these may seem like a counsel of despair. They are not meant to be. An answer to stagnation lies in the bold actions of such men as the "agitators" of Saskatchewan, who are not satisfied with anything but utopia. These men are often destined, as Vanzetti once said, to "live out their lives speaking on street corners to scornful men." They may, on the other hand, like E. A. Partridge, be destined to help form mighty social movements to advance human welfare. As long as there are social organizations that produce men who do not accept the *status quo*, who see "the inhumanity of man to man" as a crime, there will be hope in the human race.

Notes

NOTES TO CHAPTER I

[1] Harry W. Laidler, *Social-Economic Movements* (New York, Thomas Y. Crowell Co., 1949).

[2] "[The Americans] are born conservatives—just because America is so purely bourgeois, so entirely without a feudal past." Karl Marx and Friedrich Engels, Letter 209, "Engels to Sorge," *Correspondence, 1846–1895* (New York, International Publishers, 1936), p. 467.

[3] Gunnar Myrdal, *An American Dilemma* (New York, Harper and Brothers, 1944), p. 714.

[4] "[The weakness of Marxism in America] is not a function of some immaterial national spirit, but a product of material conditions. A nation rapidly growing rich has sufficient reserves for conciliation between hostile classes and parties. . . . America was free of . . . [Marxism] only because it had a plethora of virgin areas, inexhaustible reserves of national wealth and, it would seem, limitless opportunities for enrichment." Leon Trotsky, *The Living Thoughts of Karl Marx* (New York, Longmans, Green and Co., 1939), p. 34.

[5] Myrdal, *op. cit.*, p. 714.

[6] "The huge immigration through the decades has constantly held the lower classes in a state of cultural fragmentation. They have been split in national, linguistic and religious sub-groups, which has hampered class solidarity and prevented effective mass organization." *Ibid.*, p. 713.

[7] Frederick J. Turner, *The Significance of Sections in American History* (New York, Henry Holt and Co., 1932).

[8] "The Voice of the Farmer," *The Nation*, Vol. 50, p. 329, quoted in John D. Hicks, *The Populist Revolt* (University of Minnesota Press, 1931), p. 80.

[9] *Ibid.*, p. 95.

[10] S. J. Buck, "Independent Parties in the Western States, 1873–1876," in *Essays in American History Dedicated to Frederick Jackson Turner* (ed. by Guy Stanton Ford; New York, Henry Holt and Co., 1910), pp. 137–164.

[11] Buck, *The Granger Movement* (Harvard University Press, 1913), p. 100.

[12] *Ibid.*, p. 53.

[13] *Ibid.*, pp. 238–239.

[14] Fred E. Haynes, *Third Party Movements since the Civil War* (State Historical Society of Iowa, Iowa City, 1916), p. 123.

[15] *Ibid.*

[16] *Ibid.*, pp. 124, 142.

[17] C. O. Ruggles, "The Economic Basis of the Greenback Movement in Iowa and Wisconsin," *Mississippi Valley Historical Society, Proceedings,* Vol. 5, p. 160.

[18] Hicks, *op. cit.,* p. 35.

[19] *Ibid.,* p. 124.

[20] *Ibid.,* pp. 155–158.

[21] *Ibid.,* p. 115.

[22] *Ibid.,* p. 125.

[23] Harlen P. Crippen, "Conflicting Trends in the Populist Movement," *Science and Society,* Vol. 6 (1942), p. 134.

[24] In "1888–1891, the farm price of wheat was 82 cents a bushel; for 1892–1895 it had declined thirty-three per cent and was 55 cents a bushel. The average aggregate farm value of wheat crops in the two periods showed a decline of thirty-one per cent; from 393 million to 249 million dollars." Nathan Fine, *Labor and Farmer Parties in the United States* (Rand School of Social Science, New York, 1928), p. 73.

[25] *Ibid.,* pp. 77–78.

[26] *Ibid.,* p. 76.

[27] Hicks, *op. cit.,* pp. 321–379.

[28] *Ibid.,* pp. 299–300.

[29] Haynes, *op. cit.,* p. 51.

[30] Ruggles, *op. cit.,* p. 160.

[31] *Ibid.,* p. 157.

[32] *Ibid.,* p. 165.

[33] Crippen, *op. cit.,* p. 142.

[34] *Ibid.,* p. 134.

[35] Benton H. Wilcox, "An Historical Definition of North-Western Radicalism," *Mississippi Valley Historical Review,* December, 1939, p. 381.

[36] *Ibid.,* p. 386.

[37] Raymond C. Miller, "The Economic Basis of Populism in Kansas," *Mississippi Valley Historical Review,* Vol. 11 (1925), p. 481.

[38] Wilcox, *op. cit.,* p. 386.

[39] Walter E. Nydegger, "The Election of 1892 in Iowa," *Iowa Journal of History and Politics,* Vol. 25 (1927), p. 466.

[40] Herman C. Nixon, "The Populist Movement in Iowa," *Iowa Journal of History and Politics,* Vol. 24 (1926), pp. 103–104.

[41] Editorial, December 12, 1914, p. 11.

[42] Robert F. Hoxie, "The Rising Tide of Socialism: A Study," *Journal of Political Economy,* Vol. 19, p. 625.

[43] Oscar Ameringer, *If You Don't Weaken* (New York, Henry Holt and Co., 1940), p. 269.

[44] Fine, *op. cit.,* p. 210.

[45] *Ibid.,* p. 272.

[46] Herbert G. Gaston, *The Non-Partisan League* (New York, Harcourt, Brace and Co., 1920), p. 54.

[47] *Ibid.,* p. 59.

[48] W. B. Bizzell, *The Green Rising* (New York, Macmillan Co., 1926), p. 180.

[49] Paul Fossum, *The Agrarian Movement in North Dakota* (Baltimore, Johns Hopkins Press, 1925), pp. 85–86.

[50] Andrew A. Bruce, *The Non-Partisan League* (New York, Macmillan Co., 1921), p. 56.

[51] Fred E. Haynes, *Social Politics in the United States* (New York, Houghton Mifflin Co., 1924), p. 309.

[52] Gaston, *op. cit.,* pp. 285–287.

[53] Arthur LeSeur, in *The Call*, March 2, 1917, quoted in Bruce, *op. cit.*, p. 141.

[54] Gaston, *op. cit.*, pp. 237–238.

[55] Wilcox, *op. cit.*, p. 391.

[56] Quoted in S. Roy Weaver, *The Non-Partisan League in North Dakota* (Canadian Reconstruction Association, Toronto, 1921), p. 44.

[57] *Ibid.*, p. 43.

[58] *Ibid.*, p. 45.

[59] *Ibid.*

[60] Fossum, *op. cit.*, p. 124.

[61] Stuart A. Rice, *Farmers and Workers in American Politics* (New York, Longmans, Green and Co., 1924), p. 162; see also Wilcox, *op. cit.*, p. 372.

[62] Rice, *op. cit.*, p. 174.

[63] The presidential elections of 1924 in the United States witnessed the most successful third-party movement since the Civil War. Robert M. La Follette, running as an independent candidate for president, succeeded in polling over five million votes.

La Follette's candidacy, however, was not the result of a genuine new-party movement. It was organized by a coalition of the A. F. of L., the Railroad Brotherhoods, the Socialist Party, and the agrarian reformers who had supported the Non-Partisan League. The trade-unions supported La Follette because of repeated legislative rebuffs by both of the old parties and their nomination of conservative presidential candidates. The Socialists and agrarians backed La Follette in the hope of building the new national party which they had long wanted.

The La Follette candidacy did not create an organized new party. The campaign was conducted around the personality of La Follette, and no attempt was made to set up a permanent party organization. "The progressive campaign concentrated upon attaining success for the national ticket to the exclusion of state and local contests. La Follette supporters for local offices were encouraged to seek places on the Democratic or Republican tickets." William B. Heseltine, "Third Parties: The Progressives of 1924," *The Progressive*, August 25, 1947, p. 4.

Soon after the election, La Follette and the trade-unions withdrew from attempts to establish a new party. This left the agrarians and Socialists to continue the fight alone. The prosperity of the 'twenties made the effort impossible, and the movement soon disappeared.

Heseltine, *The Rise and Fall of Third Parties* (Washington, D.C., Public Affairs Press, 1948), pp. 28–33.

[64] Thorstein Veblen, *Absentee Ownership* (New York, Viking Press, 1945), p. 130.

NOTES TO CHAPTER II

[1] Arthur S. Morton, *History of Prairie Settlement* (Toronto, Macmillan Co. of Canada, Ltd., 1938); Chester Martin, *"Dominion Lands" Policy* (Toronto, Macmillan Co. of Canada, Ltd., 1938); C. A. Dawson and Eva A. Younge, *Pioneering in the Prairie Provinces* (Toronto, Macmillan Co. of Canada, Ltd., 1940); *Report of the Saskatchewan Royal Commission on Immigration and Settlement, 1930* (Regina, 1930).

[2] Martin, *op. cit.*, p. 519.

[3] *Report of the Royal Commission on Dominion-Provincial Relations: Canada, 1867–1939* (Ottawa, 1940), Book I, p. 68.

[4] Charles Cecil Lingard, *The Autonomy Question in the Canadian North-West* (University of Chicago Press, 1942).

[5] Claris Edwin Silcox, *Church Union in Canada* (New York, Institute of Social and Religious Research, 1933); Dawson and Younge, *op. cit.*, pp. 237–241.

[6] Interviews with former members of the S.G.G.A.

[7] Hopkins Moorhouse, *Deep Furrows* (Toronto, George J. McLeod, Ltd., 1918), pp. 231–232.

[8] Interviews with leaders of the U.F.C.

[9] Frontier Oklahoma, which had the strongest Socialist Party before the First World War, also had been settled by many former working-class radicals. See Oscar Ameringer, *If You Don't Weaken* (New York, Henry Holt and Co., 1940), p. 260.

[10] Bank of Canada, *Report of the Financial Position of the Province of Saskatchewan* (Ottawa, 1937), p. 2. (Italics mine.)
"The composition of freight loaded on cars in Saskatchewan in 1936 was: agricultural products, 79.5 per cent; mineral products, 8.8 per cent; forest products, 5.1 per cent; manufacturing and miscellaneous, 6.6 per cent." G. E. Britnell, *The Wheat Economy* (University of Toronto Press, 1939), p. 33.

[11] R. E. Motherwell, "A Study of Crop Insurance," *Report of the Saskatchewan Reconstruction Council* (Regina, 1944), p. 30.

[12] Wilmer J. Hansen, "Economic Aspects of Crop (Yield) Insurance with Reference to the Province of Saskatchewan," Ninth Annual Meeting, Canadian Agricultural Economic Society, *Proceedings*, 1937, p. 49.

[13] Dominion Bureau of Statistics, *Canada Year Book, 1922–1923*, pp. 282, 283; *ibid., 1932*, p. 1061.

[14] Jean Burnet, "Town-Country Relations and the Problem of Rural Leadership," *Canadian Journal of Economics and Political Science*, August, 1947, pp. 395–397.

[15] Thorstein Veblen, *Essays in Our Changing Order* (New York, Viking Press, 1934), pp. 286–293.

[16] Burnet, *op. cit.*, pp. 404–405.

[17] Province of Saskatchewan, Department of Coöperation and Coöperative Development, *Third Annual Report* (Regina, 1948).

[18] Burnet, *op. cit.*, pp. 405–407.

[19] Dominion Bureau of Statistics, *Eighth Census of Canada, 1941*, Bulletin A-6, p. 6.

[20] Britnell, *op. cit.*, p. 23.

[21] Jim Wright, "Saskatchewan," *Canadian Geographic Magazine*, March, 1947, p. 120.

[22] *Farms and Farmers in Canada: Facts from the Census, 1941 and 1931* (Sanford Evans Statistical Service, Winnipeg, 1944), p. 8.

[23] The provincial government assesses the relative worth of parcels of land and assigns to each an index number that is used as the basis for computing the tax rate.

[24] Provincial Mediation Board, *A Survey of Agriculture Land Debt and of Ownership and Tenancy in Saskatchewan, as at December 31, 1943* (Regina, 1944), p. 31.

[25] Wright, *op. cit.*, pp. 117–120.

NOTES TO CHAPTER III

[1] Max Weber, *Essays in Sociology* (ed. by H. H. Gerth and C. W. Mills; New York, Oxford University Press, 1946), pp. 183–184.

[2] Harold S. Patton, *Grain Growers' Coöperation in Western Canada* (Harvard University Press, 1928), p. 14; Hugh Boyd, *New Breaking: An Outline of Coöperation among the Farmers of Western Canada* (Toronto, J. M. Dent and Sons, Ltd., 1938), pp. 19–20; W. A. Mackintosh, *Agricultural Coöperation in Western Canada* (Toronto, Ryerson Press, 1924), p. 8; Hopkins Moorhouse, *Deep Furrows* (Toronto, George J. McLeod, Ltd., 1918), pp. 37–38.

[3] L. A. Wood, *Farmers' Movements in Canada* (Toronto, Ryerson Press, 1924), p. 170. See also Boyd, *op. cit.*, pp. 24–25; Moorhouse, *op. cit.*, p. 45; Patton, *op. cit.*, p. 31.

[4] Boyd, *op. cit.*, p. 21.

[5] *Ibid.*, pp. 30–31.

[6] Moorhouse, *op. cit.*, pp. 29–52; Boyd, *op. cit.*, pp. 26–29; Patton, *op. cit.*, pp. 32–34.

[7] Patton, *op. cit.*, p. 34; Boyd, *op. cit.*, pp. 29–30; Wood, *op. cit.*, pp. 174–175.

[8] Moorhouse, *op. cit.*, p. 230.

[9] "The government was impressed, and the Grain Growers' resolutions were incorporated in almost the very language of the petitioners [the Territorial Grain Growers' Associations] in amendments to the shipping clauses of the Manitoba Grain Act." Patton, *op. cit.*, p. 35.

[10] *Ibid.*

[11] *Ibid.*, p. 33.

[12] *Ibid.*, pp. 35–36; Moorhouse, *op. cit.*, pp. 55–58; Wood, *op. cit.*, p. 180; Mackintosh, *op. cit.*, p. 15.

[13] Patton, *op. cit.*, p. 37; Boyd, *op. cit.*, p. 36.

[14] Mackintosh, *op. cit.*, p. 19.

[15] Boyd, *op. cit.*, pp. 41–47.

[16] Letter of Grain Growers' Grain Company to Premier R. P. Robbin, December 20, 1906, quoted in Mackintosh, *op. cit.*, p. 23.

[17] *Ibid.*, pp. 25–26; Moorhouse, *op. cit.*, pp. 119–121; Patton, *op. cit.*, pp. 53–58.

[18] See Manitoba *Free Press*, December, 1906, to April, 1907.

[19] Wood, *op. cit.*, p. 183.

[20] Quoted in Mackintosh, *op. cit.*, p. 34.

[21] Moorhouse, *op. cit.*, pp. 61–72, 85–92, 133.

[22] A. J. Muste, "Factional Fights in Trade Unions," and J. B. S. Hardman, "Problems of a Labor Union Somewhere in the U. S.," *American Labor Dynamics* (ed. by J. B. S. Hardman; New York, Harcourt, Brace and Co., 1928).

[23] See E. A. Partridge, *A War on Poverty* (Winnipeg, Wallingford Press, Ltd., 1926), for a statement of his long-range views.

[24] Mackintosh, *op. cit.*, p. 27.

[25] Moorhouse, *op. cit.*, p. 133.

[26] *Grain Growers' Guide*, June, 1908, and *passim*.

[27] Mackintosh, *op. cit.*, p. 157.

[28] Patton, *op. cit.*, pp. 73–74.

[29] Editorial quoted in Moorhouse, *op. cit.*, p. 60.

[30] United Grain Farmers, Ltd., *Farmers in Business for Ten Successful Years, 1906–1916*, p. 6.

[31] Moorhouse, *op. cit.*, pp. 155–156.

[32] Patton, *op. cit.*, p. 75.

[33] Mackintosh, *op. cit.*, p. 34.

[34] Pamphlet of Manitoba Grain Growers' Association, cited in *Grain Growers' Guide*, June, 1908, p. 6. (This issue was edited by E. A. Partridge.)

[35] Patton, *op. cit.*, p. 82–83.

[36] Moorhouse, *op. cit.*, pp. 169–170.

[37] Wood, *op. cit.*, p. 211.

[38] A Grain Growers' candidate had contested a provincial by-election on the issue of government ownership of elevators and won it not long before the Manitoba government agreed to support government ownership.

[39] Wood, *op. cit.*, p. 212; Patton, *op. cit.*, pp. 86–87; Boyd, *op. cit.*, p. 58.

[40] Wood, *op. cit.*, p. 220.

[41] *Report of the Elevator Commission of the Province of Saskatchewan* (Regina, 1910). "This [Saskatchewan Royal] commission was headed by Robert Magill, Professor of Political Economy at Dalhousie. The scholarly reasoning by means of which he demonstrated in his report that public ownership of elevators would not work suggests strongly that he was opposed to public ownership in principle, and an inference hard to escape is that the Saskatchewan government was aware of that opposition before he was appointed." V. C. Fowke, "Royal Commissions and Canadian Agricultural Policy," *Canadian Journal of Economics and Political Science*, May, 1948, p. 171.

[42] Wood, *op. cit.*, p. 214.

[43] Patton, *op. cit.*, pp. 110–111.

[44] Moorhouse, *op. cit.*, pp. 110–111.

[45] *Ibid.*, pp. 134–135.

[46] *Report of the Elevator Commission of the Province of Saskatchewan*, pp. 19–22.

[47] Moorhouse, *op. cit.*, p. 209.

[48] Minutes of the 1907 S.G.G.A. Convention, pp. 60–61.

[49] *Ibid.*, p. 23.

[50] *Ibid.*, p. 19.

[51] Minutes of the 1909 S.G.G.A. Convention, p. 13.

[52] Minutes of the 1913 S.G.G.A. Convention, p. 34.

[53] *Grain Growers' Guide*, March 2, 1910, p. 8.

[54] "The Central [S.G.G.A.] is handling a full line of staple groceries and is about to greatly extend this field of operation.... It is a well known fact that the west is outrageously overloaded with retailers, so that coupled with poor service, the rural consumer has to pay in many cases exorbitant prices for inferior goods, and by purchasing in wholesale quantities it is obvious that the farmers can effect and are effecting material savings." *Prairie Farms and Homes*, April 12, 1916, p. 2.

[55] Moorhouse, *op. cit.*, p. 230.

[56] Wood, *op. cit.*, pp. 125–128; Morton, *op. cit.*, pp. 115–116.

[57] Minutes of the 1909 S.G.G.A. Convention, pp. 21–22.

[58] Fowke, *op. cit.*, pp. 170–171.

[59] W. L. Morton, an unpublished study of the Progressive Party.

[60] Minutes of the 1909 S.G.G.A. Convention, pp. 29–30.

[61] *Grain Growers' Guide*, July 12, 1911, p. 5.

[62] See letter by "Marieta," *ibid.*, August 7, 1909, p. 11. "I am pretty sure if they [the farmers] had a party in the [legislative] houses of Alberta, Saskatchewan and Manitoba, the Premier's reply respecting the elevator question would be entirely different and until the farmers have their representatives in the different parliaments of the provinces and at Ottawa, legislation in their favor will move very slowly indeed."

[63] Minutes of the 1913 S.G.G.A. Convention, pp. 25–28.

[64] *Ibid.*, p. 31.

[65] Minutes of the 1914 S.G.G.A. Convention, pp. 20–26.

[66] See Minutes of the S.G.G.A. Board of Directors, 1916, p. 100, for discussion and report on the N.P.L.; Wood, *op. cit.*, p. 340.

[67] Minutes of the S.G.G.A. Board of Directors, October 7, 1916, pp. 108–109; November 24, 1916, pp. 55–56.

[68] Minutes of the 1919 S.G.G.A. Convention, p. 4.

[69] Wood, *op. cit.*, p. 348.

[70] Minutes of the 1917 S.G.G.A. Convention, pp. 46–48.

[71] Minutes of the S.G.G.A. Executive Board, March 26, 1919, p. 105; May 21, 1919, p. 111.

[72] *Canadian Parliamentary Guide, 1921* (ed. by E. J. Chambers; Ottawa, Mortimer Co., Ltd.), p. 279; Wood, *op. cit.*, pp. 349–350.

[73] Wood, *op. cit.*, pp. 329–331.

[74] *Ibid.*, pp. 339, 341–343.

[75] *Ibid.*, pp. 351–355.

[76] *Ibid.*, p. 358; interviews.

[77] *Canada Year Book, 1941*, p. 181; *ibid., 1945*, pp. 52, 235.

[78] *Canadian Parliamentary Guide, 1922*, pp. 204–290.

[79] Wood, *op. cit.*, pp. 293–294.

[80] *Ibid.*, pp. 357–360; interviews with former Progressive leaders.

[81] *Ibid.*, p. 364.

[82] The Provincial Treasurer, Charles Dunning, told the convention that "as a government, the Saskatchewan government does not support the party led by Mackenzie King [Liberals] or T. A. Crerar [Progressives] or Meighen [Conservatives]. As an aggregation of individuals there may be one or two who support King. I am dead sure there are some who will support Crerar, but I do not know one who will support Meighen." Minutes of the 1921 S.G.G.A. Convention.

[83] Wood, *op. cit.*, pp. 340–341.

[84] *Canadian Parliamentary Guide, 1922*, pp. 547–550.

[85] S. W. Yates, *The Saskatchewan Wheat Pool*, U.F.C. (Saskatchewan Section), (Saskatoon, 1947), pp. 32–36.

[86] *Ibid.*, p. 57. "The new movement [the Farmers' Union] had its roots in the post-war agricultural depression and in a growing reaction against the alleged domination of the conventions and policies of the Saskatchewan Grain Growers' Association by a group who also variously shared office in the Saskatchewan Coöperative Elevator Company and the Saskatchewan government." Patton, *op. cit.*, pp. 213–214.

[87] Yates, *op. cit.*, p. 89.

[88] *Ibid.*, p. 90.

[89] Saskatchewan Coöperative Wheat Producers, Ltd., *Handbook* No. 2 (Regina, 1927).

[90] See "Open Forum," *Western Producer*, 1924, for repeated criticisms of Coöperative Elevator officials by local farm leaders.

[91] Yates, *op. cit.*, pp. 116–128; Patton, *op. cit.*, p. 233.

[92] Patton, *op. cit.*, p. 405.

[93] Saskatchewan Coöperative Wheat Producers, Ltd., *Annual Report* (Regina), 1925–1948.

[94] Saskatchewan Coöperative Producers, Ltd., *Handbook* No. 1 (Regina, 1944).

[95] "Open Forum," *Western Producer*, 1924–1948.

[96] George F. Stirling, "Mind Your Own Business," U.F.C. (Saskatchewan Section), *Pamphlet No. 1* (Saskatoon, n.d.), pp. 12–13.

[97] U.F.C. (Saskatchewan Section), *Constitution and By-Laws.*

[98] Stirling, *op. cit.*, p. 13.

[99] Weber, *op. cit.*, p. 186.

[100] Stanley B. Mathewson, *Restriction of Output among Unorganized Workers* (New York, Viking Press, 1931).

[101] Weber, *op. cit.*, pp. 183–184.

NOTES TO CHAPTER IV

[1] From a letter to the author by a former Wheat Pool leader.

[2] "They tell us the larger the institution the more economically it can be managed, and by the amalgamation of capital a concern similar to our Canadian Pacific Railway can be better managed and give better service and be more profitable to its shareholders because of its magnitude. If this be so, is it not possible for such an institution to be managed in a similar manner for all the people; and to an even much greater advantage when the principle of self-help and coöperation had been planted in the heart of every workman in the system; and when those who perform the labor are receiving an equitable share in the proceeds. If such a gigantic institution can be so successfully worked for a corporate few, what might we not hope for from it when all the workers have an equitable share in the wealth they create." *Grain Growers' Guide*, May 4, 1910, p. 9.

[3] "Farmers' Union Page," *Western Producer*, September 25, 1924, p. 8.

[4] *Ibid.*, October 9, 1924, p. 8.

[5] J. S. Woodsworth, "Labor in the Canadian Parliament," in H. W. Laidler and Norman Thomas (eds.), *The Socialism of Our Times* (New York, Vanguard Press, 1929), pp. 134–143.

[6] Minutes of the 1924 Farmers' Union Convention, p. 5.

[7] Minutes of the U.F.C. Board of Directors, March, 1928, p. 10.

[8] E. A. Partridge, *A War on Poverty* (Winnipeg, Wallingford Press, Ltd., 1926), p. 80.

[9] S. W. Yates, *The Saskatchewan Wheat Pool*, U.F.C. (Saskatchewan Section), (Saskatoon, 1947), pp. 137–145.

[10] H. A. Innis (ed.), *The Diary of Alexander James McPhail* (University of Toronto Press, 1940), pp. 185–189.

[11] *Saskatchewan Coöperative Wheat Producers, Ltd.: Its Aims, Origins, Operations and Progress, June, 1924–January, 1928* (Regina, 1928), p. 7.

[12] *Western Producer*, February 21, 1928, p. 13.

[13] Minutes of the U.F.C. Board of Directors, March 5–13, 1929.

[14] *Summary of Resolutions Passed at the 1929 Convention of the U.F.C.*, p. 10.

[15] Paul F. Bredt, *Submission on Behalf of the Pool Organization of Alberta, Saskatchewan and Manitoba to Royal Grain Inquiry Commission, 1937*, p. 27.

[16] Saskatchewan Coöperative Producers, Ltd., *The Wheat Pool and Its Accomplishments to 1946* (Regina, 1946), p. 10.

[17] Saskatchewan Coöperative Producers, Ltd., *Submission of Saskatchewan Coöperative Producers Limited and Its Subsidiaries to Commission on Taxation of Coöperatives* (Regina, 1945), p. 9.

[18] *The Wheat Pool and Its Accomplishments to 1946*, p. 9.

[19] *Western Producer*, July 31, 1930, p. 9.

[20] *Ibid.*, February 26, 1931, pp. 2–3.

[21] Minutes of the U.F.C. Convention, 1926–1929..

[22] Minutes of the 1930 U.F.C. Convention, p. 19.

[23] *Ibid.*, p. 231.

[24] *U.F.C. Official Record of Resolutions, 1930 Convention*, p. 2.

[25] Regina *Leader-Post*, May 23, 1930, pp. 1, 12.

[26] *Ibid.*, July 12, 1930, p. 12.

[27] *Ibid.*, July 7, 1930, p. 1.

[28] *Ibid.*

[29] *Canadian Parliamentary Guide, 1930*, pp. 215–314.

[30] Regina *Leader-Post*, January 24, 1931, p. 1.

[31] Partridge, *op. cit.*, pp. 197–202.

[32] Regina *Leader-Post*, February 7, 1931, p. 2.

[33] Minutes of the 1931 U.F.C. Convention, p. 211.

[34] *Ibid.*, p. 168.

[35] *Ibid.*, pp. 124, 210. (Italics mine.)

[36] *Ibid.*, p. 312.

[37] *Ibid.*, pp. 328–329.

[38] *Ibid.*, p. 360.

[39] Interviews with founders of the I.L.P.

[40] Interviews with founders of the I.L.P.

[41] Minutes of the Joint Conference of U.F.C. and I.L.P. Delegates in Regina, June 26–27, 1931.

[42] U.F.C. (Saskatchewan Section), *Another Explanation of Clause No. 8 of the Provincial Economic Policy* (Saskatoon, 1932), p. 1.

[43] Minutes of the Joint Conference of U.F.C. and I.L.P. Delegates in Regina, June 26–27, 1931, p. 9.

[44] Interviews with leaders of the U.F.C.

[45] Letter from a U.F.C. supporter to a U.F.C. official, Mrs. Louise Lucas, 1931.

[46] Letter from Frank Eliason to Mrs. Louise Lucas, April 1, 1932.

[47] "United Farmers' Page," *Western Producer*, 1931–1932.

[48] Regina *Leader-Post*, January 25, 1932, p. 12. See also *ibid.*, December 2, 1932, p. 2. The more conservative United Farmers of Ontario also voted late in 1932 to support the socialists.

[49] *Canadian Parliamentary Guide, 1933*, p. 302.

[50] League for Social Reconstruction, *Social Planning for Canada* (Toronto, Thomas Nelson and Sons, Ltd., 1935).

[51] J. King Gordon, "Socialism and Christianity," *Saskatchewan C.C.F. Research Review*, May, 1934, pp. 4–9.

[52] F. R. Scott, "The C.C.F. Convention," *Canadian Forum*, September, 1933, pp. 447–449.

NOTES TO CHAPTER V

[1] Bank of Canada, *Report of the Financial Position of the Province of Saskatchewan* (Ottawa, 1937), p. 3.

[2] *Prairie Population Possibilities—A Study Prepared for the Royal Commission on Dominion-Provincial Relations* (Ottawa, 1939).

[3] William Allen, and E. C. Hope, *The Farm Outlook for Saskatchewan* (University of Saskatchewan, 1934), p. 2.

[4] *Ibid.*, 1935, p. 2.

[5] *Ibid.*, 1936, p. 2.

[6] *Ibid.*, 1938, pp. 1–2.

[7] *Ibid.,* 1939, p. 1.

[8] *Ibid.,* 1940, p. 1. (Italics mine.)

[9] University of Saskatchewan, College of Agriculture, "Changes in Farm Income and Indebtedness in Saskatchewan during the Period 1929 to 1940," *Agricultural Extension Bulletin 105* (Saskatoon, 1940), p. 13.

[10] Province of Saskatchewan, *A Submission by the Government of Saskatchewan to the Royal Commission for Dominion-Provincial Relations* (Regina, 1937), p. 187; G. E. Britnell, *The Wheat Economy* (University of Toronto Press, 1939), p. 97.

[11] *Report of the Royal Commission on Dominion-Provincial Relations: Canada, 1867–1939* (Ottawa, 1940), Book I, p. 164.

[12] Britnell, *op. cit.,* p. 170.

[13] *Ibid.,* p. 171.

[14] D. B. MacRae and R. M. Scott, *In the South Country: A Reprint of a Series of Articles Which Appeared in the Winnipeg Free Press, Regina Leader-Post and Saskatoon Star-Phoenix in September, 1934, as a Result of a Tour of the Drouth-Stricken Districts of Saskatchewan and Manitoba* (Saskatoon *Star-Phoenix,* 1934), pp. 18–20.

[15] *Ibid.,* pp. 7–14.

[16] Province of Saskatchewan, Department of Telephones, *Annual Report* (Regina), 1930–1939.

[17] Gertrude S. Telford, "Livingstone: A Social Survey" (unpublished master's thesis, McMaster's University, 1931), p. 34, quoted in Britnell, *The Wheat Economy,* pp. 179–180.

[18] Dominion Bureau of Statistics, *The Prairie Provinces in Their Relation to the National Economy of Canada* (Ottawa, 1934), p. 109.

[19] *Ibid.,* p. 115.

[20] Legislative Assembly of Saskatchewan, *Journals* (Regina, 1937), p. 174.

[21] MacRae and Scott, *op. cit.,* p. 18.

[22] G. E. Britnell, "Economic Conditions in Rural Saskatchewan," *Canadian Forum,* March, 1934, p. 210.

[23] Carolyn Rose, unpublished manuscript in possession of author.

[24] Britnell, *The Wheat Economy,* p. 202.

[25] Quoted in *ibid.,* p. 212.

[26] *Report of the Saskatchewan Reconstruction Council* (Regina, 1944), p. 115.

[27] Province of Saskatchewan, Department of Agriculture, *Fortieth Annual Report* (Regina, 1945), p. 167.

[28] *Report of the Saskatchewan Reconstruction Council,* p. 80.

NOTES TO CHAPTER VI

[1] Minutes of the First Convention of Delegates Representing U.F.C. Lodges, Branches of I.L.P., and Provincial Constituency Organizations, 1932, p. 14.

[2] Saskatoon *Star-Phoenix,* July 28, 1932, p. 4.

[3] Regina *Leader-Post,* June 8, 1934, p. 9.

[4] *Ibid.,* September 15, 1931, p. 4.

[5] See esp. Regina *Leader-Post,* Regina *Star,* and Saskatoon *Star-Phoenix,* 1931–1934.

[6] Regina *Leader-Post,* March 3, 1934, p. 2.

[7] *Ibid.,* May 13, 1935, p. 8.

[8] *Ibid.,* May 17, 1934, p. 3.

[9] *Official Election Results,* Secretary of Executive Council, Province of Saskatchewan.

[10] *Ibid.*

[11] J. A. Irving, "The Evolution of the Social Credit Movement," *Canadian Journal of Economics and Political Science,* August, 1948, pp. 321–341.

[12] October 9, 1935.

[13] *Canadian Parliamentary Guide, 1937,* pp. 234–357.

[14] Minutes of the 1936 C.C.F. Convention, pp. 13–14.

[15] *Ibid.,* p. 20.

[16] Regina *Leader-Post,* July 17, 1936, pp. 1–2.

[17] Minutes of the 1936 C.C.F. Convention.

[18] Interviews with C.C.F. leaders.

[19] Letter from C.C.F. Provincial Council, October 6, 1937.

[20] "A Challenge to Reaction" (editorial), *New Era,* February 16, 1938, p. 2.

[21] B. T. Richardson, "C.C.F. in Saskatchewan Would Pull with Social Credit, Not So in Alberta," Regina *Leader-Post,* October 14, 1937, p. 4.

[22] Regina *Daily Star,* May 14, 1938, p. 9.

[23] See 1938 campaign literature, Liberal Party file, Regina.

[24] Interviews with C.C.F. leaders. Unlike the campaign of 1934, in the 1938 campaign there were no newspaper accounts of statements of Catholic leaders opposing the C.C.F. See Regina *Leader-Post* and Saskatoon *Star-Phoenix,* January–June, 1938.

[25] *Canadian Parliamentary Guide, 1939.*

[26] Irving, *op. cit.,* p. 333.

[27] Minutes of the 1939 C.C.F. Convention (Saskatchewan Section), p. 12.

[28] Unpublished address before the C.C.F. National Convention, 1937.

[29] Interviews with C.C.F. leaders.

[30] Interviews with C.C.F. leaders.

[31] Interviews with C.C.F. leaders.

[32] *Canadian Parliamentary Guide, 1941.*

[33] Data from Secretary of Statistics, Department of Agriculture, Regina.

[34] Saskatchewan Coöperative Producers, Ltd., *Submission Made to Prime Minister King and His Cabinet in Support of the Saskatchewan Agricultural Petition Bearing 185,000 Signatures* (Regina, 1942). See also Saskatchewan Coöperative Producers, Ltd., *Eighteenth Annual Report* (Regina, 1942).

[35] Saskatchewan Coöperative Producers, Ltd., *The Wheat Pool and Its Accomplishments to 1946* (Regina, 1946).

[36] In August, 1941, according to the membership and financial records of the Saskatchewan C.C.F., there were 4,460 paid members. In July 31, 1942, the paid membership rose to 9,813. The financial report also indicates a growth of the C.C.F. In 1933 the revenues collected were $2,134; in 1934, $3,053; in 1941, $6,325; in 1942, the year of the March on Ottawa, $13,605.

[37] Interviews with C.C.F. leaders.

[38] Interviews with C.C.F. leaders.

[39] Canadian Institute of Public Opinion, *Report* (Toronto).

[40] *Ibid.,* 1943.

[41] Records of C.C.F. National Office, Ottawa, 1945.

[42] See the Canadian and the American Institute of Public Opinion, *Report,* October, 1943.

[43] "A Big Job for the Tories" (editorial), *Saskatchewan Commonwealth,* January 19, 1944, p. 4.

[44] According to the records of the Saskatchewan C.C.F., membership in 1944 was 25,925; it rose to 31,858 in 1945.

[45] *Official Election Results,* Secretary of Executive Council, Province of Saskatchewan.

[46] Datus C. Smith, Jr., "North Dakota Seeks a Demagogue," *New Republic,* October 3, 1934, p. 205.

[47] *World Almanac* (New York *World-Telegram*, 1947), p. 170. Lemke obtained less than 2 per cent of the national vote.

[48] John Gunther, *Inside U.S.A.* (New York, Harper and Brothers, 1947), p. 241.

[49] Irving, *op. cit.*, pp. 336–341.

[50] Gunther, *op. cit.*, p. 244.

NOTES TO CHAPTER VII

[1] Interview with a C.C.F. member.

[2] Interview with a C.C.F. leader.

[3] C.C.F. campaign leaflet (Regina, 1934).

[4] C.C.F. (Saskatchewan Section), *The Coöperative Commonwealth—Conservative and Liberal Objections Answered* (Regina, 1936), p. 2; *The Most Frequent Objections to Socialism Answered* (Regina, 1934).

[5] *New Era*, February 3, 1948, p. 2. (Italics mine.)

[6] Saskatchewan Farmer-Labor Group (C.C.F.), *Handbook for Speakers* (Regina, 1933), p. 21.

[7] *Ibid.*, p. 12.

[8] *Handbook to the Saskatchewan C.C.F. Platform and Policy* (Regina, 1938), p. 1.

[9] C.C.F. (Saskatchewan Section), *The Growth of the Provincial Platform* (Regina, 1938), p. 2.

[10] George Williams, *Social Democracy in Canada* (Regina, 1938), pp. 40–41. (Italics mine.)

[11] Federal program adopted by the Saskatchewan Farmer-Labor Group, 1933.

[12] *Provincial Platform*, 1938.

[13] *Ibid.*, 1944.

[14] Williams, *op. cit.*, p. 39.

[15] Gertrude S. Telford, *What Happened to David Jones?* C.C.F. (Saskatchewan Section), (Regina, 1939), p. 39.

[16] T. C. Douglas, *Towards a United Canada* (Regina, 1944), p. 5.

[17] Saskatchewan Farmer-Labor Group (C.C.F.), *Economic Policy* (Regina, 1933), p. 4.

[18] *Handbook for Speakers*, p. 14.

[19] Regina *Leader-Post*, June 16, 1934, pp. 1–2.

[20] *Provincial Platform*, 1944.

[21] See Franz Lindner, *Sozialismus und Religion* (Leipzig, Tauchnitz, 1932), for a discussion of the British Labor Party's attitudes on religion.

[22] C.C.F. (Saskatchewan Section), *Religion and the C.C.F.* (Regina, n.d.).

[23] "Youth and the New Day," *Research Review*, June, 1934, p. 2.

[24] *Religion and the C.C.F.*, pp. 1–4.

[25] Regina *Leader-Post*, December 3, 1938, p. 1.

[26] Excerpt from radio speech, April 20, 1943.

[27] *Economic Policy*, p. 4.

[28] C.C.F. (Saskatchewan Section), *The Farmer and the C.C.F.* (Regina, n.d.), p. 3.

[29] C.C.F. (Saskatchewan Section), *The C.C.F. Program for Saskatchewan* (Regina, 1944), pp. 2, 3.

[30] Ottawa, House of Commons Debates: "The Address and Purchasing Power," *Speeches of M. J. Coldwell* (1937), pp. 4–5; M. J. Coldwell and T. C. Douglas, *Saskatchewan Conditions* (1938), pp. 3–4; also, by the same authors,

A *Plea for Democratic Government* (1944), pp. 6–7; and C.C.F. Parliamentary Group, *Fighting for Democracy on All Fronts* (1940), pp. 5, 8–10, 26–28.

[31] *The C.C.F. Program for Saskatchewan*, p. 3.

[32] C.C.F., *Provincial and Federal Program* (Saskatoon, 1933).

[33] *The Growth of the Provincial Platform*, p. 4. (Italics mine.)

[34] C.C.F. (Saskatchewan Section), *Labor and Urban Security* (Regina, 1944), pp. 2–4.

[35] Andrew A. Bruce, *The Non-Partisan League* (New York, Macmillan Co., 1921), pp. 142–144.

[36] Minutes of the 1923 Farmers' Union Convention.

[37] Interviews with U.F.C. leaders.

[38] *Handbook for Speakers*, p. 13.

[39] C.C.F. (Saskatchewan Section), election leaflet (Regina, 1935).

[40] Saskatchewan Liberal Party, *The C.C.F. Platform* (Regina, 1938), p. 3.

[41] George Williams, *Problems Confronting the Retail Merchants of Western Canada* (Regina, January 4, 1939), pp. 2–3. A published address.

[42] "The Coöperatives" (editorial), *Saskatchewan Commonwealth*, February 12, 1944, p. 4.

[43] *Ibid.*, January 11, 1944, p. 4.

[44] Interviews with members of *Leader-Post* staff.

[45] "A Big Job for the Tories" (editorial), *Saskatchewan Commonwealth*, January 19, 1944, p. 4.

[46] Karl Mannheim, *Ideology and Utopia* (London, Routledge and Kegan Paul, Ltd., 1936), p. 187.

[47] Rosa Luxemburg, *The Russian Revolution* (New York, Workers Age Publishers, 1940), pp. 17–22.

[48] Julius Braunthal, *In Search of the Millennium* (London, Victor Gollancz, Ltd., 1945), pp. 267–268.

[49] Gelo and Andrea, "French Letter: The November Elections," *Politics*, December, 1946, pp. 378–379.

[50] See W. E. Walling, *Socialism As It Is* (New York, Macmillan Co., 1912), for a discussion of ideological shifts of socialist parties before the First World War. See also Franz Borkenau, *Socialism, National or International* (London, G. Routledge and Sons, Ltd., 1942).

[51] Toronto *Star*, June 14, 1948, p. 1.

[52] Sir John Maynard, *The Russian Peasant and Other Studies* (London, Victor Gollancz, Ltd., 1947), pp. 180–183, 279–288.

NOTES TO CHAPTER VIII

[1] Stuart A. Rice, *Farmers and Workers in American Politics* (New York, Longmans, Green and Co., 1924), p. 165.

[2] The election results of a number of Saskatchewan towns were analyzed with political leaders of these towns. They invariably indicated that the poorer and working-class areas supported the C.C.F., whereas the business-class districts backed the old parties.

[3] Jean Burnet, unpublished doctoral thesis, University of Chicago, 1948; Jim Giffen, unpublished master's thesis, University of Toronto, 1947.

[4] Rural municipalities are about eighteen miles square. The province is divided into more than 300 municipalities of this size. Their population varies from about 800 to 5,000. The municipalities average six election polls each. The election results were calculated for each municipality by adding the results for the polls within municipalities. When a poll overlapped municipal boundaries, each municipality was assigned a proportionate part of the vote.

[5] The Lazarsfeld latent attribute is a method of analyzing the relationships among a number of variables. It indicates the presence or absence of a common underlying factor.

[6] J. H. Kolb and E. de S. Brunner, *A Study of Rural Society* (New York, Houghton Mifflin Co., 1935), p. 353.

[7] Letter of the Rev. Eugene A. Cullinane, C.S.B., Professor of Economics, University of Saskatchewan.

[8] England has a similar pattern. The Methodists, who are the largest group in the United Church of Canada, were the backbone of the British labor movement.

". . . it seems to me that it still remains true that, in the silent solid membership of every popular movement in the country, from Trade-Unionism and Coöperation, from Friendly and Temperance Societies, right up to the rapidly growing Labour Party itself—no less than among their active local organizers and leaders—perhaps the largest part is contributed by the various branches of the Methodist community." Sidney Webb, *The Story of the Durham Miners, 1662–1921* (London, Labour Publishing Co., 1921), p. 24.

"The training in self-expression and in the filling of offices and the control of public affairs which these [Methodist] Societies provided for a great host of working men and women was invaluable as a preparation for industrial combination and for the future work of Trade-Unionism. The Dissenting Chapel and the Methodist Society were the pioneer forms of the latter self-governing labour organizations, and they became the nurseries of popular aspirations after place and power in civic and national government." A. D. Belden, *George Whitefield the Awakener* (London, S. Low, Marston and Co., Ltd., 1930), pp. 247 ff.

[9] G. E. Britnell, *The Wheat Economy* (University of Toronto Press, 1939), p. 188.

[10] Thorstein Veblen, *The Theory of the Leisure Class* (New York, Modern Library, 1934), p. 193.

[11] G. D. H. Cole explained the failure of English socialism in the 1930's as a result of the fact that "distress is to a great extent now localized in the so-called 'special areas,' and affects comparatively little the major portion of the population, or even of the working class. Over most of the South, indeed, the sense of crisis was only acute for a few months at most; and actually a majority of the British people, including nearly all those who have been able to keep in regular work, has enjoyed a higher purchasing power during the depression than ever before . . . so great was the effect of this fall [in the price of foodstuffs] that even the reduced wages paid to the employed workers enabled them to buy more than they could afford when times were better." *Socialism in Evolution* (London, Penguin Books, Ltd., 1938), p. 224.

[12] "I assumed the role of one who was out of work and had become a communist because I couldn't get a job. I was told frankly and with great emotion that I could get work if I wanted it, that I was simply lazy and wanted a handout from people who had energy enough and ambition enough to work for a living even though it meant twelve to sixteen hours a day." E. Wight Bakke, *Citizens without Work; A Study of the Effects of Unemployment upon the Workers' Social Relations and Practices* (Yale University Press, 1940), p. 61.

[13] C. O. Ruggles, "The Economic Basis of the Greenback Movement in Iowa and Wisconsin," Mississippi Valley Historical Society, *Proceedings*, Vol. 5; Benton H. Wilcox, "An Historical Definition of North-Western Radicalism," *Mississippi Valley Historical Review*, December, 1939; Raymond C. Miller, "The Economic Basis of Populism in Kansas," *ibid.*, Vol. 11 (1925); Rice,

op. cit.; Jerry Nepresh, *The Brookhart Campaigns in Iowa: 1920–26* (Columbia University Press, 1932).

[14] Marie Lazarsfeld-Jahoda (Paul Lazarsfeld), *Die Arbeitslosen von Marienthal* (Leipzig, S. Hitze, 1933), pp. 35–37.

[15] Emile Durkheim, *Selected Readings of Anomie* (trans. by W. C. Bradbury, Jr., from *Le Suicide, étude de sociologie*), Part V, reprinted from *University Observer*, Winter, 1947.

[16] The greatest gains in the Socialist Party vote in the United States were in 1902, 1904, and 1912—periods of economic expansion. "On the other hand, the panics of 1907 and 1913 did not make it possible for the party to get recruits or money in abundance and to wage as good a campaign as during better times. Workingmen are not militant if they are out of work or threatened with loss of work, unless the condition lasts for a long time. . . . The Socialist Party made no gains in 1908 and lost votes in 1914." Nathan Fine, *Labor and Farmer Parties in the United States* (Rand School of Social Science, New York, 1928), p. 217.

[17] A random sample of 549 Saskatchewan farmers made after the federal election of 1945 tends to confirm the interpretation that the poorer farmers are now the farthest to the left.

DIFFERENCES IN SUPPORT RECEIVED BY SASKATCHEWAN
POLITICAL PARTIES IN 1945*

(Percentage)

	C.C.F.	Liberal	Conserva-tive	Others
Socioeconomic status:				
Above average............................	42.6	31.3	22.7	4.4
Average...................................	45.5	32.3	19.3	3.9
Below average............................	49.3	27.6	19.2	4.9
Religion:				
Catholic..................................	38.1	48.7	1.9	2.3
United Church...........................	52.0	23.7	24.6	0.7
Anglican.................................	36.4	31.5	28.8	4.3
Ethnic Origin:				
Anglo-Saxon..............................	47.4	37.7	32.2	3.7
Central European and French.............	45.3	42.9	7.2	5.6

SOURCE: Sample of 549 farmers interviewed.
* Original data in files of Canadian Institute of Public Opinion, Toronto, Ontario.

[18] Interviews with leaders of the U.F.C. (Saskatchewan Section).

NOTES TO CHAPTER IX

[1] "By the very nature of their role reform leaders tended to be people devoid of 'respectable' attributes. . . . The influences which prompted people to break from established institutions and to take up the case of reform often increased opposition against them. Desire to escape from the boredom of routine tasks, inability to secure a living or recognition in any other way, love of power which was experienced in swaying large audiences or large reading publics, and personal 'grudges' against persons in authority, may have mingled, along with other motives, with the sincere conviction of doing good." S. D. Clark, *The Social Development of Canada* (University of Toronto Press, 1942), pp. 14–15.

[2] A study of members and leaders of Communist organizations suggested that they come from marginal groups, i.e., they tend to be members of minor-

ity, foreign-born, or ethnic groups, or people who are personally insecure. Harold Lasswell and Dorothy Blumenstock, *World Revolutionary Propaganda* (New York, Alfred A. Knopf, 1939), pp. 277–300.

[3] The findings in this study of rural coöperative and C.C.F. leadership in Saskatchewan are similar to those of other sociological studies of rural leadership. In the United States, higher economic status and farm ownership are correlated with active participation and leadership in farmers' organizations. Dwight Sanderson, *Rural Sociology and Social Organization* (New York, John Wiley and Sons, 1942), pp. 598–600. "Coöperatives are more successful in enlisting the better educated, the more experienced, wealthier farmers than the others, and farm owners will join more readily than tenants. . . . In the main, coöperators belong to more organizations like churches, farm bureaus, lodges, and have a higher standard of living, more conveniences and more equipment than noncoöperators." J. H. Kolb and E. de S. Brunner, *A Study of Rural Society* (New York, Houghton Mifflin Co., 1935), p. 353.

Ethnic influences in the United States are similar to those in Saskatchewan. Segregated ethnic colonies participate much less in organizations such as the Farm Bureau and coöperatives than do the Anglo-Saxons. Farmers of Scandinavian and Teutonic origin participate more than those coming from Slavic or Latin countries. E. de S. Brunner, *Immigrant Farmers and Their Children* (New York, Doubleday, Doran and Co., 1929), chap. v.

[4] Letter from Frank Eliason to William Thomson, president, Wynyard Local Council, U.F.C., August 6, 1931, p. 2.

[5] Jim Giffen, unpublished master's thesis, University of Toronto, 1947.

[6] *Ibid.*

[7] Robert Michels, *Political Parties* (New York, Hearst's International Library Co., 1915), pp. 260–261.

[8] Escott Reid, "The Saskatchewan Liberal Machine before 1929," *Canadian Journal of Economics and Political Science*, February, 1936, pp. 27–40.

[9] Thorstein Veblen, *The Theory of the Leisure Class* (New York, Modern Library, 1934), pp. 195–196.

[10] Paul Lazarsfeld, Bernard Berelson, and Hazel Gaudet, *The People's Choice* (2d ed.; Columbia University Press, 1948), pp. 145–147.

[11] *Ibid.*, pp. 148–149.

[12] The sources of this study, based on a random sample of the Saskatchewan population, are confidential.

NOTES TO CHAPTER X

[1] Gunnar Myrdal, *An American Dilemma* (New York, Harper and Brothers, 1944), p. 714.

[2] Nathan Fine, *Labor and Farmer Parties in the United States* (Rand School of Social Science, New York, 1928); John D. Hicks, *The Populist Revolt* (University of Minnesota Press, 1931), p. 80; Paul Fossum, *The Agrarian Movement in North Dakota* (Baltimore, Johns Hopkins Press, 1925), pp. 85–86.

[3] The coöperative organizations of the province have 477,000 members, though there are only 125,000 farmers. See Saskatchewan *News*, March 22, 1948, p. 3; also Department of Municipal Affairs, *Report* (Regina, 1948).

[4] G. E. Britnell, *The Wheat Economy* (University of Toronto Press, 1939), p. 188.

[5] Jean Burnet, "Town-Country Relations and the Problem of Rural Leadership," *Canadian Journal of Economics and Political Science*, August, 1947, pp. 395–419.

[6] Hugh Boyd, *New Breaking* (Toronto, J. M. Dent and Sons, Ltd., 1938); Saskatchewan Coöperative Producers, Ltd., *Annual Report* (Regina), 1924–1947.

[7] Saskatchewan Coöperative Producers, Ltd., *The Wheat Pool and Its Accomplishments to 1946* (Regina, 1946), p. 12.

[8] George Robson, "Letter to Editor," *Western Producer*, January 30, 1943, p. 2.

[9] In the past, many agrarian protest movements succeeded despite the initial opposition of the top officials of the organized farmers. The Grain Growers' Grain Company was organized in spite of the fact that the heads of the Saskatchewan Grain Growers' Association opposed it. After the First World War, independent political action was forced on the leaders of the S.G.G.A. The Wheat Pool succeeded despite the early reluctance of the officials of the S.G.G.A. and the Saskatchewan Coöperative Elevator Company. The 100 per cent pool plan was adopted in 1929 and 1930, though the leaders of the U.F.C. and the Wheat Pool were opposed to it. See chaps. iii and iv.

[10] Records of Saskatchewan C.C.F.

[11] C. Rufus Rorem, *The Municipal Doctor Scheme in Rural Saskatchewan* (University of Chicago Press, 1931).

[12] *Ibid.*, pp. 83–84.

[13] C.C.F. (Saskatchewan Section), *Handbook* (Regina, 1946).

[14] Commission of the Central Committee of the Communist Party of the Soviet Union, *History of the Communist Party of the Soviet Union* (New York, International Publishers, 1939), pp. 46–49.

[15] C.C.F. (Saskatchewan Section), *Provincial Convention Delegates' Handbook* (Regina, 1945), p. 33.

[16] *Ibid.*

[17] *Ibid.*, 1946, p. 51.

[18] *Ibid.*, p. 45.

[19] *Ibid.*, p. 51. It should be noted that the last two resolutions were passed at constituency conventions at which cabinet ministers were present.

[20] The Saskatchewan Liberal Party held a convention in 1947.

[21] C.C.F. Convention, *Handbook*, 1945, 1946, 1947.

[22] Hopkins Moorhouse, *Deep Furrows* (Toronto, George J. McLeod, Ltd., 1918), pp. 230–233, 265.

[23] From interviews with C.C.F. leaders.

[24] Myrdal, *op. cit.*, p. 714.

[25] S. Roy Weaver, *The Non-Partisan League in North Dakota* (Canadian Reconstruction Association, Toronto, 1921), p. 13.

[26] John Gunther, *Inside U.S.A.* (New York, Harper and Brothers, 1947), p. 242.

[27] Henry Wallace, "Report on the Farmers," *New Republic*, June 30, 1947, p. 12.

[28] Myrdal, *op. cit.*, p. 717. (Italics in original.)

[29] Similar results were found in an unpublished study of a small, self-contained housing community in an industrial area. Craftown, a community of 2,500, was found to be much more active politically than neighboring urban areas. The community, like rural Saskatchewan, was a small, relatively homogeneous town, with four-fifths of its population industrial workers. Similarly, it faced a series of problems that demanded organized action. Because of the lack of public services, the working-class citizenry had to start volunteer police and fire departments and a coöperative store. These associations provided opportunities for learning collaborative techniques and leadership skills which were also put to use in political action.

"Joined in an interlocking complex, these factors of the manageable size of the local community, a new and flexible social structure, a continuing flow of problems visibly common to the group and a nucleus of men and women equipped through experience with skills of collaboration all contributed to the building of an actively participating citizenry." Robert K. Merton and Patricia Salter, *An Interim Report: The Lavenburg-Columbia Research on Human Relations in the Planned Community. The First Year's Work—1945–1946* (New York, 1946). Mimeographed.

[30] John Dewey, *Freedom and Culture* (New York, G. P. Putnam's Sons, 1939), p. 159.

NOTES TO CHAPTER XI

[1] "Britain, Decay of the Conservatives," *Time*, April 21, 1947, p. 3. See Marquis W. Childs, *Sweden: The Middle Way* (New York, Penguin Books, Ltd., 1948), pp. 142–147, for a description of compromise attitudes of Swedish parties.

[2] "Scandinavia—Between Two Worlds," *New Republic*, May 5, 1947, p. 14.

[3] See provincial platforms of Saskatchewan Liberal and Conservative parties, 1929.

[4] "And the People Are Watching," Regina *Daily-Star*, March 15, 1937, p. 4.

[5] Quoted in Regina *Leader-Post*, August 7, 1931, p. 12.

[6] The prairies have provincially owned telephone systems, widespread coöperatives, and local rural systems of socialized medicine.

[7] Stuart A. Rice suggested the "existence of a radical culture area in northwestern North Dakota, with lines of diffusion extending eastward and southward and again bending westward." See his *Farmers and Workers in American Politics* (New York, Longmans, Green and Co., 1924), p. 181. If we extend Rice's "radical culture area" directly northward, we enter Saskatchewan.

[8] *Statutes of Saskatchewan, Second Session, 1944* (Regina, 1945).

[9] Interviews with H. K. Warren, chairman of Provincial Mediation Board.

[10] Unpublished address by Premier Douglas.

[11] Province of Saskatchewan, Department of Agriculture, *Annual Report* (Regina), 1944–1948.

[12] Interviews with C.C.F. leaders.

[13] The proposal to limit the size of farm holdings has never come before a C.C.F. provincial convention.

[14] Province of Saskatchewan, Department of Coöperation and Coöperative Development, *Annual Report* (Regina), 1946–1948.

[15] An unpublished study by a private research organization in 1947 indicates clearly that the members of Saskatchewan coöperatives are upper-income farmers.

[16] Interviews with members of the Economic Planning Board.

[17] The shift in one decade in rural opinion in New Zealand has been significant.

RURAL ELECTIONS

	1935	1938	1943	1946
Labor	20	15	10	4
Opposition	17	22	27	27

SOURCE: "New Zealand, the General Election," *Round Table*, No. 146 (March, 1947), p. 202.

[18] David T. Bazelon, "The Faith of Henry Wallace," *Commentary*, April, 1947, p. 314.

[19] Maurice Dobb, *Russian Economic Development since the Revolution* (London, G. Routledge and Sons, Ltd., 1928).

[20] *Western Producer*, August 19, 1946, p. 1; and interviews with leaders of the U.F.C. (Saskatchewan Section).

[21] This was written before the 1949 elections, which saw the C.C.F. lose support in the rural areas of the province.

[22] *Statutes of Saskatchewan*, 1945, 1948.

[23] Regina *Leader-Post*, November 2, 1945, p. 1.

[24] *Statutes of Saskatchewan*, 1947.

[25] Interviews and attendance at the 1946 C.C.F. Convention.

[26] Interviews with labor leaders and members of the Department of Labor.

[27] "The Issue at Grimethorpe" (editorial), London *Economist*, September 6, 1947, p. 393.

[28] Province of Saskatchewan, Department of Education, *Annual Report* (Regina), 1945–1949.

[29] Unpublished address, p. 3.

[30] See provincial platforms of Liberal and Conservative parties, 1938, 1944.

[31] Dr. Hugh McLean, *An Address on Medical Health Services* (Regina, 1944), p. 2.

[32] Testimony of representatives of Saskatchewan College of Physicians and Surgeons before special subcommittee of Saskatchewan legislature, 1946.

[33] *Handbook to the Saskatchewan C.C.F. Platform and Policy* (Regina, 1937), pp. 34–35. (Italics mine.)

[34] Health Services Planning Commission, *Report on Regional Health Services: A Proposed Plan* (Regina, 1945), Part II, p. 2.

[35] *Ibid.*, Part III, p. 7.

[36] Dr. Lloyd Brown, president of Regina Medical Services, unpublished address on Saskatchewan Health Plan, April 26, 1946.

[37] Dr. J. G. K. Lindsay, registrar of Saskatchewan College of Physicians and Surgeons, quoted in Regina *Leader-Post*, March 16, 1946, p. 1.

[38] Interviews with members of the Department of Health and Saskatchewan physicians.

[39] "Medical Rackets Grip New Zealand," New York *Times*, October 7, 1945; "Medical Care Criticized by New Zealand Hospital Head," *Christian Science Monitor* (Boston), September 29, 1945.

[40] "Saskatchewan Executive Meets Government," *Trades and Labor Congress Journal*, February, 1946, p. 12.

[41] See note 36.

[42] Dr. C. J. Houston, president of the Council of the Saskatchewan College of Physicians and Surgeons, quoted in Regina *Leader-Post*, August 7, 1947, p. 13.

[43] Province of Saskatchewan, Department of Social Welfare, *Social Welfare in Saskatchewan* (Regina, 1948).

[44] O. W. Valleau, *Saskatchewan Government Insurance* (Regina, 1945), p. 1. Mimeographed radio speech.

[45] *Report of the Saskatchewan Reconstruction Council* (Regina, 1944), p. 113.

[46] C. M. Fines, Provincial Treasurer, *Budget Speech* (Regina, 1948), pp. 12–13.

[47] The shoe factory and the tannery were forced to shut down in December, 1948.

[48] Oskar Lange and Fred M. Taylor, *On the Economic Theory of Socialism* (University of Minnesota Press, 1938).

[40] H. V. Evatt, *Australian Labour Leader* (Sydney, Angus and Robertson, Ltd., 1945), pp. 306, 395, 431, 496–497, 501–511.

[50] Felix Morrow, *Revolution and Counter-Revolution in Spain* (New York, Pioneer Publishers, 1933).

[51] "No labor leader would repudiate the socialist objective; but none could honestly argue that in practice his socialism had gone beyond a tendency toward using governmental controls as a method of dealing with immediate problems; and toward expanding social services for the mass of the Australian people. We have accepted socialism as a goal, but we have seldom planned a legislative program of rapid and widespread steps toward socialism." Lloyd Ross, *Labor in Australia* (American Council, Institute of Pacific Relations, New York, 1943), p. 17. See also Childs, *op. cit.*, p. 147; Harry W. Laidler, *Social-Economic Movements* (New York, Thomas Y. Crowell Co., 1944), pp. 563–570.

NOTES TO CHAPTER XII

[1] Interview data.

[2] "Resolution Submitted by Canora Constituency," C.C.F. Convention, *Handbook*, 1945, p. 63.

[3] "Resolution Submitted by Qu'Appelle-Wolseley Constituency," *ibid.*, pp. 67–69.

[4] "Resolution Submitted by Saskatoon Constituency," *ibid.*, p. 70.

[5] "Resolution Submitted by Redberry Constituency," *ibid.*, p. 67.

[6] "Resolution Submitted by Regina Constituency," *ibid.*, 1946, p. 79.

[7] "Resolution Submitted by Regina Constituency," *ibid.*, 1947, p. 71.

[8] "Resolution Submitted by Notukeu-Willowbunch Constituency," *ibid.*

[9] "Resolution Submitted by Maple Creek Constituency," *ibid.*

[10] Harold Laski, *Democracy in Crisis* (London, Allen and Unwin, 1933), pp. 99–104; Max Weber, *Essays in Sociology* (New York, Oxford University Press, 1946), pp. 232–235; Herman Finer, *The Future of Government* (London, Methuen and Co., 1946), pp. 12–13.

[11] J. Donald Kingsley, *Representative Bureaucracy* (Yellow Springs, Ohio, Antioch Press, 1944), pp. 287–305.

[12] *Ibid.*, pp. 42–77.

[13] Marx characteristically expressed this idea in a letter to Kugelmann: "If you look at the last chapter of my *Eighteenth Brumaire* you will find that I say that the next attempt of the French Revolution will be no longer, as before, to transfer the bureaucratic-military machine from one hand to another, but to smash it." Karl Marx and Friedrich Engels, *Correspondence, 1846–1895* (New York, International Publishers, 1936), p. 309. See also Marx, "The Civil War in France," *Selected Works* (Moscow, Publishing Society of Foreign Workers in the U.S.S.R., 1936), Vol. 2, pp. 498–505.

"To destroy officialism immediately, everywhere, completely—of this there can be no question. That is a utopia. But to *break* up at once the old bureaucratic machine and to start immediately the construction of a new one . . . this is not a utopia, . . . it is the direct and necessary task of the revolutionary proletariat." V. I. Lenin, *The State and Revolution* (New York, Vanguard Press, 1926), p. 155.

[14] "Bureaucratic Sabotage," American Academy of Political and Social Science, *Annals*, January, 1937, p. 5.

[15] London *Daily Herald*, October 23, 1933; quoted in Edgar Lansbury, *George Lansbury, My Father* (London, S. Low, Marston and Co., Ltd., n.d.), p. 197.

[16] Charles Aikin, "The British Bureaucracy and the Origin of Parliamentary Policy," *American Political Science Review,* February, 1939, pp. 40–41.

[17] V. G. Childe, *How Labour Governs* (London, Labour Publishing Co., Ltd., 1923), p. 16.

[18] Kingsley, *op. cit.,* p. 274. Leon Blum himself suggested that the conservative attitudes of the civil service were an obstacle to reform. Blum, *For All Mankind* (London, Victor Gollancz, Ltd., 1946), p. 59.

[19] Escott Reid, "The Saskatchewan Liberal Machine before 1929," *Canadian Journal of Economics and Political Science,* February, 1936.

[20] *C.C.F. Election Manifesto, 1944,* p. 1. (Italics mine.)

[21] "The C.C.F. and the Civil Service," *Saskatchewan Commonwealth,* December 1, 1943, p. 8. Radio address.

[22] Interviews with leaders of the C.C.F. and of the Liberal Party, and members of the civil service.

[23] Interviews; Minutes of the C.C.F. Provincial Convention, 1945–1948.

[24] "Consider the tasks which fall upon an important minister in the modern state. He has his own departmental business to get through. He has to make himself acquainted with at least the outlines of the bigger issues before the cabinet. He has to pay all necessary attention to the legislative assembly. . . . He must make party speeches, realizing that from the position he occupies every word he says will be narrowly scrutinized. Ceremonial functions, also, will take up hours of precious time." Laski, *op. cit.,* p. 63.

[25] Interviews with civil servants.

[26] Information based on interviews with civil servants. These reports are composite pictures of actual cases.

[27] "Bureaucracy," *Encyclopaedia of the Social Sciences* (ed. by Edwin R. A. Seligman; New York, Macmillan Co., 1935), Vol. 3, p. 72.

[28] Weber, *op. cit.,* p. 234.

[29] " . . . [Socialist] ministers are likely to arrive in office, not with a complete body of specific plans, but with some general principles which the departments will be asked to test against the facts before they are given the share of a concrete measure. The inevitable tendency of the departments will be for the minister's own sake, to minimize the break with tradition. . . . They will be passionately and laudably anxious to save him from failure. Unless they share his own outlook—and this is unlikely enough—they will want time where he demands speed, the attack on the narrow front, where his instruction is for comprehensiveness.

" . . . this attitude in the civil service is wholly compatible with its tradition of neutrality. . . . My point is the quite different one that . . . the whole ethos of the service becomes one of criticism which looks towards delay instead of encouragement which looks toward action." Laski, *Democracy in Crisis,* pp. 103–104.

[30] Speech before panel on civil service at C.C.F. Provincial Convention.

[31] Michels, *op. cit.;* James Burnham, *The Managerial Revolution* (New York, John Day Co., Inc., 1941).

[32] Bendix's study of the origins of American federal administrators is the first such study in the United States. He reports that only one similar study was made in Europe. Reinhard Bendix, *Higher Civil Servants in American Society* (University of Colorado Press, 1949). See also Philip Selznick, *T.V.A. and the Grass Roots* (University of California Press, 1949).

[33] Kingsley, *op. cit.,* pp. 42–77.

[34] In defending a merit civil service, Leonard D. White and T. V. Smith suggest that it is possible to have a neutral bureaucracy in the United States because "the battles between Democrats and Republicans are fought on a

narrow stage, with far greater areas of agreement between them than of disagreement." White and Smith, *Politics and Public Service* (New York, Harper and Brothers, 1939), pp. 132–133.

[35] Kingsley, *op. cit.*, pp. 304–305.

[36] Quoted in White and Smith, *op. cit.*, p. 44.

[37] *Ibid.*, p. 57.

[38] *Ibid.*, p. 92.

[39] Kingsley, *op. cit.*, p. 274.

[40] White and Smith, *op. cit.*, p. 53.

[41] Max Weber, *The Theory of Social and Economic Organization* (trans. by Talcott Parsons and A. K. Henderson; New York, Oxford University Press, 1947), p. 128.

NOTES TO CHAPTER XIII

[1] Province of Saskatchewan, Department of Coöperation and Coöperative Development, *Annual Report* (Regina, 1949).

[2] J. A. Irving, "The Evolution of the Social Credit Movement," *Canadian Journal of Economics and Political Science*, August, 1948, pp. 321–341.

[3] Regina *Leader-Post*, July 24, 1948, p. 1.

[4] *Ibid.*, November 22, 1948, p. 11.

[5] *Ibid.*, August 20, 1948, p. 10.

[6] Harold Laski, *Democracy in Crisis* (London, Allen and Unwin, 1933); Leon Trotsky, *Stalin* (New York, Harper and Brothers, 1941); Adolf Sturmthal, *The Tragedy of European Labor* (London, Victor Gollancz, Ltd., 1944).

[7] Leon Blum, *For All Mankind* (London, Victor Gollancz, Ltd., 1946), p. 59.

[8] Quoted in Sturmthal, *op. cit.*, p. 71.

[9] Daniel Guérin's description of these events bears quoting here:

". . . immediately after the March on Rome he [Mussolini] invited the general secretary of the Federation [of Labor], D'Aragona to enter his government. D'Aragona accepted. If Mussolini finally had to give up this plan, it was only because his intimates objected. But the union leaders continued to offer themselves. The organ of the railway workers, the *Tribuna del Ferrovieri*, published under the title, 'Without Reservations,' an editorial offering the fascist government the 'collaboration' of the railway unions. For a few months direct negotiations were carried on between the union leaders and Mussolini. In August, 1923, D'Aragona explained to the national committee of the Federation of Labor that the 'collaboration' would not be in any case *political*, but only *technical*. The Federation of Labor would participate in the advisory bodies of the state and in all bodies where problems of labor and production were to be discussed. 'The Federation's policy cannot follow preconceived ideas. . . .' In the meantime, it broke with the Socialist Party.

". . . At the end of 1926, it had to dissolve. Then its leaders substituted for it a Center for cultural association—intended to 'assist by its advice and criticism the social action of the government.' They published a manifesto in which they declared: '*The fascist regime is a reality, and any reality must be taken into consideration.*' The union movement in the past, they explained, could not decide itself either in favor of, or against, the state. However, it was necessary to choose and either wage a struggle for the destruction of the state or collaborate with, and integrate itself within it. They had decided on the second alternative—an alternative that 'implies naturally the abandonment of the principle of the class struggle.' . . .

"When Hitler took power, the Federation's [of Labor] executive committee declared that it 'will await the government's actions.' First of all the Federation broke with the Socialist party, and on March 20th it published a manifesto: 'The union organizations are the expression of an indisputable social necessity, an indispensable part of the very social order. . . . As a result of the natural order of things, they are increasingly integrated into the state. The social task of the unions must be carried out, *whatever the nature of the state regime.* . . . Union organizations make no claim to influence state power directly. *Their task here can be merely to put at the disposal of the government and parliament knowledge and experience acquired in this field.* . . .'

"On April 7, Leipart raised his bid and declared that the unions '*are pursuing the same end as the government, namely to found freedom of the nation at home and abroad on the productive forces of the whole people.*' On April 20, the national committee of the Federation invited unionists to take part in the May 1st celebration as a symbol of the incorporation of the working class into the National Socialist state." Daniel Guérin, *Fascism and Big Business* (New York, Pioneer Publishers, 1939), pp. 126–128. (Italics in original.)

[10] *Ibid.,* p. 14.

Index

Aberhart, William, 108, 112, 122
Agriculture, Canadian Council of, 56
Alberta, 21, 22, 31, 93, 108, 114, 121, 122, 124, 125, 178, 216, 279; C.C.F. in, 108, 113, 122, 123. *See also* Social Credit Party
American Federation of Labor, 7
Anderson, J. T. M., 113, 224
Anglican Church, 137, 173, 186, 194
Anglo-Saxons, 34, 163, 165–169 *passim*, 184, 185, 189, 191
Anti-Catholicism, 35, 185–186
Apristaism, 124
Australia, 27, 28, 155, 178, 245, 246, 250, 251, 259
Austrian Social Democrats, 155, 176

Background, 1 ff.
Bankers' Association (N. Dakota), 15–16
Banks, 4, 9, 15–16, 31, 50, 67, 68, 81, 105, 122, 133, 140, 154, 281, 283
Bela Kun, 155
Bellamy, Edward: *Looking Backward*, 74; *Equality*, 74
Benson, "Jake," 109
Blum, Leon, 259; quoted, 284–285
Brecht, Arnold, quoted, 258
British Columbia: Socialist Party, 86, 137; C.C.F. in, 108, 111, 213
British Commonwealth, 135, 156, 259, 284
British Labor Party, socialism in, 23, 25, 54, 74, 83, 87, 104, 136, 138, 155, 156, 157, 178, 222, 235, 246, 259, 260, 269–270, 273

Bryan, William Jennings, 9
Bureaucracy and bureaucratization, 43–44, 62, 64, 70, 76, 204, 208–209, 211 ff., 234–235, 255–275, 278, 279, 285–286
Burnham, James, 271
Burton, Joseph W., 138, 172

Cabinet ministers, and C.C.F., 261–266, 269. *See also* Bureaucracy; Civil Service
Calgary Conference, 87, 104
Canadian Pacific Railway (C.P.R.), 38, 40, 41, 79, 128
Canadian Parliamentary Guide, 193
Catholic Church and Catholics, 34–35, 106–107, 114, 135, 137, 138, 163, 165, 166, 169–173 *passim*, 185–187, 189, 194
Childe, V. G., 259
Civil Service, 231, 255–275
Class and class consciousness, 2, 12, 17–18, 29 ff., 32, 37 ff., 48–49, 61, 63, 64, 68–69, 71, 74–75, 82, 87, 143, 145–146, 152–153, 154, 161 ff., 174, 178, 187 ff., 191, 197–198, 202, 208, 214–215, 222, 227–228, 268
"Clear Grits," 3
Coalition, 111–113, 115, 278
Coldwell, M. J., 83, 84, 104, 106, 110, 111, 116, 129, 134, 138
Community organization, 58, 174–175, 201 ff., 218–219
Communist Party, 105, 106, 112, 155, 157, 178, 198, 208, 234, 285; in Russia, 153, 155, 157, 230; in